KT-460-456

A Daughter's Choice

MARGARET FORD

WITH JACQUIE BUTTRISS

HIGH LIFE HIGHLAND LIBRARIES	
38001900292040	
BERTRAMS	18/06/2019
B.FOR	£7.99
ANF	

PAN BOOKS

First published 2019 by Pan Books
an imprint of Pan Macmillan
20 New Wharf Road, London N1 9RR
Associated companies throughout the world
www.panmacmillan.com

ISBN 978-1-5098-9192-4

Copyright © Margaret Ford 2019

The right of Margaret Ford to be identified as the
author of this work has been asserted by her in accordance
with the Copyright, Designs and Patents Act 1988.

All photographs courtesy of the author.

All rights reserved. No part of this publication may be reproduced,
stored in a retrieval system, or transmitted, in any form, or by any means
(electronic, mechanical, photocopying, recording or otherwise)
without the prior written permission of the publisher.

Pan Macmillan does not have any control over, or any responsibility for,
any author or third-party websites referred to in or on this book.

1 3 5 7 9 8 6 4 2

A CIP catalogue record for this book is available from the British Library.

Typeset by Palimpsest Book Production Ltd, Falkirk, Stirlingshire
Printed and bound by CPI Group (UK) Ltd, Croydon, CR0 4YY

This book is sold subject to the condition that it shall not, by way of
trade or otherwise, be lent, hired out, or otherwise circulated without
the publisher's prior consent in any form of binding or cover other than
that in which it is published and without a similar condition including
this condition being imposed on the subsequent purchaser.

Visit www.panmacmillan.com to read more about all our books
and to buy them. You will also find features, author interviews and
news of any author events, and you can sign up for e-newsletters
so that you're always first to hear about our new releases.

A.M.D.G.

With everlasting love for my mother, Ray, Les and Jim

Contents

Prologue

The pavement was hidden under a sparkling white blanket of snow as I stepped out of the front door of our house on Robinson Street for my long-awaited wedding day. Uncle John, who had reluctantly agreed to walk me down the aisle, sat in the back seat of the hired car, waiting for me. I took a deep breath and got in next to him. We sat in silence as we drove through the snow and the slush to St Alban's Church, watching the glittering rooftops and trees go by.

I should be happy and smiling, I thought, but instead I was full of anxiety that things would not go to plan: would tension bubble up between our families? Would my older brother Bobby try to stop the wedding? Or even worse, would Joe find a way to ruin everything? At that moment, it seemed to me that the whole world was against us having the perfect day we'd dreamed of.

Perhaps I'd had too long to think. Maybe I wasn't ready. Conflicting thoughts raced around my brain. By the time we reached the entrance to the church, as I saw him standing there, stamping his feet in the snow, waiting for me with a wide grin on his face, I felt overwhelmed by doubts . . . I couldn't do it.

'Drive away please,' I said suddenly.

'Are you sure, miss?' the driver replied.

'I need to get away.'

Uncle John gave me a sideways look, but he didn't say a word – just tutted and turned back, staring straight ahead.

As we reversed out of the drive I watched my fiancé's smile drop, replaced with a look of baffled dismay, then shock. How could I do this to him? But wouldn't it be worse to subject him to a shattered dream? And it wasn't just about him. I knew he loved me completely, but what if I didn't love him enough? What if I lost my independence? I could see a future stretch ahead of me that I wasn't sure I wanted . . .

1

Playing with Otters

1926–1929

> Born blue, the baby was slapped and swung round
> in the air by her ankles till she cried.

I was that baby. I started life loudly amidst the silenced mills of Blackburn following the General Strike of May 1926. I was born in our two-up, two-down terraced house in Goldhey Street, Little Harwood and was weaned on Oxo. These were hard times for working families in Blackburn, but, although we were cash-poor, both sets of grandparents made sure we always had enough to eat.

Our house was on top of a hill, about fifteen minutes' walk from the centre of the city and not far from where my mother's parents lived. Grandad Harrison was a master builder and had his own building company, with a large yard near to their home. They lived in a detached house near Daisyfield Station, about two hundred yards from Goldhey Street.

Grandad had bought our house for my parents when they got married, so we occasionally stayed there, but most of the time we lived at the Tanners' Arms in Dinckley, a village about six miles away from central Blackburn. The Tanners' was a popular pub which was owned and run by my father's parents, Grandma and Grandpa Holden, with the help of my father, Horace, and his brother, Uncle Eddie. They both worked full-time because Grandpa Holden also had another job as a mills inspector, touring all the local cotton mills to check they didn't break any laws. He was a stern man with dark, greying whiskers, a moustache and a bushy beard. He wouldn't tolerate any bad behaviour.

His wife, my grandma, was just as stern. I once heard one of their customers calling her 'a cantankerous woman'. She always wore long, dark clothes and was fierce in her mission for cleanliness. She had a temper and I remember her snapping at my mother if she didn't do something the way she wanted it. She was often cross with her sons too. Uncle Eddie was never quick enough for her, and Father was too generous when he measured out the drinks. Everyone had to jump to, or there'd be trouble.

Although all seven of us lived together on the first floor of the pub, it was a large building and I didn't spend much time with my Holden grandparents. I shared a room upstairs with my brother Bobby who was five years older than me. Downstairs was all to do with the pub. In the main room, there was a big open fireplace and a long bar with a wooden top that had to be polished every day. I think that was my father's favourite place, drinking with his friends at the bar. Along the back was a row of wooden barrels with low taps on them.

One day, as a toddler, I was sitting on the stone slabs of the floor behind the bar and I turned on one of the taps. The brown liquid poured out all over me and I screamed because I couldn't stop it. I was sitting in a spreading pool of ale, crying my eyes out, when Uncle Eddie rushed across and turned the tap off, then roughly lifted me up and bundled me upstairs.

'You must never do that again,' he scolded as he handed me over to my mother. I didn't like Uncle Eddie much as he wasn't very kind or friendly. I don't think he liked me either. He ignored me most of the time.

The bar area led to two smaller rooms filled with curved-back chairs around tables, each with a heavy ashtray. There was also a kitchen on the ground floor. Most of the customers were local agricultural workers, passers-by or travellers during the week, but at weekends, high days and holidays people from Blackburn came in their droves to the countryside for a day out, especially in good weather.

The Tanners' Arms was surrounded by acres of open fields and farmland. Veevers Farm, across the road, had land that stretched out in all directions with a long walk from the road to the large stone farmhouse. It was a wonderful place to grow up.

Grandpa Holden also used to keep animals, like pigeons and hens, on some ground outside. At the time I thought they were pets but we sometimes used to eat pigeon pie and I never thought to ask where the filling came from! I only realized one Sunday, when Grandad wrung a chicken's neck so that we could cook and eat it for lunch. I had watched this chicken and her friends running carefree around their pen in our garden just an hour before. Now the hen squawked and screeched in her death throes. I was horrified, but none of the grown-ups comforted me. This was not a demonstrative family. Only Bobby put his arm round me, which cheered me up.

Apart from the chicken incident, I have only happy recollections of my early childhood, not then knowing or even sensing the frictional undercurrents that existed across my extended family.

My two earliest memories were of being with my gentle mother, Alice – a pretty young woman with thick chestnut curls, a round face and a thin waist. The first was at our Goldhey Street house, where Mother was always more relaxed. Perhaps that's why we went there, away from the pub, just the two of us. I was sitting on her knee in her rocking chair in the living room, rocking to and fro in front of the coal fire in the hearth just as the klaxon was sounding for the mill workers to go home. I watched the flames leap in the fire and I remember the cosy, warm feeling I had, feeling safe in her company. The other was on a bright, sunny day when she took me half a mile down the lane from the Tanners' to the river Ribble in my big pram.

When we reached her favourite spot, she lifted me out of the pram and held my hand as I toddled down to the water's edge and sat on the patch of sand that she called 'Little Blackpool'. While she sat next to me and did her crocheting, I splashed about with my stubby fingers in the puddles on the sand. Slowly, a baby otter approached and dared to come out of the water, followed by his more timid siblings. I remember watching them as they played with each other, turning and tumbling on the sand around my legs as if they trusted me. I think the brave one let me touch him. Mother laughed with me at their antics. I've loved otters ever since. It's just as well that I knew nothing then about the annual Boxing Day gathering of otter hounds and their masters, along that very stretch of the river. I was always happiest with my mother. Unlike Father and some of the other grown-ups, she was never raucous or unpredictable, angry or upset when it was just the two of us – always calm and happy.

During the day at the Tanners', everyone in the family had their jobs and Bobby was at school, so I was very happy to be left to my own devices. Looking back, I expect the adults were happy to get me out from under their feet. It might seem strange now, but in those days nobody worried about young children playing unsupervised in the countryside, which seemed so safe. I became a very independent child and loved making up my own games to keep myself occupied.

Outside the pub, the farmer from Veevers Farm stood his milk-kits every morning, on two platforms at the side of the building, one higher than the other. I sat and waited to watch them being collected by a man driving his horse and wagon. This carthorse was a gentle giant, with its long fetlocks and glossy mane – it gave a friendly whinny whenever it saw me.

Across the road from the Tanners' was a small, rectangular red postbox on a wooden pole, next to a grassy mound.

There was very little traffic passing down the road then – just the odd, lumbering horse-drawn cart or pushbike, as very few people had motor cars yet in Blackburn – so it was safe to let me play out there. In fact, it was an exciting occasion if ever we did see a motor car, and everyone would go outside to have a look.

Every morning, after breakfast, I used to wander across the road to the postbox, and scramble up the grassy mound. Then I could grab hold of a branch that jutted out of the overgrown hedge to pull myself up to reach the slit. I spent many happy hours carefully picking grasses and gathering stones, roots, pebbles, twigs, nuts – anything I could find – from around the Tanners'. I started to build a pile of them on top of the bank, so that I could have a lovely time posting them all through the slit of the postbox until I had filled it right up to the top.

Having finished this task, I would potter off a few yards down the road to talk to the horse that lived in the field. He always came to the fence as soon as I arrived and listened intently to whatever story I told him that day, while he patiently munched on the tufts of long grass in my hand, plucked from the verge on my side of the fence.

After I'd filled up the postbox for three days in a row, it began to cause some alarm at the Tanners'.

'Somebody has blocked up the postbox!' complained one rather large lady who popped into the pub with her letters in her hand. 'Who could have done such a thing?'

'Don't ask me,' was my grandpa's curt reply, though I think he might have guessed the small vandal's identity. 'Just put your letters up on the bar for now and I'll tell the postman to call in for them.' As I continued with my mischief, he put a table outside where people could leave their post. Then, at the right time, he would go out and bring all the letters and parcels in to put on the bar, ready for the postman's visit. Well, anyone who came inside would stay for a drink, wouldn't they?

So, each day, the postman pedalled up to the Tanners' to collect the letters . . . and stayed for a pint to 'wet his whistle'. Sometimes he stayed for two!

It wasn't long before the local policeman, patrolling on his clattering bike, took to popping in as well. It was always at about the same time, just to make sure everything was all right . . . and to have a drink while he was there. Some days he stayed so long that the inspector came to join him! When I was old enough to think about it, I realized I must have done my family a favour by filling up that postbox so efficiently.

The Tanners' Arms was quite an old building, probably Victorian. It had no flush lavatories or hot water. Consequently, we had outside latrines and chamber pots that were emptied into 'tubs' with carrying handles at each side. At the end of each day, after I'd gone to bed, Father and Uncle Eddie had to empty them somewhere outside. I never knew where. It was only when I was older that I realized why we so often ate mushrooms for breakfast!

Down the side of the Tanners' there was a long, narrow tea room, which was a glass-fronted extension. It had a lovely garden where people brought their children to have free lemonade and play, while the adults sat on old school benches and paid for their drinks. Even when I was very

small, I always joined in the fun and games, though many
of the children were older than me.

Beside the tea room there were lots of sheds and the
area of ground where my grandfather kept his hens,
pigeons and doves. There was one smelly shed I was
forbidden to go into. One day I asked my mother why.

'That's where they make gas for the lights,' she explained.
'So it's dangerous. You haven't to go anywhere near it.'
For once, I did as I was told.

As an independent three-year-old, I continued to seek out
new adventures. One very hot day, whilst Mother and I
were at our Goldhey Street house, with all the windows
and doors open to let the air through, I couldn't resist the
chance to have a little wander, as I often did at the Tanners'.
As soon as Mother noticed I was missing, she went round
to all our neighbours, looking for me. They came out to
help search the street, gardens and alleyways, whilst Alice
Fish, from the shop over the road, ran down to the police
station.

'They're sending a policeman out to help us find
Margaret,' Alice told my mother. 'They said for you to
stay at home, in case she turns up again.'

Mother must have been very worried about me, waiting
at home for news. But I was having a whale of a time . . .
until our friendly local policeman looked over the school
railings half an hour later and recognized me sitting in
the middle of a circle of children in the playground, as
they took turns to roll a ball to me. He tried to pick me
up, but I struggled and kicked and screamed.

'Let me go,' I wailed, tears running down my cheeks. 'Go away!'

So in the end he had to go and ask my mother to come and fetch me. When she arrived, she walked across and took my hand.

'Come home now, Margaret,' she said in as calm a voice as she could, highly relieved, no doubt. But I was completely oblivious to all the worry and upheaval I had caused. Despite her anxiety, she was such an easy-going person, kind and considerate to everybody, that she didn't tell me off that afternoon. In fact, I don't ever remember her telling me off for anything. Thinking back now, I know I was quite a handful for my mother to manage. I often led her a merry dance, but she was as stoical as a saint.

I was glad my father wasn't there that day. He would have been furious!

One day, I can remember my mother dressing me up in a pale-blue outfit, trimmed with white fur. 'Your father wants to take you on an outing,' she smiled brightly, in an attempt to give me confidence. But I was not so sure, as I was not close to my father and feared his temper. Now I realize Mother must have had her qualms about this 'outing' too, particularly as my father had never taken me anywhere alone without the rest of the family. I wasn't excited about the trip but he did make a fuss of me sometimes, giving me sweets and once buying me a doll.

So off we went. I don't know where we went or what we did, except for a vague memory of walking across Blackburn and going into a big house with a wide doorway, up the stairs, and being left in a room on my own. It was a small, pretty bedroom and I lay down on the pink candlewick bedspread. It was so comfy that I must have fallen asleep. After a little while, Father woke me up and we walked to another noisier building, where he left me sitting outside while he went in. Much later in the afternoon, my father arrived back home without me.

My mother frantically asked him where I was but he was so drunk he couldn't remember where he'd left me. Exasperated with him and worried about me, she had to send for the police again. He was probably too drunk to care. This time the search was much wider, as Father couldn't even remember where he'd been. There were a lot of pubs in Blackburn, so I could have been anywhere. I suppose I was always such a happy child that I must have amused myself in some way while I was waiting for him – playing with stones or making patterns with leaves, maybe.

All I remember is a kind policeman coming to find me, sitting on the bench where I suppose Father had left me, outside one of the pubs. I don't think I would have been tempted to wander away in a strange place. The policeman took me back to our house in Goldhey Street, where my mother rushed up to me, bent down and looked at my face. 'Are you all right?' she asked, stroking my tangled hair with relief.

I nodded. I was fine. Knowing me, I probably wondered what all the fuss was about. Mother made me something for tea and then helped me wash and put me to bed. I don't know what happened between the grown-ups after that. However, I do know that Mother was 'not pleased', as she told me years later, when relating the tale to me.

As I grew older, my mother started to talk to me about her past. She used to tell me how, as a young girl of about fifteen, at the end of the First World War, she used to bake cakes or shortbreads and take them in a basket down to the railway station at Daisyfield. There she distributed them to the returning wounded soldiers, some of whom had been prisoners of war.

'They were all bloodied and dirty from the trenches,' she explained.

One of those men was my father. Horace Holden was only fifteen when he joined up in the Sherwood Foresters Regiment during the First World War, and just sixteen when he was wounded in France and taken as a prisoner to Germany.

When he returned home to Blackburn, skin and bone from being a prisoner of war, he and my mother met at the railway station and started courting. She soon fell pregnant and in 1920 they were forced by both sets of parents to marry. He was nineteen and Mother was seventeen. He took a job in a cotton factory – it was a terrible place to work but he had no choice as he now had a wife to keep and my brother Bobby was on the way. Fortunately, two or three years later, his father was able to give him a better job, working in the Tanners' Arms. By the time I came along, five years after Bobby, we lived in at the Tanners' most of the time. I suppose it was easier that way.

I didn't usually go into the pub part of the Tanners' in the evening when it was very busy, but I often walked through at quieter moments in the morning or afternoon.

There were two or three regular drinkers I came to recognize, who used to smile or wave if they saw me. One of these was a lovely man called David Furness. Mother told me he had a large house overlooking the river Ribble but he spent most of his days at the Tanners'. He always had a skiver bag with him – a small bag, made of the finest leather. He laid it on the table, next to his pint, while he talked with his mates. Or sometimes he sat on his own.

One day, when he sat alone, I asked him what was in his bag.

'Why don't you look and see?' he grinned and pulled a chair round for me to sit on.

I clambered up and knelt on the chair, so that I could reach his bag. He opened the tab for me and I looked inside.

'What is it?' I asked.

'Empty it out and see,' he suggested.

So I gently poured the contents out onto the tabletop. 'Oooh,' I exclaimed as I saw the gold coins glinting in the sunlight from the window. 'Is it money?'

'Yes, in a way,' he agreed. 'But it's old money.'

I pulled the coins across the table so that I could see them better.

'They're gold sovereigns,' he said.

I turned one over to see both sides. Pointing at the head engraved on its surface, I asked him, 'Is this you?'

He laughed kindly. 'No, it's the king. He's better-looking than me.'

Whenever I saw him in the pub after that, he always let me play with his sovereigns. I would pile them up carefully to make a tower, or place them side by side in a row, making a pattern with them on the table. My mother even gave me some paper and a crayon so that I could make rubbings of them to keep in my room.

Like most small children, as I approached school age my life was exciting and carefree. I had no idea that frictions between my mother's staunchly Protestant family and my father's equally devout Roman Catholic family had existed even before they got married. In those days, Catholics were not allowed to enter a Protestant church or marry a non-Catholic, so my parents had to go to a registry office. Both sets of grandparents were very wary and critical of each other's religion. But that wasn't all. The animosity between them was much more to do with the circumstances of my parents' marriage, as my mother had fallen pregnant so young and out of wedlock.

As a young girl I was ignorant of these troubles so their sometimes strange interactions with each other just made me laugh. Grandma Holden used to peg a large sheet on the washing line at the Tanners'. I thought it was so the two sets of grandparents couldn't see each other across the fields. I found this funny, especially when Grandad Harrison got out his telescope while I was at their newly built bungalow in Salesbury and looked through it in the garden to annoy them at the Tanners'. Later my mother told me that the real reason for the sheet was to signal when we left the Tanners' to walk over to my Harrison grandparents' bungalow, so that they knew we were on the way. But I liked my version of the story better! Grandma and Grandpa Holden were older, stricter and mostly ignored me but Grandma and Grandad Harrison always welcomed me into their home and loved to watch me playing in their garden. I knew who I preferred.

There were growing tensions, too, of a different kind, between my mother and father. After my mother's frustrated reaction on the day my father got drunk and came home without me, things never really felt the same. Though they did try to shelter me from all that most of the time. I know now that there must have been a lot of pressures on their marriage, having been made to wed so young, when they had hardly had time to form a true relationship. I never witnessed any arguments between them but sometimes heard raised voices when I was tucked up in bed at night. One such night, in our Goldhey Street house, there was a knock on the door and I heard my cousin Billy's voice.

'I was passing a pub just as Uncle Horace came out,' he explained to my mother. 'He looked as if he'd drunk too much, so I thought I'd better bring him home, or there'd be no knowing what he'd 'a done next.'

I heard my mother thanking Billy in a tired voice as my father stumbled into the house and shouted gibberish back at him. That wasn't the last time Billy brought him home.

2

Family Frictions

1930

As my fourth birthday came and went, Father's mood and his drinking didn't seem to be getting any better. One morning, we were all sitting round the table in our Goldhey Street house – Father, Mother, Bobby and me, eating our breakfast. I can't remember who was talking, but suddenly Father made a rude noise. It made me burst into a fit of giggles. Mother gulped as Father's face turned red with anger.

I suppose I should have seen the signs and stopped there, but I was too young to pre-empt the consequences.

'You trumped,' I said in my innocence.

This enraged him even further. He shoved back his chair, scraping the quarry-tiled floor, thumped his fist on the old wooden table and stood up, towering over us. We all fell silent, unsure what he would do next.

'Don't you dare use rude words against me!' he shouted, pointing his finger at me, his eyes bulging with anger. He grabbed his belt, undid the buckle and pulled it off, winding part of it round his hand. As he took a step towards me I heard Mother cry out.

'You can't hit little girls!' She looked alarmed and upset. I'd never seen her show this kind of emotion before. Suddenly I was afraid.

'Right,' barked Father, turning to my nine-year-old brother, Bobby. 'I'll punish you instead.' Father took hold of his ear and propelled him outside into the yard, where he thrashed him with several lashes of his belt, till his anger ran out.

I cried and cried, but Mother held me back, gently but firmly. Finally Father let Bobby go, so he stumbled back inside and, with his hand on his sore back, he gave me a wink.

'It's all right,' he said, trying to reassure me. From that moment, I feared my father's unpredictability, especially his anger, and avoided him whenever I could. It took a long time for me to get over what had happened that day, but Bobby and I bonded more closely than ever as a result.

My father's drinking pals started coming to the Tanners' every weekend. He didn't believe in taking money from them . . . and he had a lot of 'friends', so it was free drinks all round. I used to stay away from the bar area when it was busy, so I never got to know any of them personally. I could often hear how loud and rowdy they were, though.

Grandpa and Grandma Holden, landlords of the pub, started to worry about the growing number of 'friends' arriving every week, so thought up a solution to avoid losing so much drinks money. They arranged for us to go away at weekends, when the weather wasn't too cold. We used to take the train either to Southport, Blackpool or

Morecambe, where we stayed in boarding houses. To keep the cost down, we used to take some food with us and the landlady would cook it for our tea.

I always liked those family weekends by the sea – Mother, Father, Bobby and me. Mother, Bobby and I played on the beaches, visited the piers, watched Punch and Judy shows and went for walks. Father would sometimes tag along but mostly went off in search of the pubs.

We used to take the train back on Sunday evenings, sometimes after dark. One moonless night, on our way back from Blackpool, Father had had quite a bit to drink. It was a long walk back to the Tanners' from Langho Station, along York Lane, which was unlit. About halfway along, Father suddenly tripped over a cow lying in the middle of the road. He said a funny word which I'd never heard before. Wanting to show off that I'd learned this new phrase I repeated it again and again as I skipped along. Suddenly, his temper flared and he motioned for me to come and stand in front of him. 'Don't you dare use a word like that!' he scolded. Surprised and hurt, I kept walking at a distance from him. Mother came and took my hand gently and I knew to keep quiet the rest of the way home.

I enjoyed our trips, but I was always glad to get back to the Tanners' on a Sunday evening. Even I could tell that things seemed to be changing, though. Instead of going to the pub, my father started playing cards for money with his friends at the kitchen table in our Goldhey Street house. Mother was 'not pleased', as she told me later, and I tried to keep out of their way as much as possible. So, if it was fine weather, I would go and play out on the street with the other children while Bobby kept a close eye on me. If Father had an evening off from the pub, I would usually be in bed asleep by half past six when his 'friends' came, though I often woke to hear male voices talking or laughing. Mother also had to stay out of their way, so she went into the front room, furthest away from the kitchen, and did some sewing or knitting. She seemed rather subdued around my father and his 'friends', but was always careful to hide her true feelings when I was in the room. I'm sure she must have shed tears when she was on her own. She certainly had a lot to cry about.

As tensions grew at home, my big brother, Bobby, used to go and help out at Veevers Farm over the road from the Tanners' after school and in the holidays, to avoid my father. He helped the farmer and his wife all through the year in their big creameries, stirring the vats to separate the cream, then the curds from the whey to make cheese. Through the winter he helped to feed the cattle in the barns and in the summer he collected the eggs laid by their free-range hens and joined the vegetable and fruit pickers. He loved it at the farm and spent all his time there, which is why I didn't see him much during the day. Every evening, though, without fail, he told me a bedtime story in the room we shared or sang me to sleep.

Bobby's favourite time, and mine too, was haymaking. That summer, he asked me if I would like to come with him to help.

I didn't hesitate. 'Yes please.' I idolized Bobby, so I felt proud that he wanted to show me the things he did at his favourite place. He took me across the road from the pub and I said hello to the friendly farmer and his wife, who always waved at me when they saw me in the lane. Their children were grown-up, so they seemed genuinely pleased to see me.

As they did at this time every year, the merry haymakers had come over from Ireland to work at the farm. I loved their laughter, their lilting accents and the Irish songs they sang as they worked. I remember giggling one lunchtime as I watched them eating slithery white tripe with their fingers. After lunch one of them lifted me right up to the top of the hay wagon for a ride, trundling along on the uneven ground with the prickly hay scratching the backs of my legs – I can almost feel it now. But I laughed and laughed at their antics, which I'm sure they put on especially for me. They let me join in their songs too, like the last bit of the chorus to 'Molly Malone' – I used to love singing 'Alive, alive oh!' That made them all laugh. Those were wonderful, fun-filled, carefree days – some of the best of my childhood.

Just after I turned five, my mother's brother, Uncle George, suddenly took me to stay in Blackpool with his wife's family, who lived there. Maybe it was to give Mother a break. He was the most successful of Grandma and Grandad Harrison's three children, as he helped Grandad to run the building business and was also an alderman in Blackburn Town Council. His wife Evelyn was often poorly, but she seemed better than usual on this holiday, perhaps because we were staying with her parents in the seaside air.

My mother had given me some spending money for the first time ever, so, on my first day there, I decided to buy some small presents to take home for everyone. There was a shop across the road from their house, so I went there to choose what to buy, paid and carefully took everything back to my room, where I put them in my own little case. It's amazing how clear that time is to me now. I can recall every detail – the colour of my leather suitcase, a patch where it had been mended underneath and a scuffed corner; the flowery cotton dress I was wearing, made by my mother.

Auntie Evelyn's sister Norma also came to stay at her parents' house for that week. She was very pretty, I remember, and her boyfriend Connor was Irish. The weather was so sunny on that second day that we all went to the Pleasure Beach to make the most of it. We had sandwiches and ice cream for lunch and Uncle George bought me some Blackpool rock. But later that day, when we returned from the beach, the happy atmosphere of the morning turned sour. My aunt and uncle told me to go and sit in my room and I knew something was wrong. I felt nobody wanted me there any more.

What I didn't know then was that while Uncle George took me for a stroll to the nearby park with swings, Norma and Connor had told her parents and Auntie Evelyn that she was pregnant. Well, that was a terrible shock for them. It was quickly agreed that, like it or not, Norma and Connor would 'have to' get married. Auntie Evelyn must have told Uncle George when we got back, as he went quiet, no doubt recalling the exact same situation between my parents . . . and the repercussions.

Sensing the tense atmosphere around the house, I got out my case from under the bed and packed my few possessions in it. Then I tiptoed down the stairs and out of the back door without anyone hearing me. My plan was to walk home to Blackburn. I didn't know how far it was or how long it would take, but I was quite confident I would find the way.

Of course, it wasn't long before someone noticed I was missing, and Uncle George came after me. He soon spotted me, a small child carrying a case and striding along on my own. He took me back to the house, but it was no longer a happy stay in Blackpool. I couldn't wait to get home.

A few months later, Norma and Connor's baby boy was born. Sadly, Norma died in childbirth. The family were devastated, particularly Auntie Evelyn and Uncle George. Regardless of their connection to the new baby, they snubbed Connor because of the stigma of unmarried pregnancy and his Catholic religion. Norma's parents really felt it was Connor's fault their daughter had died, so he was left to bring up his son alone. We never saw the new baby boy.

While Bobby escaped to Veevers Farm, I used to love going to my maternal grandparents' house in the countryside at Salesbury, about an hour's walk from the Tanners'. I went to see them at every possible opportunity. They were much easier to be with than my father's parents. I loved their house, a spacious bungalow built by Grandad's workmen, all beautifully decorated and furnished. The rural area that surrounded it was perfect for long walks through the woods and I would bake biscuits or play card games with Grandma when it was wet. I loved them. I thought the world of them. But I didn't love Grandad's silence punishment.

I don't know what I'd done to deserve it, but I do remember that, every Sunday afternoon, after tea, I had to sit on the chair in front of the clock on the mantelpiece and not move or speak for a whole hour. I wonder now whether perhaps they just wanted a rest. I tried to sit still and watch the minute hand as it hardly moved at all. I began to count the seconds in my head, up to sixty each time, and then see if I was right – had the hand moved a minute? I was frightened I might cough or sneeze – would that count? And what if I had an itchy foot? It was a terrible trial for a small, energetic child like me. After a while I stopped watching the clock and started making up stories in my head. When the hour was over, Grandad used to give me a shiny new penny. I wouldn't do that to a child. But, after that, whenever I couldn't get to sleep, I started counting seconds and minutes . . . and soon nodded off.

As I've said, this was not a family who openly showed affection. Neither side gave me hugs or kisses. The only time I can recall my mother being affectionate was when she cuddled me in her rocking chair when I was a toddler.

I don't remember it happening again. Regardless, Bobby always looked out for me and cheered me up if I hurt myself, and Mother was always making me clothes and taking me for walks, so I knew I was loved. They just chose to show it in different ways. With my father spending less and less time with us and my parents not being close, the idea of adults hugging or kissing each other never occurred to me. But one morning, while I was staying at Grandma and Grandad Harrison's house, Grandma was cleaning out the fireplace. She was on her knees in front of the grate and Grandad was ready to go out. I came into the room and stopped still as I saw him bend down to kiss her. I thought that was marvellous, absolutely wonderful. I was awestruck. I have never forgotten that moment. It was the only time I ever saw anyone in my family kiss.

Grandma and Grandad Harrison had three children: Mother, George and Elsie. We saw Uncle George every week and sometimes his wife Auntie Evelyn, when she was well enough. Mother's sister, Auntie Elsie, never married and lived with Grandma and Grandad throughout my childhood, though I didn't see much of her, except when she wanted me to help clean her shoes.

My father's parents were, coincidentally, born with the same surname, Holden, and came from Hurst Green, quite close to the river where my mother would take me and I would play with the otters. Father was the youngest of their four sons – Percy, John, Eddie and Horace, my father, but we only regularly saw Uncle Eddie, who lived and worked at the Tanners'. He was not the friendly sort and kept to himself because he was shy.

The other two brothers led more separate lives. Uncle John and his family lived in Little Harwood, close to our Goldhey Street house, and he was the manager of Bastfield Mill in Blackburn. He was always busy with work and lived a grander life than we did. He had a wife, Auntie Frances, and two children, older than me, but I hardly ever saw them. Father's other brother was Percy, who lived in London with his wife and his daughter Iris. I only ever remember meeting her once, when she came to stay at the Goldhey Street house and we went to the swimming baths.

Apart from religious differences, money was the cause of all the problems on both sides of my family. Grandad Harrison made a lot of money from his successful building business, but he was very careful with it, which would later cause rifts within the family. For Grandpa Holden, things were more of a struggle. He had to do his extra mills inspector job to keep the Tanners' going, so there was only just enough to go round.

Mother often used to tell me about Grandma Holden's brother Richard, who was my great-uncle. He started out home-brewing beer in his kitchen for himself and friends. As it grew in popularity they started to sell it from behind the bar at the Tanners'. Then other pubs in the area wanted it too. Very soon he expanded his little kitchen industry into a thriving business – the Nova Scotia New Brewery, well loved across the whole of Blackburn. The business was so successful that he made a lot of money and sold his company for a fortune to Lion Brewery on Coniston Road in 1920. As a Roman Catholic, he was a great supporter of the Church, but he also wanted to benefit his family with his new wealth. However, a bitter falling out with his sister, my stern 'cantankerous' Grandma, jeopardized his plan.

'Uncle Richard was so cross,' Mother told me, 'that he went red in the face. He said he had come to see her to give her and the family some of his money, but now he would give it away to where it would be more greatly appreciated.'

Mother paused as she recalled the scene. 'And do you know what Grandma said?'

'No,' I replied in wonder, hearing all this for the first time. 'What did she say?'

'She turned on him and shouted: "You can keep your money. I don't want it. I wouldn't have it even if I was penniless." Then she stormed out of the room and they never spoke to each other again.'

This was one of the first times in my life that I was party to such family gossip. Knowing Grandma Holden's reputation, and having seen her occasional fits of anger, I believed it all. A small part of me had to admire her too, for sticking up for herself, even though it left our family without a share of Great-Uncle Richard's wealth.

Mother pursed her lips. She seemed quietly aggrieved about it, particularly when money was always short in our household.

So Great-Uncle Richard gave all his profits away to the Blackburn Royal Infirmary, to pay for new wards to be built and more beds to be put into use. He also gave money to a few small charities and to the Catholic Church, who bestowed on him the honorary title of 'Papal Knight'. Shortly after this, he fell gravely ill and the nuns made good use of their enhanced facilities to nurse him through his final days.

It was generally understood that young children didn't go to funerals or burials, so on the day of Great-Uncle Richard's service – a Catholic Requiem Mass – Mother, Father, Bobby and the rest of the Holdens went to the church, while Auntie Frances took me for a walk instead, picking bluebells in Sale Wheel Woods. Later that day, as Auntie Frances and I joined everyone gathered in the Tanners' for Great-Uncle Richard's wake, I eavesdropped on snippets of conversation from under the tables.

'Do you know?' began one rather frumpy woman to a more elegant relative: 'Richard wrote in his will that he wants to have a solid stone slab, with a marble statue on top of it.' She paused for a quick breath. 'Would you believe it?'

'Well, that will keep him down all right!' said the other with a high-pitched laugh.

What a family!

A few weeks after the wake, Mother became ill with rheumatic fever. She had to go to the Infirmary for some treatment and children weren't allowed to visit. She was a patient there for quite a long time and I missed her every day. I worried about her too. What if she never came back? When Bobby was at school, nobody really bothered about me, but when he came home he did his best to cheer me up. Eight weeks later, Mother was allowed out and I was very glad to have her back home again.

'Was it horrid in the infirmary?' I asked.

'No. I felt quite at home there,' she told Bobby and me with a smile. 'The ward was full of beds with Great-Uncle Richard's name on the end of them, including mine.' She paused, with a look of surprise. 'And nearly everyone knew who he was.'

3

Gandhi in Blackburn

1931–1934

Not long after Mother came back home from the Infirmary, just after my fifth birthday, Grandpa Holden died suddenly. It was a great shock for the whole family. What would happen to the Tanners' Arms? While the solicitors tried to sort out what to do, Father and Uncle Eddie took over the day-to-day running of the pub. They rubbed along somehow, though they were never close as brothers and neither of them was much good at the management side of things. They must have felt uncertain about their future but they carried on as best as they could.

Grandma Holden could have taken over – she was bossy enough. But, only days after Grandpa Holden's funeral, Grandma Holden fell ill and was confined to her bed upstairs in the Tanners'. Mother took over the nursing of her difficult mother-in-law with enormous patience and care.

'You must eat,' scolded Mother, as kindly as she could.

Grandma just shook her head, with her lips firmly sealed.

'You won't get better unless you eat something nourishing,' persisted Mother. 'Is there anything you would like, anything at all?'

Grandma paused to think, then came out with a surprising answer.

'Oysters.'

'Really?' My mother patted Grandma's wrinkly hand.

Grandma nodded and added, in a weak voice: 'I always loved oysters.'

'Then oysters it shall be,' nodded Mother.

'Thank you.' A big smile lit up Grandma's weary face as she lay back to rest.

Somebody must have given Mother some money, as she bought a piece of the finest silk from the market. I remember watching her cut the material into squares before sewing two together with tiny stitches to make little pouches, with one side open on each. I couldn't understand why she'd made them. When they were finished, she took me with her to Langho Station, where we caught the train to Blackburn, then on to the fishmonger's stall at the big, bustling indoor market to buy a bag of oysters. As Mother paid, I looked around with wonder at all the colourful stalls, selling everything from fresh fruit to clothing. The different sounds and smells muddled together – I'd never been to a place like it! When we got back home to the Tanners', Mother removed one of the oysters from its shell, put it into a home-made pouch and gently placed it in Grandma's mouth for her to suck on. It seemed such a strange thing to do.

I can still picture the look on Grandma's face – a smile

of bliss at the delicious taste as she sucked the silk bag to savour the sensation and nourish her thin, weakened body with this very special delicacy. The protein from the oyster juice was what her body needed to keep her going a little longer.

As Grandma sucked on her oysters, she beckoned me and pointed weakly at a special little cupboard she had in the corner of her room, with silk curtains drawn across the glazed part of the door. I had noticed it before, but never knew what was in it. I would never have dared to look inside.

'Go and see,' whispered Grandma.

I went over to the cupboard, opened the door and looked inside, to find a large, decorated box. I turned to Grandma to see if this was what she meant.

She nodded her head with a slight smile of encouragement, so I lifted the big, heavy box out of the cupboard and put it down on a nearby rug. I was still a bit hesitant as I had never seen a gentle side to Grandma Holden before. Perhaps it was because she was ill. She watched as I opened the lid to see the most astonishing collection of golden jewellery and precious stones sparkling in the light from the half-curtained window.

'You can play with them if you like,' she said. Every day from then on, while Mother cared for Grandma, I played with these special jewels. There was an array of necklaces, rings and brooches, each embedded with shiny, colourful stones. I would inspect and arrange them into patterns on the rug before trying them on as if I was going to a grown-ups' party. It never occurred to me that they were valuable. They might as well have been penny-stall trinkets to me.

Grandma soon became too ill to speak and slept all the time. A few weeks after Grandad had died, I was sent out of Grandma's room while Father and Uncle Eddie came to sit beside her bed. It was just in time as she took her last breath.

Both Grandma and Grandpa Holden were buried in a private graveyard in the grounds of Stonyhurst College, alongside their parents and ancestors, just a mile from where they were both born.

After their deaths, everything seemed to change. While their belongings were distributed among the family and the inheritance was paid, it became clear that not everyone was happy. One day, arguments suddenly erupted between my father and his brothers. Accusations and raised voices were flying to and fro between the grown-ups in the bar area about 'messy dealings' and anger at the fact that the Tanners' had been left to Father and Eddie only. It wasn't a happy atmosphere for a child. Mother took me out of the way upstairs while all the shouting was going on and sat with me until Bobby came home. By the evening, things were simmering down and it was quiet again. Bobby read me the story of The Three Billy Goats Gruff and tucked me into bed. But as I lay down under the covers, I worried what would happen next.

It was just Uncle Eddie, Father, Mother, Bobby and me at the Tanners' Arms now. Without my grandparents it didn't feel right, and Mother was expected to cook, clean, mend clothes and tidy for all of us while helping with customers too. Before long, she fell ill again. This time I was told it was a very serious illness and I overheard Uncle Eddie telling Bobby: 'Your mother's rheumatic fever has returned and this time it's affected her heart.'

'Oh,' said Bobby in a shocked voice.

I was worried when I heard it was her heart. What if she didn't come back this time?

She was taken back to the Blackburn Royal Infirmary for about three months and I missed her terribly. When she came home, she had to stay in bed for several weeks. I was still worried about her. Would she die, like Grandma? I was so relieved to have her back at the Tanners' that I helped to look after her. I brought her a drink of water every morning and helped Bobby to make her meals each day. I took my favourite books into her room for her to read and I sang her some of the children's hymns we learned at church. She was still very weak but her face lit up whenever I came to spend time with her.

She did slowly start to get better but was far too fragile to take on the chores around the pub any more.

Instead, Uncle Eddie decided to take on a pretty young woman called Jenny from St Alban's Church to live in at the Tanners' and be our cleaner, cook, housekeeper and childminder. I didn't take to her at all.

Well, she started out all right, doing a few chores, but she soon set her sights on Uncle Eddie. Even I could see that. Consequently, she did precious little cleaning, housekeeping or childminding. Especially not the child-minding. I think I just looked after myself, as I had done most of the time since I was a toddler.

Jenny wheedled Uncle Eddie round and made merry with him. They got married and drank together so much that it didn't take them long to drink the pub dry. Customers stopped coming and there was no money to pay the bills or restock the pub. Eventually they had no choice but to sell up and find somewhere else to live.

Mother had recovered and was up out of bed just as the pub had to be sold. This left us without a home and my father without a livelihood. Luckily we were able to move back into our house on Goldhey Street, but Father still needed an income. So Grandad Harrison stepped in. He offered Father a job in his building company and, regardless of the animosity between them, Father didn't have much choice, so he took the job.

Following the sale of the Tanners', Father's friends continued to come round to our house to play cards for money every weekend. Father started building up debts, which he failed to tell Mother about.

'The insurance man called yesterday,' she said to Father at breakfast one Saturday morning. I was about to ask what an insurance man was, but I hesitated when I saw Father's stormy expression.

He mumbled something under his breath and carried on eating.

'He says we owe him three months' payments.'

'Who needs insurance?' he replied, avoiding her gaze.

'They're all money-grabbers. We're healthy enough. Let's keep it that way.'

Mother pursed her lips and looked away, keeping her thoughts to herself, probably because she didn't want to worry Bobby and me. But I could tell she was anxious.

We finished our breakfast and carried the plates through. Bobby started washing up and I dried, while Father clattered the chairs as he rearranged them.

The door was open a crack, wide enough for us to hear Mother's quiet voice.

'Are your friends coming this morning?'

'Yes, of course,' he snapped. 'What of it?'

She said nothing more, but joined us in the kitchen to put things away. She had her back to us, but as she turned to reach for something I caught a glimpse of her sad face. It looked as if she was close to tears.

Fortunately for Father, when the Tanners' Arms was sold there was a share of the remaining money left for him. He was able to pay off his gambling debts, much to Mother's relief. He then made the decision to sell our Goldhey Street home. I had some wonderful memories of living on the street, particularly of the times Mother and I had spent there in each other's company, so I was sad to leave it.

Father bought a slightly bigger house on the much busier Whalley Old Road, only five minutes' walk away from Goldhey Street. We all settled in there quite quickly and things seemed better for a while. Mother didn't have to worry so much about Father's debts and he was happier too.

'Now, we've got out of that house your father gave us,' he said to Mother. 'We're living in our own home at last.'

So they were both more relaxed . . . for a while.

One sunny September day, not long after we'd moved into the new house, my mother took me to see my godmother, Auntie Maggie, who lived nearby and had a sweet shop. I loved going to see her because she always gave me a scoop of her delicious home-made ice cream – a great treat, and while I ate that I could look at all the different jars of sweets on the shelf behind the counter. My favourites were aniseed balls and spearmint balls, both twenty for a penny or ten for a ha'penny, or you could have them mixed. I liked humbugs too, and chocolate bonbons. Her window was always beautifully arranged with sweets of all colours, including marzipan ovals, little Pontefract cakes, sherbet dips, liquorice sticks and coconut ices. Sometimes she would let me choose a few of each in a little bag to take home and I made them last as long as I could, which usually wasn't very long at all! Because it was so warm that day, I took my ice cream outside to eat, just as a group of people were approaching down the middle of Florence Street. This was unusual as it was a quiet road, but I didn't take much notice at first.

As they came closer, I saw that in the centre of this group of men, mostly in suits and some of them writing in notebooks, there was a small, skinny old man, draped in what looked like a white sheet. I'd never seen anyone like that before, so I watched as they came closer. At first, it looked as if he didn't have anything on his feet, but then I realized he had sandals on, with his toes poking out. He looked as if he must be very poor. I didn't really understand what was going on, but Mother and Auntie Maggie came out of the shop and stood with me to see what was happening.

The whole group walked on past, turned the corner and went off towards Bastfield Mill, on the corner of Church Hill, where Uncle John was the manager. Could they be going there?

That evening I heard Mother telling Father about it: 'We saw a little man wearing a sheet and sandals walking down Florence Street when we went to Maggie's shop today.'

Father looked up from his newspaper.

'On his own?'

'No, he was surrounded by several men and some of them were taking notes. I suppose they wrote down what he was saying to them.'

'He must be very poor,' I interrupted, 'if he has to wear a sheet!'

Mother smiled but Father tutted and ignored me.

'Which way were they going?'

'They turned the corner towards Bastfield Mill. Isn't that strange?'

'Not really,' said Father.

'What do you mean? Who could it be?' asked Mother.

'It says here,' he said, pointing at the front page of the morning paper. 'It says that Mahatma Gandhi was due to visit Blackburn and Darwen today, visiting mills, because of the Lancashire mill workers' letter to him. Gandhi is a very important man in India and he sticks up for the poor all over the world. He has come especially to respond to their letter.'

'What is the letter about?'

'Telling Gandhi about the damage India's embargo on imports of cotton from England is doing to our mills, especially to the workers being laid off because of it.'

I didn't know what the words 'imports' or 'embargo' meant, but I liked the sound of them, so I tried to remember to ask Bobby later.

'So that was Mahatma Gandhi?'

'Yes, I expect he was on his way to visit John's mill. What an honour.'

'Yes, it must be. You'll have to ask him about it.'

As I went off to play, I kept repeating that name: 'Mahatma Gandhi'. It sounded so funny to me!

That September also marked a milestone for me – my first day at school. I was very excited. Ever since I had gone wandering that day as a toddler and the policeman had found me in a school playground, I had longed to be part of all that.

I was five years old when I proudly waved goodbye to my mother that first morning as I set off with Bobby to St Alban's School in Birley Street. I was starting at the mixed infants' school, while Bobby, aged ten, was in the top class of the junior school, on the same site. We were divided into separate classes and playgrounds, one for boys and another for girls. From that very first day, I was in my element at St Alban's and made lots of friends.

I quickly found I loved learning too. From that moment, school was always a happy place for me.

A couple of months later, on Bonfire Night, my father was upstairs for a long time with Mother and another lady. Then he came down the stairs to see us.

'You've got a little brother,' he said, with a weary smile.

I couldn't believe it at first. Of course, I had no idea how babies came about. I grinned at Father, then turned to Bobby, who looked less surprised than me, but very pleased all the same.

'Another boy, eh?' he said to Father.

'Yes. Isn't that grand?'

The birth of my little brother Jeffrey was an exciting event and I loved him from the first time I saw him, when we were allowed upstairs to meet him that evening. Baby Jeffrey helped us feel more like a family again, for a while at least. I would play with him every day when I came home from school, so I didn't take much notice of the underlying friction that continued between my parents. Only a few days after Jeffrey was born Father's friends came round and money became an issue again. Mother would give him a look when Father handed over the housekeeping money.

'It's short this week,' she said.

'Well, it's all I've got left,' he replied, then turned his back and marched out of the house, slamming the door behind him.

Mother looked at the back of that door, hiding her face from us.

I know now that the missing money went on Father's gambling habit, but I don't believe I thought much about it that day. Times were hard for most people and there was a lot of poverty in Blackburn, as I suppose there was everywhere else too. I don't remember ever going hungry myself, but I did know people who were, including other children in my class.

Mother was always knitting, crocheting, sewing or mending clothes for us. Sometimes, neighbours and friends who liked her designs and knew her expertise as a seamstress would ask her to make an outfit for them, or perhaps to mend or darn something. She was also very good at making new outfits out of old clothes, perhaps a blouse from a torn summer dress, or shorts from trousers. She could turn cuffs and collars with ease. These commissions gave her a little extra income, on top of Father's wages, to put towards the housekeeping bills. Though money was tight, that helped us get by.

As the school term progressed, I grew in confidence and made a wide circle of friends. St Alban's School had a cobbled playground on a slope. All the older girls used to skip in the playground, so I watched how they did it and picked up a rope abandoned by the wall to try and do it myself. After several days of effort and a lot of tangles round my ankles I eventually learned to skip. This was a big milestone for me. Gradually my friends learned to skip as well and one of them brought a long length of rope to school so that we could have our own group skipping games. The only trouble was that two of us at a time had to miss out on the fun, and swinging the heavy rope round was hard work, which I hated.

Mother used to put an apple in my satchel every day. I would eat it at morning break. One of the 'Cottage Home' girls came up to me one breaktime and asked if I could 'stump' her and she would take my turn at 'twisting' or swinging one end of the rope, in return for my apple. I was very happy with that arrangement.

So I gave her my apple and watched as she devoured it, core, pips and all. I could see she was hungry, so it seemed a fair exchange.

What we called 'stumping' was more like a bribe, I suppose, looking back on it now. But I didn't see anything wrong with it at the time, as we both benefited. In fact, it still doesn't seem wrong to me; two children swapping for each other's gain. But I do feel bad that this girl was obviously not fed well enough at the children's home and I never thought to tell anybody about it.

Father was building up debts again and Mother protested in her own, silent way. If she ever voiced her complaints I didn't hear them. The atmosphere was becoming very tense again in our house, so Bobby often took me out with him, especially on Sundays, when the card-players came.

Bobby had the responsibility of going down to Grandma and Grandad Harrison's every Sunday afternoon to give their hen cabins a thorough clean-out, so he often took eighteen-month-old Jeffrey and me with him. Grandad was a lovely man, but a strong character who liked the boys best. Grandma was always gentle and kind. She used to take me for walks along the lanes, telling me the names of flowers and pointing out the different birds' songs, while Bobby worked. When it was time to learn the times tables at school, I told Bobby, so every time we went down to see Grandma and Grandad Harrison, I practised them. It was quite a long way to their house in Salesbury from Little Harwood – over three miles, so we used to catch the tram to Wilpshire, and then we walked the rest of the way, down the hill to their house. Bobby would carry Jeffrey while I skipped along, chanting whichever of the tables I was learning as I went.

Jeffrey seemed to find it funny, laughing a lot while watching me from his perch in Bobby's arms. I told him that when it was his turn, I would teach him the same way, though I don't suppose he understood what I was saying. It was an easy way to learn and I practised all my tables that way. They are still as fresh now as they were then.

Father's growing debts soon meant we had to move house again. This time he sold our Whalley Old Road house to Uncle Eddie and his awful wife Jenny and bought a smaller one in Whalley New Road for us to live in, so that he could pay back the money he owed. This meant we were living on a shoestring, with Mother often counting out her pennies, but once again it felt happier there for a while.

Grandma and Grandad Harrison used to come every Saturday for tea, so Father would go out after lunch for the rest of the day.

'Right, I'm off,' he called out as he slammed the door.

Mother rarely reacted, though I'm sure his attitude must have affected her. Father and her parents used to avoid each other as much as they could, but it was always a happy, relaxed day when they came to visit.

They used to bring with them a big ham for Mother to cook, that would last us a few days afterwards, and a whole basket of eggs, vegetables and cheese from their hens, their garden and a local farm. Their generosity helped Mother to keep food on the table.

When I had just turned eight, Bobby was injured when a motorbike ran into him as he walked along the pavement to school and knocked him over. After a couple of days in hospital he came home and Mother nursed him, but then she fell ill with another recurrence of rheumatic fever. With the doctor worried about her heart, the decision was made for Bobby, Jeffrey and me to spend some time away from her to aid her recovery. Bobby was taken down to Salesbury for Grandma Harrison to look after him while his injuries healed, and Jeffrey, still a toddler, was taken in by Mother's brother, Uncle George, and his wife Auntie Evelyn.

I suppose I didn't need as much looking after, and the school holidays had just started, so I was sent to stay with an Irish family who lived near Liverpool. I can't remember how long I stayed, but these people were very kind and made a lot of fuss over me. While I was there, they took me and their two children, of similar ages to me, on a special outing in their car to the opening of the new

Mersey Tunnel. It was 15 July 1934, and there was a lot of cheering when the ribbon was cut. After the opening ceremony, I think we were one of the first cars to drive right through the tunnel from Liverpool to Birkenhead . . . and back again. It was all very exciting.

It does seem strange as I think back now. The thing is, I had never seen these people before or since and cannot work out who they were. I do know they were Catholics and they took me to Mass on Sunday mornings, so I assume they must have been friends of my father's family. I never did find out, but they were lovely people and were kind enough to treat me as one of their own when our family was in need.

4

Kidnapped!

1935–1936

By the time I got back home to Little Harwood, my father's money problems had loomed large again. He had carried on with his card-playing friends in our absence, no doubt drinking with them as well. Money was so tight we had to sell up once again and move to a rented house back in Whalley Old Road, this time with a shop attached. I don't know what Father did with any money he had left over from the house sale, but I'm sure Mother never saw any of it. He was still working for Grandad Harrison, building new houses, but I don't know where his wages went either.

With the few things Mother already had, or could make quickly, such as baby clothes, cushions and gifts, she started up the shop, whilst also minding Jeffrey, who was then three or four years old and quite a handful.

With virtually no money, Mother could not buy in enough stock to set up a shop properly, so she tried to expand her dressmaking business, designing and making clothing on commission. She was a talented seamstress and designer, but in those days there was very little money about in Blackburn for such luxuries, so she took in mending as well. Sadly, business was only spasmodic and she didn't have enough time to do all her sewing and knitting while looking after Jeffrey, so the income barely paid the bills.

There was also another problem. Right from when we moved to the new rented house, my parents stopped talking to each other. It was a strange atmosphere. It made us all feel uncomfortable, as if something might happen at any time. It was always better when Father was out – which was most of the time – as Mother could relax for a while, though her sadness spread to Bobby and me as well. But things were about to change.

We suddenly started to have a lot of visits from a woman with bleached blonde hair who seemed to be a friend of Father's. She would arrive at different times throughout the day and was always wafting around our house and shop in a red dressing gown, smoking. I don't think Mother liked her and they hardly said a word to each other. I felt confused about the whole situation and nobody told me anything, not even Bobby. I think he must have known the truth, but he was very protective of me. I was like a mushroom – always kept in the dark. I just tried to ignore it and carry on as if nothing was happening.

A strange thing happened one Saturday afternoon, just after Father and the blonde had gone out and my Harrison grandparents were due to arrive for tea. I must have been playing in my bedroom and I opened my door to catch sight of my mother emerging from the bathroom, trying to disperse a mist of smoke clinging around and behind her. The smell was the same as the blonde's smell when she smoked her cigarettes. Was Mother secretly smoking? I could hardly believe it. But when I thought about this, I worried about the stress she was under. I wondered whether smoking would maybe calm her down. Perhaps she had smoked before and was trying to keep it a secret. I'd never seen her do this before.

One morning, when I went to clean my teeth before school, I noticed a grey pumice stone next to my nail brush. I'd never seen it before, so I knew it must be the blonde's. Was she living here? By now, it must have been two or three months after she first came to our house, and I didn't like her. I don't think she liked me either, as she never once talked to me and I had to spend all my time in my room, outside or at friends' houses. Bobby would go out with his own friends and Mother kept out of the way with Jeffrey. We all seemed to be living separate lives during this period.

I used to go to bed at half past six. Bobby would come up to my room and read stories to me – always about flying. His favourite book was called *Flying Aces,* about Baron somebody and other famous pilots from the Great War. Bobby was so keen on aeroplanes that the porch and the front room, where he slept on a pull-out bed, were full of model aeroplanes, hanging from the ceilings. He was always explaining them to me – what models they were and what they were used for. Some nights he used to tell me funny stories – jokey things, but never anything rude. Occasionally, for a change, he would sing to me to send me to sleep. The song I liked him singing best was 'Drink to Me Only with Thine Eyes'.

One night, after Bobby finished reading to me, he put out the light and left. I was halfway to sleep when there was a sudden explosion of noise from downstairs. I remember a lot of shouting and banging about. I got out of bed and tiptoed out onto the landing, but somebody, I think maybe Bobby, told me to go back to bed and stay there, so I did. I never found out what happened that night, but it sounded like a fight and the next day my father had broken ribs. I wasn't allowed to watch the nurse putting bandages on him, round his chest, but I could hear the awful fuss he was making about the pain.

A few days later, my father disappeared. In the morning he was there with his lady friend at the breakfast table, but when I got back from school he had gone. At first, I took no notice. I thought he would just come back again later that day. But he didn't. A few days later, while having breakfast with my mother and Jeffrey, I plucked up the courage and asked her about it.

'Where is Father?'

'He's gone off with the blonde,' said my mother. 'Together with all the money from selling our old house.' She pursed her lips with a firm expression, which suggested that I should not ask her any more, so I didn't.

I could only remember him going away once before and that was on a business trip to Jersey, for Grandad Harrison. So this sudden disappearance with the blonde did seem unusual. Though, thinking about it now, the blonde might have gone with him on that trip . . .

That night, when Bobby came to tuck me up, I asked him about it.

'Do you know that Father has gone off with the blonde?'

'Yes, Mother told me.'

'Where has he gone?'

'I don't know where,' he said. 'But I reckon it's good riddance.'

I was shocked. 'But why did he leave us?'

'You mustn't worry your pretty head about it,' was his only answer. 'Now tell me about what you did at school today.'

And that was that. Nobody told me anything else about it. I never saw Father much when he did live with us anyway, so I didn't really miss him. In fact, the tension seemed to have left with him. Mother was more relaxed than I'd seen her for a long time, despite her immediate money worries. I was old enough now just to get on with my life, both at school and with my friends. I tried not to think about what had happened at home. The landlord allowed us all to stay, as long as we paid the rent. This proved almost impossible for my mother, with so little income from the shop. Jeffrey would be starting school soon, giving her more time to work, so being the positive person she was, she soldiered on for a while, but it was a struggle to earn enough to make ends meet.

Despite her best efforts, Mother had no choice but to give up the shop. The rent for the house with the shop included was too high for her to manage, so we moved again and took on the rent of a more affordable small two-up, two-down terraced house, just nearby in Robinson Street. There she could continue making things for people privately, as she had often done in the past.

Even with less rent to find, she had three of us to provide for and virtually no income apart from the odd seamstress job, so it was tough for her. She had never had a job since she met my father, and of course she had Jeffrey still at home to look after for a few more weeks before school started.

Bobby was now fourteen, so he decided to be the man of the house and left school to work for Grandad Harrison, as an apprentice carpenter. Though relatively meagre, his weekly wage made all the difference for Mother. At last she could pay the rent and all the household bills without having to juggle one against the other. There was precious little left over, but Bobby's contribution removed a lot of her anxiety for the first time in years. Finally, we all felt happier in our new home.

Luckily, despite all the house moves, we had always been within walking distance of St Alban's School, so I was able to remain with my old friends.

I had quite a walk to get to school each day and home again at lunchtime, then back for the afternoon before my return journey at the end of the school day. On the coldest winter days, when the ground was covered in snow, Mother used to give me a basin of food, covered with a lid, for my lunch. All I had to do was to ask the caretaker if I could heat it up on his stove. Fortunately, he was a very kind man with lots of grandchildren and he always said yes. I loved his cosy little cubbyhole and warming myself by the stove. I mainly walked down a long road called Cob Wall, which ran along a high wall around the buildings and grounds of the Convent of Notre Dame, the best girls' school in the area. I was in awe of the girls and their smart uniforms when I saw them in the streets. Being a Catholic, I would have loved to go to the convent when I was older, but I knew it was an impossible dream. For a start, you had to be very clever to get in there, and I also knew we couldn't afford it.

One of my best friends at school, Winnie Binnington, used to walk part of the way home with me. Like many people in Blackburn in those days, Winnie always wore clogs. I suppose they were more hard-wearing than shoes. One day I was curious.

'What does it feel like to wear clogs?' I asked.

'Quite comfortable really,' she replied. 'Do you want to try them on?'

'Ooh, yes please.'

We were about the same size, so we swapped. She wore my shoes and I wore her clogs. They were much more comfortable than I thought, but it took me a few minutes to get used to them. Then I discovered something. I found that if I walked in a certain way, I could strike sparks off the flagstones beside the road. This was an exciting discovery and I loved doing it, so we often exchanged footwear after that. But I had to make sure that I changed back into my own shoes before I reached Robinson Street, as the first time I did it, Mother was surprisingly upset.

'I know a lot of people wear clogs in Blackburn,

including some of your lovely friends, but I don't want *you* to wear them,' she explained. 'We may not have much money, but my days of working in the cotton mills were long ago, before you were born, and I don't want to be reminded of them.' She paused. 'Now, Uncle John is a highly respected mill manager and of course Grandpa Holden was an inspector of mills, not to mention Uncle George being an alderman, so I don't want you looking like a little mill girl, wearing clogs.'

'But . . .'

'I don't like you wearing Winnie's clogs where anyone will see you,' she continued. 'Please don't wear them home again.'

'Yes, Mother.' I was quite shocked – I had never before heard her speak so vehemently.

One very hot afternoon, as I was returning to school after lunch, I noticed little bubbles, hundreds of them, rising up from between the tarred wooden cobbles that made up the road surface of Cob Wall. These bubbles were gas rising from the tar, which was melting in the warmth of the sunshine. I stopped, mesmerized, to watch them rising from the cracks. I just couldn't resist the temptation to pop some of them. As soon as I stepped on one or two, another five would appear in their place. Well, once I'd started, I couldn't stop. It was compulsive. I just had to pop every bubble. I stepped from one to another and another . . . hearing the sticky 'pop' as I stamped each bubble out. It was such fun, almost like a dance.

I was enjoying myself so much and was so intent on

popping every single bubble, that I completely lost track of time. It was only when I heard the voices and laughter of my friends approaching that I looked up and realized it was the end of the school day.

'What are you doing, Margaret?' asked Winnie.

'Popping bubbles,' I said. 'What are you doing here? What time is it?'

'It's home time,' replied Theresa. 'Have you been out here all afternoon?'

'I suppose so,' I replied, suddenly feeling guilty. 'Did anyone notice I was missing?' I asked, hoping they hadn't.

'Yes, the teacher asked where you were.'

'Am I in trouble?'

'Well, you might be,' said a quite serious friend, Agnes, with a worried face. 'But Melanie said she thought you had a headache this morning . . .'

'Oh, that was kind of her.' I knew in a way it was wrong, but I was pleased she liked me enough to stick up for me.

'The teacher might write a letter to your mother,' suggested another friend.

'Oh dear,' I sighed. 'I suppose I'd better tell her, then, just in case. I expect I'll be in trouble whatever I do!'

When I got home, I told Mother what had happened. I thought she would be cross, and she was. But she had a hint of a smile as she told me off. I wondered if maybe she had done something like that herself when she was at school. I was dying to ask her, but I didn't dare.

Sure enough, I did get into trouble at school the next day. I had to own up about why I had missed the whole afternoon and had to stay in at breaktimes that day to make up for the lessons I'd missed. Still, it was worth it.

A few months later, when the weather had turned cold and there were council workmen replacing some of the worn wooden blocks on Cob Wall that I had been jumping on, I saw a pile of the old ones that had been rejected and took a few of them, as many as I could carry, home to put on our fire. We burned one of those tarred blocks on our fire each evening for the next few days and they made a wonderful smell throughout the house.

The following year, on a beautiful spring day, the four of us were walking home from school in a dawdling sort of way, chatting and laughing. We came to the point where I had to walk on in a different direction from Winnie, Theresa and Agnes, so we stopped and chatted some more before I said goodbye and continued following Cob Wall. Only a hundred yards on, I was walking past some houses when a man came out of an alleyway and grabbed me – a big, ugly man with a beer belly and tattoos all up his arms.

'Help!' I yelled. 'Let me go,' I shrieked, as he held my arm in a vice-like grip. I tried to shake him off, but I had no chance against his strength. His face was set as he dragged me, kicking and screaming, down the alleyway and into a double garage in the 'backs' – a narrow roadway along the back of the houses. I kept hollering as loudly as I could, till he growled at me to stop. I was so frightened that I did. Why had he grabbed me? I didn't have any money. He plonked me down to sit on a large and

very rusty Nuttall's Mintoes tin. There was a horrible
smell – all oily and something else I didn't recognize,
probably paraffin or petrol, but it was very strong. I was
so scared that I didn't dare move. I started to cry.

'Shut up!' he bellowed at me.

'I can't,' I sobbed. It wasn't so much because I was
frightened for myself, though I was, but mainly because
I was wearing my mother's favourite scarf and she didn't
know I had borrowed it. It was pale blue, with darker
blue spots. But now it was all creased and dirty, the blue
so dark that the spots didn't show.

Suddenly, there was a huge commotion of shouting
outside and people kicking the garage doors. I froze with
fear. Were these more men who were going to come in
and hurt me? I realized I was in danger and couldn't see
any way to escape.

My kidnapper's jowly face turned bright red with fury.
The racket outside continued a little longer and the wooden
garage door was nearly splitting at the joints with all that
kicking and battering. I could hear adults' voices now, as
well as children, and someone called my name.

Finally, the hinges gave way and the doors burst inwards,
followed by my three friends, who had seen what happened,
and a lot of adults who lived near the garages. They had
heard my friends' shouts and joined the fray. I was moment-
arily surprised to see that one of them was my godfather,
George Watson – my father's cousin. But I didn't stop to
wonder how he came to be there. I just ran straight outside
and breathed in the fresh air, with my friends gathered
round me, as if protecting me. They were so kind. Everyone

was. As I left, there were some men still wrestling with my assailant and pinning him down, but I don't know what happened after that – whether anyone called the police or reported him. I suppose they probably did, but I don't remember being interviewed about it, or anything like that. Still concerned for me, my friends accompanied me back home, by which time I had calmed down a lot and could walk into my house as usual, as if nothing had happened.

When my mother found out about it from our neighbours, she must have told the rest of the family and there was a lot of fuss made, especially by Bobby, who told me to walk home by a different route in future. I was so naive that I had no idea then just how much danger I had been in that day. Thank goodness my lovely friends had witnessed my kidnap and rescued me.

That evening I rinsed out my mother's scarf. I knew how special it was to her as we didn't have a lot of money to buy pretty clothes. It was dry by the next morning and the pattern had come back, so I never had to tell her about that part of the story.

Only weeks after Bobby had started his apprenticeship with Grandad Harrison, I had a bad toothache so had to go and see a dentist for the first time in my life. He took one look in my mouth and sent me to the clinic to have a lower back tooth taken out. I knew the tooth was bad, but dentists cost money and I didn't want to bother Mother with it, just when she'd got straight. But finally the pain was too strong and I had to go.

I remember being asked to sit down in the chair, but I

don't recall being given any anaesthetic or pain relief. The dental surgeon started poking about in my mouth and every time he touched the rogue tooth I felt a sudden sharp pain. I flinched several times and once or twice cried out, as he tried to get a grip on the tooth. Finally, he put something on it and twisted it. Parts of the tooth came out in the tool and he used tweezers to pull out a few more.

Outside in the street, my school friend Winnie was walking past the clinic with her mother when they heard a piercing scream. 'That's Margaret,' she said to her mother. 'I'm sure it's her.' And it was.

I couldn't take any more, so I jumped off the dentist's chair, ran screaming through the waiting room, which must have caused some consternation, out of the door and straight home. I could feel with my tongue that I still had jagged shards of tooth sticking out and a sort of string hanging from it.

My mother was cross and wanted to go back with me, but I downright refused. I didn't want anybody to touch my tooth. Not long after, Bobby came home from work and he was furious, but I still refused to see any dentist to put it right, so he helped me work the tooth fragments free, little by little, over the following days. And whatever the string thing was, it was stuck fast, so I just chewed at it on and off all through the week and finally it fell away. I later discovered the 'string' had been a nerve – no wonder it hurt so much.

This episode put me off going to the dentist for many years, well into my adult life. I'm very glad that today's dental care is so entirely different and nobody has to suffer like I did that day.

I don't believe we ever got a bill for that tooth disaster, so we continued to scrape by with reasonable comfort . . . until the next big expense.

5

A Pinch of Snuff

1937

I was now in my final year at St Alban's Junior School, enjoying it and doing well, but I wasn't sure where I would go from there. I just hoped I could continue to have the kind of teachers I'd had so far, who would help me to go on learning new things and do my best in every subject. And, no matter what school I went to, I looked forward to keeping the friends I had as well as making new ones.

I was delighted when I was invited to try for a scholarship and I straight away said yes. That year, there were only two scholarships on offer for a free place at the Convent of Notre Dame, and I wanted one of them. I knew it was a very hard school to get into, and we couldn't afford to pay for me to go, so the scholarship would be my only chance. I didn't know whether I was good enough, but I had no qualms about trying my hardest to succeed.

When the time came, the whole of the top class at St Alban's Junior School sat the scholarship exam. I never liked doing tests but I worked my way through the English and maths papers methodically. I don't remember anything that was in the exam, except the final maths question. There was a diagonal line, with a complicated sum to do and instructions showing how I should work it out. But I noticed there were two numbers on the side, when the question said there was only one. I had just enough time left, so I worked it out both ways, first using one number, then the other, with a written explanation that I had done both versions to make sure one would be the answer they wanted. I closed the paper and put my pen down with just one minute to spare.

After that, we all just carried on for our last two terms at St Alban's. Nobody knew when the results would come out, giving the names of the lucky pupils who had won those two scholarships. So, after a couple of weeks, I stopped thinking about it.

On the way to St Alban's, I used to pass a tiny shop every morning on the other side of Cob Wall. One day, out of curiosity, I crossed over to have a look in the window. It was full of all sorts of tins of tobacco, things in tubes, cigarettes and snuffboxes. I'd heard somewhere that people take a pinch of snuff to make them sneeze. An idea formed in my mind. Wouldn't it be a lot of fun to make everyone sneeze in class? I only had a term or so left at St Alban's, so I went into the shop and asked how much snuff I could buy for a penny.

The shopkeeper laughed. 'What do you want snuff for?' he asked.

'As a joke,' I explained. 'To make the people in my class sneeze.'

He grinned. 'Well, how much money have you got?'

I put my hand in my gymslip pocket, took out the penny and placed it on his counter.

'That will do.' He obviously liked my idea, as he measured a teaspoonful of snuff onto a piece of white paper, then twisted it. 'There you are, love,' he said with a grin. 'I hope you have some fun with it.'

I placed it in my pocket and carried on to school. In the top class, our teacher was Miss Baldwin. She was lovely and enjoyed a laugh, so I told my best friends, Winnie, Theresa and Agnes, what I was going to do. They all liked the idea and, once we got to the bit of the lesson when we were doing some writing, I opened the twist of white paper in my lap, took a tiny bit, put it to my nose and sniffed. Then I passed it on. Within seconds I started sneezing, and so did the girl next to me. Before long the whole class was sneezing. Miss Baldwin was sympathetic when I sneezed, but her expression soon changed to confusion at the uproar of sneezing and laughter all round the room. We had tears rolling down our cheeks.

Gradually the sneezing subsided and Miss Baldwin regained our attention, so the lesson continued as normal. I always wondered whether she guessed what had set us all off. But the thing that really hurt me was that she didn't even ask who started it!

The weekend after this escapade, my mother received an official-looking letter in an embossed envelope with a typed address through the post. I watched her as she opened it and then read it through with a straight face.

Was this the one? She reread it, making me impatient to know.

'Who is it from?' I asked, as casually as I could manage. But she must have known I had guessed as I never usually took any interest in her letters.

'See for yourself,' she replied, showing me the letter heading. She was unable to conceal a hint of a smile, yet also had some slight hesitancy as she handed me the letter.

It was from the Convent of Notre Dame and, with trepidation, I started to read the first paragraph. Straight away it said I had been awarded the only scholarship for the convent this year. It was written by Sister Josephine, the headmistress, and asked Mother to pass on her congratulations to me for doing so well in the exam. I could hardly believe it. She even said they were looking forward to having me in their school. I was thrilled.

'Well done, Margaret,' said Mother, with her usual measured response. 'It says you scored nearly top marks in the scholarship exam.'

'I'm so excited,' I said with a grin. I felt like my insides were doing cartwheels. 'I expect I only got it because I did two alternative answers to the last question.' I paused, trying to take it in, after the long wait. 'I can't quite believe it. Isn't it wonderful?'

'Yes, it is very good,' she said. 'Clever girl. You have worked hard and you deserve it,' she continued. There was a pause while she read through the other sheets of paper that came with the letter.

'What is that all about?' I asked.

'The first page is the dates of school terms for the year

and the special days for religious closures, so that's fine,' she said, going through the letter. 'The second page is about the class you will be in and what you are to do on the first day of term. The third is about the uniform and other things you will need.' I noticed her smile disappearing as she quickly scanned the long list. 'The uniform is all supposed to be bought from a particular shop – Johnny Forbes.' She gulped. 'Or if I want to make your summer dress for next year, the material for that is only stocked by Porritts, so I expect that won't be cheap.' She paused. 'And all your stationery has to be bought at Seed and Gabbutts. Well, I expect we can buy some of it cheaper at the market.' Mother's smile had turned to a worried frown as she shuffled to the last page, about extra activities, which again had to be paid for.

From such initial excitement, I now doubted whether I would even be able to take up this precious scholarship. How strict would the nuns be about the uniform? Did I have to have all of it?

'I don't care about the activities,' I reassured her. 'But do you think we can afford to buy the uniform?'

'I don't know,' she replied with a shrug, then attempted a slight smile. 'But we'll go and find out the prices and I expect I can make some of it.' She paused. 'Don't worry, Margaret, I will do everything I can to try and make it possible.' I suddenly felt like Cinderella. Would I be able to go to the ball? And if I did, would I have to go home early?

Up to now, I hadn't considered any potential obstacles that might get in the way of my ambition, but now I knew these strict requirements could change everything.

I fervently crossed my fingers, prayed like mad and hoped for a miracle.

It was a Saturday, so Mother suggested that after lunch we should at least go to the uniform shop and look at the clothes and their prices. I sent up a few prayers that afternoon as we walked towards Johnny Forbes, the school outfitters.

I looked at the uniforms in the window – all very smart and expensive-looking. I was almost shaking with nerves. My mother opened the door and strode confidently in. I followed her through the doorway and was immediately hit by a strong smell. At first I couldn't work out what it was, then Mother leant over me to whisper, 'Mothballs.'

I couldn't help wondering: did all the convent girls smell like that? I hoped not.

Inside Johnny Forbes's shop, there were rails of uniforms for all the local senior schools, all with different colours and designs. I was sure that everyone in Blackburn must be able to recognize the uniform of the Convent of Notre Dame. We certainly did. Mother led the way over to the display in the middle of the shop, while I hung back, fearing the worst.

I held my breath as Mother picked up the first item – a dark-green gymslip. She didn't flinch as I had feared, but took a careful look at the fabric and the way it was made. Watched by the shop assistant, she then had a quick look at the price, as if that was of secondary importance. Next she picked up some of the other items of uniform, studying each in turn. She left the green blazer till last and asked me to try it on. 'How does it feel?' asked Mother.

'A bit stiff,' I answered.

'It would soften with wear,' she said.

I noticed that she said 'would', so maybe the cost wasn't an impossible demand. How could Mother afford any of this, even with Bobby's contributions? I was downcast. But then she did an unexpected thing. She picked up a school tie, dark green with pale-blue and yellow stripes, and took it to the polished wooden counter.

'I'll take this now,' she said. 'How much?' I knew she had already looked at the price, so I assumed she must have brought enough money with her. She took a note and some coins from her purse and handed it over. The assistant wrapped the tie in tissue paper and Mother gave it to me to carry as she led the way out of the shop.

I was puzzled by her purchase of the tie. Did that mean I could take up the convent scholarship? On the way home I plucked up courage and asked her.

'Why did you buy the tie?'

'Because it's made of a specially woven fabric, so it would be difficult for me to copy if I made it.'

'So does that mean I can go to the convent?'

'I hope so,' she said with a smile. 'But only if I can save up enough money to buy the material and make all the rest of your uniform; well, most of it, anyway.'

'How long will that take?'

'I don't know, but I'll do my best. I've got a few months before you need it, so I hope I'll get it done in time.' She paused. 'Now let's get back home and rescue Bobby from looking after Jeffrey.'

I was full of joy for days after that. I would have liked

to give my mother a hug, to show her how relieved and grateful I was, but we didn't hug in my family.

Over the years, my mother had learned to be very thrifty. That week, she walked into town and scoured the indoor and outdoor markets to see if she could find affordable materials. She saw just the right colour of dark-green wool at a knock-down price, bought it and straight away started knitting me a cardigan for school. She also put a deposit on a length of dark-green worsted to make my gymslip, adding a bit more each week till it was hers. She unpicked an old cream shirt of Bobby's to make into a school shirt for me, and we already had the tie, so I began to feel a little more confident that I might indeed be able to take up my scholarship place at the convent. I couldn't wait!

We had now settled well in our rented house in Robinson Street. It was a stone-clad terraced house in a row of thirteen, all joined together. It had iron railings in front, the same as all the ones in the row, a gate, a small front garden with a path and two steps up to the front door. It was a nice house, with sash windows. I've no idea how old it was. Quite likely Victorian or Edwardian. Inside, there was a vestibule going down. On the right when you came in through the front door was the front room, where Mother slept with Jeffrey on fold-down beds. Then down the tiled passage was the sitting room, with a lovely coal fire in the fireplace that warmed the walls all around and made the house cosy. The fire had a stand over it to boil a kettle or pan on.

The kitchen and the scullery beyond it were built out on the back of the house. We thought it was a good kitchen, with a new gas stove and a dresser. But, of course, it would be almost unrecognizable as a kitchen these days.

Beyond the scullery, we had a yard, surrounded by a wall, with our outside lavatory and a back gate that linked us to the 'backs', a narrow passageway between our neighbours' houses and the back gates of those on the next street.

Upstairs, there were two bedrooms. Mine was on the right and Bobby's was on the left, both with their own wardrobes. Straight ahead was the bathroom, with plenty of hot water from the sitting-room fire's back boiler. But it had no lavatory. The only one we had was outside in the back yard, so if you needed to go in the night, you had to brave all weathers in the dark to use it. Woe betide you if you needed it on a freezing night, when the water in it had turned to ice.

We had flower-patterned wallpaper on all the walls. The sitting room had a big leaded-light window. To the left of the fireplace was Mother's rocking chair, and a large, comfy fireside chair on the right. The mantelpiece was wooden, covered with ornaments, with a big mirror over the top.

My bedroom was my favourite place. It was a pretty room, quite big for one person, with chintzy curtains and bedcover and a rug beside my bed. I put lots of pictures up on my wall, so Mother called it 'the gallery'. Whenever any of my friends came round, she would tell them: 'Margaret is up in the gallery.'

At that time, Robinson Street was a road that petered out into a path at one end, so it was like a cul-de-sac, and children used to play outside in the street. It wasn't tarmacked or anything like that. The ground was just black and gritty. We played games like hopscotch and sack races. The coalman gave us a pile of sacks and we took one each to step inside and pull up to have races in. I always tried to be first and to pick the cleanest sack.

Across the road from the houses, on what seemed like spare land, were 'Howarth's Pens', with rails and wire fencing all round. Lots of chickens were kept here, out in the open in the daytime and in their huts overnight. Imagine, all the thirteen houses in Robinson Street had open land opposite them to look out on. The other two-thirds of the land had nothing on it at all, so we used to go over there and play. At one end, there was a gate to the Conservative Club, with a bowling green alongside it.

Mother's brother, Uncle George, was a town councillor and alderman for the Conservatives and one day he took me inside the Club building and showed me round. First, he showed me the Mayor's portrait in the hall.

'Haven't you been the Mayor?' I asked him.

'No, I'm afraid not. I was asked, several times, but Auntie Evelyn is not a well woman and she doesn't want me to leave her on her own in the evenings.'

I remember there was a grand staircase, with old men's portraits on the wall all the way up, including a large one of Uncle George. The upstairs landing led to a posh ball-room where they held their Conservative parties and dances.

I liked Robinson Street. It was a lively and safe place to live, with friendly neighbours and lots of space to play with my friends. After all the moves we'd made, and all the previous family troubles, this was a calm and secure house. It felt like a proper home.

For a reason I never understood, it was important to have our doorstep donkey-stoned. This was my job every day before school. Looking back on it now, it was really just keeping up with the neighbours. Everybody seemed to take great pride in what the fronts of their houses looked like, so each household felt the need to outshine every other . . . as if the world would fall apart if they missed a day. I thought it was a crazy thing to do.

'Why do we have to do this?' I once asked my mother.

'Because it looks nice,' she replied. And that was that.

The 'donkey stone' was a hard, rectangular greyish-yellow block, like a small brick, that we used to scrub the stone steps.

'Who started all this?' I asked.

'Oh, I think it was in the cotton mills, in Blackburn and all the other towns that had mills. I think it was to stop the stone steps in the mills from being slippery. It probably has the same effect on our steps.'

'Do I really have to do it every day?'

'Yes,' was her curt reply.

So each morning I went out with the donkey stone and some water to scrub and scour the two stone steps up to the front door till they were almost sparkling clean and a light shade of yellow. When I'd done it, I stood back and had a good look to make sure I hadn't missed a bit. I was usually quite proud of how well I'd done them, particularly as you could see the contrast with the boards round the steps. But not content with doing just the minimum, I often went round to our yard and donkey-stoned the back doorstep too, and all around the drains. Was that one-upmanship? Or maybe just me being a perfectionist.

Finally it was July 1937 and time to leave St Alban's Junior School behind. I had always enjoyed my time there and I knew I would go on seeing my friends, but I was especially sad to say goodbye to my favourite teacher. I loved Miss Baldwin. She was a very good teacher, and, oh! . . . that green hat with a feather! Unforgettable.

6

New Challenges

1937–1938

The summer holidays flew by, and as September began my mother had just managed to finish knitting and sewing all the uniform she thought I would need. She carefully laid out the various items on the eve of my starting at the Convent of Notre Dame. I was proud that she had done all that work for me, but a little worried that I had no blazer, since that was supposed to be an essential item. However, she had made a very good copy of the dark-green coat and saved up to buy me a new bonnet-style hat. Some more of the items had to be bought, such as the five pairs of shoes (outdoor, indoor, gym, sports and formal) and the essential 'extras' too.

I got up early on the first day and started to get dressed. Three days a week we were to wear a dark-green dress with white collar and cuffs. The other two were gym or sports days, and this was one of them. First my regulation dark-green knickers (which had to be bought from Marks & Spencer), my new liberty bodice, my crisp cotton shirt and then my home-made gymslip. Bobby had taught me how to fasten my tie, so I did that without much trouble. Then I put on my knitted green cardigan and finally my dark-brown stockings, which had to be attached to a suspender belt, worn round my waist.

Standing in front of the mirror to see how I looked, I couldn't help but feel proud. I had seen some of the convent girls walking to and from school in their smart uniforms. Mine didn't look quite the same, but nearly, and with my home-made but beautifully tailored green coat and my shiny brown leather lace-up shoes on, nobody would know. I was just so happy to be going on this new adventure that I thought it would do. Indeed, I knew it would have to do.

I gladly set off on that first morning, with Mother, Bobby and Jeffrey waving me off from the doorstep, wearing my satchel and clutching the expensive art port-folio Mother had had to buy for me. As I neared the school, I was conscious of not having a blazer to wear, but it was a warm day and I hoped nobody would notice.

I had reread the first day instructions the evening before and my first job on entering the school building was to unlace my outdoor shoes, place them in a locker by the entrance and put on my softer indoor shoes. Everyone else also took their blazers off and hung them on their allotted pegs, so now I felt less conspicuous. There was a nun who greeted all the new girls in the hallway and she pointed us down a corridor.

I soon found the right classroom, went in and sat down in a space next to a girl who smiled at me. All the other girls were new like me. And, like me, they all looked nervous but also curious; eager to begin our first day at the convent. I think I was rather more apprehensive than the others, who were all wearing their posh and proper uniforms.

A smiling nun entered the room, followed by a little terrier dog on a lead. This was a nice touch as it made many of us feel more at home. He was a lovely dog, friendly and well trained.

'I am Sister Magdalene and I shall be your form mistress for this year. Your class is called Lower III German and we will meet here every morning for the register, before you go to your lessons. First today, after the register, we will go to the hall to meet our headmistress, Sister Josephine.'

As we soon discovered, Sister Josephine was an imposing woman. She must have been over six feet tall. We stood in our straight rows across the polished wooden floor as she spoke to us about the history of the school. But I didn't hear much of it that day, as I was mesmerized by her height. To me, close to the front, it was like looking up a tree trunk. She terrified me.

Back in our classroom, Sister Magdalene told us which houses we would each be in. I was put in Ward House. This was specifically for when we were playing sports or competing for something. The girls in each house played against the other houses.

By the end of that first day, I had found my way around most of the school and learned the rules the nuns told us – don't run in the corridors, no hair loose below the collar, hems below the knees, only brown shoes, no loud voices (except for the teachers) and, most important of all, it seemed: when you see a nun, always stand still and curtsey. We all had to practise the right kind of curtsey, which caused some merriment and broke the ice. By home time, I had already got to know several other girls and a few of them walked part of the way home with me. My school life from then on was timed by the ringing of bells.

The twin-gabled stone frontage of the Convent of Notre Dame was an imposing building. Inside, I thought it was beautiful. The walls of the corridor to the chapel were covered in tiny, multicoloured pieces of ceramic tile, with a predominantly blue effect. I loved walking along it, running my finger lightly over the fragments. The chapel itself had such a calm, peaceful feel too. But if I was late for the morning service and ended up sitting near the altar, I sometimes had to leave because of the powerful aroma from the incense. On one occasion the fumes knocked me out – it was quite dramatic. Then there was the embarrassment when I came to, lying on the hard floor, with nuns and pupils gathered round me, looking anxious. But it conveniently got me out of prayers, because one of the nuns took me to a quiet room with soft chairs where she gave me a thin slice of buttered bread, then sat and talked to me.

Over those first few days, I settled into the different routines. There were new subjects to learn about and new ways to learn. Most of the teaching involved listening to the teacher, reading from books and a certain amount of rote-learning. But in some lessons we were also encouraged to think for ourselves. The convent homework of essays and equations was more interesting than the spellings and

sums I used to have at St Alban's, and we knew that high
standards were expected of us all.

There were thirty-two pupils in my class and several
of them came from abroad, so we had lovely long school
holidays. The teachers themselves were inspiring, kind and
always willing to help.

Miss McAvoy taught maths and geography – my
favourite. I loved learning about other countries and I was
always asking questions, quite often to get a laugh from
my friends. But she always had a sort of smile for me. Of
course, I was always near the top for arithmetic, though
I could never see the point of algebra or geometry.

One day I asked her: 'Miss McAvoy?'

'Yes, Margaret.'

'Can you tell me,' I asked as politely as I could. 'What
use will algebra and geometry be to me when I grow up?'

She paused, and for a moment I feared she might be
cross, but then her expression softened and she smiled.

'This is a school of social etiquette,' she explained,
decisively.

A fat lot of good that would be to me, I thought, but
I had enough social etiquette not to say it.

Miss Finnegan taught us French and German. I loved
French, but German was too guttural and full of declen-
sions. Besides, my mother told me about the awful things
going on in Germany at that time, so I didn't really want
to learn it. Being in a 'German' form, we had to say prayers
in German at the beginning of every lesson, so, with Latin
as well, at least I can pray in four languages! But I still
prefer French.

There was a story going around the convent that Sister Mary Brendan, our needlework (or 'knickers') teacher, was a titled lady. Apparently she came from an aristocratic family, and she did sometimes act as if she was from another world. She was obsessed with cleanliness, especially hands, so she was always dashing off to wash them.

Miss Wren, the art mistress, was quite a large lady. She could be strict, if necessary, but I think she just tolerated me as, although I was no good at art, I did try.

Miss Binks taught gym and games and I adored every minute with her. We all had to learn the old ballroom dances. I suppose that was part of our social etiquette training, but I loved it. The tall girls had to be boys and they had to ask us 'petite' girls to dance. At the end of each term we had a dance afternoon and wore party dresses. Mother, of course, excelled herself and made me a beautiful dress with a blue silk top and layers of net for the skirt, scattered with butterflies. Everyone crowded round me to admire this dress. Philomena McDermot, a close friend of mine, loved it so much that I gave it to her. She was thrilled.

As well as Philomena, I made several good friends and, from the start, I was very happy there. Every day in the convent's chapel, I thanked God for helping me to win that scholarship.

One day in the second or third week, my form teacher, Sister Magdalene, asked me to stay behind after school and have a chat with her. I hoped I hadn't done anything wrong. There were so many rules that I was almost sure to have broken one or two already. But it wasn't anything bad. Apparently she was speaking to each of us in turn, to make sure we had settled in all right.

'Now, Margaret, how have you enjoyed your first few weeks here?'

'I love it,' I said with obvious enthusiasm. 'I love everything about it.'

'Good. I can already see that you are doing very well . . . in most of your subjects.'

'Except in art?' I grinned. 'I can't draw for sixpence.'

'Not everyone can be a talented artist,' she reassured me with an understanding smile.

'I enjoy all the other lessons,' I said eagerly. 'I always want to know new things.'

'That's excellent, Margaret,' she said with a smile. 'Keep it up and you could go far with your studies.' She paused. 'Now off you go home. I don't want your mother worrying about you being late.'

I felt like dancing all the way back to Robinson Street, but I knew my responsibility as a pupil at the Convent of Notre Dame was to be demure and behave in a modest way, to keep the school's good name. We had been told this every day since I arrived, so I just walked as fast as I could, to get home and tell Mother what Sister Magdalene had said.

Every day, just like at St Alban's, I walked home for lunch and back again. The convent was very close to Robinson Street and school lunches were expensive, so it made more sense for me to eat at home. It had the additional advantage that I then wasn't free to take up any of the extra activities, like art club or piano lessons. They all had to be paid for and I knew we couldn't possibly afford it. I was useless at art and couldn't sing a note, so I didn't mind missing all that.

To my great relief, no one ever mentioned my home-made uniform during those first few weeks. A few of my fellow students may have made comments when I was out of earshot, but, if they did, I wasn't aware of them. I would have ignored them anyway.

As the dark, cold evenings drew in and there was less light to play outside, I started doing handiwork and making things. One of my jobs was to cut up Mother's old dress-making patterns into squares and thread them on a string that we hung up and used in the outside lavatory as toilet paper. As I did this boring task, while five-year-old Jeffrey played with a toy train by the fire, I had an idea.

'Come here, Jeffrey,' I said, in what I hoped was an encouraging voice. 'I want to show you something.'

Not wanting to miss out, Jeffrey came over and sat on the chair next to me.

'What is it?'

'We all have jobs in this house,' I began. 'Now that you're getting bigger, would you like to have a job too?' I asked him.

'Yes, please.'

'It's a very important job,' I explained. 'Because you have to learn to use scissors safely, and I'm going to teach you how.' So I showed him, then gave him the scissors to try. They were our smallest scissors, but it still took a couple of days before he could use them properly. Then I showed him how to cut squares and soon he was building up a pile of his own. One less job for me!

After tea one evening, Mother said to me: 'I'm going to teach you how to do corkwork.'

'What's that?' I asked. 'I've never heard of it.'

'I'll show you,' she explained. 'First you need this special bobbin.'

She handed me a cotton reel with a hole down through the middle of it, and four nails hammered into the top. It didn't look very special to me, but I'd never seen one before, so I watched as Mother took one end of a ball of wool and started to wind it round the nails, using a thick needle to hook the strands over each time. I was fascinated to watch as this started to make a sort of woollen string. She added in other colours as well to make a pattern down the 'string' that turned into more of a snake.

'Can I have a go?' I asked.

'Yes, here you are. Just continue to wind it round like I did and you can make a piece as long as you like.'

So that's what I did. It was quite exciting to watch the pattern change as I chose the order of colours to use. Soon I had a 'snake' that trailed halfway across the sitting-room floor.

'You can stop it there if you like,' she said. 'I'll show you how to finish it off, then you can coil it to make a mat or pot-holder, or even a teapot stand if you like. Later you could think of some other things to make with it.'

So, that first evening, I followed Mother's instructions

and carefully coiled the snake into a tight circle on the table and pinned it, so that I could put in some stitches to keep it coiled flat.

After that, I made lots of things we could use around the house or give as presents, keeping my biggest and best circle of rainbow colours to put on the dressing table in my bedroom.

Bobby was out a lot with his friends, so most evenings it was just Mother and me, sewing or making things together.

I had not seen my father since he had left that night and hardly ever thought about him. One evening though, I became curious.

'What happened to Father?' I asked her. 'Have you seen him since he left?'

'No,' replied Mother with a shrug. 'He's too busy with his blonde.'

'I wonder whether Jeffrey remembers him,' I said.

'I shouldn't think so, love.'

Jeffrey was growing fast now and it was fun to see more of him, to read him stories and to teach him things like the alphabet. He was so excited about his first day at St Alban's Mixed Infants' School, following in the footsteps of both Bobby and me.

While living in Robinson Street we'd taken in a stray cat called Gerry, who loved sunning himself in the street. One Saturday, Mother took Jeffrey with her and went to the local shops. Meanwhile, I was playing across the road with some of my friends, when something made me look back towards the house. I saw Gerry lying down near our front gate as usual, and I was about to turn back when I noticed something odd. It looked like there was a movement by his tail. I didn't know what it was so I edged closer for a better look. What I saw really frightened me. It looked like another animal – maybe a rat. What was it doing to Gerry?

I rushed round the corner to the little grocer's shop, where I found my mother talking with one of her friends at the counter.

'Mother!' I yelled as I burst into the shop. 'Come quickly. You've got to come.' I was out of breath from running.

My mother looked alarmed. 'Why, what's the matter? Is there something wrong? Is someone hurt?'

'It's Gerry. Please, you have to come. The rat is eating Gerry. It's eating his tail.'

Mother and Jeffrey ran back with me to see. I was frightened that we might be too late, that the cat wouldn't survive. But he was still there. As we approached and could see more clearly what it was, Mother's expression changed from anxious to smiling.

'That cat is good at keeping secrets,' she said with a laugh in her voice. 'So Gerry isn't Gerry. She's Geraldine, and she's had kittens!'

'Oh,' I gasped in confusion. 'So it wasn't a rat?'

'No. It was probably the first kitten.'

'I didn't know,' I said, confused.

'No, I didn't know either. I thought he was getting fat, so I cut down his food ration – and now, this.' She laughed again.

But what I meant was that I really didn't understand. I didn't know about kittens or any kinds of babies. Nobody ever told me anything, so I had no idea how they came to be or how they were born. I wasn't even allowed to watch.

Geraldine had four kittens that day, all tiny and cute. But that was the first and last I saw of them. I never knew where they went or what happened to them, and I didn't dare ask. But we kept Gerry and carried on calling her by her familiar name, as that's what we were all used to.

So, despite almost having witnessed the kittens' birth, I still knew nothing. I don't think any of my friends did either. It wasn't that, as children, we were missing anything. We just didn't know what there was to miss. We were all in the same position. Nobody ever explained anything.

The first time I saw Raymond Nash he was wearing shorts and riding a shiny red bike down Robinson Street and back again. He had medium-brown straight hair, a strong jaw and looked quite sporty. Raymond was thirteen, a year older than me, and almost a neighbour, living at the bottom of Coniston Road. I was friends with a lot of the local children, most of them boys, but Raymond was special. We just liked all the same things. His father was the manager of the main butcher's shop across from Blackburn Market. Ray would help out at a local butcher's in Rydal Road after school, and I'd see him in a striped apron delivering meat on the shop bike to houses all over Little Harwood.

We were a happy group of children, playing together

in the street or in the 'rec', the recreation ground down the road. There wasn't much on it, just some patchy grass and a small play area, with a see-saw for the little ones, which Jeffrey loved, roundabouts, a slide, swings of different sizes, some bars to climb, and ropes, knotted at the bottom, to climb or swing on. Through the summer the council employed a man to watch over the playground, to make sure children stayed safe.

For going to the rec, which I did nearly every day after school, Mother would never let me wear a frock. I always wore shorts. I lived in shorts and jumpers. And I was never allowed to wear my school shoes, so I had to change as soon as I got in, before she would let me out to play.

Ray and I were always the adventurous ones – especially me. My favourite thing was to swing on the ropes. As soon as I climbed halfway up a rope, the watchman would wag his finger at me and tell me off.

'Don't climb so high,' he used to shout at me. 'Or there's going to be an accident!' I always pretended not to hear him as I climbed right up to the top.

'Hold on tight, Margaret,' shouted Ray, the steadying influence to my impulsive nature, sounding just a little concerned.

Then I'd come down a bit, grab the next-door rope and start to swing. The girls used to move out of the way, whilst the boys stood in a circle under the rope as I swung round over their heads. I used to love playing on the bars too. It was good practice for the gym at school, and I was the only one who could pull myself over the top bar.

*

These were some of the happiest times in my childhood, both at home and at school, and, with no notion yet of what might occur beyond our little world, I looked forward to every day, having fun with the people I loved.

7

A Royal Visit

1938

We were sitting in class on the morning of 16 May 1938 when Sister Magdalene gave us some exciting news.

'As some of you may already know, King George and Queen Mary will be coming on a royal visit to Blackburn tomorrow. And the whole of the school has been invited to come out together and line one of the streets along which they will pass.'

There was a collective gasp around the classroom.

'So we are relying on every girl in the school to look her best, in full, pressed uniform with blazers over your summer dresses and immaculate panama hats. I'm afraid that anyone not in full uniform will not be able to join the reception line. Those properly attired and neat will have the privilege of seeing and maybe even meeting the king and queen themselves.'

I thought she was going to look straight at me when she said we needed to be in full uniform, but she was sympathetic enough not to show me up in that way and I was very grateful.

At breaktime that morning, the whole playground was buzzing with excitement . . . all except for me. I didn't have either a blazer or a panama hat – both far too expensive. So presumably that meant I couldn't see the king and queen. What could I do? I thought it all through over and over again during lessons, but couldn't see a way to take part, so I was very subdued for the rest of the day. I did consider hanging back at the end of school and asking at the school office if there was any spare uniform, but I didn't. I was too proud to explain my plight to any of the staff.

I came from a good family, a well-established Blackburn family, with both sets of grandparents running successful businesses, one of them also a mills inspector; two uncles were mill managers and another a councillor, plus a great-uncle was a Papal Knight who had endowed various institutions in the town. Mother might have fallen on hard times through no fault of her own, but she never dropped her standards and brought us all up very well.

However, none of this helped me when it came to the question of whether I would be able to go and see the king and queen. Philomena was worrying for me too.

'I wish I had a spare panama hat,' she said, as we started to walk home after school. 'But I haven't.'

'I'd need a blazer as well,' I reminded her.

'Not necessarily,' she replied. 'You're quite small, so if we squeezed you in at the back nobody would see you weren't wearing a blazer . . .'

'Hmm,' I mumbled. 'That's not a bad idea. Do you think we could pull it off?'

'Yes, I do . . . if you had the panama hat. That's all that would need to show.'

'Thank you,' I said. 'It's a brilliant idea and I'm going to think about it.'

That night, after tea, I played with Jeffrey and put him to bed, then went to my bedroom to read . . . and think.

When I got up in the morning, I knew what I had to do.

'Mother, did you know that the king and queen are coming to Blackburn today?'

'Yes, Alice told me.'

'Well, all the convent girls have been invited to line part of their route.'

'How exciting for you,' she said, pouring milk into Jeffrey's glass.

'Yes, it would be, but I need to beg or borrow a panama hat or I won't be allowed to be there. So, Philomena thought up a good idea.'

'What's that?'

'Do you have any spare change at all? I've got about a shilling left of what Grandad gave me for my birthday. If I can scrape together enough money and run down to Johnny Forbes, I can ask if they will lend me a panama, or sell me a damaged one for whatever money I have.'

Mother went straight to the tin where she kept the housekeeping money and gave me another four shillings.

'That's all I can spare,' she said. 'I hope it's enough.'

I ran all the way to Johnny Forbes's shop and stopped outside all breathless, looking in the window while I caught my breath. The shop had just opened and was empty of customers, so I walked in and spoke to the man at the counter – the same one we'd seen the previous summer.

'I can't afford a brand-new panama hat for the convent,' I began, in a rush. 'And I can't go and line the royal visit route with all the other girls if I don't have one. I've brought all our spare housekeeping money – five shillings. I know it won't be enough to buy a new one, but I wondered whether maybe you have a damaged or stained panama hat that you can't sell? Would five shillings be enough?'

I was breathless again now, but more out of nerves than anything else.

'We don't have any faulty stock,' said the man, in a snooty voice. 'So we won't have an unsaleable panama hat.'

'Are you sure?'

'Yes.'

'Couldn't you even go and look? Please.'

'It wouldn't be any use.'

I could feel the tears coming, so I ran out of the shop. But I didn't want to leave altogether. This was my only chance, so I knew I had to swallow my pride and go back in. I stood by the display of convent uniform and tried on the new panama hat on the stand. The man disappeared into an area behind the counter and I stayed put, hoping against hope that he might come back with something.

Sure enough, five minutes and a lot of rustling later, he reappeared, holding a panama with the convent's colours on it.

'Here we are,' he said with a smile. 'I can see you really

want to see the king and queen, so I've found you a reject that I wouldn't be able to sell in the shop. Look.' He held it out for me to see. 'It has a few darker pieces of straw, so you can have it for five shillings.'

'Oh, yes please!' I could have kissed him. I saw that the faults were hardly noticeable, unless you looked really close up. I handed over the money and looked at the clock on the wall. The girls would all be assembling at the school about now, so I had to rush.

'Thank you, thank you, thank you,' I yelled as I raced out of the shop. Breaking all the rules about behaving decorously in public, I all but flew to the convent, where I joined the girls in my form, wearing my hat and the green coat that Mother had made. I stood well away from the nuns, walking behind some taller girls, and, in the rush, they didn't notice my lack of blazer. When we reached our places on the royal route, we shuffled into place. True to her word, Philomena stood right in front of me so that only my head and my panama hat were showing over her shoulder.

Sister Magdalene walked along our part of the line, stopped in front of Philomena and looked over her shoulder at me. She fixed her eyes on the hat for a moment, then back at my face with a smile and a nod of approval.

As we stood waiting, someone distributed red roses, one to each of us – red for Lancashire – so we all had one to wave when the royal cavalcade drove down our street on the way to the town hall, where our head prefect had a space in the specially erected stand outside.

The king and queen were in an open-topped car, moving

slowly along as they waved to the onlookers at either side. When they reached us, they both looked and smiled in our direction. I felt so proud to be there.

It was the most exciting event in my life up to then. I couldn't believe it was real. Our school magazine later said we *made quite a stir with our light-green dresses, dark-green blazers and panamas, each carrying a rose*. If only they'd known!

At regular intervals in the convent, we had to have 'inspections'. They were nothing to do with our learning or our safety, but they had everything to do with the convent's strict rules about uniform. (Here we go again!)

Every morning, as we arrived at school and took our outdoor shoes off, we had to line them up with all our other pairs for a prefect to check that we had the right number and type of shoes, in good order.

When it came to the end of my first year at the convent, this worried me a lot. My feet were growing too fast! I had the right number and styles of shoes, but some of them were too small for me, so I had to push and squeeze my feet into them, with increasing discomfort. I knew that by the beginning of the new term in September, I might not be able to get them on at all.

I also realized that I couldn't ask Mother for so many pairs of new shoes so soon. She had enough trouble affording more than one thing at a time. Five pairs at once would be an impossibility – especially as the convent decreed that four out of the five could only be bought at Johnny Forbes, who charged accordingly. The only exception was our outdoor shoes, which had to be bought from a proper shoe shop. So I decided to ask, as soon as we had broken up, for just one new pair to replace my outdoor shoes, which were the tightest. Mother gulped, but immediately started saving what she could, so that by the end of August she had enough money and we went to have my feet measured, ready to buy the appropriate size, with room to last.

'Wait a minute,' said Mother. 'I've just realized. Your feet are now the same size as Grandma's and I think she has a pair of brown shoes she hardly ever wears. Let's ask her first if you can wear her shoes for school.'

'All right,' I agreed, my heart sinking a bit as I hoped they were not too old-fashioned.

'I suppose all your other shoes are too small as well?' asked Mother as we walked back home.

I nodded. 'Yes, they're getting a bit tight, but not quite as bad.'

'All right, I'll have to take on some more work,' she sighed. 'But don't worry. Now that Jeffrey is nearly six, you could look after him some days while you're on your school holidays. You can take him to Grandma and Grandad's to visit, one day a week. That way I'll be able to do more dressmaking during the day and I'll save up gradually so that we can buy one pair at a time.'

'Thank you, Mother. That will be fine.'

I would have done almost anything to help Mother buy my shoes, but Jeffrey turned out to be more of a handful on the tram to Grandma and Grandad's house than I expected. He made faces at other passengers and climbed over the seat to stroke a very hairy dog before pinching an apple from an old lady's basket when she wasn't looking. I felt awful about that and had to apologize for him. Fortunately I'd stopped him taking a bite out of it.

'Don't worry,' she said with a twinkle in her eye. Then she handed it back to me. 'Here, love. I've got plenty. Let him have this one.'

'Thank you,' I said, and I made Jeffrey thank her too.

The trouble was, he was such a bright child that he was inquisitive about everything. On one trip he even asked the tram driver how old he was. I was always apologizing for him, but people were very kind in those days.

On the last part of the journey, walking to their house, I used to get him skipping along down the hill while I taught him to chant the times tables, just as Bobby had taught me. He was younger than I had been and wasn't doing the tables at school yet, but he was clever enough to pick them up, starting with the easiest ones: two, five and ten.

At the convent, we had our hair length checked every now and then, to make sure any girl with hair touching her shoulders tied it back. Mine was short enough, but always curling round my hat. I tried to tuck it away underneath, but it kept popping out again. One particular nun, Sister Bernadette, didn't like that.

'There's one way to make sure your hair will stay put, Margaret,' she said, getting out her wire brush and using it vigorously. With my hair, I knew this wasn't a wise thing to do. The whole class watched as she brushed and brushed. Finally she stood back to examine the results – only to realize that my hair was now extremely frizzy and standing on end. The other girls could hardly suppress their laughter!

The length of our gymslip skirts were also regularly checked. The sight of Sister Magdalene with her long wooden ruler would fill me with dread. Each pupil had to kneel down on the floor, while she measured to make sure that our gymslips were no shorter than our knees. In the summer our dress hems also had to be below our knees, and as soon as I saw that ruler I used to start pulling my dress down as far as I could. It had worked so far, but for how much longer? At the last inspection at the end of my first year, I only just passed.

'Margaret, I think you'll have to tell your mother that you'll soon be needing some new uniform.'

I nodded, feeling forlorn, but determined not to show it. 'Yes, Sister Magdalene.' But I didn't tell my mother, not till I really had to. She was already saving up for my new shoes, after all.

Sunday was always a busy day for me as I went to Mass at St Alban's Church. I was a Roman Catholic, like all the Holdens, and having spent my early childhood living mostly at the Tanners' Arms with my Catholic grandparents, Sunday morning Mass was a way of life for me. My mother never came with us to church, as she was from a strongly C. of E. background; hence the past animosity between the two families.

I know my father was not the best example of what a

Roman Catholic should be, but praying in the chapel at the convent, and watching the nuns every day, my faith developed and grew. Gradually I passed it on to Jeffrey as well. I'd take him with me to Sunday morning Mass, then we caught the tram and walked the rest of the way down to Grandma and Grandad Harrison's house. As well as visiting them, my weekly task, unpaid, was to clean all of Auntie Elsie's shoes. Elsie was my mother's younger sister, who had never married and still lived with Grandma and Grandad. She had shoes of many colours and I had to clean them all for her. I don't know why she didn't clean them herself.

We stayed for a lovely roast lunch, then took the tram back home to Blackburn. Bobby didn't come with us because he was now a dedicated member of the local model aeroplane club. Every Sunday afternoon they would all go to the flying field, which was on the farm at the side of the New Inn pub, or in one of their barns if it rained. One weekend at breakfast time, Bobby had an idea.

'You're good at arithmetic, Margaret. We need an official timekeeper at the flying field. Why don't you come with me one Sunday and see what it's like?'

I adored my big brother Bobby, so the fact that he thought I could do something like that for him and his friends was a tremendous boost to my self-esteem.

'Yes please. I'd love to come and keep the times.'

So, from then on, I went to join him and his pals every Sunday afternoon. I loved it. At the end of my first session, Ernie Aspinall gave me the title of 'official timekeeper' and enrolled me as the only female in their club. Every week, the boys brought along the model aircraft they had made. Each of them in turn wound up their plane with rubber bands, set it off and I timed its flight.

One rainy Sunday afternoon in 1938, when we were messing around in the barn, the boys seemed to notice that I was growing up. It was quite funny really, as they started to be polite and actually talk to me.

Most of the model aircraft were quite small, but once someone brought along a petrol model with a six-foot wingspan. Off it went, soaring into the air like an eagle . . . but it flew so well and so far that we quickly lost track of it. Later in the afternoon, we discovered that it had flown off towards Accrington, where the military defence chaps spotted it and, knowing that an international conflict was looming, and suspecting it might be an alien spy plane, followed it with their binoculars, but it crashed before they could shoot it down.

The plane had to be accounted for and collected from its crash site in a farmer's field. Bobby, Ernie and the other boys were working late on the Monday, so Bobby's great pal Gordon Fudge brought his tandem and I agreed to go with him. I had always liked Gordon, although he was six years older than me. He was tall, with curly reddish hair and a friendly smile. He worked at the tea warehouse in Blackburn and used to bring me stickers off the crates from India, Ceylon and other countries. Gordon was born and brought up in Scotland, but his grandmother lived in Blackburn, so he had moved south to keep her company. He must have been such a help to her.

We set off at teatime and arrived half an hour later at the farm, where we were taken to the site of the crash. There, in a forlorn heap on the ground, was the suspect model-kit plane. Only its nose and parts of the wings were recognizable. Everything else had fallen apart.

We loaded all the smaller pieces into the large basket on the front and the panniers at the back and got back on the tandem. If I hadn't been so anxious not to drop or damage anything, I would have seen the funny side of it – Gordon pedalling away as hard as he could to carry both our weights as well as the smashed-up plane, with me sitting on the back seat, trying desperately to hold on to all the larger parts, all the way back to Blackburn.

Despite the five-year difference in our ages, that was when Bobby started to see me as not just a child to protect, but also a part of his world, if only for a relatively short time.

That year, 1938, I spent most of the summer holidays outside playing with my friends, particularly Ray, who always used to call for me. He was good fun. We laughed at the same things, so when the rest of the group weren't there, we would just go for walks or bike rides together, and we got to know each other's parents quite well, so they were happy for us to visit each other's houses when it rained. In fact, Ray was at our house so often that Mother was quite amused.

'He's like another son,' she said with a laugh.

Ray was a dab hand at most of the dice games, like 'Snakes and Ladders', that we always played with Jeffrey.

One day Ray brought round a brand-new board game called 'Monopoly' and Mother joined us to play, helping five-year-old Jeffrey to 'buy' houses. Ray also loved card games and he even taught Jeffrey to play poker, just for fun of course, though I'm not sure what Mother thought of that.

These were good times and, still only twelve, I was hardly aware that Britain's relationship with Hitler's Germany was fractious and that a war was becoming more and more likely. Unlike my parents, I had never lived through a war, so I had little idea how that might change our lives. For now, I let it all simmer in the background while I enjoyed the rest of my summer break.

8

'Look, Duck and Vanish'

1938–1939

Five empty lockers, with names removed; five empty spaces in the classroom. Most of us had come back to school chattering nineteen to the dozen, but now our voices were hushed. What could have happened? Our new form teacher, Miss Wilson, came in and, before we had the chance even to speculate about this mystery, she gently broke it to us:

'Good morning, girls, and welcome back for the new school year.' She paused, taking a deep breath. 'As you can see, we have some empty desks. I'm very sad to have to tell you that five of your friends have died during the summer holidays. I'm afraid I don't know any more, but I'm sure you will want to remember them all in your prayers.'

One of the girls, Anastasia Long, was quite small and was not very good at games, but excelled in her other subjects. Another was Eileen Parkinson, who was very, very good at drawing. They were both lovely girls and I couldn't believe they were gone. It was a subdued atmosphere that first day of term as we all went to the chapel to pray for their souls. Most of us had not previously experienced the death of someone we knew in our own age group, someone who was part of our everyday life.

I was now in Upper III German and continued to do well – usually near the top of the class, especially in arithmetic. But I was also the class joker. I loved acting and was in all the plays we put on, including *A Midsummer Night's Dream*. With so much going on, this term seemed to go by quickly, now that it was my second year at the convent.

Walking to and from school each day I passed Plane Street, where there was a row of shops. One of them was Sellers' Butcher's, where a boy called Clarence Charnley worked. Most people called him Clarry and he was three years older than me.

It seemed that Clarry was well aware of me going to school, backwards and forwards each day. I was only twelve, but I must have looked older, despite the uniform. Four times a day I went past that shop and it felt as if Clarry was always standing outside, waiting for me to walk by. Initially, he just smiled at me, but then he started to whistle, wave and call out to me every time. I used to put my head down and walk swiftly past, trying to ignore him, but with a small smile on my face.

As I eased myself back into school rules and routines after our carefree summer, my brother Bobby and his pal Gordon Fudge joined the Civil Air Guard at weekends so that they could learn to fly. Every Saturday morning, they cycled the twenty-five miles to Squires Gate airfield near Blackpool, making the same journey back again in the evening. Before long, both of them applied to join the RAF. Gordon gained his wings, but his medical found him slightly deaf in one ear and the RAF turned him down. Poor Gordon. I did feel sorry for him as it must have been quite a stigma at that time, especially since Bobby passed the medical, and was in training to gain his wings. He was soon accepted by the RAF.

Bobby had completed five years of his carpentry apprenticeship, so just before he turned eighteen he joined up. He was extremely excited at the thought of becoming an RAF pilot but his happiness was short-lived, as they refused him pilot training. When he asked his commanding officer why, he was told that it would take only six weeks to train him as an RAF pilot, whereas it takes five years or more to train a carpenter. They were desperately in need of fully trained carpenters to build and repair their wooden Mosquito aircraft and he was already well on the way to having the relevant qualifications.

Once he was reconciled to his initial disappointment, Bobby made some new friends, in particular one called Arthur Isherwood, who was training to be an aerial photographer. The RAF certainly kept my brother busy from the outset and he made good use of the excellent carpentry skills he had learned in Grandad Harrison's workshop and building sites. He was always away from home now, either at his base or working on airfields around the country. I worried about him and I know Mother did

too, in case anything should happen to him. I missed him
terribly. It was a miserable time. My father had left us
and now I had lost my big brother as well. But Bobby
was very good, as he continued to send part of his RAF
pay to Mother every month and wrote letters to both of
us. The letters he sent to me were full of questions about
what I had been doing and instructions on what I shouldn't
be doing, such as not going out except with Mother or
to school or church. It was as if he had put me in a tin
when he left and he didn't want me to get out of it till
he got home again. I knew it was because he loved me,
but I didn't tell him half of what I did. Bobby came home
on leave whenever he could, often with a toy for Jeffrey
and a bracelet or other special present for me. We were
all glad to have him home each time, but it was difficult
for me as, now I was older, he just wanted to follow me
around all the time, keeping an eye on me.

As the new year of 1939 dawned, tensions were rising in
political circles, if the headlines on newspaper sellers' boards
were anything to go by. Many of the younger working men
were being put on the army's reserve lists, and some began
to enlist in the forces, to train in earnest. Several of the
men of Blackburn, conscious of the talk of a coming war,
got together at weekends or during the evenings to start
training, just in case. Every now and then, on fine days, we
used to see these middle-aged men marching up and down
the streets or lanes practising drills, old brooms on their
shoulders, always with at least one of them woefully out
of step. They called themselves the Local Defence Volunteers.

It looked quite comical to Ray and me as we sat on a wall and watched them passing by, whilst others with enormous tubas, French horns and drums played them on, seriously out of tune. We giggled at their uncoordinated efforts, but I don't think the prospect of war troubled us much at that stage, if at all. We couldn't imagine it would ever really happen.

More worrying for me was my shrinking convent uniform – I was growing too fast! So, to help Mother out with our finances, I decided it was time for me to take on some part-time jobs. On Friday nights, I went round collecting payments for a dentist. I recognized the irony of that, having had such trouble with my teeth when I was younger, but I quite liked the job as I could chat to people.

On Saturday afternoons I'd taken a job covering buttons for the 'Holidays' stall in the market hall in the centre of Blackburn. It was run by two glamorous sisters, selling haberdashery such as ribbons, threads, buttons and zips. My task was to sit at the stall and cover buttons to order. Customers would bring me a piece of their dress material and ask me to make buttons out of it. I had a little gadget that helped me punch the fabric over each of the little metal discs and they looked lovely when I'd finished. It was just the one afternoon each week and for that I was paid five shillings, which was half a week's wages for some people, so I did very well. The market hall was always so full of life, with its little cafes, high-class groceries and butchers.

*

In the summer of 1939, during Blackburn's Wakes Week, when the mills and factories were closed for their annual maintenance, Bobby and his pal Arthur had a week's leave, so he paid for Mother, her friend Alice, Jeffrey and me to join the two of them for a week's holiday in Blackpool. It was excellent timing, as it turned out. We stayed at a good boarding-house and the friendly land-lady was happy for us to buy our own food, which she cooked for us. We had done the same thing in previous childhood visits, to keep the costs down. It had rained a lot in Blackpool for the two weeks before our visit, but the week we were there it was dry every day, so we took Jeffrey on the beach and he had a ride on a donkey for the first time. Knowing this might be the last carefree holiday we could all have for a while, we made the most of the time together. War was becoming almost inevitable now.

As soon as we were back home again, Mother was suddenly in demand. This time not as a dressmaker, but rather a blackout-curtain maker. We had various neigh-bours' and friends' bales of blackout material stacked all over the house, ready for Mother to make up into curtains to fit their windows snugly.

Nobody knew quite when the war might happen, but the talk was non-stop and there seemed little doubt that it would, so the government was urging all citizens to be prepared. We were allocated rolls of gummed brown paper to tape up our windows with diagonals or criss-cross lines making diamond or square shapes, so that if a bomb fell nearby, it might not shatter the glass and injure anyone.

Well, that was the idea, anyway, but I couldn't see how a few strips of thin brown paper could block out the lethal power of an exploding bomb.

It was rather worrying in a way, but I was such an optimist that I really didn't think it would affect us in Blackburn. Mother must have been anxious, however, even though she didn't show it. I once overheard her talking about the coming war with one of her friends. They were discussing what might happen if the Germans came over to Blackburn and tried to take their daughters away. I didn't like the sound of that!

By late August the Local Defence Volunteers were out every day practising their marching, and generally making a nuisance of themselves.

'Look at their medals,' I said to Ray as we stopped to watch them in the square. 'Some of them must have fought in the First World War.'

'Yes, and some of them are so old, they were probably in the Boer War too!'

We watched them getting in a bit of a muddle, doing some sort of manoeuvre.

'Do you know what my father calls the Local Defence Volunteers?' he asked.

'No, what does he call them?'

'Well, their initials are L.D.V., so he and his friends call them "Look, Duck and Vanish". Don't you think that's a good name for them?'

'Yes.' We laughed and walked on.

As war loomed, the LDV became the Home Guard,

which Ray's father was in and Ray had just joined as well. Some of them were also training to become air-raid wardens, preparing themselves for the worst so that they could do 'save and rescue' duties. But few of them had been issued with their uniforms yet, or any proper equipment.

On Friday, 1 September, I was walking into town when I passed a newspaper hoarding which said Germany had invaded Poland. I didn't know much about politics, but I knew that was serious.

Later in the day, on my way home, I saw a forlorn group of children with labels around their necks and their gas-mask boxes across their chests, carrying small suitcases. Some of the youngest were holding older siblings' hands and carrying teddy bears. There were a few adults with them, leading them into a big building.

When I got home, I asked Mother if she knew about them.

'They must be evacuees,' she said. 'I think they arrived today at the station and now they have to be found places to stay. When I went to the shop, some of the locals were talking about it. Apparently, most of these children come from Manchester . . . or was it London? They will be given temporary homes in farms and country houses outside Blackburn.'

'Like Grandma and Grandad's?'

'No. Their house is probably too small, with Elsie living in their main spare room.'

'Why not in the town?' I was curious.

'Because Blackburn is a city and the Germans will probably target urban areas, so it might not be much better than where they came from.'

'But we're not even at war yet, are we?'

'No, but Hitler has invaded Poland now . . .'

'Yes, I saw that on the newspaper seller's board this morning.'

'So, it can't be long,' she said quietly, putting on our tea, while I read a book with Jeffrey.

That Sunday morning, 3 September 1939, I took Jeffrey to Mass at St Alban's Church as usual, completely unaware that this day would be different from any other Sunday. I did notice that there seemed to be a few of the regular congregation missing, but that was all . . . till we came out of the church and saw the street full of Home Guard men, including Ray himself and his father, out on parade.

I was amazed. It was the first time I'd seen Ray in that role, alongside some of the other boys from the neighbourhood, and the grown-ups. He looked across and gave me a rueful smile. It was quite amusing really, after all the fun we had made of these would-be soldiers, often called 'Dad's Army'. Now he was one himself.

There was a buzz of conversation and I kept hearing the words, 'war with Germany', 'Hitler' and 'Chamberlain'.

'Why are there so many soldiers?' asked Jeffrey, watching them with evident excitement. 'I want to be a soldier too.'

Before I could say anything, one of the church ladies

standing nearby said: 'I think we must be at war, dear. And you're too young to be a soldier.' And then she turned to me. 'I just heard somebody saying that Neville Chamberlain was on the radio, talking about it.' She paused, looking distracted. 'Perhaps we'd all better go home and find out for ourselves.'

Sure enough, instead of standing and talking for ages outside the church as some of the grown-ups usually did, they moved away very quickly, hurrying off in search of news.

From that day on, almost every time I went into the town, I was stopped by one of the LDV or the Home Guard, checking that I was carrying my gas mask and my identity card. Mother had had to fill in a form about how many lived in our house and the children's ages. Once she'd sent that in, we had our gas masks in their boxes and identity cards delivered to the house, including a small gas mask for Jeffrey. At the beginning, I often got into trouble because I had forgotten to bring them with me wherever I went. I'm sure I wasn't the only one.

Early the next week we had a leaflet through our door about what to do if the sirens went. Both Mother and I read it through, but hoped we wouldn't need it. However, days later, the sirens sounded loudly across Blackburn and we all had to follow the instructions to 'take cover'. This wasn't very helpful, but we knew that under the stairs must be the safest place, so that's where we went, all squeezing into the cupboard and closing the door. We didn't know it was only a practice run, but at least now we'd done it. We'd be ready for a real air-raid warning, if it came.

As we hid under the stairs, I asked Mother, 'Surely the war won't last long? It's a real nuisance, having to leave everything and rush to take shelter.'

'Yes, I was about your age when the Great War started, and we thought that one would be over quickly, but it lasted more than four years,' she explained. I knew she didn't want to worry me, but her voice did sound a little higher than usual. 'And Hitler seems to be an even worse enemy than the Kaiser.'

On the following Saturday, 7 September, we heard that the first air raids had been carried out in Britain. They were in Kent, so a long way from Blackburn, but it showed that the Germans were serious. The war was a reality. I wasn't so concerned for us, but I did worry that our poor fighter pilots might have to put themselves in danger. All I could do was think of Bobby, working on the airfields, and hope he'd be safe.

Throughout that autumn term of 1939, although the war was an ever-present threat, it still seemed distant as not much had happened so far in Blackburn. Personally, I had more pressing concerns at that time – in particular, I was still growing too fast. I only just managed to avoid some of the uniform inspections that term, and had a close shave with others. But by Christmas, I was being told more and more often that I must have a new gymslip, new shoes and all the rest. In fact, I didn't need to be told by the nuns. It was getting hard to do up my shirt buttons, but luckily Mother had enough material to make me another shirt, which she did over the Christmas holidays. Other items were not so easy to replace or conceal. I dreaded the day I would be told to buy new everything . . . or else.

9

New Beginnings

1940

On 6 January 1940, food rationing was introduced for every person in Britain. It started with bacon, butter and sugar. Other foods were gradually added to the list, including meat (the equivalent of just over a pound in weight or half a kilo per person per week), tea, jam, biscuits, cereals, cheese, eggs (one per person per week) and milk. To make the rations go further, powdered egg and powdered milk also became available. Sausages were not rationed at this time, but they began to contain less meat, and bread was used to fill them out. 'National' bread, a filling wholemeal loaf, was freely available but wasn't very nice.

Mother had to nominate the shops she would use to buy each type of food and could only buy our rations there. If they ran out of something, we had to do without. We had a ration book each and the shopkeepers had to cancel each coupon as the item was purchased.

This was all quite strange at first, but soon everybody got used to it. Luckily for us, Grandma and Grandad

Harrison had their own hens, laying plenty of eggs, and we were able to buy or barter for dairy products from neighbouring farms, so, between us, we made sure we had enough healthy food most weeks of the year.

Clothing was rationed on a points system, equal to one whole outfit a year to start with, though it was gradually reduced. That's where Mother's dressmaking skills came into their own.

Despite my contributions, our finances didn't improve much in early 1940. Through that school term, I continued to dread more uniform inspections, but somehow they didn't happen so often. I think because of the war they were a little more lenient, so I got by for a while longer. I desperately wanted to talk to Mother about my concerns, but I didn't want to upset her. Bobby was always away, so I couldn't talk to him, and anyway, he sent as much of his RAF pay home as he could. I dreaded the day the nuns would give me the ultimatum – buy new uniform or else – but I never told Mother how bad I felt.

One Sunday, when we were all at Grandad and Grandma's house for lunch, I was playing a game with Jeffrey on the rug while the grown-ups talked. I wasn't really listening to the conversation, but Mother must have said something and I heard her mention my name so I listened for what would come next. There was a brief silence, then Grandad responded.

'She'll only get married,' he said.

There was another silence and then Grandad changed the subject. I had my back to them, but I was pretty sure that Grandad had said that about me. What did he mean? Maybe I would get married one day, but there were a lot of other things I wanted to do as well.

In bed that night, I couldn't sleep for thinking about it and wondering about my future. What had Mother said to Grandad? Might it have been about money? I would probably never know. But it was Grandad's comment that had stayed in my mind. Was marriage the only thing Grandad expected of me? I loved him dearly and I knew he loved me, but that throwaway remark had upset me. Here I was at the best girls' school in town, with the best teachers and so many opportunities. I loved the convent. When I won that scholarship, it was for all my schooling up to the age of eighteen. But now we had so little money that I had to give all I earned to Mother and there was hardly anything left to buy the necessary extras, especially the books I needed. Only the day before I had taken the few pennies Mother could spare into town to see if I could buy a copy of *Nos Amis Français* that I needed for my French lessons. It had cost two shillings, and that was just one of the books I needed, so it was out of the question to buy it. How would we manage if anything happened to Bobby? I felt like I might be losing something special . . . all my hopes and dreams were crashing to the ground. What if I had to give up school for good? I sobbed myself to sleep.

One Saturday in March 1940, I was mopping my bedroom floor when Mother called me. Her voice sounded urgent so I went to the top of the stairs.

'I want you to go to the phone and speak to Auntie

Elsie. Tell her, "This is the time." She'll know what you mean,' explained Mother.

It didn't make much sense to me, but I knew not to ask questions, so I ran up the road to the phone box and asked the operator for my grandparents' number. Luckily, it was Auntie Elsie who answered, so I told her exactly what Mother had said.

'All right, love,' she said, without a hint of surprise. 'Now you go home and collect Jeffrey, then bring him here to Grandma's. I'll come and join your mother, so we might pass on the way.'

I ran straight home and in through the door, which was never locked during the day.

Mother was in the vestibule, looking a bit flustered.

'Auntie Elsie said I should take Jeffrey down to Grandma's house,' I told her. 'And she is coming here.'

'Good,' nodded Mother. 'Now I've packed you both a bag and here's the tram fare. You're to stay overnight. I want you to play lots of games with Grandma . . . and let her win!'

She briefly waved from the front step, but then a neighbour popped round and ushered her inside. By the time we reached the end of the road, she had gone in. I didn't really think anything of it.

After lunch the next day, we were allowed to go home again, so we skipped and sang our way along the lanes, took the tram to Bastwell and walked the rest of the way back along Plane Street, under Star Bridge and past the memorial clock, to Robinson Street.

When we arrived home, Jeffrey went straight out to

play in the street with his friends, while I went in and called out for Mother to tell her we were back.

'In the living room,' she replied.

I walked through the door to a wonderful surprise. Mother was sitting in her rocking chair by the fire, gently cradling a baby.

'Come and meet your new brother,' said Mother, stroking the baby's tiny hand. 'This is Alan.' She passed him over to me.

'Hello, Alan,' I whispered, full of love and pride, as I took him into my arms. From that moment, I was totally smitten. Looking back on all this now, I hadn't noticed my mother gaining weight. She normally had a tiny waist and was such a skilful dressmaker that she probably concealed her pregnancy well.

I never heard any of our relatives or friends questioning who the father was, though they might have done amongst themselves. Being very naive about such things, I don't think I even knew there had to be a father!

But now I remember that the previous summer, when we'd spent that week in Blackpool with Bobby and Arthur, just before the war started, there was one evening when Mother went out somewhere with her friend Alice. I had taken Jeffrey to the cinema. I knew my mother was not a drinker. However, she always liked peppermint, so I can put two and two together and surmise that Mother and Alice might have met a couple of RAF men – there were plenty of those about in Blackpool, because of the airfield. Perhaps they encouraged her to have a drink or two of peppermint liqueur.

Looking back, the only difference I can recall after that was her withdrawal from going anywhere and her friends coming round more often to spend time with her at our house.

What the real story was I will never know, but I was delighted to have Alan to fuss over. What I wanted more than anything was a real baby to look after . . . and now, here he was. From that moment on, whenever I could, I cared for him, sang to him, bathed him and played with him. I even carried him all the way to his christening at St Alban's Church. I often argued with Mother because I wanted to be the one to look after him – for Alan to be *my* baby, and she couldn't allow that.

Regardless, his addition to the family was a wonderful surprise and I couldn't have been happier about it.

With another mouth to feed and only a few days left of the Easter term, I had to face the truth. Although I dreaded the idea and still hoped for a miracle, I was realistic enough to know that I might have to leave the convent soon. I just couldn't let Mother struggle any more. In a few weeks I would turn fourteen, so I could at least postpone thinking about it till then . . . or that's what I thought.

A few days later, I bumped into one of my local friends, Hilda, who was a couple of years older than me and worked as a secretary at Hodgson and Taylor's Dye Works. We stopped for a chat.

'I think I could get you a job,' she said. 'Where I work. They're looking for somebody bright like you to test the yarns.'

'But I don't have an insurance card,' I told her.

'Don't worry about that. I work in the office, so I can help you get away with it. I'll just put you through without it. Nobody at the Works will ask about that. But you'll have to come and meet my boss. I'll introduce you. He just wants to fill the position, so if he offers it to you, then you'll probably have to start straight away.'

'All right,' I said, with hardly a thought. 'I'm leaving school anyway, so what difference will a couple of weeks make?' I had my practical head on now – no looking back.

I went for an interview with a middle-aged manager, but he didn't ask me much. I can't remember his name, but he seemed like a nice man, with a friendly face, and I knew Hilda was happy there, so when he asked me, 'Will you take the job, starting next Monday?' I gulped, smiled and said 'Yes.'

So that was it. The decision was made. Deep down, I was immensely sad about leaving the convent, but this was an opportunity I could not turn down. It would solve all our money problems. I became quite excited at the thought of it as I walked down the street and in at our front door.

'It's only me,' I called out, as usual, closing the door behind me and walking through to Mother in the kitchen. 'I've got a job.'

'Oh yes?' she said, as if I'd told her I'd brought the washing in. She looked round at me while she carried on stirring. 'Where?'

'At the dye works,' I said. 'It's a full-time job and I'll be earning ten shillings a week.'

'Really?' She sounded surprised. 'When do they want you to start?'

'Monday.'

'What, during the Easter holidays?'

'No, this coming Monday.'

'But . . .' she gasped, 'it's Friday today.'

'Yes, so I won't be going back to school. I would have had to leave at the end of next week anyway, right?'

Mother nodded. 'Yes, I suppose so. But you're still only thirteen.'

'I know, but I'll be fourteen in May, and then I'll be legal, so nobody will worry about a few weeks, will they?'

I never went back to the convent again after that weekend and never told any of my teachers I was leaving. I didn't know then, but the convent always checked up on their pupils, so they did write to Mother to ask where I was a few weeks later and to see if I was all right. She must have replied that I'd had no choice but to leave.

Early on the Monday morning, I started my working life. The company was housed in a big building on the corner of Willow Street and Bay Street, with several different sections. The noise from all the machines hit me as I walked in through the factory entrance. Everyone looked up and smiled at me when I arrived and went through to the winding shop, where the machines thinned the yarn and wound it onto spools. The workforce were mostly young girls close to my age and all seemed very friendly, so that was a good start. Just like at school, I settled in easily.

At the end of my first week, we were all told that Mr

Hodgson, the owner of the dye works, was coming on a visit and he wanted to talk with us on his rounds. I saw a gleaming Rolls-Royce convertible pull up outside and our manager striding out to meet Mr Hodgson and escort him in. I rushed down to meet them with a smile as they entered the building and the manager took Mr Hodgson's hat and coat.

'Hello,' said the very small man with blond hair and a bristly moustache. 'I haven't seen you before. What's your name?'

I told him my name and what job I was doing.

'Yes, and I've noticed what a quick learner you are, Margaret,' said the manager. 'Well done. You've made an excellent start.'

'Thank you,' I said with a smile at them both.

'Haven't we got a job coming up soon for a bright young woman like this?' asked Mr Hodgson, turning to the manager.

'Yes, as a matter of fact, I was only talking to Hilda about that yesterday. She suggested Margaret for the job.' He turned to me. 'Hilda tells me you won a scholarship to the convent and you're very good at maths. Is that right?'

'Yes, it is.' I tried to look a bit modest.

'And writing too?' asked Mr Hodgson.

'Yes, sir.'

'It's a much more challenging job,' continued the manager. 'And Hilda thinks you're just the right person to take it on. What do you think?'

'What job is it?' I asked.

'You'll still be testing the yarns,' replied the manager.

'But also in sole charge of recording all the results and writing reports about them. It's a job with a lot of responsibility, testing and comparing the various yarns' strength and other properties on the machines and then filling in the results on mathematical tables to attach to your reports. Do you think you could do that?'

'Yes,' I said straight away. 'I love working with figures.'

'Good. You will have your own office and . . . let me see . . .'

'What wage are you on now?' interrupted Mr Hodgson, twisting his moustache.

'Ten shillings a week.'

'Oh,' he continued. 'I think we could change that, couldn't we?' he asked the manager, who nodded with a smile.

Mr Hodgson turned back to face me, with a twinkle in his eye. 'Make it fifteen shillings. What do you say?'

'I say yes please!'

Before we left for home, Hilda took me up to show me my new office. I was astonished. It was fabulous – a large, spacious room, beautifully clean and tidy, with huge windows letting in lots of light. I had never imagined I would have my own office, and such a beautiful one, after such a short time . . . and still only thirteen years old!

I went home that evening with a light heart, my first pay packet and a strong temptation to skip up our street, like I did as a small child.

I couldn't wait to tell Mother all about it.

'Well, that's a great turn-up,' she said with a smile. 'I

always knew you were a worker, and a clever one at that. Half again added to your salary, eh? What a difference that will make.'

'Yes, I was very surprised when he told me.'

'Does he know you're under age?'

'I'm not sure.' I hesitated. 'Why? Does it make any difference?'

'I shouldn't think so, now that he values your work.' She went to the mantelpiece and took down an official-looking brown envelope and handed it to me. It was addressed to her and she had already opened it.

I took the letter out of its envelope and started to read.

'What's a summons?' I asked. 'And why do you have to go to court?'

'It's because it's illegal for anyone under fourteen to leave school. And because of your age, it's the parent who has to take the blame. The summons means I have to go to court on that day and explain. Then they will fine me.'

'Really?' I was shocked. 'I had no idea that could happen.' I paused, but she didn't look too worried. 'It's so unfair,' I continued. 'How can they expect you to pay a fine, when the reason for my leaving school early is that we don't have enough money?'

Mother shrugged. 'Well, they can't get blood out of a stone!'

Things began to look up for Mother, the boys and me, now that there were two of us contributing to the house-keeping – no more scrimping to pay the rent, buy fresh food or pay for a bus ride.

Mother carried on with her sewing as well. I don't want to sound vain, but it was true – I was always the best dressed girl in the town. With the war on, other people were buying clothes where they could, but there wasn't much choice and nobody had enough clothing coupons in their ration book, so Mother came to their aid. She was very clever and resourceful, mending as well as dress-making. Every dress she made was different. I never saw any two customers in a similar style. She even made coats, and it didn't stop there. She treated me to her wonderful creations as well. With a piece of extra material she had she made me a raincoat, with some ruching at the top and a matching bag. Everyone admired what she made and she became even more sought-after as the war went on. No wonder she had so many kind friends, giving us free fruit from Blackburn Market or an extra couple of slices of bacon at no charge and ration-free.

However, I never had stockings. They were very scarce during the war because the military was given priority over the nylon supply, so we all used to paint our legs with something out of a bottle, specially made for that purpose. You could buy the liquid at a chemist or Woolworths. Some people used to do it with tea or coffee. Mine came from a bottle. I can remember one day, when Ray was round at our house; I was going upstairs and he was walking up behind me, when Mother saw us.

'Where are you two going?' she asked.

'Ray is going to draw the seams down my legs.'

'Oh no, he's not!' she said, with the tone of a policeman about to arrest someone.

'But he's good at painting and decorating, so he's the best one at drawing lines,' I explained.

'Not on you,' she insisted. 'If anyone is going to do that for you, it will be me, so give me the crayon and I'll do it now.'

Although fourteen and thirteen respectively, Ray and I were so innocent that we had no idea why Mother was so intent on stopping us going upstairs. The trouble was, we didn't know what we didn't know. Nobody had ever mentioned anything about how babies came to be. They just seemed to arrive in people's families. One weekend, Ray and I were at the rec, sitting and chatting on a bench, watching a mother and her little ones, who were playing on the toddlers' slide. I said something about how sweet they all looked and it went from there.

'I don't understand it,' I murmured.

'What don't you understand?' he asked, with a quizzical smile.

'I'm not sure,' I replied. 'Babies, I suppose . . . I've always wondered. Where do babies come from?' I paused. 'Do you know?'

'Yes.' He nodded. 'One of my pals in the Home Guard told me.'

'What did he say?'

'It's all to do with the atmosphere,' he began. 'The atmosphere in the bedroom has to be a certain temperature for several nights in a row. I've forgotten how many nights.'

'Oh, is that all?'

'I think so.'

We sat in silence while we both tried to puzzle it out. My first thought was for those of my convent friends who were boarders, all sleeping in the same dormitory. What if it was the right temperature for babies and they all had them . . . and I was the only one without? Wouldn't the nuns have a fright? Or even better, what if the nuns were in the same room?

I decided to ask Bobby the next time he came home on leave. But I knew he wouldn't answer a straightforward question – he was too protective of me and still saw me as his innocent little sister. He wasn't far wrong. So I decided to try a different angle, inspired by a book I had on African wildlife.

'Where do baby elephants come from?' I asked him, as we did the washing-up together one evening.

He gave me a quizzical grin. 'From eggs, of course,' he said.

Well, I knew that baby birds came from eggs, but I didn't know animals and humans did too. I also knew Bobby could be a bit of a joker and liked to tease me sometimes, but I couldn't tell if he was teasing me now.

I tried again another day.

'Elephant egg shells must be very hard,' I said. 'How do their babies break out?'

'Don't tell me you're still on about that elephant!' he replied, without giving me an answer.

And that's the way it stayed. I never did get another explanation, so it remained a big mystery.

*

Now that we had enough income to pay all our bills, with a little left over for treats, we could relax a bit more and enjoy occasional outings.

I had always loved going to the pictures as a small child, and now that I had a few pennies to spare, I occasionally treated Mother to a trip to the cinema, leaving seven-year-old Jeffrey and baby Alan with her friend Alice or one of our neighbours. In fact, I only had to pay the first time at the Star Cinema in Little Harwood, because the projectionist was the grandfather of one of my old school friends and he recognized me.

'Hello. It's Margaret, isn't it?' He paused. 'Do you remember me?'

'Oh yes. You're Sheila's grandpa.'

'That's right.' His face lit up, as if he'd had a good idea. 'Did you pay to come in today?'

'Yes.'

'Well, you won't have to pay again. Just say my name at the box office and they'll let you in free.'

'Thank you. That's very kind of you,' I said with a smile, just as my mother had taught me. He was true to his word. From then on that cinema was always free for me and a relative or friend. And even better, once they knew me, an usherette would come and take me and whoever was with me out of the queue for downstairs and up to the best seats in the balcony. So that was lucky – we could splash out on snacks instead.

I was always hungry at the pictures. If I went with Mother we would take some sandwiches with us, or sweets if they were available. If not, my mother always took a brown-paper bag full of cornflakes for us to munch. I don't suppose the people sitting near us were too pleased about that.

The only thing I ever made was a sort of humbug, with dried milk. It was surprisingly good and minty. I'd bake a batch of them and take them to the cinema to share with anyone who wanted one.

Sometimes I used to go to the cinema with Ray, after we'd both finished work. In fact we went to most places together in those days. We liked the same films and we chatted and laughed all the way home afterwards.

I can still remember some of the things we saw. They were nothing like the old silent films. These were 'talkies', mostly black-and-white, of course, like *Goodbye Mr Chips* and *Wuthering Heights*. But the first colour movies were coming out too, and they were wonderful. The two I remember best were both American: *The Wizard of Oz* and *Gone with the Wind*. I loved the costumes in that, as well as the story. But it was such a long film that we were very glad we had brought sandwiches with us that night.

My favourite movie actor was Walter Pidgeon. I loved going to see his films most of all. He always made me cry. I suppose it was because he was the father I had always wanted, the father I wished I had.

10

A Scary Warning

1940

I'd been working for about three months when Bobby came home again on leave.

'Can I come and see you at the dye works today?' he said at breakfast.

'Why do you want to come to my work?' I asked, feeling rather annoyed that I couldn't go anywhere without him checking up on me.

'Just to make sure it's a good sort of place where they treat you right.'

'Well, all right,' I sighed. Much as I loved Bobby being home, I did find him restrictive sometimes, but I was resigned to it.

'When can I come?' he asked.

'Lunchtime,' I suggested. 'You can come straight up to my office. One of the girls will tell you where I am.'

He looked rather pleased . . . and I suddenly realized why.

'Do you know a girl called Nellie?' he asked.

'Do you mean Nellie Forrester?'

'Yes, that's her. Will she be there today?'

'Yes, she works in the winding room. She's a pretty girl,' I added. 'About two or three years older than me. How do you know her?'

'I met her once while she was visiting her brother, who's one of the mechanics at my RAF base,' he explained. 'I'd like to just pop in and say hello.'

So, as promised, Bobby arrived during my lunch break.

'What a big office,' he said, looking around the room. 'You've done well for yourself here, Margaret.'

'Yes, it's not bad, is it?'

By now I'd worked out that Bobby had a crush on Nellie Forrester, so I took him to her machine, where he could casually bump into her, and left them to it. He didn't have long before she had to get back to her yarn-winding, but it was long enough for him to arrange to meet her at the end of her shift and walk her home.

Some of the girls at work became good friends of mine and, all of them being older than me, they used to talk a lot about boyfriends and going to dances. I'd never been to a dance and it sounded like fun, so when Hilda and the Snape sisters, Irene and Edna, asked if I'd like to go with them, I didn't hesitate. Of course, I had to ask, or rather tell, Mother. I was a bit worried about that, so Irene and Edna came with me. Mother had met them a couple of times before and said what nice girls they were.

'Hello, Mrs Holden,' said Irene with a smile. 'We would very much like to take Margaret with us to a dance on Friday night. We'd collect her from the house and take her there. She'd be with us all evening and we'd bring her straight back here as soon as the dance finishes,' she explained.

'What time would that be?' asked Mother.

'Oh, about midnight, I expect.'

Mother turned to look at me. 'Do you want to go?' she asked.

'Yes, I do. I've got enough money to pay to get in and buy a lemon drink. I promise I won't drink anything else.'

'Well, you're a working girl now,' said Mother. 'So if you are paying, you can go.'

I was surprised that she agreed so readily, but she seemed to have confidence in Irene's promise and I knew she didn't want to spoil my evening. She even offered to make a dress for me out of the leftover blackout material.

'At least you know how to dance,' she added. 'That's one good thing the convent taught you.'

'That's true.' In those days, dancing was a big thing, but it was always the ballroom classics, such as the waltz, the quickstep or the foxtrot that were the most popular. I remembered those lessons at the convent when my tall friends had to be the 'boys'. Luckily, I was small, so I was used to taking the girl's part.

There were a few days to go before the dance on the Friday night, so Mother rustled up this beautiful black dress for me – I would never have believed that such a special-looking dress, with a bit of lace at the neck and some sequin trimmings round the waist and hem, could be made out of the same material as our blackout curtains!

She helped me put it on and it fitted perfectly.

'I'll just put in this pin over the zip to stop it falling,' she said. 'Now let's look at you.'

I stood back. She looked me up and down and turned me round, then stepped back. 'You'll do,' she said with a nod. 'You look very nice, Margaret.'

One of the girls called for me and I picked up my dance shoes to go out. 'Don't forget,' Mother called after me. 'Be home by midnight. Don't be late.'

Blackburn had three main dance halls: St George's Hall, the Pal de Dance and – most popular with the girls from the dye works – Tony's New Empress Ballroom, or Tony's for short. I didn't know at that time who Tony Billington was, but I soon found out.

'Hello, Margaret,' said a cheery voice across the entrance hall, and a small round man walked towards me. I recognized him from my time at the convent – I sometimes used to go and call for his daughter Josephine, a year younger than me, to walk to school together in the mornings.

'Hello, love,' he used to call cheerily as I arrived at their gate, before we set off together. They only lived a few streets away in Little Harwood, and his cousin lived a few doors down from our house in Robinson Street.

'Have you paid to get in?' asked Tony.

Thinking he was checking to make sure, I said yes and showed him my ticket. Irene, Edna and Hilda gathered round me protectively.

'Well,' he said with a smile. 'Our Josephine always liked it when you walked to school with her, so you won't have to pay next time you come. Just tell the doorman, "Tony says I can come in for free." Do that every time and you'll never need to pay again. The same with the cloakroom.'

I was amazed at people's generosity. After all, I didn't know him very well, but I always used to smile and say hello. I later found out that he and his wife had been a professional dancing couple.

My friends were impressed. 'You lucky thing,' said Hilda as she led the way up the beautiful wide and shallow curved steps into the dance hall. It was an enormous room, with a column just by the entrance door and triangular seats at its base. There was a huge mirror ball hanging from the high ceiling and uplighters all round the ballroom that sometimes dimmed or brightened. The band were in their place on the stage at the front of the room, smiling at all the girls. The dance floor was shiny polished wood and the rest of the room was carpeted, with a small bar tucked away in the corner. I had a marvellous evening. The band played a mixture of tunes and it was a joy to dance to their music.

Many of the boys at Tony's were in uniform and looked so much more exciting than the ones I knew, who were far too young to join up. I recognized several of the soldiers, sailors and airmen as Bobby's pals. They all came over to talk to me, and some even asked me to dance. I knew that would get back to Bobby and wondered how he might react. He was always overprotective of me. I had liked that when I was young, but now I had turned fourteen and, much as I loved him, I wanted a life of my own.

Suddenly I realized it was time to go home and I would have to dash to get back by midnight. One of the boys offered to escort me, which was kind of him. I checked with Irene and she knew him so she said that would be fine. But she and her dance partner would come with us, in case Mother objected. Not far from Tony's, we were stopped by an LDV volunteer who asked for our identity cards. Luckily I had tucked mine into my pocket before coming out.

'Where's your gas mask?' he asked.

'I couldn't bring it,' I replied. 'Because I had to carry my dance shoes and I couldn't manage both.'

Irene laughed, but he gave her a look as she tried to straighten her face. He insisted on looking at my dance shoes, with a sneer of disapproval. 'Make sure you always carry your gas mask,' he said with suitable emphasis. 'Your dance shoes won't save you from a gas attack.'

We continued on our way, this boy and me chatting as we walked, and he gave me a peck on the cheek as he left me at the front gate.

I was elated with my evening. This was the start of the rest of my life.

From then on, I went dancing at Tony's a lot, and loved to see even the plainest boys made handsome by their uniforms. Hilda, Irene and Edna were often there, so we had a lot of fun. I danced with several of the boys and there was always somebody to walk me home if Ray couldn't be there. He came whenever he could, but some nights he was on duty, practising drills or helping out with the Home Guard. He was happy that some of his or Bobby's old friends walked me home when he wasn't around to do it himself. But Ray and I were best pals and I loved it when he could come with me. Most people assumed we were a pair, and always would be. We assumed it too.

One by one, the boys Bobby's age donned their uniforms and went away on training, a few of them all the way to Canada, before joining the action. Many of them were posted overseas, mostly to Europe, but some much further away. Those who were based near home would come back on leave whenever they could. They were always renewing acquaintances for a few days, before they disappeared again.

It was June or July 1940 when one of the RAF boys, Ernie Aspinall, who had been a member of the model aeroplane club, came back to Blackburn on his last leave before joining the bombing raids across Europe. I bumped into him at Tony's where we sat and chatted light-heartedly for quite a while, reminiscing about the old days. We laughed at the memory of me and Gordon on the tandem, carrying home bits of the wrecked model plane that was nearly shot down in Accrington.

'Those were happy days, weren't they?' he said. But then he turned a little more serious. 'Do you remember how excited you were when I told you I was going to be an RAF pilot?' he asked. 'I think you assumed I would be piloting Spitfires.'

'Yes,' I replied.

'I don't want you to be disappointed, Margaret,' he continued. 'But I'm going to pilot bombers.'

I tried not to show it, but I was disappointed. Being a Spitfire pilot sounded so much more glamorous.

'They asked me to be on the bigger planes,' he told me, 'because they consider me to be steadier than most, which is what they need for taking charge of a crew, rather than flying a fighter.'

'Well, that's quite a compliment, isn't it?' I said. 'They obviously have faith in you.'

'Thanks.' He smiled with a look of relief that I had taken it well.

Within days, Ernie was flying on his first operation of what later became known as the Battle of Britain. Not long after, I had a letter from Bobby. He started by telling me about his imminent posting to the Sudan. But when I turned to the second page, it changed:

I'm sorry to tell you some sad news, Margaret. Ernie flew on a raid the night he saw you, after he got back to the base. He and his crew, and several other planes, went off to bomb German cities. A few hours later, our bombers started to come back. I watched and counted them as they landed, but there was no sign of Ernie's plane. The next morning we heard the plane had been shot down with the loss of all lives. Ernie didn't make it. But it may help you to remember that he was doing what he wanted to do. Ernie always loved planes, ever since those happy days with our model aircraft in the club.

That was a terrible shock – the first of our friends to be killed in action. Now the war was not just about handsome uniforms. This war was real. It had come close to home. It was deadly. I looked again at Bobby's words, stunned . . . but then the tears came, welling up and trickling down my cheeks. I was miserable for days afterwards.

It was a warm summer's evening, the sun just going down, when Ray and I came out of the Palace Cinema on Blackburn Boulevard. Across the road was a familiar figure, Clarence Charnley, the butcher's boy who used to wave at me, now dressed in a smart blue uniform.

'Oh, there's Clarry. He's in the navy!' I said as I ran across to see him. The boys in blue were always my favourites, and I was particularly fond of Clarry. I wanted to talk to him and find out more about his training, whether he'd got a ship yet and when he would have to leave for active service.

'Hold on,' I told him. 'I'll just go and tell Ray.' Then I ran back to Ray, whose face was a picture!

'I've got to walk home with Clarry,' I said. 'He's in the navy and I expect he'll be leaving soon.' We were such close friends, Ray and I that I didn't think he'd mind, but he did. I could tell he was upset but I ignored it. I felt bad about that afterwards.

So I left Ray and walked away with Clarry. We walked and we talked. He told me about his naval posting and wanted to know about what I'd been up to.

'Where have you been all these months?' he asked. 'I've

missed seeing you with your short skirt and your cheeky smile.' Well, I didn't think I had ever been cheeky, but it was fun being teased like that, by an older man – all of eighteen years old.

I told Clarry about having to leave the convent. 'And I got a good job with good pay and my own office.'

'That's a turn-up,' he said with a grin. 'So now you could stand me a fish-and-chip supper!'

'Not yet,' I replied, mirroring his smile. 'I've got to help Mother out with the housekeeping and I want to try and save up too.'

'Very sensible,' nodded Clarry. He stopped me and took a good look at me. 'You're a pretty girl, Margaret,' he said. 'You'll have all the boys after you, like bees to a honeypot.'

I wasn't sure what to say to that so, as usual, I made light of it. 'I've got three brothers,' I said with a smile. 'So I'm used to boys.'

'Hmm.' Clarry paused, just as we reached my front steps. 'That's not quite what I meant.'

Well, I had no idea what he meant, but I felt a moment-ary tinge of apprehension.

He leant down and kissed me – an exciting kiss, like none I'd ever had before. With Ray it was just innocent pecks on the cheek or lips, but Clarry's was my first grown-up kiss. The next day was Saturday. I did think of going to see Ray to apologize, but he was at a Home Guard meeting, so I was in when Clarry knocked on our door.

'Hello, Margaret,' he said. 'I've come round to see if

you'd like to go for a walk with me. There's something I want to talk to you about.'

I was intrigued, so I agreed and we went off across the spare ground towards the country lanes beyond. It was a sunny day and at just fourteen I was rather in awe of Clarry. What did he want to talk to me about?

I soon discovered.

'Let's go and sit down on that wall,' he suggested. 'It's time somebody warned you about boys, and what they might want to do.'

'What do you mean?'

'Well, it's all right to be friends with boys, but you have to have limits.'

'What limits?'

'Well, you can let a boy kiss you, but you mustn't allow any touching of flesh.'

I wasn't sure I liked this sudden stern warning of his.

Clarry proceeded to give me the only grown-up talk I've ever had. He told me what was likely to happen with boys. He told me what I could allow, which wasn't much, and what I couldn't.

'There's a sort of line,' he said. 'And it's flesh.' He paused. 'You haven't to have flesh. No touching of flesh . . . and you certainly haven't to have anybody touch you under your skirt.' He carried on talking about this 'line'. I knew it wasn't a real line, of course, but I found it all quite shocking . . . and confusing.

The more he talked the more uncomfortable I felt at the thought of it all, and I was still trying to take in everything he had told me.

'I'm sorry if I've upset you, Margaret. But you needed to know.'

I nodded.

'It's very important, you see. There is this line, and you haven't to cross it until you are certain. It's only once in your life that you can cross this line, and then it's permanent. So there's no going back. It's forever. Do you understand?'

I nodded. In my mind I was thinking back to the nuns and their warnings to us about sin. I think flesh came into that somewhere. A Bible passage we once had to learn flashed into my head: *If you live by the deeds of the flesh, you will die.*

I never forgot what Clarry said to me that afternoon, but sometimes I did wonder if I'd have been better off without his advice.

One day at work, when Hilda and I were chatting during a break, she told me about her cousin who had recently joined up in the navy.

'The trouble is, Wilfred is feeling very low. He's at home on leave, staying with us for a couple of days, before he is posted overseas.'

'They're all coming and going, aren't they?' I said. 'As soon as I meet someone at Tony's and dance with him a couple of times, he's gone again. It must be very disruptive for them.'

'Yes. Wilfred is only young and he says that all the lads his age have sweethearts at home who write them letters, but he's the only one who doesn't have that. He says it doesn't have to be a sweetheart, just someone who is willing to write to him.'

'Like a pen pal, you mean?'

'Yes.' She paused, looking at me. 'I don't suppose you would write him a letter or two, would you? It would cheer him up tremendously if you could.' She smiled.

I knew she was hoping that I would agree and I did feel sorry for the poor boy, facing homesickness as well as the dangers and discomforts of war.

'All right,' I agreed.

'Oh, thank you, Margaret. You are such a good friend.'

'Well, I can't promise to write very often,' I warned her. 'You'd better tell him I'll write when I have time.' Then I thought how he would feel. 'I'll try to write once a week,' I added. 'I have other letters to write too, you see. There's Bobby, of course, but some of the other boys I've danced with also like me to write them letters when they're away.'

'I'm sure that will be fine, Margaret. He'll be grateful for anything, and I know this will cheer him up no end.'

'Did you say his name is Wilfred? What is he like?'

'I tell you what,' replied Hilda. 'He's coming to meet me to walk me home after work. If we leave together you'll see him.'

The afternoon rolled on, and I was so busy with a backlog of testing that I was surprised when Hilda came into my office.

'Are you ready?'

'Is it that time already? I'll just put these away and I'll be with you. Why don't you go and meet him and I'll join you in five minutes?'

By the time I left the building, Hilda was deep in conversation with a medium-height young man in uniform, with a rather earnest expression. I walked over to them and Hilda turned to give me a smile. 'This is Wilfred,' she said. 'I've just told him what we were talking about.'

'I'm pleased to meet you,' I said with a warm smile that made him seem a little more at ease as he gave me a tentative smile back.

That was it – less than two minutes. We said goodbye and went our separate ways home. The next day, Hilda gave me the address I should write to. 'And I've given Wilfred your address too,' she said.

So that was that. Over the next few weeks I wrote regular letters to this boy I hardly knew, and each time he wrote back. It did seem strange that we had only spent two minutes together, but he showed his gratitude in every letter, saying how much better he felt, just knowing that he would have regular letters from me, and thanking me every time.

'All the lads are teasing me now about my mystery sweetheart!' he wrote.

I was pleased that just by sending him the occasional letter I could cheer him up so much.

11

Red Alert!

1940

While Bobby was based in England, repairing damaged Mosquito fuselages, he continued to have occasional leave.

One time he met up with his old pal Maurice Haslam of the Inniskilling Dragoon Guards, or 'Skins' as he called them. He brought Maurice back to our house to join us for tea. Just as Bobby had been fed up because he wasn't allowed to fly the planes, Maurice had his own problems, but worse. He had been wounded at Dunkirk and was officially still recuperating from his injuries.

'I've got bits of shrapnel all over my body, but I'd better not tell you where!' he said with a grin. 'Here, feel my hands.' He held them out in front of me.

I felt gingerly across the back of one hand, till I came to a lumpy-looking area and found something hard and quite sharp embedded under his skin. I flinched. It made me feel quite weird.

'And try this one,' he said, attempting to encourage me.

I didn't really want to, but I didn't wish to upset him, so I couldn't refuse. I lightly touched where he was pointing, on the palm of his other hand. As soon as I felt the shrapnel, I recoiled again. It felt so wrong – a solid piece of metal lodged in his flesh. A part of me wanted to be sick, but I managed to control it and tried to smile with genuine sympathy.

'Does it hurt?' I asked him.

'Not so much now,' he replied. 'More of an ache. The wounds are healing well. But I still have a shock every morning, the first time I feel one of these pieces. It takes me right back to Dunkirk.'

'Was it terrible there?'

'I don't want to talk about it.'

'Couldn't they take the bits of shrapnel out?' I asked, curiosity getting the better of me, as usual.

'No, the medics said they were best left in for the time being. They did remove the largest pieces, in my back and one leg, but they told me it could cause more damage if they tried to dig out the smaller fragments, so they were best left alone. Some of them might give me trouble one day, but hopefully not.'

On another occasion, Bobby came back on leave with three of his pals. His main focus was to meet up with Nellie Forrester again at the dye works, and he knew I could get him in. The courtship had been continuing through letters and he was keen to see her on this trip, so he came in at lunchtime, as before, and they found a quiet place to chat and share their sandwiches. But things were not as he thought. Nellie had a sailor boyfriend as well, so he wasn't happy about that.

After he'd headed back to his base, Bobby wrote me a

letter to say that Nellie had turned him down and chosen her sailor boyfriend instead, because she thought he would be 'more settled' than Bobby. I could tell he was aggrieved about it. I worshipped my big brother Bobby, so I was almost as upset as he was.

Gordon Fudge was down in Blackburn at this time as well, visiting his grandmother, and came round to see us. It made me think back to those days when Gordon and Bobby were about the age I was now, and Gordon was always around at our house. For their holidays, Gordon and Bobby used to pack up the panniers on each side of the back wheels of Gordon's tandem, load up their cooking gear and cycle from Blackburn to Paisley in Scotland to stay with his sister. It was just under two hundred miles to ride each way, but they stopped and camped at points along the route, there and back, having a wonderful time. I used to wish they could take me with them, but, 'No room on the tandem,' as Bobby used to say, and I'm sure Mother would have forbidden it. After we'd chatted over a cup of tea, Gordon asked me if I would like to come with him back to Paisley to stay with his sister for a short holiday.

'On your tandem?' I asked him with a grin.

'Not this time, love. Let's travel in luxury!'

I had some leave owing from the dye works, so I agreed. It would be lovely to meet his family and to visit a new place. I'd never been further north than Blackpool. Gordon took me all the way on the train and I stared out of the window, fascinated to see how much the landscape changed along the way. The close-packed urban areas of

Lancashire gave way to lush green countryside, followed by the wild beauty of the Yorkshire Dales – its rolling hills, crags and streams. I kept asking Gordon where we were and he was very patient, trying to tell me, as best he could, what we were seeing out of the windows.

'What are those high hills?' I asked him.

'That's the Pennines,' he explained. 'They run down the middle of England.'

The train rumbled and clattered on northwards, clouds of steam shrouding our view every now and then. As we emerged from one such burst of steam, Gordon said, 'I think this is Otterburn, where the English fought the Scots about 5,550 years ago.'

'Who won?' I asked. 'The English?'

'No, the Scots,' he replied with a grin. 'They had fewer fighting men, but they still managed to win the battle.'

We sat in a companionable silence as we moved on through Settle and Appleby, after which Gordon told me about his and Bobby's favourite camping spot in the Lake District, which we were passing to our left.

'We used to put up the tent above a fast-running brook, get out our Primus stove and cook up a corned beef hash.' He paused. 'That makes me hungry. Shall we eat our sandwiches now?'

I got out the waxed-paper parcel and untied the string so that we could share the packed lunch Mother had made for us early that morning.

As we ate, Gordon told me about his family. 'My sister is deaf,' he told me. 'But she plays the piano beautifully.'

'How can she play the piano if she can't hear it?' I asked.

'She can hear it very faintly and she says she can feel the vibrations.'

He explained that she and her husband lived in a tenement building. I had never heard of such a thing, so I was looking forward to seeing it.

It was a long, rattling journey, stopping at Carlisle, crossing the border and on through the Galloway hills, grazed by the peculiar Belted Galloway cattle, past forests and heathlands to Glasgow station, where we got out of the train at last and caught a bus for the last leg of the journey.

At last we reached Paisley and arrived at the tenement building. I'd never seen anything like it before. It was one huge, long grey building, with four flats on each floor. On the ground floor there were alleyways, called ginnels, between each pair of flats. We went up to their flat on the third floor, and through their front door straight into the living room, which had a lovely view over the park. Gordon introduced me to his sister Isla and brother-in-law Robert, who were very kind and friendly and had a tea of scones and cake ready for us to eat. After our day-long travels and a pleasant evening, I was ready for bed. But what I didn't realize was that I was already in my bedroom! My bed was in an alcove in the living-room wall, with a curtain across it. There was no bathroom, toilet or kitchen in the flat, they were all out of the front door and down the corridor, shared with other tenants on this landing. So I would have to undress in the living room, where anyone could walk through to go for a wash or to use the toilet.

I was horrified at the thought and just couldn't do it. I could not get undressed in that situation knowing anyone could burst in. Maybe it was because I was so tired, and still only fourteen, but I'm afraid I caused something of a fuss. So, in the end, Gordon took me and my things round the corner, from 19 Cochrane Street to 23 Green Road, where his aunt lived, in a house more like ours. I was to stay here to sleep and felt a lot more comfortable.

The next morning, back in Cochrane Street, Isla and Robert went off to work and Gordon suggested we should go on a coach trip to Troon. We were dropped off right by the sea and decided to hire a boat. As we rowed around, enjoying ourselves, I suddenly caught sight of something away in the distance.

'Is that the top of a submarine?' I asked.

'Yes, it could be,' agreed Gordon. 'Let's row across and have a closer look.' So that's what we did. He took some photos with his box Brownie camera, but I wanted to go nearer.

'Closer, closer,' I said as we approached.

Finally we reached it and I particularly wanted to have a photograph taken of me and the submarine, so Gordon had his camera ready.

But just then, we realized we couldn't manoeuvre our boat at all. We were stuck, half on the top of the submarine! As we tried unsuccessfully to push ourselves off again, several heads popped out of the conning tower, shouting at us.

'Go away, get out of here!' yelled one.

'You're in dangerous waters,' added another.

'Don't you know there's a war on?' shouted the third.

Their voices were rising in anger and they continued to call things out at us.

Luckily they were on our side in the war, but they sounded furious as they produced a long pole and tried to push us off their deck. They kept yelling and shrieking and all the noise became really frightening, as they rocked our boat to dislodge it.

Eventually they succeeded in freeing us, but our boat rolled over and tossed us both into the sea. I was afraid because I couldn't swim far, but as I floundered about, Gordon took hold of me and helped me grab on to the upturned hull. Just then we spotted a larger boat on its way out from the shore to pick us up. As it approached, we realized this rescue boat had men in uniforms on it. They pulled us out of the water and righted our boat, tying it behind theirs. Soaking wet, we were taken back to the shore.

But that wasn't the end of the story. When we reached the beach, there were two policemen waiting for us. They caused a kerfuffle, grabbing hold of Gordon and pointing out a big sign that said 'Cameras not allowed.'

'But we didn't see that,' protested Gordon, still holding his dripping camera.

'It's quite hidden,' I added, helpfully . . . or otherwise.

The first thing the policemen did was to take Gordon's camera from him. We watched as they deliberately pulled all the film out of it. Then they took us to a hut-like building – more like a large shed, with some chairs in it – and asked us a lot of questions. Gordon answered most of them.

One of them turned to me and asked: 'Can we see your identity card?'

Well, I was so flustered, I searched my usual pocket but it wasn't there. 'I don't have it,' I said. 'I don't know why, but I suppose I must have forgotten it, or perhaps it fell into the sea.'

They were cross about that and they took all my details. I feared what would happen next. Would they arrest me, or both of us? Would we be able to get away?

I was worried about what could happen to Gordon as well. Being an officer in the Home Guard and an adult, he was responsible for me, so would he get into trouble because I couldn't show them my identity card? At that point, I don't think it had occurred to me that the real problem was much worse.

'I hope you both realize how serious this incident is,' scolded the senior police officer. 'You caused a red alert, rowing out to the submarine like that.'

'Sorry, Officer,' said Gordon, in a conciliatory voice. 'We didn't mean to cause any trouble.'

'I just wanted to see if it was a submarine,' I added.

The police officer gave us a strict telling-off and a lecture about the waters around Britain in wartime. I can't remember most of it. I was too worried to concentrate. But finally they let us go and took us back to the coach, which was waiting for us. By this time, we had dried out completely in the warmth of the day and were keen to get away.

So off we went after our day's adventure, with all the people on the coach singing to me: 'She's a Lassie from Lancashire'. That really cheered me up.

We talked about it all when we got back to Paisley and wondered whether they would summons us, but fortunately we never heard any more about it. And when I finally looked in my other pocket, there was my slightly water-damaged identity card. I'd had it all the time!

After a good night's sleep at Gordon's aunt's house again, I went back to the flat. Just as we were discussing what to do that day, the air-raid siren blared out and we all had to run downstairs.

Everybody in the building gathered in the ginnel, which was like a tunnel between the flats, open at each end. We had to wait, all huddled together, and this is where I met Cathy Renfrew, who also lived in the building and was almost my age.

'Do you think this is a real air raid?' I asked her tentatively.

'Och, I expect so,' she replied in a whisper. 'But maybe not here. Most of the raids have been dropping bombs on Glasgow, especially the shipyards on the Clyde.'

I was relieved to hear that. I could almost feel the tension as we all waited, without really knowing what for. It helped to have someone to talk to.

'Can you see the shipyards from here?' I asked.

'Aye,' nodded Cathy. 'When it's the night raids and the fires light up the sky.' She paused as some of the other residents, late arrivals, jostled to pack themselves in amongst us, under cover. 'What about you?'

'Our air-raid sirens only go off when the planes are flying low enough, but most of the warnings are for groups of German bombers or stray planes flying overhead,' I explained. 'On their way to Manchester and Liverpool. That's where the real raids are.'

Just as we were beginning to feel that this might be a false alarm, we heard the drone of a fighter plane approaching. It was the first enemy plane I'd heard at close quarters, but it was an unmistakable sound and coming closer still.

In the ginnel, it was hard at first to tell what direction it was coming from or its altitude, so we all hushed and listened as it grew louder and louder. Cathy and I managed to manoeuvre ourselves so that we could peek out of the street end of the ginnel, and that's when we saw the plane itself approaching at an angle, one wing higher than the other, so low that we could just make out the black-and-white cross under the wing. I wondered if Cathy could hear my heart beating fast. Suddenly the plane opened fire, its guns shooting *rat-a-tat-a-tat-a-tat*, non-stop, as it passed along the street. It seemed almost like a war film but it couldn't have been more real . . . or frightening. Cathy and I hugged each other close as the noise got louder.

We could see the hail of bullets hitting the grass in the park opposite, and the dust they threw up into the air. The German plane zoomed to the end of the street, where it rose and soared away, higher and higher, into the distance.

We heard later that this had been a 'rogue' event and that the plane had lost its bearings and crashed over the Braes, killing the pilot.

*

On our final day, a Sunday, we all set out to go to Mass at their nearby church. On the way we noticed that there was broken glass all over the place – across the roads, on the pavements, in the shopfronts. As we passed a lovely ice-cream parlour and the chip shop, we all had to tread very carefully. Wherever I put my feet, they were crunching on glass. All the shop windows had been smashed in.

'Excuse me,' I asked a passer-by. 'Do you know what happened here?'

'It was the Italians,' she said. 'The army came for them.'

'Why?' I asked, horrified.

'Because they are changing sides in the war,' explained the passer-by. 'The government has ruled that all Italians have to be rounded up and taken to internment camps. So that's what a group of our soldiers did last night, all around Paisley I should think, though there aren't many of them here.'

'Oh,' I gasped. 'Is that why the ice-cream parlour has been smashed up?'

'Yes. It's a shame, isn't it? They were lovely people.'

I nodded sadly and we hurried on, not wanting to be late for Mass. Fortunately, we made it just in time. 'Normally the church is packed,' whispered Gordon's sister, sitting next to me. 'But look at that bench over there.' She pointed across the aisle. 'That's where the Italian families from the ice-cream parlour and the chip shop sat, but now it's completely empty.' She paused. 'They were good people – always cheerful and friendly, especially with little children. How could anyone think they would do anything to harm us?'

As the Mass began, I couldn't help thinking back to the convent. I knew that Italian people were usually Roman Catholics – after all, Rome was in Italy. Were there any Italian girls at the convent? I thought there were, higher up the school. Would the same thing happen to them back in Blackburn?

I didn't understand the ins and outs of why they had been taken away, but I felt very sad about what had happened to them.

This was meant to have been a short holiday to get away from the war, but it had turned out to be quite the opposite, so I was unexpectedly glad to board the train back home again the following morning. I was certainly ready to go home by then.

By the end of summer 1940, the air raids were stepping up to three or four a month, as the Germans increased their attacks on Britain's strategic targets. We didn't have many of those in Blackburn, so the raids weren't as intense as in the bigger cities. However, it was still becoming a cause for concern, especially since, apart from the odd cellar or home-made back-yard bunker, there were no air-raid shelters in Blackburn.

We didn't have a cellar, so Mother had followed the government instructions and made up a sort of sleeping area under the stairs, which soon became crowded. Jeffrey and Alan would go in at the end, where the stairs came lowest overhead. Mother would put in her rocking chair at the other end, which was occupied by an old lady from the end of the street. As soon as the siren went off she'd arrive in her huge white nightdress under a thick black coat, carrying an enormous handbag. That had to be wedged in too. Rather than sheltering, Mother would be busy in the kitchen – usually making snacks and drinks for everyone. We'd sometimes be joined by a boy who was training to be a pilot. He used to leave his grand-mother a few streets away and come over to see that we were all right. I never did work that one out. There certainly wasn't room for him under the stairs so he'd bed down on the couch until the all-clear sounded.

Usually, if I'd been at a dance, I couldn't be bothered to take shelter, so I'd just go up to bed. But I remember on one occasion, a bomb dropped nearby and it rattled the place so much that I fell out of bed, bleary-eyed, and opened the door to go down and join the others under the stairs. I thought I'd opened the door to the landing but I'd somehow walked into the fitted wardrobe instead, and its door shut behind me, leaving me completely in the dark. I didn't even realize what I'd done. I could feel a wall in front of me, so I thought it had fallen in and trapped me. I started scratching at it with my fingernails. Meanwhile, I could hear the muffled sounds of everybody panicking downstairs.

Then I heard Mother screaming from the bottom of the stairs: 'Margaret! Are you all right? Come down here at once!'

'I can't,' I shouted. 'I'm blocked in and I can't get out.' I wasn't sure whether she could hear me. I was still scratching at what I thought was the collapsed wall, but it wouldn't move.

'What are you doing, Margaret? For goodness sake come down.'

'Help me! I can't move.'

Just then, I realized what I'd done, turned round and found my way out of the wardrobe and stood at the top of the stairs. I must have been quite a sight, blinded by the light, embarrassed and no doubt looking rather sheepish.

This was the first of a series of bombs that fell in late August 1940 in the Blackburn area. A few dropped on Bennington Street, damaging several houses, but fortunately their occupants all escaped unharmed. Sadly, this was swiftly followed, just before midnight on 31 August, by a much more devastating raid.

Peggy, a friend from work, and I were walking home from the cinema when the air-raid siren went, wailing through the clear night air. We had nowhere to shelter, so just stepped up our pace homeward. Seconds after the siren stopped, we heard the distinctive sound of a single German plane's engine, then a whistling sound and an ear-shattering explosion a few streets away. Terrified, we started to run, trying to put as much distance between us and the area as possible. We found out later that evening that the bombing was a direct hit on two shops with residences in Ainsworth Street, in the centre of Blackburn. Two people were killed – the driver and conductor of a passing tram, which luckily was carrying no passengers as it was on its way back to the depot for the night. The explosion also injured eight others and caused a lot of structural damage to the nearby buildings.

From then on, I took the air raids a bit more seriously. A few days later a whole line of bombs fell in a field by the Livesey Branch Road, clearly intended for a large factory, but luckily they landed off course so no one was hurt. In October two more bombs fell between the power station and the gasworks, but again, very little harm was done.

In November, wanting a new challenge, I felt it was time for a change of job. I wanted to take the next step up in my career now I was the legal age, so started to scour the newspapers for opportunities. I soon found one at Philips, a big international company, with its headquarters in Holland and a factory, laboratories and offices in Blackburn. I was offered a bigger salary and had a proper contract. I had to sign the Official Secrets Act and wore a white coat, like a doctor or a scientist. The first job I had there was on the Photostat machine, making and checking copies of photographs of buildings. I never knew what for, but perhaps it was something to do with the war.

After a short while, I was moved to a research laboratory for testing the power, strength and duration of light bulbs of all shapes and sizes and some other related components. Here I had to learn to use a slide rule. I always loved learning. I liked the people at Philips and soon made several new friends.

Not long after I'd joined the company, while I was walking between rooms a rat suddenly appeared and scuttled across the floor in front of me. I screamed and leapt at the first figure coming along the corridor, who was a huge man,

very tall and wide, called Mr Bruch. As I leapt, he caught
me in his arms.

'What is it?' he asked, not unreasonably.

'A rat,' I replied. 'A huge rat just ran across in front of
me.'

'Oh dear, we can't have that,' he said with a grin, still
holding me safely. I didn't want him to let me down before
I knew that rat had gone. So there he stood, with me in
his arms, and I'd only seen him once before, at a meeting.
What must he have thought of me?

Finally he set me down and assured me that the rat
must certainly have gone into hiding by now. 'You will
be quite safe,' he said, and I did feel a little reassured, but
not altogether.

This Mr Bruch was Dutch – one of the top people from
the company's office in Holland – and we had been told
he would be joining us for the duration of the war. Just
after he'd made that decision, the Dutch factory was
bombed by the Allies to stop the invading Germans using
it for the production of German bombs and ammunition,
so he had a very lucky escape. Perhaps he was warned by
the British and got out while he could.

I saw him a few times after that, usually when he was
showing high-level visitors around, explaining to them
what we were doing. He always smiled and wagged his
finger at me, which was quite funny. I really enjoyed our
little joke.

Ray had left school at fourteen, two years before, and
now worked as a decorator in his Uncle Osbert's business.

Whenever Ray finished work early, he would come and meet me outside Philips to walk me home. We always had so much to talk about – often the funny or sad things that happened at work or at the Home Guard or to other friends round about.

He would go home for his tea, then often come back to my house to walk me to Tony's, to dance the evening away. We usually danced together, but sometimes we swapped partners. We could forget about the war and all our other troubles when we were at the dance hall.

One night, just before Christmas 1940, Ray and I were walking home from Tony's arm in arm, talking and laughing together as usual, when we noticed bright red and orange lights shining and leaping as they lit up the darkness of the night sky. It was nearly midnight and we couldn't think what it was.

'It looks like fire,' I said. 'A lot of fire. What else could it be?' We stood in silence for a few moments, taking it in.

'It must be a big fire,' said Ray quietly. 'And it looks a long way away, on the horizon.' He paused. 'I reckon that could be Manchester.'

'Yes, maybe,' I agreed. 'But what could be happening?'

It was so dramatic and, in a way, awe-inspiring, that we couldn't stop looking.

After watching the distant flames in companionable silence for ten minutes or so, we realized we couldn't stay there all night and finally went back to our own homes and went to bed. It was nearly the end of 1940, the first full year of the war, and the whole of Manchester looked to have been set alight by the bombings. As I turned off my lamp, the distant glow shone through my curtains, casting eerie lights and shadows on the opposite wall.

Sure enough, the next day I heard that we were right. It had been Manchester burning. It was something called a 'blitz' – the 'Christmas Blitz', as it came to be known, demolishing large swathes of the city and killing many people.

This was a daunting time for us all. What would the new year bring? Would we be next in line?

12

The Mystery Visitor

1941–1942

Despite the rationing, we managed to enjoy the usual Christmas lunch in 1940, thanks to Grandma and Grandad. They brought a large chicken, vegetables and eggs from neighbouring farms so we had everything we needed for a traditional lunch, and the whole family gathered together as usual for a good feast. Even Bobby was able to join us that year.

Every time Bobby came home on leave, I let him have my bedroom. A part of me was annoyed at the inconvenience but I always volunteered because he was the man and I thought the world of him. We had a settee in the sitting room that folded out into a bed, so I slept on that when he was home.

It was baby Alan's first Christmas, so there were ten of us plus the baby squashed together round my grandparents' big dining table: Granny, Grandad and Auntie Elsie of course, plus Uncle George and Auntie Evelyn with their spoilt son, Ronnie. Bobby, Mother, Jeffrey, Alan – in Mother's lap – and I made up the numbers.

Jeffrey and I arrived last, fresh from Mass, which was always a black mark against me, for being a Roman Catholic and, even worse, for making Jeffrey one as well, although that had been down to Father, who had him christened as a Catholic before he left.

After lunch, we all sat around and opened the presents from under the Christmas tree. The gifts were mostly knitted or sewn pieces of clothing from my mother to everyone, but there were also wooden animals or trains for the children and wooden boxes or ornaments for the adults, made and carved in Grandad's workshop by his workers throughout the year, whenever the building work was rained off. (He never wanted to lay the workers off because he knew they and their families needed their wages.)

In addition to the presents, Grandad always gave an envelope with money in it to each of his grandchildren . . . but not the same amounts! In his mind, the fairest way was to give the same amount to one side of the family as to the other. So if he was giving five pounds, the single child, Ronnie, seven years younger than me, would get the whole lot but Bobby, Jeffrey, Alan and I would end up with one pound five shillings each.

It was typical of the way Ronnie was treated. Although often naughty – a pest and a menace – he was never told off and had received all the help with his education that Grandad had denied me. I wasn't exactly jealous of Ronnie for this, or for the way everybody spoilt him. It wasn't his fault. But it did hurt me that those who could have helped me chose not to. Uncle George paid for Ronnie to attend all the best schools, while I, who passed the scholarship that would have funded all my years up to eighteen at the convent, couldn't even be given the uniform to stay on to the minimum school-leaving age. When Ronnie didn't reach the standard required to gain a scholarship, Grandad paid for a lot of extra tutoring to help him scrape through for a bursary, which covered only a small proportion of his school fees. Uncle George then paid the rest.

In early 1941 I had a pay rise at Philips. I was getting a bit bored with testing light bulbs all day but I did enjoy the slide-rule work, doing calculations, and of course the social side of work – chats with the girls and banter with the boys. There were a lot of girls working at Philips and they were as much in the dark as I was about how babies were made. It was the subject of many of our conversations during breaks at work. Or rather, it was the absence of any knowledge about it that we discussed. How could we find out? Who could we ask? Then Kathleen Dugdale came and sat with us one day. She had been training to become a nurse before she came to work at Philips, but for whatever reason she had given it up. We assumed she had learned about people's bodies, so we were all curious to find out what she knew.

'Where do babies come from?' I asked and we all waited, agog for her answer.

'Well,' she began, then a long pause.

'Did you learn about it in your training?' asked Vera, one of the girls.

'Ye-e-e-s,' she hesitated. 'I remember there was some-thing about it.'

'What?'

'I think they told us how people make them,' said Kathleen.

'Do you remember how?'

'They gave us a book to read about it, but I wasn't well that day, so I didn't have it.'

'Well, what do you know?' We were all becoming a bit exasperated now.

'I saw a diagram,' she said and we all leaned forward again. She must have seen how desperate we were to find out something about this mystery. 'It showed a piece that is under a woman's bottom.' We waited impatiently for further explanation. 'I think that has something to do with it.'

'What else?' someone asked.

'They told us about people having piles.'

'Can anyone get piles?' I was confused. I knew there was something below, but I couldn't see how it could have anything to do with babies.

'Yes.' Kathleen looked a bit more confident now. Perhaps she was on firmer ground talking about this condition. 'Yes,' she said. 'And I think anyone can have babies too.'

'Is that all you know?'

'Yes,' she admitted, looking rather embarrassed. 'I didn't stay on long enough to find out any more.'

From what little Kathleen had said and described, I now had the idea that I must have piles, so I went to see the local doctor.

'Hello, Margaret. What have you come to see me about?'

'I have piles,' I blurted out.

He gave me a funny look. 'And where have you got these piles?' he asked.

I explained where I thought the problem was, under my bottom.

'Well, let's have a look, shall we?' He indicated for me to undress and lie down on his high bed so that he could examine me. But I wouldn't let him. I refused to undress in front of him.

'Right,' he said. 'Front or back bottom?'

'Front.'

'Then you haven't got piles,' he said, categorically. 'You're perfectly normal, so don't worry.'

When I left his surgery I still didn't really know what piles were or where they should be, and I certainly knew nothing more about where babies came from.

This was the same doctor that came to my aid the time that Alan, now a very active toddler, tripped over on the pavement and knocked his front teeth through his tongue. He shrieked and wailed. I didn't think of going to my mother for help, I just picked him up and carried him down the road, straight to the doctor's surgery, with blood pouring out of his mouth. The receptionist took one look and sent us straight through to the doctor. I watched as he treated Alan as best he could, with all his writhing and screaming. Then I heard the doctor say: 'I think it's you that needs me now, Margaret . . .' and I don't remember anything else. I had passed out from seeing all that blood.

When I came to, lying on the couch, the doctor was

back with Alan, who was now lying down with a nurse holding him as still as possible on the bed, looking very concerned. I sat up and craned my head to get a better look at my little brother and I saw that his face was white as chalk.

'What's wrong?' I asked.

Without turning, the doctor replied: 'He's suffering from shock and a fever, so I think we'd better take him to the hospital.' He paused. 'Is your mother at home?' he asked me.

'Yes, I think so.'

'Well, I will take Alan straight to the Infirmary and you can both meet me there.' And then, as an afterthought, carrying Alan to his car, he called after me: 'Don't worry. He will be all right.'

But I did worry, and I felt awful. It was all my fault as I was supposed to be looking after him. I ran home as fast as I could, my heart pounding. Mother turned pale when I told her. For once we took the bus, impatient to get there quicker. When we reached the ward where they'd taken Alan, I almost cried to see my livewire little brother lying very still on a hospital bed. Mother went straight to him and stroked his curly hair, soothing him with soft words.

'There, there, love. Ssh, ssh,' she murmured as he cried anew on seeing her. 'You haven't to worry. The doctors and nurses will soon have you well again and then you'll be able to come back home.'

Sure enough, he came home the next day and the doctor was right; Alan did get better in the end. It took a long time, or so it seemed to me, worrying constantly at the memory of his white face, presumably the result of shock. But it was actually only about two weeks before his tongue healed and he was back to his usual self.

This was all well before the NHS was founded. But I don't remember anybody not getting the help they needed. And somehow, everyone managed to pay for it. Most workers had basic health insurance taken from their wages, but only for themselves, not their families. Others could contribute to insurance through societies such as Working Men's Clubs. Those who were self-employed could pay into an insurance scheme, with the money collected weekly or monthly at their door. I think Mother must have done that, as I know she put money by when she could and I don't remember ever having to worry about doctors' bills.

In late 1941, the government issued supplies of a new kind – an air-raid shelter for the home called a Morrison shelter. It was a huge metal table-type contraption that looked like a cage. We had to crawl into it when the air-raid sirens sounded. It was a good idea as we didn't have an outdoor shelter, but it didn't look great, taking up most of the space in our front room. At least, with the area under the stairs as well, we now had enough safe space for all of us and our two extras to shelter.

As the war ground on through 1941 and into 1942 the number of air raids seemed to increase, but the planes were usually passing over us to go somewhere more important. They had their strategic targets and, fortunately for us, these were rarely in Blackburn. There was a fair bit of superficial damage from time to time, mainly the falling debris from damaged planes that clattered onto roofs, but there were no other fatalities in town from enemy bombs and no real destruction, so we were lucky.

Meanwhile, from spring 1942, Ray was only too aware that his eighteenth birthday was approaching the following March, and that he would have to go to war himself. He started to talk to the boys in blue, from the RAF and the navy, as well as those in khaki, wanting to know what they all did. Of course, they all tried to persuade him to join whatever branch they were in, but he kept an open mind. Knowing that he would be leaving in a matter of months we became inseparable, wanting to make the most of our friendship for as long as we could. We mostly avoided talking and even thinking much about the fact that time was passing. We just wanted to enjoy our precious time together.

One day in September 1942, I came home from work for lunch as I often did and let myself in.

'I'm home,' I called out to my mother. But as I walked through the sitting room and into the kitchen, there stood a stranger – a soldier, with his sleeves rolled up, washing his hands at our sink.

'Oh!' I said in surprise.

Mother was standing there with a quizzical expression, looking at me expectantly, hoping I'd enlighten her. Jeffrey was back from school for his lunch, so both of my younger brothers looked from me to the soldier and back to me. The soldier said nothing. He looked rather dour, or maybe sad, with a set expression and sealed lips. I didn't know what to say. We were all too polite to ask what he was doing in our house, so we went through to where the table was laid. As we all took our places and the soldier sat down on the vacant chair, still nobody said a word, and I was desperately trying to work out: who the heck can this be?

We had our lunch together, with ten-year-old Jeffrey telling us about his lessons that morning. Two-year-old Alan was sitting on a couple of cushions and kept falling off. Well, the first time he did it accidentally, but it made us laugh, so he slid off again . . . and again. It helped to break the ice with the stranger, who managed a momentary smile. As I helped Mother to clear away and got ready to go back to work, our anonymous visitor started to talk to me about somebody called Wolf.

'I'm sorry,' I said. 'But I don't know anyone called Wolf.'

'No, Wilf,' he corrected me. 'Wilfred.'

'Oh, do you mean Wilfred Taylor? I—'

'That's right,' he interrupted me. 'My brother. First of all, I had hoped to come here and congratulate you . . .' He paused, looking down and fidgeting with his hands.

'Really? I didn't know I'd done anything special. May I ask what for?' I really didn't know where this conversation was going.

'I wanted to congratulate you on your engagement.'

Now he'd really flummoxed me. 'Thank you,' I said, hesitantly.

'We were all so pleased when he told us in his last letter.'

Well, I was thinking, he didn't tell me! What could I say?

'Thank you, but . . .'

'All Wilf's friends are looking forward to meeting you.' He had started this sentence with an effort to look pleased, but he now looked as if he was about to cry.

I had no idea how to respond, so I suggested we go and sit down in the front room. I waited for him to compose himself sufficiently to go on.

'In his last letter, Wilf said he was coming home and he was going to get engaged . . . to you, Margaret. He even gave us your address.'

Now I realized how he came to be here, but I was still a bit puzzled.

He took a deep breath and looked me in the eyes for the first time. 'I don't know how to say this,' he began. Another deep breath. 'I'm afraid Wilfred was killed a few days ago. First he was wounded in action when he took part in a disastrous commando raid at Tobruk.' He paused, as much for himself as for me.

'Oh, I'm sorry to hear that,' I began. 'How badly?'

'Well, I'm not sure, but I know he had treatment and survived that. He was coming home on a British hospital ship, HMS *Coventry*, through the Eastern Mediterranean. They were just passing the coast of Egypt when they were dive-bombed by several German war planes. The letter we received today from a commanding officer says they had four direct hits and the ship sank, with the loss of sixty-three lives, including Wilfred's.' His brother paused to blow his nose, which gave me time to take it all in.

'How awful,' I said, genuinely upset. Even though I barely remembered meeting Wilf, I'd been getting to know him through our exchange of letters. He was only twenty and now his life had come to this horrible end. It really hit me again how cruel this war was and how close to home it could come.

'What a terrible shock for you all,' I added. 'I'm so sorry.'

'I'm sorry too, to bring you such bad news, when this should have been a happy occasion for you both, and for all of us.'

At that moment I just couldn't bring myself to tell him that I hardly knew Wilfred and we were just pen pals.

'I'm really sorry,' I said, looking at the clock on the mantelpiece. 'But I have to go back to work. I'm going to be late.'

'My father has a very serious illness,' he blurted out. 'And my mother is so upset she won't go out. They would both love to meet you. Could I please take you to meet them at the weekend?'

What could I say? I felt a fraud. Tragic as this was, it really didn't have anything to do with me. I couldn't pretend to have been Wilfred's fiancée . . . could I? In their eyes, we were engaged, so I suppose some people would say he was the first boy I was engaged to, but I couldn't see it that way, since I was never consulted. It was all so awkward and unfair.

I felt sorry for the brother, but there was something about him I wasn't too sure of. If I'd seen him in the street I probably would have kept my distance. I really didn't want to have to go and see Wilfred's parents and share their grief. It didn't seem right.

The brother looked at me with pleading eyes. 'Will you?'

'All right,' I agreed with a sigh. What choice did I have?

So on the Saturday morning, Wilfred's brother came round and took me to his parents' house in Montague Street, an area of Blackburn I didn't know. I still didn't feel comfortable going there under such false pretences. His father was lying in a bed in their living room. I think he had tuberculosis. His mother sat in an easy chair next to the bed. They seemed glad I had come, but the conversation felt very strained. I tried to say the right things, and I stayed for an hour or so, but couldn't wait to leave. I know that sounds awful, but I couldn't just make things up, so there wasn't much I could say.

Just six weeks later, in mid November 1942, I had another shock. Clarry was serving on HMS *Avenger*, an aircraft carrier, in the western Mediterranean. Most of the men had been on deck as they passed the Rock of Gibraltar, out towards the Atlantic, where they were unwittingly heading closer to a group of enemy submarines. All it took to sink the ship was one torpedo, with the terrible loss of 516 lives. The boy who used to whistle at me on my way home from the convent, the boy who gave me my first grown-up kiss, was killed. He was only twenty-two.

What an awful thing war is, when so many young men die.

13

Bittersweet

1943

It was a dramatic start to the new year, when a loud explosion resounded across our part of Blackburn. I was on my way home from the pictures with my friend Kathleen Cronshaw, who lived above her family's chip shop round the corner on Whalley Old Road. It was about nine o'clock and we were almost home when we heard the blast. We could see people in uniforms coming and going – the police, the fire service, an ambulance – and followed to have a closer look. They were all converging on what remained of a house across the road from Kathleen's family chip shop. I didn't know much about the family who lived there, just that the mother worked at the munitions factory, filling bombs and shells with gunpowder.

A policeman stopped us going any further, just as Kathleen recognized her father, blackened from the explosion that had broken their windows and caused havoc all around. The house had been reduced to a terrible mess of rubble and Mr Cronshaw was disappearing into the site of the debris.

'What happened?' Kathleen asked one of her neighbours. 'Did you see it?'

'I was at home when it went off . . . and I assumed it was an unannounced air raid,' he explained. 'But the policeman has just told me it was an explosion that happened from inside the house. No bombs were dropped.'

'How can that be?' Kathleen asked.

'Well, it could have been some kind of gas or other explosive.'

'Could it have been gunpowder?' she asked.

'Well . . . yes, it could be, if there was any around.'

'My younger brothers go over there to play sometimes,' explained Kathleen. 'And Derek, the eldest, told me that the boy who lives there – his mother works with gunpowder, just like Guy Fawkes.'

I waited a bit longer with Kathleen, until her father and some of the other men emerged from the building, covered in soot and dust, stumbling on the bricks and bits of wood on the ground, some of them bringing out the injured. Mr Cronshaw was carrying a child. The child didn't move, so he carefully laid him down and wiped some of the black stuff from the boy's face with his handkerchief. It was only then that he realized he had been carrying his own middle son.

'Frank, Frank,' he said frantically, sinking to his knees and gently trying to wake him. 'Come on, son.'

But it was no good. An ambulance man came over and took his pulse, then slowly shook his head and stood back.

Kathleen ran over to join her father, kneeling with him and gently stroking her brother's blackened arm, desperately hoping to find he had just been stunned. From where I was standing, only a few yards away, I could see quite a lot of blood on him. Kathleen was wailing by now, and the sound brought out her mother and her youngest brother, in his pyjamas. The family spent some minutes together with Frank, inconsolable in their grief. Watching this tragic scene I felt like an intruder, so I turned away from the gathered crowd. I walked sadly home and told Mother about what had happened, but I couldn't get that image of Kathleen's grief out of my mind for several days.

I didn't see her for some time after that, but when I did, she told me about Frank's funeral.

'It was awful, as we knew it would be, having to bury our dear boy. It was comforting to see his school friends, who came in a group . . .' She paused. 'Somehow they made it both easier and harder to bear, with their singing and their memories of him.' There were tears in her eyes as she told me about Frank, and in mine too, but I think it helped her to talk to me about it.

Ray had finally opted to serve in the navy, on the submarines if he could, though there was no guarantee he would be given his first choice. He enlisted, passed his medical and in late February he received his orders. Knowing what must be in the envelope, he brought it round so that we could open it together.

'Here it is,' he said, unfolding the letter. We read what it said with a great deal of apprehension. Up to now, Raymond had been quite excited at the thought of donning a handsome uniform and joining his friends to fight for our freedom. I suppose it was a mixture of patriotic fervour and bravado, tinged with a sense of duty and also perhaps a hint of apprehension – even fear. None of the boys wanted to be left out or, even worse, shamed for not joining up. And none of them wanted to go down the coal mines, which was always a threat. They weren't afraid of the mines, but they feared being regarded as cowards because they weren't in the armed services. Mining was an essential job, as everyone needed coal, so some men were ordered to do it, but nobody wanted it to be them. This letter would seal Ray's fate. It would be the final step towards his war service.

I know we both shared a great reluctance, to say the least, to be separated for the first time. We had been almost daily companions since my family had moved to Robinson Street, about seven years before. Friends and relations always joked that we were stuck together like glue. But now it really hit us that we would have to part.

'Well, they've confirmed that I'll serve on a submarine all right,' said Raymond.

'But they don't say which one,' I added.

'No, not yet. That's because they told me I'd have to go for training first.'

'Ah, so that's what this part is about,' I said, pointing at the longest paragraph.

'Yes. That's my orders. It says I have to get a train from Blackburn on the 8th March.'

'But that's the day after your eighteenth birthday,' I interrupted.

'Yes, I didn't realize it would be as soon as that.'

We sat in silence, just staring at the stark details.

Ray broke the tension: 'Orders is orders!' he grinned.

We spent as much time together as we could over the next few days, going down to the rec to sit on the end of the slide and reminisce about those days when we all gathered here and the times when I used to swing around above him on the ropes.

We went to the cinema one night and saw *Mrs Miniver* – what a wonderful, sad film that was, and of course it starred my favourites: Greer Garson and, especially, Walter Pidgeon – the man I would have chosen to be my father. Tears were streaming down my cheeks as we filed out that night. In fact, most of the other women and girls were weeping too. It was a great film, but maybe not the right one to see just before Raymond went to war.

We carried on dancing together most evenings. 'Next time we come to Tony's,' Ray said, on the eve of his eighteenth birthday, 'I will be in my naval uniform, and then, if I'm lucky, you might even think I look handsome.'

'You know I can't resist a good-looking boy in a uniform,' I agreed, squeezing his hand. 'Especially a blue uniform.' We both laughed at the thought.

On 7 March, Raymond celebrated his eighteenth birthday with a party at his house for his close family and me. Everybody was in a good mood, wanting to wish him well, not only because it was his birthday, but because by now everyone knew it was also his last day of 'freedom'.

It was a bittersweet evening for us both. I sat next to

Ray at the dinner table and later all his family smiled and spoke to me, as I stood proudly beside him.

After everyone else had gone, he walked me home, arm in arm, for the last time before he left. We talked non-stop all the way and continued on the doorstep.

'Come in and say goodbye to my mother,' I suggested.

'Good idea.'

'Ah, Raymond,' said Mother with a smile as she opened the door.

'Hello, Mrs Holden. I just came in to say goodbye. I'm leaving early tomorrow morning.' They shook hands.

'I'm very glad you came in. I wanted to have the chance to wish you all the best. I know Margaret will miss you.'

'And I will miss her too.' He nodded. 'Very much. But I will write letters – a lot of letters.'

'That will be lovely,' said Mother. 'Maybe Margaret will be able to read some of them to us, so that we can hear your news.'

'Yes, I'll tell you how my training goes and where I'll be going next.'

'Thank you, Raymond. Now you stay safe and come back to see us as soon as you possibly can.'

'I'll try my best,' he agreed.

We went back out to the front doorstep. Neither of us wanted the evening to end, but we knew it had to, so I gave him a big hug and a long, loving kiss and waved him off as he slowly walked up the road, turning to wave one last time at the corner before he disappeared.

He was my best friend, my confidant, my childhood playmate and . . . well, we had never talked of engagement or marriage, but we had a very special bond and there was an unspoken understanding between us. I'm sure we both assumed we would always be together.

Only the war could part us . . . but hopefully not for long.

Raymond and I wrote letters to each other almost every day. But there were others too. Every time a different boy walked me home from the dance halls, he would invariably ask me to write to him while he was away. I hadn't the heart to say no, so my address book soon filled up with the names and addresses of dance partners, some of whom I could barely remember. And that wasn't the only thing that filled up.

One morning, there was a knock on the door and it was our postman with yet another pile of letters from British forces overseas.

'I'm glad I caught you, Margaret,' he began, with a flustered look on his face. 'My mail bag is full every day with all these letters for you, all with different writing on. In fact, I have to use a bigger sack now and almost half of it is letters to you!'

Well, I knew that was an exaggeration, but I could see his point. Both Mother and I were trying to keep a straight face.

'You'll give me a hernia if this carries on!'

'I'm sorry,' I said.

I did try to keep up with replying to these boys. I knew from Bobby how important letters from home were to all the boys in the forces, most of them so far away. So I did my best to reply as quickly as I could, but sometimes I did get behind with the answers. Some of the boys were so impatient that they wrote to Mother, politely enquiring about my health, or more insistently requesting her to prompt me to write back more quickly. One of them even wrote to her to ask why I hadn't replied: 'Has Margaret broken her arm?' That made us laugh, but it worked. I wrote back to him straight away.

Usually the correspondence would begin by describing ordinary things, like the weather. But gradually the letters would become more daring. Quite often the boys would declare that they loved me.

I found this quite strange, since I had rarely spent more than a few hours with some of them, or a few evenings on the dance floor. I was just having fun in the moment, enjoying their company while it lasted – all very innocent. It meant much more to them, I think, than it did to me. So professions of love didn't seem appropriate.

I never did understand this business of the word 'love'. After all, you love your mother, you love the colour green, you love the cat and you love the weather . . . sometimes! It's a much misused word.

Occasionally a boy would come back from the war, or I'd see him the night after we'd danced, and he'd say: 'Do you still love me?' What could I say to that? I loved everybody and everything in a general way. But Ray was the only one I truly loved.

He wrote me letters about all the goings-on during his training, parts of which, especially the funny stories, I used to read out to Mother and the boys during lunchtimes or

after work. I always went home for lunch in those days
and after we'd eaten, Mother and I often played word or
number games with Jeffrey and Alan. Lexicon was our
favourite and it was great at teaching both the boys to
spell, each at their own level. It was a card game and each
card had one letter on it, so it was all about making words,
a forerunner of Scrabble. Jeffrey was already quite good
at spelling and he had a wide vocabulary, but he liked to
use those skills to beat Mother and me. At the same time
we all helped little Alan to see that letters made words
and what some of the simple words looked like. Both the
boys were very bright and keen to learn.

When Ray was first posted to his submarine, he wrote
and told me they would be setting off for the Far East,
where he would be based. We had hoped that he would
have a short leave before he went, but apparently there
wasn't time.

It all happened far too quickly and now he would only
be able to write when he was on land, or in safe waters
where post could be transferred between naval craft,
which was quite sporadic. I did miss his letters on the
days I had none, but once they started again, I would
have several all at once – which was a joy. To start with,
his letters were mostly light-hearted, telling me about the
places he'd been, or giving nameless descriptions of them
at least, trying to steer on the right side of the censor. He
also described the inside of his submarine, the quirks of
his fellow submariners, and the incidents and tales of his
everyday life, all of which Mother and the boys loved to
hear.

Increasingly he would write just to me, about his hopes for the future, the plans we could make for when he came home, or when the war was ended. Neither of us mentioned marriage for some time, but it was obvious to both of us. In one letter, Ray even described a length of delicate white lace he had bought for me, and in another a beautiful ring he had purchased for me to wear on our special day. We exchanged ideas about the kind of house we would like to live in and where it might be.

All of this sustained us over the months. Of course, there was sadness too, on both sides. It was a cruel war, especially in Asia. I worried about Raymond a lot, but tried not to dwell on the risks and dangers he faced. I preferred to fix my focus on keeping up his morale . . . and to look forward to the day when he would finally come back home.

If only he could have some leave, but apparently that was not possible from where he was. All the other boys were coming back every now and then for forty-eight hours, or sometimes more, but never Ray. It was so unfair. I longed to see him.

One of the sad things I wrote about to Raymond concerned Bobby's old friend, Arthur Isherwood, who was killed in action. Bobby had written to tell us about it. Arthur had been a big part of our lives before the war accelerated. I often remembered with fondness the lovely holiday I had with Arthur, Bobby, Mother, her friend Alice and Jeffrey in Blackpool. Those happy days seemed so long ago now.

We knew that Arthur had been trained to take photographs

on aerial reconnaissance missions. I hadn't really thought too much about it, assuming he would be flying behind the lines. But the most important part of his job was to fly over enemy territory, as low as his pilot dared and evading the German fighter planes, to photograph potential industrial targets, railways and roads. Bobby wrote that, on 9 June 1943, Arthur's plane was shot down in flames over Germany and he was killed – another dear friend gone to his Maker. A very sad loss.

That July, during Blackburn Wakes Week, I was with Peggy and some other girls at a dance in King George's Hall, when we decided to go across the road to the Jubilee Inn. We went to the bar and ordered 'Spitfires'. Well, no, I probably asked for my usual orange and lemon first, but when I saw that the Spitfire had a cherry on a stick, I decided I would have that instead . . . and that again. Suddenly I was seeing two cherries, and the ashtray looked like a box of matchsticks.

Peggy was playing the piano and we were listening.

'That sounds like camels coming across the desert,' I said. I do remember that.

The next thing I remember was being back in the toilet block at the dance hall, feeling as if I was dying.

Someone shouted at me, 'If your brother could see you now!' It was Nellie Forrester, Bobby's old crush.

Then I was staggering and stumbling along with Peggy holding me up and somehow getting me home, where Mother put me to bed. I was there for at least a week. The doctor called one day and checked me over.

'I think you've got some sort of flu, Margaret,' he said. Did I imagine that he winked ever so slightly at my mother?

'That's strange,' I said. 'I had the new flu injection at Philips last week.'

'What's that?' Mother asked in surprise.

'It's a trial,' I replied. 'I think it's the first time they've done it. They said it would stop me getting the flu, so how do I have it now?'

'Perhaps it's a different kind of flu,' suggested the doctor.

Luckily, I'd fully recovered in time for a family trip to Blackpool in August. We were in the Tower Ballroom at the 'tea dance', when a Polish officer came over to our table and clicked his heels together.

He turned to my mother. 'May I ask your daughter to dance?'

She was impressed by his good manners. 'Yes, you may,' she agreed with a smile.

He turned to me. 'May you dance with me?'

We went out together onto the dance floor. He was a good dancer and I was glad to have him as a partner. He spoke reasonably good English, so we were talking as we danced. He told me his name was Ivan and when I said my name was Margaret, he said 'Marishka', which sounded lovely.

Suddenly there was a commotion, as Alan pulled himself away from Mother and trotted onto the dance floor, straight towards me. He pulled at the Polish airman's trousers, then started smacking his legs. Well, by this time, everyone in the place was laughing, including the band who had seen it all and could hardly play another note, so the music petered out and everyone stopped dancing to look.

I was so embarrassed that I just picked up Alan and took him back to our table, to get us both out of trouble. It was at least two or three more minutes before everyone calmed down and the band struck up again.

I assumed that would be the last I would see of Ivan, but he came over to the table again and asked me if I would see him that evening.

'There will be party,' he said with a smile. 'You come with me? I bring you back after?' He looked from me to my mother and back again.

Then I looked at my mother. 'May I?'

'Yes, as long as you're back where we're staying by ten.'

So we all went back and I changed into a different dress, made by my mother. We were very lucky to have a place to stay, since so many of the boarding houses in Blackpool had been commandeered as billets for soldiers and airmen based nearby. But Auntie Evelyn's mother lived at 14 Gladstone Street and she was happy to have us for short stays.

Ivan came to call for me and we went to the party, which was held in a classy bar beneath Blackpool Tower. It wasn't at all what I expected. When we arrived, Ivan seemed to be the centre of attention. I found myself being introduced to various people, most of whose names I immediately forgot, with all the excitement going on. We were in the middle of a lot of backslapping – him, not me! Apparently, this so-called party was to celebrate Ivan being awarded the DFC (which I later found out meant the Distinguished Flying Cross, awarded for gallantry).

It was a wonderful atmosphere, but I was way out of my depth and could hardly follow what was going on – most of it in Polish. Everyone was so friendly and happy, but I was glad to get away and Ivan walked me back to where we were staying. He was the essence of politeness.

We went home the next day, so I never saw Ivan again. To this day, I have no idea whether he survived the war.

14

Making a Splash

1944

New Year 1944 burst in with a very welcome influx of glamorous American GIs to the town. Based nearby, they flocked into Blackburn and made a beeline for the dance halls most evenings, especially Tony's. They were so friendly and cheerful, which rubbed off on all of us. They loved to dance and they had money to spend. Above all, I could hardly believe how polite and courteous they were. I had watched a few wartime American films, but the GIs who came to Blackburn had very different stories and bore little if any resemblance to the actors or plots in those films.

My friends and I couldn't help flirting with our American visitors, most of whom were great dancers, good fun and very respectful of women. It was a promising start to the year and brightened up the monochrome aspects of Blackburn life in wartime.

There were more GIs than girls some nights, so we had our pick of them. Matt Karmelsky, however, was different from all the others. For a start, he didn't dance. He was a quiet man, an older American Tec. Sergeant, about twenty-eight to thirty years old, with a pale complexion, straight blond hair and blue eyes. He had his US Army pay but he was also paid a full salary by his former employer, GEC, because they wanted him back, so he had an awful lot of money.

I never went out with Matt. I never danced with him – nobody did, as he never asked. He used to watch the dancing with a benign smile as he spoke with his wonderful American drawl, telling his stories about the characters of his childhood in his home town. He was a great talker, but also a great listener. He had a way of making a girl feel she was the only person in the room. However, not surprisingly, there were always a lot of girls around him, including Peggy and Hilda. He was part of the crowd I was involved with. I knew he liked me, but then again, he liked a lot of other girls who were around him and they knew him a great deal better than I did. I realized he was generous, but I was surprised when, one evening, he came up to me and quietly slipped something into my hand, something wrapped in tissue paper, and gave me a smile, then a tilt of his head, suggesting he wanted me to open it. There was no box or anything showy; just the tissue paper. I gently unwrapped and opened it out. When I saw it for the first time, it took my breath away. It was the most beautiful thing I'd ever seen, let alone held in my hand.

It was a pretty golden watch, with what looked like diamonds around its face, but I knew they couldn't be real diamonds or real gold. It had a delicate black strap with a decorative loop. It was just perfect. I turned it over and saw, engraved on the back, the word 'Switzerland'.

'That's where I went to buy it for you,' he said. I was astonished. This was wartime and he was telling me that he'd flown over to Switzerland especially to buy a watch for me? He hardly knew me. It was like a fairy tale – even more so when he told me they were all real diamonds and the best-quality gold.

'How did you do this?' I whispered, overawed.

'Can you keep a secret?' he asked.

'Yes,' I replied. In fact, I was good at keeping secrets, so that was true.

'Well,' he continued. 'It's all very hush-hush. I work on something called radar, so I had to fly over to Switzerland for a meeting about it. That's the main reason I was there. But I had some time to spare, so I went round the jewellery shops to find a gift for you.'

'Why me?'

'Because I like you. You're different – special.'

'Thank you . . . thank you very much. It's a beautiful gift.'

We sat and chatted a while, then he walked me home, but that was all. He was very charming, very polite. It was just a walk with a friend.

'It's only me,' I called as I opened the door, in a happy mood and happier still to see Bobby, who had unexpectedly come home for a couple of days. He saw the gift, still in my hand, and questioned me about it. I didn't know what to say, except what actually happened. It was all very innocent. But Bobby took it the wrong way and he said some awful things. As much as I loved him, I was a little frightened of his cold, hard voice, accusing me of things and making me feel cheap. Looking back on it now, I realize that Bobby felt he was being protective of me. He must have assumed that Matt's gift was a bribe to lure me into the wrong kind of relationship. But he made me feel it was my fault – that I had flirted with Matt and led him on. Of course, that was far from the truth, so I didn't understand why he was so cross with me. I had done nothing wrong. After about half an hour of this, I was in floods of tears.

'But you don't understand,' I wailed, one last time.

'Oh yes, I do understand,' he shouted, pointing his finger at me in his rage. 'I understand only too well what men like him want, and you're the kind of silly girl who falls for it.' He paused for breath. 'But you can't keep that monstrosity of a watch,' he told me. 'If you want a watch, I'll buy you a watch.'

'But . . .'

'No buts. Tomorrow I insist that you give it straight back to this man, and that's final.'

I looked again at Matt's beautiful gift when I was alone that night. Not in my bedroom, of course, because Bobby had that, but on the fold-out sofa downstairs. I turned the watch over in my hand and watched the diamonds sparkle in the light coming from the embers in the grate. I sighed with sadness that things had turned out this way.

The next day, with great reluctance, I wrapped the watch up again in the tissue paper, took it to the dance hall with me and handed it back to Matt Karmelsky.

'I think it is a very beautiful gift,' I explained. 'But I'm afraid my family said I haven't to accept it.'

Matt gave me a disappointed look, then turned round and gave it to the girl next to him.

I had worked at Philips for a couple of years and I felt like a change – something that could lead to a proper career. So in spring 1944 I went to work for an accountant in Richmond Terrace. He was a big, hefty, middle-aged man with a ruddy complexion. He told me that he would pay me a wage and train me for free to become an accountant myself. That sounded good to me and it all started off all right. But gradually it became a little uncomfortable. It was a small office; just him and me working in the same room, and no other employees. It began with him asking me to come over to look at something, then I would feel his knee squeezing mine against the drawers of his big old-fashioned desk. I tried to avoid this as much as possible, but I didn't know what to do to stop him. Maybe he didn't realize. However, the training tailed off and I became more uncomfortable as his interest in me grew. I used to look up from my work to find he was staring at me.

At the end of each working day, my task was to lock the filing cabinets. The lock was right down at the bottom, so I had to kneel down and lean forward to put the key in the lock and turn it. He often watched me do this and I tried to ignore him. But one day, he stood so close behind me that as I got to my feet, awkwardly trying to lean away from him, I still couldn't avoid our bodies touching.

He took my chin in his hand and turned my face to his, trying to kiss me on the mouth, but I managed to jerk myself away and avoid it. So that was the end of that job.

In need of new employment quickly, I found out that the General Post Office was looking for a new telephonist, so I went to see the manager and I got the job. It might not have been a professional career, but it was a secure job. I was supposed to do six weeks' training, but they moved me on after three, perhaps because I was always making my fellow trainees laugh. I was put straight on the switchboard, so I had to learn the rest on the job. It was good fun: a new set of people and more contact with the public, which I enjoyed.

The 7th March was Ray's nineteenth birthday and I sent him a beautiful card with his letter, though I could not tell when or where he would be when he received it, possibly several days late. I thought a lot about him that day, as I did most days. The next day, the 8th, he had been gone for exactly a year. I was forlorn without him. Everybody else's sweethearts came home on leave, but not Ray. I longed for him to come back, even for just a short while. I just wanted him to hold me. It seemed most unfair to be separated for so long.

I knew I should not dwell on missing Ray, so instead I threw myself into my busy social life.

The next evening at Tony's, there was a tall, handsome boy with blond wavy hair. His name was Arnold Rouston, he told me, and he was in naval uniform – my favourite. We danced most of the evening and at the end he asked if he could walk me home. I liked his friendliness as well as his good looks, so I agreed.

'I've not seen you at Tony's before,' I said as we strolled along.

'No, I've not been before, but one of my friends suggested coming along to see what it was like. We don't live in Blackburn, you see.'

'Oh?'

'I live in Accrington . . . when I'm home, that is.'

'I suppose you're on leave? How long are you here?' I asked.

'It should be only forty-eight hours, but they're doing something to the railway track, so I can't go back till after the weekend.'

'Well, it's Thursday today, so that's another three evenings at the dance hall!'

'Yes,' he laughed. 'I suppose it is. What about the daytimes, though? Are you doing anything on Saturday and Sunday?'

'I am now,' I replied with a grin.

It was all light-hearted banter and friendship. Over that long weekend, Arnold Rouston and I became good pals. I was quite sorry when he had to go back, but there were plenty of other dance partners to choose from, so that was fine. I did stop and worry sometimes though about all these boys, going back to their terrible experiences in the war. I had already lost a number of friends. I couldn't even think about losing any more, yet I couldn't help fearing what news each passing day might bring.

*

The day after Arnold's leave ended, I took my mother to a private dance at Tony's, where I spotted another new face – a good-looking airman with wavy brown hair, a steady gaze and a confident manner. He came over and introduced himself to Mother and me.

'I'm Leslie Fielding. I'm a flight sergeant in the RAF – 576 Squadron.'

'I'm Margaret Holden.' I echoed his introduction. 'And I love dancing.'

'Well, that's good, because I was just going to ask you for a dance!'

As we danced we chatted.

'Are you home on leave?' I asked.

'Yes, just a short leave this time, but now I've met you, I think I might come again.'

I told him about my life, my family and my work. He told me about his work, his crew and some of his recent sorties in his Lancaster bomber – the regular ones he could talk about.

'I'm currently training on a new wireless system at Lindholme airbase near Doncaster,' he told me. 'But my home airfield is Elsham Wolds in Lincolnshire.'

I was eighteen and he was twenty-two. We danced a lot and we talked a lot more. In the break, Leslie came and sat down with us and Mother told him about Bobby being in the RAF and repairing Mosquitoes and I mentioned I had been the timekeeper at Bobby's model aircraft club.

The band struck up, so we walked out onto the dance floor again.

'What did you do before the war?' I asked.

'I worked in a tax office.'

'Well, that's a coincidence. I worked for a tax accountant in Blackburn.'

'We do have a lot in common,' he said with a smile.

We got on really well and by the end of the evening we felt like we'd known each other for ages.

'Let me walk you two ladies home,' he suggested, with a twinkle in his eyes, which seemed to impress my mother. Of course, once she had gone into the house, there was also the first, gentle kiss on the doorstep before he left.

The rest of the weekend we strolled along country lanes, arm in arm, and talked about our lives before the war, stopping every now and then for a kiss, and again when we ate our picnic, behind a hedge in one of the fields. I always loved kissing, but Leslie's kisses were special. There was something about him that really appealed to me and we quickly became closer than I had with any new dance partner since Ray had gone to war. But he had to go back to his temporary base at Lindholme, near Doncaster, so we exchanged addresses and kept in touch by letter. Our poor postman's bag must have been bulging more than ever.

When I opened the door a few days later, I was amazed to see Les back quite so soon.

'How did you manage to get more leave?' I asked.

'Why? Don't you want me?' he grinned.

'It's not that. I'm really glad to see you. But nobody else I know in the forces gets two lots of leave so close together.'

'Are you going to Tony's?' he asked. He knew it was a rhetorical question. 'Why don't we go down there together and I'll tell you all about it.

'Every time we fly off on a raid over Europe,' he explained, 'I come back and have nothing to do until the next raid, so I thought I'd come over and see you again.' We kissed outside the dance hall. 'I can only stay a few hours, but you're worth it.'

That made me feel good, and I liked his cheeky grin. 'Is it a few hours of my stimulating company? Or is it the dancing?'

'Yes,' he said with a lopsided smile. 'Something like that.'

'Which?' I put him on the spot.

'Both.' We laughed.

Now that we had arrived in the well-lit dance hall I could see his pallor and the lines of fatigue on his face.

'You look tired,' I said, with concern.

'Yes, I'm whacked. We've been on a raid over Germany today and I came straight here to see you.'

'Well, thank you,' I said with a smile. 'But you must try to get enough sleep.'

'Maybe I can just lie down on this settee for a bit of shut-eye, and then I'll be the life and soul of the party.'

For the rest of the evening, Les slept as if he hadn't been to bed for months. Perhaps he hadn't, with so many sorties. I woke him when it was time to leave and he walked me home, before going back to his airbase at Elsham Wolds.

Over the next few weeks, after most raids, Les used to

turn up at Tony's and slump down on a settee to sleep, still in his white roll-neck flying jersey, until it was time for him to walk me home. It was always lovely to see him, but he spent a lot more time catching up on lost sleep than we had awake together.

I wondered how long this could continue. Surely he would be missed at his base? But it wasn't long before the pattern changed.

'When an aircraft is shot down or any of the crew members are injured, the rest of the crew are "laid down" until the pilot forms a new crew,' he explained to me one evening, as he walked me home, arm in arm. 'Well, that has just happened to us. Our gunner was hit by a stray German bullet, so now, until we have a new gunner, we're all at a loose end. We spend pretty well all our time sitting at our base, watching and waiting as other crews take off and seeing who returns.' He paused. 'Well, that wasn't what we signed up for, doing nothing for days on end, so one of my pals, an officer, hatched a plan for me. He got hold of a batch of leave passes and signed them all for me to go home when I wasn't needed and just come back every other Tuesday for a briefing and to draw my pay.'

This went on for several weeks, so it was the perfect opportunity for us to spend time together, growing closer every day. However, one Tuesday he didn't return and I later found out from one of his letters that the RAF had discovered the ruse with the leave passes, so they arrested Les and confined him to his quarters at Elsham Wolds, awaiting trial.

I was very worried about him and wrote to him every

day. I couldn't wait to find out the date of the trial, or the court martial, and what the outcome would be. I found I really missed him, which surprised me. I couldn't believe he would be convicted of anything. Yet I knew it must be a possibility.

One evening, I heard from another RAF sergeant who knew him that Les had been tried and acquitted. More than that, he had been awarded an extra fourteen days' leave as a reward for 'the outstanding performance of his duties'. This 'punishment' was hilarious, and amazing. I was thrilled with the outcome and wondered when next he would be able to come over to see me.

Halfway through that evening, when I was dancing with one of my GI friends, the music abruptly changed to Ray McKinley's 'My Guy's Come Back'. We all looked at the band and followed their gaze to the door, just as Les walked in, with a big grin on his face. Everyone surrounded him, patting him on the back and making a fuss of him. Only ten or fifteen seconds later, though it seemed a lot longer, the crowd parted so that he could come over and give me a long kiss, to the enthusiastic applause of all our audience.

It was great news and we made the most of it. During those two weeks of extra leave, we walked arm in arm and talked, about our families and friends, news of the war, our pasts and our futures.

'If I survive this awful war, I'd like to go back to accountancy and settle down here in Blackburn,' he said with a smile. 'What about you?'

'Well, I'm younger than you, so I haven't really thought

about the future. But I'd like to get a better job, with my own office again, and I suppose I might like to settle down too one day, with the right man.'

'And do you think that man could be me?'

'Well,' I laughed, 'you never know. It might be!' I didn't want him to think it wasn't . . . but although I was beginning to realize that Leslie meant a lot to me, I hadn't told him about Ray, who was so far away, but still in my thoughts. I couldn't think about the future yet. I wasn't sure how I felt. I needed time to think it all through . . . and I hadn't seen Ray for so long.

Les and I both loved the cinema and musicals. His favourite song was 'You'll Never Know How Much I Love You'. Even now I can't hear it without thinking back to those times.

We talked about everything, but only rarely would he talk about his fears, though sometimes it just came out.

'My worst fear is being burned,' he told me, with a pained expression. 'I've been on raids where I've seen planes being shot out of the sky, their whole fuselages alight, and knowing there were men inside. I could almost hear them screaming.' His face contorted and I was afraid he was going to say more, but he stopped, as if suddenly aware that he'd said more than enough.

'How awful.' I really felt for him and all those brave airmen.

'Yes, this is an awful war, but I've come to see you for a break from all that.' He tried to make light of it, protecting me from any more horror stories.

We packed in a lot of fun and a good deal of serious

courting as well, though, while I felt a lot for him, I tried to keep it as light-hearted as possible most of the time.

There was one funny incident that stood out, though Les didn't notice. It happened one night, when we were coming down the stairs at the Rialto and I suddenly spotted Glen Douglas, an Australian pilot I'd been out with. His aunt lived near me in Little Harwood. I hadn't seen him for a while and I was glad he was all right, but I realized this could be awkward if he saw me. What would Les think?

But I needn't have worried, as when Les caught sight of Glen, he called out his name to attract his attention. Well, I might as well not have been there. They were the ones who were embracing. It turned out that they were old pals from their RAF training and so glad to see each other that they made a big noise and show of it. Everyone in the place must have noticed. When Les 'introduced' us and Glen saw my face, he just winked and we went our separate ways. I never saw him again.

Our two weeks were nearly up and we talked quite a lot about our feelings for each other, in a restrained way, neither of us being certain what lay ahead. But before he went back to Elsham Wolds, Les started a serious conversation.

'You're a very special girl, Margaret. I've fallen in love with you, and I think you may feel the same about me.'

I opened my mouth to respond, though I'm not certain what I was going to say, but he stopped me.

'Let me have my say first, because it's important that we are both honest with each other. These are dangerous days for aircrewmen like me, so any kind of commitment is unreliable. Two of my close friends on the base were killed in separate raids last week. So I know at first hand how risky it is to make any kind of plan for the future.'

'Yes, I know,' I said, with genuine sadness, for him even more than for me. 'You are special to me too,' I said. 'We've been together longer than I have with any of my previous boyfriends, apart from my childhood sweetheart. But we had been friends for years as children, so that was different.'

'Where is he now?'

'On a submarine in the Far East. I haven't seen him since he enlisted.'

'I hope perhaps I will meet him one day,' said Les. I suppose it was his kindest way of saying he hoped they both survived.

How could I know how I felt? I was so confused that I just had to separate them in my thoughts. Right now I had to focus on Les. I didn't know when Ray would be coming home.

Les's expression became more sombre. 'There is so much I want to say . . .'

'There is still a war on,' I interrupted. 'It's not the time for making promises. Let's just carry on as we are for now. We're happy, aren't we?'

'Yes, of course.' He smiled, reluctantly. 'That's decided, then.'

Finally, it was the last night before Les had to return to his base and his crew.

'You know my favourite song?' he asked as he walked me home.

'Yes, it's our song now.'

'It's how I feel about you . . . and about our situation.'

'I know. I feel the same.'

'But do you?' He cupped his hands gently round my face and looked into my eyes for a few silent seconds, as I returned his gaze.

'Yes,' I confirmed. 'We've had a wonderful time, haven't we? And I hope we'll have many more, but it isn't the right time to make plans.'

'But we do have an agreement, don't we?' he asked. 'If we . . .'

I put my finger to his lips. 'You don't have to say it. We do have an agreement and I look forward to what the future may bring.'

I think we both knew the odds were against us with every new raid he flew on, but neither of us put it into cold, hard words that night.

'We have some major missions coming up,' he told me. 'A big project, any day now, so I may not be able to see you for a while.'

'You will still be able to come over sometimes, won't you?' I asked.

'If I can.' He gave me a wistful smile. 'So you'd better behave yourself while I'm away!'

We kissed, a long kiss, and I waved him off as he left. I watched him stride down the road and stop again at the corner for another heartfelt wave.

That night in bed, I did think about what I would have said if he had asked me outright to marry him. It was difficult to know. Les and I had grown very close, and I did love being with him. Perhaps I was in love with him. But the war was a dangerous place to live. One of our friends, who was part of our group, was tall, thin, doll-faced Isobel. She had a very pale complexion, with the most gorgeous dark hair. One day she didn't turn up and for the next two weeks we wondered what had happened to her. When she did reappear, even thinner and paler than before, she told us that, following a whirlwind courtship with a dashing pilot, she had married her man. They had a wonderful weekend's honeymoon, after which he returned to the war. Four days after their wedding he was gone – killed in action. It was awful! My gosh . . . She looked like death on a stick.

Inevitably, I thought of Les and was glad we had agreed not to make any promises, yet. In peacetime it might have been different, but then I would have had Ray as my companion and would probably never have met Les.

I didn't know it then, but all the aircrews, and all the other services, were preparing for a huge Allied operation that could change the course of the war.

Sunday, 27 May 1944 was my eighteenth birthday. Instead of a party, I had arranged to have a short holiday with Jenny Bolton, who was a farmer's daughter and a good friend from Tony's. She was always up for a lark. I got up early, joining Jenny on her milk round, which was great fun. We chatted as we went along, and all the customers were so friendly, coming out to greet us with their jugs, some of them paying with eggs or vegetables instead of money. When we returned to the farm, Jenny's mother had baked us some potatoes, which we ate with lashings of home-made butter. This was a delicious treat, at a time when butter in the shops was strictly rationed.

My mother had made me a special outfit for my birthday. She had managed to get hold of some gabardine material, so she made me a raincoat, with the back like a battledress top and a band drawing in the waist over quite a full skirt, and with a hat and holdall bag to match. Under this I wore a tight-fitting black woollen dress she had recently made me.

We collected our tickets and set off on the train to Leamington Spa. It was quite a long journey, so when we arrived we checked in at our boarding house and had a brief walk around the town with its elegant buildings, before having something to eat at a riverside cafe.

After our late lunch we strolled along the bank of the river Avon and met two pilots, Maurice and Ted, who joined us and chatted until we reached a little jetty where a man was renting out rowing boats.

'Let's hire a boat and row downstream,' said Maurice.

We all agreed, they paid and helped us into the boat. It was a warm afternoon, so Jenny and I were just in our dresses. We sat on the wooden seat at one end as the boys rowed us around and bantered with us, showing off the skills they didn't seem to have.

'Let's row over to that sunny glade,' suggested Ted.

'Good idea,' agreed Maurice. 'How do you steer this thing?'

They managed to row us in the general direction, but before we reached it, disaster struck. Ted stood up, for a better view of the glade I suppose, just as another boat bumped into us from behind. Our boat wobbled, then overturned and we all fell in! Fortunately, I managed to hang on to my handbag, with both our train tickets and our money in it, or it would have sunk into the murky depths never to be seen again. It was a weedy stretch of the river so Jenny and I got our legs a bit tangled up as we flailed about and tried to swim towards the nearest bank. I wasn't a strong swimmer, so I was anxious that I wouldn't make it without help. Meanwhile, the boys had swum back towards the jetty on the other side.

As we neared our bank, we saw that this was where the fire station was situated. Three burly firemen ran out and leapt into the water, wading out to rescue us. By this time, Jenny and I were shivering from the cold water, and perhaps from shock as well.

As we stood on the bank, we must have been a comical sight, both of us squelching in our sodden clothes, with weeds hanging from our arms and our hair bedraggled.

The firemen led us into their fire station. 'What you need,' said one of them, 'is a good cup of hot, sweet tea and a chance to warm up.'

That sounded good to me. The friendly firemen led us through to a cosy room at the back of the station, made us some sweet tea, then gave us a blanket each and a heater to dry our clothes on.

There was even a lock on the inside of the door, so we were able to take off our sopping wet clothes and put them on a rack in front of the heater. After drying ourselves with towels we draped the firemen's blankets round us to drink our tea. We sat and laughed about our escapade and the pilots. Which one did we each like best? Where had they gone? Would we ever see them again?

Finally, our dresses were dry. I helped Jenny into hers, then she helped me slip mine over my head . . . but that's when my troubles began. The short back zip was undone, so it went over my head all right, but it was a struggle getting my arms into it. That was as far as it went. When I tried to pull it down, it wouldn't go. I couldn't get it over my bust.

'Here, let me help you,' said Jenny, and we both pulled and tugged, in fits of giggles, to no avail.

'My mother made it out of a woollen material,' I said. 'It must have shrunk.' It seemed the more we pulled, the worse it got.

'You are not going to get this dress on,' said Jenny. 'You'll have to go back to the boarding house with a fireman's blanket round you.'

The thought of me in nothing but my underwear and a fireman's blanket sent us off into more fits of giggles. Finally, the firemen asked where we were staying and one of them drove us back there in a fire engine.

'I'll go in first,' said Jenny. 'Just to make sure the coast is clear. Then you can run in when I wave at you.'

'I don't think I'd better run. The blanket might fly up or slip off.'

The lovely fireman, grinning all the way, parked right outside and everything went to plan. The coast was clear, with nobody in the street or in the hallway of the house.

I was so relieved to get back into our room at last and put on the other dress I had brought with me. Phew.

We thought that would be the end of the story, but somehow the pilots found out where we were staying, maybe from the fireman, and they turned up a couple of hours later to take us out dancing. It was their last night of leave and we had a great evening with them. The next day Jenny and I strolled around Leamington again, then we went into a bar and ordered a drink each, to celebrate my birthday. The barman served Jenny all right, but he wouldn't serve me at first.

'You don't look old enough,' he said.

'Well, I am. I was eighteen years old yesterday.'

'If you want me to believe that, you'll have to show me your identity card.'

So I did. 'There, see? I'm now eighteen years old.'

'Sorry, madam,' he said with a rueful smile. 'And happy birthday for yesterday.'

We took our drinks to a table and sipped them while we decided what to do next. We got through the drinks quicker than we'd expected, so we decided to order another – perhaps a cocktail this time. After that, my mind went blank. I don't remember anything, until I woke up in my narrow bed in our room in the boarding house.

Was I dreaming it? I rubbed my eyes, but yes, that's where I was. Jenny was with me and so was the landlady and a middle-aged man wearing a spotted bow tie.

'Thank goodness you've woken up at last,' said Jenny, looking anxious. 'This is the doctor and he's come to see what made you collapse in the bar.'

'What?' I asked in a weak voice that didn't sound at all like me.

'Ssh, don't fret,' said the landlady, a kindly soul.

Now it was the doctor's turn. 'Your friend Jenny tells me you had a couple of drinks to celebrate your eighteenth birthday. Do you remember that?'

'Yes, I remember the first one, but I don't remember whether I drank the second one, or anything after that.' I turned to Jenny. 'How did I get back here?'

'I was so worried about you. I didn't know quite what to do, but the barman called the landlord and he brought us both back here in his car.'

'That was kind.' I tried to smile, to stop her worrying so much. But when I tried to sit up, it was too much of a struggle and I had to lie flat again. The room was spinning.

'You'll need to stay in bed for the rest of the day,' said the doctor. 'And maybe longer.'

'What's the matter with me?' I asked.

'I think it's some kind of flu,' replied the doctor. Did I imagine his slight wink towards the landlady?

Now where had I heard these words before? Some kind of flu . . . Was it a coincidence? I couldn't quite remember.

'Your friend tells me that you both fell in the river yesterday, then went dancing all the evening,' continued the doctor. 'So that might have something to do with it too.'

'Maybe you swallowed some water?' suggested the landlady.

'I wouldn't be surprised,' agreed Jenny.

Well, whatever it was, I had collapsed and been unconscious for several minutes, so the doctor would not let me take the train home until I was well enough. Jenny couldn't stay with me. She had to return the next day as planned, as she had her duties on the farm to get back to.

'Can this young lady stay an extra day or two?' the doctor asked the landlady.

'Yes, I won't charge you for an extra day in the circumstances,' she assured me.

'Thank you,' I replied. 'That's very kind.'

As soon as Jenny got back to Blackburn the next morning, she went straight round to my mother's to explain what had happened. Mother got her friend Alice to have Jeffrey and Alan, so that she could get the train to Leamington Spa to look after me and accompany me back home again. What a palaver it all was, but it certainly turned out to be a memorable eighteenth birthday trip!

15

Let Me Go!

June–December 1944

One day they were at Tony's and the next day they were gone. What had happened? Where did they go? For months now, the GIs had lit up the dance hall, and one evening, without any warning, the place was almost empty. The Americans had been the life and soul of the dance floor, for me anyway. They livened up every party. But now, my friends and I found ourselves competing for the few men in uniform who were left. A few days later, some of those had also disappeared.

The previous weekend, I had overheard Uncle George telling Grandad that there was something going on, some sort of 'campaign to turn around the war'. But then they started whispering and I didn't hear the rest.

The build-up and preparation for something big was unmistakable, but I had no idea what. Even Les, when he had said goodbye that night a week or so ago, had only hinted at some big project coming up, but said nothing more.

*

One evening at the beginning of June 1944, I was walking home with one of the few boys remaining, when the low sound of several planes grew louder and louder.

'There's no air-raid warning,' he said. 'So they must be our planes.'

'They're getting much louder now, like a grinding, unstoppable flood,' I panicked. 'It sounds like they're heading straight for us.'

'Not for us,' he said. 'Beyond us.'

We looked up as the sky grew black with planes.

'There must be hundreds of them,' I gasped in wonderment. 'Where have they come from? Where are they going?'

'Perhaps there are planes flying across other parts of Britain too, going south like these.' He sounded as awestruck as I was.

As we stood there, watching them passing endlessly overhead, my thoughts turned to Les. Maybe he too would be flying his plane southwards. I said a fervent prayer for him and for all of them. It was a night to remember.

It was only days later that I discovered why: 6 June was D-Day – the beginning of our huge campaign to take back Normandy on the way to repelling the Germans from France. It wasn't just RAF and US bombers going south; there were Canadians, Australians and other Allies too. The navy sent troop ships, landing craft, floating bridges and all kinds of seagoing vessels, packed full of men, mostly army, ready with their packs and rifles to land on the beaches of northern France and run for their lives, dodging artillery fire as they headed inland if they could.

I learned all this with interest from the newspaper

hoardings and the radio news bulletins that Mother listened to avidly every night, while she knitted jumpers for the boys. As I sat with her on these evenings, I heard the newsreaders heaping praise on the huge and efficient organization of the Normandy landings, the largest seaborne invasion in history. They told how it involved all three armed services, with backup from US Coast Guards to rescue soldiers wounded or stranded on the beaches or in the water. They also said that the RAF had been bombing the beaches and inland in preparation for D-Day and I wondered whether Les or any of Bobby's friends were involved.

Now he was getting older, twelve-year-old Jeffrey was taking much more interest in the military operations and he was eager to talk about it to Bobby, the next time he came home.

A few days later, I heard on the grapevine, with great sadness, that most of our GI friends had been killed on the D-Day beaches. What lovely men they were. I felt sure I would never forget them.

One evening I was having a quiet night in, catching up on all the letters I had to write to boys in the services, and doing a bit of Fair Isle knitting, which Mother had recently taught me. I was just getting the hang of it when there was a loud, insistent knock on our front door.

'I'll get it,' said Mother. I immediately recognized Peggy's voice, faster and higher than usual.

'Hello, Mrs Holden.' She sounded out of breath. 'Is Margaret in?'

'Yes, she's in the sitting room.'

Peggy burst through. 'Oh Margaret, you'll have to come. It's awful, truly awful . . . and he's asking for you. You'd better come . . . quick.'

Peggy wasn't usually like this, so I knew it must be something serious, but she hadn't given any clues.

'What is it, Peggy? I'll put my cardigan on and come with you. Do I need anything else?'

'No, he's waiting for you . . .' She was so breathless that I thought she must have run all the way here. 'And I had to talk to you first.'

This was becoming more and more mysterious. Even my mother seemed curious and gave me a look as I went out.

'We'll have to hurry, Margaret,' said Peggy as I closed the front door behind us. 'He's been looking for you, so I said I'd come and find you for him.'

I stopped. 'Who is looking for me?'

'Come on, don't keep him there too long. He's waiting for you outside Tony's. I'll tell you as we go.'

'Right, but first tell me who is waiting for me.'

'Arnold Rouston,' she finally managed.

'Ah, that's the good-looking sailor that I made friends with last winter. He's a good dancer too, and . . .'

'Stop, Margaret.' She was strangely insistent. 'You can't think about all that now.'

'Why not?'

'Oh dear. I have to warn you – his face has been badly burned, and his hands, and other parts . . .'

I stopped in disbelief. 'Oh no! How dreadful. He's one of the most handsome boys I know.'

'Was,' she said. 'But you'll have to brace yourself now. Try not to look too shocked when you see him. You must look him in the eyes and try not to appear too upset.'

'Yes, of course. You're right, Peggy.' I paused to think. 'Is it bad? Very bad?'

'Yes, although he's still having treatment, so it will get a bit better over time. But he won't be as you remember him.'

'Well, he has a great personality,' I said, determined to look on the positive side. 'That's what I like most about him.'

Peggy walked part of the way back with me and left me at the corner so that I could go alone to meet Arnold. There he stood, outside Tony's, still wearing his uniform and lit only by the moonlight. He had his back to me. I was determined not to act any differently, so I called his name as I came close and he turned round.

'Hello, Arnold. Peggy came and told me you were back and looking for me, so here I am,' I said, in as bright a voice as I could. He pulled back slightly, as if to protect me from too close a look. His face was a terrible shock, but I didn't turn away. Instead, I tucked my arm in his. 'Let's go inside and have a dance.'

'Are you sure?' he asked. 'I look even worse with the lights on,' he added, with a smile in his voice.

'Not to me,' I reassured him. 'It's you I'm here for, not your face or your hands. Oh, come on, Arnold, let's dance!'

We went inside and spent the rest of the evening on the dance floor. He had always been a nifty dancer and he still was. He might have lost some of his confidence, but he still had his sense of humour, so we had a good evening, catching up with each other as we danced the night away. Other people may have given him looks, or talked behind his back, but I didn't notice.

In the band's break, we went to sit down and Arnold told me about his accident. The fire was caused by one of the giant boilers on his ship and he'd been rescued and taken for treatment, but not before he'd sustained these terrible burns.

'It was just after I saw you in January,' he said. 'I've been in and out of the military hospital ever since. It's not so painful now, and they say they can do some more work on my face to make it look better. I think I may have to go down south for that. I'll never be handsome again, but better than this would be a good start.' He gave me a one-sided smile.

'You'll always be handsome on the inside,' I said. 'What about your hands?'

'I think they're going to do some more work on them too,' he explained. 'Don't worry. They look worse than they feel. And I have some lovely nurses looking after me, so I can't complain!'

I waved Arnold off at the station on 24 July 1944 and went to work with a heavy heart. He needed his friends right now, but I was glad he was going back to the nurses he was so fond of.

Later that day, Leslie Fielding turned up unannounced at Tony's, as he had so often done earlier in the year. We hadn't seen each other since before D-Day, though we had exchanged a lot of letters, so I knew he had lived through it. What a huge relief that was.

The only problem on this evening at Tony's was that when Les arrived, I was dancing and laughing with one of the Americans who had come back from D-Day and I didn't see him come in. In the old days, he would just have lain down to have a sleep. But this evening was different.

When the music stopped, I turned around and there he was, standing watching me from the edge of the dance floor, with a scowl on his face. I went straight over to give him a hug, and he did return it briefly.

'Come on,' he said in a gruff voice, which I'd never heard before. 'Let's get your jacket and I'll walk you home.' Normally I would have said it was too early, or maybe made a quip to cheer him up, but he seemed preoccupied, so I just nodded and collected my jacket. We stepped out into the warm evening air, I tucked my arm into his and we walked along, talking about nothing very much. I was making most of the conversation, as he was unusually quiet.

I felt as if I'd upset him somehow, but couldn't think how unless he was upset to find me dancing and laughing with my American dance partner. Did Les feel jealous? No, I didn't think so – it wasn't like him. Or maybe he thought I should have seen him come in. I assumed it was something I'd done or said and it made me feel guilty. I certainly never wanted to upset him.

He had his head down as we walked and seemed very unhappy. Had he stopped loving me? Was he preparing to 'dump' me? I was really worried and stopped talking, as he didn't seem in the mood for everyday conversation. We turned into Robinson Street and stopped outside my house, as we always did. But Leslie was still distant and it unnerved me.

We kissed outside my door but it seemed different when he pulled away. He stood back and took both my hands in his.

'I can't tell you anything,' he began, 'but I'm sure this is the last time I will see you.' His eyes looked loving for a moment, then steely cold. Something was very wrong and I was trying not to tremble.

'Is it because of the American I was dancing with?' I asked him.

'You can think that if you like,' he replied.

I felt so hurt I couldn't speak.

'This is our last goodbye,' he said with a solemn expression, still holding my hands in his. He kissed me strongly, then abruptly pulled away, turned and strode off down the road. I was bewildered as I watched him walk heavily down Robinson Street. I waited to wave him off at the corner, as usual, but he didn't turn round. He just quickened his pace round the corner and out of sight. Selfishly, I felt let down and very hurt.

As I went to bed that night, I thought it all through and couldn't work it out. Was it really the last time? Why? Les was not a petty sort of man. He'd never complained before when I danced with all the boys while he was resting on Tony's couch. Why now? Perhaps he'd just gone off me.

*

Three days later, when I'd just got back from work, there was an urgent-sounding knock at our door. It was Jackie Fielding, Leslie's brother, with a letter in his hand. As soon as I saw the official envelope I had a horrible premonition. My heart was racing, as Jackie read out the letter to us, announcing the death of Flight Sergeant Leslie Fielding on 29 July 1944. He had been on a major raid to bomb Stuttgart when his Lancaster plane was shot down over Northern France, exploding in the air before any of the crew had a chance to escape, other than the pilot, who was the only survivor and was taken prisoner.

I turned cold. Mother had come in and heard most of what Jackie read out.

'I'm so sorry, Margaret,' he said. 'But Les told us that if anything happened to him, we were to come round and tell you straight away.'

'Thanks, Jackie,' I said, numb with shock. 'I appreciate that.'

After he left, I confided in Mother how I felt about Les. I told her about his last visit, suddenly realizing that it was just the evening before that final night's raid, only hours before he was killed. At that moment, I had a great urge to be on my own and ran up the stairs to my bedroom, closed the door and lay on my bed.

How could I have been so heartless? It was as if he knew he was going to be killed. He clearly knew that he would be on a massive mission, involving thousands of Allied planes bombing all German cities repeatedly over five nights. Les had been killed on the fifth and last night. Could he have known he would be killed? A premonition, perhaps? Is that why he was so quiet and distant with me? Or was he deliberately trying to make me cross with him, perhaps to cushion the inevitable outcome? I wouldn't put it past him. He was always so caring and protective of me. Maybe he thought his aloofness would make it less painful for me to hear he'd been killed. He'd once told me the average life expectancy of aircrew in bombers at that time was four raids. I knew he had done over one hundred.

I had so many thoughts going round and round in my head that evening. My emotions too were all over the place – shock and grief, of course, but also a great sadness that our final goodbye had been so unsatisfactory and upsetting for us both. Why was I so thoughtless as to leave him feeling insecure, and maybe even unloved, the very day above all others when he needed to feel confident and positive? I was ashamed of myself. He must have felt so miserable walking home alone that night and then travelling back to the airfield. He must have felt even more miserable on that flight. And it was all my fault. I wasn't quite sure how it had happened, but I had to take at least some of the blame.

If only he had survived that raid and come back. I was certain that all would have been forgiven and forgotten. We would have been back to normal and happy again . . . but it wasn't to be. Only he knew the ending and he did his best to prepare me for it.

Thus my close companion for several intense weeks – the man who wanted to marry me one day, and yes, the man I was in love with – Flight Sergeant Leslie Fielding, had been killed on a clear summer's night, 29 July 1944.

I gulped and the tears came. He was only twenty-two, a great friend and companion who could have had a fine future. I wasn't quite as sure as he was that we would have married after the war, but he was very special to me and I would never forget him.

Losing Leslie like that made me feel restless. I couldn't settle at anything. All these boys were going off to fight for our benefit, but what was I doing to help the war effort?

It came to me one day. I should give up my cosy job at the Post Office and go and do 'war work'. Quite what kind of war work I could do, I didn't know, but I asked around and found out what there was in the Blackburn area.

I worked out my notice at the Post Office, had a good send-off, and the following day I turned up to clock in – or was it clock on? – for the first time in my life, at the fuse factory.

I'd never seen anything like it. I had to wear a green overall and a green hat thing pulled over my head to keep my hair away from the machinery. It clearly wasn't designed to hold my curly hair, which kept bursting out. We made lorry-doll fuse light strips, whatever they were. I never saw the finished product as I only worked on one part. It was nearly all women in the factory, but there were a few men. The manager, Mr Greenwood, went to the same church as me and knew my father and his side of the family. He also knew I had been a pupil at the convent, which was rather unusual in his factory.

Mr Greenwood would go around the factory floor every day, talking to all the staff. I worked on the capstan lathe machine. I stood on a box, with a wheel to my right that I had to spin, which sent a rod through the machine, then it was washed and cooled by some white, soapy liquid. In my first break, one of the girls told me that I hadn't to do it too well, or they would be out of a job, so I tried to keep that in mind. It wasn't difficult, because I really struggled to make the machine work properly and was always catching my fingers on the rough bits, so it wasn't long before I had pretty well all of them bandaged up! I had a great time there chatting to the other girls, but I was hopeless with all the mechanical bits and pieces. I'm just not cut out for that sort of thing. But I did persevere, and finally got the knack of it.

One night at Tony's, in autumn 1944, my friend Kathleen Brown introduced me to her latest boyfriend, Joe, the most handsome boy in the room. He spent most of the evening with her and walked her home. A few days later, however, Kathleen and Joe had split up and he came and asked me to dance. Well, I thought that was great. Joe had it all. He was in the Coldstream Guards, a talented athlete, the life and soul of any party, a good singer . . . and he seemed able to do anything one could want. He was so good-looking, with his blond hair and bright-blue eyes, that he had all the girls gravitating around him. Tony Billington's wife used to call him a 'Greek god'. She would say, 'Where's the Greek god tonight?' But from that evening on, he seemed to have eyes only for me. I was very flattered.

All my friends, especially Peggy and Irene, would have loved Joe to dance with them, but he always asked me. When he started to take me out on dates or to any of the dance halls, Peggy and my other friends admitted they were all envious of me. His dancing was very good. He did everything better than most and he could be great fun, but there turned out to be a darker side to him too.

I could soon tell Joe was getting serious. He was about Bobby's age, so five years older than me, and I thought it was probably the war that made him think it was time for him to settle down. But what about me? I was only eighteen, and, crucially, I didn't love Joe. I don't know what it was. I liked him. I liked the idea. Let's be honest, he was an Adonis, wanted by everyone, and I liked the idea of 'he's mine!' But I didn't want a serious relationship and Joe did, though I didn't realize it until he pretended to ask me to marry him – at least, I thought he was pretending.

We were standing on my doorstep at the end of an evening.

'Did you know that Tony's wife calls you "the Greek god"?' I asked him.

'Does she?' he said with a grin, then got down on one knee, still laughing. 'In that case, will you marry me and be my Greek goddess?' he asked with what I took to be mock seriousness.

I was embarrassed in case anyone came along or my mother came out, and I was sure he was joking, so I said, 'Oh, all right. Now get up off our step and say goodnight.'

'Let's go to Manchester tomorrow and buy you a ring,'

he suggested with a grin. 'And we could have a nice lunch there to celebrate, then go and see a film.'

'All right,' I agreed – anything to get him away home!

But as I went in, it sounded like a good day out, so I was glad. It just didn't occur to me that he really meant any of it. I thought that if we bought a ring, it would be a penny ring from Woolworths, just for fun.

So that's what we did, except it was a jeweller's, which surprised me. I chose the cheapest pretty ring they had and, with what I took to be mock ceremony, he put it on my finger. I always liked jewellery, so that's how I saw it really, as enjoying ourselves rather than as a serious commitment. In my mind it was nothing more than carrying on the joke with, at most, a temporary 'engagement' until Ray returned.

We had a lovely lunch and found a cinema that was showing *Meet me in St Louis*. Being Manchester, it cost us five shillings each, so it was an expensive day, but it was fun.

'Let's go in and tell your mother,' he said, when we got back home that evening.

'Tell her what?' I asked, laughing.

'About our engagement, of course.'

'Oh, all right. If we must.' I was obviously very naive, as I still thought this a continuation of the charade. But it turned quite serious when we got inside.

'Hello, Mrs Holden,' he began. 'I've asked Margaret to marry me and she has said yes. Will you give us your blessing?'

Mother looked at me with a surprised expression. I

gave a slight shrug, hoping to suggest I wasn't necessarily in agreement.

She turned back to Joe.

'Well, Joe, Margaret can get engaged as often as she likes, but she hasn't to marry till she's twenty-one.'

Looking back, I can see I should have made clear that this was all a misunderstanding, but at the time I failed to take the initiative . . . and then it was too late.

Once it was in his mind that we were engaged, Joe changed. He became very possessive and jealous. He seemed to want to control me, but I wasn't having any of that. I already had a possessive brother, which I could cope with because I knew he had always been like that, out of love for me. But I couldn't take it from Joe.

When he saw me talking with my old crowd the next evening at Tony's, including a couple of boys home on leave, Joe erupted: 'You've got to stop talking to other boys.'

'But they're just old friends,' I explained.

'I will not have you talking with any other boys. I don't care who they are. You're mine now and you do as I say. You only talk to me.'

I wasn't going to let anybody stop me from talking with my friends, so I decided I had to try and break off this engagement. However, knowing him better now, I was afraid he might be angry if I just told him that I wanted to call it off and gave back his ring. So I came up with an idea that I thought would put him off me.

We still used to meet at Tony's a lot, so instead of walking in on my own, or just with my girlfriends, I thought I could occasionally arrange to meet up with other boys, big, strong ones, who were good friends and who understood my predicament, so that they could walk me in. With luck, Joe might realize I wasn't serious about him, or anyone else.

So one evening I asked Bert Cave, a Lancaster pilot who had been a prisoner of war, to come with me. He had recently arrived back from Germany following an exchange of prisoners. Bert was good fun and I enjoyed his company. I walked to Tony's with him and I was laughing with him as we walked in. I looked across at Joe, whose expression changed to a black look . . . and not just at me. At that moment I feared for Bert and maybe even for myself, as Joe raced across the room, took my arm and pulled me aside, before picking a fight with Bert.

'Quick, hurry,' I said to Bert, 'you've got to get away.' But he only took a few steps outside, then hesitated and turned, worried about me. Joe flashed across the road, socked him a punch and knocked Bert right over the wall. I realized I couldn't try that again.

The relationship was all very on–off, as far as I could make it. I hadn't meant to get engaged to Joe and hadn't recognized his mercurial nature, nor his jealousy and possessiveness. In his good moments, I liked him and enjoyed his company, especially amongst a crowd of friends. I liked seeing strangers turn their heads at his chiselled good looks and his confidence. I liked all the girls being impressed that I was going out with him, engaged or not. But I didn't love him and couldn't help flirting with other boys from time to time – it was just part of my nature. I should have realized, though, after what happened to Bert, how it would make Joe's anger boil up to the surface.

One night, at a special dance, his frustrations came to a head. I remember I was wearing a long pale-blue evening dress at the time, and was dancing and flirting with an American GI, while Joe was with my crowd of friends, entertaining them with one of his stories. Joe saw me and stepped onto the dance floor towards us. My partner saw him coming and rushed off to the gents, followed hotfoot by Joe, who cornered him there and started a fight with him. The band played as loudly as they could, but they couldn't drown the shouts. I knew it was all about me, and I felt bad about it, but I couldn't do anything. Feeling trapped, I slipped away and set off for home. It was a moonlit night and I was walking as quickly as I could, but my evening dress and shoes slowed me down. I hadn't got far when I heard a man's running footsteps behind me. Joe caught up with me, took hold of my arm and pushed me roughly into a doorway.

'No, Joe. Let me go!' I shrieked. 'You're hurting me.'

He had his hands round my neck and tightened his grip. I froze, but I knew I had to get away, somehow. I remember the terrible fear as I tried to struggle, but he wouldn't let me go.

'If I didn't love you so much,' he said, 'I would kill you.'

He held me like that for what seemed like several minutes, his steely eyes staring into mine, piercing right through me. I wanted to shout for help, but I could barely breathe and I felt like I was going to faint. I suppose he must have realized . . . and loosened his grip. I saw my chance and, with a supreme effort, I pulled myself loose, but slipped on the doorstep. Realizing I was trying to escape, he put his foot firmly on the hem of my dress. I struggled as he pinned me to the door again and expressed his fury. 'Did you hear me?'

I nodded.

'You are engaged to me now, so I don't want you to go out with any other boy, or even dance with them. You should not even speak to any other boy, unless you are with me. We are engaged, so you belong to me now; remember that!' He paused again for my answer.

'Yes,' I said, trying to stall him, as I looked for an opportunity to escape. Finally, he let go of my neck and I slipped right down to the ground. To help me up, he took my hand, more gently this time, but I summoned enough strength and pulled free of his grip at last. I ran and ran, all the way home. I think he may have been following me, to make sure I was all right, but I didn't dare stop till I got through our front door, to the safety of our fireside, where my mother was sewing in her rocking chair.

She must have realized something was wrong. I was out of breath, dishevelled, and I noticed her gaze went straight to the large footprint on the bottom of my pale-blue dress, then back up at my face with a silent question mark.

'It's all right,' I said. 'It was just Joe, having a tantrum.'

I don't know why I tried to make light of the danger I had been in. Perhaps because it already seemed unreal. We never spoke about it again, but I knew for certain now that I had to break up with Joe.

I stayed away from Tony's the next day, but the day after I met Joe there and told him that, instead of dancing, I wanted to get a drink of lemonade and sit down at a table. I had thought about what I wanted to say, so I plucked up my courage and began by taking off my ring.

'Joe, I'm really sorry,' I started. 'I didn't know you were serious when you asked me to marry you. Because you were joking around, I thought it was just a stunt, a bit of fun.' I could see his face reddening and his mouth open to speak. 'Please just let me finish,' I said. 'I never meant for all this to happen and I certainly didn't want to upset you. But in the circumstances, I am asking you to accept that our engagement is off.' I placed the ring on the table and slid it across towards him. 'It's a beautiful ring, but I'm sorry I didn't realize you meant it to be an engagement ring.'

He looked as if he was going to explode at me. I was a bit scared, but determined not to show it.

'I'm really sorry, Joe,' I repeated.

He opened his mouth, but said nothing . . . Then he dropped his shoulders and gave in. He just nodded. He must have realized that shouting in a place like this would do no good.

'Keep the ring,' he suddenly said, shoving it back towards me. Then he got up, pushed past the table and walked away.

I felt as if a huge weight had been lifted from my shoulders.

At the end of his leave, Joe went back to the war and I went back to the dance hall, feeling free again.

In late 1944, Kathleen Cronshaw and I decided to go on a short trip to Blackpool. On the first evening, we were dancing in the Tower Ballroom when we met George Slack, who was a singer with the RAF Entertainment Troupe. He sang brilliantly, but he was also a good dancer, so we got on well and started to write to each other.

A few weeks later he wrote that his troupe were bringing their show to the Grand Theatre in Blackburn as part of an evening performance. With this advance notice, I was able to buy tickets for the front row downstairs, for Kathleen, me, Mother and her friend Alice Westwell. I had recently found out that Alice's brother Sydney was serving on HMS *Maidstone*, the mother ship for Raymond's submarine. I could hardly believe this coincidence as I knew him well, and it definitely brought me closer to Ray. It's a small world, isn't it?

On the night of the show, we dressed up and went to settle in our seats, ready for it to start. Alex Munro, a well-known popular Scottish comedian, was the host of the show, introducing each act. It was what was called a variety show, so it included comedians, magicians and all sorts of other performers.

Finally it was George's moment, as he came onto the stage and started straight into a medley of Italian songs. He had a beautiful, lilting voice. For his final number he came to the front of the stage, dropped on one knee right in front of me and sang an Italian love-song, looking straight at me. Then he produced a single red rose and leant across to pass it to me.

'For you, Margaret.'

Embarrassed in front of this large audience, which included many people I knew, I stood up, reached across and took it.

Alex Munro strode onto the stage and said, for all to hear: 'Come on, Margaret. Put him out of his misery and say "yes".'

This was all good-natured fun, but it was never serious. I described it all to Ray in my letter that evening. Throughout his time away – nearly two years now without seeing him – we had kept up our correspondence almost daily, and our affection for each other had grown into a pure and abiding love. We both treasured plans for the future – the rest of our lives together. Why had he still not been allowed any leave? And when would we finally meet again? I yearned for him to come home and hold me close.

16

The Worst Tragedy

1945

Christmas 1944 was more upbeat than the earlier wartime Christmases. Since D-Day, things had been progressing well for the Allies, who were driving back the enemy. We really felt this might be our last wartime Christmas.

But in the meantime we had to maintain our patience and frugality for just a little while longer, or so we thought. Rations had been gradually reduced throughout the war and were now at their lowest levels. As a family, we continued to receive fresh food grown by Grandma and Grandad Harrison or procured by them from nearby farms: all surplus to rations, of course, but it was a very different story for most people in Blackburn. Even if they had a ration coupon for butter (two ounces per person per week), or eggs (one egg per young or elderly person per week), there was no guarantee they would be available at their designated shop. Every individual was entitled to a maximum of one shilling and two pennies' worth of meat – the equivalent of two chops – per week, which was much lower than when rationing started in 1940, and there was often little choice of meat. I don't know how we would have managed without the dozen eggs from Grandad's hens or the pound of butter and the slab of cheese made at their friends' farm. Businesses too were suffering more than at any previous time during the war, especially from the rationing of paper and petrol.

On the morning of New Year's Day 1945, I had an unexpected visit at home from Arnold Rouston. This was a very welcome surprise and I could see considerable improvements to the scars on his face and hands. They were still badly disfigured and always would be, but it was wonderful to see what the medics had done to help him.

'I've had some more operations at a specialist burns unit in East Grinstead, where everyone is in the forces, and we made a jolly crowd while we were there, all bandaged up and cracking jokes nineteen to the dozen.'

'Your scars certainly look less angry than last time I saw you,' I said. 'It's quite a miracle really, how much better and more comfortable your face looks. Does it feel better for you?'

'Yes, and they say they can still do a bit more here and there.'

'I do admire your positive attitude, Arnold.'

'Thank you. But I reckon it's the only way.'

'How long are you here for?' I asked, thinking we might go out somewhere.

'For a couple of days, mainly with the family,' he replied. 'But we could maybe go dancing at Tony's one night if you like?'

'Yes please, that would be great – just like old times.'

'Well, not quite!'

'Oh, I'm sorry . . .'

'It's fine. Don't worry. I was only teasing.' He took a deep breath and told me the real reason for his visit. 'I'm not on my own this time. I've brought someone special with me to meet my family. In fact, she's with them now. And you've been such a good friend to me, Margaret, over the past few months, that I'd like to introduce her to you as well. Can I bring her round at four-ish this afternoon?'

Ooh, that sounds exciting, I thought. Could it be? Well, I'd soon find out. 'Yes please, that will be a perfect time to come. If she's special to you, I'd love to meet her. What a lovely start to the new year.'

'Yes, very special. She nursed me with great care and dedication for several months in the hospital, after I was first wounded . . . and now she's agreed to marry me!'

'That's wonderful,' I exclaimed, giving him an impromptu hug.

'Yes, isn't it? I'm the luckiest man alive.'

As I waited to greet them with scones and tea that afternoon, I was still feeling delighted at Arnold's wonderful news. This nurse had obviously grown to know and love him for what he was, a remarkable individual, without any comparisons to his good looks before. What a wonderful person the woman must be.

And indeed she was. They arrived arm in arm.

'This is Eunice, my fiancée,' Arnold said as they came in. She was a pretty girl – petite like me, with auburn hair.

'I'm so glad to meet you, Eunice. Come on through to the front room.'

'It's lovely to meet you too,' she said, giving Arnold's arm a squeeze before they sat down close to each other on the sofa.

'Show Margaret your engagement ring,' he suggested, and grinned as she held out her hand.

'Arnold chose it before he asked me to marry him,' she explained. 'And he couldn't have chosen better.' She gave him a conspiratorial smile. 'Did you tell Margaret how we met?'

'Yes, but I didn't tell her how I proposed.'

'Oh yes,' she giggled. 'Well. He did it the old-fashioned way, in a tea room, down on one knee,' she told me.

'And some of the other customers started clapping,' said Arnold with a grin.

'Only he lost his balance and toppled over.'

'Yes, and I dropped the ring,' he added. 'It rolled across the floor, under the tables, and before long we had nearly everyone on the floor searching for it!'

'Did you find it all right?'

'Yes, we did,' replied Arnold. 'And a good job too, or we might not be engaged now!' They exchanged loving glances.

Eunice was a lovely girl and I was so pleased for Arnold. They evidently adored each other, but I couldn't help feeling pangs of deep sadness. The way they were with each other reminded me of the special closeness Ray and I had shared in those last months before he left for the war. It wasn't that I was jealous – not at all. I was delighted for Arnold in his new happiness, but if only Ray could come home. I longed for that time . . . for his handsome smile and his loving kisses.

I'd had time now to think about things and I knew that my love for Leslie had been different from what I felt about Ray. Yes, I loved them both, but whilst Leslie was the serious wartime romance, which was very real for a time, Ray was the one I always knew would be there for me in the long term, the one who would love me unconditionally, and I him . . . even if we had to wait till the end of the war. But it was a long time. If only he could be allowed some leave . . .

The following day, I had a long, loving letter from Ray, from somewhere under the Indian Ocean. That was all he could tell me about his location, of course. He wrote about the fantastic Christmas lunch they had been given on his submarine. By the sound of it, they were eating a lot better than we were in Britain, with our meagre rations! Later in the day, he wrote, the whole crew put on a talent show for themselves and each other. Ray was good at so many things that I wondered what he had chosen to do for it. I sat down straight away to write back and ask him. I could also tell him about Arnold and the lovely news about his engagement.

Ray had written this letter on the evening of Christmas Day and he said that they were going on special exercises, so he would keep writing me letters, as always, but I was not to worry if I didn't hear from him for a couple of weeks or so, as they would be out of contact for at least that long. This seemed to be nothing unusual for submariners, so I looked forward to an avalanche of letters all at once, whenever they finally arrived.

'But what about his leave?' I wanted to scream across the oceans at his commanding officer. I knew Ray had put in several written requests for leave over the nearly two years that he'd been away, but he said that he wasn't the only one who had been refused, so there wasn't much we could do. It seemed that the best we could hope for would be an early end to the war.

The days passed slowly, with no news from Ray; then, in the last week of January, I heard the letter box bang and found two letters on the mat. I picked them up, puzzled to recognize my own handwriting and Raymond's address. Then I saw the words stamped across them in black: *Missing, presumed dead.*

'What?' I gasped, and turned cold. I must have cried out, because Mother hurried through to the hall to see what had happened. By now I was shaking, so I handed her the letters.

'What does that mean?' I asked her, in a confusion of fear and disbelief. 'Surely they can't presume someone is dead? If they don't know he's dead, he could easily still be alive . . . couldn't he?' I was clutching at straws, because I needed to. 'Surely there's a good chance that some junior clerk has stamped this on a lot of envelopes, without checking if they are all correct?' I could hear my voice rising to a near-hysterical pitch. 'It must be wrong . . . mustn't it?'

'Well . . .' Mother paused, as she led me to sit down

and sat with me, wondering how to respond. 'I very much hope it's wrong,' she said. 'But I'm afraid you must try to steel yourself . . .' Uncharacteristically, she put her arm round me. That meant a lot, but it couldn't change the words.

That awful phrase, 'missing, presumed dead', might as well have been a knife to my heart. I couldn't think of anything else.

'I wonder whether Alice could find out,' she suggested. 'I'll be seeing her tomorrow. If you remember, Alice's brother is on the supply ship for Raymond's submarine, HMS *Porpoise*.'

'Yes, maybe she can ask?'

'But he might not be able to tell us anything, if it was a secret mission, or something like that.'

I was desperate to know now, but of course it might take time. 'Do you think Ray's parents would know anything?' I asked.

'They may do, if the War Office has contacted them direct.'

I tossed and turned in my bed nearly all night, the dreaded phrase continually running through my mind, along with all the possible ways I desperately hoped it could be wrong. Maybe tomorrow I would get a letter from him, to show he was alive . . . but I didn't. I went to work as I always did, but I was in a state all day and probably got everything wrong. I walked back home in a daze. Not knowing was surely even worse than knowing, except that there was a small chink of hope.

Poor Ray, far from home and desperate to get back to see me again, while I had been able to carry on dancing with all the boys in uniform. This thought made me feel terribly guilty. But in the months since Les's tragic death, I had focused my thoughts and future hopes back on Ray, who had never wavered in his love for me, nor I in mine for him. We both wrote of our longing for the war to end, bringing nearer the time when we could be together again at last. Now that dream was turning into a nightmare.

I let myself in, calling out, 'It's only me.' I could hear voices in the front room, but I didn't feel like talking to visitors. As I took off my coat, Mother came out into the hall.

'Ray's father is here,' she said.

My heart leapt with hope. 'Have they found him? Is he alive?'

My mother looked stunned, then gave a very slight shake of her head . . . and my hopes plummeted.

'Come and join him. I'll go and make us all some tea.'

I walked into the front room, just as Raymond's father stood up. We took one look at each other and hugged. Neither of us spoke at first. It was a great comfort for me, and I think for him too, that we could share that moment without the need for words.

Ever since Ray and I first played together, we had often been to each other's houses and came to know each other's parents well. Mr Nash felt more like family to me than some of my blood relations.

'Is it true?' I asked him as we both sat down. 'Can he be dead?'

'Yes, Margaret. I'm afraid it is true,' he said in a gentle voice.

The shock was like a physical punch to the stomach. I could barely breathe.

'That's why I wanted to come round straight away to tell you what we know.'

'Thank you,' I whispered.

'Your mother tells me you had a couple of letters returned with that terrible message stamped on them?'

'Yes. I thought it must be wrong,' I said.

'So did we.'

'I was so shocked when I saw it – I couldn't believe it. I still can't,' I added. 'I suppose that's because I don't want to.'

'You've put that very well,' he said. 'We feel just the same. Raymond's mother would have liked to come with me to see you, but she is so distraught that she cannot leave the house at the moment. I'm sure you of all people can understand that, Margaret.'

'Yes,' I nodded, with tears in my eyes. 'It must be terrible for her.'

He put his hand in his jacket's inside pocket and took out a buff-coloured envelope. 'We received the telegram from the War Office yesterday afternoon, but we were all so upset that I couldn't even come round to let you know, and anyway, we didn't know anything about what had happened.' He paused to open the envelope. 'This is the official letter we received today from the War Office. It doesn't say much.' He unfolded it to show me, but the print seemed to swim in front of my eyes.

'Could you please just tell me what it says?' I asked him.

'Yes. It seems that HMS *Porpoise* travelled on the surface to this position and submerged for Raymond and the rest of the crew to lay mines in the sea. It doesn't say where, but I think it was probably somewhere off Malaya. When they had finished, they surfaced again and a lone Japanese fighter pilot saw the submarine. His crew loosed a bomb. That was all it took – one plane with one bomb. It was a direct hit and badly damaged the submarine, which sank below the surface, leaking oil. Then two more attacks followed and dispatched the ailing submarine, which sank with all hands. It now lies on the bottom of the ocean.'

He looked up to see if I was all right. 'The only nugget of comfort I take from this,' he said, 'is that if there was an explosion, Raymond and all the crew could not have had time to realize what was happening. They almost certainly would have died immediately.'

I wasn't sure whether Mr Nash was just saying that to give me some consolation, but I could see that it might have been true. I desperately wanted it to be true.

'This letter also says,' continued Mr Nash, 'that Raymond's personal possessions, which he left on the support ship, will be gathered together, listed and sent back to us.' He paused. 'I will let you know, Margaret, when they arrive. I've talked about this with my wife, and we would both like you to choose something of his to keep.'

'Thank you,' I said. 'That is very kind, but . . .'

'We insist,' he interrupted. 'It's what Raymond would have wanted.'

I nodded, the tears trickling silently down my face.

As I closed the front door after him, I knew I had to accept the facts. John Raymond Nash, aged twenty, had been killed in action. It was a shock of immeasurable proportion. I went up to my bedroom to be alone for a while. I was devastated by this terrible news and needed time to myself to think.

Throughout the two years since Ray had gone to war, we had corresponded as often as his submarine's locations would allow, growing ever closer, sharing an understanding that we would be back together again for good one day. I'd known Ray since he was in short pants. He was my first love, my best friend and my sweetheart – the child I played with, the boy I danced with and the young man I had assumed I would marry one day.

When Les died, I told Ray all about it, pouring out some of my sadness and sense of guilt in my letters to him, all of which Ray nobly understood. He really was a very special person. He knew me so well. We were always together and expected to stay that way. Our families and friends knew we were inseparable . . . or had been, until the day after his eighteenth birthday, when Ray went to war. And now I would never see him again.

A few days later, Mr Nash came round again and I took him through to the front room.

'A box of Raymond's possessions has arrived from the

War Office,' he told me. 'And there is a package with a label on it for you. We haven't opened it. I was going to bring it with me, but my wife would especially like to give it to you herself.'

'Thank you.'

'She still refuses to go out. She is too upset and the doctor has said she should stay at home and rest.' He paused, with a worried frown. 'I'm afraid she doesn't want to see anybody . . . except for you. She particularly asked me to invite you to visit her at our house, when you are free.' He paused. 'It would mean so much to her to see you and share her memories of him with you.'

'Yes, I will come,' I promised. 'Perhaps after work tomorrow – about half past five?'

'Yes. Thank you, Margaret. That will be perfect. We'll see you then.'

The path from our house to Raymond's was so familiar to me and as I walked it once more, down Robinson Street and round the corner, it was impossible to believe my childhood sweetheart would never again be there to greet me. I knocked on the door and it was opened almost immediately. Mr Nash welcomed me into their sitting room, where his wife was sitting in an easy chair by the fire. 'Hello, Mrs Nash,' I said with a sympathetic half-smile as she wiped away her tears and held her arms out. I gave her a long hug. Finally, as she loosened her grip, I sat down on the chair beside her.

She turned to pick up a long brown-paper package in her trembling hands and showed it reverently to me. 'There,' she said with a weak smile. 'Look,' she added, pointing at a label. I saw my name, Margaret Holden, written very carefully in Raymond's best handwriting. My heart lurched. I would have recognized his handwriting anywhere.

I hesitated to take it.

'Please,' urged his father. 'He left it especially for you.'

This time I let his mother pass it to me and I held it in my hands, knowing that he had held it too. I gently traced his writing with my fingertip, gulping the air, my tears trickling down my cheeks. 'If you don't mind, Mrs Nash, I'll open it later.'

'Yes, quite right,' she said kindly. 'Best to open it on your own.'

'Thank you for being so understanding.'

I could tell from their expressions they were disappointed I didn't want to open it whilst there with them. But I didn't think I could cope with that. I stayed and had a cup of tea with them, however, and we reminisced about the days when Ray and I played, carefree, around the neighbourhood, coming back into one or other of our houses at regular intervals for refuelling with snacks and drinks.

Finally, it was time to go, so I said my goodbyes and promised to visit them both again soon.

I went straight home, where I took the package upstairs to my bedroom and shut the door. I placed it gently on the bed and sat next to it, just looking at it. I don't know how long it was before I touched it again. It was long and soft on the outside, with something small and hard in the middle. As I traced my name again, I imagined him writing this himself, in his quarters on the submarine. I touched the wrapping where he must have touched it himself, when he was doing up the string. A shiver went through my body. This was torture.

Finally I decided to open the parcel. I suddenly had an idea of what might be inside it, something that he had written about in one of his letters, to form part of our future plans.

I took a little while to unknot the string, as I didn't want to tear the paper, especially where he had so lovingly written my name. I set aside the string and unfolded the brown paper, inside which I found another layer of tissue paper. I carefully opened that out to reveal the most beautiful white lace I had ever seen. Unlike some of the English lace I'd touched, this was feather-soft and delicate, intricately patterned in what I guessed was an oriental style.

The tears fell once again as I gently opened out the lace, one fold at a time, to reveal a small, separately wrapped package between the layers. This was the hard item I had felt earlier . . . and now I knew what it was.

Raymond wrote in a letter that he had bought a length of white lace for my wedding dress and I sobbed as I held it against me. What a beautiful dress my mother could have made out of it . . . but it was not to be. Exquisite as it was, I could never wear it now.

I hesitated for a moment when it came to the small package, but I knew it held the rings that Raymond had also written about buying for me, for our special day. Part of me thought I'd rather not see them, but my curiosity got the better of me and I undid the box to reveal two gold rings. One plain, and the other a solitaire diamond, beautifully cut and sparkling, set on a matching band of gold. I tried them on. They were a perfect fit. How did he manage that? I wore them for only a few sad seconds, then put them away again and wrapped the package up to look as it was before.

It upset me too much to have this in my room, so I asked Mother to look after it for me. When I came back from work the following day, I collected that precious package and took it back to Raymond's parents.

'I'm really sorry,' I said as I handed it back to Mrs Nash. 'But I did undo it all to see what it was. It was a length of beautiful white lace that he told me in one of his letters he had bought for my wedding dress. And inside that were two rings – engagement and wedding rings.' The tears were running down my cheeks again. 'It was lovely to see it all, but I'll never feel able to wear them, so I'd rather you look after it for me, or use the material for something else.'

They both looked sadly at me. 'But why, Margaret?' asked Raymond's mother.

'Because it would upset me too much to keep it in my house,' I explained. 'I hope you understand.'

'I see – yes, of course we understand,' she assured me.

'Yes, I can see how much these things must have upset you, but Raymond left them for you, so we shall be their keepers, until you want to take them back again,' said his father. 'You'll always be welcome here,' he added. 'We always thought of you as our future daughter-in-law, and I see no need to change that.'

'And I agree,' echoed Mrs Nash.

I was relieved that they had taken it so well and grateful for their encouragement to come and see them whenever I wanted.

Walking home, however, I felt lost and guilty. I had lived for the day, having fun, while he was imprisoned in a large metal box under the sea, far from everyone and everything he loved. And now that metal box had become his tomb.

Although Raymond's body would never be recovered, his parents still wanted to have a proper funeral for him. I too felt bereft. So when I received a note from them, asking me to attend his funeral, I knew I had to be there. In those days, it was not permitted for a Roman Catholic to attend a service in any other Christian church, so I went to see the priest at my church and explained the situation. It was wartime, and he understood. He approached the bishop and I was given special dispensation to attend the C. of E. church for Raymond's funeral.

Raymond's funeral service was conducted at St Stephen's Church in Little Harwood, by our friend George Heaton's father. I was close to tears throughout the service, but especially when the vicar mentioned my name with Raymond's, as always being inseparable, until the war parted us. That went straight to my heart. It was very hard, but also very special. He was always with me as we grew up, and I have thought of him every day, ever since. This hasn't stopped me living my life, enjoying my days, but I have never forgotten my first love.

Although Raymond Nash had no grave, other than the submarine in which he lived and died, his name is remembered, engraved on the Royal Naval Memorial on Plymouth Hoe.

17

The Palais Glide

1945

It was January 1945. The snow fell and lay thick on the ground, bringing the buses and trams to a halt. But the most urgent requirement for us was our outside lavatory. It was the only lavatory we had for up to five people, when Bobby was home on leave.

One Friday night the snow was particularly heavy, with a strong wind. When I got up the next morning and opened the back door, leading into the yard, the snow had drifted so high that it was over the door. This was not funny when the lavatory was at the far end of the yard, next to the coal bunker.

Thank goodness for a good fire, despite the scarcity of coal. It also heated the water in our back boiler. Mother and I first had to dig out a path to get to the lavatory, which we had to make sure didn't become slippery. We then had to heat up extra bucketfuls of water on the fire to carry out to the lavatory to melt the ice in it, before anyone could use it.

Jeffrey came down and helped us dig, while Alan, who

was still only five and full of mischief, decided the best way to help would be to make snowballs and pelt his brother with them. Meanwhile, Mother swept the path as clean and dry as she could while I brought through the containers of steaming water, trying my best not to slip nor to slop any of it out to scald any of us.

Once we had the lavatory in working order, temporarily at least, we could then get on with our day. It wasn't too bad if the snow fell on a weekend, but I do remember one snowy week when there was no bus running to my war-work factory in Lower Darwen. I had to muffle myself up in the warmest clothes I had, pull on my thickest socks, my stoutest shoes and hat, then set off to trudge all the way – about four miles – through the snow to work. My legs, bare above my socks, smarted from the biting cold. Some days, the snow was so thick that I didn't arrive till nearly lunchtime. I did maybe an hour or two of work, and then had to set off back home to Blackburn again. On one frightening day everything was so white, like a fantasy land, that I got lost, walking in circles until I finally found a landmark to steer me back in the right direction.

My mother sometimes listened to the radio and kept me up to date with whatever was going on – mostly news of the war. I didn't take too much notice, now that Ray would never come back. I had lost the two most important loves of my life, so now I put my energies into enjoying the dances and my friends – anything to brighten my days, and other people's too.

*

In the spring, Joe came home on leave. He came round to our house, hoping to pick up where he thought we had left off. I had written the occasional letter to him while he was away, just because I wrote to all the boys to cheer them up . . . and perhaps also, in a strange way, because I felt guilty that I couldn't return his love. But my letters to Joe were all about Blackburn gossip and people he knew and nothing about anything personal or about the future, which I certainly didn't intend to spend with him.

He still refused to accept that we were not engaged and insisted on my wearing his ring. He got so cross if I didn't that he frightened me. He would grasp my left wrist and tighten his grip till I winced. I feared he might lose control, so it was safer to go along with it. But I never wore it when he wasn't there. I agreed to go dancing with him one night, afraid of him flying into a rage if I didn't, but when I talked to any of my friends, especially Bert, or the other boys, he made his jealous anger clear.

'When I take you dancing, as my fiancée, I expect you to have eyes only for me,' he said as he walked me home. I hadn't wanted him to walk me home, but he gave me no choice.

I took a sly look at his face. Even when cross, he was undeniably handsome – he could have been a film star walking down the street. But I could not shake off the memory of the night when he tried to strangle me. I chose to say nothing, to avoid another such scene, but once he had gone I breathed a huge sigh of relief and just carried on as usual.

*

On Monday, 7 May 1945, everyone seemed to be smiling. At first I didn't know why, but I met an air force boy, Peter, at the dance that night and he told me.

'Now that Hitler is dead, most of the chaps at my base think the war will be ending very soon. We are having a sweepstake on what day we think it will be.'

'Do you have a ticket?' I asked.

'Yes, I went for Friday this week.'

'As soon as that?' I was astonished. But then I hadn't listened to any news bulletins lately, so I didn't even know that Hitler was dead. Mother must have forgotten to tell me.

'It's quite a big thing,' he explained as he walked me home. 'Even some of the officers have joined in the sweepstake!'

As we reached my house and were stood on the doorstep saying goodbye, the front door burst open and Mother came out with a triumphant look.

'The war in Europe is over!' she exclaimed. 'Well, it will be in a few minutes, just after midnight. It was announced on the wireless this evening. I can't believe it! We're free! No more blackouts.'

I don't think I'd ever seen my mother look so delighted about anything.

'Yes, it's great. But what . . . How do you know?' I asked, catching her enthusiasm.

'It was a short announcement,' she explained. 'The Germans signed the surrender today! Winston Churchill will give a speech tomorrow, followed by King George.' She paused for me to take it in. 'Isn't that wonderful?

We're going to have a national holiday tomorrow to celebrate. VE Day, for victory in Europe. So you'll have a day off from work.'

'Let's not wait till tomorrow,' I suggested to Peter. 'We have to celebrate right now!' I knew Mother had to stay in as Jeffrey and Alan were asleep, but I was too thrilled and now much too wide awake to go to bed, so Peter and I turned around and walked, full of joy, back into town.

'Close, but no cigar,' he said with a grin.

'What do you mean?'

'I was out by two days,' he said. 'On the sweepstake, I mean. But I don't care – this is the best evening I've had in years. Let's go and live it up!'

As we walked past the empty spaces where the iron railings had been, some of them now replaced by other makeshift barriers, people were coming out of their houses, laughing and joking with each other, pulling down their wooden fences to pile up on a big celebration bonfire. The mood was joyous as complete strangers talked with each other and worked together in their preparations for the big day. Some of them put up bunting that had been stored away since the war began. Others blew up balloons.

We were jubilant as we walked along, meeting Bert, Kathleen, Peggy and most of my other friends, who joined us along the way so that by the time we reached the Market Square in the centre of Blackburn we were already a large party. We were all standing there, thinking what we could do to mark this special occasion, when the clock struck midnight. Suddenly all the street lights came on, for the first time since 1939. It was magnificent.

'Let's light a bonfire,' I shouted out, clambering onto a market table. 'Who's got some matches?'

'What can we light a fire with?' yelled a voice from the back of the square.

Bert got up and joined me. 'Let's gather all the stalls and tables together and fire up the market to celebrate!'

'Yes, that's all we've got.' I was always inclined to be mischievous when I could, but now I was really charged up with euphoria and keen to do something extraordinary. In all the excitement, we didn't even think about the damage we would cause.

Everyone dragged the tables and stalls together and some matches were found, so I struck one and tried to light the stall nearest to me. Everyone else soon joined in. But try as we might, we couldn't get them to stay alight.

By this time, a band had arrived and set up their instruments, and jolly music filled the square. As we gathered round they started to play familiar, morale-boosting songs from both the world wars for us to join in with. Songs like 'Bluebirds over the White Cliffs of Dover' and 'Pack up your Troubles' were the most popular. It was marvellous to hear everyone sing so happily. By now we had gathered a huge crowd. The whole square was packed with hundreds of people – mostly young like us.

While the band took a rest, I suddenly had another idea. 'Everyone get into long lines,' I shouted, climbing on top of one of the stalls to be heard over the crowd.

Somebody found me a megaphone and I shouted it out again, even louder. 'Let's do the old "Palais Glide"!' I suggested, and looked over at the band to see if they were ready. They were all smiling and nodding as they sorted out their sheet music. Bert, Peter and some of the other boys, still in their uniforms, organized the lines, so that we would all have enough space if we went the same way.

The band started to play and everyone laughed and cheered as they joined in, draping arms round each other and doing the steps . . . or any steps, as long as they managed to keep upright and in line, which most did.

I have no idea what time I got home, but there wasn't much sleep for anyone that night!

The next day, I went back into the centre of town again, where I had arranged to meet with all my friends. Kathleen and Peggy were there, along with Hilda, Bert, Peter and Jenny from the farm. I even met up with Philomena, my old friend from the convent. It was wonderful to catch up with her after so long.

Almost every building I saw was festooned with flags, bunting or some sort of colourful decorations – even Christmas-tree baubles. The whole of Blackburn had erupted in a frenzy of joyous celebrations. The day was packed with impromptu, bring-your-own street parties across the town. Bands were playing, there were games for the children, a bonfire in the Market Square and a happy fairground atmosphere.

It was a great community celebration of the freedom

we had gained. We were drunk on relief and hope. It was a day never to be forgotten.

Now at last we could burn the blackout curtains, tear up the ration books, get back our iron railings, switch on the lights and live! Well, not entirely, as it turned out. The blackout material could go, but the ration books had to stay, temporarily we thought, but in fact they were still needed for another nine years for some shortage items. Our beautiful railings wouldn't be back for some time either, if ever, but it was a joy to be able to switch on our lights whenever we wanted and especially good to see the warm glow in other people's windows again as I walked home from the Market Square.

One of the GI boys I used to dance with quite a lot at this time was called Hank, and we started to go out together for a while as friends. Of course, we knew that he would have to go back home to the USA soon with his pals, just as our boys would soon start coming home. But we made the best we could of that time between, when he didn't have too many duties and the light evenings beckoned us to explore the English countryside that he liked so much.

My family was not strong on shortening names, except for Bobby's. However, Hank used to call me Margie, and I quite liked it when he said it, with his American drawl. So it was always Margie . . . but not in front of my mother.

I had never visited an American base, so I was looking forward to going with Hank to a special dance they were holding at Bamber Bridge near Preston, before the GIs started to leave, either for the Far East, where the war still raged, or for home. My friend Peggy and I received our special invitations and were taken there, about twelve miles, in a huge army truck, which was quite a novelty for us. Hank and Peggy's partner Omar were waiting to greet us on our arrival.

The dance was a lot of fun and a great success. We each had some time to kiss and say goodbye – me with Hank and Peggy with Omar – and we were all very happy as we went to board the truck taking us back home, which was parked next to another large truck going somewhere else. I don't know how it happened. We were obviously not concentrating and, as Peggy boarded first, I suddenly realized that she was on the wrong truck. I was gesturing to her, trying to explain and reaching to grasp her arm and pull her down, while Omar was standing beside me, encouraging her to get out and change trucks. Suddenly Hank grabbed me and dragged me away from the vehicle. A van flashed past us, missing me by inches, and smashed into Omar, pinning him to the truck.

Being a medic, Hank quickly turned to a bystander and rasped, 'Take her away . . . and quickly. Take her back inside – anywhere away from here!' As I was ushered away by another GI, Hank took his jacket off and turned back towards the scene of the accident. 'I'm a medic! I'll stay with him.'

It was so fast that I didn't see much of what happened to Omar, which was just as well. I knew that he'd been hurt and Hank would be busy treating him, but it wasn't till later, as an officer drove us home, that I found out how awful it had been. Peggy was in a terrible state as she had seen it all. She sat with me in the back seat shaking with shock and inconsolable. I put my arm round her, trying to soothe her.

Omar was taken to hospital where he survived, unconscious, for two days before he died of his internal injuries. Peggy was distraught. He must have meant a lot to her, but I think she felt guilty as well, because he was trying to help her down from the truck when he was hit.

The Americans were preparing to leave, while our boys were beginning to come back and being demobbed. Every day I wished Ray could have been among them. It was hard to be cheerful, but I knew I must be.

They came to the dances in their civvies with big smiles on their faces, visibly relieved to be home at last. But within days their good moods had faded as many of them failed to find work and couldn't settle back into their old lives as easily as they had expected. Everybody they left behind had moved on, whilst all these boys wanted to do was to get married, settle down and have families.

Some of the boys I'd played with as a child, and grown up with, came back to the neighbourhood, and when they met my mother in the street, they were all asking her: 'Has Margaret made her mind up yet?' What they were keen to know, of course, was whether I'd decided who I wanted to marry, or if I wanted to marry and therefore whether I was still eligible.

To which Mother would give her usual answer:

'Margaret can get engaged as often as she likes, but she hasn't to get married till she's twenty-one.'

Well, that was telling them. They didn't want to wait that long so they looked for potential marriage partners elsewhere, which suited me.

Many of us shared a depressed, let-down feeling after the euphoria of VE Day, only a few weeks before. Things hadn't improved as quickly as we expected. There were still long queues outside shops and shortages of all sorts. Unemployment of ex-servicemen was high and there was not much prospect of work for most of them. It would take some time for the factories and businesses to adjust their plans and return to their pre-war production. Many returning men also suffered from physical wounds, and they had witnessed terrible traumas on the front line but were unable or unwilling to talk about their inner turmoil. A lot of young couples had sudden short courtships, marrying quickly in the months following VE Day, and there were then not enough houses and flats to go around, which was another source of discord.

During the war, women had taken on many of the men's jobs – finding exhilarating and fulfilling work, with new social networks which they were reluctant to forego. They too were affected by the expectation that they would give up their work to provide employment for their menfolk and go back to what some thought of as the drudgery and boredom of their former lives, always taking second place.

As someone who had been independent from an early age, I agreed with them. I had always enjoyed working so I wouldn't have wanted to stop either. I decided to leave my 'war work', however, now that we were no longer at war in Europe, so I approached the Post Office and they offered me my old job back from the following Monday. That meant I would now be working nearer home again, and I was doing work that suited me better – I never was any good at machines and physical work. First, though, I decided to have a break. A couple of days in Scotland was just what I needed, so I arranged to take the train up to Paisley on Thursday to stay with Gordon and his new wife Betty.

'Hank came to see me this afternoon,' said my mother while we were having tea on the Wednesday.

'Really? What did he want?' It was a surprise to me and I couldn't think why he would have come.

'The usual,' she replied, with a smile.

'What do you mean?'

'He wants to marry you and take you back with him to America.'

'Oh . . . I had no idea!'

'Well, I did wonder. I know you're friends, but I wasn't expecting that, were you?'

'No, he hasn't asked me. I knew he would have to go back sometime soon, but we haven't even talked about the future.' I was genuinely astonished. 'What did you say?'

'The usual, that you can get engaged as many times as you like, but you haven't to marry till you're twenty-one.'

I smiled. 'Yes, that's fine.'

'Would you want to go and live in America?'

'I don't think so. I wouldn't even want to marry him. He's a good man and I enjoy his company, but he's a friend. There isn't that spark. It would never work.'

'He said to tell you he'll see you at Tony's tonight.'

'Thanks for warning me,' I smiled. 'But I wasn't thinking of going dancing tonight.' I needed to iron some things and pack my bag, so that I could leave for Paisley straight from work tomorrow. It was my last day at the factory, so they were letting me go at lunchtime. 'I'll see Hank when I get back and sort it all out with him,' I added.

It was lovely to get away on the train, winding through all the different patches of countryside. Gordon and Betty were at the station to meet me and we had a good chat over supper that evening at their house. 'Tomorrow night, if it's all right with you, we've all been invited to a ball.'

'Oh yes. It will be lovely to dance somewhere new and meet different people.'

Sure enough, we went to the ball on the Friday evening and I met a good-looking English captain, in uniform. We danced most of the evening and arranged to meet the next day, Saturday. His name was Alastair and he had a car, so we drove over to Glasgow for the day. He had it all planned out. He took me to a lovely restaurant where we had lunch and, unusually for me, some wine. Then we went to the cinema and afterwards we strolled up Sauchiehall Street.

Unexpectedly, we bumped into another officer who was an old friend of Alistair's and he joined us, so now we were a threesome. While we were deciding what to do next, I came up with an idea.

'I know what we can do. I've heard such a lot about dancing at the Barrowland Ballroom. Why don't we go there?'

I noticed that they gave each other strange looks.

'Why not?' said my escort.

So off we went. I was quite excited to see this place that I'd heard people rave about at Tony's. But when we got there, the vast size of the dance hall, the crowded floor and the famous band playing stopped me in the doorway. For the first time ever at a dance hall, I felt frightened. Here I was in an unfamiliar city, with two men I hardly knew. What if they preferred to dance with other girls and left me on my own, or if someone else came up and asked me to dance? Would we be able to find each other again if we were parted in the crowd?

I wished I hadn't had all that wine at lunchtime. I was sure I was going to be sick. But where was the cloakroom? Now the captain wanted to dance, so we took to the floor, but I knew I wasn't much company; I felt awful and I just wanted to get back to Paisley. I couldn't say so straight away, so we stayed for a short while and then I asked to go. I could see my captain was disappointed that I seemed to have changed so much from the brave, vivacious girl I was in the morning, to the timid, uncertain mouse I had become in that place.

He drove me back to Gordon's house in Paisley and we parted as friends. I was so relieved the following day to be on the train home, to security and an evening with

Hank, dancing at good old Tony's on the Monday evening.

I did go dancing on Monday, but couldn't find Hank anywhere. I asked around and one of our friends told me he had gone.

'He had no choice,' she said. 'He so much wanted to see you before he left, but we found out you were away in Scotland, so he had to leave without saying goodbye.'

'Where did he go?' I asked, knowing it could either be to another posting or back to the States.

'He went home. Back to his mom's cooking, he said. But he asked me to tell you he would miss you and would write soon.'

Indeed, Hank did write me a letter. He was very sad to have missed me, he wrote. But would I consider getting engaged, and going out to visit him when I could get the time off work?

He was a lovely guy, and would make someone a funny, kind and loyal husband, but not me, and especially not in America. It wasn't going to happen.

In August 1945 the surrender of Japan was officially announced, giving us another public holiday and a new excuse for celebrations, with all the bunting back up for the street parties and merrymaking across Blackburn. This lifted the mood for a few days. The war was over across the whole world now and our prisoners of war from the Far East might at last be able to come home. But once again, many families would be disappointed and dispirited. Most of their POW boys were so close to death that it would take up to two years before they were allowed back, since they needed so much medical treatment following their long starvation and the accompanying diseases.

In the autumn, Bobby came home for a rare two weeks' leave, as possessive as ever, wanting to escort me wherever I went. By coincidence, only a day or two later Joe was also back for forty-eight hours and he came straight round to see me, once again insisting we were still engaged. Sitting with him at our kitchen table, I tried to tell him, yet again, that it was over.

'Joe, it's really good to see you again, but it would be so much better and easier for me if you could accept that we are just friends – good friends. I tried to make it clear when I told you I didn't want to be engaged any more. Will you please accept that our engagement is over? It was finished when I tried to give you back your ring.'

'I never agreed to that.' He raised his voice and his whole face turned to anger. 'You cannot be serious about this, Margaret. I will not hear of it. We are engaged to be married because we are made for each other . . . and that's that!' He slammed his hand palm-down on the table.

I gulped, then looked steadily at him as I tried to keep my voice calm. 'I've always liked you, Joe, and I'm glad of your friendship . . .' I took a deep breath. 'But I'm afraid I don't love you.'

He pushed the table roughly and stood up, towering over me. 'I don't believe you, Margaret. I'm not standing for any more of this. Come on.' He grasped my wrist tightly and pulled me up. 'You're coming with me to the cinema this afternoon.' And that was it.

He just wouldn't listen to what he didn't want to hear, and I was too fearful of his temper to push him any further this time, so for his two days of leave I had no choice but to go along with what he wanted to believe. But I was determined to change his mind about going to the cinema and at least I got my way over that.

I told Joe I had arranged to meet some of my friends that evening down at the George and Dragon, where our newly formed choir were having a practice, and I wanted to wash my hair first.

'My older brother Bobby is on leave too, so I've already agreed to let him walk me down town tonight, and I'll meet you there.'

Joe reluctantly agreed to this change of plan. 'Well, all right,' he said, letting go of my wrist. 'But you're my fiancée, so you will sit with me.'

Bobby chatted all the way as we strolled down to the pub together that evening.

'There will be quite a few people there that you know,' I said.

'What about your fiancé?' he asked.

'Joe? He's not my fiancé,' I explained. 'The engagement was over ages ago, when I told him and gave him back his ring. But Joe wouldn't accept it.'

Not having met Joe yet, he shrugged, but looked quietly pleased. I expect he wanted to keep on protecting me himself, at least until I met someone who would protect me as well as he did, which he no doubt thought would never happen.

By the time we arrived, the choir had finished singing and were settling themselves down with a drink to chat. Joe was there and made a big thing of standing and greeting me with a kiss, though I turned my head to make sure it was only a peck on the cheek.

'Joe, this is my brother Bobby, home on leave for a fortnight.'

'Lucky man,' said Joe as they shook hands. 'I've only got a couple of days, so I want to make the most of it.'

Joe had saved me a seat next to him, which he signalled to me, but before I could sit down, Bobby took my place. Good old Bobby! For a moment I thought Joe was going to make a scene about me sitting there instead, but Bobby got straight in, talking to him, and it was as if all Joe's momentary resentment just dissipated.

I left the two of them to talk together and went over to chat with the girls. Later, when I looked back at them, Bobby and Joe were still deep in conversation together, as if they were good pals. How strange, I thought, since they didn't have that much in common . . . other than me. Were my ears getting red?

We all met up again the following night, including Bobby and Joe who once again were getting on like a house on fire, standing by the bar and exchanging banter most of the evening. I was getting worried now that they might gang up on me. Thank goodness Joe would be leaving the next day and they probably wouldn't be at home at the same time again for quite a while, since Bobby was staying on in the RAF at his base in Africa.

From then on, for the rest of his leave, Bobby seemed

to turn up almost everywhere I went, whether at the George and Dragon or at Tony's. Had he made a pact with Joe? Or was I imagining it? Perhaps he was just being his usual protective self . . . but I had the distinct feeling that Bobby's ulterior motive was to make sure I didn't pick up with any of the other boys.

Little did he know!

18

The Bush Hat

1946

It was 22 March 1946, the day of the Annual Northrop Ball at King George's Hall, Blackburn, which was always a big occasion for my mother and her extended family. I was expected to be there, of course, whether I wanted to go or not. This year was a not. I tried everything to get out of going.

'Why do I have to go?' I asked over breakfast that morning. 'It's a stuffy dance for the old folks.'

'So are you saying I'm an "old folk"?'

'No, of course not. But what's wrong with wanting to be with my friends?'

'Nothing, but you're with your friends every night of the year, except this one.' Mother paused. 'I'd like you to be there. I've made you a beautiful new dress, so you'll be the star of the ball, and all the family will be proud of you. I will be proud of you. I know everyone would be very disappointed if you were missing.'

'But it's Friday. All my friends will be at Tony's. I'll have the pick of dance partners there. Friday's the best night at Tony's and I don't want to miss the fun. I could wear my new dress there instead.'

'No. I made it for the Northrop Ball. I'm sure there will be young men there too. You'll enjoy it once you're there.'

My mother could be very determined and this was one of those occasions. So, with great reluctance, I gave in.

That evening, when I got in from work, I laid out on the bed the dress Mother had made me, along with my new bra, stockings and dancing shoes. I admired the dress – Mother really had excelled herself. It was a beautiful black ballgown, with short sleeves, a sweetheart neckline and a v-shape from each side of my waist coming to a point at the back, made to one of my designs. Nobody would know that parts of it were made from our redundant blackout curtains. It was so elegant and close-fitting that when I put it on and did up the zip, it reminded me of what an old boyfriend had once said to me: 'Oh Margaret, you look like you've been poured into that frock!'

This was one dance where I wasn't really bothered what I looked like, so instead of taking time to put my hair up as usual, I left it curly and loose on my shoulders. I was sure there would not be anybody there to impress. But I did put on some lipstick and a bit of mascara, just to please my mother.

I went downstairs for her to put the finishing touch to my dress, as she always did. She had a way of putting a pin in that meant nobody could find it and undo the dress except her. 'There,' she said as she stood back. 'That will keep it all in place.'

I think I must have been a bit dim about that pin, as it was quite some time later that it finally occurred to me she had an ulterior motive for this!

It was time to leave and Grandad Harrison – whose business had the contract for building works at the Northrop Loom Company – had sent a car for us, so off we went in style. When we arrived at King George's Hall, the foyer was brightly lit, like a public square. We went through to the hall itself and there were all my relations on my mother's side, sitting in a long row along the far wall. I smiled nicely at all the old aunts and uncles but my heart sank. This was going to be a terrible evening, sitting there like birds on a telegraph wire hour after hour, with all the fuddy-duddies gossiping amongst themselves. The hall was dimly lit and the band hadn't started yet, so I was bored already, and there would be three or four hours of this.

I recognized a lot of the people coming and going, fetching their drinks. Mother waved at them now and then, but mostly she was chatting with her friend Alice.

My attention switched to the musicians setting up. It was Oscar Rabin's band, who had an excellent reputation, so at least I would be able to listen to their music to while away the time.

The main doors to the foyer were still open, with more people coming in . . . and that's when I saw, silhouetted against the bright light behind him, a tall, uniformed soldier, wearing a bush hat. As he walked away from the door, I could make out his face enough to see his fair good looks. I was fascinated by his bush hat. I had only ever seen those in wartime films.

'Ooh,' I said to my mother. 'I wonder if he's Australian.' The band started up, the noise drowning her reply.

I looked around and by now there were some other men still in uniform. I saw a naval officer, an airman and a couple of soldiers, but my eyes were on the man in the bush hat as he took it to check in at the cloakroom counter, then returned to the hall. After a quick look round the room, he made a beeline for me. As he walked towards me, I noticed his thick blond wavy hair, his sky-blue eyes and his rugged, sunburnt skin. But the features that stood out most were his big smile and the twinkle in his eyes. I must have smiled back as he approached and asked me to dance.

As soon as we stepped onto the dance floor, my heart sank. I wasn't the best dancer ever, but I was very good, thanks to the convent, and I realized this clodhopper had probably never danced in his life. He hadn't a clue. After we'd introduced ourselves and he told me his name was Jim, we shared a bit of small talk and he told me he had a month's leave before he had to go back to India. I knew I liked him, but I couldn't go on with this embarrassing charade, with him struggling over every step and everyone looking at us. I'd never live it down if any of my friends came in now.

Then, to make it worse, because of the sweetheart neckline of my dress, he'd somehow, unintentionally got part of my new bra strap in his hand and it started to unravel.

'What's this?' he asked.

I was mortified.

'Oh, Mother!' She always had pins, so when she saw

what had happened she came over and did something to sort it out.

'Phew! Let's sit down and have a drink,' I suggested firmly, already pulling him away from the dance floor.

He ordered a beer and I had my usual orange and lemonade that cost the princely sum of fourpence.

'Well, you're very cheap!' said Jim and we both laughed.

I didn't want to have to sit down with the family again, so I suggested we go and sit up in the balcony instead.

We went up the stairs and there was nobody there, so we had our pick of the seats, choosing two overlooking the dance floor, but far enough up that the music wasn't too loud, and we chatted away. If I went to a dance I expected to dance all night – this was the first time, the one and only time, that I'd sat down for the whole evening! But the hours flew by as we talked and talked, just getting to know each other.

'I went to St Mary's College,' he told me.

'Really? That's where my brother Jeffrey is now.'

'Where did you go to school?' asked Jim.

'The Convent of Notre Dame.'

'Well, how strange. We're both Catholics, then? And my sister is at the same convent. She'll be leaving this year.'

'So she must be a couple of years younger than me?'

'How old are you?'

'Nineteen. I'll be twenty in May. What about you?'

'Just a year older than you. I'll be twenty-one in July.'

Jim was very easy to talk to and, with three brothers, I was used to talking with boys. We chatted mostly about our families, our early childhoods and our first memories.

'So if your grandfather was the landlord at the Tanners'

Arms, and my father used to take me with him when he
went for a drink in their beer-garden, and I think we
children had free lemonades, do you think we might have
met, playing in the garden?'

'Yes!' I was quite excited at the thought. 'I played with
all the children who came and, being almost the same age,
we probably did play together in those days. Isn't that
amazing?'

'Yes, quite a coincidence, but a shame we don't
remember each other.'

'We must have been very young.'

The longer we chatted, the more coincidences we discovered. It was as if we were meant to meet. Maybe we
were.

'I won our section of the Border Regiment's lottery in
India to come here tonight,' Jim told me. 'We put all our
names in a hat and mine was picked out, so I won my
passage home for a whole month's leave! Now I feel as
if I was meant to meet you on my very first evening.'

Before we knew it, the taxi arrived to take us home. My
mother had to come up to find me.

'Sorry to end your evening,' she said. 'But we have to
go now. Our taxi is waiting.'

Not for the first time in my life, I felt a bit like Cinderella,
having to rush away before the clock struck twelve.

'Can't we stay a bit longer?' I asked her.

'No, we can't keep him waiting, or Grandad might
make us pay!'

'Hello, Mrs Holden,' said Jim. 'I'm James Ford of the

Border Regiment.' Then he took me by surprise. 'We're only just getting to know each other,' he explained. 'And we have so much more to talk about. I'd like to walk your daughter home, if that's all right with you. I promise I'll look after her.'

Mother hesitated for only a couple of seconds. 'All right,' she said, then turned to me. 'Mind you come in by midnight.' Now I really was like Cinderella.

Jim got that too. 'I'll make sure she doesn't turn into a pumpkin!' We all smiled at that and off she went to the waiting taxi, while we went down to collect my coat and his bush hat, which he put on as we left the building.

We must have talked for at least four hours already that evening, and we carried on talking all the long walk home. When we arrived back at my house, we went up the path. There were two steps in front of our front door, so he stood at the bottom and I was on the first step. He was six foot two inches, you see, and I was only five foot three. I always loved the six-footers.

Neither of us wanted the evening to end, although it was very late. I was probably being a bit coy, not wanting to seem too keen, and we must have annoyed the man who lived next door. He pulled open his upstairs window and shouted down.

'For goodness sake, Margaret, let him kiss you and then we can all get some sleep!'

It was difficult with the bush hat in the way, but he managed to kiss me. Just then Mother, having heard the neighbour's voice, opened the door.

'Will you bring him in?' she said. It was more of an order than a question.

So we followed her in. Mother sat back down in her rocking chair in front of the fire and picked up her crocheting to finish off, while Jim sat in my chair, to the side, and I perched on the stool in front of him. While we talked quietly he started to play with my hair. I didn't like anyone fiddling with my hair, so I pulled my head away a bit to give him the hint. After a few minutes, Mother put her crocheting down and rested her head back, eyes down, but still gently rocking.

We sat silently, watching the glowing embers, and when it looked like Mother had fallen asleep, Jim leant over to me.

'Does she never go to bed?' he asked me in a whisper.

'Not until you've gone, Jim,' she said, without opening her eyes.

As I lay in bed that night, still wide awake, I relived the evening. If I'd gone to Tony's, as I wanted, I probably wouldn't have met Jim, so I was very glad Mother had persuaded me to go with her and the family instead.

I'd known Jim for less than a day, so far. It seemed so strange that we'd only met a few hours before and yet already I felt very much at ease with him. There was definitely a spark between us.

I knew Jim felt it too when the next day, a Saturday, he was back at our house unexpectedly, just after breakfast, eager for us to go out for a walk.

'I don't want to waste one minute of my leave,' he explained.

The sun shone and I looked forward to a lovely day out with him. If it went as well as I thought, we would have a whole month to enjoy after that.

I made some sandwiches to take with us and we set off together for a tour of our childhood haunts, starting with the sandy patch we called 'Little Blackpool' on the bank of the river Ribble, where I had played with otters as a toddler. We didn't see any otters that day, so we walked on, hand in hand, along the river bank, past the ferryman who took paying passengers across the river to Hurst Green and Stonyhurst College, where my Holden grandparents were buried.

'We never took the ferry,' said Jim. 'I used to swim across the river, with my friends.'

'With your clothes on?' I laughed.

'No, we used to take them off and wind them round our heads, with our snake-clip belts fastened round to keep them there.'

'Did they ever fall off?'

'Only once,' said Jim with a grin. 'Luckily they floated, but I had to go home in wet clothes that day.'

We walked on to Sale Wheel Woods, with its wild spring flowers, then sat on a log to eat our sandwiches and watched the birds rooting around for comfy twigs which they took up into the trees to make their nests.

There was so much to talk about and so much to see on that first day, so we walked on and talked about the eccentricities of our families. I told Jim about my two sets of grandparents being at loggerheads with each other and putting up a sheet to hide their houses from each other.

I told him about my father, all the trips to the coast at weekends and the time he fell over a cow coming back one Sunday night.

Jim told me stories of his family too, but none quite as eccentric as mine. I learned that his father was Irish and served in the Connaught Rangers. He had been wounded in the Great War, shot in the eye.

'He was on the way home on a hospital ship when it was sunk,' said Jim. 'He survived and was taken onto another hospital ship which was also sunk. He was rescued again. It was a case of third time lucky for him and he finally got back to England, where he was classified as disabled, so he's been unable to work for most of his life.'

'Oh dear. But thank goodness he survived.'

'Yes, but I nearly didn't.'

'What do you mean?'

'You see this scar?' asked Jim, pointing to a red-and-white mark on his neck.

'Yes. What happened?'

'When I was about eleven, I was knocked down by a car. I don't remember it, but they told me about it afterwards. In fact, I didn't know anything as I was lying unconscious in hospital for a week before I woke up.'

'Your parents must have been very worried.'

'Yes, it was touch and go, the doctor told them. But I survived it all right. In fact, it probably knocked some sense into me!' He grinned.

'What about your family? Do you have any brothers and sisters?'

'Yes, three brothers and one sister. Jack is a chief petty officer in the navy, with a medal for gallantry. He's four years older than me. Then there's Louis in the air force, three years older than me. I'm in the middle, with David two years younger and Margaret, the youngest, still at school.'

He then told me about some of the antics he and his brothers got up to as children. In fact, there were so many stories to tell that we spent most of Sunday, after church, carrying on with our reminiscences. We took a tram to Wilpshire and walked the country lanes near where my Harrison grandparents still lived.

It was on this route that we bumped into a character from my childhood at the Tanners' Arms. I saw him walking towards us and thought I recognized him, but I wasn't certain till he came close. There was something about his face that looked familiar . . . and then I noticed it: the skiver bag that he always kept with him at the Tanners' Arms, and obviously still had – the bag that contained the big, gold sovereign coins that I loved playing with. He gave me a puzzled look, then uncertain recognition dawned.

'Margaret?' he said.

'Yes, that's right. How lovely to see you after all these years . . . and you still have your skiver bag.' I smiled with fondness for those days, and for the man. 'David Furness, isn't it?'

'Spot on, love,' he said. 'What a memory you have. You must have only been about three or four when you used to climb onto that high stool at the Tanners' Arms.'

'Yes, I remember. And you said that the head on the coins was better-looking than yours! But I didn't agree.'

We laughed.

'This is my friend Jim,' I said, introducing them to each other.

'I'm delighted to meet you, Jim. Anyone who has this girl for a friend is a lucky man. I always felt she would be a catch for someone special when she grew up.'

'Hey, enough of that,' I said with a grin. 'I only met Jim yesterday.'

'Well, you look like you already make a happy couple,' he said.

'Yes, I think we are,' agreed Jim, squeezing my hand.

'I'm so glad to have bumped into you, Margaret, after all this time,' said David. 'Hopefully it won't be so long before we meet again.'

We said our farewells and each walked on our separate ways, happier for having had that brief encounter with our past. Jim too was pleased to have met him and amused by what he said about us.

That evening, Jim joined us for tea at our house and met my younger brothers. Luckily, Bobby was still in the RAF, away overseas, but I dreaded what he would have said if he saw me walking out with Jim, instead of his new pal Joe, who was now serving in Germany. I could see trouble brewing. I knew I should warn Jim about this potentially tricky situation, but not tonight. Not yet. First I just wanted to enjoy some relaxed happiness – a happiness I didn't expect to find so soon after losing so much to the war.

19

Tickling Trout

1946

I had just finished my breakfast on Monday morning when there was a knock at the door. I opened it and there stood Jim on the doorstep, with a big grin and a bunch of flowers.

'Good morning, Margaret. I've come to escort you to work!'

Well, that was a happy surprise. I picked up my bag and off we went, chatting while we walked.

'I'm going to ask for the rest of the week off,' I said. 'Then we can go for more days out.'

'Good idea. Will they let you?'

'Oh, I think they will. They're very good, and anyway they owe me some holiday.'

We walked as slowly as we dared and I got there with only a minute to spare.

'Just time for a kiss?' asked Jim with a cheeky grin.

I stood on tiptoes – it was definitely a 'kiss and run' situation.

'I'll come for you after work,' he called after me as I

ran in through the door, holding my hat on and ready to apologize. A couple of the post girls had seen and shared a giggle.

True to his word, when I came out at the end of the day, Jim was there, standing to the side of the building, not wanting to show me up, but I'm sure it was noticed. I didn't mind. I felt quite spoilt, having a handsome man to walk me home.

'Did you get the time off?' he asked as we crossed the road.

'Yes, that was fine, so we've got the whole week to do what we like.'

'That's great.'

'What have you been doing today?'

'Well, I spent most of my day looking forward to coming to meet you.' He smiled. 'But I also helped my parents with a few things and did some errands of my own, like going into the bank and the dentist.'

'I thought the army had its own doctors and dentists?'

'Yes, it does, when we're living on an army base, but there aren't any dentists in the jungles of Burma.'

'You didn't tell me last night that you'd served in Burma.'

'You didn't ask,' he said with a smile. 'I wanted to hear all about you first.'

'It must have been awful, fighting out there.'

'Yes, for quite a while. It was tough, and the terrain made it harder, not to mention the poisonous wildlife and the tropical climate – like an inferno at times, carrying our packs and beating our way through with machetes.'

'That sounds terrible.'

'It's all part of the job.' He shrugged modestly. 'At least I just avoided the worst thing.'

'What was that?'

'Well, after two years in the Burmese jungle, we had orders to prepare to invade Japan. A lot of our troops were rerouted from Europe to join us for this massive invasion to try and end the war in Asia.'

'I thought the bombs on Hiroshima and Nagasaki did that?'

'Yes, they did. And that was what saved us. If those atom bombs hadn't been dropped on Japan, or if the Emperor had refused to surrender, our invasion would have gone ahead. If that had happened, millions would have died . . . and I might not have survived to meet you at the Northrop Ball!'

We carried on talking, happy to know that we had the whole week to continue learning about each other.

'Come and have some tea at our house,' I suggested. 'Then let's go and see what's on at the cinema.'

That first week together went by in a happy haze of sharing memories, walking and talking: strolling by the river, round the park or visiting the places we knew as children. Jim spoke quite a bit more about his time in Burma, which I knew from what other soldiers had told me was one of the most feared postings in the army, and any man who came through that was one to admire. Jim said very little about any of the worst things that happened, or the terrible things he saw. I suppose he didn't want to upset me – like my brother Bobby, always protecting me from anything bad.

We grew closer every day, though there was a part of me that wanted to keep it all light – nothing too serious. I had lost too many special people during the war, and if Jim was going away to fight or put himself in any more danger, I feared finding myself in that position again.

One day we took a walk through our childhoods, going to see all our old schools and sharing stories of our schooldays. As we went from one school to another we found out that we both knew quite a few of each other's school friends – yet more coincidences.

At the end of each afternoon, we walked back home up Robinson Street, past the playground where Ray and I had played as children, past Howarth's Pens, where hundreds of chickens roamed before the war, in large wood and wire-mesh pens. The hens went when war was declared, the wire went soon after to the ammunition factories and the wooden frameworks were ripped up to fuel the VE Day bonfires. So now it was bare ground, but we still called it Howarth's Pens.

The surface of our road hadn't been kept up during the war. It remained a black and rather sooty-surfaced asphalt, with random potholes and wagon tracks. Now that the weather was warming up, most of the children were playing outside after school, skipping and playing hopscotch, or its variation, 'airplane hopscotch', just like my friends and I used to play in the St Alban's Junior School playground.

Even after the war, there still wasn't much traffic along Robinson Street, but tradesmen came on their rounds, some of whom we hadn't seen since the early days of the war, before rationing took over. We had a twice-daily milk cart. The first visit was early morning and the other late afternoon. The milk was in 'kits' or churns and we had to bring our own jugs for the milkman to pour the milk into. The children had great fun with the horse-drawn coal wagon, petting the coalman's beautiful shire horse and running after him with buckets, some for loose coals and others for manure to nourish their parents' tomatoes.

We had missed our rag-and-bone man during the war, poor chap, with the metal all taken for the war effort and the 'rags' or old clothes going to the WVS (Women's Voluntary Service), where the volunteers would unpick the seams and unravel knitted garments to make new ones – a helpful way to stretch the clothing coupons in our ration books, except that Mother was an expert at that in our house. I don't remember any of our neighbours giving our rag-and-bone man bones, but still he called out 'Rag and bone' in a gruff, sing-song voice as he rounded the corner into our street. 'Any old metal. Bring out yer rags.' We were pleased to see him back again. I suppose it was a sign that all was well with the world once more. He smiled as we passed him. 'Hello, love. Tell yer mother I'm back,' he said.

'Yes, I will.' I returned his smile. 'I expect she heard you.'

On our second weekend I managed to persuade Jim to come to a dance – the first time since the Northrop Ball.

'You know I don't like dancing,' complained Jim. 'And, as I remember, you didn't like my style.'

'What style?'

'Whatever it was, you certainly pulled me off the dance floor quickly enough!'

'Yes, before anyone I know saw us.'

'So why do you want us to go tonight?'

'I haven't been to Tony's all week! Besides, I want you to meet some of my friends. But you don't have to dance. You could always talk to them while I'm dancing – I'm sure you'll like them.'

'All right, then. I'm not going to get any peace if I don't!'

With reluctance, Jim came into Tony's with me and I introduced him to all the gang. He talked a bit to Kathleen, Peggy and Jenny, plus Bert and the other boys, while I danced with various partners, until finally he'd had enough.

'Come on, Margaret. Let's go back to your mother's.'

So I agreed and we walked back home again. 'How did you like my friends?' I asked him.

'They were all right,' he said, but the messages were obvious – he didn't like me dancing with other boys and he didn't like having to make polite conversation with my friends, of whom he didn't seem particularly enamoured. Perhaps it was just how he felt that evening. But I noticed that, as he relaxed a bit, he was very charming with the girls and I was dying to find out what they thought of him. I'd have to wait to ask them, though I was sure they appreciated his tall good looks.

He soon livened up when it was just the two of us again, walking home. Mother invited him in, as always. I think she was already growing rather fond of him. So was I, but rather more than just fond, despite his moodiness tonight. On the Sunday, Jim's parents had invited me to come and meet them for tea, so we walked over there, taking some flowers that I'd bought with Jim on the Saturday. Although his house wasn't very far as the crow flies, it was a long walk to Mary Street in Eanam, with there being only one way of going under the railway line. We set out in good time and, as always, talked non-stop all the way.

Finally we arrived at a neat-looking terraced house, smaller than ours and without a garden, but inside it was immaculate. All the furniture was polished to a high shine. Jim's parents were welcoming and friendly, so it was lovely to meet them. His mother cooked a delicious tea, despite the continuation of rations, and we all had a good chat about the latest post-war news and our childhoods.

'What do you think, Ma?' Jim said as we all sat down together after tea. 'Wasn't I right?'

His mother turned to me and smiled warmly. 'Yes, you were right. But I'm not going to embarrass Margaret while she is here by praising her.'

'Why do you think none of your brothers or your sister were at home?' I asked after we left.

'Just as well,' said Jim. 'You'll get to know them soon enough.'

I sensed a slight note of tension in his voice, but thought it better to say nothing.

On the long walk back to my house, I asked Jim whether he knew Joe Walker.

'Vaguely, but I don't think I've ever spoken to him.'

'I was sort of engaged to him for a short while last year. I thought he was pretending to propose, but he was being serious. Not only that, he was terribly jealous if I even looked at another man, let alone danced with any of the boys at Tony's, especially the Americans. I didn't like that and I didn't like the way he tried to control me,' I explained. I decided not to mention his near-strangulation attempt. 'I had to break the engagement.'

'Good,' said Jim with a sigh of relief, although I think he was already confident in my growing relationship with him.

'The only trouble is, Joe wouldn't accept it. He still calls me his fiancée, tries to get back with me and won't acknowledge that it's over.'

'Well, it takes two to be engaged, so if you don't want to be, there can't be an engagement to Joe any more,' Jim said with certainty. I just wasn't sure Joe would see it that way.

Every working day, Jim turned up at breakfast time, walked me to work, then often went back to my mother's for a bit. Mother liked Jim and seemed happy to have him around, whether I was there or not. He might go back to his parents' house for the afternoon, then he walked all the way back to pick me up at the end of my working day. We rarely went to Tony's in the evenings as Jim didn't enjoy it, but there would be plenty of time for me to make up for that when his leave was over.

Time was running out, however. It was a Saturday morning, the third and last weekend of his leave, and we

strolled through the park, enjoying the spring bulbs, the
newly mown lawns and the blossom on some of the trees.

We sat down together on a nearby bench to relax.

'It's such a lovely time of the year in England,' said Jim.
'I shall miss it when I go back to the sweltering heat, this
time in India.' He paused, turning to face me. 'And that
won't be the only thing I will miss.'

'I should hope not!' I replied. 'If you mean me.'

'Will you miss me too?'

I pretended to think about it . . . but not for too long.
'Yes,' I agreed. 'I will miss you and all our walks and
chats. It's going to seem very strange without you, and
yet we've only known each other for three weeks.'

'I know. I feel as if I've known you for months or years
– not just weeks. But we still have six days to fill before
I have to leave.'

'Will you write to me when you are away?' I asked,
thinking back to all those letters I used to receive from
boys abroad during the war, and the struggle I had to find
time to reply to them. The special ones, particularly Ray,
I always answered first. They were the ones I looked out
for when the postman came, but now there were no more
letters from Ray or Les, Clarry or even Wilfred. I told Jim
all about these boys and how much I felt for them, but
I'm sure he also knew now that he was special to me too.
I found it strange, in a way, that we had become a couple
in such a short time, but it felt right.

'You bet I'll write to you – every day. What else will I
have to do?' He grinned. 'You'd better make sure you
write back and tell me everything you've been doing.'

'Everything?' I teased.

'Well, you know what I mean.'

Jim was due to leave from the station on Friday morning, so we made the best we could of the few remaining days, until midweek, when I suddenly developed a rash. As soon as she saw it, Mother dabbed gentian violet on the spots, leaving mauve blotches all over my face. I looked such a sight that I didn't dare go to work that day. I'd have frightened away the customers' children!

So I sent Jeffrey before school to tell a girl round the corner who worked at the Post Office to let them know that I couldn't come to work today.

As soon as he left, there was a familiar knock on the door and Mother opened it, to let Jim into the vestibule.

'Where's Margaret?' he asked. 'Isn't she ready yet?'

'Don't let him in,' I cried.

'She's got a rash on her face,' explained Mother.

'You can't see me like this,' I called out to him. 'I'm covered in gentian violet.'

'What?' I don't suppose he had a clue what I meant. 'Please let me in to see you. I want to talk to you.'

'Well, I'm not going out anywhere,' I said as he came through the door to our sitting room. I held up a cushion to hide part of my face.

'Nobody will see you if we just go for a walk.'

'Why can't you talk to me here?'

'Because I'd like to have a serious talk with you and . . .' He looked around. Jeffrey had just come back to collect his school bag. Alan was trying to chop up an apple on the tablecloth with a blunt knife and Mother was clearing the breakfast things.

'It's time you left for school, Jeffrey,' she told him. 'Alan, put that knife down and help me clear up. We have to get you to school too or you'll be late.'

Jim and I sat together yet apart on the sofa, watching all this with some amusement and, in Jim's case, frustration.

'Come on, Margaret. It's a lovely day. Let's go out for a walk.'

'But somebody might see me.'

'Who are you afraid of seeing you?'

'Anyone from the Post Office.'

'But how can they see you if they're at work?'

'Oh . . . all right, then, but maybe later, when my face isn't such a bright colour.'

Of course, we could have had the talk that Jim wanted at home, but he was unusually determined that nobody should interrupt us, even my mother who would return shortly. So I went and washed my face to try and remove some of the vivid colouring, then cut us some sandwiches and off we went.

'Let's go to Corporation Park first,' he suggested.

'We went there the other day, why don't we go somewhere in the country instead?'

'Well, we've got all day – we can do both.'

As we walked through Little Harwood, I remember feeling guilty not to be at work. After all, it was only a rash . . . but it was on my face, except that it seemed better now.

'I feel a fraud,' I confessed. 'I hope nobody sees me.'

'Never mind. If anyone should recognize you, they will probably just assume you're having a day off.'

'Y-e-s, maybe.' I wasn't too certain about that.

As we approached the grand Victorian entrance to the park, Jim slowed me down to a stop. 'Have you heard the song "Macushla"?' he asked.

'Yes. I've heard it on the radio, when Mother listens to songs in the evenings.'

'It's one of my favourites.' He paused. 'Because of what the word "Macushla" means.'

'Oh yes? Is it a real word, then?'

'Yes, it's an Irish word. In Gaelic, "Macushla" means "my pulse" or "pulse of my heart". Isn't that wonderfully romantic?'

'Yes, it is rather.'

'Sometimes people in Ireland use "Macushla" instead of "Darling", so that's what I'm going to call you.'

We walked through the gateway and along the paths round the park, then came to the seat we'd sat on last time. Jim seemed a bit tense and I was just about to ask him if he was all right, when he put his hand in his pocket and brought something out, then opened it to show me. I could see it looked like gold, but it was quite unusual.

'What is it?' I asked.

'It's called a rosary ring,' said Jim. 'Try it on.'

So I slipped it onto the ring finger of my right hand, held it away and admired it. 'It looks very pretty,' I said. 'I've never seen one of these before. Why is it called a rosary ring?'

'Because . . . can you see these ten little knobs on it? They're the rosary.'

'Oh, that's clever.'

'It used to belong to my grandmother when she was young.'

'Oh. Shouldn't your sister have it?'

'No, she has another of our grandmother's rings.'

'Well, I really like it, thank you.'

So there we were, sat on a bench in Corporation Park, when Jim shuffled himself forward and got down on one knee. He took my hand and said, 'Will you agree to become engaged to me?'

Out of the corner of my eye, I noticed there were some people walking down the path towards us. 'Will you ask me again, so that these people can see?'

Jim looked a bit surprised, then smiled, kissed the back of my hand and asked me again, a little louder this time, 'Will you agree to get engaged to me?'

'Yes,' I replied in a clear voice.

The elderly couple smiled at us as they walked past.

'Good luck,' said the woman.

'Be happy,' added the man.

'We will,' responded Jim. 'Won't we, Margaret?'

'Yes,' I said again. 'I really think we will.'

Jim gave me a big hug, lifting me off my feet and twirling me round.

'Why did you make me do it again?' he asked with a quizzical expression.

'I just wanted other people to see.' I paused. 'I'm a terrible show-off, aren't I?'

'Yes, even with your gentian violets.'

'Oh, I had forgotten about that!' We had a giggle together.

'So we're engaged?' asked Jim, as if wanting to make sure he hadn't dreamt it.

'Yes, we're engaged,' I confirmed. 'Isn't it great?' It wasn't a surprise, but it was exciting, though I didn't take it too seriously at the time after the fracas with Joe, although this was entirely different. Everybody wanted to get married after the war, but my friendship and easy familiarity with Jim had grown into love, rather as it had with Ray, though this time it had been over a much shorter time and still needed developing.

'I'll save up and buy you a proper engagement ring as soon as I can,' he said. 'But I'll just put the rosary ring on your left hand for now.' It fitted perfectly.

'Let's go and tell someone,' I suggested. 'We could go and tell my mother. I think I know what she will say.'

'What's that?' He looked a bit worried.

'I'll let you find out. But don't worry, it's nothing bad,' I laughed.

When we got back to the house and told her, she seemed genuinely pleased. Then she turned to Jim: 'I'll tell you what I've told all the others. Margaret can get engaged as many times as she likes, but she hasn't to marry till she's twenty-one.'

He turned to me. 'Have there been a lot of others, then?'

'Not many,' I said. 'I've already told you about them,

but I was younger then and most of them were lost in the war.'

'But will you give us your blessing to marry after that, Mrs Holden?'

'Yes,' she said with a nod of her head. 'I can see that Margaret thinks a lot of you, Jim, and so do I. But I'm afraid you may have a different response from other people.'

'Do you mean Joe?' he asked.

'Yes, I'm sure Joe won't be happy. But also, more importantly, I'm thinking of Bobby. You know how protective he's always been of you, Margaret. And he still thinks of you as his little sister – far too young to make your own decisions. He wants to make them for you. I think he may have something to say about it, but you'll have to tell him yourself, not me.'

I knew Bobby's next leave wasn't till after Jim had gone, so I would have time to work out the best way to tell him. And at least Jim wouldn't be there to complicate things.

The next stop was Jim's parents and they were delighted for us, though I found out later that his brothers were not so happy. I didn't know why. Perhaps because they hardly knew me, and it had all happened so quickly.

We spent our last two days visiting other relatives and meeting up with friends to announce our engagement. Everyone seemed happy for us. Of course, it would be more than a year before we could marry, as I would only be twenty the next month, and Jim could be away in India for up to two years before his next leave. My emotions were all over the place as these idyllic four weeks came to an end.

As I lay in bed that last night before Jim's departure, I was in quite a state – a mixture of happiness, sadness and anxiety. Our four weeks together had been a blur of happiness and I knew that Jim was the one I loved. But now he was going off, far away, and leaving me for goodness knows how long without him.

I dreaded having to tell Bobby. I was frightened of angering or upsetting him. I knew he had my best interests at heart, but he didn't always have a clear view of what my best interests might be. I desperately wanted his blessing. I hoped for the best, but feared the worst.

In the end, whatever Bobby said, it was Jim that mattered most now. If only I could be sure he would not be killed.

I slept fitfully that night.

20

A Long Goodbye

1946

The dreaded day dawned – Friday, 19 April 1946. I met Jim at the station, as planned. He was back in his uniform, complete with the bush hat that had first attracted my attention just four weeks before. He dropped his kitbag and gave me a long embrace, twirling me off my feet and right round.

'Didn't your parents want to come and see you off?' I asked, once he'd put me down.

'Yes, but I told them I wanted it just to be you and me and I think they understood. I said all my family goodbyes at home.'

We went straight to the platform, sat on a bench and waited for the train, holding hands and chatting non-stop, trying to be cheerful for each other's sake, but feeling the opposite inside.

Far too soon, the train pulled into the station, then screeched and clattered to a halt in front of us. One last kiss and Jim climbed aboard. He sat by the window next to where I stood, and as the guard blew his whistle and waved his green flag, the train slowly clanked and trundled into action. As it began to move out along the track, he waved as furiously as I did, through the clouds of steam, until well after he and the train were out of sight. How long till we could be together again?

I don't remember doing as much work that day as I should have done. I couldn't stop thinking about Jim, watching the clock for the time he would change trains and then when he was due to arrive at Southampton. I wondered what his quarters would be like and how long it would be before he embarked on the troop ship, bound for India.

By the end of Friday afternoon, I felt drained. On my walk home, I weighed up the alternatives – stay in and mooch about Jim not being around any more, or go out on the town. So I went dancing at Tony's, caught up with my old friends and told them about Jim's proposal. They all seemed very pleased for me, but perhaps also a bit uncertain.

'Do you think it's serious this time, Margaret?' one of the boys grinned. 'Or do we still have a chance?'

The music, the fun and of course the dancing lifted my spirits and a funny lad I used to play with in the rec walked me home, telling me jokes all the way back to my house.

The weekend stretched out ahead of me, but I went back to my Fair Isle knitting, playing Lexicon with Jeffrey and Alan, plus of course dancing in the evenings.

On Tuesday I received my first letter from Jim. He was still in Southampton, awaiting his ship. It was a very long letter – several pages, so he must have been bored . . . or besotted with me! Perhaps both, judging by what he wrote.

I took it unopened up to my bedroom and shut the door before I looked at the envelope with his neat writing and the Southampton postmark, then slit the envelope and took out the letter, written on several pages of thin white paper. I began to read it:

Transit Camp,
Southampton.
Sunday morning, 10 a.m.

My own darling Macushla,
I have just had my breakfast after coming back
from Church. The atmosphere in the Church just
suited my mood, peaceful and quiet. I was waiting
in the Church for quite a while before Mass
started and as I was waiting, you were in my heart
and talking to me, just as if you were sitting beside
me, telling me of the day we will be joined
together in Holy Matrimony, and of the joy and
happiness we will be experiencing on that day.
Macushla, I love you with all my heart and
soul, and the day of our reunion cannot come too
fast. That Heavenly day when time stands still and
everything is hushed . . . We shall be oblivious to
everything else, time and people.

Jim had written each page in the same vein as the first – very loving and longing. I felt that too as I read it, right the way through to his last paragraph.

The clock on the civic building outside has just struck four. Every four hours the clock chimes out a few bars from a hymn. I know the tune, but I can't name it. With every chime that sounds, I am coming nearer to you, Macushla. I may be sailing vast oceans or in foreign lands, but I am always with you in Blackburn, as you will always be by my side. We shall be waiting patiently and saving and planning for the happy and joyous day we are together again.

I will close to catch the early post of the day, so until this evening, au revoir, my darling Macushla. I am yours, body and soul.

Your loving Jim x x x x x x x x x x x x x x x x

I shall love you and keep on loving you till my breath fails me, and my heart stops beating. From my heart to your heart, Macushla.

'I'll walk beside you through the world today' [written entirely in kisses]

Letters from Jim arrived daily, sometimes two or three a day. I used to take some of them to work with me to read extracts out to the other girls. I also read out the more descriptive parts of them to Mother, as she liked to hear about the things he had to do while he waited for his ship to come. I wrote to him too, almost as often as he wrote to me.

As Jim was still in Southampton the following weekend, I took the train down to see him. This was how I knew he was different from all the others. I really wanted to spend more time with him, while we still could. I left early on Saturday morning and bought a return ticket to arrive back home again on Sunday evening. The night in between I was booked in to stay at the Girls' Friendly Society in Southampton.

I got up very early, boarded the Blackburn 'milk train' to London and settled down for a long journey. At first I seemed to be the only person in my carriage, but a few stops later a young RAF lad got on. We said hello to each other and, being me, I started chatting, asking him about himself and where he was based. His name was David.

'Why are you going to Southampton?' I asked. 'Are you on leave?'

'Yes.' He nodded. 'I'm going home to stay the weekend with my parents.' He paused. 'What about you?'

'I'm going to Southampton for the weekend too,' I said. 'To visit my fiancé.'

We carried on chatting and looking out of the windows at the passing countryside. It helped pass the time, but we were glad when we arrived at Euston station in London. Then we had to find our way to Waterloo station. I was relieved I didn't have to navigate London on my own. It seemed such a huge, busy, noisy city and we had to walk, of course, carrying our overnight bags, as neither of us could afford buses on top of the train fares. It was quite a long walk, but on the way I was amazed to find we were crossing London Bridge, the one in the rhyme, but it wasn't falling down at all.

By the time we had reached Waterloo, found the

platform and boarded the train, I was tired out. Before long, with the movement of the train, I felt more and more sleepy. David seemed to notice it.

'You look tired,' he said.

'Yes, it's been a very long journey, all the way from Blackburn.'

'Why don't you just lie down across the seat and have a sleep. I'll keep guard.'

I was a bit unsure at first . . . would I be putting myself in danger? But he was such a nice, innocent-looking young man that I had the feeling I could trust him . . . and I did need a nap.

'Thank you,' I said with a smile, as I lay down along the bench seat and put my coat over me as a cover. The rhythmic sounds of the train lulled me straight to sleep and I only woke up as it slowed to a stop.

'That was well timed,' David said with a grin. 'I hope you enjoy your weekend.'

'You too,' I said as we parted ways.

He turned, put his kitbag over his shoulder and strode off towards his home.

It was wonderful to see Jim in the station forecourt, waiting for me with a huge smile. He ran towards me and, being a whole foot taller than me, swept me off my feet.

'I can't tell you how wonderful it feels to have you in my arms again,' he said. We walked on a few paces, arm in arm. 'Are you hungry?'

'A bit,' I admitted. 'But I've got two rounds of sandwiches with me. Shall we find somewhere to sit and share them?'

After we'd eaten and I'd told Jim how I'd fallen asleep on the train he suggested going to the pictures. 'It's nice and dark in there,' he said with a twinkle in his eyes. 'And we could sit on the back row.'

'Yes, let's,' I agreed. So we did. I can't remember what the film was – I don't think we watched much of it. But I do remember the lovely time we had in the interval, when the organ played and the whole place was in an uproar, singing 'Deep in the Heart of Texas'.

At the end, we all poured out of the cinema into the street. By now it was about teatime and Jim carried my bag for me. 'What time do you have to be at the Girls' Friendly Society hostel?' he asked.

'Well, they close the doors at ten and apparently they don't let anyone in after that, no matter what. So I guess I should be there by around quarter to ten.'

'Right, that gives us a few hours,' said Jim. 'Let me show you the sights of Southampton,' he said with a grin.

'What sights are those?'

'You're right. You're the only sight I wanted to see,' he said, giving me another kiss, right there in the street. Luckily there was nobody around to see us. I was afraid he might be court-martialled for kissing a girl in the street while he was in uniform.

'Let's just go and walk around the port and the town,' I suggested, so that's what we did.

We hadn't got far when, heading along the pavement in the opposite direction, I saw a familiar face.

'Who's that smiling at you?' asked Jim, sounding suspicious.

'It's all right,' I said. 'It's David, the RAF boy I told you about – the one who guarded me while I slept on the train. And that must be his father with him.'

We stopped and did the introductions and then the father invited us back to their house.

'Do come back and have a cup of tea with us.'

I glanced at Jim, whose face told a story.

'Well,' I began. 'I'm afraid we . . .'

'I insist,' interrupted the father. 'Just for a cup of tea and some of my wife's cake. You needn't stay long.'

'Well . . .' Jim hesitated.

'That's decided, then. Come along with us. It's only five minutes' walk away.'

So we walked along with David and his father to a sweet little house in a quiet street, where we were invited to sit down in their comfortable living room, while his cheery wife brought tea and cake on a tray.

I've never known anyone to talk as much as David's father. He talked and talked. A fresh tray of teas appeared after the first hour, with biscuits this time and delicious home-made crumpets.

Jim was asked about his war service in Burma, which astonished them and took us well into the evening. Darkness fell and the blackout curtains were drawn tight across the windows, even though the war was over, and still David's father was talking and talking. I looked at my watch as obviously as I could, but he didn't take the hint. A few minutes later Jim too looked at his watch but there was still no break in the conversation to allow us to stand up. Neither of us wanted to be rude to these lovely people, but Jim was worried about losing the opportunity to have time alone with me, and I was becoming increasingly anxious about getting to the GFS hostel before they locked up at ten.

In the end, we just had to insist on leaving so that both of us could get back in time to where we were meant to be. After hurried goodbyes, we finally left their house at 9.30 in the evening. As soon as they closed their front door, we ran through the streets of Southampton. Luckily, Jim had already been to find out where the GFS hostel was and we just made it, arriving with only two minutes to spare.

On the Sunday morning, as early as allowed, Jim came to meet me and this time we really did walk around the port and the town, talking all the time we had – only a few hours before I had to catch my train back. I desperately didn't want to go. The relationship was becoming more and more special to me with every moment I spent with Jim. We shared our thoughts and feelings as we planned for the day we could marry and the future that would lie ahead. I was rather pensive on the journey back to London and then onwards to Blackburn. I was pretty certain of my feelings for him, the spark we had for each other, the loving letters he wrote every day. When would I see Jim again?

By the end of the next week, surprisingly, Jim's ship still hadn't arrived, so I travelled down to Southampton again. This time the Girls' Friendly Society was full, so I had to stay at the YWCA. That was a novelty! It was clean and had what I needed, but was a little less genteel. The previous weekend we had walked around the city, but this time we took a packed lunch with us and kept going till we came to the countryside, where we found a stretch of open woodland. We picked our way between the tall trees and found a little clearing where perhaps only animals gathered. Here we sat on a fallen tree trunk and ate our lunch – sandwiches first, then a small cake each. I bit into my piece, but the sponge was so dense that I couldn't eat it all.

The forest was green and peaceful, save for the natural orchestra of lively birdsong. Jim laid down his army coat and we lay side by side, holding hands and looking up through the branches to the blue sky, enjoying the spring warmth. The weekend was too brief and the parting was painful, but it had to be. We knew this might be the beginning of many months apart, with half the world between us.

Jim continued writing his letters after that brief but glorious weekend. Towards the end of the next week, I received three letters on the same day, all written on the Wednesday and recalling the carefree time we had spent together. The first was written in the early hours, when Jim couldn't sleep.

Transit Camp,
Southampton.
Wednesday morning, 2 a.m.

Dearest Macushla,

We have parted for a while, but compared with the happy lifetime we are going to spend together it is but a few seconds. We were made for each other . . .

In this letter, Jim told more of his love for me and his dreams for our future. He urged me to keep in touch with his mother and visit her whenever I could.

I am going on the BOAT tomorrow, Margaret, for my long ocean journey and long train rides. Through Monsoons, sweat and glaring sunshine, you will always be with me. Just one thought of you and I can take everything else in my stride.

I have just been paid and this afternoon we have an FFI (do you know what that is?). We cannot leave Camp as Guards have been placed at the gates.

I am thinking of you all the time. Our love for each other is like a fierce fire which will never be quenched.

I don't suppose I will get any mail from you until I get off the Boat, but I know you will be thinking of me and writing as often as you can . . .

The second letter I received that day was written at 11 a.m., just a few hours after the first, and included four lines of a popular song: 'Happy Days, Happy Hours, Happy Years', which expressed his love for me.

The third letter was also written on the same date.

Wednesday, 8.30 p.m.

My dearest Macushla,

It is getting dark here and I have just left the NAAFI Canteen, where a soldier was playing the piano. He played 'our' tune and it was just as if my stomach was coming up through my mouth, dragging my heart with it.

I told you in my previous letter that we could not leave Camp because of the Guards, but I sneaked out.

I went to the bench where we had been sitting on Saturday and stayed there for half an hour. I would have given my right arm to have had you there by my side. Then I wandered off to where we had been in the woods on Sunday. The foot-marks were still there and the grass was still flat where my overcoat had been. Then, can you remember giving me part of a cake which you couldn't eat? We put it into a paper bag in the bushes. I found it – the piece of cake you had bitten was in the bag. I kissed it and fed it to the birds which were surging from the bushes beyond. I know you would have liked it that way . . .

They are telling us to put out the lights now, Margaret, so I must close. I will write again before the boat sails away.

So goodbye until tomorrow.

You are always in my heart forever.
My body and soul are yours to cherish for ever
and ever.
Goodnight my sweetheart.
Jim xxxxxxxxxxxxxxxxxxxxxxxxxxx

That night, after reading his three letters, I lay in bed and imagined Jim boarding the ship, pausing to look back as he climbed the gangway, thinking of me here in Blackburn, thinking of him. By now he would be ever farther away at sea. If I knew where he was I could plot it in Jeffrey's school atlas.

It wasn't till the next day that I found out where he was, when another three letters arrived from Jim. The first of these began with an explanation:

Transit Camp, Southampton
Thursday morning, 10 a.m.

My dearest Macushla,
I have just returned from the Parade Ground.
Many of the soldiers were taken to the Boat, but
we were told to wait for another Boat, as that one
was full. I don't know when I shall go. Everything
is so uncertain. I do wish I could have you down
here, but I might have left by the time you arrive.
I should die if that were to happen . . .

The second letter, written at 2.30 that afternoon, began by saying:

I am glad more than ever now that I did not catch the boat. I can write you a nice, long letter whilst I am still in England . . . I am alone in the barrack room, with all your photos spread around me. You fill the room, Margaret, and tears come to my eyes when I think of the happy times we have spent together and will spend together. Remember when we cooked our meal over the open fire? And I dropped the egg on the grass. Clumsy of me. When I saw you leaning over the fire frying the eggs and you kissed me for being successful with the fire? That fire is still burning, only a different type of fire, Margaret, the fire of our love which will never die . . .

In the third letter of that batch Jim explained that, not knowing when the next ship would come, he had been trying to get leave, but unsuccessfully so far. It was so hard for both of us still to be in the same country, only 200 miles apart, and unable to be together.

On the following Monday, 13 May, I arrived home from work to the surprise of my life. I let myself in as usual and walked into the living room to find Jim sitting on the sofa, talking to my mother.

'What are you doing here?'

'What do you think?' He stood and we embraced – a wonderful warm feeling.

'Don't you want me, then?'

'Of course I do. It's great to see you here, but how . . .

did they give you some leave after all? Or have you absconded?' I smiled, sitting down next to him.

'The second ship didn't come, so they're sending me to London to fly me and some others out to India instead, once they've arranged everything. I pleaded with my lieutenant to let me come here before London and he managed to fix it for me. I didn't hesitate. I didn't even have time to send you a telegram. I just packed my kitbag, caught the first train to Blackburn . . . and here I am!'

'That's marvellous. How long is your leave?'

'Only forty-eight hours, but we can do a lot in that time. Can you get the day off tomorrow . . . and maybe the next day?'

'I'll certainly try, but I won't know till tomorrow morning.'

Mother had cooked plenty, so we all had tea together.

'As it's my first evening, let's spend it here with your mother, if that's all right with her,' he said. 'It's already my second home and it's so cosy being here with you.'

Mother had come through into the living room again and nodded her head.

'That will be fine, Jim,' she agreed with a smile.

As it happened, I had told Kathleen and Jenny that I would meet them at Tony's that night to have some fun. So when I saw Jim there, looking so pleased to have surprised me and, I suppose, assuming I would drop everything to be with him, well, yes, I was delighted . . . but I wasn't going to let my friends down.

So I told him, 'I've arranged to go to the dance tonight, at Tony's, with my friends.'

'Well, you didn't know I was coming. I'm sure they'll understand your change of plans, now that I have come home on such a short leave.'

'But I don't want to cancel the dancing. You could come with me?'

'I don't want to go dancing. I don't like going to Tony's and I don't much want to be with your friends tonight either. I just want to be with you.' That's how Jim was. He wanted his entire life to be just the two of us. But I had other plans, and I felt like being awkward, just so that he knew I was the independent type.

'I don't want to go dancing,' he repeated.

'Well, I don't want to be engaged,' I replied, in a mock huff, and flounced out of the room. I went upstairs to change and went to the dance.

I had a lovely evening with my friends. Much later, when I arrived back home, I was amazed and very relieved to find Jim was still there, with Mother and Jeffrey, waiting for my return. As I came into the room, he stood up from the sofa and said: 'Do you want to get engaged again, now?'

'Oh, well,' I replied. 'Might as well.' And it was back on again.

I took the next day off and we explored more of the country lanes together, dreading the moment we would have to say goodbye again.

The time went far too quickly, and early in the morning of Wednesday, 15 May, I went with him to the station. We embraced and he boarded the train bound for London. It was so packed with troops and travellers that he had to stand in the corridor and, as it wasn't quite time for it to go yet, he opened the door again so that we could continue talking and kissing. He didn't want to go and I didn't want him to go. I had tears pouring down my face and the guard was trying to get me to stand back, away from the train, but I didn't want to. Jim pretended to close the door. Then the guard turned round and blew his whistle, just as Jim and I were locked in a kiss.

'Stand back,' called the guard along the platform as he waved his flag and I was about to obey, when Jim took hold of me and lifted me up right into the train with him, slamming the door closed behind me, just as the train started to pull away.

As I realized what was happening, I gathered myself together and said, 'I'll just get the train back from the next stop.' I hadn't realized there were no stops till at least halfway to London, and by that time I had decided I didn't want to go back.

All the compartments were full so we sat on Jim's kitbag in the corridor, giggling together most of the way, then standing when the train became more crowded as it approached London. I had nothing with me except my handbag. I was expecting to go straight to work after I'd seen Jim off, and to go home as usual at the end of the day, working through my lunch hour to catch up on the hour I would have lost earlier . . . but I couldn't do any of that now, and I couldn't even let them know till I found a phone kiosk.

When we arrived in London, it didn't seem that easy to leave again, so I decided to stay. The first thing was for Jim to sign in at his London HQ in the Hotel Grand

Central in Marylebone. So we found the place and he did the paperwork. They expected him to sleep there, but they didn't allow women, now that it had been taken over by the army, so I couldn't stay there with him. And it was too late for me to get a train back home that day.

We didn't know what to do. We were still in the hotel reception area, so we asked where the nearest Girls' Friendly Society or YWCA were, but nobody seemed to know. Not surprising really, since they were all men.

So we left the hotel and bumped into an army pal of Jim's. He was a Londoner and knew this area well, so that was a lucky break. We all went back into the Hotel Grand Central and his pal used the hotel phone and found us a place to go. Jim came back to where I was sitting and told me he had rented a room for the night.

'I can't,' I said in alarm. 'I haven't got a nightie.'

I had my ration book with me, in my handbag, so off we went to find a shop selling nightdresses. I felt really bad about this, as Mother usually made all my nighties. I had to use six precious clothing coupons out of my ration book for the nightie I chose. It was a long, thick, granny-type thing that I'd picked, with long sleeves and a high neck with a neat collar and a ribbon bow. I was already thinking of what Clarry had said: 'No touching of flesh,' and 'No crossing the line.' I still had no idea what that meant, but I had the feeling it was something to do with Jim and me sharing a room in London together.

'I have to phone them at work,' I said. 'Or I'll lose my job.'

'Well, we'd better find a phone box, then,' he agreed. 'And what about your mother?'

We found the familiar red kiosk and I got my pennies out to make the call.

'The General Post Office switchboard please, in Blackburn,' I told the operator, and soon got through. I was relieved to hear a friendly voice at the other end. It was Margaret Abbott, a good friend of mine. She sounded quite excited at the intrigue, but went to get the supervisor, who was anything but excited.

I explained the situation: 'The train pulled away while I was still on it, saying goodbye to my army sweetheart. So I'm afraid I couldn't get back to Blackburn in time for work this morning,' I said.

'This isn't good enough, Margaret. Everyone has had more work to do because we didn't know you would be absent. If I'd known, I could have got a temporary replacement for you.'

I talked her round to letting me keep my job.

'Well, all right, Margaret. You are a good worker and we wouldn't want to lose you. When do you think you will be back?'

'We-e-ll . . .' I told her about Jim's flight leaving soon for India and asked if I could use up all the rest of my holiday allocation to stay in London for the rest of the week.

Gradually, I gained her sympathy and her reluctant agreement.

Next I somehow needed to let my mother know. I had the idea of calling the phone box at the end of Robinson

Street and hoping someone would answer it and go to fetch her to the phone, but that might not work. I was just about to put the phone down from calling the GPO, when:

'Hello, you're back to me now,' came Margaret Abbott's cheery voice. 'Would you like me to go round to your house after work and give your mother a message?'

'Oh, would you? That would be a great help.'

I knew she might be tempted to spread the news, so I tried to be careful. I told her the simple truth: that I was stuck in London with a friend and wouldn't be back till the weekend. I'm sure that must have set her wondering, but at least Mother would know I was safe.

Jim was waiting outside the kiosk, holding a scrap of paper with the address of our lodgings on it, so we went off to find where we would be staying. We soon found it – an ordinary house, with a small, sparse room and one bed in it. I started praying as soon as I saw it. I'd never slept with anybody in the same bed. I was the only daughter, the only granddaughter.

'I can see you praying,' Jim said with a grin. Then he took on a more concerned expression. 'Perhaps I'd better sleep on the floor?'

'No, I can't let you do that,' I replied. But from then on I was a nervous wreck.

We stayed together in that room, with its one bed, for all five nights and I felt confused, hovering between heaven and hell. It was a wonderful time and also a fearful time. Without quite realizing it, we crossed the line . . . and I can't begin to describe how I felt. It was marvellous –

great. But I went through a whole range of emotions. It was a cross between terrified and gloriously happy, I suppose, but also with a lot of guilt. Clarry's words kept coming back to me; his warnings plagued me. My expectations got all mixed up. I didn't know what to think. Clarry had said: *once you've crossed the line, there is no going back.* Would I always be haunted by that? Jim went and told his senior officer what we had done and asked whether that would make a baby. We didn't have a clue. I was very worried about it, so was glad when he asked, but there wasn't a clear answer.

During the days we went walking and out to eat together. Jim had to sign in at the Grand Central Hotel every morning, and we could never go too far from there in case he was needed, either for his plane to India or, as on one day, to take part in a parade. But the rest of the time was ours. We strolled in the parks and we walked around the shops, looking in their huge windows, choosing what furniture we might like to have in our first home, after we were married. We started to make plans for our future life together.

Finally the time came – the heartbreaking time of going to the station, having to leave him and come home alone. When I got back to Blackburn, I was still confused about what we'd done together. I couldn't talk to any of my friends about it and especially not to Mother.

In fact, I thought Mother would blow a fuse when I got back but she seemed her usual calm self. 'I'm sorry if you were worried about me,' I said.

'I didn't know you had gone. I assumed you were at work all day, as usual, until Margaret came round to tell me.'

'She gave you my message, then?'

'Yes, and I got Jim's too.'

'Jim's?' I was incredulous.

'Yes, didn't you know? He wrote a letter to tell me what had happened with the train moving before you could get off.' She paused. 'And he said he would look after you, and I trusted him . . . and here you are, safely back home again.'

I didn't know what to say . . . I was so proud of Jim for doing such a caring thing. It was just like him.

Jim continued writing to me morning, noon and night, so that his letters poured though our letter box, two or three a day. He had little else to occupy him while he waited for his transport to India, other than to revisit all the places we had been during those wonderful five days in London.

Despite my employers being cross with me for taking leave without notice or permission, I somehow convinced them that it would never happen again. But I had to work even harder and longer than before, to show them I meant it. So I could only write once a day back to Jim, except at weekends.

While we were in London we had talked about our future life together, even down to what kind of clock we would have on the mantelpiece. Jim wrote in one of his letters that his preference was for 'a Westminster chimer, which will give a peal every quarter.' I hated the things myself!

A few letters later, he wrote to paint a word picture of what our lives would be like:

> *I can picture us now, Margaret, me getting up first to light the fire and getting ready for work, looking forward to my breakfast, cooked by you, because I can't for the life of me cook bacon and eggs, as you already know. Then I can picture me returning home to you at night after work is done, to sit down to tea, just you and me to be together until the following morning. I think I shall enjoy looking after the chickens and the small garden. We can't help but be the happiest couple in the whole wide world.*

When I read this paragraph, I naturally assumed it meant that Jim would leave the army before our wedding. After all, everything we had talked about in London depended on that, so we carried on with planning how we would have our house.

On 27 May, I spent my twentieth birthday without Jim. It was a subdued celebration with my friends at Tony's, and nearly all the boys danced with me, including possessive Joe – I couldn't say no as I worried about his reaction, but it was difficult for me and even more so for him. I could see the pain in his eyes as I did my usual flirting with everyone. He clearly hadn't got over me yet. But none of the other boys were special to me now. I only had that real spark with Jim and he would be gone, maybe, for a very long time.

At the end of the evening, Joe came up to me with a small, slim gift-wrapped box. I didn't know what to do or say, other than, 'Thank you very much.'

'Open it when you get home,' he said.

I did, and it was a very pretty box with a bottle of perfume inside called Elle Elle. When I dabbed a spot of it on my wrist, it gave off a beautiful scent. I know it seems strange, but it immediately became my favourite perfume and I used it for a long time, until it ran out. A couple of years later, when I was throwing out some rubbish and started tearing up the pretty box that Joe had given me the perfume in, I found a little groove under where the perfume bottle had been and under that was a note: *I love you. I always have and I always will. Joe 1946.*

Can you imagine how I felt? Even now, I still feel guilty that I'd let him down so badly.

Jim's time finally came on 3 June to fly off to India, by way of Cairo.

I have now left England, flying over the English Channel. I did experience some sort of thrill when the plane left the ground and I knew I was on my way, but the thrill I am living to experience is the one when I hold you in my arms again, never to be parted . . .

With every thrust of the propeller, with every

beat of my heart, with every second that passes,
my love for you is growing within me . . .

By the time I received this letter, he would be settled
into his new barracks, with half the world dividing us.
He'd never felt so far away before.

21

A World Apart

1946–1947

Almost as soon as Jim had gone, in June 1946, Bobby wrote to tell us that he would be coming back to Britain for good in early August. Normally I would have been very glad to see him after all his time away, but I feared having to tell him about my engagement to Jim. How would he react? Not well, I was sure, especially if he ever found out about my five days in London with him. Should I tell him myself, or wait till someone else did?

As the weeks passed and a particularly rainy summer gripped the town, I longed for Jim to come back and felt as if some essential part of me was missing. Every day, except when the situation in India held up the post, I had his loving letters to maintain the thread between us. They were our lifeline. Reading his latest letter, I could tell he yearned to be back in Blackburn as he wrote of trying to cope with his new living conditions:

They have dumped us here, right in the middle of a hot, dusty desert – a fitting introduction to the

*land of torment . . . It is very hot here and
sweaty and I am very uncomfortable. The sun is
glaring down and the dust almost obscures it.
Boy would I love a cup of tea made by your
mother. We used to drink a lot of tea, didn't we?
That is the only thing you can drink here. Beer is
unknown. The water is always putrid and
warm . . .*

At night, when he finally arrived in his new barracks,
he described as much of his surroundings as he was allowed
to:

*The incessant racket made by the bullfrogs and
mosquitoes is enough to drive anybody off his
head. I have had enough of this place . . . dirt,
bad smells and discomforts. At night, when
everyone is in bed under their mosquito nets, as if
by a signal, all the jackals and hyenas begin their
incessant howling and shrieking. As soon as I get
into my bed, I shall hear the big rats nosing
around the room in search of food. Heaven knows
what I shall do if any of them jump into bed with
me.*

At the letter's close, his thoughts turned, as they always
did, to home and our future, where his heart was:

*Each time I write your address on the envelope,
my mind fills with cherished memories of the many*

*times I have come down to your house to call on
you. Remember when I used to stumble down the
high step at the corner of the back street, and how
many times have I come round the corner to find
you playing with Alan and the children? I can
picture it now, as I came down one Sunday after
dinner and you were giving Alan a donkey ride on
your back. You were wearing a green dress and
afterwards we walked to Hurst Green. That was a
marvellous day, Macushla. I would give anything
just to relive any one of those hours of glad-
ness . . . It reminds me of the poem, which I'm
sure must be about the Ribble Valley and Hurst
Green:*

   *There is not in the wide world a valley so sweet,
   As that vale in whose bosom the bright waters
meet.*

   *(From 'The Meeting of the Waters' by Thomas
Moore)*

On 23 August 1946, only two and a half months into his
posting, Jim wrote a scrawling letter to say that he was
in the camp hospital, down with malaria for the fifth time.
He had it very badly this time and had to be injected with
all sorts of things. Although he underplayed how ill he
felt, I was worried. I knew it could be life-threatening and
was always relieved when another letter arrived. Within
a few days of starting treatment, though, he began to rally
and was soon back to his duties again.

In early September, however, I was even more anxious:

My own darling Macushla,

You must excuse the terrible writing as the place where I am now isn't what you would call an ideal writing desk – namely the street cart. You see, there is trouble again in Bombay and we are here on the outskirts of the city in case the military is called in. I am browned off . . . I have been wet through all day, the place stinks and I have no bed to go back to tonight.

To make matters worse, I haven't had a letter from you for nine days . . . I keep wondering if you are ill and I am worried to death . . . To be without mail from you is almost driving me crazy . . . You mean everything to me . . .

Gosh, but I'll be glad when I am away out of this hole, back in England where everything is clean and the air is pure, where everybody isn't waiting around the next corner to stick a knife in your back . . .

I was always fearful of his being killed, just as so many others had been before him. As I read his description of men with knives standing round corners ready to attack, I wondered whether he had even survived that day. Fortunately, his letter the next day showed him back on form again, having received three of my letters at once.

As Bobby's return loomed closer, I felt more and more anxious about how to tell him and what he would say. I tried to think of various ways to start the conversation . . .

but almost as soon as he entered the house, Bobby demanded to know everything about Jim. Somebody must have told him already!

It was as tricky as I feared. He was not happy that I had got engaged to a man I'd spent so little time with (as far as he knew) and that it was someone he had never even met.

'I expect you have met him,' I said.

'Oh yes? When?'

'When we were children, he used to come and play at the Tanners'.'

'Well, that's not exactly a recommendation, is it? Lots of children came to play at the Tanners'. The whole of Blackburn probably came there at one time or another, but you don't have to marry one of them.'

I bit my lip. He was clearly worried about me.

'And what about Joe? Aren't you still supposed to be engaged to him?'

'No, I told you, remember, on your last leave, that it was already over then.'

'Well, that's not what Joe told me. You still had his ring, so you were still engaged to him the last time I was here. You can't be engaged to two people at once.'

'I've tried several times to give him back his ring, but he won't take it.'

'If you want to get married,' continued Bobby, 'how can you possibly not want to marry Joe? He's handsome, he's a good dancer, he's generous . . . and he loves you. At least if you marry Joe, I get on with him well and I will make sure he looks after you properly.'

'But I don't love Joe,' I said, trying to stay calm. 'I like him as a friend, but I don't love him.'

'I don't want you marrying a stranger,' he continued.

'Jim's not a stranger. Mother likes him.'

'Huh! Mother likes everybody. And anyway, it's you I'm worried about.'

'Well, I love Jim,' I said, defiantly. 'He's a good, kind man. We're a couple and we love each other, so I am going to marry him.'

'You're too young to know what love is. I'm the head of this household and you have to have my permission to marry anyone. So I say you can't marry Jim.'

'Not yet, maybe,' I said, trying to stand my ground. 'But I can after I'm twenty-one.'

'Well, that's not going to happen. You'll probably have a few more engagements yet before then, knowing you!' he sneered.

I decided not to take the bait and kept my mouth shut. One step at a time.

It had been an uncomfortable conversation, and others followed over the next few days and weeks. I didn't dare mention anything about my trips to Southampton . . . and especially my week in London with Jim.

While Jim was away I had continued with all my favourite activities, including the regular evenings I spent at the George and Dragon with some of my old friends, Kathleen and Peggy, plus some new ones from the GPO and Tony's, including Margaret Abbott, Frank Best and Bob Tyson, who was courting Doris Smith, so she came too. None of us had a lot of money; none of us drank much, but we would often all get together to sing. Well, I didn't sing, because I was terrible! Joe was a good singer, though, and he had now been demobbed, so he joined us. I continued to be friends with him, in a reserved way, but made sure I was never alone with him.

'If you haven't got anything better to do,' I suggested to Bobby as I was leaving for work a few days later, 'why don't you come and join us down at the George and Dragon tonight?'

'Well, I might,' he said with a shrug.

About halfway through the evening, in walked Bobby. He ordered a pint at the bar and came over. As luck would have it, the only empty seat was next to my friend Margaret Abbott from the Post Office, so Bobby sat there and they started chatting. They hit it off really well, which led to them going out together and soon they were courting. Bobby stayed in the RAF and was posted to Stornaway, from where they continued their courtship, writing letters to each other. I was relieved he had something else to think about, to take his mind off my engagement to Jim.

Jim's letters kept coming, all of them full of ardent love, expressed in every way he could think of. He said he understood about me carrying on a social life as before with my friends, both girls and boys. But I was beginning to feel that our relationship was becoming too intense, especially as we might not see each other for many months and India wasn't the safest place for him to be. I suggested to him that we should think of our relationship as more of a friendship while he was away. I suppose I was protecting myself in case he came back in a coffin. I'd been there before with Ray and Les – committing myself, only for it to end in tragedy.

'I'm young,' I wrote to him in one of my letters. 'And I think it's getting too serious. I think we should give it a rest for a while.'

Jim wrote back to say that, for 'whatever happiness we have, we will have to pay a high price.' We had talked about this before, when we had been in London. But we both agreed that this didn't mean we should avoid being happy, as long as we accepted there might be some kind of payment laid at our door.

But now, that's what I was afraid of: we'll have to pay for this. I'd been this happy before and I'd been hurt. I didn't want to rush into it again. I wrote to him that evening to explain how I was feeling.

But Jim's response in his next letter was, 'I could not live without you,' and, 'You are my life, my heart and soul. Without you, I could not continue.'

Was he insinuating something? Was this emotional blackmail? Or was I imagining it? I couldn't be sure, but he wrote similar phrases in several letters, so I didn't dare mention my concerns again. In my head, I stopped planning our future home and life together. Jim carried on with all his suggestions, but it seemed so far ahead of us that I didn't have the enthusiasm to do anything tangible about all that yet. I was uncertain in some ways, but not in others. I still had that spark for him. In some ways, Jim was still an unknown quantity and yet not one of the men coming back from the war measured up to him. He was everything right to me, and he showered his love on me through his letters. I had made a promise to him and I didn't intend to go back on a promise, especially when he was halfway across the world. I just didn't know what to do.

Jim was still firmly on my mind the next day as I walked to meet Mother at the cinema. As I was crossing Darwen Street, outside the Post Office, I suddenly caught sight of a figure I recognized. It was my father. I was so shocked – I had no idea he was living locally. I could hardly believe it. I hadn't seen him for more than ten years, not since the night he left with his blonde, who I noticed was walking slowly behind him. I ran over to speak to him and when she saw me she stayed well back, out of the way.

'Hello, Father,' I said, stepping in front of him.

'Hello, love,' he replied, looking as surprised as me. Perhaps more so. I was a little girl the last time he saw me, so I wasn't sure he even recognized me immediately. He looked puzzled for a few seconds, then realized. 'Hello, Margaret,' he said, without even a smile.

'How are you?' I asked him.

'Fair,' he replied. 'Well enough.'

I waited for him to ask me, but he didn't, so I told him my news. 'I'm going to get married in a few months' time,' I explained.

'Oh no, you're not!' he growled. 'Who is he?'

'Jim Ford' I said, dismayed at his reaction.

'Never heard of him. Where does he live?'

'Mary Street.'

'Never heard of it.'

'It's in Eanam, and they're a good Catholic family,' I added, hoping that would please him. 'Will you come to the wedding and give me away?'

'No. You're not marrying him,' he repeated. 'So I won't give you away . . . and that's that.' Without another word, he turned and walked off down the street. He'd barely been involved in my life and he'd still managed to make me feel ashamed and upset.

When I got to the cinema, I told Mother what had happened.

'So I don't really feel like watching a film this evening,' I explained.

'We'd better go home,' she nodded. 'You never know what he's going to do.' So off we went, back to Robinson Street, to the safety of our house, in the knowledge that he didn't even know where we lived.

I never saw him again.

Jim had asked me before he left for India to go and visit his mother while he was away. He wanted us to get to know each other better. Jim's parents were always welcoming, especially his mother, but his brothers were still not happy about our engagement, particularly the eldest, Jack, so he and Louis would always make themselves scarce when I came. In fact, I rarely saw any of them, so we never actually talked to each other. It was only Jim who got it in the neck from Jack for being too young to marry, and he took no notice. It seems the brothers were not that close and, in temperament and looks, Jim was the odd one out. As Christmas 1946 approached, I reflected on the long seven and a half months Jim and I had been apart already and how much I missed sharing such occasions with him. If only he could come back again soon.

Christmas in India for Jim was very different in some ways, but alike in others. On 24 December he wrote:

I'm afraid that nothing exciting has happened for me this Christmas Eve. There has been a kind of party in the Mess, with singing, etc., the beer being finished by nine o'clock, as there were only three bottles per man . . . We are having turkey and goose for dinner tomorrow, so I hope the cook makes a good job of it. We will only have a light snack at lunchtime, then the big feed at seven p.m. The food is the only reminder of Christmas around here. The weather is so warm one could fry eggs on the pavement (if there was a pavement) . . . Gosh, they could have all the turkeys and geese and good cheer in the world, if I could be sitting down somewhere with you, eating some of your mother's chips . . .

I can picture the dance halls and the parties of crowds and merrymakers. Still, if they enjoyed themselves a million times more than they are doing now, they would still be unhappy, compared to how happy we two will be from that heavenly and glorious moment when we meet again. Every day will be Christmas Day, every second complete with love and happiness . . .

New Year 1947 heralded much soul-searching for me as I once again felt insecure about what this year would bring. Would Bobby come to accept my engagement with Jim? Would Jim survive to leave the army and come home this year? If he did, would we be married?

Jim was looking ahead too. Despite 'crossing the line' in London, we were both still very hazy about how things worked. I knew that my two younger brothers were both born in my mother's bedroom, but how did they get there? Nobody ever told me. Jim was equally confused, as he wrote in one of his letters: 'How wonderful it will be if, when we are married, we wake up one morning to find our own little baby at the bottom of our bed.'

The months passed and my twenty-first birthday approached. Uncle George arranged for me to have my party in the posh ballroom at the Conservative Club, with a small band playing my favourite music. My mother had the invitations printed and I gave them to all my friends and relations. I also invited Jim's family. Bobby, still stationed in Stornoway, managed to get leave to come home for the party. All my aunts and uncles were there, and my Harrison grandparents, Jim's parents and all my friends came. Some of the boys came in uniform, which was lovely for me. It seemed so much brighter – just like during the war.

Sadly, I couldn't help noticing a slight sense of discomfort amongst the older generations, between my Grandma and Grandad Harrison, who were both staunchly Protestant, and some of the older Catholic guests on both sides. They sat apart from each other in the hall and avoided talking to one another where they could. I was worried that Jim's parents might hear a whisper or notice any tension there might be. But if they did, they certainly didn't show it, smiling and enjoying the evening, to my great relief.

The party itself went very well and I had a great time with everyone, despite Jim's absence. There was one particularly awkward moment, however, when Uncle Eddie's wife Jenny came over to speak to me.

'Happy twenty-first birthday, Margaret,' she began, in a loud voice. 'How do you like your jewellery?'

'What jewellery?' I asked. I noticed that the guests around us had suddenly gone quiet and there were some loud intakes of breath nearby.

'Grandma Holden's jewellery,' she said. 'Do you remember, when you were little and played with all of Grandma's gold jewellery?'

I nodded, but was too surprised to speak, uncertain as to why she had asked me. I was just about to say that her jewels hadn't been in her cupboard any more after she died, but then I realized that might suggest I was accusing someone of taking them.

Just then I caught Mother giving Jenny a black look.

'He got rid of that years ago,' Mother said, then turned away.

Somebody must have told the band to play something loud and this incident was soon forgotten. In bed that night, I began to puzzle out what had happened from my mother's reaction. Why had nobody told me that Grandma had left me her jewellery? How come Jenny knew about it and I didn't? And who had got rid of it? My father, perhaps? Surely he hadn't thrown it all away? I assumed he must have sold it when he was losing at cards.

When the party was over, some of us went back to our house, more or less across the road, where Kathleen, Peggy, Jenny, Margaret Abbott, Bert, my brother Bobby and I stayed up and talked the night away. Bobby was now quite serious with Margaret so he was in a good mood that night. It was a flash of the old Bobby who always wanted the best for me and took that thrashing for me when I was little. But how long would it last?

Sure enough, the next day he asked me: 'Are you still carrying on your correspondence with Jim?'

'Yes.' I was going to say more, but something told me the least said the better.

'Well, you needn't think you are going to marry him if he ever comes back here.'

'Why not?'

'Because I won't give my permission.'

'But I don't need your permission,' I said. 'Now that I'm twenty-one.'

'I'm head of this household, the man of the house, so I have to make the decisions.'

Not my decisions, I thought . . . not any more.

In fact, I was feeling rather disillusioned. It was more than a year since Jim had gone to India, and there was no sign of him being allowed to come home. In the weeks following my birthday I made a confusing discovery when

Jim let a clue slip in one of his letters. Instead of working out the last few months of his army service and coming home to start a new life in our own home, as we had planned, he had actually signed on, from the start, for a term of nine years in the regular army, plus another three in the Reserves. Through all our letters, he had somehow neglected to tell me this. Whether he forgot or preferred not to tell me, I don't know. But it made a charade of all this planning for how we wanted our own house to look and what to have in it. We would have to live in married quarters wherever we were sent, with no home to call our own, or else live separately. This was not the life I had planned.

I knew he still loved me very much, and I loved him too, but I felt unsettled and insecure. Disappointed because the excitement had gone out of my life, I was restless and felt it was time for me to make some sort of decision of my own. I needed to feel as if I was taking back control of my life.

Because I worked with Bobby's girlfriend, Margaret, I knew she was also feeling at a bit of a crossroads as things were heating up between them. Bobby was becoming too possessive, so she wanted out of the relationship.

With both Jim and Bobby away, Margaret and I talked it through and we decided, on a whim, that we would both give up our Post Office jobs to go and join the WAAF (the Women's Auxiliary Air Force).

I wrote and told Jim our plan, thinking he would be pleased for me, so I was very disappointed to read his response:

Naturally I have been shaken by what you told me
as regards joining the WAAF . . . You want my
honest feelings – here they are. I know you want
to be doing something to pass the time away. In
that respect, it will favour us admirably. You won't
be in long enough for your number to dry (army
wisecrack to young soldiers). I hope that you have
found out that you will definitely get your
discharge when we are married. So you see, sweet
darling, you will only be wearing uniform for a
few months at the most.

Despite Jim's lukewarm reply, I was determined to do this for myself. So off we went to sign up, but first we had to have medicals. Margaret passed hers, but sadly I didn't. I had to go back twice for further investigation into an old hearing problem I'd had.

Meanwhile, Bobby found out what we'd done. I don't know what he said to Margaret to dissuade her, but he made it very clear what he had in mind for me.

'As I'm in the RAF, if you join the WAAF, I can claim you, as my sister, to come to be with me on my base.'

Well, I didn't know whether that was true or if he was making it up, but the thought of being stuck with Bobby on an island in the North Atlantic put me off completely. So, all in all, the whole idea just fizzled out.

Jim was very pleased with that outcome and in his letters he seemed optimistic that he might, at last, be able to have some leave. Though it was exciting for both of us, I didn't dare get my hopes up.

22

Ship Ahoy!

1947

On 27 August 1947, from New Delhi, Jim wrote the best
letter yet:

> I have been told that I will be 'standing by' to
> move out from the 3rd September . . . I only hope
> the fact that so many troops and civilians are
> leaving India, due to independence, doesn't make
> shipping scarce. I am like a cat on hot bricks. I do
> want to see you so very much and to be with
> you . . .
>
> I have all my clothing ready now, darling . . .
> just this afternoon I bought some dark brown
> corduroy slacks, which will be just the thing for
> going on our long hikes together – they won't
> wear out due to lying on the grass so many
> times!!!

With Jim's return in sight, I realized just how much I
had to do. However, the major stumbling block remained:

how could I arrange a wedding, without knowing when it would be? Even so, I began to feel excited again, and started to organize what I could at this stage.

I loved my bedroom at Robinson Street. But now I needed to think about it from Jim's point of view, as we didn't know where or when he would be posted after his leave so we might be staying in it for a while. I needed a new bed anyway, so the first thing I did was go out and buy a new double bed, which was duly installed. It wasn't just a mattress, like so many of our friends were using in those days, after the war. It was a proper bed and it had to be double for after we got married, though of course when Jim first came home he would sleep at his parents' house.

Next, one night, I wrote out a list of all the people we would like to invite to the wedding. It was a long list of more than fifty, so it might have to be shortened to about thirty. I would have to consult Jim about that.

Meanwhile, an idea formed itself in my mind. I had been saving money ever since I started work at thirteen, and more regularly after we had that week in London, sixteen months ago – I wanted us to have enough to buy our own little house in Blackburn. When I checked with the bank, it looked as if I'd saved quite a healthy amount, but it was nowhere near enough.

Mother had moved into our house, with Bobby, Jeffrey and me, when she was a newly abandoned single mother, scrimping and scraping, sewing and mending to pay the rent as well as keep and feed her hungry young family, soon increased with the arrival of Alan. It had been a tremendous struggle for her, with no help from anyone, especially not our father. It was only when first Bobby and then I felt obliged to leave education and start work to help pay the bills that she could breathe a little more easily. Bobby and I had paid the rent between us for years. But Bobby was still in the RAF, so was only home for a few days occasionally. I might soon be leaving as well, to goodness knows where, so now this idea came to the fore. Instead of leaving the money in the bank, doing nothing, I could perhaps buy our house for Mother to live in, so that she would never have to worry again. We might even need to live in it ourselves sometimes, between postings, or when Jim left the army, so it seemed the sensible thing to do.

I went to see the bank manager and asked about a mortgage. I didn't really know much about such things, so he explained it all for me. I found that, with the deposit I had saved and my good income from the GPO, as well as Jim's army income, the bank would agree to provide me with a mortgage on Mother's house.

I had to persuade a friend and neighbour, Albert Bennett, to come with me to see the landlord, who had once followed me round and round the table when he came to collect the rent and I was alone in the house. (Dear Ray had appeared at just the right moment to save me that day.) I didn't trust him without a chaperone, and Albert was the perfect person. He owned the shuttle factory and he was in the Home Guard throughout the war, so he was well known and wouldn't stand any nonsense.

I had a plan up my sleeve. Our house needed a lot of

work doing to it, so I started with a long list of repairs that were needed. The landlord looked very shifty, trying to get out it.

'I can't afford all that,' he complained.

'I could go to the council and get someone round.'

'They wouldn't be interested!'

'Oh, I think they would,' I insisted. 'My Uncle George is a councillor and an alderman . . .'

He looked as if he was starting to take me a bit more seriously now.

'Of course, if you can't afford the repairs . . . I'll tell you what,' I continued. 'I'll not report you to the council for being a bad landlord, if you let me buy the house.'

I was very determined and I could see Albert nodding his approval. The landlord thought about it but not for long.

'All right,' he said with a shrug. 'But I'll want the full price. It must be worth at least £800.'

'The *market* price,' I emphasized. 'I've had it valued, by Harrison's.' (This was my grandfather's company, but I didn't tell him that.) 'And they've said it's worth £500 in the current market,' I said.

He looked surprised, not so much at the value, but at my daring to do all this.

'£650,' he said. 'And not a penny less.'

'We have to leave a margin for the repairs,' I replied. 'And the builders have estimated at least £100 for those.' I paused to give him a few seconds to think. 'So I won't pay a penny more than £550. That's my absolute maximum.'

He cleared his throat, looking distinctly uncomfortable.

'£550 and it's a deal, or I go home and we forget about it.'

Now both the men looked surprised.

The landlord looked cornered. He swallowed hard. 'You drive a hard bargain,' he said in a whining voice.

'Yes. I like everything to be fair.'

'Right,' he mumbled. 'You win. You can have it for £550.'

With great reluctance, he shook hands with me and we left.

I was quietly pleased at how this meeting had gone. I didn't tell him, but I would have gone up to £650 if I'd had to.

Next I went to a solicitor to sort out all the paperwork. I didn't want to mention it to Mother until it was all finalized and the house was in Jim's and my names. I just assumed she would be pleased that she would never again have to worry about paying the rent.

A few weeks later, when it had been completed, I explained to Mother what I had done.

'I wanted to have a chat with you about the house,' I began.

'This house?'

I nodded.

'What about it?'

'Well, you know there is a lot of work and repairs needed?'

'Yes, love, that's all been building up since before the

war, since we first moved in. I've asked the landlord to get going with some of the most urgent repairs, but he said he can't afford it. He's always been a right miser.'

'He said the same to me,' I agreed with a smile.

'When did you see him?' she asked, rather alarmed. 'The rent's not due till next week.'

'Yes, I know it would be . . . but now it's not due any more.'

'What do you mean?' she interrupted.

I took a deep breath. 'I had a letter from the solicitor this morning and he said that the house is now ours, mine and Jim's, so you never need to pay rent again.'

Her normally placid face showed a mixture of shock and confusion. Her mouth opened to speak, but nothing came out.

'I'm sorry to take you by surprise, but I didn't want to tell you till it was done and completed. You see, Jim and I have been wondering where to live when we are married. Of course, we will mostly have to live in married quarters, away from home, but when he's on leave and if he gets posted abroad again, we need a house that is our base, here in Blackburn. It struck me that if I went to see the landlord, he might sell it to me.'

'How?' she asked. 'Where will the money come from?'

'Well, it's all been arranged. I used some of my savings as a deposit . . . and the bank manager kindly gave me and Jim a mortgage, based on both our salaries, so we managed it. It's paid for and, from today, it's our house – your house, for you and the boys too. Nothing will change, except for Jim sometimes living here with us. And we'll gradually do the repairs as well.' I smiled nervously as she rocked her chair to and fro in thoughtful silence. I suppose she was trying to take it all in.

After a few seconds I asked her, 'What do you think, Mother? It will help you because we'll still contribute to the food and bills.'

'Well,' she said, giving me a curious look. 'Does this mean you are now my landlord?'

I laughed. 'I would be,' I replied, 'if you were paying rent, but you won't be.'

'You always were a clever girl, Margaret, but how you've done all this without me knowing about it . . . well . . . I don't know what to think.'

Mother sat back and said nothing more, but she seemed happy enough.

When I woke up early the next morning, however, I sat up with a jolt at the realization that I had forgotten one very important detail. I should have consulted Bobby, or at least told him my plans early on. The house was Bobby's home too and he expected to come back and live in it again himself when he left the RAF, which he would shortly do. So, quite rightly, he was entitled to know and have his say before I went ahead. But I never even mentioned it to him. I just went ahead regardless. Talk about single-minded! I'd forged ahead with my plan and left him out of it completely. Now I was in fear of his reaction, but I would have to tell him, somehow.

So, on his next leave, I tried to tell him and explain, but he was in no mood to listen. He was furious.

'How dare you go ahead without even consulting me? This is MY house you are talking about. I am the head of this household . . . and now you try to make your pathetic excuses.'

'I'm very sorry, Bobby.' I took a gulp of air. 'It was foolish of me, I know, but it's done now and all I can do is apologize.'

'How dare you decide to take over like that? How dare you do anything without my permission?' His face was bright red and he was marching up and down the living room, berating me with a continuous flow of invective.

I had clearly misjudged the whole situation. But I had no idea that he would be quite so angry. I had assumed he would be pleased at no longer having to contribute to Mother's rent, but how wrong I was!

'How could you even think of making such an important decision behind my back? I'm sure it will all go wrong. And are you telling me that Jim is going to come and live in MY house? No, I can't allow it. I am the man of this house and I make the decisions round here.'

I didn't necessarily go along with that, but I did accept that I'd gone about it all wrong.

'I'm sorry, Bobby,' I apologized again. 'I can see now that I should have discussed it with you. It's your home too. I just thought you would be pleased that—'

'Well, I'm not,' he interrupted. 'How could I be? You've gone completely over my head and now it's too late to put things right. You should never have done this, Margaret. I blame it all on Jim. I expect he put you up to it, pushing me out of my own house so that you two can have it to yourselves. Well, that's not going to happen!' He paused, his face reddened. 'I will not let it. This is my home and it always will be.'

'Yes, I agree that it's your home – the home of all our family. But don't blame Jim. He had nothing to do with it. It was all my idea . . . and my fault.'

He looked very cross and, if I hadn't known he loved me, I might have been frightened at that moment but I knew him well enough to know that his anger hid his disappointment. He was more upset than he would ever show, and I couldn't blame him for that. But I did have to stick up for Jim.

'I know you are upset . . .'

'And it's all your so-called fiancé's fault.'

'No, Bobby, it's all my fault. Jim had nothing to do with it. He's still in India and took no part in it. So I must take the blame. Nobody else.'

'Well then, YOU should have asked my permission to do this. And MY name is the one that should be on the deeds, not yours.'

I wanted so much to explain to Bobby that I'd done it for Mother, and for all of us, but he refused to listen to anything I could say. I had to get away from his ranting, so I put my head down and left the room. I went outside to try and calm down, watching Alan play airplane hopscotch with his friends in the street, just as Ray and I had done all those years ago. As I tried to hide my tears, I went over and over what Bobby had said.

I don't know what had made me cry most. Bobby's fury, of course – the strength of his reaction and all that shouting at me – but also a great sense of frustration. I had tried to do everyone a good turn; it had all seemed such a good idea, but now I wished I'd never thought of it.

As I sat there on the edge of the pavement, I suddenly realized that the thing that had probably hurt Bobby the most was the prospect of having to share his house with Jim, whom he'd never even met.

Of course, Jim was the last person Bobby wanted in his house. Although Bobby was a few years older than Jim and they had both gained campaign medals in the war, Jim was senior in rank and he had the Burma Star. Jim was taller than Bobby too. He had been to the top school for boys in the area and, cruellest of all, he was generally admired for having fought in Burma, the fiercest and most dangerous theatre of war, where fighting was often hand-to-hand. Bobby, meanwhile, had travelled from one airfield to another, in Britain, Italy or in African war zones, building Mosquitoes and repairing their war-damaged fuselages. It was very important work, and nobody ever reproached Bobby for it, because it wasn't his choice, but I'm sure he was hurt that he couldn't be the pilot he dreamed of being. I began to realize that he probably knew some of these things about Jim and that he was perhaps a little in awe and maybe jealous of him, which might have played its part in his dislike of the whole idea of my marrying Jim.

He was obviously affronted too that his role as 'man of the house' might be threatened, or at the least shared, which Bobby wouldn't like at all. Whoever's name was on the deeds, to him, it would always be Bobby's house. I did understand.

Finally, Jim had a date for his return, 15 December, so at last we could set a date for our wedding. I booked the church for Boxing Day, 26 December 1947. Now I had to arrange everything else – flowers, reception, invitations. Mother offered to make my wedding dress, so I did a drawing of what I wanted it to look like. She had a length of beautiful white crêpe de Chine, under which she would make a slip out of unused blackout material which she had bleached white. Every now and then she needed me for another fitting and I could see her finest stitching and the shape of the dress developing into a perfect fit. It was going to look beautiful.

I was desperate to be there, on the dockside, to meet Jim as soon as he touched English soil. I wouldn't miss that for anything . . . and he would have been bitterly disappointed if I wasn't there, waiting. So on 14 December I took the train down to Southampton, arriving the night before Jim's ship was due to dock. I stayed at the Girls' Friendly Society hostel and got up very early, so excited to see him, as if arriving early would bring his ship in sooner. I took a taxi down to the dockyard and showed my papers before being allowed through. I thought it would be packed with people meeting their loved ones. Perhaps they were already there, lining the dockside.

I found my way to the correct quay. Not having seen

a large troop ship coming in before, I expected it to be anchored in the harbour, with the men being ferried ashore in small boats. But I was wrong. As I rushed round the last corner I nearly ran too far. One more step and I'd have fallen in.

There was a vast steel wall alongside the empty quay. I looked up and there was the side of the ship right in front of me, so tall and wide that I had to stand back to see it properly. As I did so, all I could hear was a loud chorus of shouts and wolf whistles. I'd never heard anything like it. The troop ship had three long tiers of uniformed soldiers, all hanging out and waving. I looked around . . . but I was the only person there. Were they all waving at me? I waved back. There must have been hundreds of them, perhaps thousands, all cheering and whistling at me.

As I waved, I ran my eyes along each tier, trying to look at all the faces, but it was an almost impossible task. I thought I saw Jim on the top deck and directed my waves and smiles at him. I was the only girl on the quay, so I had whistles, cheers, everything. It was an amazing, exhilarating experience. I kept on waving at the soldier I thought was Jim, and all those around him were patting him on the back and shaking his hand. Then, as I waved, something made me turn to my right and there was Jim, running along the quay towards me!

He picked me up, swung me around and kissed me . . . to the sound of even louder cheers and whistles. We were still locked together in our first embrace for nineteen long months when two policemen appeared and tried to pull us away behind some huge cargo crates.

'If you carry on like that,' said one of them with a gruff voice and a wide grin, 'we'll have a riot on our hands.'

'Yes,' said the other. 'Keep out of sight.'

So, still entwined, we sat down behind the crates and talked and talked, while the policemen kept guard.

'I'll have to go back to join the others,' said Jim.

'Why?' I asked, incredulous. 'We've waited long enough to be together, I don't want to lose you after just ten minutes!'

'You can't go back now, sir. You'll be killed by the crush. You'll have to stay here, out of the way, till the majority of them have disembarked. Then we'll escort you back and explain why we made you wait.'

'Yes, officer,' said Jim and we kissed again.

I thought we would just go straight to the station and back to Blackburn. But no.

'We'll have to sign out first,' explained Jim. 'Then we have to get a train to London and change to another train going to Scotland. I have to report to the depot at Buchanan Castle to sign for my new orders, passes and money for my leave.'

By the time we'd got out of the dockyard, onto the train and arrived in London, it was mid afternoon, so we decided to go to the pictures at a cinema in Tottenham Court Road that we had been to before. Then it had been a new American film – *Gilda*, with Rita Hayworth and Glenn Ford. This time they were showing a Marlene Dietrich and Charles Boyer film – something about a garden, I think it was. We didn't see much of the film. We were just locked in each other's arms. Then we went to

King's Cross and got tickets on the overnight train to Stirling, then a taxi to the castle. I had to stand and wait outside, looking at this amazing building with its tall, round turrets, while Jim went in and completed his paper-work. He came out with his money and passes and we then had to make our way back to Stirling. We walked out of the grounds and must have looked rather lost and forlorn by the side of the road. Jim was still in uniform, which is perhaps why a lorry stopped.

'Do you want a lift?' asked the driver.

We were so tired by then that we would have gone with anyone. So we got in and the driver talked to us as he drove us all the way to the station in Stirling – prob-ably well out of his way. He was a cheery, helpful soul and dropped us off by the station entrance. We gathered ourselves and walked in. It wasn't until we got to the ticket office to buy a train ticket to Blackburn for me that Jim made the awful discovery.

'Oh no!' he said, his tanned face turning pale. We looked at each other in alarm.

'What is it?' I asked.

'My money is gone. Everything – money, passes, the lot!'

'But you only just collected it all. I saw them in your hand when you came out of the castle. Then you put them in your pocket.'

'I know, but they're not in my pocket now.' He frantic-ally checked all his pockets. 'No, not in any of my pockets.'

'What are we going to do?' I asked. 'I've got *some* money.'

'Yes, but we need to find . . .'

Just then, who should come running towards us but the lorry driver, with the whole package held triumphantly aloft in his hand.

'Here, you left these in my cab,' he said with a cheery grin. 'Lucky I spotted them on my way out. They must have fallen out of your pocket when you got in. I'm glad I caught you.'

'Thank you so much,' we chorused.

'It was very kind of you to bring them back here for us,' I added. 'We are so grateful.'

'Yes, pal,' said Jim. 'You're one in a million.'

We were very lucky that morning and desperately tired. At last we were going home to Blackburn and our plans to start our new life together.

We had talked it through on the train and decided to split up when we got back, so that Jim could go and see his family while I dealt with the upset I was sure I would have to face when I got home.

In fact, I was right. All hell was let loose in both our houses. Jim's parents welcomed him home as if he were the Prodigal Son. But his two older brothers were furious with him for wanting to get married so young, they told him, and would barely talk to him. I think they steered clear of him as much as possible. I couldn't understand why at the time, but I wonder now whether it was something to do with me and where we lived – two different areas of Blackburn. People could be quite sensitive about that in those days.

Meanwhile, at my house, Mother was suspicious about how I'd spent my extra night and day away. I could understand that and I tried to explain. But Bobby was furious. I know my delay had made him think the worst and he therefore didn't believe me.

'You're too young to get married,' he said later that day. 'I want you to cancel this fiasco of a wedding. I've always promised myself that I would take you travelling with me all around the world. Now is the time. I'm leaving the RAF and you can leave the GPO, then we'll set off on our travels. Won't that be wonderful? We'll see all the sights and do lots of new things in every country we visit.'

'No, Bobby,' I interrupted him. 'I'm sorry, really I am, but I can't come with you round the world. I hate travelling. I thought you knew that. Anyway, I love Jim and I am going to marry him. Nothing will make me change my mind.'

At this point Bobby stormed out of the house and I sat down in the living room, my head in my hands.

Within half an hour, the last person I wanted to see, Joe, was knocking at our door.

'I'm back for good now,' he said. 'So let's get married.' He stepped forward to kiss me, but I moved to the side. Had Bobby sent him? Or was it a coincidence? Either way, I knew where my heart lay.

'I'm sorry, Joe, but I thought you would have realized by now – I am not going to marry you. I hope you have a happy life, but I will not be a part of it. I am engaged to marry Jim Ford and we will soon be wed. So please leave now.'

He looked shocked and confused.

'But . . .' He tried to step inside.

'No. Goodbye, Joe.' I firmly closed the front door.

When Jim and I were comparing notes, later that afternoon, out for a walk in the fast-fading light, he told me about his brothers' reaction against him marrying and asked me what Bobby had said about our wedding.

'Was Bobby happy for us?'

'I'm afraid not. He was angry too because I am disobeying him to get married.' I didn't want to say how furious he really was, as it would have worried Jim. 'I expect he'll come round to it.'

We were both glad to be walking together, wrapped up well on this cold winter's day. We kept on the move as I told him more details of our wedding plans and who I'd sent invitations to. He described the suit he'd had made in New Delhi to wear at our wedding, but admitted he wasn't sure whether to wear that or his uniform.

'Definitely your uniform,' I said.

We discussed what would happen after his two and a half weeks off, just after New Year, when he would be based at Chester, with married quarters for us both to live in.

'But what about my job?' I asked.

'You can give your notice in now,' he replied. 'There's no need for you ever to work again.'

I stopped in my tracks. 'But I want to work. I love working. I know I'll have to leave this job, but I can find a new one in Chester.'

'Why?' he asked, with a hurt look. 'Isn't it enough for you to look after our home and me?'

'No!' I replied, rather too sharply. 'I don't want to sit around all day, doing not very much. I'd be bored to death.'

He was clearly disappointed in me. He had been building up his dreams and hopes over all those nineteen months, and me working wasn't in his picture of our happy domestic future together. But it was in mine.

There were only a few days left until the wedding now and I still hadn't found anybody willing to give me away. Bobby had downright refused.

'I'm not giving you away to anyone but Joe,' he said. 'In fact, I don't even want to come to your fiasco of a wedding.'

'All right, then. I won't invite you,' I replied.

My father had already refused when I had met him by chance that day in Darwen Street. He probably didn't want to meet any of the relatives. Next I asked my mother's brother, Uncle George, but he said no, because the wedding was going to be in a Catholic church. Well, of course, both Jim and I were Catholics, so that was also a black mark to some of my family and that was why Grandad Harrison also declined to give me away. I wondered about Jeffrey, but Mother said no, he was too young at fifteen.

I was unsure what to do next. Bobby was visibly pleased that I'd failed so far. Then, however, I had a brainwave and asked Uncle John, my father's older brother. I had never liked him, but he did agree, so that was a relief.

Now the wedding could go ahead and we had only the last-minute things to sort out.

Meanwhile, Jim and I spent as much time together as we could, out walking in all weathers in the daytime to get away from our families and just be the two of us, making up for lost time. We spent some of our evenings at Tony's so that I could dance, and Jim even occasionally joined in too, with a bit of tutoring from me.

Sometimes in the evenings we went to the cinema and a couple of times we joined the group in the George and Dragon. One night, though, Jim and I went to the Jubilee Inn, just across the road from the George and Dragon. Peggy must have seen us go in, because the next thing was that we could hear the sound of singing, wafting across the road and coming closer. Then in through the door of the Jubilee Inn came the choir, all of them, including Joe, all filing in and lining up right in front of us, singing, 'With someone like you, a pal good and true . . .'

It was as if they were saying goodbye to me. I suppose they were. I looked along the line, all of them smiling – even Joe, who looked directly at me as he sang. Of course, he could have meant that this was what he wanted himself, but that night I thought he was saying through this song that he now accepted the situation, that he really meant it for me. Was that wishful thinking?

When they finished the song, some of them bought drinks and they all came to join us in a large group. Knowing how volatile Joe could be, I suddenly felt nervous and was on the brink of suggesting we leave, when the strangest thing happened.

I had told Jim everything about all my old boyfriends. This naturally included my engagement with Joe and his refusal to let me go. So Jim knew all about Joe, but Joe didn't know that he did. Jim went straight over to where Joe was sitting. I dreaded to think what he would do, but I needn't have worried. Jim put out his hand to Joe and he took it. They shook hands.

'Thank you for taking such good care of Margaret while I was away,' said Jim, with a genuine smile.

I held my breath and waited, fearing the worst, but I was amazed to see that Joe was a real gentleman about it and took what Jim said at face value, though I thought I detected a slightly quizzical expression on his face afterwards.

It was a brave and caring gesture of Jim's, but would it make any difference? I could only wait and see.

23

Best Laid Plans

December 1947

Boxing Day 1947 dawned with thick snow on the ground, the rooftops and the trees. Jim and I had been to midnight Mass together to hear our banns being read for the final time. Now everything had been done and it was time to get ready for our special day.

This day was the culmination of all of Jim's dreams – everything he had written in his letters and all that he wanted in life. My fervent hope early that morning was that it would all go to plan, with no upsets, so that it could be a wedding day to remember.

Mother came in with the wedding dress she had lovingly made for me and laid it out on my bed. First I helped her to get ready. Then I went back to my bedroom, put on some make-up and brushed my hair. Normally I put it up, but not today. Jim had especially asked me to wear it loose for our wedding, as he always preferred it that way, with my natural curls down to my shoulders.

I put on my dress, with Mother's help, as it fitted perfectly to my shape. It had quite a high stand-up collar, puff-topped sleeves tapering down to a point at each wrist, a full skirt down to my feet and a frilly bit draped from the point at the back, right around.

Jim had once written to me from India, saying he'd seen the most beautiful white material for my wedding dress . . . but then he'd remembered Ray and his white lace, and Jim thought he'd better not buy it for me, in case it upset me. In those days of rationing, it would have been sensible to bring material from India, but I think Jim was right. I probably would have refused it. Anyway, as always, Mother had done a brilliant job of the dress with what she had.

When I went downstairs in my wedding dress, Bobby was nowhere to be seen.

Oh dear, I thought. Where was he? I knew he had refused to come to 'this fiasco of a wedding'. But I had hoped he would be there to see me in my wedding dress. I just prayed that his absence at this moment was not something I should be anxious about. Perhaps it was his way of showing he loved me by finally accepting the situation and refraining from marring my happiness. I hoped so. I knew that, deep down, Bobby would not have wanted to hurt me. He had always been my protective big brother because he loved me and he knew I thought the world of him. We were very, very close – too close, I suppose.

It was Joe's unpredictability that I feared the most. What if he decided to crash the wedding and tried to halt it? If only Bobby could be there to prevent him. I couldn't bear it if anything happened to scupper Jim's dreams.

*

Fifteen-year-old Jeffrey came to join us, looking very smart, with his hair brushed as flat as he could make it. Mother decided that, at seven, Alan was too young to come to a wedding, so he was spending the day with a neighbour but would join us afterwards.

Uncle John arrived, smartly dressed. 'You look nice, Margaret. I'll wait in the car for you. Don't be long.' Mother adjusted my dress.

'You look lovely,' she said with a smile. 'I'm sure Jim will be proud of you.' She and Jeffrey went off to the church, so I locked up and went out to the hired car.

'Are you ready to go?' asked the driver.

I nodded. 'Yes, I think so,' and off we went, at a stately pace, through the snow. Uncle John didn't speak so as we drove along there was nothing to distract me from the conflicting thoughts chasing round my brain. I knew I loved Jim, but was I really ready to settle down with a regular soldier, to move from place to place like a nomad, to give up my job, to lose my independence? By the time we reached the turning for St Alban's Church, I was wracked with doubt. My hands were sweating inside my gloves, but my throat was dry and my heart was racing.

The driver turned into the drive and continued slowly upwards towards the church entrance. Outside, stamping their feet in the snow to keep their circulation going, stood Jim and his younger brother, David.

I don't know why, but on the spur of the moment I decided.

'Stop and turn round,' I told the driver in a resolute voice, though I certainly didn't feel resolute. 'I can't go in.'

The driver looked surprised, but attempted to turn the car – more tricky than usual on the carpet of snow, trying not to let his wheels spin. Uncle John said nothing.

'Back out and go round again,' I said to the driver.

As we receded backwards down the drive, I glanced at the two figures, expectantly waiting for us to stop. I saw Jim's beaming face as it crumpled into disbelief. That's an image I shall always remember.

The driver took us on a tour of the nearby roads, while I imagined Jim being distraught. Why had I done this to him? I didn't know the answer myself.

'Are you ready to go back now?' the driver asked in a kindly voice.

'Yes please,' I said, fearful that I'd ruined the whole day. Would Jim still be there? Would everyone have gone home? What could I say to them?

Our lovely driver turned in towards the church again. I shifted forward on my seat to get a better look and, to my great relief, Jim and David were still there, looking baffled as we approached. A huge smile spread across Jim's face before they dashed into the church. Now I knew it would all be all right.

Jim's Uncle Nicholas married us in St Alban's Church – a beautiful building with a special atmosphere. Yes, it was Roman Catholic. It was a nuptial mass; the whole congregation was there as well as all our guests and the church was packed. My parish priest attended too. He knelt, holding the big black Bible on his head for Father Ford, alias Uncle Nicholas, to read from. The marriage ceremony went well, up to the part where the priest asked whether there were any objections. This was the bit I was dreading. What if Joe had crept in at the back of the church, ready to shout out at this moment? I looked round at my mother and she looked at me, knowing what I was thinking, and we both held our breath. I'm sure Jim did too. The seconds seemed like minutes but the silence certainly was golden that day. With huge relief and no interruptions or hitches, we were pronounced man and wife.

We smiled at each other and kissed, then went to sign the register. We came back out and stood for a few seconds as the organist started to play. Instead of some classical anthem or hymn, the melody that came out was 'The Bells of St Mary's' – a Bing Crosby song. I tried my best not to laugh. The organist, I discovered later, was from St Mary's College, where Jim had gone to school and where Jeffrey was now a pupil. He obviously had the same impish sense of humour as Jim, whose idea it was to depart from tradition as a kind of joke for my benefit. Everybody loved it, except perhaps one or two of the older members of the congregation who may have muttered their displeasure to each other.

Jim and I went in the wedding car and everyone waved us off before coming to join us at the Grosvenor Hotel in Blackburn, where our wedding breakfast would take place.

The hotel itself looked absolutely beautiful, with white ribbons draped from the picture rails, starched white linen tablecloths, silver cruets and cutlery, crystal glasses and gold-rimmed plates. All of Jim's family were there, except for Jack and Louis, his older brothers. All of my usual family members were there too, except for Auntie Elsie, who said she had a cold. I didn't understand that, as one of the uncles or cousins would have given her a lift, I'm sure, and she needn't have stayed all day.

Of course, my father and Bobby were obvious by their absence, for different reasons. I had nurtured this little hope that Bobby might change his mind at the last minute and come. But he didn't. I refused to be sad on my wedding day so I didn't dwell on it and neither did Jim.

Nearly all our close friends were there to help us celebrate and everyone seemed to be in a good mood when they arrived, though if there was any slight nuance of tension, it could only have been the old sore point of religion. After all, the wedding had been a Catholic service in a Catholic church, led by a Catholic priest. I expect that might have been hard for the Protestants to swallow.

We all found our places at the table for the sit-down meal. Grandad Harrison had supplied the Grosvenor Hotel with a dozen chickens and they cooked them a special way, which was delicious in that time of rations and shortages. The speeches passed me by in a whirl. We had a pianist who played all the popular tunes of the day while a lot of the younger guests danced. It was all very celebratory. This was our day – Jim and me. We had been separated for so long and we were very happy to be wed at last.

Ever since Ray's father came round to our house that day, to tell me Ray had been killed by a bomb sinking his submarine, I had kept in touch with his parents. I used to go and have a cup of tea with them every now and then. I had invited them to my twenty-first birthday party the previous year, but I wasn't sure whether they would come to the wedding, as to them I suppose it should have been Ray's wedding to me. But I sent them an invitation anyway and they accepted. I was so pleased to see them there.

I know that, without a body to bury or a grave to visit, nor any irrefutable proof of their son's death, they still nurtured some tiny germ of hope that it was all a mistake, and Ray would come back one day. His father could not shake this notion and often told me he felt he was still alive. Meanwhile, Ray's mother had been to several seances and she always used to come round to our house to tell me what the spiritualist had said. It was always just a bit more each time, to keep her going back, I suppose.

'Ray's alive!' she said the last time. 'He's alive and living on an island, but he's gone blind – he can't see at all.'

Every time I had tried to be sympathetic, but it was all very unsettling for me, as I had accepted Ray must be dead. I'm sure she told me with the hope that maybe I would not marry Jim, or anyone else, but wait for Ray to come home. I didn't know what to do to stop her, so finally I had written to Jim about it and he wrote to Ray's father, asking him to stop his wife coming round to me with all this. He put it very well, saying how much I loved to see them – they had been part of my life for so long.

On the day I married Jim, Ray's father came over and hugged me, as if it was Ray I was marrying. But Mr Nash knew Jim too, as Jim and Ray were the same age when they joined the Home Guard together, where Mr Nash was their sergeant. Ray and Jim even went to join up for the war together as they both wanted to be in the navy, though Jim soon after changed his mind in favour of the army.

Both Ray's parents were very good about me marrying Jim. As well as the warm hugs, they gave me a wedding present.

'Open it,' suggested Ray's father, with a tear in his eye.

I unwrapped it to find a lovely photograph frame.

'Look,' he said. 'You can swing it like this,' and he showed me how it swivelled.

'It takes two photos,' said Ray's mother. 'You could put Raymond's photo in that if you like. I'm sure Jim wouldn't mind.'

At the end of the wedding reception, we had the hired car again to take us back to my house to change and go away. We'd booked to stay in Ireland for a few days. I can still remember the address: Clontarf Street, Dublin.

'Are you really looking forward to this honeymoon trip?' I asked Jim as we sat in the back of the car, going home.

'Yes,' he beamed, then gave me a look of concern. 'Why? Aren't you?'

'We-e-ell.' I hesitated. 'It's so cold – just imagine how freezing it will be on that ferry to Ireland this afternoon.' I shivered. 'I'm not sure I want to go anywhere today.'

'I hadn't thought of that,' he said. 'The ferries might not even run in this weather.'

'As long as we're together,' I continued, 'wouldn't it be cosier just to stay at home and be warm? Then we can go out for lots of walks, just like we used to do, to all the places we love.'

So that's what we decided. We arrived back in Robinson Street, where all our relatives were also converging. The hotel had been marvellous in giving us all the uneaten food to take away with us – very useful, with so much still rationed in the shops. I had been bottling peaches for weeks, so I got those down from the pantry shelf and I started preparing a splendid tea for all the family. But as I was doing the finishing touches . . . oh, the horrible aunts! Like gannets on sparse feeding grounds, they rebelled against so many years of short rations, brazenly uploaded various amounts of food and went off home.

I had invited our next-door neighbours to come round, so now they sat down at our table tucking into everything that was left.

'Who is going to help me with the washing-up?' I asked, as they moved off, back to their house.

'I'll help you,' offered Jim.

'No, it's all right,' I whispered. 'What I'd really like you to do is to take Mother and Alice out somewhere.'

'Where?'

'I don't mind; anywhere will do,' I replied. 'As long as you give me enough time to have a huge wash-up and to clear away all this mess.'

Dear Jim. I have no idea to this day where he took them, but they were out for quite a while and by the time they got back, it was all clean and tidy. So that was our wedding day, right down to the bride doing all the washing-up!

There was one disturbing footnote to the day. When Jim came back with Mother and Alice, they told me what they had heard from a man down the street, who was on his way home from a lunchtime drink.

'Apparently, Bobby and Joe smashed all the glasses in the George and Dragon,' said Mother.

'Oh no!' My heart sank. 'What, both of them?'

'Yes,' said Alice. 'We heard they made a real mess of the pub, so it will be the talk of the town!'

'It's such a shame,' added Mother. 'Two nice young men, good boys, both of them. I know our Bobby was against the wedding,' she said. 'But I can hardly believe he did that.'

'I think they were both cross with me,' I explained. 'Joe would probably have gone into one of his rages because I wouldn't marry him. If he couldn't marry me, he couldn't stand the thought of anyone else having me . . . and Bobby didn't want me to get married at all, and especially not to Jim. I know he didn't like that.'

Everyone was silent as we all took it in.

'It wasn't how I dreamed our wedding would be,' muttered Jim. Then he turned to me. 'But we've had a lovely day and I've married the best girl in the world, so that's all that really matters.'

The way my beloved brother Bobby behaved on my wedding day caused a rift between us that sadly didn't heal fully for many years. Indeed, it was another sixty years before Bobby wrote me a letter out of the blue that told me a lot of family secrets and explanations I had never known or understood, including the real reason why he didn't come to the wedding. He said it was so that he could stop Joe's plans to ruin everything, to burst into the church and object to the marriage, to start something, perhaps a fire, so that the church would have to be evacuated. Joe had been determined to stop the service before we were officially wed. Although Bobby succeeded in preventing him from ruining our wedding, he did it by steering him into making his protest in the pub instead. Bobby couldn't stop him smashing the glasses in his fury and frustration. Joe had started it and goaded Bobby into joining in.

Finally, after a long day of ups and downs that saw us married at last, we could relax and warm ourselves in front of the sitting-room fire before bed. In so many of his letters, Jim had written about how he couldn't wait to get into our bed together on our wedding night. At last it was really happening.

The following morning, we got up and dressed, feeling rather embarrassed about going downstairs to see everyone. I opened our bedroom door a little, just as someone knocked at the front door.

'Is Margaret in?' asked the voice.

It must have been Alan who opened the door, as I heard him say, 'She's in bed with Jim. I don't know what they're doing.'

We cracked up laughing. Now we really didn't know

how to get out of the bedroom! In the end, we just had to walk down the stairs as if it were any normal day.

Despite the snow, we had several idyllic days of being together and knowing that nothing could part us for a long time now. Jim would be posted to Chester after New Year, where we could start our new life together in married quarters. We hadn't seen the place yet, but I already had ideas about how we could make it our own.

As midnight struck on New Year's Eve, Jim opened a bottle of champagne. I never drink alcohol – well, hardly ever – but this was a special occasion: the beginning of what we hoped would be our bright future, together at last. When the chimes finished and it was the first minute of 1948, Jim proposed a toast:

'To us, to our future together – long life, love and happiness, looking forward to travels with the army to foreign lands, new friends and starting our own family. You never need to work again.'

We clinked glasses and I sipped that first fizzling taste.

Smiling at Jim, I silently added my own personal wish: that whatever Jim thinks and wherever we go, I will have a good job of my own . . . and I will carry on dancing.

Epilogue

We never did have our honeymoon, but our lives were packed with travels and adventures; highs and lows in equal measure. When Jim was posted to Chester, soon after our wedding, there were no married quarters available, so I had to stay behind in Blackburn. Mother and the boys went down to Southsea on the south coast to stay with an uncle, so I was all alone in our house in Robinson Street. I carried on my job at the Post Office and started on much-needed repairs to the house. Here I was, newly married, yet living apart and lonely. I had serious doubts whether I had done the right thing.

But things did get better and I soon joined Jim in Chester, where we had two and a half happy years in army accommodation. From there followed many excitements and challenges as we embarked on a series of postings abroad. We went all over the world, first to Egypt and then to Cyprus and Singapore. I never thought, after growing up in Blackburn, I would get to visit and live in so many exciting and exotic places. We had such adventures together and I have such fond memories of those times. Wherever we were, I always tried to work and get stuck in with the social life. We adopted a stray Alsatian in Egypt, escaped a ship fire on the way to Cyprus and I opened the first two bookshops in the Union Jack Club for all servicemen in Singapore. I was in my element!

In 1974, when I was based back in the UK, something happened during a posting in Northern Ireland that affected Jim badly. When he came home he was very moody and changeable, so I felt I was always walking on eggshells. I never did find out what happened, but I looked after him and tried to do my best for him. Looking back, I know that he must have been suffering from PTSD. But there was no name for it then and no help, so it affected him for the rest of his life.

After Jim left the army, we lived in Morecambe for a while before we finally settled in a small bungalow near Carnforth. We enjoyed sixty-seven happy years together but sadly he died, clinging to me, on 26 November 2013. Despite my grief, I was relieved that after so many years of suffering, Jim was at last free.

Bobby broke his silence three years after my wedding by writing me a letter, in which he apologized for not attending the ceremony. He explained that he only ever wanted to protect me. However, it would be several more decades before he gave me a full explanation of everything – not just his behaviour on my wedding day, but all the mysteries I had never understood about my family. We kept up a lovely correspondence over the years, and there were meetings too, with him, his wife Phyllis and their four sons. It brought Bobby and me close again through the rest of our lives.

Just after writing this book, I saw a plea in the *Lancashire Telegraph* for anyone who might have known Flight Sergeant, Wireless Operator/Air Gunner Leslie Fielding to make contact with a man who lives in France, near the Second World War crash site of Leslie's Lancaster bomber, shot down by the enemy.

Benoit Howson has installed a memorial to all those five men who were killed that night. It included their names, ranks and portraits, but there was no picture for Leslie. Benoit was looking for a family member or anyone else who could give him a photo of Leslie to inlay on the memorial beneath his name.

I contacted Benoit through the newspaper editor and he called me direct from France. He was delighted when I told him that I do have a good photo of Leslie, a copy of which I emailed to him straight away. I was also able to tell him a lot about Leslie and how close we had become during the months leading up to his death that fateful night.

Benoit immediately emailed me some pictures of the memorial, now with Leslie's portrait in place. He also posted to me, seventy-four years after the event, some fragments of the very aeroplane itself – the Lancaster bomber shot down that night.

It all came back to me again, as vivid as if it was now – that evening when he told me I would not see him again. He knew it was our last embrace and I know now that he was releasing me, not rejecting me, when he said, 'This is the last time.'

I am now aged ninety-two and still live in our bungalow

in a quiet village south of the Lake District, within sight of the sea. Here I still love talking to people, whether it be Kim, my technician nephew who visits to upgrade my computer, or occasional phone calls with nieces. Jim's niece Susanna, who had always written letters to him when he was overseas, now regularly keeps up with me and takes me out for enjoyable lunches and shopping trips from time to time. Sadly, all my old friends have died.

I spend most of my time these days rereading Jim's 630 love letters from all over the world and listening to our favourite music from the Forties; living in the past, when times were harder and people so much friendlier.

Acknowledgements

My husband Jim, for sixty-seven years of love and adventure.

My mother, who never confided or complained.

Raymond and Leslie, for their love.

Jacquie Buttriss, for her interest in writing this story.

Clare Hulton, my literary agent.

Ingrid Connell, Charlotte Wright and everyone at Macmillan.

Mum, Dad and toddler Bobby riding in a landau in Blackpool.

Me with Grandma Harrison.

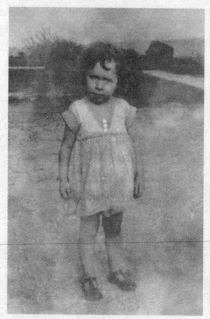

Aged four playing outside.
Independent as ever!

My older brother Bobby, aged eighteen. I idolized him.

Our rented house in Robinson Street.

Childhood sweetheart Ray, aged sixteen, in the Home Guard.

Me, aged eighteen, with a bow in
my hair!

Leslie Fielding in his RAF uniform.
He really meant a lot to me.

Enjoying a day out with a friend in Blackpool.

Handsome Joe who soon became too possessive.

Jim in Burma, wearing the bush hat I love.

Jim and me on our wedding day in December 1947.

David Baldacci attended law school at the University of Virginia, and went to work as a trial lawyer, and later as a corporate lawyer, in Washington D.C. He is now a full-time writer whose bestselling novels include *Absolute Power*, *Total Control*, *The Winner* and *Saving Faith*. He lives in Virginia with his wife and two children.

Praise for *Wish You Well*

'A touching tale . . . a love letter to a rural world' *Entertainment Weekly*

'. . . reveals his talent as a storyteller of the highest merit' *Punch*

'Compelling . . . stirring . . . an old-fashioned coming-of-age-story . . . [with] plenty to savour' *People*

'Baldacci's fans will enjoy this entertaining detour into his past' *Washington Post*

'A moving story . . . the focus is on young people, and the message about love is heartwarming' *Booklist*

'. . . abounds with affection for the state he makes his home' *USA Today*

'Succeeds as a departure for Baldacci . . . a tender . . . inspirational story . . . some wonderfully lyric prose' *Denver Post*

'Baldacci proves he can write in any genre with this wonderful b——'

SHETLAND LIBRARY
91205565

KT-460-454

Also by David Baldacci

Absolute Power
Total Control
The Winner
The Simple Truth
Saving Faith

DAVID BALDACCI

WISH YOU WELL

WITHDRAWN
SHETLAND LIBRARY

POCKET
BOOKS

LONDON · SYDNEY · NEW YORK · TOKYO · SINGAPORE · TORONTO

First published in the US by Warner Books, 2000
First published in Great Britain by Simon & Schuster UK Ltd, 2001
This edition first published by Pocket Books, 2001
An imprint of Simon & Schuster UK Ltd
A Viacom company

Copyright © Columbus Rose, Ltd., 2000

This book is copyright under the Berne Convention.
® and © 1997 Simon & Schuster Inc. No reproduction without permission.
All rights reserved.

The right of David Baldacci to be identified as author of this work has
been asserted by him in accordance with sections 77 and 78 of the
Copyright, Designs and Patents Act, 1988.

1 3 5 7 9 10 8 6 4 2

Simon & Schuster UK Ltd
Africa House
64-78 Kingsway
London WC2B 6AH

Simon & Schuster Australia
Sydney

A CIP catalogue record for this book is available from the British Library

ISBN 0-7434-2890-0

This book is a work of fiction. Names, characters, places and
incidents are either a product of the author's imagination or are used
fictitiously. Any resemblance to actual people living or dead, events or
locales is entirely coincidental.

Book design by Giorgetta Bell McRee

Printed and bound in Great Britain by
Omnia Books Ltd, Glasgow

To my mother,
the inspiration for this novel

AUTHOR'S NOTE

The story in *Wish You Well* is fictional, but the setting, other than the place names, is not. I have been to those mountains, and also was fortunate to grow up with two women who called the high rock home for many years. My maternal grandmother, Cora Rose, lived with my family in Richmond for the last ten years of her life, but spent the prior six decades or so on the top of a mountain in southwestern Virginia. At her knee I learned about that land and the life there. My mother, the youngest of ten, lived on that mountain for the first seventeen years of her life, and while I was growing up she passed along to me many fascinating stories from her youth. Indeed, both the hardships and the adventures experienced by the characters in the novel would not be unfamiliar to her.

In addition to the stories I listened to as a child, I spent considerable time interviewing my mother in preparation for writing *Wish You Well*, and it was an enlightening time for me, on many levels. Once we reach adulthood, most of us assume we know all there is to know about our parents and other family members. However, if you take the time to ask questions and actually listen to the answers, you may find there is still much to learn about people so close to you. Thus this novel is, in part, an oral history of both where and how my mother grew up. Oral histories are a dying art, which is sad indeed, for they show appropriate respect for the lives and experiences of those who have come before. And, just as important, they document those remembrances, for once those lives are over, that personal knowledge is lost forever. Unfortunately, we live in a time now where everyone seems to be solely looking ahead, as though we deem nothing in the past worthy of our attention. The future is always fresh and exciting, and it has a pull on us that times past simply can never muster. Yet it may well be that our greatest wealth as human beings can be "discovered" by simply looking behind us.

Though I am known for my suspense novels, I have always been drawn to stories of the past in my native Virginia, and tales of people living in places that sharply limited their ambitions, yet provided them with a richness of knowledge and experience few have ever attained. Ironically, as a writer, I've spent the last twenty years or so hunting relentlessly for story material, and utterly failed to see a lumberyardful within my own family. However, while it came later than it probably should have, writing this novel was one of the most rewarding experiences of my life.

WISH YOU WELL

CHAPTER ONE

THE AIR WAS MOIST, THE COMING RAIN telegraphed by plump, gray clouds, and the blue sky fast fading. The 1936 four-door Lincoln Zephyr sedan moved down the winding road at a decent, if unhurried, pace. The car's interior was filled with the inviting aromas of warm sourdough bread, baked chicken, and peach and cinnamon pie from the picnic basket that sat so temptingly between the two children in the backseat.

Louisa Mae Cardinal, twelve years old, tall and rangy, her hair the color of sun-dappled straw and her eyes blue, was known simply as Lou. She was a pretty girl who would almost certainly grow into a beautiful woman. But Lou would fight tea parties, pigtails, and frilly dresses to the death. And somehow win. It was just her nature.

The notebook was open on her lap, and Lou was filling the blank pages with writings of importance to her, as a fisherman does his net. And from the girl's pleased look, she was landing fat cod with every pitch and catch. As always, she was very intent on her writing. Lou came by that trait honestly, as her father had such fever to an even greater degree than his daughter.

On the other side of the picnic basket was Lou's brother, Oz. The name was a contraction of his given one, Oscar. He was seven, small for his age, though there was the promise of height in his long feet. He did not possess the lanky limbs and athletic grace of his sister. Oz also lacked the confidence that so plainly burned in Lou's eyes. And yet he held his worn stuffed bear with the unbreakable clench of a wrestler, and he had a way about him that naturally warmed other's souls. After meeting Oz Cardinal, one came away convinced that he was a little boy with a heart as big and giving as God could bestow on lowly, conflicted mortals.

Jack Cardinal was driving. He seemed unaware of the approaching storm, or even the car's other occupants. His slender fingers drummed on the steering wheel. The tips of his fingers were callused from years of punching the typewriter keys, and there was a permanent groove in the middle finger of his right hand where the pen pressed against it. Badges of honor, he often said.

As a writer, Jack assembled vivid landscapes densely populated with flawed characters who, with each turn of the page, seemed more real than one's family. Readers would often weep as a beloved character perished under the writer's nib, yet the distinct beauty of the language never overshadowed the blunt force of the story, for the themes imbedded in Jack Cardinal's tales were powerful indeed. But then an especially well-tooled line would come along and make one smile and perhaps even laugh aloud, because a bit of humor was often the most effective tool for painlessly driving home a serious point.

Jack Cardinal's talents as a writer had brought him much critical acclaim, and very little money. The Lincoln Zephyr did not belong to him, for luxuries such as automobiles, fancy or plain, seemed forever beyond his reach. The car had been borrowed for this special outing from a friend and admirer of Jack's work. Certainly the woman sitting next to him had not married Jack Cardinal for money.

Amanda Cardinal usually bore well the drift of her husband's nimble mind. Even now her expression signaled good-natured surrender to the workings of the man's imagination, which always allowed him escape from the bothersome details of life. But later, when the blanket was spread and the picnic food was apportioned, and the children wanted to play, she would nudge her husband from his literary alchemy. And yet today Amanda felt a deeper concern as they drove to the park. They needed this outing together, and not simply for the fresh air and special food. This surprisingly warm late winter's day was a godsend in many ways. She looked at the threatening sky.

Go away, storm, please go away now.

To ease her skittish nerves, Amanda turned and looked at Oz and smiled. It was hard not to feel good when looking at the little boy, though he was a child easily frightened as well. Amanda had often cradled her son when Oz had been seized by a nightmare. Fortunately, his fearful cries would be replaced by a smile when Oz would at last focus on her, and she would want to hold her son always, keep him safe always.

Oz's looks came directly from his mother, while Lou had a pleasing variation of Amanda's long forehead and her father's lean nose and compact angle of jaw. And yet if Lou were asked, she would say she took after her father only. This did not reflect disrespect for her mother, but signaled that, foremost, Lou would always see herself as Jack Cardinal's daughter.

Amanda turned back to her husband. "Another story?" she asked as her fingers skimmed Jack's forearm.

The man's mind slowly rocked free from his latest concocting and Jack looked at her, a grin riding on full lips that, aside from the memorable flicker of his gray eyes, were her husband's most attractive physical feature, Amanda thought.

"Take a breath, work on a story," said Jack.

"A prisoner of your own devices," replied Amanda softly, and she stopped rubbing his arm.

As her husband drifted back to work, Amanda watched as Lou labored with her own story. Mother saw the potential for much happiness and some inevitable pain in her daughter. She could not live Lou's life for her, and Amanda knew she would have to watch her little girl fall at times. Still, Amanda would never hold out her hand, for Lou being Lou would certainly refuse it. But if her daughter's fingers sought out her mother's, she would be there. It was a situation burdened with pitfalls, yet it seemed the one destined for mother and daughter.

"How's the story coming, Lou?"

Head down, hand moving with the flourishing thrust of youthful penmanship, Lou said, "Fine." Amanda could easily sense her daughter's underlying message: that writing was a task not to be discussed with nonwriters. Amanda took it as good-naturedly as she did most things having to do with her volatile daughter. But even a mother sometimes needed a comforting pillow on which to lay her head, so Amanda reached out and tousled her son's blondish hair. Sons were not nearly so complex, and as much as Lou wore her out, Oz rejuvenated his mother.

"How're you doing, Oz?" asked Amanda.

The little boy answered by letting out a crowing sound that banged off all sides of the car's interior, startling even the inattentive Jack.

"Miss English said I'm the best rooster she's ever heard," said Oz, and crowed again, flapping his arms. Amanda laughed and even Jack turned and smiled at his son.

Lou smirked at her brother, but then reached over and tenderly patted Oz on the hand. "And you are too, Oz. A lot better than me when I was your age," said Lou.

Amanda smiled at Lou's remark and then said, "Jack, you're coming to Oz's school play, aren't you?"

Lou said, "Mom, you know he's working on a story. He doesn't have time to watch Oz playing a rooster."

"I'll try, Amanda. I really will this time," Jack said. However, Amanda knew that the level of doubt in his tone heralded another disappointment for Oz. For her.

Amanda turned back and stared out the windshield. Her thoughts showed through so clearly on her features. *Life married to Jack Cardinal: I'll try.*

Oz's enthusiasm, however, was undiminished. "And next I'm going to be the Easter Bunny. You'll be there, won't you, Mom?"

Amanda looked at him, her smile wide and easing her eyes to pleasing angles.

"You know Mom wouldn't miss it," she said, giving his head another gentle rub.

But Mom did miss it. They all missed it.

CHAPTER TWO

AMANDA LOOKED OUT THE CAR WINDOW. Her prayers had been answered, and the storm had passed with little more than annoying patches of drizzle and an occasional gust of wind that failed to motivate the park trees to much more than a skimming of limbs. Everyone's lungs had been pressed hard from running the long, curvy strips of park grass end to end. And to his credit, Jack had played with as much abandon as any of them. Like a child, he had hurtled down the cobblestone paths with Lou or Oz on his back laughing riotously. Once he had even run right out of his loafers and then let the children chase him down and put them back on after a spirited struggle. Later, to the delight of all, he hung upside down while he performed on the swings. It was exactly what the Cardinal family needed.

At day's end the children had collapsed on their parents, and they all had napped right there, a huge ball of wild-angled limbs, deep breathing, and the contented sighs of tired, happy people at rest. A part of Amanda could have lain there the rest of her life, and felt as though she had accomplished all the world could ever reasonably demand of her.

Now, as they returned to the city, to a very small but cherished home that would not be theirs much longer, Amanda felt a growing uneasiness. She did not particularly care for confrontation, but Amanda also knew it was sometimes necessary when the cause was important. She checked the backseat. Oz was sleeping. Lou's face was turned to the window; she also appeared to be dozing. Since she rarely had her husband all to herself, Amanda decided now was the time.

She said softly to Jack, "We really need to talk about California."

Her husband squinted although there was no sun; in fact the darkness was almost complete around them. "The movie studio already has writing assignments lined up," he said.

She noted that he stated this without a trace of enthusiasm. Emboldened by this, Amanda pressed on. "You're an award-winning novelist. Your work is already being taught in schools. You've been called the most gifted storyteller of your generation."

He seemed wary of all this praise. "So?"

"So why go to California and let them tell you what to write?"

The light in his eyes dimmed. "I don't have a choice."

Amanda gripped his shoulder. "Jack, you *do* have a

choice. And you can't think that writing for the movies will make everything perfect, because it won't!"

Her mother's raised voice caused Lou to slowly turn and stare at her parents.

"Thanks for the vote of confidence," said Jack. "I really appreciate it, Amanda. Especially now. You know this isn't easy for me."

"That's not what I meant. If you'd only think about—"

Lou suddenly hunched forward, one arm grazing her father's shoulder even as her mother retreated. Lou's smile was big but obviously forced. "I think California will be great, Dad."

Jack grinned and gave Lou a tap on the hand. Amanda could sense Lou's soul leaping to this slight praise. She knew that Jack failed to realize the hold he commanded over his little girl; how everything she did was weighed against whether it would please him enough. And that scared Amanda.

"Jack, California is not the answer, it's just not. You have to understand that," said Amanda. "You won't be happy."

His expression was pained. "I'm tired of wonderful reviews and awards for my shelf, and then not even making enough money to support my family. *All* my family." He glanced at Lou, and there appeared on his features an emotion that Amanda interpreted as shame. She wanted to lean across and hold him, tell him that he was the most wonderful man she had ever known. But she had told him that before, and they were still going to California.

"I can go back to teaching. That'll give you the freedom to write. Long after we're all gone, people will still be reading Jack Cardinal."

"I'd like to go somewhere and be appreciated while I'm still alive."

"You *are* appreciated. Or don't we count?"

Jack looked surprised, a writer betrayed by his own words. "Amanda, I didn't mean that. I'm sorry."

Lou reached for her notebook. "Dad, I finished the story I was telling you about."

Jack's gaze held on Amanda. "Lou, your mother and I are talking."

Amanda had been thinking about this for weeks, ever since he had told her of plans for a new life writing screenplays amid the sunshine and palm trees of California, for considerable sums of money. She felt he would be tarnishing his skills by putting into words the visions of others, substituting stories from his soul with those that would earn the most dollars.

"Why don't we move to Virginia?" she said, and then Amanda held her breath.

Jack's fingers tightened around the steering wheel. Outside there were no other cars, no lights other than the Zephyr's. The sky was a long reef of suspect haze, no punctures of stars to guide them. They could have been driving over a flat, blue ocean, up and down exactly alike. One's mind could easily be tricked by such a conspiracy of heavens and earth.

"What's in Virginia?" His tone was very cautious.

Amanda clutched his arm in her growing frustration.

"Your grandmother! The farm in the mountains. The setting for all those beautiful novels. You've written about it all your life and you've never been back. The children have never even met Louisa. My God, *I've* never met Louisa. Don't you think it's finally time?"

His mother's raised voice startled Oz awake. Lou's hand went out to him, covering his slight chest, transferring calm from her to him. It was an automatic thing now for Lou, for Amanda was not the only protector Oz had.

Jack stared ahead, clearly annoyed by this conversation. "If things work out like I'm planning, she'll come and live with us. We'll take care of her. Louisa can't stay up there at her age." He added grimly, "It's too hard a life."

Amanda shook her head. "Louisa will never leave the mountain. I only know her through the letters and what you've told me, but even I know that."

"Well, you can't always live in the past. And *we're* going to California. We will be happy there."

"Jack, you can't really believe that. You can't!"

Lou once more rocked forward. She was all elbows, neck, knees—slender limbs seemingly growing before her parents' eyes.

"Dad, don't you want to hear about my story?"

Amanda put a hand on Lou's arm even as she gazed at a frightened Oz and tried to give him a reassuring smile, though reassurance was the last thing she was feeling. Now was clearly not the time for this discussion. "Lou, wait a minute, honey. Jack, we can talk later.

Not in front of the kids." She was suddenly very fearful of where this might actually go.

"What do you mean I can't really believe that?" Jack said.

"Jack, not now."

"You started this conversation, don't blame me for wanting to finish it."

"Jack, please—"

"Now, Amanda!"

She had never heard quite this tone, and instead of making her more afraid, it made her even angrier. "You hardly spend any time with the kids as it is. Always traveling, giving lectures, attending events. Everybody already wants a piece of Jack Cardinal, even if they won't *pay* you for the privilege. Do you really think it'll be better in California? Lou and Oz will never see you."

Jack's eyes, cheekbones, and lips formed a wall of defiance. When it came, his voice was filled with a potent combination of his own distress and the intent to inflict the same upon her. "Are you telling me I ignore my children?"

Amanda understood this tactic, but somehow still succumbed to it. She spoke quietly. "Maybe not intentionally, but you get so wrapped up in your writing—"

Lou almost vaulted over the front seat. "He does not ignore us. You don't know what you're talking about. You're wrong! You're wrong!"

Jack's dense wall turned upon Lou. "You do not talk to your mother that way. Ever!"

Amanda glanced at Lou, but even as she tried to

think of something conciliatory to say, her daughter proved swifter.

"Dad, this really is the best story I've ever written. I swear. Let me tell you how it starts."

However, Jack Cardinal, for probably the only time in his life, was not interested in a story. He turned and stared directly at his daughter. Under his withering look, her face went from hope to savage disappointment faster than Amanda could take a breath.

"Lou, I said not now!"

Jack slowly turned back. He and Amanda saw the same thing at the same time, and it pulled the blood from both their faces. The man was leaning into the trunk of his stalled car. They were so close to him that in the headlights Amanda saw the square bulge of the man's wallet in his back pocket. He wouldn't even have time to turn, to see his death coming at him at fifty miles an hour.

"Oh my God," Jack cried out. He cut the wheel hard to the left. The Zephyr responded with unexpected agility and actually missed the car, leaving the careless man to live another day. But now the Zephyr was off the road and onto sloped ground, and there were trees up ahead. Jack heaved the wheel to the right.

Amanda screamed, and reached out to her children as the car rocked uncontrollably. She could sense that even the bottom-heavy Zephyr would not maintain its balance.

Jack's eyes were silver dollars of panic, his breath no longer coming up. As the car raced across the slick road and onto the dirt shoulder on the other side, Amanda lunged into the backseat. Her arms closed around her children, bringing them together, her body between them and all that was hard and dangerous about the car. Jack swung the wheel back the other way, but the Zephyr's balance was gone, its brakes useless. The car missed a stand of what would have been unforgiving trees, but then did what Amanda had feared it would all along, it rolled.

As the top of the car slammed into the dirt, the driver's door was thrown open, and like a swimmer lost in a sudden rip, Jack Cardinal was gone from them. The Zephyr rolled again, and clipped a tree, which slowed its momentum. Shattered glass cascaded over Amanda and the children. The sound of tearing metal mixed with their screams was terrible; the smell of freed gasoline and billowy smoke searing. And through every roll, impact, and pitch again, Amanda pinned Lou and Oz safely against the seat with a strength that could not be completely her own. She absorbed every blow, keeping it from them.

The steel of the Zephyr fought a fearsome battle with the hard-packed dirt, but the earth finally triumphed and the car's top and right side buckled. One sharp-edged part caught Amanda on the back of her head, and then the blood came fast. As Amanda sank, the car, with one last spin, came to rest upside down, pointing back the way they had come.

Oz reached for his mother, incomprehension the only thing between the little boy and possibly fatal panic.

With a whipsaw motion of youthful agility, Lou pulled free of the destroyed guts of the car. The Zephyr's headlights were somehow still working, and she looked frantically for her father in the confusion of light and dark. She heard footsteps approaching and started saying a grateful prayer that her father had survived. Then her lips stopped moving. In the spread of the car's beams she saw the body sprawled in the dirt, the neck at an angle that could not support life. Then someone was pounding on the car with a hand, and the person they had almost killed was saying something. Lou chose not to hear the man whose negligent actions had just shattered her family. Lou turned and looked at her mother.

Amanda Cardinal too had seen her husband outlined there in the unforgiving light. For one impossibly long moment, mother and daughter shared a gaze that was completely one-sided in its communication. Betrayal, anger, hatred—Amanda read all of these terrible things on her daughter's features. And these emotions covered Amanda like a concrete slab over her crypt; they far exceeded the sum total of every nightmare she had ever suffered through. When Lou looked away, she left a ruined mother in her wake. As Amanda's eyes closed, all she could hear was Lou screaming for her father to come to her. For her father not to leave her. And then, for Amanda Cardinal, there was nothing more.

CHAPTER THREE

THERE WAS A CALM PIETY IN THE SONOROUS ring of the church bell. Like steady rain, its sounds covered the area, where the trees were starting to bud and the grass was stretching awake after a winter's rest. The curls of fireplace smoke from the cluster of homes here met in the clear sky. And to the south were visible the lofty spires and formidable minarets of New York City. These stark monuments to millions of dollars and thousands of weary backs seemed trifling against the crown of blue sky.

The large fieldstone church imparted an anchor's mass, an object incapable of being moved no matter the magnitude of problem that assailed its doors. The pile of stone and steeple seemed able to dispense comfort if one merely drew near it. Inside the thick walls there was another sound besides the peal of holy bell.

Holy singing.

The fluid chords of "Amazing Grace" poured down

the hallways and crowded against portraits of white-collared men who had spent much of their lives absorbing punishing confessions and doling out reams of Hail Marys as spiritual salve. Then the wave of song split around statues of blessed Jesus dying or rising, and finally broke in a pool of sanctified water just inside the front entrance. Creating rainbows, the sunlight filtered through the brilliant hues of stained glass windows up and down these corridors of Christ and sinners. The children would always "ooh" and "ahh" over these colorful displays, before they trudged reluctantly into Mass, thinking, no doubt, that churches always made fine rainbows.

Through the double doors of oak the choir was singing to the very pinnacle of the church, the tiny organist pumping with surprising energy for one so aged and crumpled, and "Amazing Grace" trumpeted ever higher. The priest stood at the altar, long arms tenaciously reaching to heaven's wisdom and comfort, a prayer of hope rising from him, even as the man pushed back against the tidal wave of grief confronting him. And he needed much divine support, for it was never an easy thing explaining away tragedy by invoking God's will.

The coffin sat at the front of the altar. The polished mahogany was covered with sprays of delicate baby's breath, a solid clump of roses, and a few distinctive irises, and yet that sturdy block of mahogany was what held one's attention, like five fingers against one's throat. Jack and Amanda Cardinal had exchanged their wedding vows in this church. They had not been back since, and no one present today could have envisioned their return being for a funeral mass barely fourteen years later.

Lou and Oz sat in the front pew of the full church. Oz had his bear crushed to his chest, his gaze cast down, a collection of tears plunking on the smooth wood between skinny legs that did not reach the floor. A blue hymnal lay unopened beside him; song was really beyond the boy right now.

Lou had one arm around Oz's shoulders, but her eyes never left the casket. It did not matter that the lid was closed. And the shield of beautiful flowers did nothing to obscure for her the image of the body inside. Today she had chosen to wear a dress for one of the few times in her life; the hated uniforms she had to wear to meet the requirements of the Catholic school she and her brother attended did not count. Her father had always loved her in dresses, even sketching her once for a children's book he had planned but never got around to. She pulled at her white socks, which reached uncomfortably to her bony knees. A pair of new black shoes pinched her long, narrow feet, feet that were quite firmly on the floor.

Lou had not bothered to sing "Amazing Grace." She had listened to the priest say that death was merely the beginning, that in God's enigmatic way this was a time for rejoicing, not sorrow, and then she did not listen anymore. Lou did not even pray for the lost soul of her father. She knew Jack Cardinal was a good man, a wonderful writer and teller of tales. She knew he would be deeply missed. No choir, no man of the cloth, no god needed to tell her these things.

The singing stopped, and the priest once more took up his ramblings, while Lou picked up on the conversation of the two men behind her. Her father had been a shameless eavesdropper in his search for the authentic ring of conversation, and his daughter shared that curiosity. Now Lou had even more reason to do so.

"So, have you come up with any brilliant ideas?" the older man whispered to his younger companion.

"Ideas? We're the executors of an estate with nothing in it" was the agitated response from the younger man.

The older man shook his head and spoke in an even lower tone, which Lou struggled to hear.

"Nothing? Jack did leave two children and a wife."

The younger man glanced to the side and then said in a low hiss, "A wife? They might as well be orphans."

It was not clear whether Oz heard this, but he lifted his head and put a hand on the arm of the woman sitting next to him. Actually, Amanda was in a wheelchair. A wide-bodied nurse sat on the other side of her, arms folded across her flop of bosom; the nurse was clearly unmoved by the death of a stranger.

A thick bandage was wrapped around Amanda's head, her auburn hair cut short. Her eyes were closed. In fact, they had never once opened since the accident. The doctors had told Lou and Oz that their mother's physical side had been mostly repaired. The problem now apparently was only a matter of her soul's having fled.

Later, outside the church, the hearse carried Lou's father away and she did not even look. In her mind she had said her good-byes. In her heart she could never do so. She pulled Oz along through the trenches of somber suit coats and mourning dresses. Lou was so tired of sad faces, moist eyes catching her dry ones, telegraphing sympathy, mouths firing off broadsides of the literary world's collective, devastating loss. Well, none of *their* fathers lay dead in that box. This was *her* loss, hers and her brother's. And she was weary of people apologizing for a tragedy they could not begin to understand. "I'm so sorry," they would whisper. "So sad. A great man. A beautiful man. Struck down in his prime. So many stories left untold."

"Don't be sorry," Lou had started saying right back. "Didn't you hear the priest? This is a time to rejoice. Death is good. Come on and sing with me."

These people would stare, smile nervously, and then move on to "rejoice" with someone else of a more understanding nature.

Next, they were to go to the grave-site service where the priest would no doubt say more uplifting words, bless the children, sprinkle his sacred dirt; and then another six feet of ordinary fill would be poured in, closing this terribly odd spectacle. Death must have its ritual, because society says it must. Lou did not intend to rush to it, for she had a more pressing matter to attend to right now.

The same two men were in the grassy parking lot. Freed from ecclesiastical confines, they were debating in normal voices the future of what remained of the Cardinal family.

"Wish to God Jack hadn't named us as executors," said the older man as he pulled a pack of cigarettes from his shirt pocket. He lit up and then pressed the match flame out between his thumb and forefinger. "Figured I'd be long dead by the time Jack checked out."

The younger man looked down at his polished shoes and said, "We just can't leave them like this, living with strangers. The kids need someone."

The other man puffed his smoke and gazed off after the bubble-topped hearse. Up above, a flock of blackbirds seemed to form a loose squadron, an informal send-off for Jack Cardinal. The man flicked ash. "Children belong with their family. These two just don't happen to have any left."

"Excuse me."

When they turned, they saw Lou and Oz staring at them.

"Actually, we do have family," Lou said. "Our great-grandmother, Louisa Mae Cardinal. She lives in Virginia. It's where my father grew up."

The younger man looked hopeful, as though the burden of the world, or at least of two children, might still be shed from his narrow shoulders. The older man, though, looked suspicious.

"Your great-grandmother? She's still alive?" he asked.

"My parents were just talking about us moving to Virginia to be with her before the accident."

"Do you know if she'll take you?" the younger man eagerly wanted to know.

"She'll take us" was Lou's immediate reply, though in truth she had no idea at all if the woman would.

"All of us?" This question came from Oz.

Lou knew her little brother was thinking of their wheelchair-bound mother. She said in a very firm voice to the two men, "All of us."

CHAPTER FOUR

As LOU STARED OUT THE WINDOW OF THE train, it occurred to her that she had never really cared that much for New York City. It was true that during her childhood she had sampled many of its eclectic offerings, filling her days with trips to museums, zoos, and theaters. She had towered over the world on the observation deck of the Empire State Building, laughed and cried at the antics of the city dwellers trapped in glee or doom, observed scenes of emotional intimacy and witnessed passionate displays of public outcry. She had made some of these treks with her father, who had so often told her that the choice to be a writer was not the mere selection of an occupation, but rather the choice of an all-consuming lifestyle. And the business of a writer, he carefully pointed out, was the business of life, in both its uplifting glory and its complex frailty. And Lou had been privy to the results of such observations, as she had been enthralled by the readings and musings of some of the most skillful writers of the day, many in the privacy of the Cardinals' modest two-bedroom walkup in Brooklyn.

And their mother had taken her and Oz to all the boroughs of the city, gradually immersing them in various economic and social levels of urban civilization, for Amanda Cardinal was a very well-educated woman intensely curious about such things. The children had received a well-rounded education that had made Lou both respect and remain ever curious about her fellow human beings.

Still, with all that, she had never really become that excited about the city. Where she was going now, that she was very eager about. Despite living in New York City for most of his adult life, where he was surrounded by a large supply of story material that other writers had culled with critical and financial success over the years, Jack Cardinal had chosen to base all his novels upon the place the train was carrying his family to: the mountains of Virginia that rose high in the toe of the state's topographical boot. Since her beloved father had deemed the place worthy of his life's work, Lou had little difficulty in deciding to go there now.

She moved aside so that Oz could look out the window too. If ever hope and fear could be compressed into one emotion and displayed on a single face, they were now on the little boy's. With any given breath, Oz Cardinal looked like he might either laugh till his ribs pushed through his chest, or else faint dead away from utter terror. Lately, though, there had only been tears.

"It looks smaller from here," he commented, inclining

his head at the fast-receding city of artificial lights and concrete blocks stacked around welded threads of steel.

Lou nodded in agreement. "But wait until you see the Virginia mountains—now, they're big. And they stay like that, however you look at them."

"How do you know? You've never seen those mountains."

"Of course I have. In books."

"Do they look all that big on paper?"

If Lou hadn't known better, she would have thought Oz was being smart, but she knew her brother did not possess even a mildly wicked bone in his whole being.

"Trust me, Oz, they're big. And I've read about them in Dad's books too."

"You haven't read all of Dad's books. He said you weren't old enough."

"Well, I've read one of them. And he read parts of all the others to me."

"Did you talk to that woman?"

"Who? Louisa Mae? No, but the people who wrote to her said she really wanted us to come."

Oz pondered this. "That's a good thing, I guess."

"Yes, it is."

"Does she look like Dad?"

This stumped his sister. "I can't say I've ever seen a picture of her."

It was clear this answer troubled Oz. "Do you think she's maybe mean and scary-looking? If she is, can't we come back home?"

"Virginia is our home now, Oz." Lou smiled at him.

"She won't be scary-looking. And she won't be mean. If she were, she never would have agreed to take us."

"But witches do that sometimes, Lou. Remember Hansel and Gretel? They trick you. Because they want to eat you. They all do that. I know; I read books too."

"So long as I'm there, no witch is going to be bothering you." She gripped his arm, showing off her strength, and he finally relaxed and looked over at the other occupants of their sleeper compartment.

This trip had been financed entirely by the friends of Jack and Amanda Cardinal, and collectively they had spared no expense in sending the children off in comfort to their new lives. This included a nurse to travel with them, and to stay with them in Virginia for a reasonable length of time, to care for Amanda.

Unfortunately, the hired nurse seemed to have taken it upon herself to act as the disciplinarian of wayward children as well as overseer of motherly health. Understandably, she and Lou had not particularly seen eye to eye. Lou and Oz watched as the tall, bony woman tended to her patient.

"Can we be with her for a bit?" Oz finally asked in a small voice. To him the nurse was part viper, part fairytale evil, and she scared him into the next century. It seemed to Oz that the woman's hand at any moment could become a knife, and he the blade's only target. The idea of their great-grandmother having witchlike qualities had not come entirely from the unfortunate tale of Hansel and Gretel. Oz held out no hope that the nurse would agree to his request, but, surprisingly, she did.

As she slid closed the door to the compartment, Oz looked at Lou. "I guess she's not so bad."

"Oz, she went to take a smoke."

"How do you know she smokes?"

"If the nicotine stains on her fingers hadn't clued me in, the fact that she reeks of tobacco would've been enough."

Oz sat next to his mother, who lay in the lower bunk bed, arms across her middle, eyes closed, her breath shallow but at least there.

"It's us, Mom, me and Lou."

Lou looked exasperated. "Oz, she can't hear you."

"Yes, she can!" There was a bite to the boy's words that startled Lou, who was used to virtually all of his ways. She crossed her arms and looked away. When she glanced back, Oz had taken a small box from his suitcase and was opening it. The chain necklace he pulled out had a small quartz stone at the end.

"Oz, please," his sister implored, "will you stop?"

He ignored her and held the necklace over his mother.

Amanda could eat and drink, though for some reason unfathomable to her children she could not move her limbs or speak, and her eyes never opened. This was what bothered Oz greatly and also gave him the most hope. He figured some small thing must be out of sorts, like a pebble in a shoe, a clog in a pipe. All he had to do was clear this simple obstruction and his mother would join them again.

"Oz, you are so dumb. Don't do this."

He stopped and looked at her. "Your problem is you don't believe in anything, Lou."

"And your problem is you believe in *everything*."

Oz started to swing the necklace slowly back and forth over his mother. He closed his eyes and started saying words that could not be clearly understood, perhaps not even by him.

Lou stood and fidgeted, but finally could not take this foolishness any longer. "Anybody sees you doing that, they'll think you're loony. And you know what? You are!"

Oz stopped his incantations and looked at her crossly. "Well, you ruined it. Complete silence is necessary for the cure to work."

"Cure? What cure? What are you talking about?"

"Do you want Mom to stay like this?"

"Well, if she does, it's her own fault," Lou snapped. "If she hadn't been arguing with Dad, none of this would've happened."

Oz was stunned by her words. Even Lou looked surprised that she could have said something like that. But true to her nature, Lou wasn't about to take any of it back once it was said.

Neither one looked at Amanda right at that moment, but if they had, the pair would have seen something, only a tremble of the eyelids, that suggested Amanda had somehow heard her daughter, then fallen deeper into the abyss that had held her so very tightly already.

Although most of the passengers were unaware, the train gradually banked left as the line curved away from the city on its way south. As it did so, Amanda's arm slid off her stomach and dangled over the side of the bed.

Oz stood there stunned for a moment. One could sense that the boy believed he had just witnessed a miracle of biblical dimension, like a flung stone felling a giant. He screamed out, "Mom! Mom!" and almost dragged Lou to the floor in his excitement. "Lou, did you see that?"

But Lou could not speak. She had presumed their mother incapable of such activity ever again. Lou had started to utter the word "Mom" when the door to the compartment slid open, and the nurse filled the space like an avalanche of white rock, her face a craggy pile of displeasure. Wisps of cigarette smoke hovered above her head, as though she were about to spontaneously combust. If Oz had not been so fixated on his mother, he might have jumped for the window at the sight of the woman.

"What's going on here?" She staggered forward as the train rocked some more, before settling into its arrow path through New Jersey.

Oz dropped the necklace and pointed at his mother, as if he were a bird dog in search of praise. "She moved. Mom moved her arm. We both saw it, didn't we, Lou?"

Lou, however, could only stare from her mother to Oz and back again. It was as though someone had driven a pole down her throat; she could form no words.

The nurse examined Amanda and came away even more sour-faced, apparently finding the interruption of her cigarette break unforgivable. She put Amanda's arm back across her stomach and covered her with the sheet.

"The train went around a curve. That's all." As she bent low to tuck in the bedcovers, she saw the necklace on the floor, incriminating evidence of Oz's plot to hasten his mother's recovery.

"What's this?" she demanded, reaching down and picking up Exhibit One in her case against the little boy.

"I was just using it to help Mom. It's sort of"—Oz glanced nervously at his sister—"it's sort of magic."

"That is nonsense."

"I'd like it back, please."

"Your mother is in a catatonic state," the woman said in a cold, pedantic tone designed to strike absolute terror in all who were insecure and vulnerable, and she had an easy target in Oz. "There is little hope of her regaining consciousness. And it certainly won't happen because of a necklace, young man."

"Please give it back," Oz said, his hands clenched together, as though in prayer.

"I have already told you—" She was cut off by the tap on her shoulder. When she turned, Lou stood directly in front of her. The girl seemed to have grown many inches in the last several seconds. At least the thrust of her head, neck, and shoulders seemed emboldened. "Give it back to him!"

The nurse's face reddened at this abuse. "I do not take orders from a child."

Quick as a whip Lou grabbed the necklace, but the nurse was surprisingly strong and managed to pocket it, though Lou struggled hard.

"This is not helping your mother," the nurse snapped,

puffing out the odor of Lucky Strikes with each breath. "Now, please sit down and keep quiet!"

Oz looked at his mother, the agony clear on his face at having lost his precious necklace over a curve in the track.

Lou and Oz settled next to the window and spent the next several rolling miles quietly watching the death of the sun. When Oz started to fidget, Lou asked him what was the matter.

"I don't feel good about leaving Dad by himself back there."

"Oz, he's not alone."

"But he *was* in that box all by himself. And it's getting dark now. He might be scared. It's not right, Lou."

"He's not in that box, he's with God. They're up there talking right now, looking down on us."

Oz looked up at the sky. His hand lifted to wave, but then he looked unsure.

"You can wave to him, Oz. He's up there."

"Cross your heart, stick a needle in your eye?"

"All of that. Go ahead and wave."

Oz did and then smiled a precious one.

"What?" his sister asked.

"I don't know, it just felt good. Think he waved back?"

"Of course. God too. You know how Dad is, telling stories and all. They're probably good friends by now." Lou waved too, and as her fingers drifted against the cool glass, she pretended for a moment that she was certain of all that she had just said. And it did feel good.

Since their father's death, winter had almost given over

to spring. She missed him more each day, the vast emptiness inside her swelling with every breath Lou took. She wanted her dad to be fine and healthy. And with them. But it would never be. Her father really was gone. It was an impossibly agonizing feeling. She looked to the sky.

Hello, Dad. Please never forget me, for I won't ever forget you. She mouthed these words so Oz couldn't hear. When she finished, Lou thought she might start bawling herself, but she couldn't, not in front of Oz. If she cried, there was a strong possibility that her brother might also cry, and keep right on going for the rest of his life.

"What's it like to be dead, Lou?" Oz stared out into the night as he asked this.

After a few moments she said, "Well, I guess part of being dead is not feeling anything. But in another way you feel everything. All good. If you've led a decent life. If not, well, you know."

"The Devil?" Oz asked, the fear visible in his features even as he said the terrible word.

"You don't have to worry about that. Or Dad either."

Oz's gaze made its way, by steady measures, to Amanda. "Is Mom going to die?"

"We're all going to die one day." Lou would not sugarcoat that one, not even for Oz, but she did squeeze him tightly. "Let's just take it one step at a time. We've got a lot going on."

Lou stared out the window as she held tightly to her brother. Nothing was forever, and didn't she know that.

CHAPTER FIVE

I T WAS VERY EARLY MORNING, WHEN THE BIRDS had barely awoken and thumped their wings to life, and cold mists were rising from the warm ground, and the sun was only a seam of fire in the eastern sky. They had made one stop in Richmond, where the locomotive had been changed, then the train had cleared the Shenandoah Valley, the most splendidly fertile soil and temperate climate for growing virtually anything. Now the angle of land was far steeper.

Lou had slept little because she had shared the top bunk with Oz, who was restless at night under the best circumstances. On a swaying train heading to a new, terrifying world, her little brother had been a wildcat in his sleep. Her limbs had been bruised from his unconscious flailing, despite her holding him tight; her ears were hurting from his tragic screams, in spite of her whispered words of comfort. Lou had finally climbed down, touched the cold floor with bare feet, stumbled to the window in the darkness, pulled back the curtains, and been rewarded by seeing her first Virginia mountain face-to-face.

Jack Cardinal had once told his daughter that it was believed that there were actually two sets of Appalachian mountains. The first had been formed by receding seas and the shrinkage of the earth millions of years before, and had risen to a great height that rivaled the present Rockies. Later these ridges had been eroded away to peneplain by the pounding of unsettled water. Then the world had shaken itself again, Lou's father had explained to her, and the rock had risen high once more, though not nearly so high as before, and formed the current Appalachians, which stood like menacing hands between parts of Virginia and West Virginia, and extended from Canada all the way down to Alabama.

The Appalachians had prevented early expansion westward, Jack had taught his ever-curious Lou, and kept the American colonies unified long enough to win their independence from an English monarch. Later, the mountain range's natural resources had fueled one of the greatest manufacturing eras the world had ever seen. Despite all that, her father had added with a resigned smile, man never gave the mountains much credit in shaping his affairs.

Lou knew that Jack Cardinal had loved the Virginia mountains, and had held high-angled rock in the deepest awe. He had often told her that there was something magical about this stretch of lofty earth, because he believed it held powers that could not be logically explained. She had often wondered how a mixture of dirt and stone, despite its elevation, could impress her father so. Now, for the first time, she had a sense of how it could, for Lou had never experienced anything quite like it.

The bumps of tree-shrouded dirt and slate piles Lou had initially seen really qualified only as small offspring; behind these "children" she could see the outlines of the tall parents, the mountains. They seemed unlimited by sky or earth. So large and broad were they that the mountains seemed unnatural, though they had been born directly from the planet's crust. And out there was a woman Lou had been named for but had never met. There was both comfort and alarm in that thought. For one panicked moment, Lou felt as though they had passed right into another solar system on this clickety-clack train. Then Oz was beside her, and though he was not one to inspire confidence in others, Lou did feel reassurance in his small presence.

"I think we're getting close," she said, rubbing his small shoulders, working out the tension of another round of nightmares. She and her mother had become experts in this. Oz, Amanda had told her, had the worst case of night terrors she had ever seen. But it was something neither to pity, nor to make light of, she had taught her daughter. All one could do was be there for the little boy and work out the mental and physical snarls as best one could.

That could have been Lou's own personal scripture: *Thou shalt have no greater duty than taking care of Thy brother Oz.* She meant to honor that commandment above all else.

The little boy focused on the landscape. "Where is it? Where we're going to be?"

She pointed out the window. "Somewhere out there."

"Will the train drive right up to the house?"

Lou smiled at his remark. "No. Someone will be wait-ing for us at the station."

The train passed into a tunnel slashed through the side of one of the hills, throwing them into even greater dark-ness. Moments later they shot clear of the tunnel and then how they climbed! Their degree of ascent made Lou and Oz peer out anxiously. Up ahead was a trestle. The train slowed and then eased carefully onto the bridge, like a foot at cold water's edge. Lou and Oz looked down, but could not see the ground below in the poor light. It was as though they were suspended in the sky, somehow carried aloft by an iron bird weighing many tons. Then suddenly the train was back on firm ground, and the climb was on again. As the train picked up speed, Oz took a deep breath inter-rupted by a yawn—perhaps, Lou thought, to stifle his anx-iety.

"I'm going to like it here," Oz suddenly proclaimed as he balanced his bear against the window. "Look out there," he said to his stuffed animal, which had never had a name that Lou knew of. Then Oz's thumb nervously probed the insides of his mouth. He'd been diligently trying to stop sucking his thumb, yet with all that was happening he was finding it tough going.

"It'll be okay, right, Lou?" he mumbled.

She perched her little brother on her lap, tickling the back of his neck with her chin until Oz squirmed.

"We're going to be just fine." And Lou somehow forced herself to believe that it would be so.

CHAPTER SIX

THE TRAIN STATION AT RAINWATER RIDGE was no more than a glorified pine-studded lean-to, with a single cracked and spider-webbed window and an opening for a door but no door to fill the space. A narrow jump separated this wreck of nail and board from the railroad track. The channeled wind was fierce as it fought its way through the gaps in rock and tree, and the faces of the few folk hanging about, along with the runted trees, evidenced the blunt force of its chisel.

Lou and Oz watched as their mother was loaded into an ancient ambulance. As the nurse climbed into the vehicle, she scowled back at her charges, the confrontation of the day before obviously still rankling her.

When the doors of the vehicle closed, Lou pulled the quartz necklace from her coat pocket and handed it to Oz.

"I slipped into her room before she got up. It was still in her pocket."

Oz smiled, pocketed the precious item, and then reached on tiptoe to give his sister a kiss on the cheek. The two stood next to their luggage, patiently awaiting Louisa Mae Cardinal.

Their skin was scrubbed raw, each hair on their heads assiduously brushed—Lou had taken extra time with Oz. They were dressed in their very best clothes, which managed barely to conceal their pounding hearts. They had been there for a minute when they sensed someone behind them.

The Negro man was young and, in keeping with the geography, ruggedly built. He was tall and wide of shoulder, deep-chested, with arms like slabs of ham, a waist not small but not soft either, and legs long but one oddly pushed out where calf met knee. His skin was the color of deep rust and pleasing to the eye. He was looking down at his feet, which necessarily drew Lou's gaze to them. His old work boots were so big a newborn could have slept in them with some room to spare, the girl observed. His overalls were as worn as the shoes, but they were clean, or as clean as the dirt and wind would allow anything to be up here. Lou held out her hand, but he did not take it.

Instead, with one impressive move, he picked up all their bags, then flicked his head toward the road. Lou interpreted this as "hello," "come on," and "I'll tell you my name maybe later," all wrapped into one efficient motion. He limped off, the bulging leg now revealed to be a bum one. Lou and Oz looked at each other and then trudged after him. Oz clutched his bear and Lou's hand. No doubt the boy would have tugged the train after them if he could have somehow managed it, so as to effect a quick escape if needed.

The long-bodied Hudson four-door sedan was the color of a sweet pickle. The car was old but clean inside. Its tall, exposed radiator looked like a tombstone, and its two front fenders were missing, as was the rear window glass. Lou and Oz sat in the backseat while the man drove. He worked the long stick shift with an easy skill, nary a gear ever left grinding.

After the woeful state of the train station, Lou had not expected much in the way of civilization up here. However, after only twenty minutes on the road they entered a town of fair size, though in New York City such a meager collection of structures would hardly have filled one sorry block.

A sign announced that they were entering the township of Dickens, Virginia. The main street was two-laned and paved with asphalt. Well-kept structures of wood and brick lined both sides of it. One such building rose five stories, its vacancy sign proclaiming it to be a hotel at fair rates. Automobiles were plentiful here, mostly bulky Ford and Chrysler sedans, and hefty trucks of various makes adorned with mud. All were parked slantwise in front of the buildings.

There were general stores, restaurants, and an open-door warehouse with box towers of Domino sugar and Quick napkins, Post Toasties and Quaker Oats visible inside. There was an automobile dealership with shiny cars in the window, and next to that an Esso gas station sporting twin pumps with bubble tops and a uniformed man with a big smile filling up the tank of a dented La Salle sedan, with a dusty Nash two-door waiting behind it. A big Coca-Cola soda cap was hanging in front of one café, and an Eveready Battery sign was bolted to the wall of a hardware shop. Telephone and electrical poles of poplar ran down one side of the street, black cables snaking out from them to each of the structures. Another shop announced the sale of pianos and organs for cash at good prices. A movie theater was on one corner, a laundry on another. Gas street lamps ran down both sides of the road, like big, lit matchsticks.

The sidewalks were crowded with folks. They ranged from well-dressed women with stylish hairdos topped by modest hats, to bent, grimy men who, Lou thought, probably toiled here in the coal mines she had read about.

As they passed through, the last building of significance was also the grandest. It was red brick with an elegant two-story pediment portico, supported by paired Greek Ionic columns, and had a steeply pitched, hammered tin roof painted black, with a brick clock tower top-hatting it. The Virginia and American flags snapped out front in the fine breeze. The elegant red brick, however, sat on a foundation of ugly, scored concrete. This curious pairing struck Lou as akin to fine pants over filthy boots. The carved words above the columns simply read: "Court House." And then they left the finite sprawl of Dickens behind.

Lou sat back puzzled. Her father's stories had been filled with tales of the brutish mountains, and the primitive life there, where hunters squatted near campfires of hickory sticks and cooked their kill and drank their bitter coffee; where farmers rose before the sun and worked the land till they collapsed; where miners dug into the earth, filling their lungs with black that would eventually kill them; and where lumberjacks swept virgin forests clean with the measured strokes of ax and saw. Quick wits, a sound knowledge of the land, and a strong back were essential up here. Danger roamed the steep slopes and loamy valleys, and the magisterial high rock presided over both men and beasts, sharply defining the limits of their ambition, of their lives. A place like Dickens, with its paved roads, hotel, Coca-Cola signs, and pianos for cash at good prices, had no right to be here. Yet Lou suddenly realized that the time period her father had written about had been well over twenty years ago.

She sighed. Everything, even the mountains and its people, apparently, changed. Now Lou assumed her great-grandmother probably lived in a quite ordinary neighborhood with quite ordinary neighbors. Perhaps she had a cat and went to have her hair done every Saturday at a shop that smelled of chemicals and cigarette smoke. Lou and Oz would drink orange soda pop on the front porch and go to church on Sunday and wave to people as they passed in their cars, and life would not be all that much different than it had been in New York. And while there was absolutely nothing wrong with that, it was not the dense, breathtaking wilderness Lou had been expecting. It was not the life her father had experienced and then written about, and Lou was clearly disappointed.

The car passed through more miles of trees, soaring rock and dipping valleys, and then Lou saw another sign. This town was named Tremont. This was probably it, she thought. Tremont appeared roughly one-third the size of Dickens. About fifteen cars were slant-parked in front of shops similar to those in the larger town, only there was no high-rise building, no courthouse, and the asphalt road had given way to macadam and gravel. Lou also spotted the occasional horse rider, and then Tremont was behind them, and the ground moved higher still. Her great-grandmother, Lou surmised, must live on the outskirts of Tremont.

The next place they passed had no sign naming its location, and the scant number of buildings and few people they saw didn't seem enough to justify a name. The road was now dirt, and the Hudson swayed from side to side over this humble pack of shifting earth. Lou saw a shallow post office building, and next to that was a leaning pile of boards with no sign out front, and steps that had the rot. And finally there was a good-sized general store with the name "McKenzie's" on the wall; crates of sugar, flour, salt, and pepper were piled high outside. In one window of McKenzie's hung a pair of blue overalls, harnesses, and a kerosene lamp. And that was about all there was of the nameless stop along the poor road.

As they drifted over the soft dirt, they passed silent, sunken-eyed men, faces partially covered by wispy beards; they wore dirty one-piece overalls, slouch hats, and lumpy brogans, and traveled on foot, mule, or horse. A woman with vacant eyes, a droopy face, and bony limbs, clothed in a gingham blouse and a homespun woolen skirt bunched at the waist with pins, rocked along in a small schooner wagon pulled by a pair of mules. In the back of the wagon was a pile of children riding burlap seed bags bigger than they were. Running parallel to the road here a long coal train was stopped under a water tower and taking in big gulps, steam belching out from its throat with each greedy swallow. On another mountain in the distance Lou could see a coal tipple on wooden stilts, and another line of coal cars passing underneath this structure, like a column of obedient ants.

They passed over a large bridge. A tin sign said this was the McCloud River flowing thirty feet underneath them. In the reflection of the rising sun the water looked pink, like a miles-long curvy tongue. The mountain peaks were smoke-blue, the mists of fog right below them forming a gauzy kerchief.

With no more towns apparent, Lou figured it was time to get acquainted with the gentleman up front.

"What's your name?" she asked. She had known many Negroes, mostly writers, poets, musicians, and those who acted on the stage, all her parents' friends. But there had been others too. During her excursions through the city with her mother, Lou had met colored people who loaded the trash, flagged down the cabs, heaved the bags, scooted after others' children, cleaned the streets, washed the windows, shined the shoes, cooked the food, and did the laundry, and took, in amicable measures, the insults and tips of their white clientele.

This fellow driving, he was different, because he apparently didn't like to talk. Back in New York Lou had befriended one kindly old gentleman who worked a lowly job at Yankee Stadium, where she and her father would sometimes steal away to games. This old man, only a shade darker than the peanuts he sold, had told her that a colored man would talk your ear off every day of the week except the Sabbath, when he'd let God and the women have their shot.

The big fellow just continued to drive; his gaze didn't even creep to the rearview mirror when Lou spoke. A lack of curiosity was something Lou could not tolerate in her fellow man.

"My parents named me Louisa Mae Cardinal, after my great-grandmother. I go by Lou, though, just Lou. My dad is John Jacob Cardinal. He's a very famous writer. You've probably heard of him."

The young man didn't grunt or even wiggle a finger. The road ahead apparently held fascination for him that a dose of Cardinal family history simply could not compete with.

Getting into his sister's spirited attempt at conversation, Oz said, "He's dead, but our mom's not."

This indelicate comment drew an immediate scowl from Lou, and just as quickly Oz looked out the window, ostensibly to admire the countryside.

They were thrown forward a little when the Hudson came to an abrupt stop.

The young boy standing there was a little older than Lou, but about the same height. His red hair was all crazy-angled cowlicks, which still failed to cover conical ears that could easily have caught on a nail. He wore a stained long john shirt and dirty overalls that didn't manage to hide bony ankles. His feet were bare even though the air wasn't warm. He carried a long, hand-whittled cane fishing pole and a dented tackle box, which appeared to have once been blue. There was a black-and-tan mutt of a dog next to him, its lumpy pink tongue hanging out. The boy put his pole and box through the Hudson's open rear window and climbed in the front seat like he owned it, his dog following his relaxed lead.

"Howdy-howdy, Hell No," the stranger boy said amiably to the driver, who acknowledged this newcomer with an ever-so-slight nod of the head.

Lou and Oz looked at each other in puzzlement over this very odd greeting.

Like a pop-up toy, the visitor poked his head over the seat and stared at them. He had more than an adequate crop of freckles on his flat cheeks, a small mound of nose that carried still more freckles, and out of the sun his hair seemed even redder. His eyes were the color of raw peas, and together with the hair they made Lou think of Christmas wrapping paper.

"I bet I knowed me what, y'all Miss Louisa's people, ain'tcha?" he said in a pleasant drawl, his smile endearingly impish.

Lou nodded slowly. "I'm Lou. This is my brother, Oz," she said, with an easy courtesy, if only to show she wasn't nervous.

Swift as a salesman's grin, the boy shook hands with them. His fingers were strong, with many fine examples of the countryside imbedded in each of them. Indeed, if he'd ever had fingernails, it was difficult to tell under this remarkable collection of dirt. Lou and Oz both couldn't help but stare at those fingers.

He must have noted their looks, because he said, "Been to digging worms since afore light. Candle in one hand, tin can in the other. Dirty work, y'all know." He said this matter-of-factly, as though for years they all had knelt side by side under a hot sun hunting skinny bait.

Oz looked at his own hand and saw there the transfers of rich soil from the handshake. He smiled because it was as though the two had just undertaken the blood brother ritual. A brother! Now that was something Oz could get excited about.

The red-haired young man grinned good-naturedly, showing that most of his teeth were where they were supposed to be, though not many of them were what one could call either straight or white.

"Name's Jimmy Skinner," he said by way of modest

introduction, "but folk call me Diamond, 'cause my daddy say that how hard my head be. This here hound's Jeb."

At the sound of his name Jeb poked his fluffy head over the seat and Diamond gave each of the dog's ears a playful tug. Then he looked at Oz.

"That a right funny name fer a body. Oz."

Now Oz looked worried under the scrutiny of his blood brother. Was their partnership not to be?

Lou answered for him. "His real name is Oscar. As in Oscar Wilde. Oz is a nickname, like in the Wizard of."

His gaze on the ceiling of the Hudson, Diamond considered these facts, obviously searching his memory.

"Never tell of no Wildes up here." He paused, thinking hard again, the wrinkles on his brow crazy-lined. "And wizard'a what 'xactly?"

Lou could not hide her astonishment. "The book? The movie? Judy Garland?"

"The Munchkins? And the Cowardly Lion?" added Oz.

"Ain't never been to no pitcher show." Diamond glanced at Oz's bear and a disapproving look simmered on his face. "You right big fer that, now ain'tcha, son?"

This sealed it for Oz. He sadly wiped his hand clean on the seat, annulling his and Diamond's solemn covenant.

Lou leaned forward so close she could smell Diamond's breath. "That's none of your business, is it?"

A chastened Diamond slumped in the front seat and

let Jeb idly lick dirt and worm juice from his fingers. It was as though Lou had spit at the boy using words.

The ambulance was far ahead of them, driving slowly.

"I sorry your ma hurt," said Diamond, in the manner of passing the peace pipe.

"She's going to get better," said Oz, always nimbler on the draw than was Lou with matters concerning their mother.

Lou stared out the window, arms across her chest.

"Hell No," said Diamond, "just plop me off over to the bridge. Catch me anythin' good, I bring it fer supper. Tell Miss Louisa?"

Lou watched as Hell No edged his blunt chin forward, apparently signaling a big, happy "Okay, Diamond!"

The boy popped up over the seat again. "Hey, y'all fancy good lard-fried fish fer supper?" His expression was hopeful, his intentions no doubt honorable; however, Lou was unwilling just now to make friends.

"We all shore would, Diamond. Then maybe we can find us a pitcher show in this one-horse town."

As soon as Lou said this, she regretted it. It wasn't just the disappointed look on Diamond's face; it was also the fact that she had just blasphemed the place where her father had grown up. She caught herself looking to heaven, watching for grim lightning bolts, or maybe sudden rains, like tears falling.

"From some big city, ain'tcha?" Diamond said.

Lou drew her gaze from the sky. "The biggest. New York," she said.

"Huh, well, y'all don't be telling folks round here that."

Oz gaped at his ex–blood brother. "Why not?"

"Right chere's good, Hell No. Come on now, Jeb."

Hell No stopped the car. Directly in front of them was the bridge, although it was the puniest such one Lou had ever seen. It was a mere twenty feet of warped wooden planks laid over six-by-six tarred railroad ties, with an arch of rusted metal on either side to prevent one from plummeting all of five feet into what looked to be a creek full of more flat rock than water. Suicide by bridge jumping did not appear to be a realistic option here. And, judging from the shallow water, Lou did not hold out much hope for a lard-fried fish dinner, not that such a meal sounded particularly appealing to her anyway.

As Diamond pulled his gear from the back of the Hudson, Lou, who was a little sorry for what she had said, but more curious than sorry, leaned over the seat and whispered to him through the open rear window.

"Why do you call him Hell No?"

Her unexpected attention brought Diamond back to good spirits and he smiled at her. " 'Cause that be his name," he said in an inoffensive manner. "He live with Miss Louisa."

"Where did he get that kind of a name?"

Diamond glanced toward the front seat and pretended to fiddle with something in his tackle box. In a low voice he said, "His daddy pass through these parts when Hell No ain't no more'n a baby. Plunked him right on the dirt. Well, a body say to him, 'You gonna come back, take that child?' And he say, 'Hell no.' Now, Hell No, he never done nobody wrong his whole life. Ain't many folk say that. And no rich ones."

Diamond grabbed his tackle box and swung the pole to his shoulder. He walked to the bridge, whistling a tune, and Hell No drove the Hudson across, the structure groaning and complaining with each turn of the car wheels. Diamond waved and Oz returned it with his stained hand, hope welling back for maybe a friendship of enduring degree with Jimmy "Diamond" Skinner, crimson-crowned fisherboy of the mountain.

Lou simply stared at the front seat. At a man named Hell No.

CHAPTER SEVEN

T HE DROP WAS A GOOD THREE THOUSAND feet if it was an inch. The Appalachians might pale in size if leveled against the upstart Rockies, but to the Cardinal children they seemed abundantly tall enough.

After leaving the small bridge and Diamond behind, the ninety-six horses of the Hudson's engine had started to whine, and Hell No had dropped to a lower gear. The car's protest was understandable, for now the uneven dirt road headed up at almost a forty-five-degree angle and wound around the mountain like a rattler's coils. The road's supposed twin lanes, by any reasonable measurement, were really only a single pregnant one. Fallen rock lay along the roadside, like solid tears from the mountain's face.

Oz looked out only once at this potential drop to heaven, and then he chose to look no more. Lou stared off, their rise to the sky not really bothering her any.

Then, suddenly flying around a curve at them was a farm tractor, mostly rust and missing pieces and held together with coils of rusty wire and other assorted trash. It was almost too big for the narrow road all by itself, much less with a lumbering Hudson coming at it. Children were hanging and dangling every which way on the bulky equipment, as if it were a mobile jungle gym. One young boy about Lou's age was actually suspended over nothing but air, hanging on only by his own ten fingers and God's will, and he was laughing! The other children, a girl of about ten and a boy about Oz's age, were clamped tight around whatever they could find to hold, their expressions seized with terror.

The man piloting this contraption was far more frightening even than the vision of out-of-control machinery holding flailing children hostage. A felt hat covered his head, years of sweat having leached to all points of the material. His beard was bristly rough, and his face was burnt dark and heavily wrinkled by the unforgiving sun. He seemed to be short, but his body was thick and muscular. His clothes, and those of the children, were almost rags.

The tractor was almost on top of the Hudson. Oz covered his eyes, too afraid even to attempt a scream. But Lou cried out as the tractor bore down on them.

Hell No, with an air of practiced calm, somehow drove the car out of the tractor's path and stopped to let the other vehicle safely pass. So close were they to the edge that a full third of the Hudson's tires were gripping nothing but the chilly brace of mountain air.

Displaced rock and dirt dribbled over the side and were instantly scattered in the swirl of wind. For a moment Lou was certain they were going over, and she gripped Oz with all her strength, as though that would make a difference.

As the tractor roared by, the man glared at them all before settling on Hell No and shouting, "Stupid nig—"

The rest, thankfully, was covered by the whine of the tractor and the laughter and whoops of the suspended-in-air boy. Lou looked at Hell No, who didn't flinch at any of this. Not the first time, she imagined—the near fatal collision and the awful name calling.

And then like a strike of hail in July, this rolling circus was gone. Hell No drove on.

As she got her nerves settled down, Lou could see loaded coal trucks far below them inching down one side of a road, while on the other side empty trucks flew hell-bent back up, like honeybees, to gorge some more. All around here the face of the mountains had been gashed open in places, exposing rock underneath, the topsoil and trees all gone. Lou watched as coal trolleys emerged from these wounds in the mountains, like drips of blackened blood, and the coal was tippled into the truck beds.

"Name's Eugene."

Lou and Oz both stared toward the front seat. The young man was looking at them in the mirror.

"Name's Eugene," he said again. "Diamond, he fergit sometime. But he a good boy. My frien'."

"Hi, Eugene," said Oz. And then Lou said hello too.

"Ain't see folks much. Words ain't come easy for me. I sorry for that."

"That's okay, Eugene," said Lou. "Meeting strangers is hard."

"Miss Louisa and me, we real glad you come. She a good woman. Take me in when I ain't got no home. You lucky she your kin."

"Well, that's good because we haven't been very lucky lately," said Lou.

"She talk 'bout y'all much. And your daddy and momma. She care for your momma. Miss Louisa, she heal the sick."

Oz looked at Lou with renewed hope, but she shook her head.

More miles went by, and then Eugene turned the car down a lane that wasn't much more than twin ruts in the dirt spread over with still dormant grass and bracketed by thick wild brush. As they were obviously drawing near to their destination, Oz and Lou exchanged a glance. Excitement, nervousness, panic, and hope competed for space on the small landscapes of their faces.

The dirt lane nudged over to the north as it cleared a rise. Here the land splayed out into a broad valley of simple beauty. Green meadows were bracketed by vast forests of every wood the state boasted. Next to the meadows were cleared patchwork fields that yielded to split-rail corrals, weathered gray and wrapped with naked rambler rose vines. Anchoring the corrals was a large two-story plank barn, topped by a gambrel roof with rain hood, all covered by cedar shingles fashioned with froe and maul. It had large double doors at each end, with a set of hay doors above. A projecting timber was immediately above this portal and used to support the hay fork dangling from it. Three cows lay in the grass in one protected space, while a roan horse grazed alone in a small snake-rail corral. Lou counted a half dozen sheared sheep in another pen. And behind that was another fenced space where enormous hogs rolled in a wallow of mud, like giant babies at play. A pair of mules were doubletreed to a large wagon that sat by the barn, the sun reflecting off its tin-wrapped wooden wheels. Near the barn was a farmhouse of modest proportion.

There were other buildings and lean-tos, large and small, scattered here and there, most of plank. One structure situated in an overhang of maple trees looked to be formed from logs chinked with mud and seemed half-buried in the earth. The cleared fields, which sloped at their ends like the curl of hair, sprang outward from the central farm buildings like spokes on a wheel. And rising high behind all of this were the Appalachians, making this good-sized farm property seem but a child's model by comparison.

Lou was finally here, the place her father had spent much of his life writing about yet had never returned to. She drew in several quick breaths, and sat very erect as they drove on to the house, where Louisa Mae Cardinal, the woman who had helped to raise their father, awaited them.

CHAPTER EIGHT

INSIDE THE FARMHOUSE THE NURSE WAS ADVIS-
ing the woman as to Amanda's condition and other
essentials, while the woman listened intently and
asked pointed questions.

"And we might as well get *my* requirements out of
the way," said the nurse finally. "I suffer from animal
and pollen allergies, and you need to make sure that
their presence here is kept to a minimum. Under no circumstances should animals be allowed in the house. I
have certain specific dietary needs. I will provide you
with a list. I will also require a free reign in overseeing
the children. I know that falls outside my formal duties, but those two obviously need discipline, and I intend to so provide it. That girl, in particular, is a real
piece of work. I'm sure you can appreciate my frank-
ness. Now you can show me to my room."

Louisa Mae Cardinal said to the nurse, "I *appreciate*
you coming out. Fact is, we ain't got room for you."

The tall nurse stood as erect as she could, but she was still shorter than Louisa Mae Cardinal. "Excuse me?" she said with indignation.

"Tell Sam out there to take you on back to the train station. Another train north be coming through. Rare place for a walk while you wait."

"I was retained to come here and look after my patient."

"I look after Amanda just fine."

"You are not qualified to do so."

"Sam and Hank, they need get on back, honey."

"I need to call somebody about this." The nurse was so red-faced that she looked as though *she* might become a patient.

"Nearest phone on down the mountain in Tremont. But you can call the president of these United States, still my home." Louisa Mae gripped the woman's elbow with a strength that made the nurse's eyes flutter. "And we ain't got to bother Amanda with this." She guided the woman from the room, closing the door behind them.

"Do you seriously expect me to believe that you don't have a telephone?" the nurse said.

"Don't have that electricity thing neither, but I hear they right fine. Thank you agin, and you have a good trip back." She placed three worn dollar bills in the nurse's hand. "I wish it was more, honey, but it all the egg money I got."

The nurse stared down at the cash for a moment and said, "I'm staying until I'm satisfied that my patient—"

Louisa Mae once more gripped her elbow and led her to the front door. "Most folk here got rules 'bout trespassing. Warning shot's fired right close to the head. Get they's attention. Next shot gets a lot more personal. Now, I'm too old to waste time firing a warning shot, and I ain't never once used salt in my gun. And now I can't give it no straighter'n that."

When the Hudson pulled up, the ambulance was still parked in front of the farmhouse, which had a deep, cool porch and shadows elongating across it as the sun rose higher. Lou and Oz got out of the car and confronted their new home. It was smaller than it had appeared from a distance. And Lou noted several sets of uneven add-ons to the sides and back, all of which were set on a crumbling fieldstone base with stepstone rock leading from ground to porch. The unshingled roof had what looked to be black tar paper across it. A picket-fence railing ran along the porch, which also sagged in places. The chimney was made of hand-formed brick, and the mortar had leached over parts of it. The clapboard was in need of painting, heat pops were fairly numerous, and wood had buckled and warped in places where moisture had crawled inside.

Lou accepted it for what it clearly was: an old house, having gone through various reincarnations and situated in a place of unforgiving elements. But the front-yard grass was neatly cut, the steps, windows, and porch floor were clean, and she tallied the early bloom of flowers in glass jars and wooden buckets set along the porch rail and in window boxes. Climbing rose vines ran up the porch columns, a screen of dormant maypops covered part of the porch, and a husky vine of sleeping honeysuckle spread against one wall. There was a rough-hewn workbench on the porch with tools scattered across its surface and a split-bottom hickory chair next to it.

Brown hens started singing around their feet, and a couple of mean-looking geese came calling, sending the hens off screeching for their lives. And then a yellow-footed rooster stomped by and scared the geese off, cocked its head at Lou and Oz, gave a crow, and stomped back from whence it had come. The mare whinnied a greeting from its corral, while the pair of mules just stared at nothing. Their hairy skin was cave black, their ears and snout not quite balanced with each other. Oz took a step toward them for a better look and then retreated when one of the mules made a noise Oz had never heard before yet which clearly sounded threatening.

Lou's and Oz's attention shifted to the front door when it was thrown open with far more thrust than was necessary. Their mother's nurse came clomping out. She stalked past them, her long arms and legs cocking and firing off rounds of silent fury.

"Never in all my life," she wailed to the Appalachians. Without another word or grimace, flap of arm or kick of leg, she climbed into the ambulance, closed the doors, which made two modest thunks as metal hit metal, and the volunteer brigade beat a timid retreat.

Beyond perplexed, Lou and Oz turned back to the house for answers and found themselves staring at her.

Standing in the doorway was Louisa Mae Cardinal. She was very tall, and though also very lean, she looked strong enough to strangle a bear, and determined enough to do so. Her face was leathern, the lines creasing it the etch of wood grain. Although she was approaching her eightieth year, the balls of her cheeks still rode high. The jaw was also strong, though her mouth drooped some. Her silver hair was tied with a simple cord at the nape, and then plunged to her waist.

Lou was heartened to see that she wore not a dress, but instead baggy denim trousers faded to near white and an indigo shirt patched in various places. Old brogans covered her feet. She was statue-like in her majesty, yet the woman had a remarkable pair of hazel eyes that clearly missed nothing in their range.

Lou boldly stepped forward while Oz did his best to melt into his sister's back. "I'm Louisa Mae Cardinal. This is my brother, Oscar." There was a tremble to Lou's voice. She stood her ground, though, only inches from her namesake, and this proximity revealed a remarkable fact: Their profiles were almost identical. They seemed twins separated by a mere three generations.

Louisa said nothing, her gaze trailing the ambulance.

Lou noted this and said, "Wasn't she supposed to stay and help look after our mother? She has a lot of needs, and we have to make sure that she's comfortable."

Her great-grandmother shifted her focus to the Hudson.

"Eugene," Louisa Mae said in a voice possessed of negligible twang, yet which seemed undeniably southern still, "bring the bags in, honey." Only then did she look at Lou, and though the stare was rigid, there was something prowling behind the eyes that gave Lou a reason to feel welcome. "We take good care of your mother."

Louisa Mae turned and went back in the house. Eugene followed with their bags. Oz was fully concentrating on his bear and his thumb. His wide, blue eyes were blinking rapidly, a sure indication that his nerves were racing at a feverish pitch. Indeed, he looked like he wanted to run all the way back to New York City right that minute. And Oz very well might have, if only he had known in which direction it happened to be.

CHAPTER NINE

✥

THE BEDROOM GIVEN TO LOU WAS SPARTAN and also the only room on the second floor, accessed by a rear staircase. It had one large window that looked out over the farmyard. The angled walls and low ceiling were covered with old newspaper and magazine pages pasted there like wallpaper. Most were yellowed, and some hung down where the paste had worn away. There was a simple rope bed of hickory and a pine wardrobe scarred in places. And there was a small desk of rough-hewn wood by the window, where the morning light fell upon it. The desk was unremarkable in design, yet it drew Lou's attention as though cast from gold and trimmed by diamonds.

Her father's initials were still so vivid: "JJC." John Jacob Cardinal. This had to be the desk at which he had first started writing. She imagined her father as a little boy, lips set firm, hands working precisely, as he scored his initials into the wood, and then set out upon his career as a storyteller. As she touched the cut letters, it was as though she had just put her hand on top of her father's. For some reason Lou sensed that her great-grandmother had deliberately given her this room.

Her father had been reserved about his life here. However, whenever Lou had asked him about her namesake, Jack Cardinal had been effusive in his answer. "A finer woman never walked the earth." And then he would tell about some of his life on the mountain, but only some. Apparently, he left the intimate details for his books, all but one of which Lou would have to wait until adulthood to read, her father had told her. Thus she was left with many unanswered questions.

She reached in her suitcase and pulled out a small, wood-framed photograph. Her mother's smile was wide, and though the photograph was black and white, Lou knew the swell of her mother's amber eyes was near hypnotic. Lou had always loved that color, even sometimes hoping that the blue in hers would disappear one morning and be replaced with this collision of brown and gold. The photo had been taken on her mother's birthday. Toddler Lou was standing in front of Amanda, and mother had both arms around her child. In the photo their smiles were suspended together for all time. Lou often wished she could remember something of that day.

Oz came into the room and Lou slipped the photograph back into her bag. As usual, her brother looked worried.

"Can I stay in your room?" he asked.

"What's wrong with yours?"

"It's next to hers."

"Who, Louisa?" Oz answered yes very solemnly, as though he was testifying in court. "Well, what's wrong with that?"

"She scares me," he said. "She really does, Lou."

"She let us come live with her."

"And I'm right glad you did come."

Louisa came forward from the doorway. "Sorry I was short with you. I was thinking 'bout your mother." She stared at Lou. "And her needs."

"That's okay," Oz said, as he flitted next to his sister. "I think you spooked my sister a little, but she's all right now."

Lou studied the woman's features, seeing if there was any of her father there. She concluded that there wasn't.

"We didn't have anyone else," Lou said.

"Y'all always have me," Louisa Mae answered back. She moved in closer, and Lou suddenly saw fragments of her father there. She also now understood why the woman's mouth drooped. There were only a few teeth there, all of them yellowed or darkened.

"Sorry as I can be I ain't made the funeral. News comes slowly here when it bothers to come a'tall." She looked down for a moment, as though gripped by something Lou couldn't see. "You're Oz. And you're Lou." Louisa pointed to them as she said the names.

Lou said, "The people who arranged our coming, I guess they told you."

"I knew long afore that. Y'all call me Louisa. They's

chores to be done each day. We make or grow 'bout all we need. Breakfast's at five. Supper when the sun falls."

"Five o'clock in the morning!" exclaimed Oz.

"What about school?" asked Lou.

"Called Big Spruce. No more'n couple miles off. Eugene take you in the wagon first day, and then y'all walk after that. Or take the mare. Ain't spare the mules, for they do the pulling round here. But the nag will do."

Oz paled. "We don't know how to ride a horse."

"Y'all will. Horse and mule bestest way to get by up here, other than two good feet."

"What about the car?" asked Lou.

Louisa shook her head. "T'ain't practical. Take money we surely ain't got. Eugene know how it works and built a little lean-to for it. He start it up every now and agin, 'cause he say he have to so it run when we need it. Wouldn't have that durn thing, 'cept William and Jane Giles on down the road give it to us when they moved on. Can't drive it, no plans to ever learn."

"Is Big Spruce the same school my dad went to?" asked Lou.

"Yes, only the schoolhouse he went to ain't there no more. 'Bout as old as me, it fall down. But you got the same teacher. Change, like news, comes slowly here. You hungry?"

"We ate on the train," said Lou, unable to draw her gaze from the woman's face.

"Fine. Your momma settled in. Y'all g'on see her."

Lou said, "I'd like to stay here and look around some."

Louisa held the door open for them. Her voice was gentle but firm. "See your momma first."

✣

The room was comfortable—good light, window open. Homespun curtains, curled by the damp and bleached by the sun, were lightly flapping in the breeze. As Lou looked around, she knew it had probably taken some effort to make this into what amounted to a sick-room. Some of the furniture looked worked on, the floor freshly scrubbed, the smell of paint still lingering; a chipped rocking chair sat in one corner with a thick blanket across it.

On the walls were ancient ferrotypes of men, women, and children, all dressed in what was probably their finest clothing: stiff white-collared shirts and bowler hats for the men; long skirts and bonnets for the women; lace frills for the young girls; and small suits and string ties for the boys. Lou studied them. Their expressions ran the gamut from dour to pleased, the children being the most animated, the grown women appearing the most suspicious, as though they believed their lives were to be taken, instead of simply their photographs.

Amanda, in a bed of yellow poplar, was propped up on fat feather pillows, and her eyes were shut. The mattress was feather-filled too, lumpy but soft, housed in a striped ticking. A patchwork quilt covered her. A faded drugget lay next to the bed so bare feet wouldn't have to touch a cold wood floor first thing in the morning.

Lou knew her mother would not be needing that. On the walls were pegs with items of clothing hung from them. An old dresser was in one corner, a painted china pitcher and bowl resting on it. Lou wandered around the room idly, looking and touching. She noted that the window frame was slightly crooked, the panes of glass filmy, as though a fog had infiltrated the material somehow.

Oz sat next to his mother, leaned over, and kissed her.

"Hi, Mom."

"She can't hear you," Lou muttered to herself as she stopped her wandering and looked out the window, smelling air purer than any she had before; in the draft were a medley of trees and flowers, wood smoke, long bluegrass, and animals large and small.

"It sure is pretty here in . . ." Oz looked at Lou.

"Virginia," Lou answered, without turning around.

"Virginia," Oz repeated. Then he took out the necklace.

From the doorway, Louisa watched this exchange.

Lou turned and saw what he was doing. "Oz, that stupid necklace doesn't work."

"So why'd you get it back for me then?" he said sharply.

This stopped Lou dead, for she had no ready answer. Oz turned back and began his ritual over Amanda. But with each swing of the quartz crystal, with each softly spoken utterance by Oz, Lou just knew he was trying to melt an iceberg with a single match; and she wanted no part of it. She raced past her great-grandmother and down the hall.

Louisa stepped into the room and sat down next to Oz. "What's that for, Oz?" she asked, pointing to the jewelry.

Oz cupped the necklace in his hand, eyed it closely, like it was a timepiece and he was checking what o'clock it was. "Friend told me about it. Supposed to help Mom. Lou doesn't believe it will." He paused. "Don't know if I do either."

Louisa ran a hand through his hair. "Some say believing a person get better is half the battle. I'm one who subscribes to that notion."

Fortunately, with Oz, a few seconds of despair were usually followed by replenished hope. He took the necklace and slid it under his mother's mattress. "Maybe it'll keep oozing its power this way. She'll get well, won't she?"

Louisa stared at the little boy, and then at his mother lying so still there. She touched Oz's cheek with her hand—very old against very new skin, and its mix seemed pleasing to both. "You keep right on believing, Oz. Don't you never stop believing."

CHAPTER TEN

THE KITCHEN SHELVES WERE WORN, KNOT-holed pine, floors the same. The floorboards creaked slightly as Oz swept with a short-handled broom, while Lou loaded lengths of cut wood into the iron belly of the Sears catalogue cook-stove that took up one wall of the small room. Fading sunlight came through the window and also peered through each wall crevice, and there were many. An old coal-oil lamp hung from a peg. Fat black iron kettles hung from the wall. In another corner was a food safe with hammered metal doors; a string of dried onions lay atop it and a glass jug of kerosene next to that.

As Lou examined each piece of hickory or oak, it was as though she was revisiting each facet of her prior life, before throwing it in the fire, saying good-bye as the flames ate it away. The room was dark and the smells of damp and burnt wood equally pungent. Lou stared over at the fireplace. The opening was large, and she guessed that the cooking had been done there before the Sears cookstove had come. The brick ran to the ceiling, and iron nails were driven through the mortar all over; tools and kettles, and odd pieces of other things Lou couldn't identify but that looked well-used, hung from them. In the center of the brick wall was a long rifle resting on twin braces angled into the mortar.

The knock on the door startled them both. Who would expect visitors so far above sea level? Lou opened the door and Diamond Skinner stared back at her with a vast smile. He held up a mess of smallmouth bass, as though he was offering her the crowns of dead kings. Loyal Jeb was beside him, his snout wrinkling as he drew in the fine fishy aroma.

Louisa came striding in from outside, her brow glistening with sweat, her gloved hands coated with rich dirt, as were her brogans. She slipped off her gloves and dabbed at her face with a sweat rag pulled from her pocket. Her long hair was pulled up under a cloth scarf, wisps of silver peeking out in spots.

"Well, Diamond, I believe that's the nicest mess of smallmouth I ever seen, son." She gave Jeb a pat. "How you doing, Mr. Jeb? You help Diamond catch all them fish?"

Diamond's grin was so wide Lou could almost count all his teeth. "Yes'm. Did Hell No—"

Louisa held up a finger and politely but firmly corrected, "Eugene."

Diamond looked down, collecting himself after this blunder. "Yes'm, sorry. Did Eugene tell you—"

"That you'd be bringing supper? Yes. And you'll be staying for it seeing you caught it. And get to know Lou and Oz here. Sure y'all be good friends."

"We've already met," Lou said stiffly.

Louisa looked between her and Diamond. "Well, that's right good. Diamond and you close in years. And be good for Oz to have another boy round."

"He's got me," Lou said bluntly.

"Yes, he does," Louisa agreed. "Well, Diamond, you gonna stay for meal?"

He considered the matter. "I ain't got me no more 'pointments today, so yep, I set myself down." Diamond glanced at Lou, and then he wiped at his dirty face and attempted to tug down one of a dozen cowlicks. Lou had turned away, however, completely unaware of his effort.

※

The table was set with Depression glass plates and cups, collected over the years by Louisa, she told them, from Crystal Winter oatmeal boxes. The dishes were green, pink, blue, amber, and rose. However pretty they might be, no one was really focusing on the dishes. Instead, tin fork and knife clashed as they all dug into the meal. When Louisa had said the meal prayer, Lou and Oz crossed themselves, while Diamond and Eugene looked on curiously but said nothing. Jeb lay in the corner, surprisingly patient with his portion. Eugene sat at one end of the table, methodically chewing his food. Oz absorbed his entire meal so fast Lou seriously considered checking to make sure his fork had not disappeared down his throat. Louisa dished Oz the last piece of lard-fried fish, the rest of the cooked vegetables, and another piece of cooked-in-grease cornbread, which, to Lou, tasted better than ice cream.

Louisa had not filled her plate.

"You didn't have any fish, Louisa," Oz said, as he stared guiltily at his second helping. "Aren't you hungry?"

"Meal by itself seeing a boy eating his way up to a growed man. Et while I cooked, honey. Always do."

Eugene glanced questioningly at Louisa when she said this and then went back to his meal.

Diamond's gaze kept sliding between Lou and Oz. He seemed eager to make friends again, yet seemed unsure how to accomplish it.

"Can you show me some of the places my dad would go around here?" Lou asked Louisa. "The things he liked to do? See, I'm a writer too."

"I know that," she said, and Lou gave her a surprised look. Louisa put her cup of water down and studied Lou's face. "Your daddy he like to tell 'bout the land. But afore he done that he done something real smart." She paused as Lou considered this.

"Like what?" the girl finally asked.

"He come to unnerstand the land."

"Understand . . . dirt?"

"It got lots of secrets, and not all good ones. Things up here hurt you bad if you ain't careful. Weather so fickle, like it break your heart 'bout the time it do your back. Land don't help none who don't never bother to learn it." On this she glanced at Eugene. "Lord knows Eugene could use help. This farm ain't going one minute more without his strong back."

Eugene swallowed a piece of fish and washed it down with a gulp of water he had poured directly into his glass from a bucket. As Lou watched him, Eugene's mouth trembled. She interpreted that as a big smile.

"Fact is," Louisa continued, "you and Oz coming here is a blessing. Some folk might say I helping you out, but that ain't the truth. You helping me a lot more'n I can you. For that I thank you."

"Sure," said Oz gallantly. "Glad to do it."

"You mentioned there were chores," Lou said.

Louisa looked over at Eugene. "Better to show, not tell. Come morning, I commence showing."

Diamond could contain himself no longer.

"Johnny Booker's pa said some fellers been looking round his place."

"What fellers?" asked Louisa sharply.

"Ain't know. But they's asking questions 'bout the coal mines."

"Get your ears on the ground, Diamond." Louisa looked at Lou and Oz. "And you too. God put us on this earth and he take us away when he good and ready. Meantime, family got to look out for each other."

Oz smiled and said he'd keep his ears so low to the ground, they'd be regularly filled with dirt. Everyone except Lou laughed at that. She simply stared at Louisa and said nothing.

The table was cleared, and while Louisa scraped dishes, Lou worked the sink hand pump hard, the way Louisa had shown her, to make only a very thin stream of water come out. No indoor plumbing, she had been told. Louisa had also explained to them the outhouse arrangement and shown them the small rolls of toilet paper stacked in the pantry. She had said a lantern would be needed after dark if the facilities were required, and she had shown Lou how to light one. There was also a chamberpot under each of their beds if the call of nature was of such urgency that they couldn't make it to the outhouse in time. However, Louisa informed them that the cleaning of the chamberpot was strictly the responsibility of the one using it. Lou wondered how timid Oz, a champion user of the bathroom in the middle of the night, would get along with this accommodation. She imagined she would be standing outside this outhouse many an evening while he did his business, and that was a weary thought.

Right after supper Oz and Diamond had gone outside with Jeb. Lou now watched as Eugene lifted the rifle off its rack above the fireplace. He loaded the gun and went outside.

Lou said to Louisa, "Where's he going with that gun?"

Louisa scrubbed plates vigorously with a hardened

corncob. "See to the livestock. Now we done turned out the cows and hogs, Old Mo's coming round."

"Old Mo?"

"Mountain lion. Old Mo, he 'bout as old as me, but that durn cat still be a bother. Not to people. Lets the mare and the mules be too, 'specially the mules, Hit and Sam. Don't never cross no mule, Lou. They's the toughest things God ever made, and them durn critters keep grudges till kingdom come. Don't never forget one smack of the whip, or slip of a shoeing nail. Some folks say mules 'bout as smart as a man. Mebbe that why they get so mean." She smiled. "But Mo does go after the sheep, hogs, and cows. So we got to protect 'em. Eugene gonna fire the gun, scare Old Mo off."

"Diamond told me about Eugene's father leaving him."

Louisa glanced at her sternly. "A lie! Tom Randall were a good man."

"What happened to him then?" Lou prompted when it appeared Louisa was not inclined to go on.

Louisa finished with a plate first and set it down to dry. "Eugene's mother die young. Tom left the baby with his sister here and went on over to Bristol, Tennessee, for work. He a coal miner here, but lot of folks started coming round to do that too, and they always let the Negroes go first. He got kilt in an accident afore he could send for Eugene. When Eugene's aunt passed on, I took him in. The other's just lies by folks who have hate in their hearts."

"Does Eugene know?"

"Course he does! I told him when he were old enough."

"So why don't you tell people the truth?"

"People don't want'a listen, ain't no good what you try tell 'em." She shot Lou a glance. "Unnerstand me?"

Lou nodded, but in truth she wasn't convinced she did.

CHAPTER ELEVEN

WHEN LOU WENT OUTSIDE, SHE SAW Diamond and Oz over by the split-rail corral where the horse was grazing. When Diamond saw Lou, he pulled a sheet of paper and a tin of tobacco out of his pocket, rolled the smoke, licked it closed, struck a match against a rail, and lit up.

Oz and Lou both gaped, and she exclaimed, "You're too young to do that."

Diamond casually waved off her protest, a pleased smile on his face. "Aww, I all growed up. Man a man."

"But you're not much older than me, Diamond."

"Different up here, you see."

"Where do you and your family live?" asked Lou.

"On down the road a piece afore you get somewhere."

Diamond pulled a cover-less baseball from his pocket and tossed it. Jeb raced after the ball and brought it back.

"Man give me that ball 'cause I tell him his future."

"What was his future?" asked Lou.

"That he gonna give a feller named Diamond his old ball."

"It's getting late," Lou said. "Won't your parents be getting worried?"

Diamond stubbed out the homemade smoke on his overalls and stuck it behind his ear as he wound up to throw again. "Naw, like I say, all growed up. Ain't got to do nothing if'n don't want to."

Lou pointed to something dangling on Diamond's overalls. "What's that?"

Diamond looked down and grinned. "Left hind foot of a graveyard rabbit. Aside fur heart'a calf, luckiest thing they is. Shoot, don't they school you nuthin' in the city?"

"A graveyard rabbit?" Oz said.

"Yessir. Caught and kilt in graveyard in black of night." He slipped the foot off its string and gave it to Oz. "Here, son, I always get me 'nuther, anytime I want I can."

Oz held it reverently. "Gosh, thanks, Diamond."

Oz watched Jeb race after the ball. "Jeb sure is a good dog. Gets that ball every time."

When Jeb brought the ball and dropped it in front of Diamond, he picked it up and tossed it over to Oz. "Prob'ly ain't much room to throw nuthin' in the city, but give it a whirl, son."

Oz stared at the ball as though he'd never held one. Then he glanced at Lou.

"Go ahead, Oz. You can do it," she said.

Oz wound up and threw the ball, his arm snapping like a whip, and that ball sprang forth from his small hand like a freed bird, soaring higher and higher. Jeb raced after it, but the dog wasn't gaining any ground. An astonished Oz just stared at what he'd done. Lou did the same.

The cigarette fell off a startled Diamond's ear. "God dog, where'd you learn to toss like that?"

Oz could only offer up the wonderful smile of a boy who had just realized he might be athletically gifted. Then he turned and raced after the ball. Lou and Diamond were silent for a bit and then the ball came sailing back. In the gathering darkness they couldn't even see Oz yet, but they could hear him and Jeb coming, a total of six spirited legs flying at them.

"So what do you do for excitement in this place, Diamond?" asked Lou.

"Fishing mostly. Hey, you ever skinny-dip in a gravel pit?"

"There are no gravel pits in New York City. Anything else?"

"Well"—he paused dramatically—"course, there's the haunted well."

"A haunted well?" exclaimed Oz, who had just run up, Jeb at his heels.

"Where?" asked Lou.

"Come on now."

Captain Diamond and his company of infantry cleared the tree line and plunged across an open field of tall grass so fine and uniformly placed, it looked like combed hair. The wind was chilly, but they were much too excited to be bothered by that slight discomfort.

"Where is it?" asked Lou, running beside Diamond.

"Shhh! Getting close, so's we got to be real quiet. Spooks round."

They kept moving forward. Suddenly Diamond called out, "Hit the ground!"

They all dropped as though attached by taut rope.

Oz said in a trembling voice, "What is it, Diamond?"

Diamond hid a smile. "Thought mebbe I hear something, is all. Can't never be too careful round spooks." They all rose.

"What y'all doing here?"

The man had stepped from behind a stand of hickory trees, the shotgun in his right hand. Under the moonlight Lou could make out the glow of an evil pair of eyes staring dead at them. The three stood frozen as the fellow approached. Lou recognized him as the crazy man on the tractor recklessly flying down the mountain. He stopped in front of them and his mouth delivered a shot of chew spit near their feet.

"Got no bizness round here," the man said, as he lifted up the shotgun and rested the barrel on his left forearm such that the muzzle was pointed at them, his forefinger near the trigger.

Diamond stepped forward. "Ain't doing nuthin',

George Davis, 'cept running round, and ain't no law agin that."

"You shet your mouth, Diamond Skinner, afore I put my fist to it." He peered over at quaking Oz, who drew back and clutched his sister's arm.

"You 'em chillin Louisa take in. Got the crippled ma. Ain'tcha?" He spit again.

Diamond said, "You ain't got no bizness with 'em, so leave 'em be."

Davis moved closer to Oz. "Mountain cat round, boy," he said, his voice low and taunting. And then he cried out, "You want it *git* you!" At the same time he said this, Davis feigned a lunge at Oz, who threw himself down and huddled in the high grass. Davis cackled wickedly at the terrified boy.

Lou stood between her brother and the man. "You stay away from us!"

"Gawd damn you, girl," Davis said. "Telling a man what to do?" He looked at Diamond. "You on my land, boy."

"T'ain't your land!" said Diamond, his hands making fists, his anxious gaze fixed on that shotgun. "Don't belong nobody."

"Calling me a liar?" snapped Davis, in a fearsome voice.

Then the scream came. It rose higher and higher until Lou figured the trees must surely topple from the force, or the rocks would work loose and slide down the mountain and maybe, with luck, crush their antagonist. Jeb came around growling, his hackles up. Davis stared off anxiously into the trees.

"You got you a gun," said Diamond, "then go git your old mountain cat. 'Cept mebbe you scared."

Davis's gaze burned into the boy, but then the scream came again, and hit them all just as hard, and Davis took off at a half-trot toward the trees.

"Come on now!" cried out Diamond, and they ran as fast as they could between trees and along more open fields. Owls hooted at them, and a bobwhite bobwhited at them. Things they couldn't see ran up and down tall oaks, or flitted in front of them, yet none of it came close to scaring them as much as they already had been by George Davis and his shotgun. Lou was a blur, faster even than Diamond. But when Oz tripped and fell, she rounded back and helped him.

They finally stopped and squatted in the high grass, breathing heavy and listening for a crazy man or a wildcat coming after them.

"Who is that awful man?" asked Lou.

Diamond checked behind him before answering. "George Davis. He got a farm next Miss Louisa's. He a hard man. A bad man! Dropped on his head when he were a baby, or mebbe mule kicked him, don't know which. He got a corn liquor still up here in one of the hollows, so's he don't like people coming round. I wish somebody just shoot him."

They soon reached another small clearing. Diamond held up his hand for them to stop and then proudly pointed up ahead, as though he had just discovered Noah's Ark on a simple mountaintop in Virginia.

"There she is."

The well was moss-crusted brick, crumbling in places, and yet undeniably spooky. The three glided up to it; Jeb guarded their rear flank while hunting small prey in the high grass.

They all peered over the edge of the well's opening. It was black, seemingly without bottom; they could have been staring at the other side of the world. All sorts of things could have been peering back.

"Why do you say it's haunted?" Oz asked breathlessly.

Diamond sprawled in the grass next to the well and they joined him.

" 'Bout a thousand million years ago," he began in a thick and thrilling voice that made Oz's eyes widen, fast-blink, and water all at the same time, "they was a man and woman live up chere. Now, they was in love, ain't no denying that. And so's they wanted to get hitched o'-course. But they's family hated each other, wouldn't let 'em do it. No sir. So they come up with a plan to run off. Only somethin' went bad and the feller thought the woman had done got herself kilt. He was so broke up, he came to this here well and jumped in. It's way deep, shoot, you seed that. And he drowned hisself. Now the girl found out what was what, and she come and jumped in herself too. Never found 'em 'cause it was like they was plopped on the sun. Not a durn thing left."

Lou was completely unmoved by this sad tale. "That sounds a lot like Romeo and Juliet."

Diamond looked puzzled. "That kin of yours?"

"You're making this up," she said.

All around them sounds of peculiar quality started up, like millions of tiny voices all trying to jabber at once, as though ants had suddenly acquired larynxes.

"What's that?" Oz said, clinging to Lou.

"Don't be doubting my words, Lou," Diamond hissed, his face the color of cream. "You riling the spirits."

"Yeah, Lou," said Oz, who was looking everywhere for demons of hell coming for them. "Don't be riling the spirits."

The noises finally died down, and Diamond, regaining his confidence, stared triumphantly at Lou. "Shoot, any fool can see this well's magic. You see a house anywhere round? No, and I tell you why. This well growed up right out of the earth, that's why. And it ain't just a haunted well. It what you call a wishing well."

Oz said, "A wishing well? How?"

"Them two people lost each other, but they's still in love. Now, people die, but love don't never die. Made the well magic. Anybody done got a wish, they come here, wish for it, and it'll happen. Ever time. Rain or shine."

Oz clutched his arm. "Any wish? You're sure?"

"Yep. 'Cept they's one little catch."

Lou spoke up, "I thought so. What is it?"

" 'Cause them folks died to make this here a wishing well, anybody want a wish, they's got to give up somethin' too."

"Give up what?" This came from Oz, who was so excited the boy seemed to float above the supple grass like a tethered bubble.

Diamond lifted his arms to the dark sky. "Like just the most grandest, importantest thing they got in the whole dang world."

Lou was surprised he didn't take a bow. She knew what was coming now, as Oz tugged at her sleeve.

"Lou, maybe we can—"

"No!" she said sharply. "Oz, you have got to understand that dangling necklaces and wishing wells won't work. Nothing will."

"But, Lou."

The girl stood and pulled her brother's hand free. "Don't be stupid, Oz. You'll just end up crying your eyes out again."

Lou ran off. After a second's hesitation Oz followed her.

Diamond was left with the spoils of something, surely not victory, judging by his disappointed face. He looked around and whistled, and Jeb came running. "Let's get on home, Jeb," he said quietly.

The pair ran off in the opposite direction from Lou and Oz, as the mountains headed for sleep.

CHAPTER TWELVE

THERE WAS NO TRACE OF OUTSIDE LIGHT AS yet, when Lou heard the creak of foot on stair. The door to her room opened and Lou sat up in bed. The glow of lantern light eased into the space, followed by Louisa, already fully dressed. With her flow of silver hair and the gentle illumination around her, the woman seemed a messenger from heaven to Lou's sleepy mind. The air in the room was chilly; Lou thought she could see her own breath.

"Thought I'd let you and Oz sleep in," Louisa said softly as she came and sat next to Lou.

Lou stifled a yawn and looked out the window at the blackness. "What time is it?"

"Nearly five."

"Five!" Lou dropped back against her pillow and pulled the covers over her head.

Louisa smiled. "Eugene's milking the cows. Be good you learn how."

"I can't do it later?" Lou asked from under the blanket.

"Cows don't care to wait round for us people," Louisa said. "They moan till the bag's dry." She added, "Oz is already dressed."

Lou jolted upright. "Mom couldn't get him out of bed before eight, and even that was a fight."

"He's right now having a bowl of molasses over cornbread and fresh milk. Be good if you'd join us."

Lou threw off the covers and touched the cold floor, which sent a shiver directly to her brain. Now she was convinced she could see her breath. "Give me five minutes," she said bravely.

Louisa noted the girl's obvious physical distress. "Had us a frost last night," Louisa said. "Stays cold up here longer. Works into your bones like a little knife. Be warm afore long, and then when winter comes, we move you and Oz down to the front room, right by the fire. Fill it with coal, keep you warm all night. We'll make it right good for you here." She paused and looked around the room. "Can't give you what you had in the city, but we do our best." She rose and went to the door. "I put hot water in the washbowl earlier so's you can clean up."

"Louisa?"

She turned back, the arc of lantern light throwing and then magnifying her shadow against the wall. "Yes, honey?"

"This was my dad's room, wasn't it?"

Louisa looked around slowly before coming back to

the girl, and the question. "From time he was four till he gone away. Ain't nobody use this room since."

Lou pointed to the covered walls. "Did my dad do that?"

Louisa nodded. "He'd walk ten miles to get ahold of a paper or a book. Read 'em all a dozen times and then stuck them newspapers up there and kept right on reading. Never saw a boy that curious in all my life." She looked at Lou. "Bet you just like him."

"I want to thank you for taking Oz and me in."

Louisa looked toward the door. "This place be good for your mother too. We all pitch in, she be fine."

Lou looked away, started to fumble with her nightdress. "I'll be down in a minute," she said abruptly.

Louisa accepted this change in the girl's manner without comment and softly closed the door behind her.

Downstairs, Oz was just finishing the last of his breakfast when Lou appeared, dressed, as he was, in faded overalls, long john shirt, and lace-up boots Louisa had laid out for them. A lantern hanging on a wall hook, and the coal fire, gave the room its only light. Lou looked at the grandmother clock on the fireplace mantel, itself a six-by-six timber of planed oak. It was indeed a little past five. Who would have thought cows would be up so early? she thought.

"Hey, Lou," Oz said. "You've got to taste this milk. It's great."

Louisa looked at Lou and smiled. "Those clothes fit real good. Said a prayer they would. If'n the boots too big, we fill 'em with rags."

"They're fine," said Lou, though they were actually too small, pinching her feet some.

Louisa brought over a bucket and a glass. She put the glass on the table, draped a cloth over it, and poured the milk from the bucket into it, foam bubbling up on the cloth. "Want molasses on your cornbread?" she asked. "Real good that way. Line your belly."

"It's great," gushed Oz as he swallowed the last bite of his meal and washed it down with the rest of his milk.

Lou looked at her glass. "What's the cloth for?"

"Take things out the milk you don't need in you," answered Louisa.

"You mean the milk's not pasteurized?" Lou said this in such a distressed tone that Oz gaped at his empty glass, looking as though he might drop dead that very instant.

"What's pastures?" he asked anxiously. "Can it get me?"

"The milk's fine," Louisa said in a calm tone. "I've had it this way all my life. And your daddy too."

At her words, a relieved Oz sat back and commenced breathing again. Lou sniffed at her milk, tasted it gingerly a couple of times, and then took a longer swallow.

"I told you it was good," Oz said. "Putting it out to pasture probably makes it taste bad, I bet."

Lou said, "Pasteurization is named after Louis Pasteur, the scientist who discovered a process that kills bacteria and makes milk safe to drink."

"I'm sure he were a smart man," said Louisa, as she set down a bowl of cornbread and molasses in front of Lou. "But we boil the cloth in between, and we get by just fine." The way she said this made Lou not want to wrestle the issue anymore.

Lou took a forkful of the cornbread and molasses. Her eyes widened at the taste. "Where do you buy this?" she asked Louisa.

"Buy what?"

"This food. It's really good."

"Told you," said Oz again smugly.

Louisa said, "Don't buy it, honey. Make it."

"How do you do that?"

"Show, remember? A lot better'n telling. And best way of all is doing. Now, hurry up and you get yourself together with a cow by the name of Bran. Old Bran's got trouble you two can help Eugene fix."

With this enticement, Lou quickly finished her breakfast, and she and Oz hurried to the door.

"Wait, children," Louisa said. "Plates in the tub here, and you gonna need this." She picked up another lantern and lit it. The smell of working kerosene filled the room.

"This house really doesn't have electricity?" Lou asked.

"Know some folks down Tremont got the dang thing. It go off sometimes and they got no idea what to do with theirselves. Like they forgot how to light kerosene. Just give me a good lantern in hand and I be fine."

Oz and Lou carried their plates to the sink.

"After you done in the barn, I show you the spring-house. Where we get our water. Haul it up twice a day. Be one of your chores."

Lou looked confused. "But you have the pump."

"That just for dishes and such. Need water for lots of things. Animals, washing, tool grinder, bathing. Pump ain't got no pressure. Take you a day to fill up a good-sized lard bucket." She smiled. "Sometimes seems we spend most our breath hauling wood and water. First ten years'a my life, I thought my name was 'git.' "

They were about to go out the door again, Lou carrying the lantern, when she stopped. "Uh, which one's the cow barn?"

"How's 'bout I *show* you?"

The air was bone-hurting cold and Lou was grateful for the thick shirt, but still wedged her bare hands under her armpits. With Louisa and her lantern leading the way, they went past the chicken coop and corrals and over to the barn, a big A-frame building with a wide set of double doors. These doors stood open and a solitary light was on inside. From the barn Lou heard the snorts and calls of animals, the shuffling of restless hoofs on dirt, and from the coop came the flapping of skittish wings. The sky was curiously darker in some places than in others, and then Lou realized these ebony patches were the Appalachians.

She had never encountered night such as this. No streetlights, no lights from buildings, no cars, no illumination of any kind granted by battery or electricity.

The only lights were the few stars overhead, the kerosene lamp Louisa was carrying, and the one Eugene presumably had on in the barn. The darkness didn't frighten Lou at all, though. In fact she felt oddly safe here as she followed the tall figure of her great-grandmother. Oz trailed close, and Lou could sense he was not nearly so comfortable right now. She well knew that, given time to think about it, her brother could imagine unspeakable terror in just about anything.

The barn smelled of stacked hay, wet earth, large animals and their warm manure. The floor was dirt covered with straw. On the walls hung bridles and harnesses, some cracked and worn out, others well oiled and supple. There were single- and doubletrees stacked on top of each other. A hayloft was reached by a wooden ladder with a broken second step. The loft took up most of the upper level and was filled with both loose and baled hay. There were center poles of poplar, which Lou assumed helped hold up the building. The barn had small wings built onto it on the sides and rear. Stalls and pens had been constructed there, and the mare, mules, hogs, and sheep loitered in their respective areas. Lou could see clouds of cold air erupting from warm animal nostrils.

In one stall, Eugene sat on a small three-legged stool that was barely visible under his bulk. Right next to him was a cow, white with black patches. Her tail twitched back and forth, her head dipping into the manger box.

Louisa left them there with Eugene and returned to the farmhouse. Oz crowded close to Lou as the cow in the next stall bumped into the partition and let out a moo. Eugene looked up at them.

"Old Bran got the milk fever," he said. "Got to hep Old Bran out." He pointed to a rusty tire pump in one corner of the stall. "Hand me that there pump, Miss Lou."

Lou gave it to him, and Eugene held the hose tightly against one of Bran's teats.

"Now g'on pump."

Oz pumped while Eugene went about holding the hose end against each of the four teats and rubbing the cow's udder, which was inflating like a ball.

"That a good girl, never held your milk afore. We take care of you," Eugene said soothingly to Bran. "Okay, that's right good," he said to Oz, who stopped pumping and stepped back, waiting. Eugene set the pump aside and motioned for Lou to take his place on the stool. He guided her hands to Bran's teats and showed her how to grip them properly and also how to rub them to get them supple to help the flow.

"We done pumped her up, now we got to get her dry. You pull hard, Miss Lou, Old Bran ain't caring none. Got to get her milk to run. That what be hurting her bad."

Lou pulled tentatively at first, and then started to hit her stride. Her hands worked efficiently, and they all heard the air escaping from the udder. It made small, warm clouds in the cold air.

Oz stepped forward. "Can I try?"

Lou got up and Eugene moved Oz in, set him up.

Soon he was pulling as well as Lou, and finally drips of milk appeared at the ends of the teats.

"You doing good, Mr. Oz. You done pulled cow teat up there in the city?"

They all laughed over that one.

Three hours later, Lou and Oz were no longer laughing. They had milked the other two cows—one heavy with calf, Louisa told them—which had taken half an hour each; carried four large buckets of water into the house; and then lugged four more from the springhouse for the animals. That was followed by two loads of wood and three of coal to fill the house's wood and coal bins. Now they were slopping the hogs, and their chore list only seemed to be growing.

Oz struggled with his bucket and Eugene helped him get it over the top rail. Lou dumped hers and then stepped back.

"I can't believe we have to feed pigs," she said.

"They sure eat a lot," added Oz, as he watched the creatures attack what appeared to be liquid garbage.

"They're disgusting," said Lou, as she wiped her hands on her overalls.

"And they give us food when we need it."

They both turned and saw Louisa standing there, a full bucket of corn feed for the chickens in hand, her brow already damp with sweat, despite the coolness. Louisa picked up Lou's empty slop bucket and handed it to her. "Snow come there's no going down the mountain. Have to store up. And they're *hogs*, Lou, not pigs." Lou and Louisa held a silent stare-down for a half dozen heartbeats, until the sound of the car coming made them look toward the farmhouse.

It was an Oldsmobile roadster, packing all of forty-seven horsepower and a rumble seat. The car's black paint was chipped and rusted in numerous places, fenders dented, skinny tires near bald; and it had a convertible top that was open on this cold morning. It was a beautiful wreck of a thing.

The man stopped the car and got out. He was tall, with a lanky body that both foretold a certain fragility and also promised exceptional strength. When he took off his hat, his hair was revealed as dark and straight, cutting a fine outline around his head. A nicely shaped nose and jawline, pleasant light blue eyes, and a mouth that had an abundance of laugh lines shimmying around it gave him a face that would prompt a smile even on a trying day. He appeared closer to forty than thirty. His suit was a two-piece gray, with a black vest and a gentleman's watch the size of a silver dollar hanging from a heavy chain riding across the front of the vest. The pants were baggy at the knee, and the man's shoes had long since given back their shine for good. He started to walk toward them, stopped, went back to his car, and pulled out a fat and battered briefcase.

Absentminded, Lou thought to herself as she watched him closely. After meeting the likes of Hell No and Diamond, she wondered what odd moniker this stranger might have.

"Who's that?" Oz asked.

Louisa said in a loud voice, "Lou, Oz, this here's Cotton Longfellow, the finest lawyer round."

The man smiled and shook Louisa's hand. "Well, since I'm also one of the very few lawyers round here, that's a dubious distinction at best, Louisa."

His voice, a mixture of southern drawl and a New England rhythm, was unique to Lou. She could not place him to a particular area, and she was usually quite good at that. *Cotton Longfellow!* Lord, she had not been disappointed with the name.

Cotton put down his briefcase and shook their hands solemnly, though there was an easy twinkle in his eye as he did so. "Very honored to meet you both. I feel like I know you from all that Louisa has told me. I've always hoped to meet you one day. And I'm right sorry it has to be under these circumstances." He said the last with a gentleness that not even Lou could fault.

"Cotton and I got things to talk about. After you slop the hogs, you help Eugene turn the rest of the livestock out and drop hay. Then you can finish gathering the eggs."

As Cotton and Louisa walked off, Oz picked up his bucket and happily went for some more slop. But Lou stared after Cotton and Louisa, clearly not thinking of hogs. She was wondering about a man with the strange name of Cotton Longfellow, who spoke sort of oddly and seemed to know so much about them. Finally, she eyed a four-hundred-pound hog that would somehow keep them from all starving come winter, and trudged after her brother. The walls of mountains seemed to close around the girl.

CHAPTER THIRTEEN

COTTON AND LOUISA ENTERED THE HOUSE through the back door. As they headed down the hallway to the front room, Cotton stopped, his gaze holding through the partially opened door and into the room where Amanda lay in bed.

Cotton said, "What do the doctors say?"

"Men . . . tal trau . . . ma." Louisa formed the strange words slowly. "That what the nurse call it."

They went to the kitchen and sat down in stumplegged chairs of hand-planed oak worn so smooth the wood felt like glass. Cotton pulled some papers from his briefcase and slid a pair of wire-rimmed spectacles from his pocket. He slipped them on and studied the papers for a moment, and then settled back, prepared to discuss them. Louisa poured out a cup of chicory coffee for him. He took a swallow and smiled. "If this don't get you going, then you must be dead."

Louisa poured herself a cup and said, "So what'd you find out from them fellers?"

"Your grandson didn't have a will, Louisa. Not that it mattered much, because he also didn't have any money."

Louisa looked bewildered. "With all his fine writing?"

Cotton nodded. "As wonderful as they were, the books didn't sell all that well. He had to take on other writing assignments to make ends meet. Also, Oz had some health problems when he was born. Lot of expenses. And New York City is not exactly cheap."

Louisa looked down. "And that ain't all," she said. He looked at her curiously. "Jack sent me money all these years, he did. I wrote him back once, told him it weren't right for him to be doing it. Got his own family and all. But he say he were a rich man. He told me that! Wanted me to have it, he say, after all I done for him. But I ain't really done nothing."

"Well, it seems Jack was planning to go write for a movie studio in California when the accident happened."

"California?" Louisa said the word like it was a malignancy, and then sat back and sighed. "That little boy always run circles round me. But giving me money when he ain't got it. And curse me for taking it." She stared off for a bit before speaking again. "I got me a problem, Cotton. Last three years of drought and ain't no crops come in. Down to five hogs and gotta butcher me one purty soon. Got me three sows and one boar left over. Last litter more runts than anythin'. Three passable milking cows. Had one studded out, but she ain't dropped her calf yet and I getting right worried. And Bran got the fever. Sheep getting to be more bother than anything. And that old nag ain't do a lick of work no more, and eats me out of house and home. And yet that old girl done worked herself to death all these years for me." She paused and drew a breath. "And McKenzie on down at the store, he ain't giving no more credit to us folk up here."

"Hard times, Louisa, no denying that."

"I know I can't complain none, this old mountain give me all it can over the years."

Cotton hunched forward. "Well, the one thing you do have, Louisa, is land. Now, there's an asset."

"Can't sell it, Cotton. When time comes, it'll go to Lou and Oz. Their daddy loved this place as much as me. And Eugene too. He my family. He work hard. He getting some of this land so's he can have his own place, raise his own family. Only fair."

Cotton said, "I think so too."

"When them folks wrote to see if'n I'd take the children, how could I not? Amanda's people all gone, I'm all they got left. And a sorry savior I am, long past being worth a spit for farming." Her fingers clustered nervously together, and she stared anxiously out the window. "I been thinking 'bout them all these years, wondering what they was like. Reading Amanda's letters, seeing them pictures she sent. Just busting with pride over what Jack done. And them beautiful children." She let out a troubled sigh, the deeply cut wrinkles on her long forehead like tiny furrows in a field.

Cotton said, "You'll get by, Louisa. You need me for anything, come up and help with the planting, the children, you just let me know. I'd be beyond proud to help you."

"G'on now, Cotton, you a busy lawyer."

"Folks up here don't have much need for the likes of me. And maybe that's not such a bad thing. Got a problem, go down to Judge Atkins over the courthouse and just talk it out. Lawyers just make things complicated." He smiled and patted her hand. "It'll be okay, Louisa. Those children being here with you is the right thing. For everybody."

Louisa smiled, and then her expression slowly changed to a frown. "Cotton, Diamond said some men coming round folks' coal mines. Don't like that."

"Surveyors, mineral experts, so I've heard."

"Ain't they cutting the mountains up fast enough? Make me sick ever' time I see another hole. I never sell out to the coal folk. Rip all that's beautiful out."

"I've heard these folks are looking for oil, not coal."

"Oil!" she said in disbelief. "This ain't Texas."

"Just what I've heard."

"Can't worry about that nonsense." She stood. "You right, Cotton, it'll be just fine. Lord'll give us rain this year. If not, well, I figger something out."

As Cotton rose to leave, he looked back down the hallway. "Louisa, do you mind if I stop in and pay my respects to Miss Amanda?"

Louisa thought about this. "Another voice might do her good. And you got a nice way about you, Cotton. How come you ain't never married?"

"I've yet to find the good woman who could put up with the sorry likes of me."

In Amanda's room, Cotton put down his briefcase and hat and quietly approached the bed. "Miss Cardinal, I'm Cotton Longfellow. It's a real pleasure to meet you. I feel like I know you already, for Louisa has read me some of the letters you sent." Amanda of course moved not one muscle, and Cotton looked over at Louisa.

"I been talking to her. Oz too. But she ain't never say nothing back. Don't never even wiggle a finger."

"And Lou?" asked Cotton.

Louisa shook her head. "That child's gonna bust one day, all she keep inside."

"Louisa, it might be a good idea to have Travis Barnes from Dickens come up and look at Amanda."

"Doctors cost money, Cotton."

"Travis owes me a favor. He'll come."

Louisa said quietly, "I thank you."

He looked around the room and noted a Bible on the dresser. "Can I come back?" he asked. Louisa looked at him curiously. "I thought I might, well, that I might read to her. Mental stimulation. I've heard of such. There are no guarantees. But if I can do nothing else well, I can read."

Before Louisa could answer, Cotton looked at Amanda. "It'll be my real privilege to read to you."

CHAPTER FOURTEEN

AS DAWN BROKE, LOUISA, EUGENE, LOU, and Oz stood in one of the fields. Hit, the mule, was harnessed on a singletree to a plow with a turnover blade.

Lou and Oz had already had their milk and cornbread in gravy for breakfast. The food was good, and filling, but eating by lantern light had already grown old. Oz had gathered chicken eggs while Lou had milked the two healthy cows under Louisa's watchful eye. Eugene had split wood, and Lou and Oz had hauled it in for the cookstove and then carried buckets of water for the animals. Livestock had been turned out and hay dropped for them. And now, apparently, the real work was about to begin.

"Got to plow unner this whole field," said Louisa.

Lou sniffed the air. "What's that awful smell?"

Louisa bent down, picked up some earth, and crumbled it between her fingers. "Manure. Muck the stalls ever fall, drop it here. Makes rich soil even better."

"It stinks," said Lou.

Louisa let the bits of dirt in her hand swirl away in the morning breeze as she stared pointedly at the girl. "You'll come to love that smell."

Eugene handled the plow while Louisa and the children walked beside him.

"This here's a turnover blade," Louisa said, pointing to the oddly shaped disc of metal. "You run it down one row, turn mule and plow round, kick the blade over, go down the row again. Throws up same furrows of dirt on both sides. It kicks up big clods of earth too. So's after we plow, we drag the field to break up the clods. Then we harrow, makes the dirt real smooth. Then we use what's called a laid-off plow. Gives you fine rows. Then we plant."

She had Eugene plow one row to show them how, and then Louisa kicked at the plow. "You look purty strong, Lou. You want'a give it a go?"

"Sure," she said. "It'll be easy."

Eugene set her up properly, put the guide straps around her waist, handed her the whip, and then stepped back. Hit apparently summed her up as an easy mark, because he took off unexpectedly fast. Strong Lou very quickly got a taste of the rich earth.

As Louisa pulled her up and wiped her face, she said, "That old mule had the best of you this time. Bet it won't next go round."

"I don't want to do this anymore," Lou said, hiding

her face with her sleeve, spitting up chunks of things she didn't want to think about. Her cheeks were red, and tears edged from under her eyelids.

Louisa knelt in front of her. "First time your daddy tried to plow, he your age. Mule took him on a ride ended in the crick. Took me the better part of a day to get him and that durn animal out. Your daddy said the same thing you did. And I decided to let him be about it."

Lou stopped brushing at her face, her eyes drying up. "And what happened?"

"For two days he wouldn't go near the fields. Or that mule. And then I come out here to work one morning and there he was."

"And he plowed the whole field?" Oz guessed.

Louisa shook her head. "Mule and your daddy ended up in the hog pen with enough slop on both choke a bear." Oz and Lou laughed, and then Louisa continued, "Next time, boy and mule reached an unnerstanding. Boy had paid his dues, and mule had had his fun, and them two made the best plow team I ever saw."

From across the valley there came the sound of a siren. It was so loud that Lou and Oz had to cover their ears. The mule snorted and jerked against its harness. Louisa frowned.

"What is that?" Lou shouted.

"Coal mine horn," said Louisa.

"Was there a cave-in?"

"No, hush now," Louisa said, her eyes scanning the slopes. Five anxious minutes passed by and the siren finally stopped. And then from all sides they heard the low rumbling sound. It rose around them like an avalanche coming. Lou thought she could see the trees, even the mountain, shaking. She gripped Oz's hand and was thinking of fleeing, but she didn't because Louisa hadn't budged. And then the quiet returned.

Louisa turned back to them. "Coal folks sound the horn afore they blast. They use dynamite. Sometimes too much and they's hill slides. And people get hurt. Not miners. Farmers working the land." Louisa scowled once more in the direction where the blast seemed to have come from, and then they went back to farming.

At supper, they had steaming plates of pinto beans mixed with cornbread, grease, and milk, and washed down with springwater so cold it hurt. The night was chilly, the wind howling fiercely as it attacked the structure, but the walls and roof withstood this charge. The coal fire was warm, and the lantern light gentle on the eye. Oz was so tired he almost fell asleep in his Crystal Winters Oatmeal plate the color of the sky.

After supper Eugene went out to the barn, while Oz lay in front of the fire, his little body so obviously sore and spent. Louisa watched as Lou went over to him, put his head in her lap, and stroked his hair. Louisa slid a pair of wire-rimmed spectacles over her eyes and worked on mending a shirt by the firelight. After a while, she stopped and sat down beside the children.

"He's just tired," Lou said. "He's not used to this."

"Can't say a body ever gets used to hard work." Louisa rubbed at Oz's hair too. It seemed the little boy just had a head people liked to touch. Maybe for luck.

"You doing a good job. Real good. Better'n me when I your age. And I ain't come from no big city. Make it harder, don't it?"

The door opened and the wind rushed in. Eugene looked worried. "Calf coming."

In the barn the cow called Purty lay on her side in a wide birthing stall, pitching and rolling in agony. Eugene knelt and held her down, while Louisa got in behind her and pried with her fingers, looking for the slicked package of a fresh calf emerging. It was a hard-fought battle, the calf seeming not to want to enter the world just yet. But Eugene and Louisa coaxed it out, a slippery mass of limbs, eyes scrunched tight. The event was bloody, and Lou's and Oz's stomach took another jolt when Purty ate the afterbirth, but Louisa told them that was natural. Purty started licking her baby and didn't stop until its hair was sticking out all over. With Eugene's help, the calf rose on tottering stick legs, while Louisa got Purty ready for the next step, which the calf took to as the most natural endeavor of all: suckling. Eugene stayed with the mother and her calf while Louisa and the children went back inside.

Lou and Oz were both excited and exhausted, the grandmother clock showing it was nearing midnight.

"I've never seen a cow born before," said Oz.

"You've never seen anything born before," said his sister.

Oz thought about this. "Yes, I did. I was there when *I* was born."

"That doesn't count," Lou shot back.

"Well, it should," countered Oz. "It was a lot of work. Mom told me so."

Louisa put another rock of coal on the fire, drove it into the flames with an iron poker, and then sat back down with her mending. The woman's dark-veined and knotted hands moved slowly yet with precision.

"You get on to bed, both of you," she said.

Oz said, "I'm going to see Mom first. Tell her about the cow." He looked at Lou. "My *second* time." He walked off.

His sister made no move to leave the fire's warmth.

"Lou, g'on see your mother too," said Louisa.

Lou stared into the depths of the coal fire. "Oz is too young to understand, but I do."

Louisa put down her mending. "Unnerstand what?"

"The doctors in New York said that each day there was less chance Mom would come back. It's been too long now."

"But you can't give up hope, honey."

Lou turned to look at her. "You don't understand either, Louisa. Our dad's gone. I saw him die. Maybe"—Lou swallowed with difficulty—"maybe I was partly the reason he did die." She rubbed at her eyes and then Lou's hands curled to fists. "And it's not like she's laying in there healing. I listened to the doctors. I heard everything all the grown-ups said about her, even though they tried to hide it from me. Like it wasn't my business! They let us take her home, because there was nothing more they could do for her." She paused, took a long breath, and slowly grew calm. "And you just don't know Oz. He gets his hopes up so high, starts doing crazy things. And then . . ." Lou's voice trailed off, and she looked down. "I'll see you in the morning."

In the fade of lantern light and the flickering coal fire, Louisa could only stare after the young girl as she trudged off. When her footsteps faded away, Louisa once more picked up her sewing, but the needle did not move. When Eugene came in and went to bed, she was still there, the fire having died down low, as thoughts as humbling as the mountains outside consumed her.

After a bit, though, Louisa rose and went into her bedroom, where she pulled out a short stack of letters from her dresser. She went up the stairs to Lou's room and found the girl wide awake, staring out the window.

Lou turned and saw the letters.

"What are those?"

"Letters your mother wrote to me. I want you to read 'em."

"What for?"

" 'Cause words say a lot about a person."

"Words won't change anything. Oz can believe if he wants to. But he doesn't know any better."

Louisa placed the letters on the bed. "Sometime older

folks do right good to follow the young'uns. Might learn 'em something."

After Louisa left, Lou put the letters in her father's old desk and very firmly shut the drawer.

CHAPTER FIFTEEN

L OU GOT UP ESPECIALLY EARLY AND WENT
into her mother's room, where she watched
for a bit the even rise and fall of the woman's
chest. Perched on the bed, Lou pulled back
the covers and massaged and moved her mother's arms.
Then she spent considerable time exercising her mother's
legs the way the doctors back in New York City had
shown her. Lou was just about finished when she caught
Louisa watching her from the doorway.

"We have to make her comfortable," explained Lou.
She covered her mother and went into the kitchen.
Louisa trailed her.

When Lou put on a kettle to boil, Louisa said, "I
can do that, honey."

"I've got it." Lou mixed some oat flakes in the hot
water and added butter taken from a lard bucket. She
took the bowl back into her mother's room and carefully spooned the food into her mother's mouth. Amanda

ate and drank readily enough, with just a tap of spoon or cup against her lips, though she could only manage soft food. Yet that was all she could do. Louisa sat with them, and Lou pointed to the ferrotypes on the wall. "Who are those people?"

"My daddy and momma. That me with 'em when I just a spit. Some of my momma's folks too. First time I ever had my pitcher took. I liked it. But Momma scared." She pointed to another ferrotype. "That pitcher there my brother Robert. He dead now. They all dead now."

"Your parents and brother were tall."

"Run in the line. Funny how that get passed down. Your daddy, he were already six feet when he weren't more'n fourteen. I still tall, but I growed down some from what I was. You gonna be big too."

Lou cleaned the bowl and spoon and afterward helped Louisa make breakfast for everyone else. Eugene was in the barn now, and they both heard Oz stirring in his room.

Lou said, "I need to show Oz how to move Mom's arms and legs. And he can help feed her too."

"That right fine." She laid a hand on Lou's shoulder. "Now, did you read any of them letters?"

Lou looked at her. "I didn't want to lose my mother and father. But I have. Now I've got to look after Oz. And I have to look ahead, not back." She added with firmness, "You may not understand that, but it's what I have to do."

After morning chores, Eugene took Lou and Oz by mule and wagon to the school and then left to continue his work. In old burlap seed bags, Lou and Oz carried their worn books, a few sheets of precious paper tucked inside the pages. They each had one fat lead pencil, with dire orders from Louisa to trim it down only when absolutely necessary, and to use a sharp knife when doing so. The books were the same ones their father had learned with, and Lou hugged hers to her chest like it was a present direct from Jesus. They also carried a dented lard bucket with some cornbread chunks, a small jar of apple butter jelly, and a jug of milk for their lunch.

The Big Spruce schoolhouse was only a few years old. It had been built with New Deal dollars to replace the log building that had stood on the same spot for almost eighty years. The structure was white clapboard with windows down one side, and was set on cinder blocks. Like Louisa's farmhouse, the roof had no shingles, just a "roll of roofing" that came in long sheets and was tacked down in overlapping sections like shingles. The school had one door, with a short overhang. A brick chimney rose through the A-frame roof.

On any given day school attendance was roughly half of the number of students who should have been there, and that was actually a high number compared to the attendance figures in the past. On the mountain, farming always trumped book learning.

The schoolyard was dirt, a split-trunk walnut tree in the center of it. There were about fifty children milling about outside, ranging in age from Oz's to Lou's. Most were dressed in overalls, though a few girls wore floral dresses made from Chop bags, which were hundred-pound sacks of feed for animals. The bags were beautiful and of sturdy material, and a girl always felt extra special having a Chop bag outfit. Some children were in bare feet, others in what used to be shoes but were now sandals of sorts. Some wore straw hats, others were bareheaded; a few of the older boys had already upgraded to dirty felt, no doubt hand-me-downs from their daddies. Some girls favored pigtails, others wore their hair straight, and still others had the sausage curl at the end.

The children all stared at the newcomers with what Lou perceived as unfriendly eyes.

One boy stepped forward. Lou recognized him as the one who had dangled on the tractor over the side of the mountain their first day here. Probably the son of George Davis, the crazy man who had threatened them with the shotgun in the woods. Lou wondered if the fellow's offspring also suffered from insanity.

"What's the matter, y'all can't walk by yourselves? Hell No got to bring you?" the boy said.

"His name is Eugene," said Lou right to the boy's face. Then she asked, "Can anybody tell me where the second- and sixth-grade classes are?"

"Why sure," the same boy said, pointing. "They's both right over there."

Lou and Oz turned and saw the listing wooden outhouse behind the school building.

"Course," the boy added with a sly grin, "that's just
for you Yankees."

This set all the mountain children to whooping and
laughing, and Oz nervously took a step closer to Lou.

Lou studied the outhouse for a moment and then
looked back at the boy.

"What's your name?" she asked.

"Billy Davis," he said proudly.

"Are you always that scintillating, Billy Davis?"

Billy frowned. "What's that mean? You call me a
name, girl?"

"Didn't you just call us one?"

"Ain't said nuthin' 'cept the truth. Yankee once is a
Yankee for life. Coming here ain't changing that."

The crowd of rebels voiced their complete agreement
with this point of view, and Lou and Oz found themselves encircled by the enemy. They were saved only by
the ringing of the school bell, which sent the children
dashing for the door. Lou and Oz looked at each other
and then trudged after this mob.

"I don't think they like us much, Lou," Oz said.

"I don't think I much care," his sister said back.

The number of classrooms was one, they immediately
discovered, which served all grades from first to sev-
enth, the students separated in discrete clusters by age.
The number of teachers matched the number of classrooms. Her name was Estelle McCoy, and she was paid
eight hundred dollars a school year. This was the only

job she had ever had, going on thirty-nine years now, which explained why her hair was far more white than mousey brown.

Wide blackboards covered three walls. A potbellied stove sat in one corner, a long pipe from it running to the ceiling. And, seeming very much out of place in the simple confines, a beautifully crafted maple bookcase with an arched top took up another corner of the room. It had glass-paned doors, and inside Lou could see a number of books. A handwritten sign on the wall next to the cabinet read: "Library."

Estelle McCoy stood in front of them all with her apple cheeks, canyon smile, and chubby figure draped in a bright floral dress.

"I have a real treat for y'all, today. I'd like to introduce two new students: Louisa Mae Cardinal and her brother, Oscar. Louisa Mae and Oscar, will you stand up please?"

As someone who routinely bowed to the slightest exercise of authority, Oz immediately leapt to his feet. However, he stared down at the floor, one foot shifting over the other, as though he had to pee really badly.

Lou, however, remained sitting.

"Louisa Mae," Estelle McCoy said again, "stand up and let them see you, honey."

"My name is Lou."

Estelle McCoy's smile went down a bit in wattage. "Yes, um, their father was a very famous writer named Jack Cardinal."

Here, Billy Davis piped in loudly, "Didn't he die? Somebody say that man's dead."

Lou glared at Billy, who made a face right back at her.

Their teacher now looked completely flustered. "Billy, please. Uh, as I was saying, he was famous, and I helped teach him. And in my own humble way, I hope that I had some influence over his development as a writer. And they do say the early years are the most important. Anyway, did you know that Mr. Jack Cardinal even signed one of his books in Washington, for the president of these United States?"

As Lou looked around the room, she could tell this meant absolutely nothing to the children of the mountain. In fact, mentioning the capital of the Yankee nation was probably not a smart thing to do. It didn't make her angry that they were not properly in awe of her father's accomplishments; instead it made Lou pity their ignorance.

Estelle McCoy was ill-prepared for the prolonged silence. "Uh, well, we welcome you, Louisa Mae, and you too, Oscar. I'm sure you'll do your father proud here, at his . . . alma mater."

Now Lou stood, even as Oz hastily dropped back into his seat, his face down, his eyes scrunched closed. One could tell he was afraid of whatever it was his sister was about to do. Lou never did anything in a small way, Oz well knew. It was either both barrels of the shotgun in your face, or you got to live another day. There was rarely any middle ground with the girl.

And yet all she said was "My name is Lou." And then she took her seat.

Billy leaned over and said, "Welcome to the mountain, Miss Louisa Mae."

The school day ended at three, and the children didn't rush to go home, since it was certain only more chores awaited them there. Instead, they milled about in small packs in the schoolyard, the boys swapping pocket knives, hand-whittled yo-yos, and homemade burley chew. The girls exchanged local gossip and cooking and sewing secrets, and talked about boys. Billy Davis did pull-ups on a sapling that had been laid across the low branches of the walnut tree, to the admiring look of one wide-hipped girl with crooked teeth, but also rosy cheeks and pretty blue eyes.

As Lou and Oz came outside, Billy stopped his workout and strolled over to them.

"Why, it's Miss Louisa Mae. You been up see the president, Miss Louisa Mae?" he said in a loud, mocking voice.

"Keep walking, Lou, please," said Oz.

Billy spoke even louder. "Did he get you to sign one of your daddy's books, him being dead and all?"

Lou stopped. Oz, sensing that further pleading was futile, stepped back. Lou turned to look at her tormentor.

"What's the matter, you still sore because us Yankees kicked your tail, you dumb hillbilly?"

The other children, sensing blood, quietly formed a circle to shield from the eyes of Mrs. McCoy a potentially good fight.

Billy scowled. "You best take that back."

Lou dropped her bag. "You best make me, if you think you can."

"Shoot, I ain't hitting no girl."

This made Lou angrier than ever a thrown fist could have. She grabbed Billy by his overall straps and threw him to the dirt, where he lay stunned, probably both at her strength and at her audacity. The crowd moved closer.

"I'll kick your tail if you don't take *that* back," Lou said, and she leaned down and dug a finger in his chest. Oz pulled at her as the crowd closed even tighter, as though a hand becoming a fist. "Come on, Lou, please don't fight. Please."

Billy jumped up and proceeded to commit a major offense. Instead of swinging at Lou, he grabbed Oz and threw him down hard.

"No-good stinking northerner."

His look of triumph was short-lived because it ran smack into Lou's bony right fist. Billy joined Oz on the ground, blood spurting from his nose. Lou was straddling Billy before the boy could take a breath, both her fists pounding away. Billy, howling like a whipped dog, swung his arms wildly back. One blow caught Lou on the lip, but she kept slugging until Billy finally stopped swinging and just covered his face.

Then the seas parted, and Mrs. McCoy poured through this gap. She managed to pull Lou off Billy, but not without an effort that left her breathing hard.

"Louisa Mae! What would your daddy think?" she said.

Lou's chest rose and fell hard, her hands still balled into mighty, boy-bashing instruments.

Estelle McCoy helped Billy up. The boy covered his face with his sleeve, quietly sobbing into his armpit. "Now, you tell Billy you're sorry," she said.

Lou's response was to lunge and take another furious swing at him. Billy jumped back like a rabbit cornered by a snake intent on eating it.

Mrs. McCoy pulled hard on Lou's arm. "Louisa Mae, you stop that right now and tell him you're sorry."

"He can go straight on to hell."

Estelle McCoy looked ready to keel over in the face of such language from the daughter of a famous man.

"Louisa Mae! Your mouth!"

Lou jerked free and ran like the wind down the road.

Billy fled in the other direction. And Estelle McCoy stood there empty-handed on the field of battle.

Oz, forgotten in all this, quietly got off the ground, picked up his sister's burlap bag, brushed it off, and went and tugged on his teacher's dress. She looked down at him.

"Excuse me, ma'am," Oz said. "But her name is Lou."

CHAPTER SIXTEEN

LOUISA CLEANED THE CUT ON LOU'S FACE with water and lye soap, and applied some homemade tincture that stung like fire, but Lou made herself not even flinch.

"Glad you got yourself off to such a good start, Lou."

"They called us Yankees!"

"Well, good Lord," Louisa said with mock indignity. "Ain't that evil!"

"And he hurt Oz."

Louisa's expression softened. "You got to go to school, honey. You got to learn to get along."

Lou scowled. "Why can't they get along with us?"

" 'Cause this their home. They act like that 'cause you're not like nobody they ever seen."

Lou stood. "You don't know what it's like to be an outsider." She ran out the door, while Louisa looked after her, shaking her head.

Oz was waiting for his sister on the front porch.

"I put your bag in your room," he told her.

Lou sat on the steps and rested her chin on her knees.

"I'm okay, Lou." Oz stood and spun in a circle to show her and almost fell off the porch. "See, he didn't hurt me any."

"Good thing, or I really would've pounded him."

Oz closely studied her cut lip. "Does it hurt much?"

"Don't feel a thing. Shoot, they might be able to milk cows and plow fields, but mountain boys sure can't hit worth anything."

They looked up as Cotton's Oldsmobile pulled into the front yard. He got out, a book cradled under one arm.

"I heard about your little adventure over at the school today," he said, walking up.

Lou looked surprised. "That was fast."

Cotton sat next to them on the steps. "Up here when a good fight breaks out people will move heaven and earth to get the word around."

"Wasn't much of a fight," said Lou proudly. "Billy Davis just curled up and squawked like a baby."

Oz added, "He cut Lou's lip, but it doesn't hurt any."

She said, "They called us Yankees, like it was some kind of disease."

"Well, if it makes you feel any better, I'm a Yankee too. From Boston. And they've accepted me here. Well, at least most of them have."

Lou's eyes widened as she made the connection and wondered why she hadn't before. "Boston? Longfellow. Are you—"

"Henry Wadsworth Longfellow was my grandfather's great-grandfather. I guess that's the easiest way to put it."

"Henry Wadsworth Longfellow. Gosh!"

"Yeah, gosh!" Oz said, though in fact he had no idea who they were talking about.

"Yes, gosh indeed. I wanted to be a writer since I was a child."

"Well, why aren't you?" asked Lou.

Cotton smiled. "While I can appreciate inspired, well-crafted writing better than most, I'm absolutely confounded when attempting to do it myself. Maybe that's why I came here after I got my law degree. As far from Longfellow's Boston as one can be. I'm not a particularly good lawyer, but I get by. And it gives me time to read those who can write well." He cleared his throat and recited in a pleasant voice: "Often I think of the beautiful town, that is seated by the sea; Often in thought go up and down—"

Lou took up the verse: "The pleasant streets of that dear old town. And my youth comes back to me."

Cotton looked impressed. "You can quote Longfellow?"

"He was one of my dad's favorites."

He held up the book he was carrying. "And this is one of *my* favorite writers."

Lou glanced at the book. "That's the first novel my dad ever wrote."

"Have you read it?"

"My dad read part of it to me. A mother loses her only son, thinks she's all alone. It's very sad."

"But it's also a story of healing, Lou. Of one helping another." He paused. "I'm going to read it to your mother."

"Dad already read all his books to her," she said coldly.

Cotton realized what he had just done. "Lou, I'm not trying to replace your father."

She stood. "He was a real writer. He didn't have to go around quoting other people."

Cotton stood too. "I am sure if your father were here he would tell you that there is no shame in repeating the words of others. That it's a show of respect, in fact. And I have the greatest respect for your father's talents."

"You think it might help? Reading to her," said Oz.

"Waste your time if you want." Lou walked off.

"It's okay with me if you read to her," said Oz.

Cotton shook the boy's hand. "Thank you much for your permission, Oz. I'll do my best."

"Come on, Oz, there's chores to do," called Lou.

As Oz ran off, Cotton glanced down at the book and then went inside. Louisa was in the kitchen.

"You here to do your reading?" she asked.

"Well, that was my thinking, but Lou made it very clear she doesn't want me to read from her father's books. And maybe she's right."

Louisa looked out the window and saw Lou and Oz disappear into the barn. "Well, I tell you what, I got lots of letters Jack wrote to me over the years. They's some he sent me from college that I always liked. He use some big words then I ain't know what they mean, but the letters' still nice. Why don't you read those to her? See, Cotton, my thinking is it ain't *what* folks read to her that's important. I think the best thing is for us to spend time with her, to let Amanda know we ain't give up hope."

Cotton smiled. "You are a wise woman, Louisa. I think that's a fine idea."

※

Lou carried the coal bucket in and filled the bin next to the fireplace. Then she crept to the hallway and listened. Murmurs of a single voice drifted down the hall. She scooted back outside and stared at Cotton's car, the curiosity bug finally getting the better of her. She ran around the side of the house and came up under her mother's bedroom window. The window was open, but it was too high for her to look in. She stood on tiptoe, but that didn't work either.

"Hey there."

She whirled around and saw Diamond. She grabbed his arm and pulled him away from the window. "You shouldn't sneak up on people like that," she said.

"Sorry," he said, smiling.

She noticed he had something behind his back. "What do you have there?"

"Where?"

"Right there behind your back, Diamond."

"Oh, that. Well, you see I was just walking down by the meadow, and, well, they was just sitting there all purty like. And swear to Jesus they was saying your name."

"What was?"

Diamond pulled out a bunch of yellow crocuses and handed them to her.

Lou was touched, but of course she didn't want to show it. She said thank you to Diamond and gave him a hard smack on the back that made him cough.

"I didn't see you at school today, Diamond."

"Oh, well." He pawed the ground with one bare foot, gripped his overalls, and looked everywhere except at Lou. "Hey, what you be doing at that window when I come up?" he finally said.

Lou forgot about school for now. She had an idea, and like Diamond, she wished to defer the explanation behind her actions. "You want to help me with something?"

A few moments later, Diamond fidgeted some, and Lou smacked him on the head to make him be still. This was easy for her to do since she was sitting on his shoulders while peering into her mother's room. Amanda was propped in the bed. Cotton was in the rocking chair next to her, reading. Lou noted with surprise that he was not reading from the novel he had brought, but rather from a letter he was holding. And Lou had to admit, the man had a pleasant voice.

Cotton had selected the letter he was reading from a number Louisa had given him. This letter, he had thought, was particularly appropriate.

"Well, Louisa, you'll be pleased to know the memories of the mountain are as strong right now as the day I left

three years ago. In fact, it is rather easy for me to transport myself back to the high rock in Virginia. I simply close my eyes, and I immediately see many examples of reliable friends parceled here and there, like favorite books kept in special places. You know the stand of river birch down by the creek. Well, when their branches pressed together, I always imagined they were imparting secrets to each other. Then right in front of me a wisp of does and fawns creep along the fringe where your plowed fields snuggle up against the hardwood. Then I look to the sky and follow the jagged flight of irascible black crows, and then settle upon a solitary hawk tacked against a sky of cobalt blue.

"That sky. Oh, that sky. You told me so many times that up on the mountain it seems you can just reach up and take it, hold it in your hand, stroke it like a dozing cat, admire its abundant grace. I always found it to be a generous blanket I just wanted to wrap myself in, Louisa, take a long nap on the porch with as I settled under its cool warmth. And when night came, I would always hold the memory of that sky tight and fast, as though an honored dream, right up to the smoldering pink of sunrise.

"I also remember you telling me that you often looked out upon your land knowing full well that it never truly belonged to you, no more than you could hold deed to the sunlight or save up the air you breathed. I sometimes imagine many of our line standing at the door of the farmhouse and staring out at that same ground. But, at some point, the Cardinal family will all be gone. After that, my dear Louisa, you take heart, for the sweep of open land across the valley, the race of busy rivers, and the gentle bumps of green-shrouded hills, with little beads of light poking out here and there, like bits of sly gold— they all will continue on. And they won't be worse off either, for our mortal dabbling in their forever existence, seeing that God made them to last forever, as you've also told me so many times.

"Though I have a new life now, and am enjoying the city for the most part, I will never forget that the passing down of memories is the strongest link in the gossamer bridge that binds us as people. I plan to devote my life to doing just that. And if you taught me anything, it's that what we hold in our hearts is truly the fiercest component of our humanity."

Cotton heard a noise, glanced toward the window, and saw a glimpse of Lou right before she ducked down. Cotton silently read the last part of the letter and then decided to read it in a very loud voice. He would be speaking as much to the daughter, who the man knew lurked right outside the window, as to the mother lying in bed.

"And from watching you all those years conduct your life with honesty, dignity, and compassion, I know that there is nothing so powerful as the emboldened kindness of one human being reaching out to another, who is held only by despair. I think of you every day, Louisa, and so I will, as long as my heart continues to beat. With much love, Jack."

Lou poked her head over the sill again. Inch by inch she turned until she was looking at her mother. But there was no change in the woman, none at all. Lou angrily pushed away from the window. Poor Diamond was teetering mightily now, for her shove against the windowsill had done his balancing efforts no kindness. Diamond finally lost the battle, and both he and Lou went tumbling over, their plummet ending in a series of grunts and groans as they sprawled on the ground.

Cotton rushed to the window in time to see the pair race around the house. He turned back to the woman in bed. "You really must come and join us, Miss Amanda," he said, and then added quietly, as though afraid that anyone other than himself would hear, "for a lot of reasons."

CHAPTER SEVENTEEN

THE HOUSE WAS DARK, THE SKY A MESS OF clouds that promised a good rain come morning. However, when skittish clouds and fragile currents bumped over high rock, the weather often changed quickly: snow became rain and clear became foul, and a body got wet or cold when he least expected to. The cows, hogs, and sheep were safely in the barn, for Old Mo, the mountain lion, had been seen around, and there had been talk of the Tyler farm losing a calf, and the Ramseys a pig. All those on the mountain handy with a shotgun or rifle were keeping their eyes peeled for the old scavenger.

Sam and Hit stood silently in their own corral. Old Mo would never prey on the pair. An ornery mule could kick just about anything to death in a matter of minutes.

The front door of the farmhouse opened. Oz made not a sound when he closed the door behind him. The boy was fully dressed and had his bear clutched tight. He looked around for a few seconds and then took off past the corral, cleared the fields, and plunged into the woods.

The night was a bucket of coal, the wind rattled tree limbs, the underbrush was thick with sounds of stealthy movement, and the tall grass seemed to clutch at Oz's pant legs. The little boy was certain that regiments of hobgoblins were roaming nearby in full terrifying splendor, he their sole target on earth. Yet something inside Oz had clearly risen superior to these horrors, for he did not once think of turning back. Well, maybe once, he admitted to himself. Or perhaps twice.

He ran hard for a while, making his way over knolls, navigating crisscross gullies, and stumbling through the jumble of dense woods. He cleared one last grove of trees, stopped, stooped low, waited a bit, and then eased out into the meadow. Up ahead he saw what he had come for: the well. He took one last deep breath, gripped his bear, and boldly walked right up to it. But Oz was no fool, so just in case, he whispered, "It's a wishing well, not a haunted well. It's a wishing well, not a haunted well."

He stopped and stared at the brick-and-mortar beast, then spit on one hand and rubbed it on his head for luck. He next looked at his beloved bear for a long time, and then laid it gently down against the base of the well and backed away.

"Good-bye, bear. I love you, but I've got to give you up. You understand."

Now Oz was unsure of how to proceed. Finally, he crossed himself and put his hands together as though in prayer, figuring that would satisfy even the most demanding of spirits who granted wishes to little boys desperately in need of them. Staring at the sky he said, "I wish that my mother will wake up and love me again." He paused and then added solemnly, "And Lou too."

He stood there with the wind slicing into him and with peculiar sounds emerging from a thousand hidden crevices, all potent with evil, he was sure. And yet with all that, Oz was unafraid; he had done what he came to do.

He concluded with "Amen, Jesus."

Moments after Oz turned and ran off, Lou stepped from the trees and looked after her little brother. She walked up to the well, reached down, and picked up his bear.

"Oz, you are so dumb." But she didn't have her heart in the insult, and her voice broke. And ironically it was iron-tough Lou and not open-souled Oz who knelt there on the damp ground and sobbed. Finally wiping her face on her sleeve, Lou rose and turned her back to the well. With Oz's bear held tightly to her chest, she started to walk away. Something made her stop though—she wasn't exactly sure what. But, yes, the fierce wind truly seemed to be blowing her backward, toward the thing Diamond Skinner had so foolishly called a wishing well. She turned and looked at it, and on a night when the moon seemed to have totally abandoned her and the well, the brick seemed to glow as though afire.

Lou wasted no time. She set the bear back down, reached in the pocket of her overalls, and pulled it out: the photo of her and her mother, still in the frame. Lou placed the precious photograph next to the beloved bear, stepped back, and taking a page from her brother's book, clasped her hands together and looked to the sky. Unlike Oz, though, she did not bother to cross herself, or to speak loud and clear to that well or to the heavens above. Her mouth moved, but no words could be heard, as though her faith in what she was doing were lacking still.

Finished, she turned and ran after her brother, though she would be careful to keep her distance. She didn't want Oz to know he'd been followed, even though she had come along only to watch over him. Behind her the bear and the photo lay forlornly against the brick, resembling nothing so much as a temporary shrine to the dead.

As Louisa had predicted, Lou and Hit finally reached middle ground. Louisa had proudly watched as Lou rose each time Hit knocked her down, the girl growing not more afraid through each tussle with the wily beast, but rather more determined. And smarter. Now plow, mule, and Lou moved with a fluid motion.

For his part Oz had become an expert at riding the big sled that Sam the mule dragged through the fields. Since Oz was lacking in girth, Eugene had piled rocks all around him. The big clods of dirt gave way and broke up under the constant dragging, and the sled eventually smoothed the field like icing on a cake. After weeks of work, sweat, and tired muscles, the four of them stood back and took stock of good ground that was ready now to accept seed.

Dr. Travis Barnes had come up from Dickens to check on Amanda. He was a burly man—red hammy face, short legs—with gray side whiskers, dressed all in black. To Lou, he looked more like an undertaker coming to bury a body than a man trained in preserving life. However, he turned out to be kindly, with a sense of humor designed to make them all comfortable in light of his bleak mission. Cotton and the children waited in the front room while Louisa stayed with Travis during his examination. He was shaking his head and clutching his black bag when he joined them in the front room. Louisa trailed him, trying to look cheerful. The doctor sat at the kitchen table and fingered the cup of coffee Louisa had poured. He stared into his cup for a bit, as though looking for some comforting words floating among the strains of beans and chicory root.

"Good news," he began, "is that far as I can tell, your momma's fine physically. Her injuries all healed up. She's young and strong and can eat and drink, and so long as you keep exercising her arms and legs, the muscles won't get too weak." He paused and set his cup down. "But I'm afraid that's also the bad news, for that means the problem lies here." He touched his forehead. "And there's not much we can do about that. Certainly beyond me. We can only hope and pray that she comes out of it one day."

Oz took this in stride, his optimism barely tarnished. Lou absorbed this information simply as further validation of what she already knew.

School had been going more smoothly than Lou had thought it would. She and Oz found the mountain children to be far more accepting of them now than before Lou had thrown her punches. Lou didn't feel she would ever be close to any of them, but at least the outright hostility had waned. Billy Davis did not return to school for several days. By the time he did, the bruises she had inflicted were mostly healed, though there were fresh ones which Lou suspected had originated with the awful George Davis. And that was enough to make her feel a certain guilt. For his part, Billy avoided her like she was a water moccasin looking to get the jump on him, yet Lou was still on her guard. She knew by now: It was right when you least expected it that trouble tended to smack you in the head.

Estelle McCoy, too, was subdued around her. It was apparent that Lou and Oz were well ahead of the others in terms of book learning. They did not flaunt this advantage, though, and Estelle McCoy seemed appreciative of that. And she never again referred to Lou as Louisa Mae. Lou and Oz had given the school library a box of their own books, and the children had slipped

by one after the other to thank them. It was a steady
if not spectacular truce all around.

Lou rose before dawn, did her chores, then went to
school and did her work there. At lunchtime she ate
her cornbread and drank her milk with Oz under the
walnut tree, which was scored with the initials and names
of those who had done their learning here. Lou never
felt an urge to carve her name there, for it suggested a
permanency she was far from willing to accept. They
went back to the farm to work in the afternoon, and
then went to bed, exhausted, not long after the sun set.
It was a steady, uninspired life much appreciated by Lou
right now.

Head lice had made their way through Big Spruce,
though, and both Lou and Oz had endured shampoos
in kerosene. "Don't get near the fire," Louisa had warned.

"This is disgusting," said Lou, fingering the coated
strands.

"When I was at school and got me the lice, they put
sulfur, lard, and gunpowder on my hair," Louisa told
them. "I couldn't bear to smell myself, and I was terrible afraid somebody'd strike a match and my head would
blow."

"They had school when you were little?" Oz asked.

Louisa smiled. "They had what was called subscrip-
tion school, Oz. A dollar a month for three month a
year, and I were a right good student. We was a hunnerd people in a one-room log cabin with a puncheon
floor that was splintery on hot days and ice on cold.
Teacher quick with the whip or strap, some bad child

standing on tippy-toe a good half hour with his nose stuck in a circle the teacher drawed on the board. I ain't never had to stand on tippy-toe. I weren't always good, but I ain't never got caught neither. Some were growed men not long from the War missing arms and legs, come to learn they's letters and numbers. Used to say our spelling words out loud. Got so the durn noise spooked the horses." Her hazel eyes sparkled. "Had me one teacher who used the markings on his cow to learn us geography. To this day, I can't never look at no map without thinking of that durn animal." She looked at them. "I guess you can fill up your head just about anywhere. So you learn what you got to. Just like your daddy done," she added, mostly for Lou's benefit, and the girl finally stopped complaining about her kerosene hair.

CHAPTER EIGHTEEN

LOUISA FELT SORRY FOR THEM ONE MORNING and gave Lou and Oz a much needed Saturday off to do as they pleased. The day was fine, with a clean breeze from the west across a blue sky, trees flushed with green swaying to its touch. Diamond and Jeb came calling that morning, because Diamond said there was a special place in the woods he wanted to show them, and they started off.

His appearance was little changed: same overalls, same shirt, no shoes. The bottoms of his feet must have had every nerve deadened like hoofs, Lou thought, because she saw him run across sharp rocks, over briars, and even through a thorny thicket, and never once did she see blood drawn or face wince. He wore an oily cap pulled low on his forehead. She asked him if it was his father's, but received only a grunt in response.

They came to a tall oak set in a clearing, or at least where underbrush had been cut away some. Lou noted that pieces of sawed wood had been nailed into the tree's trunk, forming a rough ladder. Diamond put a foot up on the first rung and started to climb.

"Where are you going?" asked Lou, as Oz kept a grip on Jeb because the hound was acting as though he too wanted to head up the tree behind his master.

"See God," Diamond hollered back, pointing straight up. Lou and Oz looked to the sky.

Far up a number of stripped scrub pines were laid side by side on a couple of the oak's massive branches, forming a floor. A canvas tarp had been flung over a sturdy limb above, and the sides had been tied down to the pines with rope to form a crude tent. While promising all sorts of pleasant times, the tree house looked a good puff of wind away from hitting the ground.

Diamond was already three-quarters up, moving with an easy grace. "Come on now," he said.

Lou, who would have preferred to die a death of impossible agony rather than concede that anything was beyond her, put a hand and a foot on two of the pieces of wood. "You can stay down here if you want, Oz," she said. "We probably won't be long." She started up.

"I got me neat stuff up here, yes sir," Diamond said enticingly. He had reached the summit, his bare feet dangling over the edge.

Oz ceremoniously spit on his hands, gripped a wood piece, and clambered up behind his sister. They sat cross-legged on the laid pines, which formed about a six-by-six square, the canvas roof throwing a nice shade, and Diamond showed them his wares. First out was a flint arrowhead he said was at least one million years old and had been given to him in a dream. Then from a cloth bag rank with outside damp he pulled the skeleton of a small bird that he said had not been seen since shortly after God put the universe together.

"You mean it's extinct," Lou said.

"Naw, I mean it ain't round no more."

Oz was intrigued by a hollow length of metal that had a thick bit of glass fitted into one end. He looked through it, and while the sights were magnified some, the glass was so dirty and scratched, it started giving him a headache.

"See a body coming from miles away," proclaimed Diamond, sweeping a hand across his kingdom. "Enemy or friend." He next showed them a bullet fired from what he said was an 1861 U.S. Springfield rifle.

"How do you know that?" said Lou.

" 'Cause my great-granddaddy five times removed passed it on down and my granddaddy give it to me afore he died. My great-granddaddy five times removed, he fought for the Union, you know."

"Wow," Oz said.

"Yep, turned his pitcher to the wall and everythin', they did. But he weren't taking up a gun for nobody owning nobody else. T'ain't right."

"That's admirable," said Lou.

"Look here now," said Diamond. From a small wooden box, he pulled forth a lump of coal and handed it to Lou. "What d'ya think?" he asked. She looked down at it. The rock was all chipped and rough.

"It's a lump of coal," she said, giving it back and wiping her hand clean on her pants leg.

"No, it ain't just that. You see, they's a diamond in there. A diamond, just like me."

Oz inched over and held the rock. "Wow" was again all he could manage.

"A diamond?" Lou said. "How do you know?"

" 'Cause the man who gimme it said it was. And he ain't ask for not a durn thing. And man ain't even know my name was Diamond. So there," he added indignantly, seeing the disbelief on Lou's features. He took the coal lump back from Oz. "I chip me off a little piece ever day. And one time I gonna tap it and there it'll be, the biggest, purtiest diamond anybody's ever saw."

Oz eyed the rock with the reverence he usually reserved for grown-ups and church. "Then what will you do with it?"

Diamond shrugged. "Ain't sure. Mebbe nothing. Mebbe keep it right up here. Mebbe give it to you. You like that?"

"If there is a diamond in there, you could sell it for a lot of money," Lou pointed out.

Diamond rubbed at his nose. "Ain't need no money. Got me all I need right here on this mountain."

"Have you ever been off this mountain?" Lou asked.

He stared at her, obviously offended. "What, you think I'a hick or somethin'? Gone on down to McKenzie's near the bridge lots of times. And over to Tremont."

Lou looked out over the woods below. "How about Dickens? You ever been there?"

"Dickens?" Diamond almost fell out of the tree. "Take a day to walk it. 'Sides, why'd a body want'a go there?"

"Because it's different than here. Because I'm tired of dirt and mules and manure and hauling water," said Lou. She patted her pocket. "And because I've got twenty dollars I brought with me from New York that's burning a hole in my pocket," she added, staring at him.

This gigantic sum staggered Diamond, yet even he seemed to understand the possibilities. "Too fer to walk," he said, fingering the coal lump, as though trying to hurry the diamond into hatching.

"Then we *don't* walk," replied Lou.

He glanced at her. "Tremont right closer."

"No, Dickens. I want to go to Dickens."

Oz said, "We could take a taxi."

"If we get to the bridge at McKenzie's," Lou ventured, "then maybe we can hitch a ride to Dickens with somebody. How far is the bridge on foot?"

Diamond considered this. "Well, by road it a good four hour. Time git down there, got to come back. And that be a tiring way to spend a day off from farming."

"What way is there other than the road?"

"You really want'a get on down there?" he said.

Lou took a deep breath. "I really want to, Diamond."

"Well, then, we going. I knowed me a shortcut. Shoot, get us there quick as a sneeze."

Since the mountains had been formed, water had continued eroding the soft limestone, carving thousand-foot-deep gullies between the harder rocks. The line of finger ridges marched next to the three of them as they walked along. The ravine they finally came to was wide and seemed impassable until Diamond led them over to the tree. The yellow poplars here grew to immense proportion, gauged by a caliper measured in feet instead of inches. Many were thicker than a man was tall, and rose up to a hundred and fifty feet in height. Fifteen thousand board feet of lumber could be gotten from a single poplar. A healthy specimen lay across this gap, forming a bridge.

"Going 'cross here cuts the trip way down," Diamond said.

Oz looked over the edge, saw nothing but rock and water at the end of a long fall, and backed away like a spooked cow. Even Lou looked uncertain. But Diamond walked right up to the log.

"Ain't no problem. Thick and wide. Shoot, walk 'cross with your eyes closed. Come on now."

He made his way across, never once looking down. Jeb scooted easily after him. Diamond reached safe ground and looked back. "Come on now," he said again.

Lou put one foot up on the poplar but didn't take another step.

Diamond called out from across the chasm. "Just don't look down. Easy."

Lou turned to her brother. "You stay here, Oz. Let me make sure it's okay." Lou clenched her fists, stepped onto the log, and started across. She kept her eyes leveled on nothing but Diamond and soon joined him on the other side. They looked back at Oz. He made no move toward the log, his gaze fixed on the dirt.

"You go on ahead, Diamond. I'll go back with him."

"No, we ain't gonna do that. You said you want'a go to town? Well, dang it, we going to town."

"I'm *not* going without Oz."

"Ain't got to."

Diamond jogged back across the poplar bridge after telling Jeb to stay put. He got Oz to climb on his back and Lou watched in admiration as Diamond carried him across.

"You sure are strong, Diamond," said Oz as he gingerly slid down to the ground with a relieved breath.

"Shoot, that ain't nuthin'. Bear chased me 'cross that tree one time and I had Jeb *and* a sack of flour on my back. And it were nighttime too. And the rain was pouring so hard God must've been bawling 'bout somethin'. Couldn't see a durn thing. Why, I almost fell twice."

"Well, good Lord," said Oz.

Lou hid her smile well. "What happened to the bear?" she asked in seemingly honest excitement.

"Missed me and landed in the water, and that durn thing never bothered me no mo'."

"Let's go to town, Diamond," she said, pulling on his arm, "before that bear comes back."

They crossed one more bridge of sorts, a swinging one made from rope and cedar slats with holes bored in them so the hemp could be pulled through and then knotted. Diamond told them that pirates, colonial settlers, and later on, Confederate refugees had made the old bridge and added to it at various points in time. And Diamond said he knew where they were all buried, but had been sworn to secrecy by a person he wouldn't name.

They made their way down slopes so steep they had to hang on to trees, vines, and each other to stop from tumbling down head-first. Lou stopped every once in a while to gaze out as she clutched a sapling for support. It was something to stand on steep ground and look out at land of even greater angles. When the land became flatter and Oz grew tired, Lou and Diamond took turns carrying him.

At the bottom of the mountain, they were confronted with another obstacle. The idling coal train was at least a hundred cars long, and it blocked the way as far as they could see in either direction. Unlike those of a passenger train, the coal train's cars were too close together to step between. Diamond picked up a rock and hurled it at one of the cars. It struck right at the name emblazoned across it: Southern Valley Coal and Gas.

"Now what?" said Lou. "Climb over?" She looked at the fully loaded cars and the few handholds, and wondered how that would be possible.

"Shoot naw," said Diamond. "Unner." He stuck his hat in his pocket, dropped to his belly, and slid between the car wheels and under the train. Lou and Oz quickly followed, as did Jeb. They all emerged on the other side and dusted themselves off.

"Boy got hisself cut in half last year doing that very thing," said Diamond. "Train start up when he were unner it. Now, I ain't see it, but I hear it were surely not purty."

"Why didn't you tell us that *before* we crawled under the train?" demanded a stunned Lou.

"Well, if I'd done that, you ain't never crawled unner, now would you?"

On the main road they caught a ride in a Ramsey Candy truck and each was given a Blue Banner chocolate bar by the chubby, uniformed driver. "Spread the word," he told them. "Good stuff."

"Sure will," said Diamond as he bit into the candy. He chewed slowly, methodically, as though suddenly a connoisseur of fine chocolate testing a fresh batch. "You give me 'nuther one and I get the word out *twice* as fast, mister."

After a long, bumpy ride the truck dropped them off in the middle of Dickens proper. Diamond's bare toes had hardly touched asphalt when he quickly lifted first one foot and then the other. "Feels funny," he said. "Ain't liking it none."

"Diamond, I swear, you'd walk on nails without a word," Lou said as she looked around. Dickens wasn't even a bump in the road compared to what she was used to, but after their time on the mountain it seemed like the most sophisticated metropolis she had ever seen. The sidewalks were filled with people on this fine Saturday morning, and small pockets of them spilled onto the streets. Most were dressed in nice clothes, but the miners were easy enough to spot, lumbering along with their wrecked backs and the loud, hacking coughs coming from their ruined lungs.

A huge banner had been stretched across the street.

It read "Coal Is King" in letters black as the mineral. Directly under where the banner had been tied off to a beam jutting from one of the buildings was a Southern Valley Coal and Gas office. There was a line of men going in, and a line of them coming out, all with smiles on their faces, clutching either cash, or, presumably, promises of a good job.

Smartly dressed men in fedoras and three-piece suits chucked silver coins to eager children in the streets. The automobile dealership was doing a brisk business, and the shops were filled with both quality goods and folks clamoring to purchase them. Prosperity was clearly alive and well at the foot of this Virginia mountain. It was a happy, energetic scene, and it made Lou homesick for the city.

"How come your parents have never brought you down here?" Lou asked Diamond as they walked along.

"Ain't never had no reason to come here, that's why." He stuffed his hands in his pockets and stared up at a telephone pole with wires sprouting from it and smacking into one building. Then he eyed a droop-shouldered man in a suit and a little boy in dark slacks and a dress shirt as they came out of a store with a big paper bag of something. The two went over to one of the slant-parked cars that lined both sides of the street, and the man opened the car door. The boy stared over at Diamond and asked him where he was from.

"How you know I ain't from right here, son?" said Diamond, glaring at the town boy.

The child looked at Diamond's dirty clothes and face,

his bare feet and wild hair, then jumped in the car and locked the door.

They kept walking and passed the Esso gas station with its twin pumps and a smiling man in crisp company uniform standing out front as rigidly as a cigar store Indian. Next they peered through the glass of a Rexall drugstore. The store was running an "all-in-the-window" sale. The two dozen or so varied items could be had for the sum of three dollars.

"Shoot, why? You can make all that stuff yourself. Ain't got to buy it," Diamond pointed out, apparently sensing that Lou was tempted to go inside and clean out the display.

"Diamond, we're here to spend money. Have fun."

"I'm having fun," he said with a scowl. "Don't be telling me I ain't having no fun."

They headed past the Dominion Café with its Chero Cola and "Ice Cream Here" signs, and then Lou stopped.

"Let's go in," she said. Lou gripped the door, pulled it open, setting a bell to tinkling, and stepped inside. Oz followed her. Diamond stayed outside for a long enough time to show his displeasure with this decision and then hurried in after them.

The place smelled of coffee, wood smoke, and baking fruit pies. Umbrellas for sale hung from the ceiling. There was a bench down one wall, and three swivel chrome barstools with padded green seats were bolted to the floor in front of a waist-high counter. Glass containers filled with candy rested on the display cabinets. There was a modest soda and ice cream fountain machine, and through a pair of saloon doors they could hear the clatter of dishes and smell the aromas of food cooking. In one corner was a potbellied stove, its smoke pipe supported by wire and cutting through one wall.

A man dressed in a white shirt with sleeves rolled to the elbows, a short wide tie, and wearing an apron passed through the saloon doors and stood behind the counter. He had a smooth face and hair parted equally to either side, held down with what appeared to Lou to be a slop bucket of grease.

He looked at them as though they were a brigade of Union troops sent directly from General Grant to rub the good Virginians' noses in it a little more. He edged back a bit as they moved forward. Lou got up on one of the stools and looked at the menu neatly written in loopy cursive on a blackboard. The man moved back farther. His hand glided out and one of his knuckles rapped against a glass cabinet set against the wall. The words "No Credit" had been written in thick white strokes on the glass.

In response to this not-so-subtle gesture, Lou pulled out five one-dollar bills and aligned them neatly on the counter. The man's eyes went to the folding cash and he smiled, showing off a gold front tooth. He came forward, now their good friend for all time. Oz scooted up on another of the barstools, leaned on the counter, and sniffed the wonderful smells coming through those saloon doors. Diamond hung back, as though wanting to be nearest the door when they had to make a run for it.

"How much for a slice of pie?" Lou asked.

"Nickel," the man said, his gaze locked on the five Washingtons on his counter.

"How about a whole pie?"

"Fifty cents."

"So I could buy ten pies with this money?"

"Ten pies?" exclaimed Diamond. "God dog!"

"That's right," the man said quickly. "And we can make 'em for you too." He glanced over at Diamond, his gaze descending from the boy's explosion of cowlicks to his bare toes. "He with you?"

"Naw, they with me," said Diamond, ambling over to the counter, fingers tucked around his overall straps.

Oz was staring at another sign on the wall. "Only Whites Served," he read out loud, and then glanced in confusion at the man. "Well, our hair's blond, and Diamond's is red. Does that mean only old people can get pie?"

The fellow looked at Oz like the boy was "special" in the head, stuck a toothpick between his teeth, and eyed Diamond. "Shoes are required in my establishment. Where you from, boy? Mountain?"

"Naw, the moon." Diamond leaned forward and flashed an exaggerated smile. "Want'a see my green teeth?"

As though brandishing a tiny sword, the man waved the toothpick in front of Diamond's face. "You smart mouth. Just march yourself right outta here. Go on. Git back up that mountain where you belong and stay there!"

Instead, Diamond went up on his toes, grabbed an umbrella off the ceiling rack, and opened it.

The man came around from behind the counter.

"Don't you do that now. That's bad luck."

"Why, I doing it. Mebbe a chunk of rock'll fall off the mountain and squash you to poultice!"

Before the man reached him, Diamond tossed the opened umbrella into the air and it landed on the soda machine. A stream of goo shot out and painted one cabinet a nice shade of brown.

"Hey!" the man yelled, but Diamond had already fled.

Lou scooped up her money, and she and Oz stood to leave.

"Where y'all going?" the man said.

"I decided I didn't want pie," Lou said amiably and shut the door quietly behind her and Oz.

They heard the man yell out, "Hicks!"

They caught up with Diamond, and all three bent over laughing while people walked around them, staring curiously.

"Nice to see you having a good time," a voice said.

They turned and saw Cotton standing there, wearing vest, tie, and coat, briefcase in hand, yet with a clear look of mirth in his eyes.

"Cotton," Lou said, "what are you doing here?"

He pointed across the street. "Well, I happen to work here, Lou."

They all stared at where he was pointing. The courthouse loomed large before them, beautiful brick over ugly concrete.

"Now, what are y'all doing here?" he asked.

"Louisa gave us the day off. Been working pretty hard," said Lou.

Cotton nodded. "So I've seen."

Lou looked at the bustle of people. "It surprised me when I first saw this place. Really prosperous."

Cotton glanced around. "Well, looks can be deceiving. Thing about this part of the state, we're generally one industry-moving-on from total collapse. Lumber folks did it, and now most jobs are tied to the coal and not just the miners. And most of the businesses here rely on those people spending those mining dollars. If that goes away, then it might not seem so prosperous anymore. A house of cards falls swiftly. Who knows, in five years' time this place might not even be here." He eyed Diamond and grinned. "But the mountain folk will. They always get by." He looked around. "I tell you what, I've got some things to do over to the courthouse. Court's not in session today of course, but always some work to be done. Suppose you meet me there in two hours. Then I'd be proud to buy you some lunch."

Lou looked around. "Where?"

"A place I think you'd like, Lou. Called the New York Restaurant. Open twenty-four hours, breakfast, lunch, or supper any time of the day or night. Now, there aren't many folk in Dickens who stay up past nine o'clock, but I suppose it's comforting to have the option of eggs, grits, and bacon at midnight."

"Two hours," repeated Oz, "but we don't have anything to tell time with."

"Well, the courthouse has a clock tower, but it tends to run a little slow. I tell you what, Oz, here." Cotton took off his pocket watch and handed it to him. "You use this. Take good care of it. My father gave it to me."

"When you left to come here?" Lou asked.

"That's right. He said I'd have plenty of time on my hands, and I guess he wanted me to keep good track of it." He tipped his hat to them. "Two hours." And then he walked away.

"So what we gonna do for two hours?" said Diamond.

Lou looked around and her eyes lit up.

"Come on," she said and took off running. "You're finally going to see yourself a picture show, Mr. Diamond."

For almost two hours they were in a place far removed from Dickens, Virginia, the mountains of Appalachia, and the troublesome concerns of real life. They were in the breathtaking land of *The Wizard of Oz*, which was having a long run at movie houses across the land. When they came out, Diamond peppered them with dozens of questions about how any of what they had just seen was possible.

"Had God done it?" he asked more than once in a hushed tone.

Lou pointed to the courthouse. "Come on, or we'll be late."

They dashed across the street and up the wide steps

of the courthouse. A uniformed deputy sheriff with a thick mustache stopped them.

"Whoa, now, where you think y'all going?"

"It's all right, Howard, they're with me," Cotton said, coming out the door. "They all might be lawyers one day. Coming to check out the halls of justice."

"God forbid, Cotton, we ain't needing us no more fine lawyers," Howard said, smiling, and then moved on.

"Having a good time?" Cotton asked.

"I just seen a lion, a durn scarecrow, and a metal man on a big wall," said Diamond, "and I still ain't figgered out how they done it."

"Y'all want to see where I do my daily labor?" asked Cotton.

They all clamored that they did indeed. Before they went inside, Oz solemnly handed the pocket watch back to Cotton.

"Thanks for taking such good care of it, Oz."

"It's been two hours, you know," said the little boy.

"Punctuality is a virtue," replied the lawyer.

They went inside the courthouse while Jeb lay down outside. There were doorways up and down the broad hall, and hanging above the doors various brass plates that read: "Marriage Registrar," "Tax Collections," "Births and Deaths," "Commonwealth's Attorney," and so on. Cotton explained their various functions and then showed them the courtroom, which Diamond said was the largest such space he had ever seen. They were introduced to Fred the bailiff, who had popped out of some room or other when they had come in. Judge Atkins, he explained, had gone home for lunch.

On the walls were portraits of white-haired men in black robes. The children ran their hands along the carved wood and took turns sitting in the witness and jury boxes. Diamond asked to sit in the judge's chair, but Cotton didn't think that was a good idea, and neither did Fred. When they weren't looking, Diamond grabbed a sit anyway and came away puff-chested like a rooster, until Lou, who had seen this offense, poked him hard in the ribs.

They left the courthouse and went next door to a building that housed a small number of offices, including Cotton's. His place was one large room with creaky oak flooring that had shelves on three sides which held worn law books, will and deed boxes, and a fine set of the Statutes of Virginia. A big walnut desk sat in the middle of the room, along with a telephone and drifts of papers. There was an old crate for a wastebasket, and a listing hat and umbrella stand in one corner. There were no hats on the hooks, and where the umbrellas should have been was an old fishing pole. Cotton let Diamond dial a single number on the phone and talk to Shirley the operator. The boy nearly jumped out of his skin when her raspy voice tickled his ear.

Next, Cotton showed them the apartment where he lived at the top of this same building. It had a small kitchen that was piled high with canned vegetables, jars of molasses and bread and butter pickles, sacks of potatoes, blankets, and lanterns, among many other items.

"Where'd you get all that stuff?" asked Lou.

"Folks don't always have cash. Pay their legal bills in barter." He opened the small icebox and showed them the cuts of chicken, beef, and bacon in there. "Can't put none of it in the bank, but it sure tastes a lot better'n money." There was a tiny bedroom with a rope bed and a reading light on a small nightstand, and one large front room utterly buried under books.

As they stared at the mounds, Cotton took off his glasses. "No wonder I'm going blind," he said.

"You read all them books?" Diamond asked in awe.

"I plead guilty to that. In fact I've read many of them more than once," Cotton answered.

"I read me a book one time," Diamond said proudly.

"What was the title?" Lou asked.

"Don't recall 'xactly, but it had lots of pictures. No, I take that back, I read me two books, if you count the Bible."

"I think we can safely include that, Diamond," said Cotton, smiling. "Come over here, Lou." Cotton showed her one bookcase neatly filled with volumes, many of them fine leatherbound ones of notable authors. "This is reserved for my favorite writers."

Lou looked at the titles there and immediately saw every novel and collection of short stories her father had written. It was nice, conciliatory bait Cotton was throwing out, only Lou was not in a conciliatory mood. She said, "I'm hungry. Can we eat now?"

The New York Restaurant served nothing remotely close to New York fare but it was good food nonethe-

less, and Diamond had what he said was his first bottle of "soder" pop. He liked it so much he had two more.
Afterward they walked down the street, peppermint
candy rolling in their mouths. They went into the five-
and-dime and 25-cent store and Cotton showed them
how because of the land grade all six stories of the place
opened out onto ground level, a fact that had actually
been discussed in the national media at one point. "Dickens's claim to fame," he chuckled, "unique angles of dirt."

The store was stacked high with dry goods, tools, and
foodstuffs. The aromas of tobacco and coffee were strong
and seemed to have settled into the bones of the place.
Horse collars hung next to racks of spooled thread, which
sat alongside fat barrels of candies. Lou bought a pair
of socks for herself and a pocketknife for Diamond, who
was reluctant to accept it until she told him that in return he had to whittle something for her. She purchased
a stuffed bear for Oz and handed it to him without
commenting on the whereabouts of the old one.

Lou disappeared for a few minutes and returned with
an object which she handed to Cotton. It was a magnifying glass. "For all that reading," she said and smiled,
and Cotton smiled back. "Thank you, Lou. This way
I'll think of you every time I open a book." She bought
a shawl for Louisa and a straw hat for Eugene. Oz borrowed some money from her and went off with Cotton
to browse. When they came back, he held a parcel
wrapped in brown paper and steadfastly refused to reveal what it was.

After wandering the town, Cotton showing them

things that Lou and Oz had certainly seen before, but Diamond never had, they piled into Cotton's Oldsmobile, which sat parked in front of the courthouse. They headed off, Diamond and Lou squeezed into the rumble seat while Oz and Jeb rode with Cotton in front. The sun was just beginning its descent now and the breeze felt good to all. There didn't seem to be anything so pretty as sun setting over mountain.

They passed through Tremont and a while later crossed the tiny bridge near McKenzie's and started up the first ridge. They came to a railroad crossing, and instead of continuing on the road, Cotton turned and drove the Oldsmobile on down the tracks.

"Smoother than the roads up here," he explained. "We'll pick it back up later on. They've got asphalt and macadam at the foothills, but not up here. These mountain roads were built by hands swinging picks and shovels. Law used to be every able-bodied man between sixteen and sixty had to help build the roads ten days a year and bring his own tools and sweat to do it. Only teachers and preachers were exempt from having to do it, although I imagine those workers could've used some powerful prayers every now and again. They did a right good job, built eighty miles of road over forty years, but it's still hard on one's bottom to travel across the results of all that fine work."

"What if a train comes?" asked an anxious Oz.

"Then I suspect we'll have to get off," Cotton said.

They eventually did hear the whistle and Cotton pulled the car to safety and waited. A few minutes later a fully loaded train rolled past, looking like a giant serpent. It was moving slowly, for the track was curvy here.

"Is that coal?" Oz said, eyeing the great lumps of rock visible in the open train cars.

Cotton shook his head. "Coke. Made from slack coal and cooked in the ovens. Ship it out to the steel mills." He shook his head slowly. "Trains come up here empty and leave full. Coal, coke, lumber. Don't bring anything here except more bodies for labor."

On a spur off the main line, Cotton showed them a coal company town made up of small, identical homes, with a train track dead center of the place and a commissary store that had goods piled floor to ceiling, Cotton informed them, because he had been inside before. A long series of connected brick structures shaped like beehives were set along one high road. Each one had a metal door and a chimney with fill dirt packed around it. Smoke belched from each stack, turning the darkening sky ever blacker. "Coke ovens," Cotton explained. There was one large house with a shiny new Chrysler Crown Imperial parked out front. The mine superintendent's home, Cotton told them. Next to this house was a corral with a few grazing mares and a couple of energetic yearlings leaping and galloping around.

"I got to take care of some personal business," said Diamond, already pulling his overall straps down. "Too much soder pop. Won't be one minute, just duck behind that shed."

Cotton stopped the car and Diamond got out and ran off. Cotton and the children talked while they waited, and the lawyer pointed out some other things of interest.

"This is a Southern Valley coal mining operation. The Clinch Number Two mine, they call it. Coal mining pays pretty good, but the work is terribly hard, and with the way the company stores are set up the miners end up owing more to the company than they earn in wages." Cotton stopped talking and looked thoughtfully in the direction of where Diamond had gone, a frown easing across his face. He continued, "And the men also get sick and die of the black lung, or from cave-ins, accidents, and such."

A whistle sounded and they watched as a group of charcoal-faced, probably bone-tired men emerged from the mine entrance. A group of women and children ran to greet them, and they all walked toward the copycat houses, the men swinging metal dinner pails and pulling out their smokes and liquor bottles. Another group of men, looking as tired as the other, trudged past them to take their place under the earth.

"They used to run three shifts here, but now they only have two," said Cotton. "Coal's starting to run out."

Diamond returned and vaulted into the rumble seat.

"You all right, Diamond?" asked Cotton.

"Am now," said the boy, a smile pushing against his cheeks, his feline green eyes lighted up.

Louisa was upset when she learned they had gone to town. Cotton explained that he should not have kept the children as long as he had, therefore she should blame him. But then Louisa said she recalled that their daddy had done the very same thing, and the pioneer spirit was a hard one to dodge, so it was okay. Louisa accepted the shawl with tears in her eyes, and Eugene tried on the hat and proclaimed it the nicest gift he had ever gotten.

After supper that night Oz excused himself and went to his mother's room. Curious, Lou followed him, spying on her brother as usual from the narrow opening between door and wall. Oz carefully unwrapped the parcel he had purchased in town and held the hairbrush firmly. Amanda's face was peaceful, her eyes, as always, shut. To Lou, her mother was a princess reclining in a deathlike state, and none of them possessed the necessary antidote. Oz knelt on the bed and began brushing Amanda's hair and telling his mother of their wonderfully fine day in town. Lou watched him struggle with the brushing for a few moments and then went in to help. She held out her mother's hair and showed Oz how to properly perform the strokes. Their mother's hair had grown out some, but it was still short.

Later that night Lou went to her room, put away the socks she had bought, lay on the bed fully dressed down to her boots, thinking about their trip to town, and never once closed her eyes until it was time to milk the cows the next morning.

CHAPTER NINETEEN

THEY ALL WERE SITTING DOWN TO DINNER A few nights later while the rain poured down outside. Diamond had come for supper, wearing a tattered piece of worn canvas with a hole cut out for his head, his homegrown mackintosh of sorts. Jeb had shaken himself off and headed for the fire as though he owned the place. When Diamond freed himself from the canvas coat, Lou saw something tied around his neck. And it wasn't particularly sweet-smelling.

"What is *that*?" Lou asked, her fingers pinching her nose, for the stench was awful.

"Asafetida," Louisa answered for the boy. "A root. Ward off sickness. Diamond, honey, I think if you warm yourself by the fire, you can give that to me. I thank you." While Diamond wasn't looking, she carried the root out to the back porch and flung the foul thing away into the darkness.

Louisa's frying pan held the dual aromas of popping lard and ribs cut thick with so much fat they didn't dare curl. The meat had come from one of the hogs they had had to slaughter. Usually a winter task, they had been compelled, by a variety of circumstances, to perform the deed in spring. Actually, Eugene had done the killing while the children were at school. But at Oz's insistence Eugene had agreed to let him help scrape down the hog and get off the ribs, middle meat, bacon, and chitlins. However, when Oz saw the dead animal strung up on a wooden tripod, a steel hook through its bloody mouth, and a cauldron of boiling water nearby— just waiting, he no doubt believed, for the hide of a little boy to give it the right spice, he had run off. His screams echoed back and forth across the valley, as though from a careless giant who had stubbed his toe. Eugene had admired both the boy's speed and lung capacity and then gone on to work the hog himself.

They all ate heartily of the meat, and also of canned tomatoes and green beans that had marinated for the better part of six months in brine and sugar, and the last of the pinto beans.

Louisa kept all plates full, except her own. She nibbled on some of the tomato chunks and beans, and dipped cornbread into heated lard, but that was all. She sipped on a cup of chicory coffee and looked around the table where all were enjoying themselves, laughing hard at something silly Diamond had said. She listened to the rain on the roof. So far so good, though rain now meant nothing; if none fell in July and August, the crop would still be dust, blown off in a gentle breeze, and dust had never lined anyone's belly. Very soon they would be laying in their food crops: corn, pole beans, tomatoes, squash, rutabaga, late potatoes, cabbage, sweet potatoes, and string beans. Irish potatoes and onions were already in the ground, and duly hilled over, frost not bothering them any. The land would be good to them this year; it was their due this time around.

Louisa listened to the rain some more. *Thank you, Lord, but be sure to send us some more of your bounty come summer. Not too much so's the tomatoes burst and rot on the vines, and not too little that the corn only grows waist high. I know it's asking a lot, but it'd be much appreciated.* She said a silent amen and then did her best to join in the festivities.

There came a rap on the door and Cotton walked in, his outer coat soaked through even though the walk from car to porch was a quick one. He was not his usual self; the man did not even smile. He accepted a cup of coffee, a bit of cornbread, and sat next to Diamond. The boy stared up at him as though he knew what was coming.

"Sheriff came by to see me, Diamond."

Everyone looked at Cotton first and then they all stared at Diamond. Oz's eyes were open so wide the boy looked like an owl without feathers.

"Is that right?" Diamond said, as he took a mouthful of beans and stewed onions.

"Seems a pile of horse manure got in the mine superintendent's brand-new Chrysler at the Clinch Number Two. The man sat in it without knowing, it still being dark and all, and he had the bad cold in the nose and couldn't smell it. He was understandably upset by the experience."

"Durn, how 'bout that," said Diamond. "Wonder how the horse done got that in there? Pro'bly just backed it-self up to the window and let fly." That said, Diamond went right on eating, though none of the others did.

"I recall I dropped you off to do some personal busi-ness right around there on our drive back from Dick-ens."

"You tell the sheriff that?" Diamond asked quickly.

"No, my memory curiously abandoned me about the time he asked." Diamond looked relieved as Cotton con-tinued. "But I spent a sorry hour over at the courthouse with the superintendent and a coal company lawyer who were all-fire sure that you had done it. Now upon my careful cross-examination I was able to demonstrate that there were no eyewitnesses and no other evidence tying you to the scene of this . . . little situation. And, fortu-nately, one can't take fingerprints from horse manure. Judge Atkins held with my side of things, and so there we are. But those coal folk have long memories, son, you know that."

"Not so long as mine," countered Diamond.

"Why would he do something like that?" said Lou.

Louisa looked at Cotton and he looked at her, and then Cotton said, "Diamond, my heart's with you on this, son, it really is. You know that. But the law's not. And next time, it might not be so easy to get out of it.

And folk might start taking matters into their own hands. So my advice to you is to get on with things. I'm saying it for your own good, Diamond, you know that I am."

With that Cotton rose and put his hat back on. He refused all further questions from Lou and declined an invitation to stay. He paused and looked at Diamond, who was considering the rest of his meal without enthusiasm.

Cotton said, "Diamond, after those coal folk left the courtroom, me and Judge Atkins had us a long laugh. I'd say that was a right good one to end your career on, son. Okay?"

Diamond finally smiled at the man and said, "Okay."

CHAPTER TWENTY

LOU ROSE EARLY ONE MORNING, EVEN BEFORE
Louisa and Eugene, she believed, for she heard
no stirring below. She had grown used to
dressing in the dark now and her fingers
moved swiftly, arranging her clothes and lacing her
boots. She stepped to the window and looked out. It
was so dark she had a vague feeling of being deep un-
derwater. She flinched, for Lou thought she had seen
something slip out from the barn. And then, like a frame
of spent lightning, it was gone. She opened the window
for a better look, but whatever it was wasn't there anymore. It must have been her imagination.

She went down the stairs as quietly as she could,
started toward Oz's room to wake him, but stopped at
the door of her mother's instead. It was partially open,
and Lou just stood there for a moment, as though something blocked her passage. She leaned against the wall,
squirmed a bit, slid her hands along the door frame,

pushed herself away, and then leaned back. Finally, Lou edged her head into the bedroom.

Lou was surprised to see two figures on the bed. Oz was lying next to their mother. He was dressed in his long johns, a bit of his thin calves visible where the bottoms had inched up, his feet in thick wool socks he had brought with him to the mountain. His tiny rear end was stuck up in the air, his face turned to the side so Lou could see it. A tender smile was on his lips, and he was clenching his new bear.

Lou crept forward and laid a hand on his back. He never stirred, and Lou let her hand slide down and gently touch her mother's arm. When she exercised her mother's limbs, a part of Lou would always be feeling for her mother to be pushing back just a little. But it was always just dead weight. And Amanda had been so strong during the accident, keeping her and Oz from being hurt. Maybe in saving her children, Lou thought, she had used up all she had. Lou left the two and went to the kitchen.

She loaded the coal in the front-room fireplace, got the flame going, then sat in front of the fire for a time, letting the heat melt the chill from her bones. At dawn she opened the door and felt the cool air on her face. There were corpulent gray clouds loitering about from a passed storm, their underbellies outlined in flaming reddish-pink. Right below this was the broad sweep of mountainous green forest that stepped right to the sky. It was one of the most glorious breakups of night she could ever recall. Lou certainly had never seen dawns like this in the city.

Though it had not been that long ago, it seemed like many years since Lou had walked the concrete pavement of New York City, ridden the subway, raced for a cab with her father and mother, pushed through the crowds of shoppers at Macy's the day after Thanksgiving, or gone to Yankee Stadium to lunge for white leather balls and gobble hot dogs. Several months ago all of that had been replaced by steep land, dirt and trees, and animals that smelled and made you earn your place. Corner grocers had been exchanged for crackling bread and strained milk, tap water for water pumped or in bucket hauled, grand public libraries for a pretty cabinet of few books, tall buildings for taller mountains. And for a reason she couldn't quite get at, Lou did not know if she could stay here for long. Maybe there was a good reason her father had never come back.

She went to the barn and milked the cows, carrying a full bucket into the kitchen and the rest to the springhouse, where she laid it in the cool stream of water. The air was already growing warmer.

Lou had the cookstove hot and the pan with lard fired up when her great-grandmother walked in. Louisa was fretting that she and Eugene had slept late. Then Louisa eyed the full buckets on the sink, and Lou told her she had already milked the cows. When she saw the rest of the work Lou had done, Louisa smiled appreciatively. "Next thing I know you'll be running this place without me."

"I doubt that will ever happen," said the girl in a way that made Louisa stop smiling.

Cotton showed up unannounced a half hour later dressed in patched work pants, an old shirt, and worn brogans. He didn't wear his wire-rim glasses, and his fedora had been replaced with a straw hat, which, Louisa said, was foresight on his part because it looked like the sun would burn a bright one today.

They all said their hellos to the man, though Lou had mumbled hers. He had come to read to her mother regularly, as promised, and Lou was resenting it more each time. However, Lou appreciated his gentle ways and courtly manners. It was a conflicted, troubling situation for the girl.

The temperature, though cold the night before, had not come close to freezing. Louisa didn't have a thermometer, but, as she said, her bones were just as accurate as bottled mercury. The crops were going in, she declared to all. Late to plant often meant never to harvest.

They trucked over to the first field to be sown, a sloped rectangle of ten acres. The vigilant wind had chased the malingering gray clouds over the ridgeline, leaving the sky clear. The mountains, though, looked markedly flat this morning, as if they were props only. Louisa carefully passed out bags of seed corn from the season before, shelled and then kept in the corncrib over the winter. She instructed the troops carefully as to their usage. "Thirty bushels of corn an acre is what we want," she said. "More, if we can."

For a while things went all right. Oz walked his rows, meticulously counting out three seeds per hill as Louisa had told them. Lou, though, was letting herself become sloppy, dropping two at some places, four at others.

"Lou," Louisa said sharply. "Three seeds per hill, girl!"

Lou stared at her. "Like it really makes a difference."

Louisa rested fists on her haunches. "Difference twixt eating and not!"

Lou stood there for a moment and then started up again, at a clip of three seeds per hill about nine inches apart. Two hours later, with the five of them working steadily, only about half the field had been laid. Louisa had them spend another hour using hoes to hill the planted corn. Oz and Lou soon had purple blood blisters in the crooks of their hands, despite the gloves they wore. And Cotton too had done the same to his.

"Lawyering is poor preparation for honest work," he explained, showing off his twin sore prizes.

Louisa's and Eugene's hands were so heavily callused that they wore no gloves at all, hilled twice as much as the others, and came away with palms barely reddened by the tools' coarse handles.

With the last dropped seed hilled, Lou, far more bored than tired, sat on the ground, slapping her gloves against her leg. "Well, that was fun. What now?"

A curved stick appeared in front of her. "Before you

get on to school, you and Oz gonna find some wayward cows."

Lou looked up into Louisa's face.

Lou and Oz tramped through the woods. Eugene had let the cows and the calf out to graze in the open field, and, as cows, like people, were wont to do, they were wandering the countryside looking for better prospects.

Lou smacked a lilac bush with the stick Louisa had given her to scare off snakes. She had not mentioned the threat of serpents to Oz, because she figured if he knew, she'd end up carrying her brother on her back. "I can't believe we have to find some stupid cows," she said angrily. "If they're dumb enough to get lost, they should stay lost."

They pushed through tangles of dogwood and mountain laurel. Oz swung on the lower branch of a scraggly pine, and then gave out a whistle as a cardinal flitted by, though most folks from the mountain would have certainly called it a redbird.

"Look, Lou, a cardinal, like us."

Keeping an eye out more for birds than cows, they quickly saw many varieties, most of which they did not know. Hummingbirds twitted over beds of morning glories and wood violets; the children scared up a mess of field larks from thick ground-cover. A sparrow hawk let them know it was around, while a pack of nasty blue jays bothered everybody and everything. Wild, bushy rhododendrons were beginning to bloom in pink and red, as were the lavender-tipped white flowers of Virginia thyme. On the sides of steep slopes they could see trailing arbutus and wolfsbane among the stacked slate and other protrusions of rocks. The trees were in full, showy form, and the sky a cap of blue to finish it off. And here they were, hunting aimless bovines, thought Lou.

A cowbell clunked to the east of them.

Oz looked excited. "Louisa said to follow the bell the cows wear."

Lou chased Oz through groves of beech, poplar, and basswood, the strong vines of wisteria clutching at them like irksome hands, their feet tripping over bumps of shallow roots clinging to uneven, shifting ground. They came to a small clearing ringed with hemlock and gum and heard the bell again, but saw no cows. A gold-finch darted past, startling them.

"Moo. Moooo!" came the voice, and the bell clunked.

The pair looked around in bewilderment until Lou glanced up in the crook of a maple and saw Diamond swinging the bell and speaking cow. He was barefoot, same clothes as always, cigarette behind his ear, hair reaching to the sky, as though a mischievous angel was tugging at the boy's red mop.

"What are you doing?" Lou demanded angrily.

Diamond gracefully swung from branch to branch, dropped to the ground, and clunked the bell once more. Lou noted that he had used a piece of twine to tie the

pocketknife she had given him to a loop on his overalls.

"Believing I were a cow."

"That's not funny," Lou said. "We have to find them."

"Shoot, that's easy. Cows ain't never really lost, they
just mosey round till somebody come get 'em." He whistled and Jeb broke through the tangle of brush to join
them.

Diamond led them through a swath of hickory and
ash; on the trunk of the latter a pair of squirrels were
having an argument, apparently over some division of
spoils. They all stopped and stared in reverence at a
golden eagle perched on a limb of a ruler-straight eighty-
foot poplar. In the next clearing, they saw the cows grazing in a natural pen of fallen trees.

"I knowed they was Miss Louisa's right off. Figger
you'd probably come traipsing through after 'em."

With Diamond's and Jeb's help, they drove the cows
back to their farm pen. Along the way, Diamond showed
them how to hold on to the animals' tails, let the cows
pull them uphill, to make them pay back a little, he
said, for wandering off. When they shut the corral gate,
Lou said, "Diamond, tell me why you put horse manure
in that man's car."

"Can't tell you, 'cause I ain't do it."

"Diamond, come on. You as good as admitted you
did to Cotton."

"Got me oak ears, can't hear nuthin' you saying."

A frustrated Lou drew circles in the dirt with her

shoe. "Look, we have to get to school, Diamond. You want to come with us?"

"Don't go to no school," he said, slipping the unlit cigarette between his lips and becoming an instant adult.

"How come your parents don't make you go?"

In response to this Diamond whistled for Jeb and the pair took off running.

"Hey, Diamond," Lou called after him.

Boy and dog only ran faster.

CHAPTER TWENTY-ONE

L OU AND OZ RACED PAST THE EMPTY YARD and inside the schoolhouse. Breathless, they hustled to their seats.

"I'm sorry we're late," Lou said to Estelle McCoy, who was already chalking something on the board. "We were working in the fields and ..." She looked around and noted that fully half the seats were empty.

"Lou, it's all right," said her teacher. "Planting time's starting, I'm just glad you made it in at all."

Lou sat down in her seat. From the corner of her eye she saw that Billy Davis was there. He looked so angelic that she told herself to be cautious. When she lifted up her desk top to put away her books, she could not stifle the scream. The snake coiled in her desk—a three-foot brown and yellow-banded copperhead—was dead. However, the piece of paper tied around the serpent, with the words "Yankee Go Home" scrawled upon it, was what really made Lou angry.

"Lou," called Mrs. McCoy from the blackboard, "is anything wrong?"

Lou closed the desk and looked at Billy, who pursed his lips and attended to his book. "No," said Lou.

It was lunchtime, and the air was cool, but with a warming sun, and the children gathered outside to eat, lard buckets and other like containers in hand. Just about everyone had something to line his or her stomach, even if it was just scraps of cornbread or biscuit, and many a hand cradled a small jug of milk or jar of springwater. Children settled back on the ground to do their eating, drinking, and talking. Some of the younger ones ran around in circles until they were so dizzy they fell down, and then older siblings picked them up and made them eat.

Lou and Oz sat under the deep shade of the walnut tree, the breeze slowly lifting the ends of Lou's hair. Oz bit heartily into his buttered biscuit and drank down the cold springwater they had brought in a canning jar. Lou, though, did not eat. She seemed to be waiting for something, and stretched her limbs as though preparing for a race.

Billy Davis strutted through the small clumps of eaters, prominently swinging his wooden lunch pail made from a small nail keg with a wire driven through it for a handle. He stopped at one group, said something, laughed, glanced over at Lou, and laughed some more. He finally climbed into the lower branches of a silver maple and opened his lunch pail. He screamed out, fell backward out of the tree, and landed mostly on his head. The snake was on him, and he rolled and pitched trying to get the serpent off. Then he realized it was his own dead copperhead that had been tied to the lid of the pail, which he still clutched in his hand. When he stopped squealing like a stabbed pig, he realized everyone in the schoolyard was belly-laughing at him.

All except Lou, who just sat there with her arms crossed pretending to ignore this spectacle. Then she broke out into a smile so wide it threatened to block the sun. When Billy stood, so did she. Oz pushed the biscuit into his mouth, gulped down the rest of the water, and scooted to safety behind the walnut tree. Fists cocked, Lou and Billy met in the very center of the schoolyard. The crowd closed around them, and Yankee girl and mountain boy went for round two.

Lou, the other side of her lip cut this time, sat at her desk. She stuck her tongue out at Billy, who sat across from her, his shirt torn and his right eye a nice purplish black. Estelle McCoy stood in front of them, arms crossed, a scowl on her face. Right after stopping the

championship bout, the angry teacher had ended school
early and sent word to the fighters' respective families.

Lou was in high spirits, for she had clearly licked
Billy again in front of everybody. He didn't look too
comfortable, though, fidgeting in his chair and glancing nervously at the door. Lou finally understood his
anxiety when the schoolhouse door crashed open and
George Davis stood there.

"What in the hell's going on here?" he roared loud
enough to make even Estelle McCoy cower.

As he stalked forward, the teacher drew back. "Billy
was in a fight, George," Mrs. McCoy said.

"You called me in here on 'count of a damn fight?"
he snarled at her, and then towered menacingly over
Billy. "I were out in the field, you little bastard, ain't got
time for this crap." When George saw Lou, his wild
eyes grew even more wicked, and then the man threw
a backhand that caught Billy on the side of his head
and knocked him to the floor.

Father stood over the fallen son. "You let a damn girl
do that to you?"

"George Davis!" Estelle McCoy cried out. "You let
your son be."

He held up a menacing hand to her. "Now on, boy
works the farm. No more this damn school."

"Why don't you let Billy decide that?"

Louisa said this as she walked into the room, Oz following closely behind her clutching at the woman's pants
leg.

"Louisa," the teacher said with great relief.

Davis stood his ground. "He a boy, he damn well do what I say."

Louisa helped Billy into his seat and comforted him, before turning to the father. "You see a boy? I see me a fine young man."

Davis snorted. "He ain't no growed man."

Louisa took a step toward him and spoke in a quiet voice, but her look was so fierce Lou forgot to breathe. "But *you* are. So don't you never hit him agin."

Davis pointed right in her face with a nail-less finger. "Don't you go telling me how to handle my boy. You had yourself one child. Had me nine, 'nuther on the way."

"Number of children fathered got little enough to do with being a good daddy."

"You got that big nigger Hell No livin' with you. God'll strike you down for that. Must be that Cherokee blood. You don't belong here. Never did, Injun woman."

A stunned Lou looked at Louisa. Yankee. And Indian.

"His name is Eugene," said Louisa. "And my daddy were part Apache, not Cherokee. And the God I know punishes the wicked. Like men who beat their children." Louisa took one more step forward. "You ever lay a hand on that child agin, best pray to whatever god *you* counsel with I ain't find you."

Davis laughed nastily. "You scaring me, old woman."

"Then you smarter than I thought."

Davis's hand curled to a fist and he looked ready to

swing until he saw big Eugene filling the doorway, and his courage seemed to peter away.

Davis grabbed Billy. "Boy, you git on home. Git!" Billy raced out of the room. Davis followed slowly, taking his time. He looked back at Louisa. "This ain't over. No sir." He banged the door shut on his way out.

CHAPTER TWENTY-TWO

SCHOOL HAD ENDED FOR THE YEAR, AND THE hard work of farming had begun. Each day Louisa rose particularly early, before the night even seemed to have settled in, and made Lou get up too. The girl did both her and Oz's chores as punishment for fighting with Billy, and then they all spent the day working the fields. They ate simple lunches and drank cold springwater under the shade of a cucumber magnolia, none of them saying much, the sweat seeping through their clothes. During these breaks Oz threw rocks so far the others would smile and clap their hands. He was growing taller, the muscles in his arms and shoulders becoming more and more pronounced, the hard work fashioning in him a lean, hard strength. As it did in his sister. As it seemed to in most who struggled to survive here.

The days were warm enough now that Oz wore only his overalls and no shirt or shoes. Lou had on overalls and was barefoot as well, but she wore an old cotton undershirt. The sun was intense at this elevation and they were becoming blonder and darker every day.

Louisa kept teaching the children things: She explained how blue lake beans have no strings, but pole beans, grown around the cornstalks, do, and they'll choke you if you don't first string them. And that they could raise most of their crop seed, except for oats, which required machinery to thresh them, machinery that simple mountain farmers would never have. And how to wash the clothes using the washboard and just enough soap made from lye and pig fat—but not too much—keeping the fire hot, rinsing the clothes properly, and adding bluing on the third rinse to get everything good and white. And then at night, by firelight, how to darn with needle and thread. Louisa even talked of when would be a good time for Lou and Oz to learn the fine arts of mule shoeing and quilting by frame.

Louisa also finally found time to teach Lou and Oz to ride Sue the mare. Eugene would hoist them, by turns, up on the mare, bareback, without even a blanket.

"Where's the saddle?" Lou asked. "And the stirrups?"

"Your saddle's your rump. A pair of strong legs your stirrups," Louisa answered.

Lou sat up on Sue while Louisa stood beside the mare.

"Now, Lou, hold the reins in your right hand like I done showed you, like you mean it now!" said Louisa.

"Sue'll let you get by with some, but you got to let her know who's boss."

Lou flicked the reins, prodded the horse's sides, generally kicked up a good row, and Sue remained absolutely motionless, as though she were sound asleep.

"Dumb horse," Lou finally declared.

"Eugene," Louisa called out to the field. "Come give me a boost up, please, honey."

Eugene limped over and helped Louisa up on the horse, and she settled in behind Lou and took the reins.

"Now, the problem ain't that Sue's dumb, it's that you ain't speaking her way yet. Now, when you want Sue to go, you give her a nice punch in the middle and make a little *chk-chk* noise. To her that means go. When you want her to turn, you don't jerk on the reins, you just glide them like. To stop, a little quick tug back."

Lou did as Louisa had shown her, and Sue started moving. Lou glided the reins to the left and the horse actually went that way. She fast-tugged back on the reins and Sue came to a slow stop.

Lou broke into a big smile. "Hey, look at me. I'm riding."

From Amanda's bedroom window, Cotton leaned his head out and watched. Then he looked to the beautiful sky, and then over at Amanda in the bed.

A few minutes later, the front door opened and Cotton carried Amanda outside and put her in the rocking chair there, next to a screen of maypops that were in full bloom of leathery purple.

Oz, who was now up on Sue with his sister, looked

over, saw his mother, and almost fell off the horse. "Hey, Mom, look at me. I'm a cowboy!" Louisa stood next to the horse, staring over at Amanda. Lou finally looked, but she didn't seem very excited to see her mother outside. Cotton's gaze went from daughter to mother, and even Cotton had to admit, the woman looked pitifully out of place in the sunshine, her eyes closed, the breeze not lifting her short hair, as though even the elements had abandoned her. He carried her back inside.

It was a bright summer's morning a few days later, and Lou had just finished milking the cows and was coming out of the barn with full buckets in her arms. She stopped dead as she stared across at the fields. She ran so fast to the house that the milk splashed around her feet. She set the buckets on the porch and ran into the house, past Louisa and Eugene and down the hall yelling at the top of her lungs. She burst into her mother's room, and there was Oz sitting next to her, brushing her hair.

Lou was breathless. "It's working. It's green. Everything. The crops are coming up. Oz, go see." Oz raced out of the room so fast he forgot he only had on his underwear. Lou stood there in the middle of the room, her chest heaving, her smile wide. As her breathing calmed, Lou went over to her mother and sat down, took up a limp hand. "I just thought you'd like to know. See, we've been working really hard." Lou sat there in silence for a minute more, and then put the hand down and left, her excitement spent.

In her bedroom that night, as on so many other evenings, Louisa worked the Singer pedal sewing machine she had bought for ten dollars on installment nine years back. She wouldn't reveal to the children what she was making, and wouldn't even let them guess. Yet Lou knew it must be something for her and Oz, which made her feel even guiltier about the fight with Billy Davis.

After supper the next evening, Oz went to see his mother, and Eugene went to work on some scythes in the corncrib. Lou washed the dishes, and then sat on the front porch next to Louisa. For a while, neither ventured to talk. Lou saw a pair of titmice fly out of the barn and land on the fence. Their gray plumage and pointed crests were glorious, but the girl wasn't much interested.

"I'm sorry about the fighting," Lou said quickly, and let out a relieved breath that her apology was finally done.

Louisa stared at the two mules in the pen. "Good to know," she said, and then said no more. The sun was starting its fall and the sky was fairly clear, with not many clouds worth noting. A big crow was sky-surfing alone, catching one drift of wind and then another, like a lazily falling leaf.

Lou cupped some dirt and watched a battalion of ants trail across her hand. The honeysuckle vine was in full, scented morning glory, filling the air along with the fragrances of cinnamon rose and clove pinks, and the purple wall of maypops dutifully shaded the porch. Rambling rose had twisted itself around most of the fence posts and looked like bursts of still fire.

"George Davis is an awful man," said Lou.

Louisa leaned her back against the porch railing. "Work his children like mules and treats his mules better'n his children."

"Well, Billy didn't have to be mean to me," Lou said, and then grinned. "And it was funny to see him fall out of that tree when he saw the dead snake I put in his lunch pail."

Louisa leaned forward and looked at her curiously. "You see anythin' else in that pail?"

"Anything else? Like what?"

"Like food."

Lou appeared confused. "No, the pail was empty."

Louisa slowly nodded, settled back against the railing once more, and looked to the west, where the sun was commencing its creep behind the mountains, kindling the sky pink and red.

Louisa said, "You know what I find funny? That children believe they should be shamed 'cause their daddy don't see fit to give them food. So shamed they'd haul an empty pail to school and pretend to eat, so's nobody catch on they ain't got nothing to eat. You find that funny?"

Lou shook her head, her gaze at her feet. "No."

"I know I ain't talked to you 'bout your daddy. But my heart goes out to you and Oz, and I love both of you even more, on 'count of I want to make up for that loss, even though I know I can't." She put a hand on Lou's shoulder and turned the girl to her. "But you had a fine daddy. A man who loved you. And I know that makes it all the harder to get by, and that's both a blessing and a curse that we all just got to bear in this life. But thing is, Billy Davis got to live with his daddy ever day. I'd ruther be in your shoes. And I know Billy Davis would. I pray for all them children ever day. And you should too."

CHAPTER TWENTY-THREE

THE GRANDMOTHER CLOCK HAD JUST struck midnight when the pebbles hit Lou's window. The girl was in the middle of a dream that disintegrated under the sudden clatter. Lou stepped to the window and looked out, seeing nothing at first. Then she spotted her caller and opened the window.

"What do you think you're doing, Diamond Skinner?"

"Come get you," said the boy, standing there next to his faithful hound.

"For what?"

In answer he pointed at the moon. It glowed more brightly than Lou had ever seen before. So fine was her view, she could see dark smudges on its surface.

"I can see the moon all by myself, thank you very much," she said.

Diamond smiled. "Naw, not just that. Fetch your

brother. Come on, now, it be fun where we going. You see."

Lou looked unsure. "How far is it?"

"Not fer. Ain't scared of the dark, are ya?"

"Wait right there," she said and shut the window.

In five minutes' time Lou and Oz were fully dressed and had crept out of the farmhouse and joined Diamond and Jeb.

Lou yawned. "This better be good, Diamond, or *you* should be scared for waking us up."

They set out at a good pace to the south. Diamond kept up an animated chatter the whole way, yet absolutely refused to divulge where they were going. Lou finally quit trying and looked at the boy's bare feet as he stepped easily over some sharp-edged rocks. She and Oz were wearing their shoes.

"Diamond, don't your feet ever get sore or cold?" she asked as they paused on a small knoll to catch their breath.

"Snow comes, then mebbe y'all see something on my feet, but only if it drifts to more'n ten foot or so. Come on now."

They set off again, and twenty minutes later, Lou and Oz could hear the quickened rush of water. A minute later Diamond put up his hand and they all stopped. "Got to go real slow here," he said. They followed him closely as they moved over rocks that were becoming more slippery with each step; and the sound of the rushing water seemed to be coming at them from all quarters, as though they were about to be confronted by a tidal wave. Lou gripped Oz's hand for it was all a little unnerving to her, and thus she assumed her brother must be suffering stark terror. They cleared a stand of towering birch and weeping willow heavy with water, and Lou and Oz looked up in awe.

The waterfall was almost one hundred feet high. It poured out from a crop of worn limestone and plummeted straight down into a pool of foamy water, which then snaked off into the darkness. And then Lou suddenly realized what Diamond had meant about the moon. It glowed so brightly, and the waterfall and pool were placed so perfectly, that the trio were surrounded by a sea of illumination. The reflected light was so strong, in fact, that night seemed to have been turned into day.

They moved back farther, to a place where they could still see everything but the noise of the falls wasn't as intense and they could speak without having to shout over the thunder of the water.

"Feeder line for the McCloud River is all," said Diamond. "Right higher'n most though."

"It looks like it's snowing upwards," said Lou, as she sat, amazed, upon a moss-covered rock. And with the frothing water kicking high and then seized by the powerful light, it did look like snow was somehow returning to the sky. At one corner of the pool the water was especially brilliant. They gathered at this place.

Diamond said very solemnly, "Right there's where God done touched the earth."

Lou leaned forward and examined the spot closely. She turned to Diamond and said, "Phosphorus."

"What?" he said.

"I think it's phosphorus rock. I've studied it in school."

"Say that word agin," said Diamond.

And she did, and Diamond said it over and over until it slipped quite easily out of his mouth. He proclaimed it a grand and pleasing word to say, yet still defined it as a thing God had touched, and Lou did not have the heart to say otherwise.

Oz leaned forward and dipped his hand into the pool, then pulled it back immediately and shivered.

"Always that way," said Diamond, "even on the hottest durn day." He looked around, a smile on his lips. "But it sure purty."

"Thanks for bringing us," said Lou.

"Tote all my friends here," he said amiably and then looked to the sky. "Hey, y'all knowed your stars good?"

"Some of them," Lou said. "The Big Dipper, and Pegasus."

"Ain't never heard'a none of them." Diamond pointed to the northern sky. "Turn your head a little and right there's what I call the bear what missing one leg. And over to there's the stone chimbly. And right there"—he stabbed his finger more to the south—"now right there is Jesus a'sitting next to God. Only God ain't there, 'cause he off doing good. 'Cause he God. But you see the chair." He looked back at them. "Ain'tcha' now? See it?"

Oz said that he could see them all, clear as day though it was night. Lou hesitated, wondering whether it was better to instruct Diamond on proper constellations or not. She finally smiled. "You know a lot more about stars than we do, Diamond. Now that you pointed them out, I can see them all too."

Diamond grinned big. "Well, up here on the mountain, we a lot closer to 'em than down to the city. Don't worry, I teach you good."

They spent a pleasant hour there and then Lou thought it would be best if they got back.

They were about halfway home when Jeb started growling and making slow circles in the tall grass, his snout wrinkled and his teeth bared.

"What's wrong with him, Diamond?" asked Lou.

"Just smells something. Lotta critters round. Don't pay him no mind."

Suddenly Jeb took off running hard and howling so loud it hurt their ears.

"Jeb!" Diamond called after him. "You come back here now." The dog never slowed, though, and they finally saw why. The black bear was moving in long strides across the far fringe of the meadow.

"Dang it, Jeb, leave that bear be." Diamond raced after the dog, and Lou and Oz ran after Diamond. But dog and bear soon left the two-legs in the dust. Diamond finally stopped, gasping for air, and Lou and Oz ran up to him and fell on the ground, their lungs near bursting.

Diamond smacked his fist into his palm. "Dang that dog."

"Will that bear hurt him?" asked Oz anxiously.

"Shoot, naw. Jeb pro'bly tree the durn thing and then

get tired and go on home." Diamond didn't look convinced though. "Come on now."

They walked briskly for some minutes, until Diamond slowed, looked around, and held up his hand for them to stop. He turned, put a finger to his lips, and motioned for them to follow, but to keep low. They scooted along for about thirty feet, and then Diamond went down on his belly and Lou and Oz did too. They crawled forward and were soon on the rim of a little hollow. It was surrounded by trees and underbrush, the limbs and vines overhanging the place and forming a natural roof, but the shafts of moonlight had broken through in places, leaving the space well illuminated.

"What is it?" Lou wanted to know.

"Shh," Diamond said, and then cupped his hand around her ear and whispered. "Man's still."

Lou looked again, and picked up on the bulky contraption with its big metal belly, copper tubing, and wooden block legs. Jugs to be filled with the corn whiskey sat on boards placed over stacked stone. A lit kerosene lamp was hooked to a slender post thrust into the moist ground. Steam rose from the still. They heard movement.

Lou flinched as George Davis appeared next to the still and flopped down a forty-pound burlap bag. The man was intent on his work and apparently never heard them. Lou looked at Oz, who was shaking so hard Lou was afraid George Davis might feel the ground vibrating. She tugged at Diamond and pointed to where they had come from. Diamond nodded in agreement and they began to slither backward. Lou glanced back at the still, but Davis had disappeared. She froze. And then she nearly screamed because she heard something coming and feared the worst.

The bear flashed by her line of sight first and into the hollow. Then came Jeb. The bear cut a sharp corner, and the dog skidded into the post holding the lamp and knocked it over. The lamp hit the ground and smashed. The bear careened into the still, and metal gave way under three hundred pounds of black bear and fell over, breaking open and tearing loose the copper tubing. Diamond raced into the hollow, yelling at his dog.

The bear apparently was weary of being chased and turned and rose up on its hind legs, its claws and teeth now quite prominent. Jeb stopped dead at the sight of the six-foot black wall that could bite him in half, and backed up, growling. Diamond reached the hound and pulled at his neck.

"Jeb, you fool thing!"

"Diamond!" Lou called out as she too jumped up and saw the man coming at her friend.

"What the hell!" Davis had emerged from the darkness, shotgun in hand.

"Diamond, look out!" screamed Lou again.

The bear roared, the dog barked, Diamond hollered, and Davis pointed his shotgun and swore. The gun fired twice, and bear, dog, and boy took off running like the holy hell. Lou ducked as the buckshot tore through leaves and imbedded in bark. "Run, Oz, run," screamed

Lou. Oz jumped up and ran, but the boy was confused, for he headed into the hollow instead of away from it. Davis was reloading his shotgun when Oz came upon him. The boy realized his mistake too late, and Davis snagged him by the collar. Lou ran toward them. "Diamond!" screamed Lou once more. "Help!"

Davis had Oz pinned against his leg with one hand and was trying to reload his gun with the other.

"Gawd damn you," the man thundered at the cowering boy.

Lou flung her fists into him but didn't do any damage, for though he was short, George Davis was hard as brick.

"You let him go," Lou yelled. "Let him go!"

Davis did let go of Oz, but only so he could strike Lou. She crumpled to the ground, her mouth bleeding. But the man never saw Diamond. The boy picked up the fallen post, swung it, and clipped Davis's legs out from under him, sending the man down hard. Then Diamond conked Davis on the head with the post for good measure. Lou grabbed Oz, and Diamond grabbed Lou, and the three were more than fifty yards from the hollow by the time George Davis regained his legs in a lathered fury. A few seconds after that, they heard one more shotgun blast, but they were well out of range by then.

They heard running behind them and picked up their pace. Then Diamond looked back and said that it was okay, it was only Jeb. They ran all the way back to the farmhouse, where they collapsed on the front porch, their breathing tortured, their limbs shaking from both fatigue and fright.

When they sat up, Lou considered taking up the run once more because Louisa was standing there in her nightdress looking at them and holding a kerosene lamp. She wanted to know where they'd been. Diamond tried to answer for them, but Louisa told him to hush in a tone so sharp it struck the always chatty Diamond mute.

"The truth, Lou," ordered the woman.

And Lou told her, including the almost deadly run-in with George Davis. "But it wasn't our fault," she said. "That bear—"

Louisa snapped, "Get yourself to the barn, Diamond. And take that dang dog with you."

"Yes'm," said Diamond, and he and Jeb slunk away.

Louisa turned back to Lou and Oz. Lou could see she was trembling. "Oz, you get yourself to bed. Right now."

Oz glanced once at Lou and fled inside. And then it was just Lou and Louisa.

Lou stood there as nervous as she had ever been.

"You could'a got yourself kilt tonight. Worse'n that you could'a got you *and* your brother kilt."

"But, Louisa, it wasn't our fault. You see—"

"Is your fault!" Louisa said fiercely, and Lou felt the tears rush to her eyes at the woman's tone.

"I didn't have you come to this mountain to die at the sorry hands of George Davis, girl. You gone off on your own bad enough. But taking your little brother too—and he follow you cross *fire,* not knowing no better—I'm ashamed of you!"

Lou bowed her head. "I'm sorry. I'm really sorry."

Louisa stood very erect. "I ain't never raised my hand to a child, though my patience run sore over the years. But if you ever do somethin' like that agin, you gonna find my hand 'cross your skin, missy, and it be somethin' you ain't never forget. You unnerstand me?" Lou nodded dumbly. "Then get to bed," said Louisa. "And we speak no more of it."

✿

The next morning George Davis rode up on his wagon pulled by a pair of mules. Louisa came outside to face him, her hands behind her back.

Davis spit chew onto the ground next to the wagon wheel. "Them devils broke up my propity. Here to get paid."

"You mean for busting up your *still*."

Lou and Oz came outside and stared at the man.

"Devils!" he roared. "Gawd damn you!"

Louisa stepped off the porch. "If you gonna talk that way, git yourself off my land. Now!"

"I want my money! And I want them beat bad for what they done!"

"You fetch the sheriff and go show him what they done to your still, and then *he* can tell me what's fair."

Davis stared at her dumbly, the mule whip clenched in one hand. "You knowed I can't do that, woman."

"Then you know the way off my land, George."

"How 'bout I put the torch to your farm?"

Eugene came outside, a long stick in his big hand.

Davis held up the whip. "Hell No, you keep your nigger self right there afore I put the whip to you just like your granddaddy had 'cross his back!" Davis started to get down from the wagon. "Mebbe I'll just do it anyway, boy. Mebbe all'a you!"

Louisa pulled the rifle from behind her back and leveled it at George Davis. The man stopped halfway off his wagon when he saw the Winchester's long barrel pointed at him.

"Get off my land," Louisa said quietly, as she cocked the weapon and rested its butt against her shoulder, her finger on the trigger. "Afore I lose my patience, and you lose some blood."

"I pay you, George Davis," Diamond called out as he came out of the barn, Jeb trailing him.

Davis visibly shook, he was so angry. "My damn head's still ringing from where you done walloped me, boy."

"You durn lucky then, 'cause I could'a hit you a lot harder if'n I wanted to."

"Don't you smartmouth me!" Davis roared.

"You want'a git your money or not?" said Diamond.

"What you got? You ain't got nuthin'."

Diamond put his hand in his pocket and drew out a coin. "Got me this. Silver dollar."

"Dollar! You wreck my still, boy. Think a damn dollar gonna fix that? Fool!"

"It done come from my great-granddaddy five times

removed. A hunnerd year old it is. Man down Tremont say he gimme twenty dollar for it."

Davis's eyes lighted up at this. "Lemme see it."

"Naw. Take it or leave it. I telling the truth. Twenty dollar. Man named Monroe Darcy. He run the store down Tremont. You knowed him."

Davis was silent for a bit. "Gimme it."

"Diamond," Lou called out, "don't do it."

"Man got to pay his debts," said Diamond. He sauntered over to the wagon. When Davis reached out for the coin, Diamond pulled it back. "Look here, George Davis, this means we square. You ain't coming round to Miss Louisa for nuthin' if'n I give you this. You got to swear."

Davis looked like he might put the whip to Diamond's back instead, but he said, "I swear. Now gimme it!"

Diamond flipped the coin to Davis, who caught it, studied it, bit on it, and then stashed it in his pocket.

"Now git yourself gone, George," said Louisa.

Davis glared at her. "Next time, *my* gun don't miss."

He turned mules and wagon around and left in a whirl of dust. Lou stared at Louisa, who held the rifle on Davis until the man was out of sight. "Would you really have shot him?" she asked.

Louisa uncocked the rifle and went inside without answering the question.

CHAPTER TWENTY-FOUR

LOU WAS CLEANING UP THE SUPPER DISHES two nights later while Oz carefully wrote out his letters on a piece of paper at the kitchen table. Louisa sat next to him, helping. She looked tired, Lou thought. She was old, and life up here wasn't easy; Lou had certainly experienced that first-hand. One had to fight for each little thing. And Louisa had been doing this all her life. How much longer could she?

By the time Lou had dried the last plate, there came a knock on the door. Oz ran to open it.

Cotton was standing at the front door, wearing his suit and tie, a large box cradled in his arms. Behind him was Diamond. The boy was dressed in a clean white shirt, face scrubbed, hair pounded down with water and maybe sticky sap, and Lou almost gasped, because the boy was wearing *shoes*. It was true she could see his toes, but still most of the boy's feet were covered. Diamond nodded shyly to all, as though being scrubbed and shod made him a circus spectacle of sorts.

Oz eyed the box. "What's in there?"

Cotton set the box on the table and took his time opening it. "While there is much to be said for the written word," he told them, "we must never forget that other great creative body of work." With a flourish to rival the best of vaudeville performances, he unveiled the gramophone.

"Music!"

Cotton took a record out of a slipcase and carefully placed it on the gramophone. Then he vigorously turned the crank and set the needle in place. It scratched the wobbly record for a moment, and then the room was filled with what Lou recognized as the music of Beethoven. Cotton looked around the room and then moved a chair against the wall. He motioned to the other men. "Gentlemen, if you please." Oz, Diamond, and Eugene pitched in, and they soon had an open space in the middle of the room.

Cotton went down the hallway and opened Amanda's door. "Miss Amanda, we have a variety of popular tunes for your listening pleasure tonight."

Cotton came back to the front room.

"Why did you move the furniture?" Lou asked.

Cotton smiled and removed his suit coat. "Because you can't simply listen to music, you must become one with it." He bowed deeply to Lou. "May I have this dance, ma'am?"

Lou found herself blushing at this formal invitation. "Cotton, you're crazy, you really are."

Oz said, "Go ahead, Lou, you're a good dancer." He added, "Mom taught her."

And they danced. Awkwardly at first, but then they picked up their pace and soon were spinning around the room. All smiled at the pair, and Lou found herself giggling.

Overcome with excitement, as he so often was, Oz ran to his mother's room. "Mom, we're dancing, we're dancing." And then he raced back to see some more.

Louisa was moving her hands to the music, and her foot was tapping against the floor. Diamond came up.

"Care to stroll the floor, Miss Louisa?"

She took his hands. "Best offer I had me in years."

As they joined Lou and Cotton, Eugene stood Oz on the tops of his shoes, and they clomped around with the others.

The music and laughter drifted down the hall and into Amanda's room. Since they had been here, winter had turned to spring and spring had given way to summer. And during all that time, Amanda's condition had not changed. Lou interpreted that as positive proof that her mother would never rejoin them, while Oz, ever the optimist, saw it as a good thing, because his mother's condition had not become any worse. Despite her bleak opinion of her mother's future, Lou helped Louisa sponge-bathe Amanda every day and also wash her hair once a week. And both Lou and Oz changed their mother's resting positions frequently and exercised her arms and legs daily. Yet there was never any reaction from their mother; she was just there, eyes closed, limbs motionless. She was not "dead," but what her mother was could surely not be called "living" either, Lou had often thought. However, something was a little odd now with the music and laughter filtering into her room. Perhaps if it was possible to smile without moving one facial muscle, Amanda Cardinal had just accomplished it.

Back in the front room a few records later, the music had changed to tunes designed to make one kick up his heels. The partners had also changed: Lou and Diamond jumped and spun with youthful energy; Cotton twirled Oz; and Eugene—bad leg and all—and Louisa were doing a modest jitterbug.

Cotton left the dance floor after a while and went to Amanda's bedroom and sat next to her. He spoke to her very quietly, relaying news of the day, how the children were doing, the next book he intended to read to her. All just normal conversation, really, and Cotton hoping that she could hear him and be encouraged by it. "I have enjoyed the letters you wrote to Louisa immensely. Your words show a beautiful spirit. However, I look forward to getting to know you personally, Amanda." He took her hands very gently and moved them slowly to the music.

The sounds drifted outside, and the light spilled into the darkness. For one stolen moment, all in the house seemed happy and secure.

※

The small coal mine on Louisa's land was about two miles from the house. There was a matted-down path leading to it, and that connected with a dirt road that snaked back to the farm. The opening of the mine was broad and tall enough for sled and mule to enter easily, which they did each year to bring out coal for the winter's heat. With the moon now shielded by high clouds, the entrance to the mine was invisible to the naked eye.

Off in the distance there was a wink of light, like a firefly. Then came another flash and then another. Slowly the group of men emerged from the darkness and came toward the mine, the blinks of light now revealed as lit kerosene lamps. The men wore hard hats with carbide lamps strapped to them. In preparation for entering the mine, each man took off his hat, filled the lamp pouch with moistened carbide pellets, turned the handle, which adjusted the wick, struck a match, and a dozen lamps together ignited.

A man bigger than all the others called the workers around, and they formed a tight huddle. His name was Judd Wheeler, and he had been exploring dirt and rock looking for things of value most of his adult life. In one big hand he held a long roll of paper which he spread open, and one of the men shone a lantern upon it. The paper held detailed markings, writing and drawings. The caption on the paper was printed boldly across the top: "Southern Valley Coal and Gas Geological Survey."

As Wheeler instructed his men on tonight's duties, from out of the darkness another man joined them. He wore the same felt hat and old clothes. George Davis also held a kerosene lamp and appeared quite excited at all the activity. Davis spoke animatedly with Wheeler for a few minutes, and then they all headed inside the mine.

CHAPTER TWENTY-FIVE

LOU WOKE EARLY THE NEXT MORNING. THE sounds of music had stayed with her through the night, and her dreams had been pleasant ones. She stretched, gingerly touched the floor, and went to look out the window. The sun had already begun its rise and she knew she had to get to the barn to milk, a task she had rapidly taken as her own, for she had grown to like the coolness of the barn in the morning, and also the smell of the cows and the hay. She would sometimes climb to the loft, push open the hay doors, and sit on the edge there, gazing out at the land from her high perch, listening to the sounds of birds and small animals darting through trees, crop field, and high grass and catching the breeze that always seemed to be there.

This was just such another morning of flaming skies, brooding mountains, the playful lift of birds, the efficient business of animals, trees, and flowers. However,

Lou was not prepared for the sight of Diamond and Jeb slipping out of the barn and heading off down the road.

Lou dressed quickly and went downstairs. Louisa had food on the table, though Oz had not yet appeared.

"That was fun last night," Lou said, sitting at the table.

"You prob'ly laugh now, but when I's younger, I could do me some stompin'," remarked Louisa, as she put a biscuit covered with gravy and a glass of milk on the table for Lou.

"Diamond must have slept in the barn," said Lou as she bit into her biscuit. "Don't his parents worry about him?" She gave Louisa a sideways glance and added, "Or I guess I should be asking if he has any parents."

Louisa sighed and then stared at Lou. "His mother passed when he was born. Happen right often up here. Too often. His daddy joined her four year ago."

Lou put down her biscuit. "How did his father die?"

"No business of ours, Lou."

"Does this have anything to do with what Diamond did to that man's car?"

Louisa sat and tapped her fingers against the table.

"Please, Louisa, please. I really want to know. I care about Diamond. He's my friend."

"Blasting at one of the mines," Louisa said bluntly. "Took down a hillside. A hillside Donovan Skinner was farming."

"Who does Diamond live with then?"

"He a wild bird. Put him in a cage, he just shrivel up and die. He need anythin', he know to come to me."

"Did the coal company have to pay for what happened?"

Louisa shook her head. "Played legal tricks. Cotton tried to help but weren't much he could do. Southern Valley's a powerful force hereabouts."

"Poor Diamond."

"Boy sure didn't take it lying down," Louisa said. "One time the wheels of a motorman's car fell off when it come out the mine. And then a coal tipple wouldn't open and they had to send for some people from Roanoke. Found a rock stuck in the gears. That same coal mine boss, he was in an outhouse one time got tipped over. Durn door wouldn't open, and he spent a sorry hour in there. To this day nobody ever figgered out who tipped it over or how that rope got round it."

"Did Diamond ever get in trouble?"

"Henry Atkins the judge. He a good man, know what was what, so's nothing ever come of it. But Cotton kept talking to Diamond, and the mischief finally quit." She paused. "Least it did till the horse manure got in that man's car."

Louisa turned away, but Lou had already seen the woman's broad smile.

Lou and Oz rode Sue every day and had gotten to the point where Louisa had proclaimed them good, competent riders. Lou loved riding Sue. She could see forever, it seemed, from that high perch, the mare's body wide enough that falling off seemed impossible.

After morning chores, they would go swimming with Diamond at Scott's Hole, a patch of water Diamond had introduced them to, and which he claimed had no bottom. As the summer went along Lou and Oz became dark brown, while Diamond simply grew larger freckles.

Eugene came with them as often as he could, and Lou was surprised to learn he was only twenty-one. He did not know how to swim, but the children remedied that, and Eugene was soon performing different strokes, and even flips, in the cool water, his bad leg not holding him back any in that environment.

They played baseball in a field of bluegrass they had scythed. Eugene had fashioned a bat from an oak plank shaved narrow at one end. They used Diamond's coverless ball and another made from a bit of rubber wound round with sheep's wool and knitted twine. The bases were pieces of shale set in a straight line, this being the proper way according to Diamond, who termed it straight-town baseball. New York Yankees' fan Lou said nothing about this, and let the boy have his fun. It got so that none of them, not even Eugene, could hit a ball that Oz threw, so fast and tricky did it come.

They spent many afternoons running through the adventures of the Wizard of Oz, making up parts they had forgotten, or which they thought, with youthful confidence, could be improved upon. Diamond was quite partial to the Scarecrow; Oz, of course, had to be the cowardly lion; and, by default, Lou was the heartless tin man. They unanimously proclaimed Eugene the Great and Mighty Wizard, and he would come out from behind a rock and bellow out lines they had taught him so loud and with such a depth of feigned anger that Oz, the Cowardly Lion, asked Eugene, the Mighty Wizard, if he could please tone it down a bit. They fought many pitched battles against flying monkeys and melting witches, and with a little ingenuity and some luck at just the right moments, good always triumphed over evil on the glorious Virginia mountain.

Diamond told them of how in the winter he would skate on the top of Scott's Hole. And how using a short-handled ax he would cleave off a strip of bark from an oak and use that as his sled to go sailing down the iced slopes of the mountains at speeds never before achieved by a human being. He said he would be glad to show them how he did it, but would have to swear them to secrecy, lest the wrong sort of folks found out and maybe took over the world with such valuable knowledge.

Lou did not once let on that she knew about Diamond's parents. After hours of fun, they would say their good-byes and Lou and Oz would ride home on Sue or take turns with Eugene when he came with them. Diamond would stay behind and swim some more or hit the ball, doing, as he often said, just as he pleased.

On the ride back home after one of these outings, Lou decided to take a different way. A fine mist hung over the mountains as she and Oz approached the farmhouse from the rear. They cleared a rise, and on top of a little knoll about a half-mile from the house, Lou reined Sue to a halt. Oz squirmed behind her.

"Come on, Lou, we need to get back. We've got chores."

Instead, the girl clambered off Sue, leaving Oz to grab at the reins, which almost made him fall off the animal. He called crossly after her, but she seemed not to hear.

Lou went over to the little cleared space under the dense shade of an evergreen and knelt down. The grave markers were simple pieces of wood grayed by the weather. And clearly much time had passed. Lou read the names of the dead and the bracket dates of their existence, which were carved deeply into the wood and were probably about as distinct as the day they were chiseled.

The first name was Joshua Cardinal. The date of his birth and death made Lou believe that he must have been Louisa's husband, Lou and Oz's great-grandfather. He had passed in his fifty-second year—not that long of a life, Lou thought. The second grave marker was a name that Lou knew from her father. Jacob Cardinal was her father's father, her and Oz's grandfather. As she recited the name, Oz joined her and knelt down in the grass. He pulled off his straw hat and said nothing. Their grandfather had died far younger than even his father. Was there something about this place? Lou wondered. But then she thought of how old Louisa was, and the wondering stopped there.

The third grave marker looked to be the oldest. It only had a name on it, no dates of birth or death.

"Annie Cardinal," Lou said out loud. For a time the two just knelt there and stared at the pieces of board marking the remains of family they had never known. Then Lou rose, went over to Sue, gripped the horse's brushy mane, climbed up, and then helped Oz on board. Neither spoke all the way back.

At supper that night, more than once Lou was about to venture a question to Louisa about what they had seen, but then something made her not. Oz was obviously just as curious, yet, like always, he was inclined to follow his sister's lead. They had time, Lou figured, for all of their questions to be answered. Before she went to sleep that night, Lou went out on the back porch and looked up to that knoll. Even with a nice slice of moon she could not see the graveyard from here, yet now she knew where it was. She had never much been interested in the dead, particularly since losing her father. Now she knew that she would go back soon to that burying ground and look once more at those bits of plain board set in dirt and engraved with the names of her flesh and blood.

CHAPTER TWENTY-SIX

COTTON SHOWED UP WITH DIAMOND A WEEK later and handed out small American flags to Lou, Oz, and Eugene. He had also brought a five-gallon can of gas, which he put in the Hudson's fuel tank. "We all can't fit in the Olds," he explained. "And I handled an estate problem for Leroy Meekins who runs the Esso station. Leroy doesn't like to pay in cash, though, so one could say I'm flush with oil products right now."

With Eugene driving, the five went down to Dickens to watch the parade. Louisa stayed behind to keep watch over Amanda, but they promised to bring her back something.

They ate hot dogs with great splotches of mustard and ketchup, swirls of cotton candy, and enough soda pop to make the children run to the public toilet with great frequency. There were contests of skill at booths set up wherever space was available, and Oz cleaned up on all those that involved throwing something in order to knock something else down. Lou bought a pretty bonnet for Louisa, which she let Oz carry in a paper bag.

The town was done up in red, white, and blue, and both townfolk and those from the mountain lined both sides of the street as the floats came down. These barges on land were pulled by horse, mule, or truck and displayed the most important moments in America's history, which, to most native Virginians, had naturally all occurred in the Commonwealth. There was a group of children on one such float representing the original thirteen colonies, with one boy carrying the Virginia colors, which were far bigger than the flags the other children carried, and he wore the showiest costume as well. A regiment of decorated war veterans from the area trooped by, including several men with long beards and shriveled bodies who claimed to have served with both the honorable Bobby Lee and the fanatically pious Stonewall Jackson.

One float, sponsored by Southern Valley, was devoted to the mining of coal and was pulled by a customized Chevrolet truck painted gold. There wasn't a black-faced, wrecked-back miner in sight, but instead, smack in the center of the float, on a raised platform simulating a coal tipple, stood a pretty young woman with blond hair, a perfect complexion, and brilliant white teeth, wearing a sash that read "Miss Bituminous Coal 1940" and waving her hand as mechanically as a windup doll. Even the most dense in the crowd could probably grasp the implied connection between lumps of black rock and the pot of gold pulling it. And the men and boys gave the expected reaction of cheers and some catcalls to the passing beauty. There was one old and humpbacked woman standing next to Lou who told her that her husband and three sons all labored in the mines. The old woman watched the beauty queen with scornful eyes and then commented that that young gal had obviously never been near a coal mine in her entire life. And she wouldn't know a lump of coal if it jumped up and grabbed her in the bituminous.

High-ranking representatives of the town made important speeches, motivating the citizens into bursts of enthusiastic applause. The mayor held forth from a temporary stage, with smiling, expensively dressed men next to him, who, Cotton told Lou, were Southern Valley officials. The mayor was young and energetic, with slicked hair, wearing a nice suit and fashionable watch and chain, and carrying boundless enthusiasm in his beaming smile and hands reaching to the sky, as though ready to snag on any rainbows trying to slip by.

"Coal is king," the mayor announced into a clunky microphone almost as big as his head. "And what with the war heating up across the Atlantic and the mighty United States of America building ships and guns and tanks for our friends fighting Hitler, the steel mill's demands for coke, our good, patriotic Virginia coke, will skyrocket. And some say it won't be long before we join the fighting. Yes, prosperity is here in fine abundance and here it will stay," said the mayor. "Not only will our children live the glorious American dream, but their children will as well. And it will be all due to the good work of folks like Southern Valley and their unrelenting drive to bring out the black rock that is driving this town to greatness. Rest assured, folks, we will become the New York City of the south. One day some will look back and say, 'Who knew the outstanding things that destiny held for the likes of Dickens, Virginia?' But y'all already know, because I'm telling you right now. Hip-hip hooray for Southern Valley and Dickens, Virginia." And the exuberant mayor threw his straw boater hat high into the air. And the crowd joined him in the cheer, and more hats were catapulted into the swirling breeze. And though Diamond, Lou, Oz, Eugene, and Cotton all applauded too, and the children grinned happily at each other, Lou noticed that Cotton's expression wasn't one of unbridled optimism.

As night fell, they watched a display of fireworks color the sky, and then the group climbed in the Hudson and headed out of town. They had just passed the courthouse when Lou asked Cotton about the mayor's speech and his muted reaction to it.

"Well, I've seen this town go boom and bust before," he said. "And it usually happens when the politicians and the business types are cheering the loudest. So I just don't know. Maybe it'll be different this time, but I just don't know."

Lou was left to ponder this while the cheers of the fine celebration receded and then those sounds were gone entirely, replaced with wind whistling through rock and tree, as they headed back up the mountain.

There had not been much rain, but Louisa wasn't worried yet, though she prayed every night for the skies to open up and bellow hard and long. They were weeding the cornfield, and it was a hot day and the flies and gnats were particularly bothersome. Lou scraped at the dirt, something just not seeming right. "We already planted the seeds. Can't they grow by themselves?"

"Lot of things go wrong in farming and one or two most always do," Louisa answered. "And the work don't never stop, Lou. Just the way it is here."

Lou swung the hoe over her shoulder. "All I can say is, this corn better taste good."

"This here's field corn," Louisa told her. "For the animals."

Lou almost dropped her hoe. "We're doing all this work to feed the animals?"

"They work hard for us, we got to do the same for them. They got to eat too."

"Yeah, Lou," said Oz as he attacked the weeds with vigorous strokes. "How can hogs get fat if they don't eat? Tell me that."

They worked the hills of corn, side by side under the fierce sun, which was so close it almost seemed to Lou that she could reach up and pocket it. The katydids and crickets scraped tunes at them from all corners. Lou stopped hoeing and watched Cotton drive up to the house and get out.

"Cotton coming every day and reading to Mom is making Oz believe that she's going to get better," said Lou to Louisa, taking care that her brother did not hear her.

Louisa wielded the hoe blade with the energy of a young person and the skill of an old. "You right, it's so terrible bad having Cotton helping your momma."

"I didn't mean it like that. I like Cotton."

Louisa stopped and leaned on her hoe. "You should, because Cotton Longfellow's a good man, none better. He's helped me through many a hard time since he come here. Not just with his lawyering, but with his strong back. When Eugene hurt his leg bad, he was here ever day for a month doing field work when he could've been in Dickens making himself good money. He's helping your ma 'cause he wants her to get better. He wants her to be able to hold you and Oz agin."

Lou said nothing to this, but was having trouble getting the hoeing down, chopping instead of slicing. Louisa took a minute to show her again, and Lou picked up the proper technique quickly.

They worked for a while longer in silence, until Louisa straightened up and rubbed at her back. "Body's telling me to slow down a bit. But my body wants to eat come winter."

Lou stared out at the countryside. The sky looked painted in oils today, and the trees seemed to fill every spare inch with alluring green.

"How come Dad never came back?" Lou asked quietly.

Louisa followed Lou's gaze. "No law say a person got to come back to his home," she said.

"But he wrote about it in all his books. I know he loved it here."

Louisa stared at the girl and then said, "Let's go get us a cool drink." She told Oz to rest some, and they would bring him back some water. He immediately dropped his hoe, picked up some rocks, and started heaving and whooping at each toss, in a manner it seemed only little boys could successfully accomplish. He had taken to placing a tin can on top of a fence post and then throwing rocks at it until he knocked it off. He had become so good that one hard toss would now send the can flying.

They left him to his fun and went to the springhouse, which clung to one side of a steep slope below the house and was shaded by leaning oak and ash trees and a wall of giant rhododendrons. Next to this shack was a split poplar stump, the tip of a large honeycomb protruding from it, a swell of bees above that.

They took metal cups from nails on the wall and dipped them in the water, and then sat outside and drank. Louisa picked up the green leaves of a mountain spurge growing next to the springhouse, which revealed beautiful purple blossoms completely hidden underneath. "One of God's little secrets," she explained. Lou sat there, cup cradled between her dimpled knees, watching and listening to her great-grandmother in the pleas-

ant shade as Louisa pointed out other things of interest. "Right there's an oriole. Don't see them much no
more. Don't know why not." She pointed to another
bird on a maple branch. "That's a chuck's-will-widder.
Don't ask me how the durn thing got its name, 'cause
I don't know." Finally, her face and tone grew serious.

"Your daddy's momma was never happy here. She
from down the Shenandoah Valley. My son Jake met
her at a cakewalk she come up for. They got married,
way too fast, put up a little cabin near here. But I know
she was all set for the city, though. The Valley was backward for her. Lord, these mountains must've seemed like
the birth of the world to the poor girl. But she had your
daddy, and for the next few years we had us the worst
drought I ever seen. The less rain there was, the harder
we worked. My boy soon lost his stake, and they moved
in with us. Still no rain. Went through our animals.
Went through durn near everything we had." Louisa
clenched her hands and then released them. "But we
still got by. And then the rains come and we fine after
that. But when your daddy was seven, his momma had
had enough of this life and she left. She ain't never
bothered to learn the farm, and even the way round a
frying pan, so's she weren't much help to Jake a'tall."

"But didn't Jake want to go with her?"

"Oh, I 'xpect he did, for she was a real purty little
thing, and a young man is a young man. They ain't 'xactly
made'a wood. But she didn't want him along, if you unnerstand me right, him being from the mountains and

all. And she didn't want her own child neither." Louisa shook her head at this painful remembrance.

"Course, Jake never got over that. Then his daddy died soon after, which didn't help matters none for any of us." Louisa smiled. "But your father were the shiny star in our days. Even with that, though, we watched a man we loved die a little more each day, and there weren't nothing we could do. Two days after your daddy was ten years old, Jake died. Some say heart attack. I say heartbreak. And then it was just me and your daddy up here. We had us good times, Lou, lot of love twixt us. But your daddy suffered a lotta pain too." She stopped and took a drink of the cool water. "But I still wonder why he never come back not once."

"Do I remind you of him?" Lou asked quietly.

Louisa smiled. "Same fire, same bullheadedness. Big heart too. Like how you are with your brother. Your daddy always made me laugh twice a day. When I got up and right afore I went to bed. He say he want me begin and end my day with a smile."

"I wish Mom had let us write you. She said she would one day, but it never happened."

"Like to knock me over with a stick when the first letter come. I wrote her back some, but my eyes ain't that good no more. And paper and stamp scarce."

Lou looked very uncomfortable. "Mom asked Dad to move back to Virginia."

Louisa looked surprised. "And what'd your daddy say?"

Lou could not tell her the truth. "I don't know."

"Oh" was all Louisa offered in response.

Lou found herself growing upset with her father, something she could never remember doing before.

"I can't believe he just left you here by yourself."

"I *made* him go. Mountain no place for somebody like him. Got to share that boy with the world. And your daddy wrote to me all these years. And he give me money he ain't got. He done right by me. Don't you never think badly of him for that."

"But didn't it hurt, that he never came back?"

Louisa put an arm around the girl. "He *did* come back. I got me the three people he loved most in the whole world."

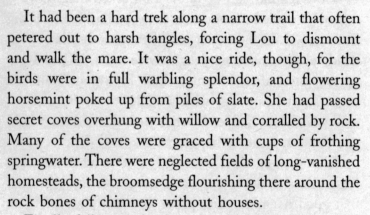

It had been a hard trek along a narrow trail that often petered out to harsh tangles, forcing Lou to dismount and walk the mare. It was a nice ride, though, for the birds were in full warbling splendor, and flowering horsemint poked up from piles of slate. She had passed secret coves overhung with willow and corralled by rock. Many of the coves were graced with cups of frothing springwater. There were neglected fields of long-vanished homesteads, the broomsedge flourishing there around the rock bones of chimneys without houses.

Finally, following the directions Louisa had given her, Lou found herself at the small house in the clearing. She looked over the property. It appeared likely that in another couple of years this homestead would also surrender to the wild that pressed against it on all sides.

Trees stretched over the roof that had almost as many holes as shingles. Window glass was missing at various spots; a sapling was growing up through an opening in the front porch, and wild sumac clung to the splintered porch rails. The front door was hanging by a single nail; in fact it had been tied back so that the door always stood open. A horseshoe was nailed over the doorway, for luck, Lou assumed, and the place looked like it could use some. The surrounding fields, too, were all overgrown. And yet the dirt yard was neatly swept, there was no trash about, and a bed of peonies sat next to the house, with a lilac behind that, and a large snowball bush flourished by a small hand-crank well. A rosebush ran up a trellis on one side of the house. Lou had heard that roses thrived on neglect. If true, this was the most ignored rosebush Lou had ever seen, since it was bent over with the weight of its deep red blooms. Jeb came around the corner and barked at rider and horse. When Diamond came out of the house, he stopped dead and looked around, seemingly for a place to hide quick, but coming up empty.

"What you doing here?" he finally said.

Lou slid off the horse and knelt to play with Jeb. "Just came to pay a visit. Where are your folks?"

"Pa working. Ma went down to McKenzie's."

"Tell 'em I said hello."

Diamond thrust his hands in his pockets, bent one bare toe over the other. "Look, I got things to do."

"Like what?" asked Lou, rising.

"Like fishing. I got to go fishing."

"Well, I'll go with you."

He cocked his head at her. "You know how to fish?"

"They have lots of fishing holes in Brooklyn."

They stood on a makeshift pier built from a few planks of rough-hewn oak not even nailed together but merely wedged into the rocks that stuck out from the bank of the wide stream. Diamond strung the line with a squirmy pink worm while Lou looked on in disgust. A tomboy was a tomboy, but apparently a worm was a worm. He handed the extra pole to her.

"G'on cast your line out there."

Lou took the pole and hesitated.

"You want hep?"

"I can do it."

"See this here's a southern pole, and I 'xpect you prob'ly used to them newfangled northern poles."

"You're right, that's all I use. Northern pole."

To his credit, Diamond never cracked a smile, but just took the pole, showed her how to hold it, and then threw a near perfect cast.

Lou watched his technique carefully, took a couple of practice tosses, and then sailed a pretty cast herself.

"Why, that was 'bout good as any I throwed," Diamond said with all due southern modesty.

"Give me a couple more minutes and I'll do better than you," she said slyly.

"You still got to catch the fish," Diamond gamely replied.

A half hour later Diamond had hooked his third smallmouth and worked it to shore with steady motions.

Lou looked at him, properly in awe of his obvious skill, but her competitive streak ran long, and she redoubled her efforts to trump her fish-mate.

Finally, without warning, her line went tight and she was pulled toward the water. With a whiplike effort, she reared the pole back, and a thick catfish came halfway out of the stream.

"Holy Lord," said Diamond as he saw this creature rise and then fall back into the water. "Biggest catfish I ever seed." He reached for the pole.

Lou cried out, "I got it, Diamond." He stepped back and watched girl and fish fighting it out on roughly equal terms. Lou appeared to be winning at first, the line going taut and then slacking, while Diamond called out words of advice and encouragement. Lou slipped and slid all over the unsteady pier, once more almost going in the water, before Diamond yanked on her overalls and pulled her back.

Finally, though, Lou grew weary and gasped out, "I need some help here, Diamond."

With both pulling on pole and line, the fish quickly was dragged to shore. Diamond reached down, hauled it out of the water, and dropped it on the boards, where it flopped from side to side. Fat and thick, it would be good eating, he said. Lou squatted down and looked proudly at her conquest, aided though it had been. Right as she peered really closely, the fish shimmied once more, then jumped in the air, and spat water, the hook working free from its mouth at the same time. Lou screamed and jumped back, knocked into Diamond, and they both went tumbling into the water. They came up sputtering and watched as the catfish flopped itself over to the edge of the pier, fell in the water, and was gone in a blink. Diamond and Lou looked at each other for a tortured moment and then commenced a titanic splashing battle. Their peals of laughter could probably be heard on the next mountain.

Lou sat in front of the fireplace while Diamond built up the flames so they could dry off. He went and got an old blanket that smelled to Lou of either Jeb, mildew, or both, but she told Diamond thank you as he put it around her shoulders. The inside of Diamond's house surprised her because it was neat and clean, though the pieces of furniture were few and obviously handmade. On the wall was an old photo of Diamond and a man Lou assumed was his father. There were no photos Lou could see of his mother. While the fire picked up, Jeb lay down next to her and started attending to some fleas in his fur.

Diamond expertly scaled the bass, ran a hickory stick through each, mouth to tail, and cooked them over the fire. Next he cut up an apple and rubbed the juice into the meat. Diamond showed Lou how to feel the rib cage of the fish and pry thick white meat from tiny bones. They ate with their fingers, and it was good. "Your dad was real nice-looking," Lou said, pointing to the picture.

Diamond looked over at the photo. "Yep, he was." He caught a breath and glared at Lou.

"Louisa told me," she said.

Diamond rose and poked the fire with a crooked stick. "Ain't right playing no tricks on me."

"Why didn't you tell me on your own?"

"Why should I?"

"Because we're friends."

This took the sting out of Diamond and he sat back down.

"You miss your mom?" Lou asked.

"Naw, how could I? Never knowed the woman." He ran his hand along the crumpling brick, mud, and horsehair of the fireplace, and his features grew troubled. "See, she died when I's born."

"That's okay, Diamond. You can still miss her, even if you didn't know her."

Diamond nodded, his thumb now idly scratching at a dirty cheek. "I do think 'bout what my momma were like. Ain't got no pitchers. My daddy told me course, but it ain't the same." He stopped, nudged a piece of firewood with a stick, and then said, "I think mostly 'bout what her voice was like. And how she smelled. The way her eyes and hair could'a catch the light just so. But I miss my daddy too, 'cause he were a good man. Schooled me all's I need to know. Hunting, fishing." He looked at her. "I bet you miss your daddy too."

Lou looked uncomfortable. She closed her eyes for a moment and nodded. "I miss him."

"Good thing you got your momma."

"No, I don't. I don't, Diamond."

"Looks bad now, but it be okay. Folks don't never leave out, less we fergit 'em. I ain't knowed much, but I knowed that."

Lou wanted to tell him that he didn't understand. His mother was gone from him, without question. Lou sat atop quicksand with her mother. And Lou had to be there for Oz.

They sat listening to the sounds of the woods, as trees, bugs, animals, and birds went about their lives.

"How come you don't go to school?" Lou asked.

"I's fourteen year old, and doing just fine."

"You said you had read the Bible."

"Well, some folks read parts of it to me."

"Do you even know how to sign your name?"

"Why, everybody up here knowed who I is." He stood and pulled out the pocketknife and carved an "X" in a bare wall stud. "That's how my daddy done it all his life, and it be good enough fer him, it be good enough fer me."

Lou wrapped the blanket around her and watched the dance of flames, a wicked chill eating into her.

CHAPTER TWENTY-SEVEN

ONE ESPECIALLY WARM NIGHT THERE came a pounding on the door about the time Lou was thinking of going upstairs to bed. Billy Davis almost fell into the room when Louisa opened the door.

Louisa gripped the shaking boy. "What's wrong, Billy?"

"Ma's baby coming."

"I knew she were getting on. Midwife got there?"

The boy was wild-eyed, his limbs twitching like he was heatstroked. "Ain't none. Pa won't let 'em."

"Lord, why not?"

"Say they charge a dollar. And he ain't paying it."

"That a lie. No midwife up here ever charge a dime."

"Pa said no. But Ma say baby ain't feel right. Rode the mule come get you."

"Eugene, get Hit and Sam doubletreed to the wagon. Quick now," she said.

Before Eugene went out, he took the rifle off the rack and held it out to Louisa. "Better be taking this, you got to deal with that man."

Louisa, though, shook her head as she looked at a nervous Billy, finally smiling at the boy. "I'll be watched over, Eugene. I feel it. It be fine."

Eugene held on to the gun. "I go with you, then. That man crazy."

"No, you stay with the children. Go on now, get the wagon ready." Eugene hesitated for a moment, and then did as she told him.

Louisa grabbed some things and put them in a lard bucket, slipped a small packet of cloths in her pocket, bundled together a number of clean sheets, and started for the door.

"Louisa, I'm coming with you," said Lou.

"No, ain't a good place for you."

"I'm coming, Louisa. Whether in the wagon or on Sue, but I'm coming. I want to help you." She glanced at Billy. "And them."

Louisa thought for a minute and then said, "Prob'ly could use another set of hands. Billy, your pa there?"

"Gotta mare gonna drop its foal. Pa said he ain't coming out the barn till it born."

Louisa stared at the boy. Then, shaking her head, she headed for the door.

They followed Billy in the wagon. He rode an old mule, its muzzle white, part of its right ear torn away. The boy swung a kerosene lamp in one hand to help guide them. It was so dark, Louisa said, a hand right in front of your face could still get the drop on you.

"Don't whip up the mules none, Lou. Ain't do no good for Sally Davis we end up in a ditch."

"That's Billy's mother?"

Louisa nodded, as the wagon swayed along, the woods close on either side of them, their only light that arcing lamp. To Lou it appeared either as a beacon, true and reliable, or as a Siren of sorts, leading them to shipwreck.

"First wife die in childbirth. His children by that poor woman got away from George fast as they could, afore he could work or beat or starve 'em to death."

"Why did Sally marry him if he was so bad?"

" 'Cause he got his own land, livestock, and he were a widower with a strong back. Up here, 'bout all it takes. And weren't nothing else for Sally. She were only fifteen."

"Fifteen! That's only three years older than me."

"People get married quick up here. Start birthing, raising a family to help work the land. How it goes. I was in front of the preacher at fo'teen."

"She could have left the mountain."

"All she ever know. Scary thing leave that."

"Did you ever think of leaving the mountain?"

Louisa thought about this for a number of turns of the wagon wheel. "I could'a if'n I wanted. But I ain't believe in my heart I be happier anywhere else. Went down the Valley one time. Wind blow strange over flat land. Ain't liked it too much. Me and this mountain get along right fine for the most part." She fell silent, her eyes watching the rise and fall of the light up ahead.

Lou said, "I saw the graves up behind the house."

Louisa stiffened a bit. "Did you?"

"Who was Annie?"

Louisa stared at her feet. "Annie were my daughter."

"I thought you only had Jacob."

"No. I had me my little Annie."

"Did she die young?"

"She lived but a minute."

Lou could sense her distress. "I'm sorry. I was just curious about my family."

Louisa settled back against the hard wood of the wagon seat and stared at the black sky as though it was the first time she'd ever gazed upon it.

"I always had me a hard time carrying the babies. Wanted me a big family, but I kept on losing 'em long afore they ready to be born. Longest time I thought Jake be it. But then Annie were born on a cool spring evening with a full mane'a black hair. She come quick, no time for midwife. It were a terrible hard birth. But oh, Lou, she were so purty. So warm. Her little fingers wrapped tight round mine, tips not even touching." Here Louisa stopped. The sounds of the mules trotting along and the turn of wagon wheel were the only noises. Louisa finally continued in a low voice, as she eyed the depthless sky. "And her little chest rose and fell, rose and fell, and then it just forgit to rise agin. It t'were amazing how quick she took cold, but then she were so tiny." Louisa took a number of quick breaths, as though still trying to breathe for her child. "It were like a bit of ice on your tongue on a hot day. Feel so good, and then it gone so fast you ain't sure it was ever there."

Lou put her hand over Louisa's. "I'm sorry."

"Long time ago, though it don't never seem it." Louisa slid a hand across her eyes. "Her daddy made her coffin, no more'n a little box. And I stayed up all night and sewed her the finest dress I ever stitched in my whole life. Come morning I laid her out in it. I would'a give all I had to see her eyes looking at me just one time. It ain't seem right that a momma don't get to see her baby's eyes just one time. And then her daddy put her in that little box, we carried her on up to that knoll, and laid her to rest and prayed over her. And then we planted an evergreen on the south end so she'd have her shade all year round." Louisa closed her eyes.

"Did you ever go up there?"

Louisa nodded. "Ever day. But I ain't been back since I buried my other child. It just got to be too long a walk."

She took the reins from Lou and, despite her own earlier warning, Louisa whipped up the mules. "We best get on. We got a child to help into the world this night."

Lou could not make out much of the Davis farm-yard or the buildings because of the darkness, and she prayed that George Davis would stay in the barn until the baby was born and they were gone.

The house was surprisingly small. The room they entered was obviously the kitchen, because the stove was there, but there were also cots with bare mattresses lined up here. In three of the beds were a like number of children, two of them, who looked to be twin girls about five, lying naked and asleep. The third, a boy Oz's age, had on a man's undershirt, dirty and sweat-stained, and he watched Lou and Louisa with frightened eyes. Lou recognized him as the other boy from the tractor coming down the mountain. In an apple crate by the stove a baby barely a year old lay under a stained blanket. Louisa went to the sink, pumped water, and used the bar of lye soap she had brought to thoroughly clean her hands and forearms. Then Billy led them down a narrow hallway and opened a door.

Sally Davis lay in the bed, her knees drawn up, low moans shooting from her. A thin girl of ten, dressed in what looked like a seed sack, her chestnut hair hacked short, stood barefoot next to the bed. Lou recognized her too from the wild tractor encounter. She looked just as scared now as she had then.

Louisa nodded at her. "Jesse, you heat me up some water, two pots, honey. Billy, all the sheets you got, son. And they's got to be real clean."

Louisa put the sheets she had brought on a wobbly

oak slat chair, sat next to Sally, and took her hand. "Sally, it's Louisa. You be just fine, honey."

Lou looked at Sally. Her eyes were red-rimmed, her few teeth and her gums stained dark. She couldn't be thirty yet, but the woman looked twice that old, hair gray, skin drawn and wrinkled, blue veins throbbing through malnourished flesh, face sunken like a winter potato.

Louisa lifted the covers and saw the soaked sheet underneath. "How long since your water bag broke?"

Sally gasped, "After Billy gone fer you."

"How far apart your pains?" Louisa asked.

"Seem like just one big one," the woman groaned.

Louisa felt around the swollen belly. "Baby feel like it want'a come?"

Sally gripped Louisa's hand. "Lord I hope so, afore it kill me."

Billy came in with a couple of sheets, dropped them on the chair, looked once at his ma, and then fled.

"Lou, help me move Sally over so we can lay clean sheets." They did so, maneuvering the suffering woman as gently as they could. "Now go help Jesse with the water. And take these." She handed Lou a number of cloth pads that were layered one over the top of the other, along with some narrow bobbin string. "Wrap the string in the middle of the cloths, and put it all in the oven and cook it till the outside part be scorched brown."

Lou went into the kitchen and assisted Jesse. Lou had never seen her at school, nor the seven-year-old boy who watched them with fearful eyes. Jesse had a wide scar that looped around her left eye, and Lou didn't even want to venture to guess how the girl had come by it.

The stove was already hot, and the kettle water came to a boil in a few minutes. Lou kept checking the outside of the cloth that she placed in the oven drawer, and soon it was sufficiently brown. Using rags, they carried the pots and the ball of cloths into the bedroom and set them next to the bed.

Louisa washed Sally with soap and warm water where the baby would be coming and then drew the sheet over her.

She whispered to Lou, "Baby taking its last rest now, and so can Sally. Ain't tell 'xactly how it lies yet, but it ain't a cross birth." Lou looked at her curiously. "Where the baby lie crossways along the belly. I call you when I need you."

"How many babies have you delivered?"

"Thirty-two over fifty-seven years," she said. " 'Member ever one of 'em."

"Did they all live?"

"No," Louisa answered quietly, and then told Lou to go on out, that she would call her.

Jesse was in the kitchen, standing against a wall, hands clasped in front of her, face down, a side of her hacked hair positioned over the scar and part of her eye.

Lou glanced at the boy in the bed.

"What's your name?" Lou asked him. He said nothing. When Lou stepped toward him, he yelled and threw the blanket over his head, his little body shaking hard under the cover. Lou retreated all the way out of the crazy house.

She looked around until she saw Billy over at the barn peering in the open double doors. She crossed the yard quietly and looked over his shoulder. George Davis was no more than ten feet from them. The mare was on the straw floor. Protruding from her, and covered in the cocoonish white birth sac, was one foreleg and shoulder of the foal. Davis was pulling on the slicked leg, cursing. The barn floor was plank, not dirt. In the blaze of a number of lanterns, Lou could see rows of shiny tools neatly lining the walls.

Unable to stand Davis's coarse language and the mare's suffering, Lou went and sat on the front porch. Billy came and slumped next to her. "Your farm looks pretty big," she said.

"Pa hire men to help him work it. But when I get to be a man, he ain't need 'em. I do it."

They heard George Davis holler from the barn, and they both jumped. Billy looked embarrassed and dug at the dirt with his big toe.

"I'm sorry for putting that snake in your pail."

He looked at her, surprised. "I done it to you first."

"That still doesn't make it right."

"Pa kill a man if he done that to him."

Lou could see the terror in the boy's eyes, and her heart went out to Billy Davis.

"You're not your pa. And you don't have to be."

Billy looked nervous. "I ain't tell him I was fetching

Miss Louisa. Don't know what he say when he sees y'all."

"We're just here to help your mother. He can't have a problem with that."

"That right?"

They looked up into the face of George Davis, who stood before them, equine blood and slime coating his shirt and dripping down both arms. Dust swirled around his legs like visible heat, as though mountain had been shucked to desert.

Billy stood in front of Lou. "Pa. How's the foal?"

"Dead." The way he said it made every part of Lou shake. He pointed at her. "What the hell is this?"

"I got them to come help with the baby. Miss Louisa's in with Ma."

George looked over at the door and then back at Billy. The look in his eye was so terrible that Lou was sure the man was going to kill her right there.

"That woman in my house, boy?"

"It's time." They all looked toward the door where Louisa now stood. "Baby's coming," she said.

Davis shoved his son aside, and Lou jumped out of the way as he stalked up to the door.

"Gawd damnit, you got no business here, woman. Get the hell off my land afore you get the butt of my shotgun agin your head, and that damn girl too."

Louisa took not one step back. "You can help with the baby coming, or not. Up to you. Come on, Lou, and you too, Billy. Gonna need both y'all."

It was clear though that George wasn't going to let

them go. Louisa was very strong for her age, and taller than Davis, but still, it would not be much of a fight.

And then from the woods they heard the scream. It was the same sound Lou had heard the first night at the well, but even more horrifying somehow, as though whatever it was, was very close and bearing down on them. Even Louisa stared out apprehensively into the darkness.

George Davis took a step back, his hand clenched, as though hoping for a gun to be there. Louisa clutched the children and pulled them in with her. Davis made no move to stop them, but he did call out, "You just make sure it's a damn boy this time. If'n it's a girl, you just let it die. You hear me? Don't need me no more gawd damn girls!"

As Sally pushed hard, Louisa's pulse quickened when she first saw the buttocks of the baby, followed by one of its feet. She knew she didn't have long to get the child out before the cord was crushed between the baby's head and Sally's bone. As she watched, the pains pushed the other foot out.

"Lou," she said, "over here, quick, child." Louisa caught the baby's feet in her right hand and lifted the body up so that the contractions would not have to carry the weight of the baby, and so as to better the angle of the head coming through. She knew they were fortunate that after so many births, Sally Davis's bones would be spread wide. "Push, Sally, push, honey," Louisa called out.

Louisa took Lou's hands and directed them to a spot on Sally's lower abdomen. "Got to get the head out fast," she told Lou, "push right there, hard as you can. Don't worry, ain't hurt the baby none, belly wall hard."

Lou bore down with all her weight while Sally pushed and screamed and Louisa lifted the baby's body higher.

Louisa called out like she was marking water depth on a riverboat. Neck showing, she said, and then she could see hair. And then the entire head showed, and then she was holding the child, and telling Sally to rest, that it was over.

Louisa said a prayer of thanks when she saw it was a boy. It was awfully small, though, and its color poor. She had Lou and Billy heat up cans of water while she tied off the cord in two spots with the bobbin string and then cut the cord in between these points with a pair of boiled scissors. She wrapped the cord in one of the clean, dry cloths that Lou had baked in the oven and tied another of the baked cloths snugly against the baby's left side. She used sweet oil to clean the baby off, washed him with soap and warm water, and then wrapped him in a blanket and gave the boy to his mother.

Louisa placed a hand on Sally's belly and felt to see if the womb was hard and small, which is what she wanted. If it was large and soft, that might mean bleeding inside, she told Lou in a small voice. However, the belly was small and tight. "We fine," she told a relieved Lou.

Next, Louisa took the newborn and laid it on the bed. She took a small wax ampule from her lard bucket and from it took out a small glass vial. She had Lou hold the baby's eyes open while Louisa placed two drops inside each one, while the child squirmed and cried out.

She told Lou, "So baby ain't go blind. Travis Barnes gimme it. Law say you got to do this."

Using the hot cans and some blankets, Louisa fashioned a crude incubator and placed the baby in it. His breathing was so shallow she kept sticking a goose feather under his mouth to see the ripple of air graze it.

Thirty minutes later the last contractions pushed the afterbirth out and Louisa and Lou cleaned that up, changing the sheets once more and scrubbing the mother down for the final time using the last of the baked cloths.

The last things Louisa took out from her bucket were a pencil and a slip of paper. She gave them to Lou and told her to write down the day's date and time. Louisa pulled an old windup pocket watch from her trousers and told Lou the time of birth.

"Sally, what you be calling the baby?" Louisa asked.

Sally looked over at Lou. "She call you Lou, that be your name, girl?" she asked in a weak voice.

"Yes. Well, sort of," said Lou.

"Then it be Lou. After you, child. I thank you."

Lou looked astonished. "What about your husband?"

"He ain't care if'n it got name or ain't got one. Only

if'n it a boy and it work. And I ain't seed him in here hepping. Name's Lou. Put it down now, girl."

Louisa smiled as Lou wrote down the name Lou Davis.

"We give that to Cotton," Louisa said. "He take it on down the courthouse so's everybody know we got us another beautiful child on this mountain."

Sally fell asleep and Louisa sat there with mother and son all night, rousing Sally to nurse when Lou Davis cried and smacked his lips. George Davis never once entered the room. They could hear him stomping around in the front for some time, and then the door slammed shut.

Louisa slipped out several times to check on the other children. She gave Billy, Jesse, and the other boy, whose name Louisa didn't know, a small jar of molasses and some biscuits she had brought with her. It pained her to see how fast the children devoured this simple meal. She also gave Billy a jar of strawberry jelly and some cornbread to save for the other children when they woke.

They left in the late morning. Mother was doing fine, and the baby's color had improved greatly. He was nursing feverishly, and the boy's lungs seemed strong.

Sally and Billy said their thanks, and even Jesse managed a grunt. But Lou noticed that the stove was cold and there was no smell of food.

George Davis and his hired men were in the fields. But before Billy joined them, Louisa took the boy aside and talked with him about things Lou could not hear.

As they drove the wagon out, they passed corrals filled

with enough cattle to qualify as a herd, and hogs and sheep, a yard full of hens, four fine horses, and double that number of mules. The crop fields extended as far as the eye could see, and dangerous barbed wire encircled all of it. Lou could see George and his men working the fields with mechanized equipment, clouds of dirt being thrown up from the swift pace of the machines.

"They have more fields and livestock than we do," Lou said. "So how come they don't have anything to eat?"

" 'Cause their daddy want it that way. And his daddy were the same way with George Davis. Tight with a dollar. Didn't let none go till his feet wedged agin root."

They rattled by one building and Louisa pointed out a sturdy padlock on the door. "Man'll let the meat in that smokehouse *rot* afore he give it up to his children. George Davis sells every last bit of his crop down at the lumber camp, and to the miners, and hauls it to Tremont and Dickens." She pointed to a large building that had a line of doors all around the first floor. The doors were open, and plainly visible inside were large green plant leaves hanging from hooks. "That's burley tobacco curing. It weakens the soil, and what he don't chew hisself, he sells. He got that still and ain't never drunk a drop of the corn whiskey, but sells that wicked syrup to other men who ought be spending their time and money on they's families. And he goes round with a fat roll of dollar bills, and got this nice farm, and all them fancy machines, and man let his family starve." She flicked the reins. "But I got to feel sorry for him

CHAPTER TWENTY-EIGHT

EUGENE WAS DRIVING THE WAGON PULLED BY the mules. Oz, Lou, and Diamond were in the back, sitting on sacks of seed and other supplies purchased from McKenzie's Mercantile using egg money and some of the dollars Lou had left over from her shopping excursion in Dickens.

Their path took them near a good-sized tributary of the McCloud River, and Lou was surprised to see a number of automobiles and schooner wagons pulled up near the flat, grassy bank. Folks were hanging about by the river's edge, and some were actually in the brown water, its surface choppy from an earlier rain and good wind. A man with rolled-up sleeves was just then submerging a young woman in the water.

"Dunking," Diamond exclaimed. "Let's have a look."

Eugene pulled the mules to a stop and the three children jumped off. Lou looked back at Eugene, who was making no move to join them.

"Aren't you coming?"

"You g'on, Miss Lou, I gonna rest my bones here."

Lou frowned at this, but joined the others.

Diamond had made his way through a crowd of on-lookers and was peering anxiously at something. As Oz and Lou drew next to him and saw what it was, they both jumped back.

An elderly woman, dressed in what looked to be a turban made from pinned-together homespun sheets and a long piece of hemp with a tie at the waist, was moving in small, deliberate circles, unintelligible chants drifting from her, her speech that of the drunk, insane, or fanatically religious in full, flowering tongues. Next to her a man was in a T-shirt and dress slacks, a cig-arette dangling like a fall leaf from his mouth. A ser-pent was in either of the man's hands, the reptiles rigid, unmoving, like bent pieces of metal.

"Are they poisonous?" whispered Lou to Diamond.

"Course! Don't work lessen use viper."

A cowering Oz had his gaze fixed on the motion-less creatures and seemed prepared to leap for the trees once they started swaying. Lou sensed this, and when the snakes did start to move, she gripped Oz's hand and pulled him away. Diamond grudgingly followed, till they were off by themselves.

"What stuff are they doing with those snakes, Dia-mond?" asked Lou.

"Scaring off bad spirits, making it good for dunk-ing." He looked at them. "You two been dunked?"

"Christened, Diamond," Lou answered. "We were

christened in a Catholic Church. And the priest just sprinkles water on your head." She looked to the river where the woman was emerging and spitting up mouthfuls of the tributary. "He doesn't try to drown you."

"Catolick? Ain't never heard'a that one. It new?"

Lou almost laughed. "Not quite. Our mom is Catholic. Dad never really cared for church all that much. They even have their own schools. Oz and I went to one in New York. It's really structured and you learn things like the Sacraments, the Creed, the Rosary, the Lord's Prayer. And you learn the Mortal Sins. And the Venial Sins. And you have First Confession and First Communion. And then Confirmation."

"Yeah," said Oz, "and when you're dying you get the . . . what that's thing, Lou?"

"The Sacrament of Extreme Unction. The Last Rites."

"So you won't rot in hell," Oz informed Diamond.

Diamond pulled at three or four of his cowlicks and looked truly bewildered. "Huh. Who'd thunk believing in God be such hard work? Prob'ly why ain't no Catolicks up this way. Tax the head too much."

Diamond nodded at the group near the river. "Now, them folk Primitive Baptists. They got some right funny beliefs. Like you ain't go and cut your hair, and women ain't be putting on no face paint. And they got some 'ticular ideas on going to hell and such. People break the rules, they ain't too happy. Live and die by the Scriptures. Prob'ly ain't as 'ticular as you Catolicks, but they still be a pain where the sun don't shine." Diamond yawned and stretched his arms. "See, that why I ain't go to church. Figger I got me a church wherever I be. Want'a talk to God, well I say, 'Howdy-howdy, God,' and we jaw fer a bit."

Lou just stared at him, absolutely dumbstruck in the face of this outpouring of ecclesiastical wisdom from Professor of Religion Diamond Skinner.

Diamond suddenly stared off in wonder. "Well, will you look at that."

They all watched as Eugene walked down to the water's edge and spoke with someone, who in turn called to the preacher out in the river, as he was pulling up a fresh victim.

The preacher came ashore, spoke with Eugene for a minute or two, and then led him out into the water, dunked him so that nothing was showing of his person, and then preached over him. The man kept Eugene down so long, Lou and Oz started to worry. But when Eugene came up, he smiled, thanked the man, and then went back to the wagon. Diamond set off on a dead run toward the preacher, who was looking around for other takers of divine immersion.

Lou and Oz crept closer as Diamond went out in the water with the holy man and was fully plunged under too. He finally surfaced, talked with the man for a minute, slipped something in his pocket, and, soaking wet and smiling, rejoined them, and they all headed to the wagon.

"You've never been baptized before?" said Lou.

"Shoot," said Diamond, shaking the water from his

hair, the cowlick of which had not been disturbed in the least, "that's my ninth time dunked."

"You're only supposed to do it *once*, Diamond!"

"Well, ain't hurt keep doing it. Plan to work me up to a hunnerd. Figger I be a lock for heaven then."

"That's not how it works," exclaimed Lou.

"Is so," he shot back. "Say so in the Bible. Ever time you get dunked it means God's sending an angel to come look after you. I figger I got me a right good regiment by now."

"That is *not* in the Bible," insisted Lou.

"Maybe you ought'n read your Bible agin."

"Which part of the Bible is it in? Tell me that."

"Front part." Diamond whistled for Jeb, ran the rest of the way to the wagon, and climbed on.

"Hey, Eugene," he said, "I let you knowed next time they's dunking. We go swimming together."

"You were never baptized, Eugene?" asked Lou as she and Oz clambored onto the wagon.

He shook his head. "But sitting here I got me a hankering to do just that. 'Bout time, I 'xpect."

"I'm surprised Louisa never had you baptized."

"Miz Louisa, she believe in God with all her soul. But she don't subscribe to church much. She say the way some folk run they's churches, it take God right out cha heart."

As the wagon pulled off, Diamond slid from his pocket a small glass jar with a tin screw cap. "Hey, Oz, I got me this from the preacher. Holy dunking water." He handed it to Oz, who looked down at it curiously.

"I figger you put some on your ma from time to time. Bet it hep."

Lou was about to protest, when she received the shock of her life. Oz handed the jar back to Diamond.

"No, thanks," he said quietly and looked away.

"You sure?" asked Diamond. Oz said he was real sure, and so Diamond tipped the bottle over and poured out the blessed water. Lou and Oz exchanged a glance, and the sad look on his face stunned her again. Lou looked to the sky, because she figured if Oz had given up hope, the end of the world must not be far behind. She turned her back to them all and pretended to be admiring the sweep of mountains.

It was late afternoon. Cotton had just finished reading to Amanda and it was apparent that he was experiencing a growing sense of frustration.

At the window, Lou watched, standing on an overturned lard bucket.

Cotton looked at the woman. "Amanda, now I just know you can hear me. You have two children who need you badly. You *have* to get out of that bed. For them if for no other reason." He paused, seeming to select his words with care. "Please, Amanda. I would give all I will ever have if you would get up right now." An anxious few moments went by, and Lou held her breath, yet the woman didn't budge. Cotton finally bowed his head in despair.

When Cotton came out of the house later and got in his Olds to leave, Lou hurried up carrying a basket of food.

"Reading probably gives a man an appetite."

"Well, thank you, Lou."

He put the basket of food in the seat next to him. "Louisa tells me you're a writer. What do you want to write about?"

Lou stood on the roadster's running board. "My dad wrote about this place, but nothing's really coming to me."

Cotton looked out over the mountains. "Your daddy was actually one of the reasons I came here. When I was in law school at the University of Virginia, I read his very first novel and was struck by both its power and beauty. And then I saw a story in the newspaper about him. He talked about how the mountains had inspired him so. I thought coming here would do the same for me. I walked all over these parts with my pad and pencil, waiting for beautiful phrases to seep into my head so I could put them down on the paper." He smiled wistfully. "Didn't exactly work that way."

Lou said quietly, "Maybe not for me either."

"Well, people seem to spend most of their lives chasing something. Maybe that's part of what makes us human." Cotton pointed down the road. "You see that old shack down there?" Lou looked at a mud-chinked, falling-down log cabin they no longer used. "Louisa told me about a story your father wrote when he was a little boy. It was about a family that survived one winter up here in that little house. Without wood, or food."

"How'd they do it?"

"They believed in things."

"Like what? Wishing wells?" she said with scorn.

"No, they believed in each other. And created something of a miracle. Some say truth is stranger than fiction. I think that means that whatever a person can imagine really does exist, somewhere. Isn't that a wonderful possibility?"

"I don't know if my imagination is that good, Cotton. In fact, I don't even know if I'm much of a writer. The things I put down on paper don't seem to have much life to them."

"Keep at it, you might surprise yourself. And rest assured, Lou, miracles *do* happen. You and Oz coming here and getting to know Louisa being one of them."

❧

Lou sat on her bed later that night, looking at her mother's letters. When Oz came in, Lou hurriedly stuffed them under her pillow.

"Can I sleep with you?" asked Oz. "Kind'a scary in my room. Pretty sure I saw a troll in the corner."

Lou said, "Get up here." Oz climbed next to her.

Oz suddenly looked troubled. "When you get married, who am I going to come get in bed with when I'm scared, Lou?"

"One day you're gonna get bigger than me, then I'm going to be running to you when *I* get scared."

"How do you know that?"

"Because that's the deal God makes between big sisters and their little brothers."

"Me bigger than you? Really?"

"Look at those clodhoppers of yours. You grow into those feet all the way, you'll be bigger than Eugene."

Oz snuggled in, happy now. Then he saw the letters under the pillow.

"What are those?"

"Just some old letters Mom wrote," Lou said quickly.

"What did she say?"

"I don't know, I haven't read them."

"Will you read them to me?"

"Oz, it's late and I'm tired."

"Please, Lou. Please."

He looked so pitiful Lou took out a single letter and turned up the wick on the kerosene lamp that sat on the table next to her bed.

"All right, but just one."

Oz settled down as Lou began to read.

"Dear Louisa, I hope you are doing well. We all are. Oz is over the croup and is sleeping through the night."

Oz jumped up. "That's me! Mom wrote about me!" He paused and looked confused. "What's croup?"

"You don't want to know. Now, do you want me to read it or not?" Oz lay back down while his sister commenced reading again. "Lou won first place in both the spelling bee and the fifty-yard dash at May Day. The latter included the boys! She's something, Louisa. I've seen a picture of you that Jack had, and the resemblance is remarkable. They're both growing up so fast. So very fast it scares me. Lou is so much like her father. Her mind is so quick, I'm afraid she finds me a little boring. That thought keeps me up nights. I love her so much. I try to do so much with her. And yet, well, you know, a father and his daughter. . . . More next time. And pictures too. Love to you. Amanda. P.S. My dream is to bring the children to the mountain, so that we can finally meet you. I hope that dream comes true one day."

Oz said, "That was a good letter. Night, Lou."

As Oz drifted off to sleep, Lou slowly reached for another letter.

CHAPTER TWENTY-NINE

LOU AND OZ WERE FOLLOWING DIAMOND AND Jeb through the woods on a glorious day in early fall, the dappled sunlight in their faces, a cool breeze tracking them along with the fading scents of summer's honeysuckle and wild rose.

"Where are we going?" asked Lou.

Diamond would only say mysteriously, "You see."

They went up a little incline and stopped. Fifty feet away and on the path was Eugene, carrying an empty coal bucket and a lantern. In his pocket was a stick of dynamite.

Diamond said, "Eugene headed to the coal mine. Gonna fill up that bucket. Afore winter come, he'll take a drag down there with the mules and get out a big load'a coal."

"Gee, that's about as exciting as watching somebody sleep" was Lou's considered opinion.

"Huh! Wait till that dynamite blows," countered Diamond.

"Dynamite!" Oz said.

Diamond nodded. "Coal deep in that rock. Pick can't git to it. Gotta blast it out."

"Is it dangerous?" asked Lou.

"Naw. He knowed what he doing. Done it myself."

As they watched from a distance, Eugene pulled the dynamite out of his pocket and attached a long fuse to it. Then he lit his lantern and went inside the mine. Diamond sat back against a redbud, took out an apple, and cut it up. He flicked a piece to Jeb, who was messing around some underbrush. Diamond noted the worried looks on the faces of Lou and Oz.

"That fuse slow-burning. Walk to the moon and back afore it go off."

A while later Eugene came out of the mine and sat down on a rock near the entrance.

"Shouldn't he get away from there?"

"Naw. Don't use that much dynamite for a bucketful. After it blow and the dust settles, I show you round in there."

"What's to see in some old mine?" asked Lou.

Diamond suddenly hunched forward. "I tell you what. I seed some fellers down here late one night poking round. 'Member Miss Louisa told me to keep my eyes open? Well, I done that. They had lanterns and carrying boxes into the mine. We go in and see what they's up to."

"But what if they're in the mine now?"

"Naw. I come by just a bit ago, looked round, threw a rock inside. And they's fresh footprints in the dirt heading out. Sides, Eugene would'a seed 'em." He had a sudden idea. "Hey, mebbe they running shine, using the mine to store the still and corn and such."

"More likely they're just hobos using the mine to keep dry at night," said Lou.

"Ain't never heard tell of no hobos up here."

"So why didn't you tell Louisa?" Lou challenged him.

"She got enough to worry 'bout. Check it out first. What a man do."

Jeb flushed out a squirrel and chased it around a tree while they all watched and waited for the explosion.

Lou said, "Why don't you come live with us?"

Diamond stared at her, clearly troubled by this question. He turned to his hound. "Cut it out, Jeb. That squirrel ain't doing nuthin' to you."

Lou added, "I mean, we could use the help. Another strong man around. And Jeb too."

"Naw. I a feller what needs his freedom."

"Hey, Diamond," said Oz, "you could be my big brother. Then Lou wouldn't have to beat up everybody by herself."

Lou and Diamond smiled at each other.

"Maybe you should think about it," said Lou.

"Mebbe I will." He looked at the mine. "Ain't be long now."

They sat back and waited. Then the squirrel broke free from the woods and flashed right into the mine. Jeb plunged in after it.

Diamond leapt to his feet. "Jeb! Jeb! Git back here!" The boy charged out of the woods. Eugene made a grab for him, but Diamond dodged him and ran into the mine.

Lou screamed, "Diamond! Don't!"

She ran for the mine entrance.

Oz shouted, "Lou, no! Come back!"

Before she could reach the entrance, Eugene grabbed her. "Wait here. I git him, Miss Lou."

Eugene fast-limped into the mine, screaming, "Diamond! Diamond!"

Lou and Oz looked at each other, terrified. Time ticked by. Lou paced in nervous circles near the entrance. "Please, please. Hurry." She went to the entrance, heard something coming. "Diamond! Eugene!"

But it was Jeb that came racing out of the mine after the squirrel. Lou grabbed at the dog, and then the concussive force of the explosion knocked Lou off her feet. Dust and dirt poured out of the mine, and Lou coughed and gagged in this maelstrom. Oz raced to help her while Jeb barked and jumped.

Lou got her bearings and her breath and stumbled to the entrance. "Eugene! Diamond!"

Finally, she could hear footsteps coming. They drew closer and closer, and they seemed unsteady. Lou said a silent prayer. It seemed to take forever, but then Eugene appeared, dazed, covered with dirt, bleeding. He looked at them, tears on his face.

"Damn, Miss Lou."

Lou took one step back, then another, and then an-

other. Then she turned and ran down the trail as fast
as she could, her wails covering them all.

Some men carried the covered body of Diamond to
a wagon. They had had to wait for a while to let the
smoke clear out, and to make certain that the mine
would not collapse on them. Cotton watched the men
take Diamond away, and then went over to Eugene, who
sat on a large rock, holding a wet cloth to his bloodied
head.

"Eugene, sure you don't need anything else?"

Eugene looked at the mine like he expected to see
Diamond walk out with his stuck-up hair and silly smile.
"All I need, Mr. Cotton, is this be a bad dream I wake
myself up from."

Cotton patted his big shoulder and then glanced at
Lou sitting on a little hump of dirt, her back to the
mine. He went to her and sat down.

Lou's eyes were raw from crying, her cheeks stained
with tears. She was hunched over in a little ball, like
every part of her was in wrenching pain.

"I'm sorry, Lou. Diamond was a fine boy."

"He was a *man*. A *fine man!*"

"I suppose you're right. He was a man."

Lou eyed Jeb, who sat mournfully at the mine entrance.

"Diamond didn't have to go in that mine after Jeb."

"Well, that dog was all Diamond had. When you love something, you can't just sit by and not do anything."

Lou picked up some pine needles and then let a few trickle out between her fingers. Minutes passed before she spoke again. "Why do things like this happen, Cotton?"

He sighed deeply. "I suppose it may be God's way of telling us to love people while they're here, because tomorrow they may be gone. I guess that's a pretty sorry answer, but I'm afraid it's the only one I've got."

They were silent for a bit longer.

"I'd like to read to my mom," said Lou.

Cotton said, "That's the finest idea I've ever heard."

"Why is it a fine idea?" she demanded. "I really need to know."

"Well, if someone she knew, someone she . . . loved would read to her, it might make all the difference."

"Do you really think she knows?"

"When I carried your mother outside that day, I was holding a living person fighting like the devil to get out. I could feel it. And she will one day. I believe it with all my heart, Lou."

She shook her head. "It's hard, Cotton. To let yourself love something you know you may never have."

Cotton nodded slowly. "You're wise beyond your years. And what you say makes perfect sense. But I think when it comes to matters of the heart, perfect sense may be the last thing you want to listen to."

Lou let the rest of the needles fall and wiped her hands clean. "You're a good man too, Cotton."

He put his arm around her and they sat there together, neither one of them willing to look at the blackened, swollen cavity of the coal mine that had taken their friend from them forever.

CHAPTER THIRTY

THERE WAS ENOUGH STEADY RAIN, AND SOME thunderstorms added to the plenty, such that virtually all the crops came in healthy and in abundance. One fierce hailstorm damaged some of the corn, but not to any great extent. A stretch of powerful rain did wash a gully out of a hill, like a scoop of ice cream, but no person, animal, or crop was hurt by it.

Harvesting time was full upon them, and Louisa, Eugene, Lou, and Oz worked hard and long, which was good, because it gave them little time to think about Diamond not being with them anymore. Occasionally they would hear the mine siren, and then a bit later the slow rumbling of the explosion would come. And each time Louisa would lead them all in a song to take their minds off Diamond's having been killed by such an awful thing.

Louisa did not speak much of Diamond's passing. Yet

Lou noted that she read her Bible a lot more often by the firelight, and her eyes swelled with tears whenever his name was mentioned, or when she looked at Jeb. It was hard for all of them, yet all they could do was keep going, and there was much to do.

They harvested the pinto beans, cast them in Chop bags, stomped them to get the husks off, and had them for dinner every night with gravy and biscuits. They picked the pole beans, which had grown up around the cornstalks, careful, as Louisa schooled them, to avoid the green stinger worms that lived under the leaves. They scythed the cornfield and bundled the cornstalks into shocks, which they stood in the field, and which would later be used for livestock feed. They shucked the corn, hauled it by sled to the corncrib, and filled it to almost overflowing. From a distance the tumble of cobs looked like yellowjackets at frenzied play.

The potatoes came in thick and fat, and with churned butter were a meal by themselves. The tomatoes came in too, plump and blood red, eaten whole or sliced, and also cut up and canned in jars in a great iron kettle on the stove, along with beans and peppers and many other vegetables. They stacked the jars in the foodsafe and under the stairs. They filled lard buckets with wild strawberries and gooseberries, and apples by the bushel, made jams and pies, and canned the rest. They ground down the cane stalks and made molasses, and shelled some of the corn and made cornmeal and fried crackling bread.

It seemed to Lou that nothing was wasted; it was an efficient process and she admired it, even as she and Oz worked themselves to near death from before sunup to long after sundown. Everywhere they turned with tool or hand, food was flying at them. This made Lou think of Billy Davis and his family having nothing to eat. She thought about it so much she talked to Louisa about it.

"You stay up tomorrow night, Lou, and you'll find that you and me thinking on the same line."

All of them were waiting by the barn late that night when they heard a wagon coming down the road. Eugene held up a lantern and the light fell upon Billy Davis as he pulled the mules to a halt and nervously stared at Lou and Oz.

Louisa approached the wagon. "Billy, I thought we might need some help. I want'a make sure you get a good load. Land been real fine to us this year."

Billy looked embarrassed for a moment, but then Lou said, "Hey, Billy, come on, I'm going to need your muscle to lift this bucket."

Thus encouraged, Billy jumped down to help. They all spent a solid hour loading bags of cornmeal, canning jars full of beans and tomatoes, and buckets of rutabagas, collards, cucumbers, potatoes, apples, plump cabbages, pears, sweet potatoes, onions, and even some cuts of salted hog meat on that wagon.

While Lou was loading, she saw Louisa take Billy to a corner of the barn and look at his face with a lantern. Then she had him raise his shirt, and she did an examination there and came away apparently satisfied.

When Billy turned the wagon around and left, the mules strained under the new weight, and the boy carried a big smile as he flicked the whip and disappeared into the night.

"They can't hide all that food from George Davis," Lou said.

"I been doing this many a year now. Man never once fretted about where the bounty come from."

Lou looked angry. "That's not fair. He sells his crop and makes money, and *we* feed his family."

"What's fair is a momma and her children eating good," answered Louisa.

"What were you checking for under his shirt?" asked Lou.

"George is smart. Most times hits where the clothing covers."

"Why didn't you just ask Billy if he had hit him?"

"Just like an empty lunch pail, children will lie when they shamed."

With all their surplus, Louisa decided the four would drive the wagon laden with crops down to the lumber camp. On the day of the trip Cotton came over to look after Amanda. The lumber folks were expecting them, for quite a crowd had gathered by the time they arrived. The camp was large, with its own school, store, and post office. Because the camp was forced to move frequently when forests had been exhausted, the entire town was on rails, including the workers' homes, the school, and the store. They were laid out on various spurs like a neighborhood. When a move was called for, the locomotives hooked up to the cars and off the entire town went in short order.

The lumber camp families paid for the crops either with cash money or with barter items, such as coffee, sugar, toilet paper, stamps, pencils and paper, some throw-off clothes and shoes, and old newspapers. Lou had ridden Sue down, and she and Oz took turns giving the camp children rides free of charge, but the patrons could "donate" peppermint sticks and other delicacies if they saw fit, and many did.

Later, from atop the sharp spine of a ridge, they looked down where a shaft of the McCloud River flowed. A splashdam of stone and wood had been created downriver, artificially backing the water up and covering boulders and other obstructions that made log transport by river difficult. Here the water was filled bank to bank with trees, mostly mighty poplar, the bottoms of the trunks scored with the lumber company's brand. They looked like pencils from this great height, but then Oz and Lou noted that the small specks on each of them were actually full-grown men riding the logs. They would float down to the splashdam, where a vital wedge would be kicked out, and the thundering water would carry the trees downriver, where they would be tied off and Virginia logs would ride on to Kentucky markets.

As Lou surveyed the land from this high perch, something seemed to be missing. It took her a moment to realize that what was absent was the trees. As far as she could see, there were just stumps. When they went back down to the camp, she also noted that some of the rail lines were empty.

"Sucked just 'bout all the wood we can from here," one of the lumberjacks proudly explained. "Be heading out soon." He didn't seem bothered by this at all. Lou figured he was probably used to it. Conquer and move on, the only trace of their presence the butts of wood left behind.

On the trip home they tied Sue to the wagon and Lou and Oz rode in the back with Eugene. It had been a good day for everyone, but Oz was the happiest of them all, for he had "won" an official baseball from one of the camp boys by throwing it farther than any of them. He told them it was his proudest possession behind the graveyard rabbit's foot Diamond Skinner had given him.

CHAPTER THIRTY-ONE

I N READING TO HER MOTHER, LOU CHOSE NOT
books, but rather *Grit* newspapers, and some copies
of the *Saturday Evening Post* they had gotten from
the lumber camp. Lou would stand against the
wall of her mother's room, the paper or magazine held
in front of her, and read of the economy, world catas-
trophes, Hitler's bludgeoning war across Europe, politics, the arts, movies, and the latest news of writing and
writers, which made Lou realize how long it had been
since she had actually read a book. School would start
again very soon; even so, she had ridden Sue over to
Big Spruce a few days before and borrowed some reading material for her and Oz from the "lending library,"
with Estelle McCoy's permission of course.

Louisa had taught Eugene to read when he was a
child, and so Lou brought a book for him too. He was
concerned he would find no time to read it, and yet he
did, late at night under lamplight, his moistened thumb

slowly turning the pages as he concentrated. Other times Lou helped him with his words as they worked the fields in preparation for the coming winter, or when milking the cows by kerosene lamp. Lou would take him through the *Grit*s and the *Post*s and Eugene particularly liked saying "Roooosevelt, President Roooosevelt," a name that appeared often in the *Grit* pages. The cows looked at him strangely whenever he said "Roooosevelt," as though they thought he was actually mooing at them in a peculiar way. And Lou couldn't help but gape when Eugene asked her why somebody would name their child President.

"You ever think about living somewhere else?" Lou asked him one morning while they were milking.

He said, "Mountain all I seed, but I knowed they a lot mo' to this world."

"I could take you to the city one day. Buildings so tall you can't walk up them. You ride in an elevator." He looked at her curiously. "A little car that pulls you up and down," she explained.

"Car? What, like'n the Hudson?"

"No, more like a little room you stand in."

Eugene thought that interesting, but said he'd probably just stick to farming on the mountain. "Want'a get hitched, have me a family, raise the chillin good."

"You'd make a good dad," she said.

He grinned. "Well, you'd be a fine ma. How you is with your brother and all."

Lou stared at him and said, "My mother was a great mom." Lou tried to recall if she had ever actually told her mother that. Lou knew she had spent most of her adoration on her father. It was a very troubling thought to her, since it was now beyond remedy.

A week after her ride to the school library, Lou had just finished reading to Amanda, when she went out to the barn to be by herself. She climbed to the hayloft and sat in the opening of the double doors and looked across the valley to the mountains beyond. Pondering her mother's depressing future, Lou finally turned her thoughts to the loss of Diamond. She had tried to put it out of her mind, but she realized she never really could.

Diamond's funeral had been a strange yet heartfelt affair. People had emerged from slivers of farms and crevices of homesteads that Lou was unaware even existed, and all these people came to Louisa's home by horse, ox, mule, foot, and tractor, and even one battered Packard with all its doors missing. Folks trooped through with plates of good food and jugs of cider. There were no formal preachers in attendance, but a number of folks stood and with shy voices offered comfort for the friends of the deceased. The cedar coffin sat in the front room, its lid securely nailed down, for no one had a desire to see what dynamite had done to Diamond Skinner.

Lou was not sure that all the older folks were really Diamond's friends, yet she assumed they had been friends of his father. In fact she had heard one old gent by the name of Buford Rose, who had a head of thick white hair and few teeth, mutter about the blunt irony of both father and son having been done in by the damn mines.

They laid Diamond to rest next to the graves of his parents, their mounds long since pulled back into the earth. Various people read from the Bible and there were more than a few tears. Oz stood in the center of them all and boldly announced that his often-baptized friend was a lock for heaven. Louisa laid a bundle of dried wildflowers in the grave, stepped back, started to talk but then couldn't.

Cotton offered up a fine eulogy to his young friend and recited a few examples from a storyteller he said he much admired: Jimmy "Diamond" Skinner. "In his own way," said Cotton, "he would put to shame many of the finest taletellers of the day."

Lou said a few quiet words, addressing them really to her friend in the box under the freshly turned dirt that smelled sweet yet sickened her. But he was not between those planks of cedar, Lou knew. He had gone on to a place higher even than the mountains. He was back with his father, and was seeing his mother for the very first time. He must surely be happy. Lou raised her hand to the sky and waved good-bye once again to a person who had come to mean so much to her, and who was now gone forever.

A few days after the burial, Lou and Oz had ventured to Diamond's tree house and took an accounting of his belongings. Lou said Diamond would naturally want Oz to have the bird skeleton, the Civil War bullet, the flint arrowhead, and the crude telescope.

"But what do you get?" asked Oz, as he examined his inherited spoils.

Lou picked up the box and took out the lump of coal, the one allegedly containing the diamond. She would make it her mission to chip carefully away at it, for as long as it took, until the brilliant center was finally revealed, and then she would go and bury it with Diamond. When she noted the small piece of wood lying on the floor in the back of the tree house, she sensed what it was before ever she picked it up. It was a whittled piece, not yet finished. It was cut from hickory, shape of a heart, the letter L carved on one side, an almost finished D on the other. Diamond Skinner *had* known his letters. Lou pocketed the wood and coal, climbed down the tree, and didn't stop running until she was back home.

They had, of course, adopted the loyal Jeb, and he seemed comfortable around them, though he would sometimes grow depressed and pine for his old master. Yet he too seemed to enjoy the trips Lou and Oz took to see Diamond's grave, and the dog, in the mysterious way of the canine pet, would start to yip and do spins in the air when they drew near to it. Lou and Oz would spread fall leaves over the mound and sit and talk to Diamond and to each other and retell the funny things the boy had done or said, and there was no short supply of either. Then they would wipe their eyes and head home, sure in their hearts that his spirit was roaming freely on his beloved mountain, his hair just as stuck up, his smile just as wide, his feet just as bare. Diamond Skinner had had no material possessions to his name and yet had been the happiest creature Lou had ever met. He and God would no doubt get along famously.

❧

They prepared for winter by sharpening tools with the grinder and rattail files, mucking out the stalls and spreading the manure over the plowed-under fields. Louisa had been wrong about that, though, for Lou never grew to love the smell of manure. They brought the livestock in, kept them fed and watered, milked the cows, and did their other chores, which now all seemed as natural as breathing. They carried jugs of milk and butter, and jars of mixed pickles in vinegar and brine, and canned sauerkraut and beans down to the partially underground dairy house, which had thick log walls, daubed and chinked, and paper stuffed where mud had fallen away. And they repaired everything on the farm that called for it.

School started, and, true to his father's words, Billy Davis never came back. No mention was made of his absence, as though the boy had never existed. Lou found herself thinking of him from time to time, though, and hoped he was all right.

After chores were done one late fall evening, Louisa sent Lou and Oz down to the creek that ran on the south side of the property to fetch balls from the sycamore trees that grew in abundance there. The balls had sharp stickers, but Louisa told them they would be used for Christmas decorations. Christmas was still a ways off, but Lou and Oz did as they were told.

When they got back, they were surprised to see Cotton's car in front. The house was dark and they cautiously opened the door, unsure of what they would find. The lights flew up as Louisa and Eugene took the black cloths from around the lanterns and they and Cotton called out "Happy Birthday," in a most excited tone. And it was their birthday, both of them, for Lou and Oz had been born on the same day, five years apart, as Amanda had informed Louisa in one of her letters. Lou was officially a teenager now, and Oz had survived to the ripe old age of eight.

A wild-strawberry pie was on the table, along with cups of hot cider. Two small candles were in the pie and Oz and Lou together blew them out. Louisa pulled out the presents she had been working on all this time, on her Singer sewing machine: a Chop bag dress for Lou that was a pretty floral pattern of red and green, and a smart jacket, trousers, and white shirt for Oz that had been created from clothes Cotton had given her.

Eugene had carved two whistles for them that gave off different tunes, such that they could communicate when apart in the deep woods or across acres of field. The mountains would send an echo to the sun and back, Louisa told them. They gave their whistles a blast, which tickled their lips, making them giggle.

Cotton presented Lou with a book of poems by Walt

Whitman. "My ancestor's superior in the arena of the poem, if I may so humbly admit," he said. And then he pulled from a box something that made Oz forget to breathe. The baseball mitts were things of beauty, well-oiled, worn to perfection, smelling of fine leather, sweat, and summer grass, and no doubt holding timeless and cherished childhood dreams. "They were mine growing up," Cotton said. "But I'm embarrassed to admit that while I'm not that good of a lawyer, I'm a far better lawyer than I ever was a ballplayer. Two mitts, for you and Lou. And me too, if you'll put up with my feeble athletic skills from time to time."

Oz said he would be proud to, and he hugged the gloves tight to his chest. Then they ate heartily of the pie and drank down the cider. Afterward Oz put on his suit, which fit very nicely; he looked almost like a tiny lawyer. Louisa had wisely tucked extra material under the hems to allow for the boy's growth, which seemed now to occur daily. So dressed, Oz took his baseball gloves and his whistle and went to show his mother. A little while later Lou heard strange sounds coming from Amanda's bedroom. When she went to check, she saw Oz standing on a stool, a sheet around his shoulders, a baseball glove on his head like a crown, and brandishing a long stick.

"And the great Oz the brave, and not cowardly lion anymore, killed all the dragons and saved all the moms and they all lived happily ever after in Virginia." He took off his crown of oiled leather and gave a series of sweeping bows. "Thank you, my loyal subjects, no trouble a'tall."

Oz sat next to his mother, lifted a book off the nightstand, and opened it to a place marked by a slip of paper. "Okay, Mom," said Oz, "this is the scary part, but just so you know, the witch doesn't eat the children." He inched close to her, draped one of her arms around his waist, and with big eyes started to read the scary part.

Lou went back to the kitchen, sat at the table in her Chop bag dress, which also well suited her, and read the brilliant words of Whitman by the glow of reliable kerosene. It became so late that Cotton stayed, and slept curled up in front of the coal fire. And another fine day had passed on the mountain.

CHAPTER THIRTY-TWO

WITHOUT EITHER LOUISA OR EUGENE knowing, Lou took a lantern and a match and she and Oz rode Sue down to the mine. Lou jumped down, but Oz sat on the horse and stared at the mouth of that cave as though it were the direct portal to hell. "I'm not going in there," he declared.

"Then wait out here," said his sister.

"Why do you want to go in there? After what happened to Diamond? The mountain might fall in on you. And I bet it'd hurt bad."

"I want to know what the men Diamond saw were up to."

Lou lit the lantern and went in. Oz waited near the entrance, pacing nervously, and then he ran in, quickly catching up to his sister.

"I thought you weren't coming," Lou said.

"I thought you might get scared," Oz answered, even as he clutched at her shirt.

They moved along, shivering from the cool air and their tender nerves. Lou looked around and saw what appeared to be new support beams along the walls and ceiling of the shaft. On the walls she also saw various markings in what looked to be white paint. A loud hissing sound reached out to them from up ahead.

"A snake?" asked Oz.

"If it is, it's about the size of the Empire State Building. Come on." They hurried ahead and the hissing sound grew louder with each step. They turned one corner, and the sound became even louder, like steam escaping. They cleared one more turn, ran forward, edged around a final bend in the rock, and stopped. The men wore hard hats and carried battery-powered lights, and their faces were covered with masks. In the floor of the mine was a hole, with a large metal pipe inserted in it. A machine that looked like a pump was attached by hoses to the pipe and was making the hissing sound they had heard. The masked men were standing around the hole, but didn't see the children. Lou and Oz backed up slowly and then turned and ran. Right into Judd Wheeler. Then they dodged around him and kept right on running.

A minute later Lou and Oz burst out of the mine. Lou stopped next to Sue and scrambled on, but Oz, apparently unwilling to trust his survival to something as slow as a horse, flew by sister and mare like a rocket. Lou punched Sue in the ribs with her shoes and took off after her brother. She didn't gain any ground on the boy, however, as Oz was suddenly faster than a car.

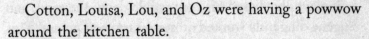

Cotton, Louisa, Lou, and Oz were having a powwow around the kitchen table.

"You crazy to go in that mine," said Louisa angrily.

"Then we wouldn't have seen those men," replied Lou.

Louisa struggled with this and then said, "G'on now. Me and Cotton need to talk."

After Lou and Oz left, she looked at Cotton.

"So what you think?" she asked.

"From how Lou described it, I think they were looking for natural gas instead of oil. And found it."

"What should we do?"

"They're on your property without your permission, and they know that we know. I think they'll come to you."

"I ain't selling my land, Cotton."

Cotton shook his head. "No, what you can do is sell the mineral rights. And keep the land. And gas isn't like coal mining. They won't have to destroy the land."

She shook her head stubbornly. "Had us a good harvest. Don't need no help from nobody."

Cotton looked down and spoke slowly. "Louisa, I hope you outlive all of us. But the fact is, if those children come into the farm while they're still under age, it'd be right difficult for them to get along." He paused and then added quietly, "And Amanda may need special care."

Louisa nodded slightly at his words but said nothing.

Later, she watched Cotton drive off, while Oz and Lou playfully chased his convertible down the road, and Eugene diligently worked on some farm equipment. This was the sum total of Louisa's world. Everything seemed to move along smoothly, yet it was all very fragile, she well knew. The woman leaned against the door with a most weary face.

The Southern Valley men came the very next afternoon.

Louisa opened the door and Judd Wheeler stood there, and beside him was a little man with snake eyes and a slick smile, dressed in a well-cut three-piece suit.

"Miss Cardinal, my name's Judd Wheeler. I work for Southern Valley Coal and Gas. This is Hugh Miller, the vice president of Southern."

"And you want my natural gas?" she said bluntly.

"Yes, ma'am," replied Wheeler.

"Well, it's a right good thing my lawyer's here," she said, glancing at Cotton, who had come into the kitchen from Amanda's bedroom.

"Miss Cardinal," said Hugh Miller as they sat down, "I don't believe in beating around the bush. I understand that you've inherited some additional family responsibilities, and I know how trying that can be. So I am most happy to offer you . . . a hundred thousand dollars for your property. And I've got the check, and the paperwork for you to sign, right here."

Louisa had never held more than five dollars cash money in her whole life, so "My goodness!" was all she could manage.

"Just so we all understand," Cotton said, "Louisa would just be selling the underlying mineral rights."

Miller smiled and shook his head. "I'm afraid for that kind of money, we expect to get the land too."

"I ain't gonna do that," said Louisa.

Cotton said, "Why can't she just convey the mineral rights? It's a common practice up here."

"We have big plans for her property. Gonna level the mountain, put in a good road system, and build an extraction, production, and shipping facility. And the longest durn pipeline anybody's seen outside of Texas. We've spent a while looking. This property is perfect. Don't see one negative."

Louisa scowled at him. " 'Cept I ain't selling it to you. You ain't scalping this land like you done everywhere else."

Miller leaned forward. "This area is dying, Miss Cardinal. Lumber gone. Mines closing. Folks losing their jobs. What good are the mountains unless you use them to help people? It's just rock and trees."

"I got me a deed to this land says I own it, but nobody really own the mountains. I just watching over 'em while I here. And they give me all I need."

Miller looked around. "All you need? Why, you don't even have electricity or phones up here. As a God-fearing woman I'm sure you realize that our creator gave us brains so that we can take advantage of our surroundings. What's a mountain compared to people making a good living? Why, what you're doing is going against the Scriptures, I do believe."

Louisa stared at the little man and looked as though she might laugh. "God made these mountains so's they last forever. Yet he put us people here for just a little-bitty time. Now, what does that tell you?"

Miller looked exasperated. "Look here now, my company is looking to make a substantial investment in bringing this place back to life. How can you stand in the way of all that?"

Louisa stood. "Just like I always done. On my own two feet."

Cotton followed Miller and Wheeler to their car.

"Mr. Longfellow," said Miller, "you ought to talk your client into accepting our proposal."

Cotton shook his head. "Once Louisa Mae Cardinal makes up her mind, changing it is akin to trying to stop the sun from rising."

"Well, the sun goes *down* every night too," said Miller.

Cotton watched as the Southern Valley men drove off.

The small church was in a meadow a few miles from the Cardinal farm. It was built of rough-hewn timbers and had a small steeple, one modest window of ordinary glass, and an abundance of charm. It was time for a down-on-the-ground church service and supper, and Cotton had driven Lou, Oz, and Eugene. They called it down-on-the-ground, Cotton explained, because there were no tables or chairs, but only blankets, sheets, and canvas; one large picnic under the guise of churchgoing.

Lou had offered to stay home with her mother so Louisa could go, but the woman wouldn't hear of it. "I read me my Bible, I pray to my Lord, but I ain't needing to be sitting and singing with folks to prove my faith."

"Why should I go then?" Lou had asked.

" 'Cause after church is supper, and that food ain't to be beat, girl," Louisa answered with a smile.

Oz had on his suit, and Lou wore her Chop bag dress and thick brown stockings held up by rubber bands, while Eugene wore the hat Lou had given him and a clean shirt. There were a few other Negroes there, including one petite young woman with remarkable eyes and beautifully smooth skin with whom Eugene spent considerable time talking. Cotton explained that there were so few Negroes up this way, they didn't have a separate church. "And I'm right glad of that," he said. "Not usually that way down south, and in the towns the prejudice is surely there."

"We saw the 'Whites Only' sign in Dickens," said Lou.

"I'm sure you did," said Cotton. "But mountains are different. I'm not saying everybody up here is a saint, because they're surely not, but life is hard and folks just trying to get by. Doesn't leave much time to dwell on things they shouldn't dwell on in the first place." He pointed to the first row and said, "George Davis and a few others excepted, that is."

Lou looked on in shock at George Davis sitting in the front pew. He had on a suit of clean clothes, his hair was combed, and he had shaved. Lou had to grudgingly admit that he looked respectable. None of his family was with him, though. His head was bowed in prayer. Before the service started, Lou asked Cotton about this spectacle.

He said, "George Davis almost always comes to services, but he never stays for the meal. And he never brings his family because that's just the way he is. I would hope he comes and prays because he feels he has much to atone for. But I think he's just hedging his bets. A calculating man, he is."

Lou looked at Davis there praying like God was in his heart and home, while his family remained behind in rags and fear and would have starved except for the kindness of Louisa Cardinal. She could only shake her head. Then she said to Cotton, "Whatever you do, don't stand next to that man."

Cotton looked at her, puzzled. "Why not?"

"Lightning bolts," she answered.

For too many hours they listened to the circuit minister, their rumps worn sore by hard oak benches, their noses tickled by the scents of lye soap, lilac water, and grittier smells from those who had not bothered to wash before coming. Oz nodded off twice, and Lou had to kick him each time to rouse him. Cotton offered up a special prayer for Amanda, which Lou and Oz very much appreciated. However, it seemed they were all doomed to hell according to this fleshy Baptist minister. Jesus had given his life for them, and a sorry lot they were, he said, himself included. Not good for much other than sinning and similar lax ways. Then the holy man really got going and reduced every human being in the place to near tears, or to at least the shakes, at their extreme uselessness and at the guilt dwelling in their awful sinned-out souls. And then he passed the collection plate and asked very politely for the cold hard cash of all the fine folks there today, their awful sin and extreme uselessness notwithstanding.

After services they all headed outside. "My father's a pastor in Massachusetts," said Cotton, as they walked down the church steps. "And he's also right partial to the fire and brimstone method of religion. One of his heroes was Cotton Mather, which is where I got my rather curious name. And I know that my father was greatly upset when I did not follow him on to the pulpit, but such is life. I had no great calling from the Lord, and didn't want to do the ministry any disservice just to please my father. Now, I'm no expert on the subject, yet a body does get weary of being dragged through the holy briar patch only to have his pocket regularly picked by a pious hand." Cotton smiled as he surveyed the folks gathering around the food. "But I guess it's a fair price to pay to sample some of these good vittles."

The food indeed was some of the best Lou and Oz had ever had: baked chicken, sugar-cured Virginia ham, collard greens and bacon, fluffy grits heaped with churned butter, fried crackling bread, vegetable casseroles, many-kind beans, and warm fruit pies—all no doubt created with the most sacred and closely guarded of family recipes. The children ate until they could eat no more, and then lay under a tree to rest.

Cotton was sitting on the church steps, working on a chicken leg and a cup of hot cider, and enjoying the peace of a good church supper, when the men approached. They were all farmers, with strong arms and blocky shoulders, a forward lean to all of them, their fingers curled tight, as though they were still working the hoe or scythe, toting buckets of water or pulling udder teats.

"Evening, Buford," said Cotton, inclining his head at one of the men who stepped forward from the pack, felt hat in hand. Cotton knew Buford Rose to be a toiler in dirt and seed of long standing here, and a good, decent man. His farm was small, but he ran it efficiently. He was not so old as Louisa, but he had said so long to middle age years ago. He made no move to talk, his gaze fixed on his crumbling brogans. Cotton looked at the other men, most of whom he knew from helping them with some legal problem, usually to do with their deeds, wills, or land taxes. "Something on your minds?" he prompted.

Buford said, "Coal folk come by to see us all, Cotton. Talk 'bout the land. Selling it, that is."

"Hear they're offering good money," said Cotton.

Buford glanced nervously at his companions, his fingers digging into his hat brim. "Well, they ain't got that fer yet. See, thing is, they ain't a'wanting to buy our land 'less Louisa sell. Say it got to do with how the gas lie and all. I ain't unnerstand it none, but that what they say."

"Good crops this year," said Cotton. "Land generous to all. Maybe you don't need to sell."

"What 'bout next year?" said a man who was younger than Cotton but looked a good ten years older. He was a third-generation farmer up here, Cotton knew, and he didn't look all that happy about it right now. "One good year ain't make up fer three bad."

"Why ain't Louisa want'a sell, Cotton?" asked Buford. "She way older'n me even, and I done all worked out, and my boy he ain't want to do this no more. And she got them chillin, and the sick woman care for. Ain't make no sense to me she ain't partial to sell."

"This is her home, Buford. Just like it is yours. And it doesn't have to make sense to us. It's her wishes. We have to respect that."

"But can't you talk to her?"

"She's made up her mind. I'm sorry."

The men stared at him in silence, clearly not a single one of them pleased with this answer. Then they turned and walked away, leaving a very troubled Cotton Longfellow behind.

Oz had brought his ball and gloves to the church supper, and he threw with Lou and then with some of the other boys. The men gawked at his prowess and said Oz had an arm like they had never seen before. Then Lou happened upon a group of children talking about the death of Diamond Skinner.

"Stupid as a mule, getting hisself blowed up like that," said one fat-cheeked boy Lou didn't know.

"Going in a mine with dynamite lit," said another. "Good Lord, what a fool."

"Course, he never went to school," said a girl with dark hair rolled in sausage curls who wore an expensive wide-brimmed hat with a ribbon around it and a frilly dress of similar cost. Lou knew her as Charlotte Ramsey, whose family didn't farm but owned one of the smaller coal mines, and did well with it. "So poor thing probably didn't know any better."

After listening to this, Lou pushed her way into the group. She had grown taller in the time she had been living on the mountain, and she towered over all of them, though they were all close in age to her.

"He went in that mine to save his dog," said Lou.

The fat-cheeked boy laughed. "Risk his life to save a hound. Boy *was* dumb."

Lou's fist shot out, and the boy was on the ground holding one of those fat cheeks that had just grown a little plumper. Lou stalked away and kept right on walking.

Oz saw what had happened and he collected his ball and gloves and caught up with her. He said nothing but walked silently beside her, letting her anger cool, surely nothing new for him. The wind was picking up and the clouds were rolling in as a storm front cleared the mountain tops.

"Are we walking all the way home, Lou?"

"You can go back and ride with Cotton and Eugene if you want."

"You know, Lou, as smart as you are, you don't have to keep hitting people. You can beat 'em with words."

She glanced at him and couldn't help but smile at his comment. "Since when did you get so mature?"

Oz thought about this for a few moments. "Since I turned eight."

They walked on.

Oz had strung his gloves around his neck with a piece of twine, and he idly tossed the ball in the air and caught it behind his back. He tossed it again but did not catch it, and the ball dropped to the ground, forgotten.

George Davis had stepped from the woods quiet as a fog. For Lou, his nice clothes and clean face did nothing to soften the evil in the man. Oz was instantly cowed by him, but Lou said fiercely, "What do you want?"

"I know 'bout them gas people. Louisa gonna sell?"

"That's her business."

"My bizness! I bet I got me gas on my land too."

"Then why don't you sell your property?"

"Road to my place goes cross her land. They can't git to me 'less she sell."

"Well, that's your problem," said Lou, hiding her smile, for she was thinking that perhaps God had finally turned his attention to the man.

"You tell Louisa if she knowed what's good for her she better sell. You tell her, she better damn well sell."

"And you better get away from us."

Davis raised his hand. "Smart-mouthed cuss!"

Quick as a snake, a hand grabbed Davis's arm and stopped it in midair. Cotton stood there, holding on to that powerful arm and staring at the man.

Davis jerked his arm free and balled his fists. "You gonna get hurt now, lawyer."

Davis threw a punch. And Cotton stopped the fist with his hand, and held on. And this time Davis couldn't break the man's grip, though he tried awfully hard.

When Cotton spoke, it was in a tone that was quiet and sent a delicious chill down Lou's back. "I majored in American literature in college. But I was also captain of the boxing team. If you ever raise your hand to these children again, I'll beat you within an inch of your life."

Cotton let go of the fist and Davis stepped back, obviously intimidated by both the calm manner and strong hands of his opponent.

"Cotton, he wants Louisa to sell her property so he can too. He's kind of insisting on it," said Lou.

"She doesn't want to sell," said Cotton firmly. "So that's the end of it."

"Lot of things happen, make somebody want'a sell."

"If that's a threat, we can take it up with the sheriff. Unless you'd like to address it with me right now."

With a snarl, George Davis stalked off.

As Oz picked up his baseball, Lou said, "Thank you, Cotton."

CHAPTER THIRTY-THREE

LOU WAS ON THE PORCH TRYING HER HAND at darning socks, but not enjoying it much. She liked working outside better than anything else and looked forward to feeling the sun and wind upon her. There was an orderliness about farming that much appealed to her. In Louisa's words, she was quickly coming to understand and respect the land. The weather was getting colder every day now, and she wore a heavy woolen sweater Louisa had knitted for her. Looking up, she saw Cotton's car coming down the road, and she waved. Cotton saw her, waved back, and, leaving his car, joined her on the porch. They both looked out over the countryside. "Sure is beautiful here this time of year," he remarked. "No other place like it, really."

"So why do you think my dad never came back?"

Cotton took off his hat and rubbed his head. "Well, I've heard of writers who have lived somewhere while young and then wrote about it the rest of their lives without ever once going back to the place that inspired them. I don't know, Lou, it may be they were afraid if they ever returned and saw the place in a new light, it would rob them of the power to tell their stories."

"Like tainting their memories?"

"Maybe. What do you think about that? Never coming back to your roots so you can be a great writer?"

Lou did not have to ponder this long. "I think it's too big a price to pay for greatness."

Before going to bed each night, Lou tried to read at least one of the letters her mother had written Louisa. One night a week later, as she pulled out the desk drawer she'd put them in, it slid crooked and jammed. She put her hand on the inside of the drawer to gain leverage to right it, and her fingers brushed against something stuck to the underside of the desk top. She knelt down and peered in, probing farther with her hand as she did so. A few seconds later she pulled out an envelope that had been taped there. She sat on her bed and gazed down at the packet. There was no writing on the outside, but Lou could feel the pieces of paper inside. She drew them out slowly. They were old and yellowed, as was the envelope. Lou sat on her bed and read through the precise handwriting on the pages, the tears creeping down her cheeks long before she had finished. Her father had been fifteen years old when he wrote this, for the date was written at the top of the page.

Lou went to Louisa and sat with her by the fire, explained to her what she had found and read the pages to her in as clear a voice as she could:

"My name is John Jacob Cardinal, though I'm called Jack for short. My father has been dead five years now, and my mother, well, I hope that she is doing fine wherever she is. Growing up on a mountain leaves its mark upon all those who share both its bounty and its hardship. Life here is also well known for producing stories that amuse and also exact tears. In the pages that follow I recount a tale that my own father told me shortly before he passed on. I have thought about his words every day since then, yet only now am I finding the courage to write them down. I remember the story clearly, yet some of the words may be my own, rather than my father's, though I feel I have remained true to the spririt of his telling.

"The only advice I can give to whoever might happen upon these pages is to read them with care, and to make up your own mind about things. I love the mountain almost as much as I loved my father, yet I know that one day I will leave here, and once I leave I doubt I will ever come back. With that said, it is important to understand that I believe I could be very happy here for the rest of my days."

Lou turned the page and began reading her father's story to Louisa.

   "It had been a long, tiring day for the man, though as a farmer he had known no other kind. With crop fields dust, hearth empty, and children hungry, and wife not happy about any of it, he set out on a walk. He had not gone far when he came upon a man of the cloth sitting upon a high rock overlooking stagnant water. 'You are a man of the soil,' said he in a voice gentle and seeming wise. The farmer answered that indeed he did make his living with dirt, though he would not wish such a life upon his children or even his dearest enemy. The preacher invited the farmer to join him upon the high rock, so he settled himself next to the man. He asked the farmer why he would not wish his children to carry on after their father. The farmer looked to the sky pretending thought, for his mind well knew what his mouth would say. 'For it is the most miserable life of all,' he said. 'But it is so beautiful here,' the preacher replied. 'Think of the wretched of the city living in squalor. How can a man of the open air and the fine earth say such a thing?' The farmer answered that he was not a learned man such as the preacher, yet he had heard of the great poverty in the cities where the folks stayed in their hovels all day, for there was no work for them to do. Or they got by on the dole. They starved—slowly, but they starved. Was that not true? he asked. And the preacher nodded his great and wise head at him. 'So that is starvation without effort,' said the farmer. 'A miserable existence if ever I heard

of one,' said the holy man. And the farmer agreed with him, and then said, 'And I have also heard that in other parts of the country there are farms so grand, on land so flat that the birds cannot fly over them in one day.' 'This too is true,' replied the other man. The farmer continued. 'And that when crops come in on such farms, they can eat like kings for years from a single harvest, and sell the rest and have money in their pockets.' 'All true,' said the preacher. 'Well, on the mountain there are no such places,' said the farmer. 'If the crops come fine we eat, nothing more.' 'And your point?' said the preacher. 'Well, my plight is this, preacher: My children, my wife, myself, we all break our backs every year, working from before the rise of sun till past dark. We work hard coaxing the land to feed us. Things may look good, our hopes may be high. And then it so often comes to naught. And we still starve. But you see, we starve with great effort. Is that not more miserable?' 'It has indeed been a hard year,' said the other man. 'But did you know that corn will grow on rain and prayer?' 'We pray every day,' the farmer said, 'and the corn stands at my knee, and it is September now.' 'Well,' the preacher said, 'of course the more rain the better. But you are greatly blessed to be a servant of the earth.' The farmer said that his marriage would not stand much more blessing, for his good wife did not see things exactly that way. He bowed his head and said, 'I'm sure I am a miserable one to complain.' 'Speak up, my son,' the holy man said, 'for I am the ears of God.' 'Well,' the farmer said, 'it creates discomfort in the marriage, pain between husband and wife, this matter of hard work and no reward.' The other man raised a pious finger and said, 'But hard work can be its own reward.' The farmer smiled. 'Praise the Lord then, for I have been richly rewarded all my life.' And the preacher seconded that and said, 'So your marriage is having troubles?' 'I am a wretch to complain,' the farmer said. 'I am the eyes of the Lord,' the preacher replied. They both looked at a sky of blue that had not a drop of what the farmer needed in it. 'Some people are not cut out for a life of such rich rewards,' he said. 'It is your wife you are speaking of now,' the preacher stated. 'Perhaps it is me,' the farmer said. 'God will lead you to the truth, my son,' the preacher said. Can a man be afraid of the truth? the farmer wanted to know. A man can be afraid of anything, the preacher told him. They rested there a bit, for the farmer had run clear out of words. Then he watched as the clouds came, the heavens opened, and the water rushed to touch them. He rose, for there was work to be done now. 'You see,' said the holy man, 'my words have come true. God has shown you the way.' 'We will see,' the farmer said. 'For it is late in the season now.' As he moved off to return to his land, the preacher called after him. 'Son of the soil,' he said, 'if the crops come fine, remember thy church in thy bounty.' The farmer looked back and touched his hand to the brim of his hat. 'The Lord does work in mysterious ways,' he told the other man. And then he turned and left the eyes and ears of God behind."

Lou folded the letter and looked at Louisa, hoping she had done the right thing by reading the words to her. Lou wondered if the young Jack Cardinal had noticed that the story had become far more personal when it addressed the issue of a crumbling marriage.

Louisa stared into the fire. She was silent for a few minutes and then said, "It be a hard life up here, 'specially for a child. And it hard on husband and wife, though I ain't never suffered that. If my momma and daddy ever said a cross word to the other, I ain't never heard it. And me and my man Joshua get along to the minute he took his last breath. But I know it not that way for your daddy up here. Jake and his wife, they had their words."

Lou took a quick breath and said, "Dad wanted you to come and live with us. Would you have?"

She looked at Lou. "You ask me why I don't never leave this place? I love this land, Lou, 'cause it won't never let me down. If the crops don't come, I eat the apples or wild strawberries that always do, or the roots that's there right under the soil, if'n you know where to look. If it snow ten-foot deep, I can get along. Rain or hail, or summer heat that melt tar, I get by. I find water where there ain't supposed to be none, I get on. Me and the land. Me and this mountain. That ain't prob'ly mean nothing to folks what can have light by pushing a little knob, or talk to people they can't even see." She paused and drew a breath. "But it means everything to me." She looked into the fire once more. "All your daddy say is true. High rock be beautiful. High rock be cruel." She gazed at Lou and added quietly, "And the mountain is my home."

Lou leaned her head against Louisa's chest. The

woman stroked Lou's hair very gently with her hand as they sat there by the fire's warmth.

And then Lou said something she thought she never would. "And now it's my home too."

CHAPTER THIRTY-FOUR

FLAKES OF SNOW WERE DROPPING FROM THE bellies of bloated clouds. Near the barn there came a whooshing sound and then a spark of harsh light that kept right on growing.

Inside the farmhouse Lou groaned in the throes of a nightmare. Her and Oz's beds had been moved to the front room, by the coal fire, and they were bundled under crazy quilts Louisa had sewn over the years. In Lou's tortured sleep she heard a noise, but couldn't tell what it was. She opened her eyes, sat up. There came a scratching at the door. In an instant Lou was alert. She opened the door and Jeb burst in, yipping and jumping.

"Jeb, what is it? What's wrong?"

Then she heard the screams of the farm animals.

Lou ran out in her nightshirt. Jeb followed her, barking, and Lou saw what had spooked him: The barn was fully ablaze. She ran back to the house, screamed out what was happening, and then raced to the barn.

Eugene appeared at the front door of the farmhouse, saw the fire, and hurried out, Oz at his heels.

When Lou threw open the big barn door, smoke and flames leapt out at her.

"Sue! Bran!" she screamed as the smoke hit her lungs; she could feel the hairs on her arms rise from the heat.

Eugene fast-limped past her, plunged into the barn, and then came right back out, gagging. Lou looked at the trough of water by the corral and a blanket hanging over the fence. She grabbed the blanket and plunged it into the cold water.

"Eugene, put this over you."

Eugene covered himself with the wet blanket and then lunged back into the barn.

Inside a beam dropped down and barely missed Eugene. Smoke and fire were everywhere. Eugene was as familiar with the insides of this barn as he was with anything on the farm, yet it was as though he had been struck blind. He finally got to Sue, who was thrashing in her stall, threw open the door, and put a rope around the terrified mare's neck.

Eugene stumbled out of the barn with Sue, threw the rope to Lou, who led the horse away with assistance from Louisa and Oz, and then Eugene went back into the barn. Lou and Oz hauled buckets of water from the springhouse, but Lou knew it was like trying to melt snow with your breath. Eugene drove out the mules and all the cows except one. But they lost every hog. And all their hay, and most of their tools and harnesses. The sheep were wintered outside, but the loss was still a devastating one.

Louisa and Lou watched from the porch as the barn, bare studs now, continued to burn. Eugene stood by the corral where he had driven the livestock. Oz was next to him with a bucket of water to dump on any creep of fire.

Then Eugene called out, "She coming down," and he pulled Oz away. The barn collapsed in on itself, the flames leaping skyward and the snow gently falling into this inferno.

Louisa stared in obvious agony at this ruin, as though she were caught in the flames herself. Lou tightly held her hand and was quick to notice when Louisa's fingers began to shake, the strong grip suddenly becoming impossibly weak.

"Louisa?"

The woman dropped to the porch without a word.

"Louisa!"

The girl's anguished cries echoed across the stark, cold valley.

Cotton, Lou, and Oz stood next to the hospital bed where Louisa lay. It had been a wild ride down the mountain in the old Hudson, gears thrashed by a frantic Eugene, engine whining, wheels slipping and then catching in the snowy dirt. The car almost went over the edge twice. Lou and Oz had clung to Louisa, praying that she would not leave them. They had gotten her to the small hospital in Dickens, and then Lou had run and rousted Cotton from his bed. Eugene had gone back up to look after Amanda and the animals.

Travis Barnes was attending her, and the man looked worried. The hospital was also his home, and the sight of a dining room table and a General Electric refrigerator had not comforted Lou.

"How is she, Travis?" asked Cotton.

Barnes looked at the children and then pulled Cotton to the side. "She's had a stroke," he said in a low voice. "Looks to be some paralysis on the left side."

"Is she going to recover?" This came from Lou, who had heard everything.

Travis delivered a woeful shrug. "There's not much we can do for her. The next forty-eight hours are critical. If I thought she could make the trip, I'd have sent her on to the hospital in Roanoke. We're not exactly equipped for this sort of thing. You can go on home. I'll send word if her condition changes."

Lou said, "I'm not leaving." And then Oz said the same.

"I think you've been overruled," said Cotton quietly.

"There's a couch right outside," Travis said kindly.

They were all asleep there, each holding the others up, when the nurse touched Cotton's shoulder.

She said softly, "Louisa's awake."

Cotton and the children eased the door open and went in. Louisa's eyes were open, but not much more than that. Travis stood over her.

"Louisa?" said Cotton. There was no answer, not even a hint of recognition. Cotton looked at Travis.

"She's still very weak," Travis said. "I'm amazed she's even conscious."

Lou just stared at her, more scared than she'd ever been. She just couldn't believe it. Her father, her mother. Diamond. Now Louisa. Paralyzed. Her mother had not moved a muscle for longer than Lou cared to think about. Was that to be Louisa's fate too? A woman who loved the earth? Who cherished her mountain? Who had lived as good a life as one could live? It was almost enough to make Lou stop believing in a God who could do such a terrible thing. Leaving a person with no hope. Leaving a person with nothing at all really.

✣

Cotton, Oz, Lou, and Eugene had just started their meal at the farmhouse.

"I can't believe they haven't caught whoever burned the barn down," Lou said angrily.

"There's no proof anybody burned it down, Lou," replied Cotton, as he poured the milk and then passed the biscuits.

"I know who did it. George Davis. Probably that gas company paid him to."

"You can't go around saying that, Lou, that's slander."

"I know the truth!" the girl shot back.

Cotton took off his glasses. "Lou, believe me—"

Lou leapt up from the table, her knife and fork clattering down and making them all jump. "Why should I believe anything you say, Cotton? You said my mom was going to come back. Now Louisa's gone too. Are you going to lie and say she's going to get better? Are you?"

Lou ran off. Oz started to go after her, but Cotton stopped him. "Let her be for now, Oz," he said. Cotton got up and went out on the porch, looking at the stars and contemplating the collapse of all he knew.

Flashing across in front of him was Lou on the mare. A startled Cotton could only stare after her, and then horse and girl were gone.

Lou rode Sue hard through the moonlit trails, tree limbs and brush poking and slapping at her. She finally came to Diamond's house and slid down, running and falling until she reached the doorway and plunged inside.

Tears streaming down her face, Lou stumbled around the room. "Why'd you have to leave us, Diamond? Now Oz and I have nobody. Nobody! Do you hear me? Do you, Diamond Skinner!"

A scuffling sound came from the front porch. Lou turned, terrified. Then Jeb raced through the open door and jumped into her arms, licking her face and breathing heavy from his long run. She hugged him. And then the tree branches started rattling against the glass, and an anxious moan came down the chimney, and Lou held especially tight to that dog. A window banged open, and the wind swirled around the room, and then things grew calm, and, finally, so did Lou.

She went outside, mounted Sue, and headed back, unsure of why she had even come here. Jeb trailed behind, tongue hanging low. She came to a fork in the road and turned left, toward the farm. Jeb started howling before Lou heard the noises herself. The throaty growls and ominous thrashing of underbrush were close upon them. Lou whipped up the horse, but before Sue could get rolling faster, the first of the wild dogs cleared the woods and came straight into their path. Sue reared up on her hind legs as the hideous creature, more wolf than dog, bared its teeth, its hackles straight up. Then another and another came from the woods, until a half dozen circled them. Jeb had his fangs bared and his hackles up too, yet he didn't stand a chance against so many, Lou knew. Sue kept rearing and neighing, and spinning in little circles until Lou felt herself slipping, as the wide body of the mare seemed to grow as narrow as a tightrope, and was also slicked, for the horse was lathered heavily after the long run.

One of the pack made a lunge for Lou's leg, and she pulled it up; the animal collided with one of Sue's hoofs and was temporarily stunned. There were too many of them, though, circling and snarling, ribs showing. Jeb went on the attack, but one of the brutes threw him down and he retreated, blood showing on his fur.

And then another beast snapped at Sue's foreleg and she went up again. And when she came down this time, she was riderless, for Lou had finally lost her grip and landed on her back, the wind knocked from her. Sue took off down the trail for home, yet Jeb stood like a stone wall in front of his fallen mistress, no doubt prepared to die for her. The pack moved in, sensing the easy kill. Lou forced herself up, despite the ache in her shoulder and back. There wasn't even a stick within reach, and she and Jeb moved backward until there was nowhere else to go. As she prepared herself to die fighting, the only thing Lou could think of was that Oz would now be all alone, and the tears welled up in her eyes.

The scream was like a net dropped over them, and the half-wolves turned. Even the largest of them, the size of a calf, flinched when it saw what was coming. The panther was big and sleek, muscles flexing under charcoal skin. It had amber eyes, and fangs showing that were double the size of the near-wolves'. And its claws too were fearsome things, like pitchfork hooked to knuckle. It screamed again when it got to the trail and headed for the wild pack with the power of a loaded coal train. The dogs turned and fled the fight, and that cat followed them, screaming with each graceful stride.

Lou and Jeb ran as hard as they could for home. About a half mile from the house they once more heard the crash of the underbrush next to them. Jeb's hackles went north again, and Lou's heart nearly stopped: She beheld the amber eyes of the cat out of the darkness as it ran parallel to them through the woods. That terrifying animal could shred both girl and hound in seconds. And yet all that thing did was run next to them, never once venturing out of the woods. The only reason Lou knew it was still there was the sounds of its paws against the leaves and undergrowth, and the glow of those luminous eyes, which looked free-floating in the darkness, as black skin blended with stark night.

Lou let out a thankful cry when she saw the farmhouse, and she and Jeb ran to the porch and then inside to safety. No one else was stirring, and Cotton, she assumed, had probably left long ago. Her chest heaving, Lou looked out the window, but never saw a sign of the beast.

Lou went down the hallway, every nerve still jangling badly. She paused at her mother's door and leaned against it. She had come so close to dying tonight, and it had been awful, more terrible than the car accident even, for she had been alone in her crisis. Lou peered inside the room and was surprised to find the window open. She went in, closed it, and turned to the bed. For one dazed moment she could not find her mother in the covers, and then of course there she was. Lou's breath became normal, the shivers of fear fading as she drew closer to the bed. Amanda was breathing lightly, her eyes closed, fingers actually curled, as though in pain. Lou reached out and touched her and then withdrew her hand. Her mother's skin was moist, clammy. Lou fled the room and bumped into Oz standing in the hall.

"Oz," she said, "you're not going to believe what happened to me."

"What were you doing in Mom's room?"

She took a step back. "What? I—"

"If you don't want Mom to get better, then you should just leave her alone, Lou. Just leave her alone!"

"But Oz—"

"Dad loved you the best, but I'll take care of Mom. Just like she always took care of us. I know Mom will get better, even if you don't."

"But you didn't take the bottle of holy water Diamond got for you."

"Maybe necklaces and holy water won't help Mom, but me believing she'll get better will. But *you* don't believe, so just leave her be."

He had never in his life talked to her this way. He just stood there and glared, his thin, strong arms dangling by his sides, like needles at the end of thread. Her little brother really angry at her! She couldn't believe it. "Oz!" He turned and walked away. "Oz," she called again. "Please, don't be mad at me. Please!" Oz never turned around. He went into his room and shut the door.

Lou stumbled to the back of the house, then went out and sat on the steps. The beautiful night, the wondrous sight of the mountains, the calls of all kind of wildlife made no impression at all on her. She looked at her hands where the sun had leathered them, the palms rough as oak bark. Her fingernails were jagged and dirty, her hair knotted and lye-soaped to death, her body fatigued beyond her years, her spirit given way to despair after losing almost all those she cared about. And now her precious Oz no longer loved her.

At that moment, the hated mine siren boomed across the valley. It was as though the mountain were shrieking in anticipation of the coming pain. The sound seemed to splinter Lou's very soul. And next the rumble of the dynamite came and finished her off. Lou looked to that Cardinal graveyard knoll and suddenly wished she was there too, where nothing else could ever hurt her.

She bent over and wept quietly into her lap. She hadn't been there long when she heard the door creak open behind her. At first she thought it might be Eugene checking on her, but the tread was too light. The arms wrapped around her and held her tight.

Lou could feel her brother's delicate breaths on her neck. She stayed bent over, yet she reached behind her and wrapped an arm around him. And brother and sister stayed there like that for the longest time.

CHAPTER THIRTY-FIVE

THEY RODE THE WAGON DOWN TO McKenzie's Mercantile, and Eugene, Lou, and Oz went inside. Rollie McKenzie stood behind a waist-high counter of warped maple. He was a little ball of a man, with a shiny, hairless head and a long grayish white beard that rested on his slack chest. He wore spectacles of great strength, yet the man still had to squint to see. The store was filled to nearly over-flowing with farm supplies and building materials of various kinds. The smell of leather harnesses, kerosene oil, and burning wood from the corner potbelly filled the large space. There were glass candy dispensers and a Chero Cola box against one wall. A few other customers were in the place and they all stopped and gaped at Eugene and the children as though they were apparitions come haunting.

McKenzie squinted and nodded at Eugene, his fingers picking at his thick beard, like a squirrel worrying a nut.

"Hi, Mr. McKenzie," said Lou. She had been here several times now and found the man gruff but fair.

Oz had his baseball mitts draped around his neck and was tossing his ball. He was never without them now, and Lou suspected her brother even slept with the things.

"Real sorry to hear 'bout Louisa," McKenzie said.

"She's going to be fine," said Lou firmly, and Oz gave her a surprised look and almost dropped his baseball.

"What can I do for you?" asked McKenzie.

"Got to raise us a new barn," said Eugene. "Got to have us some things."

"Somebody burned our barn down," said Lou, and she glared around at the people staring.

"Use some finished board, posts, nails, hardware for the doors, and such," said Eugene. "Got me a good list right chere." He pulled a piece of paper from his pocket and laid it on the counter. McKenzie did not look at it.

"I'll need cash up front," he said, finally letting his beard alone.

Eugene stared at the man. "But we good on our 'count. All paid up, suh."

Now McKenzie eyed the paper. "Lot of stuff on that list. Can't carry you for that much."

"So's we bring you crop. Barter."

"No. Cash."

"Why can't we get credit?" asked Lou.

"Hard times," replied McKenzie.

Lou looked around at the piles of supplies and goods everywhere. "Times look pretty good to me."

McKenzie slid back the list. "I'm sorry."

"But we's got to have a barn," said Eugene. "Winter come fast and we ain't keep the animals out. They die."

"The animals we have *left*," said Lou, glaring some more at the still staring faces.

A man equal in size to Eugene approached from the rear of the store. Lou knew him to be McKenzie's son-in-law, who was no doubt looking forward, she figured, to inheriting this good business one day when McKenzie squinted his last.

"Look here, Hell No," said the man, "you got your answer, boy."

Before Lou could say a word, Eugene stepped directly in front of the man. "You knowed that ain't *never* been my name. It be Eugene Randall. And don't you *never* call me nuthin' else." The big man appeared stunned, and he took a step back. Lou and Oz exchanged glances and then looked proudly upon their friend.

Eugene stared down each of the customers in the store, ostensibly, Lou thought, to make clear that this statement applied to all of them as well.

Rollie McKenzie called out, "I'm sorry for that, Eugene. It won't never happen again."

Eugene nodded at McKenzie and then told the children to come on. They went outside and climbed on the wagon. Lou was shaking with anger. "It's that gas company. They've scared everybody. Turned people against us."

Eugene took up the reins. "It be all right. We think'a somethin'."

Oz cried out, "Eugene, wait a minute." He jumped down from the wagon and ran back inside.

"Mr. McKenzie? Mr. McKenzie?" Oz called out, and the old man came back to the counter, blinking and picking at his beard.

Oz plopped his mitts and ball on the curled maple planks. "Will this buy us a barn?"

McKenzie stared at the child, and the old man's lips trembled some, and his blinking eyes grew moist through the heft of glass. "You go on home, boy. You go on home now."

They cleared all the debris from the remains of the barn and collected all the nails, bolts, and usable wood that they could from the ruins. Cotton, Eugene, and the children stood and stared at the meager pile.

"Not much there," said Cotton.

Eugene looked at the surrounding forests. "Well, we got us lot of wood, and it all free, 'cept the sweat of felling it."

Lou pointed to the abandoned shack her father had written about. "And we can use stuff from there," she said, then looked at Cotton and smiled. They had not spoken since Lou's outburst, and she was feeling badly about it. "Maybe make us a miracle," she added.

"Well, let's get to work," said Cotton.

They tore down the shack and salvaged what they could. Over the next several days they cut down trees with an ax and a crosscut saw that had been in the corn-crib and thus had escaped the fire. They pulled out the felled trees with the mules and chains. Fortunately, Eugene was a first-rate, if self-taught, carpenter. They topped off the trees and stripped the bark, and using a square and a measuring tape, Eugene cut marks in the wood showing where notches needed to be chiseled. "Ain't got 'nough nails, so's we got to make do. Notch and strap the joints best we can, mud chink 'tween. When we get mo' nails, we do the job right."

"What about the corner posts?" asked Cotton. "We don't have any mortar to set them in."

"Ain't got to. Dig the holes deep, way below the cold line, crack up the rock, pack it in good and hard. It hold. I give us some extra hep at the corners with the braces. You see."

"You're the boss," said Cotton with an encouraging smile.

Using a pick and shovel, Cotton and Eugene dug one hole. It was tough going against the hard ground. Their cold breath filled the air, and their gloved hands ached with the raw. While they were doing this, Oz and Lou chiseled out and hand-drilled the notches and insertion holes on the posts where timber mortise would meet timber tenon. Then they mule-dragged one of the posts to the hole and realized they had no way to get it in there. Try as they might, from every angle, and with every conceivable leverage, and with big Eugene straining every muscle he had, and little Oz too, they could not lift it enough. "We figger that out later," said Eugene finally, his big chest heaving from the failed effort.

He and Cotton laid out the first wall on the ground and started to hammer. Halfway through they ran out of nails. They collected all the scrap metal they could find and Eugene made a roaring coal fire for his forge. Then, using his smithy hammer, tongs, and shoeing anvil, he fashioned as many rough nails from the scrap as he could.

"Good thing iron doesn't burn," remarked Cotton, as he watched Eugene working away on the anvil, which still stood in the middle of what used to be the barn.

All of Eugene's hard work netted them enough nails to finish another third of the first wall, and that was all.

They had been at this for many cold days now, and all they had to show for it was one hole and a single finished corner post and no way to allow either to meet, and a wall without enough nails to hold it together.

They collected early one morning around the post and hole to mull this over, and all agreed the situation did not look good. A hard winter was creeping ever closer and they had no barn. And Sue, the cows, and even the mules were showing the ill effects of being out in the freezing air all night. They could not afford to lose any more livestock.

And as bad as this plight was, it was really the least of their problems, for while Louisa had regained consciousness from time to time, she had not spoken a word when awake, and her eyes appeared dead. Travis Barnes was very worried, and fretted that he should send her to Roanoke, but he was afraid she would still not survive the trip, and the fact was, there wasn't much they could do for her there anyway. She had been able to drink and eat a bit, and while it wasn't much, Lou took it as something to hold on to. It was as much as her mother was able to do. At least they were both still alive.

Lou looked around their small, depressed group, then gazed at the naked trees on the angled slopes and wished winter would magically dissolve to summer's warmth, and Louisa would rise fine and healthy from her sickbed. The sounds of the wheels made them all turn and stare. The line of approaching wagons pulled by mule, horse, and oxen teams was a long one. They were filled with cut lumber, large padstones, kegs of nails, ropes, ladders, block and tackle, augers, and all manners of other tools, that Lou suspected came in part from McKenzie's Mercantile. Lou counted thirty men in all, all from the mountain, all of them farmers. Strong, quiet, bearded, they wore coarse clothing and wide-brimmed hats against a winter's sun, and all had large, thick hands severely battered by both the mountain elements and a lifetime of hard work. With them were a half dozen women. They unloaded their supplies. While the women laid out canvas and blankets and used Louisa's cookstove and fireplace to start preparing the meals, the men began to build a barn.

Under Eugene's direction, they constructed supports for the block and tackle. Forgoing the route of post and mortar in hole, they opted to use the large, flat padstones for the barn's foundation. They dug shallow footers, laid the stones, leveled them, and then placed massive hewn timbers across the stones as the sill plates. These plates were secured together all around the foundation. Additional timbers were run down the middle of the barn floor and attached to the sill plates. Later, other posts would be placed here and braced to support the roof framework and hayloft. Using the block and tackle, the mule teams lifted the massive corner posts up and on top of the sill plates. Thick brace timbers were nailed into the corner posts on either side, and then the braces themselves were firmly attached to the plates.

With the barn's foundation set, the wall frames were built on the ground, and Eugene measured and marked and called out instructions on placement. Ladders were put up against the corner posts and holes augured into them. They used the block and tackle to raise other timbers up to be used as the crossbeams. Holes had been hand-drilled through these timbers, and they were attached to the corner posts with long metal bolts.

There was a shout as the first wall was run up, and each time after that as the remaining walls were built and run up. They framed the roof, and then the hammering became relentless as stud walls were further built out. Saws sliced through the air, cold breaths crowded each other, sawdust swirled in the breeze, men held nails in their mouths, and hands moved hammers with practiced motions.

Two meals were rung for, and the men dropped to the ground and ate hard each time. Lou and Oz carried plates of warm food and pots filled with hot chicory coffee to the groups of tired men. Cotton sat with his back against the rail fence, sipping his coffee, resting his sore muscles, and watching with a broad smile as a barn began to emerge out of nothing but the sweat and charity of good neighbors.

As Lou placed a platter of hot bread slathered with butter in front of the men, she said, "I want to thank all of you for helping."

Buford Rose picked up a piece of the bread and took a savage, if near toothless, bite. "Well, got to hep each other up here, 'cause ain't nobody else gonna. Ask my woman, ain't b'lieve me. And Lord knows Louisa's done her share of hepping folks round here." He looked over at Cotton, who tipped his cup of coffee to the man. "I knowed what I said to you 'bout being all worked out, Cotton, but lotta folk got it badder'n me. My brother be a dairy farmer down the Valley. Can't barely walk no more with all that setting on the stool, fingers done curled like some crazy root. And folk say two things dairy farmer ain't never gonna need they's whole lives:

suit'a nice clothes and a place to sleep." He tore off another bread chunk.

A young man said, "Hell, Ms. Louisa done borned me. My ma say I aint'a coming to this world what she not there." Other men nodded and grinned at this remark. One of them looked over to where Eugene was standing near the rising structure, chewing on a piece of chicken and figuring out the next tasks to be done.

"And he done help me raise new barn two spring ago. Man good with hammer 'n saw. Ain't no lie."

From under knotted plugs of eyebrows Buford Rose studied Lou's features. "I 'member your daddy good, girl. You done take after him fine. That boy, all the time pestering folk with questions. I had to tell him I done ain't got no more words in my head." He gave a near toothless grin, and Lou smiled back.

The work continued. One group planked the roof and then laid out the roll of roofing paper on top. Another team, headed up by Eugene, fashioned the double doors for both ends, as well as the hayloft doors, while yet another group planked and daubed the outside walls. When it got too dark to see what they were hitting and cutting, kerosene lamps lit the night. The hammering and sawing got to be almost pleasing to hear. Almost. None complained, though, when the final board had been laid, the last nail driven. It was well into dark when the work was done and the wagons headed out.

Eugene, Cotton, and the children wearily herded the animals into their new home and laid the floor with hay gathered from the fields and the corncrib. The hayloft, stalls, storage bins, and such still needed to be built out, and the roll of roofing would eventually need to be covered with proper wood shingles, but the animals were inside and warm. With a very relieved smile, Eugene shut the barn doors tight.

CHAPTER THIRTY-SIX

COTTON WAS DRIVING THE CHILDREN down to visit Louisa. Though they were well into winter, heavy snow had not yet come, merely dustings of several inches, though it would only be a matter of time before it fell hard and deep. They passed the coal company town where Diamond had adorned the superintendent's new Chrysler Crown Imperial with horse manure. The town was empty now, the housing abandoned, the store vacant, the tipple sagging, the entrance to the mine boarded up, and the mine superintendent's fancy, horseshitted Chrysler long gone.

"What happened?" said Lou.

"Shut down," answered Cotton grimly. "Fourth mine in as many months. Veins were already petering out, but then they found out the coke they make here is too soft for steel production, so America's fighting machine went looking elsewhere for its raw material. Lot of folks here out of work. And the last lumber company moved on to Kentucky two months ago. A double blow. Farmers on the mountain had a good year, but the people in the towns are hurting bad. It's usually one or the other. Prosperity only seems to come in halves up here." Cotton shook his head. "Indeed, the fine mayor of Dickens resigned his post, sold out his stake at inflated prices before the crash, and headed to Pennsylvania to seek a new fortune. I've often found the ones who talk the best game are the first ones to run at the earliest sign of trouble."

Coming down the mountain, Lou noted that there were fewer coal trucks, and that many of the mountainside tipples weren't even being operated. When they passed Tremont, she saw that half the stores were boarded up, and there were few people on the streets, and Lou sensed it wasn't just because of the chilly weather.

When they got to Dickens, Lou was shocked, for many stores were boarded up here as well, including the one Diamond had opened an umbrella in. Bad luck had reigned there after all, and it was no longer funny to Lou. Ill-clothed men sat on sidewalks and steps, staring at nothing. There weren't many cars slant-parked, and shopkeepers stood, idle hands on hips, nervous looks on faces, in the doorways of their empty stores. The men and women walking the streets were very few in number, and their faces carried an anxious pallor. Lou watched as a bus filled with folks slowly headed out of town. An empty coal train symbolically crept behind the line of buildings and parallel to the main road. The "Coal Is King" banner was no longer flying mighty and proud across the

Cotton looked the men over. Other than Davis, they were all men from the town, not the mountain. But he knew that didn't mean they were any less desperate than folks who tethered their survival to dirt, seed, and the fickleness of rain. These folks had just tied their hopes to coal. But coal was unlike corn; once plucked, coal didn't grow back.

"I've already been over this with you, George, and the answer hasn't changed. Now, if you'll excuse me, I've got to get these children home."

"Whole town gone to hell," said another man.

"And you think that's Louisa's fault?" asked Cotton.

"She dying. She ain't need her land," said Davis.

"She's not dying!" said Oz.

"Cotton," said a well-dressed man about fifty years old who, Cotton knew, ran the automobile dealership in Dickens. He had narrow shoulders, thin arms, and smooth palms that clearly showed he had never hoisted a hay bale, swung a scythe, or plowed a field. "I'm going to lose my business. I'm going to lose everything I've got if something doesn't replace the coal. And I'm not the only one like that. Look around, we're hurting bad."

"What happens when the natural gas runs out?" countered Cotton. "Then what will you be looking for to save you?"

"Ain't got to look that fer ahead. Take care of bizness now, and that bizness be gas," said Davis in an angry voice. "We all git rich. I ain't got no problem selling my place, hep my neighbor."

"Really?" said Lou. "I didn't see you at the barn raising, George. In fact you haven't been back since Louisa ran you off. Unless you had something to do with our barn burning down in the first place."

Davis spit, wiped his mouth, and hitched his britches, and would've no doubt throttled the girl right there if Cotton hadn't been standing next to her.

"Lou," said Cotton firmly, "that's enough."

"Cotton," said the well-dressed man, "I can't believe you're abandoning us for some stupid mountain woman. Hell, you think you'll have any lawyering to do if the town dies?"

Cotton smiled. "Don't y'all worry about me. You'd be amazed at how little I can get by on. And regarding Miss Cardinal, y'all listen up, because it's the last time I'm going to say it. She does *not* want to sell her land to Southern Valley. That's her right, and y'all better damn well respect it. Now, if you really and truly can't survive here without the gas folks, then I suggest you leave. Because you see, Miss Cardinal doesn't have that problem. Every lick of coal and gas could disappear from this earth tomorrow, and electricity and phones too, and she'd be just fine." He stared pointedly at the well-dressed man. "Now tell me, who's the stupid one?"

Cotton told the children to climb in the car, and he eased himself into the driver's seat, even as the men pushed forward a bit, crowding him. Several of them moved back and blocked the rear of the car. Cotton started the engine of the Olds, rolled down the window, and looked at them. "Now, the clutch on this thing is right peculiar. Sometimes it pops out and this old girl jumps about a country mile. Almost killed a man one time when it did that. Well, here goes. Look out now!"

He popped the clutch, and the Olds jumped backward, and so did all the men. The path cleared, Cotton backed out and they headed off. When the rock banged against the rumble seat of the car, Cotton pushed down on the accelerator and told Lou and Oz to get down and stay down. Several more rocks hit against the car, before they were safely out of range.

"What about Louisa?" asked Lou.

"She'll be fine. Travis is most always around, and he's a man not to be beat with a shotgun. And when he's not there, his nurse is just about as fine a shot. And I warned the sheriff folks were getting a bit riled. They'll keep close watch. But those people aren't going to do anything to a helpless woman in a bed. They're hurting, but they're not like that."

"Are they going to throw rocks at us every time we come to visit Louisa?" asked Oz fearfully.

Cotton put an arm around the boy. "Well, if they do, I suspect they'll run out of rocks long before we run out of visits."

When they got back to the farmhouse, an anxious-looking Eugene hurried out, a piece of paper in his hand.

"Man from the town come by with this, Mr. Cotton. I ain't knowed what it is. He say give it to you quick."

Cotton opened up the slip of paper and read it. It was a delinquent tax notice. He had forgotten Louisa had not paid her property taxes for the last three years because there had been no crops, and thus no money. The county had carried her over, as it did with all the other farmers in similar circumstances. They were expected to pay of course, but they were always given time. This notice, however, was demanding payment in full immediately. Two hundred dollars' worth of payment. And since she had been in default for so long, they could foreclose and sell the land far more quickly than normal. Cotton could feel Southern Valley's vicious stamp all over the paper.

"Is something wrong, Cotton?" asked Lou.

He looked at her and smiled. "I'll take care of it, Lou. Just paperwork, honey."

Cotton counted out the two hundred dollars to the clerk of the court and was given a stamped receipt. He trudged back to his apartment and boxed up the last pile of books. A few minutes later he looked up to see Lou standing in his doorway.

"How did you get here?" he asked.

"I got a ride with Buford Rose in his old Packard. There are no doors on the thing, so it's a fine view, but you're only one jolt away from flying out, and it's pretty cold." She stared around at the empty room. "Where are all your books, Cotton?"

He chuckled. "They were taking up too much space." He tapped his forehead. "And, leastways, I've got it all right up here."

Lou shook her head. "I went by the courthouse. I figured there was more to that paper we got than you were letting on. Two hundred dollars for all your books. You shouldn't have done it."

Cotton closed up the box. "I still have some left. And I'd like you to have them."

Lou stepped into the room. "Why?"

"Because they're your father's works. And I can't think of a better person to take care of them."

Lou said nothing while Cotton taped the box shut.

"Let's go over and see Louisa now," Cotton said.

"Cotton, I'm getting scared. More stores have closed. And another bus full of people just left. And the looks folks gave me on the street. They're really angry. And Oz got in a fight at school with a boy who said we were ruining people's lives by not selling."

"Is Oz all right?"

She smiled weakly. "He actually won the fight. I think it surprised him more than anybody. He's got a black eye, and he's right proud of it."

"It'll be all right, Lou. Things will work out. We'll weather this."

She took a step closer, her expression very serious. "Things aren't working out. Not since we've come here. Maybe we should sell and leave. Maybe it'll be better for all of us. Get Mom and Louisa the care they need." She paused and could not look at him as she added, "Someplace else."

"Is that what you want to do?"

Lou wearily stared off. "Sometimes what I want to do is go up on the little knoll behind our house, lay on the ground, and never move again. That's all."

Cotton considered this for a few moments and then said, "In the world's broad field of battle, / In the bivouac of Life, / Be not like dumb, driven cattle! / Be a hero in the strife! / Trust no Future, howe'er pleasant! / Let the dead Past bury its dead! / Act—act in the glorious Present! / Heart within, and God o'erhead! / Lives of great men all remind us / We can make *our* lives sublime, / And, departing, leave behind us . . . Footprints on the sands of time."

" 'A Psalm of Life.' Henry Wadsworth Longfellow," said Lou without much enthusiasm.

"There's more to the poem, but I've always considered those lines the essential parts."

"Poetry is beautiful, Cotton, but I'm not sure it can fix real life."

"Poetry needn't fix real life, Lou, it need just be. The fixing is up to us. And laying on the ground and never moving again, or running from trouble, is not the Lou Cardinal I know."

"That's very interesting," said Hugh Miller, as he stood there in the doorway. "I looked for you at your office, Longfellow. I understand you've been over at the courthouse paying the debts of *others*." He flashed a nasty grin. "Right good of you, however misguided."

"What do you want, Miller?" said Cotton.

The little man stepped into the room and looked at Lou. "Well, first I want to say how sorry I am about Miss Cardinal."

Lou crossed her arms and looked away.

"Is that all?" Cotton said curtly.

"I also came by to make another offer on the property."

"It's not my property to sell."

"But Miss Cardinal isn't in a position to consider the offer."

"She already refused you once, Miller."

"That's why I'm cutting right to the chase and raising my offer to five hundred thousand dollars."

Cotton and Lou exchanged startled glances, before Cotton said, "Again, it's not my property to sell."

"I assumed you would have a power of attorney to act on her behalf."

"No. And if I did, I still wouldn't sell to you. Now, is there anything else I *can't* do for you?"

"No, you've told me all I need to know." Miller handed a packet of papers to Cotton. "Consider your client served."

Miller walked out with a smile. Cotton quickly read through the papers, while Lou stood nervously beside him.

"What is it, Cotton?"

"Not good, Lou."

Cotton suddenly grabbed Lou's arm, and they raced down the stairs and over to the hospital. Cotton pushed open the door to Louisa's room. The flashbulb went off right as they came in. The man looked over at them and then he took another picture of Louisa in her bed. There was another man next to him, large and powerfully built. Both were dressed in nice suits and wore creased hats.

"Get out of here!" cried Cotton.

He raced over and tried to grab the camera from the man, but the big fellow pulled him away, allowing his partner to slide out the door. Then the big man backed out of the room, a smile on his lips.

Cotton could only stand there, breathing hard and looking helplessly between Lou and Louisa.

CHAPTER THIRTY-SEVEN

I T WAS A PARTICULARLY COLD, CLOUDLESS DAY when Cotton entered the courtroom. He stopped when he saw Miller and another man there, who was tall, portly, and very well dressed, his fine silver hair combed neatly on a head so massive it seemed hardly natural.

Cotton said to Miller, "I was pretty sure I'd see you today."

Miller inclined his head at the other man. "You probably heard of Thurston Goode, Commonwealth's attorney for Richmond?"

"Indeed I have. You argued a case before the United States Supreme Court recently, didn't you, sir?"

"More precisely," Goode said in a deep, confident baritone, "I *won* the case, Mr. Longfellow."

"Congratulations. You're a long way from home."

"The state was kind enough to allow Mr. Goode to

come down here and act on its behalf in this very important matter," explained Miller.

"Since when does a simple suit to declare a person mentally unfit qualify for the expertise of one of the finest lawyers in the state?"

Goode smiled warmly. "As an officer of the Commonwealth I don't have to explain to you why I'm here, Mr. Longfellow. Suffice it to say, that I *am* here."

Cotton put a hand to his chin and pretended to ponder something. "Let's see now. Virginia elects its Commonwealth's attorneys. Might I inquire as to whether Southern Valley has made a donation to your campaign, sir?"

Goode's face flushed. "I don't like what you're implying!"

"I did not mean it as an implication."

Fred the bailiff came in and announced, "All rise. The Court of the Honorable Henry J. Atkins is now in session. All those having business before this court draw near and you shall be heard."

Judge Henry Atkins, a small man with a short beard, thinning silver hair, and clear gray eyes, came into the room from his adjacent chambers and took his seat behind the bench. Before he got up there, he looked too small for his black robe. Once he got there, he looked too large for the courtroom.

It was at this point that Lou and Oz crept in without anyone seeing them. Wearing barter coats and thick socks stuffed into oversized boots, they had retraced their steps across the poplar-log bridge and down the mountain, catching a ride on a truck to Dickens. It had been a much harder trek in cold weather, but the way Cotton had explained it to them, the potential effect of this proceeding on all their lives was very clear. They sat slumped down at the rear, their heads barely visible over the back of the seats in front of them.

"Call the next case," said Atkins. It was his only case today, but the law court had its rituals.

Fred announced the pending matter of *Commonwealth versus Louisa Mae Cardinal.*

Atkins smiled broadly from his judicial perch. "Mr. Goode, I'm honored to have you in my courtroom, sir. Please state the Commonwealth's position."

Goode rose and hooked a finger in his lapel.

"This certainly is not a pleasant task, but one that the Commonwealth has a duty to perform. Southern Valley Coal and Gas has made an offer to purchase property solely owned by Miss Cardinal. We believe that because of her recent stroke she is not legally fit to make an informed decision on that offer. Her only relatives are both underage and thus disqualified from acting for her. And we understand that the surviving parent of these children is herself severely mentally incapacitated. We also have it on good authority that Miss Cardinal has signed no power of attorney allowing others to represent her interests."

On this Cotton cast a sharp glance at Miller, who just looked ahead in his cocksure manner.

Goode continued, "In order to fully protect Miss Cardinal's rights in this matter, we are seeking to have her declared mentally unfit, and to have a guardian appointed so that an orderly disposition of her affairs may be conducted, including this very lucrative offer from Southern Valley."

Atkins nodded as Goode sat down. "Thank you, Mr. Goode. Cotton?"

Cotton rose and stood before the bench. "Your Honor, what we have here is an attempt to circumvent rather than facilitate Miss Cardinal's wishes. She has already rejected an offer from Southern Valley to purchase her land."

"Is that true, Mr. Goode?" queried the judge.

Goode looked confident. "Miss Cardinal rejected one such offer; however, the present offer is for considerably more money, and thus must be separately entertained."

"Miss Cardinal made it very clear that she would not sell her land at any price to Southern Valley," said Cotton. He looped his finger around his coat lapel as Goode had done, then thought better of it and removed it.

"Do you have any witnesses to that effect?" asked Judge Atkins.

"Uh . . . just me."

Goode immediately pounced. "Well, if Mr. Longfellow intends to make himself a material witness in this case, I insist he recuse himself as counsel for Miss Cardinal."

Atkins looked at Cotton. "Is that what you want to do?"

"No, it's not. However, I can represent Louisa's interests until she's better."

Goode smiled. "Your Honor, Mr. Longfellow has expressed a clear prejudice to my client in full view of the court. He can hardly be considered independent enough to *fairly* represent Miss Cardinal's interests."

"I'm inclined to agree with him there, Cotton," said Atkins.

"Well, then we contend that Miss Cardinal is not mentally unfit," countered Cotton.

"Then we have ourselves a dispute, gentlemen," said the judge. "I'm setting this for trial in one week."

Cotton was astonished. "That's not enough time."

"One week's fine with us," said Goode. "Miss Cardinal's affairs deserve to be attended to with all due speed and respect."

Atkins picked up his gavel. "Cotton, I've been over to the hospital to see Louisa. Now, whether she has her senses or not, it seems to me those children are going to at least need a guardian. We might as well get it done as quick as possible."

"We can take care of ourselves."

They all looked to the back of the courtroom, where Lou was now standing. "We can take care of ourselves," she said again. "Until Louisa gets better."

"Lou," said Cotton, "this is not the time or place."

Goode smiled at them. "Well, you two sure are adorable *children*. I'm Thurston Goode. How y'all doing?"

Neither Lou nor Oz answered him.

"Young lady," said Atkins, "come up here."

Lou swallowed the lump in her throat and walked

up to the bench, where Atkins peered down at her, like Zeus to mortal.

"Young lady, are you a member of the State Bar?"

"No. I mean . . . no."

"Do you know that only members of the Bar may address the court except in the most extraordinary circumstances?"

"Well, since this concerns me and my brother, I think the circumstances *are* extraordinary."

Atkins looked at Cotton and smiled before looking back at Lou. "You're smart, that's easy to see. And quick. But the law is the law, and children your age can't live by themselves."

"We have Eugene."

"He's not a blood relative."

"Well, Diamond Skinner didn't live with anybody."

Atkins looked over at Cotton. "Cotton, will you explain this to her, please."

"Lou, the judge is right, you're not old enough to live by yourself. You need an adult."

Lou's eyes suddenly filled with tears. "Well, we keep running out of those." She turned and raced down the aisle, pushed open the double doors, and was gone. Oz fled after her.

Cotton looked back up at Judge Atkins.

"One week," said the judge. He smacked his gavel and returned to his chambers, like a wizard resting after throwing a particularly difficult spell.

Outside the courtroom, Goode and Miller waited for Cotton. Goode leaned in close to him. "You know, Mr.

Longfellow, you can make this a lot easier on everybody if you'd just cooperate. We all know what a mental examination is going to reveal. Why put Miss Cardinal through the humiliation of a trial?"

Cotton leaned even closer to Goode. "Mr. Goode, you could give a damn whether Louisa's affairs are accorded the respect they deserve. You're here as a hired gun for a big company looking to twist the law so they can take her land."

Goode just smiled. "We'll see you in court."

That night Cotton labored behind his piled-high desk. He mumbled to himself, wrote things down and then scratched them out, and paced like an expectant father. The door creaked open, and Cotton stared as Lou came in with a basket of food and a pot of coffee.

"Eugene drove me down in the car to see Louisa," she explained. "I got this over at the New York Restaurant. Figured you probably skipped supper."

Cotton looked down. Lou cleared a place on his desk, laid out the food, and poured the coffee. Finished, she made no move to leave.

"I'm pretty busy, Lou. Thank you for the food."

Cotton went to his desk and sat down, but he moved not one piece of paper, opened not a single book.

"I'm sorry about what I said in court," said Lou.

"It's all right. I guess if I were you, I would've done the same thing."

"You sounded really good."

"On the contrary, I failed utterly."

"But the trial hasn't started yet."

He took off his glasses and rubbed them with his tie. "Truth is I haven't really tried a case in years, and even then I wasn't very good. I just file papers, write up deeds and wills, that sort of thing. And I've never gone up against a lawyer like Goode." He put his glasses back on, seeing clearly for perhaps the first time all day. "And I wouldn't want to promise you something I can't deliver."

This line stood between them like a wall of flames.

"I believe in you, Cotton. Whatever happens, I believe in you. I wanted you to know that."

"Why in the world do you have faith in me? Haven't I done nothing except let you down? Quoted miserable poetry that can't change anything."

"No, all you've tried to do is help."

"I can never be the man your father was, Lou. In fact, I'm really not good for all that much, it appears."

Lou stood beside him. "Will you promise me one thing, Cotton? Will you promise you won't ever leave us?"

After a few moments Cotton cupped the girl's chin and said in a halting voice that in no way lost its strength, "I will stay for as long as all of you will have me."

CHAPTER THIRTY-EIGHT

OUTSIDE THE COURTHOUSE, FORDS, CHEVYS, and Chryslers were slant-parked next to wagons pulled by mules and horses. A dusting of snow had given pretty white toppers to just about everything, yet no one was paying any attention to that. They had all hurried into the courthouse to see a much grander show.

The courtroom had never held so many souls. The seats on the main floor were filled. Folks even stood in the back and were sandwiched five deep on the second-floor balcony. There were town men in suits and ties, women in church dresses and boxy hats with veils and fake flowers or dangling fruit. Next to them were farmers in clean overalls and felt hats held in hand, their chew stashed in their pockets. Their women were beside them, Chop dresses to the ankles and wire glasses over worn, creased faces. They looked around the room excitedly as though they were about to see a queen or movie star stroll in.

Children were wedged here and there among the adults like mortar between brick. To get a better look, one boy climbed up on the railing around the balcony and clung to a support column. A man hauled him down and sternly told him that this was a court of law and dignity was required here, not tomfoolery. The ashamed boy trudged off. And then the man climbed up on the railing for a better look-see himself.

Cotton, Lou, and Oz were heading up the steps of the courthouse when a boy in an overcoat, slacks, and shiny black shoes ran up to them.

"My pa says you're doing wrong by the whole town on account of one woman. He said we got to have the gas folks here, any way we can." The little fellow looked at Cotton as though the lawyer had spit on the boy's mother and then laughed about it.

"Is that right?" said Cotton. "Well, I respect your daddy's opinion, though I don't agree with it. Now, you tell him if he wants to discuss it with me in person later, I'd be right glad to do so." Cotton glanced around and saw someone who he was sure was the child's father, for the boy favored the man and he had been staring at them, but quickly looked away. Cotton glanced at all the cars and wagons and then said to the boy, "You and your daddy better get yourselves inside and get a seat. Looks to be a right popular spot today."

When they entered the courtroom, Cotton was still amazed at the numbers in attendance. Yet, the hard work of farming *was* over for now, and people had time on their hands. And for the townsfolk it was an accessible show promising fireworks at a fair price. It seemed they were determined to miss not one legal trick, not one semantical headlock. For many this probably would be the most exciting time of their lives. And wasn't that a sad thing, Cotton thought.

Yet, he knew the stakes here *were* high. A place dying once more only perhaps to be revitalized by a deep-pocketed company. And all he had to lay against that was an old woman lying in a bed, her senses seemingly struck from her. And there were also two anxious children counting on him; and lying in another bed a woman who maybe he could lose his heart to if only she would awaken. *Lord, how was he ever going to survive this?*

"Find a seat," Cotton told the children. "And keep quiet."

Lou gave him a peck on the cheek. "Good luck." She crossed her fingers for him. A farmer they knew made room for them in one of the rows of seats.

Cotton went up the aisle, nodding at people he recognized in the crowd. Smack in the front row were Miller and Wheeler.

Goode was at the counsel table, seeming as happy as a hungry man at a church supper as he looked around at a crowd that seemed famished to witness this contest.

"You ready to have a go at this?" said Goode.

"As ready as you are," Cotton replied gamely.

Goode chuckled. "With all due respect, I doubt that."

Fred the bailiff appeared and said his official words, and they all rose, and the Court of the Honorable Henry J. Atkins was now in session.

"Send in the jury," the judge said to Fred.

The jury filed in. Cotton looked at them one by one, and almost fell to the floor when he saw George Davis as one of the chosen.

He thundered, "Judge, George Davis wasn't one of the jurors we voir dired. He has a vested interest in the outcome of this case."

Atkins leaned forward. "Now, Cotton, you know we have a hard enough time getting jurors to serve. I had to drop Leroy Jenkins because he got kicked by his mule. Now, I know he's not the most popular person around, but George Davis has as much right to serve as any other man. Look here, George, can you keep a fair and open mind about this case?"

Davis had his churchgoing clothes on and looked quietly respectable. "Yes, sir," he said politely and looked around. "Why, y'all knowed Louisa's place right next to mine. Get along good." He smiled a black-toothed smile, which he seemed to have difficulty with, as though it were something he'd never before attempted.

"I'm sure Mr. Davis will make a fine juror, your Honor," said Goode. "No objection here."

Cotton looked at Atkins, and the curious expression on the judge's face made Cotton think twice about what was really going on here.

Lou sat in her seat, silently fuming at this. It was wrong. And she wanted to stand up and say it was, yet for once in her life she was too intimidated. This was a court of law, after all.

"He's lying!" The voice thundered, and every head in the place turned to its source.

Lou looked next to her to find Oz standing on his seat, taller now than all in the courtroom. His eyes were on fire, his finger pointed straight at George Davis. "He's lying," Oz roared again in a voice so deep Lou did not even recognize it as her brother's. "He hates Louisa. It's wrong for him to be here."

Cotton had been struck dumb like all the others. He glanced around the room. Judge Atkins stared at the little boy, none too pleased. Goode was about ready to spring to his feet. And Davis's look was so fierce that Cotton was very grateful that no gun was handy for the man. Cotton raced to Oz and swooped up the boy.

"Apparently, the propensity for public outbursts runs in the Cardinal family," Atkins boomed. "Now, we can't have that, Cotton."

"I know, Judge. I know."

"It's wrong. That man is a liar!" yelled Oz.

Lou was scared. She said, "Oz, please, it's okay."

"No, it's not, Lou," said Oz. "That man is hateful. He starves his family. He's wicked!"

"Cotton, take that child out," roared the judge. "Right now."

Cotton carried out Oz, with Lou trailing in their wake.

They sat on the cold courthouse steps. Oz wasn't crying. He just sat there and smacked his small fists against his slender thighs. Lou felt tears trickle down her cheeks as she watched him. Cotton put an arm around Oz's shoulders.

"It's not right, Cotton," said Oz. "It's just not right." The boy kept punching his legs.

"I know, son. I know. But it'll be okay. Why, having George Davis on that jury might be a good thing for us."

Oz stopped hitting himself. "How can that be?"

"Well, it's one of the mysteries of the law, Oz, but you'll just have to trust me on it. Now I suspect y'all still want to watch the trial." They both said that they would very dearly want to do that.

Cotton glanced around and saw Deputy Howard Walker standing by the door. "Howard, it's a little cold for these children to be waiting out here. If I guarantee no more outbursts, can you find a way to get them back in, 'cause I got to get going. You understand."

Walker smiled and gripped his gunbelt. "Y'all come on with me, children. Let Cotton go work his magic."

Cotton said, "Thank you, Howard, but helping us might cost you some popularity in this town."

"My daddy and brother died in those mines. Southern Valley can go to hell. Now, you get on in there and show them what a fine lawyer you are."

After Cotton went back in, Walker took Lou and Oz in through a rear entrance and got them settled at a spot in the balcony reserved for special visitors, after receiving a solemn promise from Oz that he would not be heard from again.

Lou looked at her brother and whispered. "Oz, you were really brave to do that. I was afraid to." He smiled at her. Then she realized what was missing. "Where's the bear I bought you?"

"Shoot, Lou, I'm too old for bears and thumb sucking."

Lou looked at her brother and suddenly realized that this was true. And a tear clutched at her eye, for she suddenly had an image of her brother grown tall and strong and no longer in need of his big sister.

Down below, Cotton and Goode were having a heated sidebar with Judge Atkins at the bench.

"Now look here, Cotton," said Atkins. "I'm not unmindful of what you're saying about George Davis, and your objection is duly noted for the record, but Louisa delivered two of those jurors into this world, and the Commonwealth didn't object to that." He looked over at Goode. "Mr. Goode, will you excuse us for a minute here?"

The lawyer looked shocked. "Your Honor, an ex parte contact with counsel? We don't do those sorts of things in Richmond."

"Well, damn good thing this ain't Richmond then. Now, just take yourself on over there for a bit." Atkins waved his hand like he was flicking at flies, and Goode reluctantly moved back to his counsel table.

"Cotton," said Atkins, "we both know there's a lot of

interest in this case, and we both know why: money. Now, we got Louisa laying over to hospital and most folks thinking she's not going to make it anyway. And then we got us Southern Valley cash staring folks in the face."

Cotton nodded. "So you're thinking the jury is going to go against us despite the merits of the case?"

"Well, I can't really say, but if you do lose here—"

"Then having George Davis on the jury gives me real good grounds for appeal," finished Cotton.

Atkins looked very pleased that Cotton had seized upon this strategy so readily. "Why, I never thought of that. Real glad you did. Now let's get this show on the road."

Cotton moved back to his counsel table while Atkins smacked his gavel and announced, "Jury is hereby impaneled. Be seated."

The jury collectively sat itself down.

Atkins looked them over slowly before his gaze came to rest on Davis. "One more thing now before we start. I've had my backside on this here bench for thirty-four years, and there's never been anything close to jury tampering or messing around along those lines in my courtroom. And there's never going to be such, for if there ever was, the folks that did it will think spending their whole lives in the coal mines a birthday party compared to what I'll do to them." He gave Davis one more good stare, fired similar broadsides at both Goode and Miller, and then said, "Now the parties have waived their opening statements. So Commonwealth, call your first witness."

"Commonwealth calls Dr. Luther Ross," said Goode.

The ponderous Dr. Ross rose and went to the witness stand. He had the gravity lawyers liked, when he was on *their* side; otherwise he was just a well-paid liar.

Fred swore him in. "Raise your right hand, put your left one on the Bible. Do you solemnly swear to tell the truth, the whole truth, and nothing but the truth so help you God?"

Ross said he most certainly would tell the truth and nothing but, and wedged himself into the witness chair.

Fred retreated and Goode approached.

"Dr. Ross, sir, would you state your mighty fine credentials for the jury please?"

"I'm chief of the asylum down over to Roanoke. I've taught courses in mental evaluation at the Medical College in Richmond, and at the University of Virginia. And I've personally handled over two thousand cases like this one."

"Well now, I am sure Mr. Longfellow and this court would agree that you are truly an expert in your field. In fact, you may be the number-one expert in your field, and I would say this jury deserves to hear nothing less."

"Objection, Your Honor!" said Cotton. "I don't believe there's any proof that Mr. Goode is an expert in ranking experts."

"Sustained, Cotton," said Atkins. "Get on with it, Mr. Goode."

Goode smiled benignly, as though this tiny skirmish

had been a way for him to evaluate Cotton's mettle. "Now, Mr. Ross," said Goode, "have you had occasion to examine Louisa Mae Cardinal?"

"I have."

"And what is your expert opinion on her mental competence?"

Ross smacked the frame of the witness box with one of his flabby hands. "She is *not* mentally competent. In fact, my considered opinion is she should be institutionalized."

There came a loud buzz from the crowd, and Atkins impatiently pounded his gavel. "Quiet down," said he.

Goode continued. "Institutionalized? My, my. That's some serious business. So you're saying she's in no shape to handle her own affairs? Say, for the sale of her property?"

"Absolutely not. She could be easily taken advantage of. Why, that poor woman can't even sign her own name. Probably doesn't know what her name is." He eyed the jury with a most commanding look. "Institutionalized," he said again in the projected voice of a stage actor.

Goode asked a series of carefully crafted questions, and to each he got the answers he wanted: Louisa Mae was undoubtedly mentally unfit, according to the esteemed expert Dr. Luther Ross.

"No further questions," Goode finally said.

"Mr. Longfellow?" said Atkins. "I suspect you want to have a go."

Cotton got up, took off his glasses, and dangled them by his side as he addressed the witness.

"You say you've examined over two thousand people?"

"That's correct," Ross said with a lift of his chest.

"And how many did you find incompetent, sir?"

Ross's chest immediately deflated, for he clearly hadn't expected that inquiry. "Uh, well, it's hard to say."

Cotton glanced at the jury and moved toward him. "No, it's really not. You just have to *say* it. Let me help you a little. A hundred percent? Fifty percent?"

"Not a hundred percent."

"But not fifty?"

"No."

"Let's whittle it on down now. Eighty? Ninety? Ninety-five?"

Ross thought for a few moments. "Ninety-five percent sounds about right."

"Okay. Let me see now. I think that works out to be nineteen hundred out of two thousand. Lord, that's a lot of crazy people, Dr. Ross."

The crowd laughed and Atkins banged his gavel, but a tiny smile escaped him as well.

Ross glared at him. "I just call 'em like I see 'em, lawyer."

"Dr. Ross, how many stroke victims have you examined to determine whether they're mentally competent?"

"Uh, why, none that I can recall offhand."

Cotton paced back and forth in front of the witness, who kept his gaze on the attorney as an even line of sweat appeared on Ross's brow. "I suppose with most of the people you see, they have some mental disease. Here we have a stroke victim whose *physical* incapacity may make it seem like she's not mentally fit even though she may very well be." Cotton sought out and found Lou in the balcony. "I mean, just because one can't talk or move doesn't mean one can't understand what's going on around her. She may well see, hear, and understand everything. Everything!"

Cotton swung back and looked at his witness. "And given time she may very well fully recover."

"The woman I saw was not likely to recover."

"Are you a medical doctor expert on stroke victims?" Cotton said in a sharp voice.

"Well, no. But—"

"Then I'd like an instruction from the bench for the jury to disregard that statement."

Atkins said to the cluster of men, "You are hereby instructed to take no notice whatsoever of Dr. Ross saying that Miss Cardinal would not recover, for he is most assuredly not *competent* to testify to that."

Atkins and Ross exchanged glares at the judge's choice of words, while Cotton put a hand over his mouth to hide his grin.

Cotton continued. "Dr. Ross, you really can't tell us that today, or tomorrow, or the next day, Louisa Mae Cardinal won't be perfectly capable of handling her own affairs, can you?"

"The woman I examined—"

"Please answer the question I asked, sir."

"No."

"No, what?" Cotton added pleasantly, "For this fine jury."

A frustrated Ross crossed his arms. "No, I cannot say for sure that Miss Cardinal will not recover today or tomorrow or the next day."

Goode heaved himself to his feet. "Your Honor, I see where counsel is going with this and I think I have a resolution. As of right now Dr. Ross's testimony is that Miss Cardinal is not competent. If she gets better, and we all hope she does, then the court-appointed representative can be dismissed and she can handle her own affairs from then on."

Cotton said, "By then, she won't have any land left."

Goode seized upon this opening. "Well, then Miss Cardinal can surely take comfort in the half a million dollars Southern Valley has offered for her property."

An enormous gasp went through the crowd at the mention of this ungodly sum. One man almost toppled over the balcony rail before his neighbors pulled him back to safety. Both dirty and clean-faced children looked at one another, eyes popping. And their mothers and fathers were doing the exact same thing. The jurors too looked at one another in clear astonishment. Yet George Davis just sat there staring straight ahead, not one emotion showing on his features.

Goode continued quickly, "As I'm sure others can when the company makes similar offers to *them*."

Cotton looked around and decided he would much rather be doing anything other than what he was. He saw both mountain dwellers and townsfolk gaping at him: the one man who stood in the way of their rightful fortune. And yet with all that weighing down upon him, he shook his mind clear and roared, "Judge, he's just as good as bribed this jury with that statement. I want a mistrial. My client can't get a fair shake with these people counting Southern Valley dollars."

Goode smiled at the jury. "I withdraw the statement. Sorry, Mr. Longfellow. No harm intended."

Atkins leaned back in his chair. "You're not getting a mistrial, Cotton. Because where else you going to go with this thing? Just about everybody from fifty miles around already's sitting in this courtroom, and the next nearest bench is a day away by train. And the judge there isn't nearly as nice as I am." He turned to the jury. "Now listen here, folks, you're to ignore Mr. Goode's statement about the offer to purchase Miss Cardinal's land. He shouldn't have said it, and you are to forget it. And I mean what I say!"

Atkins next focused on Goode. "I understand you have a fine reputation, sir, and I'd hate to be the one to taint it. But you pull something like that again, and I got me a nice little jail cell in this building where you'll be doing your time for contempt, and I might just forget you're even there. You understand me?"

Goode nodded and said meekly, "Yes, Your Honor."

"Cotton, you have any more questions for Dr. Ross?"

"No, Judge," Cotton said and dropped into his seat.

Goode put Travis Barnes on the stand, and though he did his best, under Goode's artful maneuvering, the good doctor's prognosis for Louisa was rather bleak. Finally, Goode waved a photograph in front of him.

"This is your patient, Louisa Mae Cardinal?"

Barnes looked at the photograph. "Yes."

"Permission to show the jury."

"Go on ahead, but be quick about it," said Atkins.

Goode dropped a copy of the photo in front of Cotton. Cotton didn't even look at it, but ripped the photograph into two pieces and dropped it in the spittoon next to his table while Goode paraded the original in front of the jurors' faces. From the clucks and muted comments and shakes of head, the photo had its intended effect. The only one who didn't look upset was George Davis. He held the photo especially long and seemed to Cotton to have to work awfully hard to hide his delight. The damage done, Goode sat down.

"Travis," said Cotton, rising and coming to stand next to his friend, "have you ever treated Louisa Cardinal for any ailments before this last one?"

"Yes, I have. A couple of times."

"Can you tell us about those instances, please."

"About ten years ago, she was bitten by a rattler. Killed the durn thing herself with a hoe, and then she come down the mountain by horse to see me. Arm swollen to about the size of my leg by that time. She took seriously ill, ran a fever higher'n I'd ever seen. In and out of consciousness for days. But she came out of it, right when we thought she wasn't going to make it. Fought like a durn mule she did."

"And the other time?"

"Pneumonia. That winter four years ago when we had more snow than the South Pole. Y'all remember that one?" he asked the folks in the courtroom and they all nodded back at him.

"No way to get up or down the mountain then. It was four days before they got word to me. I got up there and treated her when the storm ended, but she was already past the worst of it all by herself. Would'a killed a young person *with* medicine, and here she was into her seventies and not a drop of anything except her own will to live. I've never seen anything like it."

Cotton went and stood over near the jury. "So, she sounds like a woman of indomitable spirit. A spirit that cannot be conquered."

"Objection, Your Honor," said Goode. "Is that a question, or a divine pronouncement on your part, Mr. Longfellow?"

"I hope both, Mr. Goode."

"Well, let's put it this way," said Barnes, "if I were a betting man, I wouldn't bet against the woman."

Cotton looked over at the jury. "Neither would I. No further questions."

"Mr. Goode, who you calling next?" asked Atkins.

The Commonwealth's attorney rose and looked around the courtroom. He kept looking and looking until his gaze reached the balcony, moved around its edges, and then came to rest on Lou and Oz. And then finally on Oz alone.

"Young man, why don't you come on down here and talk to us."

Cotton was on his feet. "Your Honor, I see no reason—"

"Judge," broke in Goode, "now, it's the children that's going to have the guardian, and thus I think it reasonable to hear from one of them. And for a little fellow he has a mighty fine voice, since everybody in this courtroom has heard it loud and long already."

There was muted laughter from the crowd, and Atkins absently smacked his gavel while he pondered this request for six rapid beats of Cotton's heart. "I'm going to allow it. But remember, Goode, he's just a little boy."

"Absolutely, Your Honor."

Lou held Oz's hand and they slowly walked down the stairs and passed each of the rows, all eyes in the courtroom upon them. Oz put his hand on the Bible and was sworn in as Lou went back to her seat. Oz perched in the chair, looking so small and helpless that Cotton's heart went out to him, even as Goode moved in.

"Now, Mr. Oscar Cardinal," he began.

"My name's Oz, my sister's name is Lou. Don't call her Louisa Mae or else she'll get mad and punch you."

Goode smiled. "Now, don't you worry about that. Oz and Lou it is." He leaned against the witness stand. "Now, you know the court's right sorry to hear that your momma's doing so poorly."

"She's going to get better."

"Is that right? That what the doctors say?"

Oz looked up at Lou until Goode touched Oz's cheek and pointed his face toward him.

"Now, son, up here on the witness stand you got to

speak the truth. You can't look to your big sister for answers. You swore to God to tell the truth."

"I always tell the truth. Cross my heart, stick a needle."

"Good boy. So, again, did the doctors say your mother
will get better?"

"No. They said they weren't sure."

"So how do you know she will?"

"Because . . . because I made a wish. At the wishing
well."

"Wishing well?" said Goode with an expression for
the jury that clearly spelled out what he thought of that
answer. "There's a wishing well round here? I *wish* we
had one of them back in Richmond."

The crowd laughed and Oz's face turned pink and
he squirmed in his seat. "There *is* a wishing well," he
said. "My friend Diamond Skinner told us about it. You
make a wish and give up the most important thing you
have and your wish will come true."

"Sounds mighty fine. Now, you said you made your
wish?"

"Yes, sir."

"And you gave up the most important thing you had.
What was that?" Oz looked nervously around the room.
"The truth, Oz. Remember what you promised to God,
son."

Oz took a long breath. "My bear. I gave up my bear."

There were a few muffled chuckles from the on-
lookers, until all saw the single tear slide down the little boy's face, and then the snickers ceased.

"Has your wish come true yet?" asked Goode.

Oz shook his head. "No."

"Been a while since you wished?"

"Yes," Oz answered softly.

"And your momma's still real sick, isn't she?"

Oz bowed his head. "Yes," he said in a tiny voice.

Goode put his hands in his pockets. "Well, sad fact is, son, things don't come true just 'cause we wish 'em to. That's not real life. Now, you know your great-grandmother's real sick, don't you?"

"Yes, sir."

"You make a wish for her too?"

Cotton rose. "Goode, leave it be."

"Fine, fine. Now, Oz, you know you can't live by yourself, right? If your great-grandma doesn't get better, under the law, you have to go live with an adult in their home. Or else go to an orphanage. Now, you don't want to go to no old orphanage, do you?"

Cotton jumped to his feet again. "Orphanage? When did that become an issue?"

Goode said, "Well, if Miss Cardinal does not make another miraculous recovery as she did with rattlers and pneumonia, then the children are going to have to go somewhere. Now, unless they've got some money I don't know about, they're going to an orphanage, because that's where children go who don't have blood relatives to take care of them, or other persons of a worthy nature willing to adopt them."

"They can come live with me," said Cotton.

Goode looked about ready to laugh. "You? An unmarried man? A lawyer in a town that's dying? You'd be the last person on earth a court would award those children to." Goode turned back to Oz. "Now, wouldn't you like to go live in your own home with someone who has your best interests at heart? You'd like that, wouldn't you?"

"I don't know."

"Course you would. Orphanages are not the nicest places in the world. Some kids stay there forever."

"Your Honor," said Cotton, "does all this have a point other than to terrify the witness?"

"Why, I was just about to ask Mr. Goode that," declared Atkins.

It was Oz, though, who spoke. "Can Lou come too? I mean, not to the orphanage, but to the other place?"

"Why sure, son, sure," said Goode quickly. "Never break up sister and brother." He added quietly, "But there's no guarantee of that with an orphanage." He paused. "So, that'd be all right with you, Oz?"

Oz hesitated and tried to look at Lou, but Goode was too quick and blocked his view. Oz finally said quietly, "I guess so."

Cotton looked up in the balcony. Lou was on her feet, fingers wrapped around the railing, her anxious gaze fixed on her brother.

Goode went over to the jury and made a show of rubbing his eyes. "That's a fine boy. No further questions."

"Cotton?" said Atkins.

Goode sat down and Cotton rose, but then he stopped, his fingers gripping the table's edge as he stared at the ruin of a boy on the big witness chair; a little boy who, Cotton knew, just wanted to get up and go back to his sister because he was scared to death of orphanages and fat lawyers with big words and embarrassing questions, and huge rooms filled with strangers staring at him.

"No questions," said Cotton very quietly, and Oz fled back to his sister.

After more witnesses had paraded through court, showing that Louisa was utterly incapable of conscious decision, and Cotton only able to slap at bits and pieces of their testimony, the trial was adjourned for the day and Cotton and the children left the courtroom. Outside, Goode and Miller stopped them.

"You're putting up a good fight, Mr. Longfellow," said Goode, "but we all know how this is going to turn out. What say we just put an end to it right now? Save people any further embarrassment." He looked at Lou and Oz as he said this. He started to pat Oz on the head, but the boy gave the lawyer a fierce look that made Goode pull back his hand before he might have lost it.

"Look, Longfellow," said Miller, pulling a piece of paper out of his pocket, "I've got a check here for half a million dollars. All you got to do is end this nonsense and it's yours."

Cotton looked at Oz and Lou and then said, "I tell you what, Miller, I'll leave it up to the children. Whatever they say, I'll do."

Miller squatted down and smiled at Lou and Oz. "This money will go to you now. Buy anything you want.

Live in a big house with a fancy car and people paid to look after you. A right nice life. What do you say, children?"

"We already have a home," said Lou.

"Okay, what about your momma then? People in her condition need a lot of care, and it's not cheap." He dangled the check in front of the girl. "This solves *all* your problems, missy."

Goode squatted down too and looked at Oz. "And it'll keep those nasty orphanages far, far away. You want to stay with your sister, now don't you?"

"You keep your old money," said Oz, "for it's not something we need or want. And Lou and I will always be together. Orphanage or not!"

Oz took his sister's hand and they walked off.

Cotton looked at the men as they rose, and Miller angrily stuffed the check back in his pocket. "From out of the mouths of babes," said Cotton. "We should all be so wise." And then he walked off too.

Back at the farmhouse, Cotton discussed the case with Lou and Oz. "I'm afraid unless Louisa can walk into that courtroom tomorrow, she's going to lose her land." He looked at them both. "But I want you to know that whatever happens, I will be there for all of you. I will take care of all of you. Don't you worry about that. You will *never* go to an orphanage. And you will never be split up. That I swear." Lou and Oz hugged Cotton as tightly as they could, and then he left to prepare for the final day in court. Perhaps their final day on this mountain.

Lou made supper for Oz and Eugene, and then went to feed her mother. After that she sat in front of the fire for a long time while she thought things through. Though it was very cold, she led Sue out of the barn and rode the mare up to the knoll behind the house. She said prayers in front of each grave, taking the longest at the smallest: Annie's. Had she lived, Annie would have been Lou's great-aunt. Lou wished mightily that she could have known what the tiny baby looked like, and she felt miserable that such a thing was now impossible. The stars were fine tonight, and Lou looked around at the mountains painted white, the glitter of ice on branch nearly magical when multiplied as it was ten thousand times. The land could offer Lou no help now, but there was something she could do all on her own. It should have been done long ago, she knew. Yet a mistake was only a mistake if it remained uncorrected.

She rode Sue back, put the mare down for the night, and went into her mother's room. She sat on the bed and took Amanda's hand and didn't move for a bit. Finally, Lou leaned over and kissed her mother's cheek, as the tears started to trickle down the girl's face. "Whatever happens we'll always be together. I promise. You will always have me and Oz. Always." She rubbed at her tears. "I miss you so much." Lou kissed her again. "I love you, Mom." She fled the room, and so Lou never saw the solitary tear leave her mother's eye.

Lou was lying on her bed, quietly sobbing, when Oz came in. Lou did not even make an attempt to stop her weeping. Oz crawled on the bed with her and hugged his sister.

"It'll be okay, Lou, you'll see."

Lou sat up, wiped her face, and looked at him. "I guess all we need is a miracle."

"I could give the wishing well another try," he said.

Lou shook her head. "What do we have to give up for a wish? We've already lost everything."

They sat for some minutes in silence until Oz saw the stack of letters on Lou's desk. "Have you read all of them?" Lou nodded. "Did you like them?" he asked.

Lou looked as though she might start bawling again. "They're wonderful, Oz. Dad wasn't the only writer in the family."

"Can you read some more of them to me? Please?"

Lou finally said all right, she would, and Oz settled in and closed his eyes tightly.

"Why are you doing that?" she asked.

"If I close my eyes when you read the letters it's like Mom is right here talking to me."

Lou looked at the letters as though she held gold. "Oz, you are a genius!"

"I am? Why? What'd I do?"

"You just found our miracle."

Dense clouds had settled over the mountains with no apparent intention to move along anytime soon. Under a freezing rain, Lou, Oz, and Jeb raced along. Chilled to the bone, they reached the clearing, with the old well dead ahead. They ran up to it. Oz's bear and the photo still lay there, soaked and fouled by weather. Oz looked at the photograph and then smiled at his sister. She bent down and took the bear, handing it to Oz.

"Take your bear back," she said tenderly. "Even if you're all grown now."

She put the photo in the bag she carried and then reached inside and pulled out the letters. "Okay, Diamond said we had to give up the most important thing we have in the whole world for the wishing well to work. I can't think of anything more important than Mom's letters. So here goes."

Lou carefully placed the bundle on the edge of the well and set a large rock against it to hold it tight against the wind.

"Now we have to wish."

"For Mom to come back?"

Lou slowly shook her head. "Oz, we have to wish for Louisa to go down to that courthouse. Like Cotton said, it's the only way she'll keep her home."

Oz looked stricken. "But what about Mom? We might not get another chance to wish."

Lou hugged him. "I know, but after all she's done for us, we've got to do this for Louisa. She's our family too. And the mountain means everything to her."

Oz finally nodded sadly in agreement. "You say it then."

Lou held Oz's hand, closed her eyes, and he did too. "We wish that Louisa Mae Cardinal will get up from her bed and show everyone that she's just fine."

Together they said, "Amen, Jesus." And then they ran as fast as they could away from that place, both hoping and praying that there was just one wish left in that pile of old brick and stagnant water.

Late that night Cotton walked along the deserted main street of Dickens, hands stuffed into his pockets, the loneliest man in the world. Cold rain fell steadily, but he was oblivious to it. He sat on a covered bench and eyed the flicker of the street's gas lamps behind the fall of rain. The nameplate on the lamp post was bold and clear: "Southern Valley Coal and Gas." An empty coal truck drifted down the street. A backfire resounded from its tailpipe; the small explosion violently broke the silence of the night.

Cotton watched the truck go by and then slumped down. Yet as his gaze once again caught the flicker of the gas lamp, a flicker of an idea seeped into his mind. He sat up, stared after that coal truck, and then back at that gas lamp. That's when the flicker became a firm idea. And then a rain-soaked Cotton Longfellow stood tall and clapped his hands together, and it sounded like the mighty smack of thunder, for the firm idea had become a miracle of his own.

Minutes later Cotton came into Louisa's room. He stood by the bed and gripped the unconscious woman's hand. "I swear to you, Louisa Mae Cardinal, you will not lose your land."

CHAPTER THIRTY-NINE

THE COURTROOM DOOR SWUNG OPEN AND Cotton strode in with concentrated purpose. Goode, Miller, and Wheeler were already there. And along with this triumvirate, the entire population of the mountain and town had apparently managed to lever itself into the courtroom. A half-million dollars at stake had stirred feelings in folks that had not been touched in many years. Even one elderly gentleman who had long claimed to be the oldest surviving Rebel soldier of the Civil War had come to experience the final round of this legal battle. He clumped in on an oak timber-toe with a capped stump for a right arm, snowy beard down to his belt, and wearing the glorious butternut colors of the Confederate soldier. Those sitting in the front row respectfully made a space for him.

It was cold and damp outside, though the mountains had grown weary of the rain and had finally broken up the clouds and sent them on their way. In the court-room, the accumulation of body heat was fierce, the humidity high enough to fog the windows. And yet every spectator's body was tense against his neighbor, seat or wall.

"I guess it's about time to bring down the curtain on this show," Goode said amiably enough to Cotton. But what Cotton saw was a man with the satisfied look of a professional killer about to blow the smoke off his six-shooter's barrel and then wink at the body lying in the street.

"I think it's just getting started" was Cotton's bludgeoning response.

As soon as the judge was announced and the jury had filed in, Cotton stood. "Your Honor, I would like to make an offer to the Commonwealth."

"Offer? What are you getting at, Cotton?" said Atkins.

"We all know why we're here. It's not about whether Louisa Mae Cardinal is competent or not. It's about gas."

Goode lurched to his feet. "The Commonwealth has a vested interest in seeing that Miss Cardinal's business—"

Cotton interrupted. "The only *business* Miss Cardinal has is deciding whether to sell her land."

Atkins looked intrigued. "What's your offer?"

"I am prepared to concede that Miss Cardinal is mentally unfit."

Goode smiled. "Well, now we're getting somewhere."

"But in return, I want to examine whether Southern Valley is an appropriate party to acquire her land."

Goode looked astonished. "Lord, they're one of the most substantial companies in the state."

Cotton said, "I'm not talking about money. I'm talking about morals."

"Your Honor," Goode said indignantly.

"Approach the bench," said Atkins.

Cotton and Goode hurried forward.

Cotton said, "Judge, there is a long line of Virginia case law that clearly holds that one who commits a wrong shall be barred from profiting from same."

"This is nonsense," said Goode.

Cotton drew close to his adversary. "If you don't agree to let me do it, Goode, I've got my own expert who will contradict everything Dr. Ross has said. And if I lose here, I'll appeal. All the way to the Supreme Court if need be. By the time your client gets to that gas, rest assured, we'll all be dead."

"But I'm a lawyer for the Commonwealth. I have no authority to represent a private company."

"A more ironic statement I have never heard," said Cotton. "But I waive any objection and agree to be bound by the decision of this jury, even with the sorry likes of George Davis sitting on it." Goode was looking toward Miller for a cue, so Cotton gave him a shove. "Oh, Goode, go over there and talk to your client and stop wasting time."

With a sheepish look, Goode slipped over and had a heated discussion with Miller, who looked over repeatedly at Cotton. He finally nodded, and Goode came back.

"No objection."

The judge nodded. "Go ahead, Cotton."

❧

Lou had ridden down to the hospital in the Hudson with Eugene while Oz had stayed behind. He had said he wanted nothing more to do with courts and the law. Buford Rose's wife had come over to look after Oz and his mother. Lou sat in the chair staring at Louisa, waiting for her miracle to take effect. The room was cold and sterile, and it did not seem conducive to anybody's getting well, but Lou was not counting on medicine to make the woman better. Her hopes lay with a stack of old bricks in a grassy meadow and a bundle of letters that might very well be the last words of her mother she would ever have.

Lou rose and drifted to the window. She could see the movie theater from here, where *The Wizard of Oz* was still enjoying a long run. However, Lou had lost her dear Scarecrow, and the Cowardly Lion was no longer afraid. And the Tin Man? Had she finally found her heart? Maybe she had never lost it.

Lou turned and looked at her great-grandmother. The girl stiffened when Louisa opened her eyes and looked at her. There was a strong sense of recognition, a suspicion of a tender smile, and Lou's hopes soared. As though not only their names, but also their spirits, were identical, a tear trickled down the two Louisas' cheeks.

Lou went to her, slipped her hand around Louisa's, and kissed it.

"I love you, Louisa," she said, her heart so near to breaking, for she could not recall saying those words before. Louisa's lips moved, and though Lou could not hear the words, she clearly saw on her lips what the woman was saying back: *I love you, Louisa.*

And then Louisa's eyes slowly closed and did not reopen, and Lou wondered if that was to be all of her miracle.

"Miss Lou, they want us down to the courthouse."

She turned and saw a wide-eyed Eugene standing in the doorway. "Mr. Cotton want us both get on the stand."

Lou slowly let go of Louisa's hand, turned, and left.

A minute later Louisa's eyes opened once more. She looked around the room. Her expression was fearful for a moment, but then grew calm. She started pushing herself up, confused at first as to why her left side was not cooperating. She kept her gaze on the window of the room, even as she fought hard to move herself. Inch by precious inch she progressed, until she was half-sitting, her eyes still on that window. Louisa was breathing heavily now, her strength and energy nearly gone after this short struggle. Yet she lay back against her pillow and smiled. For outside the large window her mountain was now boldly visible. The sight was so beautiful to the woman, although winter had taken most of its color. Next year, though, it would surely all return. Like it always did. Family that never really left you. That was what the mountain was. And her eyes remained fixed

on the familiar rise of rock and trees, even as Louisa
Mae Cardinal grew very still.

❧

In the courtroom, Cotton stood before the bench and
announced in a strong voice, "I call Miss Louisa Mae
Cardinal."

A gasp went up from the crowd. And then the door
opened and Lou and Eugene came in. Miller and Goode
looked smug once more as they saw it was only the
child. Eugene sat while Lou went up to the witness
chair.

Fred approached. "Raise your right hand, put your
left on the Bible. You swear to tell the truth, the whole
truth, and nothing but the truth, so help you God?"

"I do," she said quietly, looking around at everyone
staring at her. Cotton smiled reassuringly. Out of sight
of anyone, he showed her that his fingers were crossed
for luck too.

"Now, Lou, what I have to ask you is going to be
painful, but I need you to answer my questions. Okay?"

"Okay."

"Now, on the day Jimmy Skinner was killed, you were
with him, right?"

Miller and Goode exchanged troubled glances. Goode
got to his feet.

"Your Honor, what does this have to do with anything?"

"The Commonwealth agreed to let me explore my
theory," said Cotton.

"All right," said the judge. "But don't take all day."

Cotton turned back to Lou. "You were at the mine entrance when the explosion occurred?"

"Yes."

"Can you describe for us what happened?"

Lou swallowed, her eyes becoming watery.

"Eugene set the dynamite and came out. We were just going to wait for it to go off. Diamond—I mean, Jimmy—ran into the mine to get Jeb, his dog, who had chased a squirrel in there. Eugene went in to get Jimmy. I was standing in front of the entrance when the dynamite went off."

"Was it a loud explosion?"

"Loudest thing I've heard in my life."

"Could you say whether you heard two explosions?"

She looked confused. "No, I can't."

"Likely as not. Then what happened?"

"Well, this big rush of air and smoke came out and knocked me down."

"Must've been some force."

"It was. It truly was."

"Thank you, Lou. No further questions."

"Mr. Goode?" said Atkins.

"No questions, Your Honor. Unlike Mr. Longfellow, I'm not going to waste the jury's valuable time with this nonsense."

"I next call Eugene Randall," said Cotton.

A nervous Eugene was on the stand. The hat Lou had given him was clutched tightly in his hands.

"Now, Eugene, you went to the mine the day Jimmy Skinner was killed to get some coal, correct?"

"Yes, suh."

"You use dynamite to get the coal out?"

"Yep, most folks do. Coal make good heat. Lot better'n wood."

"How many times you reckon you've used dynamite in that mine?"

Eugene thought about this. "Over the years, thirty times or mo'."

"I think that makes you an expert."

Eugene smiled at this designation. "I reckon so."

"How exactly do you go about using the dynamite?"

"Well, I put the stick'a dynamite in a hole in the wall, cap it, roll out my fuse, and light the fuse with the flame from my lantern."

"Then what do you do?"

"That shaft curves in a couple places, so's I sometimes wait round the curve if I ain't using much dynamite. Sometime I go outside. Noise's starting to hurt my ears now. And blast kick the coal dust up bad."

"I bet it can. In fact, on the day in question, you did go outside. Right?"

"Yes, suh."

"And then you went back inside to get Jimmy, but were unsuccessful."

"Yes, suh," Eugene answered, looking down.

"Was that the first time you'd been in the mine in a while?"

"Yes, suh. Since the first of the year. Past winter ain't that bad."

"Okay. Now, when the explosion went off, where were you?"

"Eighty feet in. Not to the first curve. Got me the bad leg, ain't moving fast no more."

"What happened to you when the explosion occurred?"

"Throwed me ten feet. Hit the wall. Thought I be dead. Held on to my lantern, though. Ain't know how."

"Good Lord. Ten feet? A big man like you? Now, do you remember where you put the dynamite charge?"

"Don't never forget that, Mr. Cotton. Past the second curve. Three hunnerd feet in. Good vein of coal there."

Cotton feigned confusion. "I'm not getting something here, Eugene. Now, you testified that on occasion you would actually stay in the mine when the dynamite went off. And you weren't injured then. And yet here, how is it that you were over two hundred feet from the dynamite charge, around not just one but *two* shaft curves, and the explosion still knocked you ten feet in the air? If you were any closer, you probably would've been killed. How do you explain that?"

Eugene too was thoroughly bewildered now. "I can't, Mr. Cotton. But it done happened. I swear."

"I believe you. Now, you've heard Lou testify as to being knocked down while she was outside the mine. Whenever you were waiting *outside* the mine, that ever happen to you when the dynamite went off?"

Eugene was shaking his head before Cotton finished his question. "Little bit of dynamite I used ain't have nowhere near that kind'a kick. Just getting me some for the bucket. Use more dynamite come winter when I take the sled and mules down, but even that wouldn't come out the mine like that. Lord, you talking three hunnerd feet in and round two curves."

"You found Jimmy's body. Was there rock and stone on it? Had the mine collapsed?"

"No, suh. But I know he dead. He ain't got no lantern, see. You in that mine with no light, you ain't know which way in or out. Mind play tricks on you. He ain't prob'ly even see Jeb pass him heading out."

"Can you tell us exactly where you found Jimmy?"

" 'Nuther hunnerd twenty feet in. Past the first curve, but not the second."

Farmer and merchant sat and stood side by side as they watched Cotton work. Miller fiddled with his hat and then leaned forward and whispered into Goode's ear. Goode nodded, looked at Eugene, and then smiled and nodded again.

"Well, let's assume," said Cotton, "that Jimmy was close to the dynamite charge when it went off. It could have thrown his body a good ways, couldn't it?"

"If'n he close, sure could."

"But his body wasn't past the second curve?"

Goode stood up. "That's easily explained. The dynamite explosion could have thrown the boy past the second curve."

Cotton looked at the jury. "I fail to see how a body

in flight can negotiate a ninety-degree curve and then proceed on before coming to rest. Unless Mr. Goode is maintaining that Jimmy Skinner could fly of his own accord."

Ripples of laughter floated across the courtroom. Atkins creaked back in his chair, yet did not smack his gavel to stop the sounds. "Go on, Cotton. This is getting kind'a interesting."

"Eugene, you remember feeling bad when you were in the mine that day?"

Eugene thought about this. "Hard to recollect. Maybe a little pain in the head."

"Okay, now, in your expert opinion, could the dynamite explosion alone have caused Jimmy Skinner's body to end up where it did?"

Eugene looked over at the jury and took his time in eyeing them one by one. "No, suh!"

"Thank you, Eugene. No further questions."

Goode approached and put the palms of his hands on the witness box and leaned close to Eugene.

"Boy, you live with Miss Cardinal in her house, don't you?"

Eugene sat back a bit, his gaze steady on the man. "Yes, suh."

Goode gave the jury a pointed look. "A colored man and a white woman in the same house?"

Cotton was on his feet before Goode finished his question. "Judge, you can't let him do that."

"Mr. Goode," said Atkins, "y'all might do that sort of thing on down *Richmond* way, but we don't in my courtroom. If you got something to ask the man about this case, then you do it, or else sit yourself down. And last time I checked, his name was Mr. Eugene Randall, not 'boy.' "

"Right, Your Honor, certainly." Goode cleared his throat, stepped back, and slid his hands in his pockets. "Now, *Mister* Eugene Randall, you said in your *expert* opinion that you were two hundred feet or so from the charge, and that Mr. Skinner was about half that distance from the dynamite and such. You remember saying all that?"

"No, suh. I says I was eighty feet in the mine, so's I was two hunnerd and twenty feet from the charge. And I says I *found* Diamond a hunnerd and twenty feet from where I was. That mean he be a hunnerd feet from where I set the dynamite. I ain't got no way to tell how far he got blowed."

"Right, right. Now, you ever been to school?"

"No."

"Never?"

"No, suh."

"So you never took math, never did any adding and subtracting. And yet you're sitting up here testifying under oath to all these *exact* distances."

"Yep."

"So how can that be for an uneducated colored man such as yourself? Who's never even added one plus one under the eye of a teacher? Why should this good jury believe you up here spouting all these big numbers?"

Eugene's gaze never left Goode's confident features.

"Knowed my numbers real good. Cipher and all. Take-away. Miss Louisa done taught me. And I right handy with nail and saw. I hepped many a folk on the mountain raise barns. You a carpenter, you got to know numbers. You cut a three-foot board to fill a four-foot space, what 'xactly have you done?"

Laughter floated across the room again, and again Atkins let it go.

"Fine," said Goode, "so you can cut a board. But in a pitch-dark twisting mine how can you be so sure of what you're saying? Come on now, Mister Eugene Randall, tell us." Goode looked at the jury as he said this, a smile playing across his lips.

" 'Cause it be right there on the wall," said Eugene.

Goode stared at him. "Excuse me?"

"I done marked the walls in that mine with white-wash in ten-foot parcels over four hunnerd feet in. Lotta folk up here do that. You blasting in a mine, you better durn sure know how fer you got to go to get out. I knowed I do 'cause I got me the bad leg. And that way I 'member where the good coal veins are. You get yourself on down to the mine right now with a lantern, mister lawyer, you see them marks clear as the day. So's you can put down what I done said here as the word of the Lord."

Cotton glanced at Goode. To him the Commonwealth's attorney looked as though someone had just informed him that heaven did not admit members of the legal Bar.

"Any further questions?" Atkins asked Goode. The

man said nothing in response but merely drifted back to his table like an errant cloud and collapsed in the chair.

"Mr. Randall," said Atkins, "you're excused, sir, and the court wants to thank you for your *expert* testimony."

Eugene stood and walked back to his seat. From the balcony Lou observed that his limp was hardly noticeable.

Cotton next called Travis Barnes to the stand.

"Dr. Barnes, at my request you examined the records pertaining to Jimmy Skinner's death, didn't you? Including a photograph taken outside the mine."

"Yes, I did."

"Can you tell us the cause of death?"

"Massive head and body injuries."

"What was the condition of the body?"

"It was literally torn apart."

"You ever treated anybody injured by a dynamite explosion?"

"In coal mining country? I say I have."

"You heard Eugene testify. In your opinion, under those circumstances, could the dynamite charge have caused the injuries you saw on Jimmy Skinner?"

Goode did not bother to rise to offer his objection. "Calls for speculation from the witness," he said gruffly.

"Judge, I think Dr. Barnes is fully competent to answer that question as an expert witness," said Cotton.

Atkins was already nodding. "Go on ahead, Travis."

Travis eyed Goode with contempt. "I well know the sorts of dynamite charges folks up here use to get a bucket of coal out. That distance from the charge and around a shaft curve, there is no way that dynamite caused the injuries I saw on that boy. I can't believe nobody figured that out before now."

Cotton said, "I guess a person goes in a mine and dynamite goes off, they just believe that's what killed him. You ever seen such injuries before?"

"Yes. Explosion at a manufacturing plant. Killed a dozen men. Same as Jimmy. Literally blown apart."

"What was the cause of that explosion?"

"Natural gas leak."

Cotton turned and looked dead-on at Hugh Miller.

"Mr. Goode, unless you care to take a shot, I'm calling Mr. Judd Wheeler to the stand."

Goode looked at Miller, betrayed. "No questions."

A nervous Wheeler fidgeted in the witness box as Cotton approached.

"You're Southern Valley's chief geologist?"

"I am."

"And you headed up the team that was exploring possible natural gas deposits on Miss Cardinal's property?"

"I did."

"Without her permission or knowledge?"

"Well, I don't know about—"

"Did you have her permission, Mr. Wheeler?" Cotton snapped.

"No."

"You found natural gas, didn't you?"

"That's right."

"And it was something your company was right interested in, wasn't it?"

"Well, natural gas is getting to be very valuable as a heating fuel. We mostly use manufactured gas, town gas they call it. You get that from heating coal. That's what fuels the streetlights in this town. But you can't make much money with town gas. And we have seamless steel pipe now, which allows us to send gas in pipelines a long way. So yes, we were very interested."

"Natural gas is explosive, right?"

"If properly used—"

"Is it, or isn't it?"

"It is."

"Exactly what did you do in that mine?"

"We took readings and did tests and located what appeared to be a huge field of gas in a trap not too far underneath the surface of that mine shaft and about six hundred feet in the mine. Coal, oil, and gas are often found together because all three result from similar natural processes. The gas always lies on top because it's lighter. That's why you have to be careful when you're mining coal. Methane gas buildup is a real danger to the miners. Anyway, we drilled down and hit that gas field."

"Did the gas come up in the mine shaft?"

"Yes."

"On what date did you hit the gas field?"

When Wheeler told them the day, Cotton said loud and clear to the jury, "One week before Jimmy Skinner's death! Would somebody be able to smell the gas?"

"No, in its natural state gas is colorless and odorless. When companies process it, they add a distinct smell so that if there's a leak people can detect it before it overcomes them."

"Or before something ignites it?"

"That's right."

"If someone set off a dynamite charge in a mine shaft where there was natural gas present, what would happen?"

"The gas would explode." Wheeler looked like he wanted to be blown up himself.

Cotton faced the jury. "I guess Eugene was real lucky he was so far away from the hole where the gas was pouring through and his lamp flame didn't ignite the gas. And he was even luckier he didn't strike a match to light that fuse. But the dynamite going off sure did the trick." He turned back to Wheeler. "What sort of explosion? Big enough to cause Jimmy Skinner's death, in the manner described by Dr. Barnes?"

"Yes," Wheeler conceded.

Cotton put his hands on the frame of the witness box and leaned in. "Didn't you ever think about posting warning signs telling people that there was gas there?"

"I didn't know they dynamited in there! I didn't know they used that old mine for anything."

Cotton thought he caught Wheeler shooting an angry look at George Davis, but he couldn't be sure.

"But if anyone went in, they might be overcome by the gas alone. Wouldn't you want to warn people?"

Wheeler spoke fast. "The ceilings in that mine shaft are real high, and there's some natural ventilation through the rock too, so the buildup of the methane wouldn't be so bad. And we were going to cap the hole, but we were waiting on some equipment we needed. We didn't want anybody to get hurt. That's the truth."

"The fact is, you couldn't post warning signs because you were there illegally. Isn't that right?"

"I was just following orders."

"You took great pains to hide the fact that you were working in that mine, didn't you?"

"Well, we only worked at night. Whatever equipment we carried in, we took out with us."

"So nobody would know you'd been there?"

"Yes."

"Because Southern Valley was hoping to buy Miss Cardinal's farm for a lot less money if she didn't know she was sitting on an ocean of gas?"

"Objection!" Goode said.

Cotton steamed right on. "Mr. Wheeler, you knew Jimmy Skinner died in that mine explosion. And you had to know the gas played some role in it. Why didn't you come forward and tell the truth then?"

Wheeler fidgeted with his hat. "I was told not to."

"And who told you not to?"

"Mr. Hugh Miller, company vice president."

Everyone in the courtroom looked at Miller. Cotton stared at Miller when he asked his next questions.

"You have any children, Mr. Wheeler?"

Wheeler looked surprised, but answered: "Three."

"They all doing well? Healthy?"

Wheeler's gaze dropped to his lap before he responded. "Yes."

"You're a lucky man."

✤

Goode was addressing the jury with his closing argument.

"Now, we've heard far more evidence than is necessary for you to find that Louisa Mae Cardinal is mentally unfit. In fact, her own lawyer, Mr. Longfellow, has conceded that she is. Now, all this talk about gas and explosions and such, well what does it really have to do with this case? If Southern Valley was somehow involved in Mr. Skinner's death, then his survivors *may* be entitled to damages."

"He doesn't have any survivors," said Cotton.

Goode chose to ignore this. "Now, Mr. Longfellow asks whether my client is an appropriate party to be buying land up here. Fact is, folks, Southern Valley has big plans for your town. Good jobs, bring prosperity back to you all."

He got real close to the jury, their best friend. "The question is, should Southern Valley be allowed to 'enrich' all of your lives as well as Miss Cardinal's? I think the answer to that is obvious."

Goode sat down. And Cotton came at the jury. He moved slowly, his bearing confident but not threatening. His hands were in his pockets, and he rested one of his scuffed shoes on the lower rail of the jury box. When he spoke, his voice leaned more southern than New England, and every single juror except George Davis hunched forward so as not to miss anything the man said. They had watched Cotton Longfellow bloody the nose of what they assumed was one of the finest lawyers from the great city of Richmond. And he had made humble a company that was as close to a monarch as one could get in a country of democracy. Now they undoubtedly wanted to see if the man could finish it.

"Let me give you good folks the legal side of the case first. And it's not complicated at all. In fact it's like a good bird dog, it points straight and true in one direction, and one direction only." He took one hand from his pocket and, like a good hound, pointed right at Hugh Miller as he spoke. "The reckless actions of Southern Valley killed Jimmy Skinner, you folks can have no doubts about that. Southern Valley's not even disputing it. They were illegally on Louisa Mae's property. They posted no warnings that the mine was filled with explosive gas. They allowed innocent people to enter that mine when they knew it was deadly. It could've been any of you. And they did not come forward with the truth because they knew they were in the wrong. And now they seek to use the tragedy of Louisa Mae's stroke as a way to take her land. The law clearly says one cannot profit from one's misdeeds. Well, if what Southern Valley did does not qualify as a misdeed, then nothing on this earth ever would." His voice up to this point had been slow and steady. Now it rose one delicate notch, but he kept his finger pointed at Hugh Miller. "One day God will hold them accountable for killing an innocent young man. But it's your job to see that they are punished today."

Cotton looked at each and every juror, stopping on George Davis; he spoke directly to him. "Now, let's get to the *nonlegal* part of this business, for I think that's where the struggle you folks are going through lies. Southern Valley has come in here swinging bags full of money in front of you, telling you that it's the savior of the whole town. But that's what the lumber folks told you. They're going to be here forever. Remember? So why were all the lumber camps on rails? How much more *temporary* can you get? And where are they now? Last time I checked, Kentucky was not part of the Commonwealth of Virginia."

He looked over at Miller. "And the coal companies told you the same thing. And what did they do? They came and took everything they wanted and left you with nothing except hollowed-out mountains, family with the black lung and dreams replaced with nightmares. And now Southern Valley's singing that same old tune with gas. It's just one more needle in the mountain's hide. Just one more thing to suck out, leaving nothing!" Cotton turned and addressed the entire courtroom.

"But this isn't really about Southern Valley, or coal or gas. It's ultimately about all of you. Now, they can cut the top of that mountain easy enough, pull out that gas, run their fine seamless steel pipeline, and it might keep going for ten, fifteen, even twenty years. But then it'll all be gone. You see, that pipeline is taking the gas to other places, just like the trains did the coal, and the river did the trees. Now, why is that, do you think?" He took his time looking around the room. "I'll tell you why. Because that's where the real prosperity is, folks. At least in the way Southern Valley defines it. And all of you know that. These mountains just got what they need to keep that prosperity going and their pockets filled. And so they come here and they take it.

"Dickens, Virginia, will never be a New York City, and let me tell you there's not a damn thing wrong with that. In fact, I believe we have us enough big cities, and a dwindling number of places like right here. Y'all will never become rich working at the foot of these mountains. Those who will claim great wealth are the Southern Valleys of the world, who take from the land and give nothing back to it. You want a *real* savior? Look at yourselves. Rely on each other. Just like Louisa Mae's been doing her whole life up on that mountain. Farmers live on the whim of the weather and the ground. Some years they lose, other years are fine. But for them, the resources of the mountain are *never* extinguished, because they do not tear its soul away. And their reward for that is being able to live a decent, honest life for as long as they so desire, without the fear that folks intent on nothing more than making a pile of gold by raping mountains will come with grand promises, and then leave when there is nothing to be gained by staying, and destroy innocent lives in the process."

He pointed to Lou where she sat in the courtroom. "Now, that girl's daddy wrote many wonderful stories about this area, and those very issues of land, and the people who live on it. In words, Jack Cardinal has enabled this place to survive forever. Just like the mountains. He had an exemplary teacher, for Louisa Mae Cardinal has lived her life the way all of us should. She's helped many of you at some point in your lives and asked for nothing in return." Cotton looked at Buford Rose and some of the other farmers staring at him. "And you've helped her when she needed it. You know she'd never sell her land, because that ground is as much a part of her family as her great-grandchildren waiting to see what's going to happen to them. You can't let Southern Valley steal the woman's family. All folks have up on that mountain is each other and their land. That's all. It may not seem like much to those who don't live there, or for people who seek nothing but to destroy the rock and trees. But rest assured, it means everything to the people who call the mountains home."

Cotton stood tall in front of the jury box, and though his voice remained level and calm, the large room seemed inadequate to contain his words.

"You folks don't have to be an expert in the law to reach the right decision in this case. All you got to have is a heart. Let Louisa Mae Cardinal keep her land."

CHAPTER FORTY

LOU STARED OUT THE WINDOW OF HER BED-room at the grand sweep of land as it bolted right up to the foothills and then on to the mountains, where the leaves on all but the evergreens were gone. The naked trees were still quite something to behold, though now they appeared to Lou to be poor grave markers for thousands of dead, their mourners left with not much.

"You should have come back, Dad," she said to the mountains he had immortalized with words and then shunned the rest of his life.

She had returned to the farm with Eugene after the jury had gone into deliberation. She had no desire to be there when the verdict came in. Cotton had said he would come tell them the decision. He said he did not expect it to take long. Cotton did not say whether he thought that was good or bad, but he did not look hopeful. Now all Lou could do was wait. And it was hard, for everything around her could be gone tomorrow, depending on what a group of strangers decided. Well, one of them wasn't a stranger; he was more like a mortal enemy.

Lou traced her father's initials with her finger on the desk. She had sacrificed her mother's letters for a miracle that had never bothered to come, and it pained her so. She went downstairs and stopped at Louisa's room. Through the open door she saw the old bed, the small dresser, a bowl and pitcher on top of it. The room was small, its contents spare, just like the woman's life. Lou covered her face. It just wasn't right. She stumbled into the kitchen to start the meal.

As she was pulling out a pot, Lou heard a noise behind her and turned. It was Oz. She wiped at her eyes, for she still wanted to be strong for him. Yet as she focused on his expression, Lou realized she had no need to worry about her brother. Something had seized him; she didn't know what. But her brother had never looked this way before. Without a word, he took her hand and drew his sister back down the hallway.

The jury filed into the courtroom, a dozen men from the mountain and the town, at least eleven of whom Cotton could hope would do the right thing. The jury had been out for many hours, longer than Cotton had thought probable. He did not know if that was good or bad. The real card against him, he knew, was that of desperation. It was a strong opponent, because it could so easily prey upon those who worked so hard every day simply to survive, or upon those who saw no future in a place where everything was being carved out and taken away. Cotton would loathe the jurors if they went against him, yet he knew they easily could. Well, at least it would soon be over.

Atkins asked, "Has the jury reached a verdict?"

The foreman rose. He was a man from the town, a humble shopkeeper, his body swollen from too much beef and potato, and from too little effort with arms and shoulders. "Yes, Your Honor," he said quietly.

Hardly a single person had left the courtroom since the jury had been given its charge from the judge and sent out. The whole population of the room leaned forward, as though they all had just been struck deaf.

"What say you?"

"We find . . . for Southern Valley." The foreman looked down, as though he had just delivered a death sentence to one of his own.

The courtroom erupted into shouts—some cheers, some not. The balcony seemed to sway with the collective weight of the decision of a dozen men. Hugh Miller and George Davis exchanged slight nods, lips easing into victorious smiles.

Cotton sat back. The legal process had had its day; the only thing absent was justice.

Miller and Goode shook hands. Miller tried to congratulate Wheeler, but the big man walked off in obvious disgust.

"Order, order in this court or I'll clear it." Atkins slammed his gavel several times, and things did quiet down.

"The jury is dismissed. Thank you for your service," he said and not very kindly. A man entered the courtroom, spotted Cotton, and whispered something in his ear. Cotton's despair noticeably deepened.

Goode said, "Your Honor, it now remains solely to appoint someone to represent Miss Cardinal's interests and assume guardianship of the children."

"Judge, I've just received some news that the court needs to hear." Cotton slowly stood, his head down, one hand pressed to his side. "Louisa Mae Cardinal has passed away."

The courtroom erupted once more, and this time Atkins made no move to contain it. Davis's smile broadened. He went over to Cotton. "Damn," he said, "this day get better and better."

Cotton's mind went blank for a moment, as though someone had smote him with an anvil. He grabbed Davis and had it in his mind to deliver him into the next county with his right fist, but then he stopped and simply heaved the man out of his way, as one would shovel a large pile of manure off a road.

"Your Honor," said Goode, "I know we're all very sorry to hear about Miss Cardinal. Now, I have a list of very reputable people who can represent these fine children in the sale of the property that has just now passed to them."

"And I hope you rot in hell for it," cried out Cotton. He raced to the bench, Goode on his heels.

Cotton pounded his fist so hard on the mighty bench of justice that Fred the bailiff took a nervous step toward them.

"George Davis tainted that whole jury," roared Cotton. "I know he's got Southern Valley dollars burning a hole in his pocket."

"Give it up, Longfellow, you lost," said Goode.

Neither man noticed the courtroom doors opening.

"Never, Goode. Never!" Cotton shouted at him.

"He agreed to be bound by the decision of the jury."

"I'm afraid he's got a point there," said Atkins.

A triumphant Goode turned to look at Miller and his eyes nearly crossed at what he was seeing.

"But Henry," pleaded Cotton, "please, the children . . . Let me be their guardian. I—"

Atkins was not paying attention to Cotton. He too was now staring at the courtroom, his mouth wide open.

Cotton slowly turned to see what Atkins was looking at, and felt himself feeling faint, as though he'd just seen God walk through that door.

Lou and Oz stood there before them all.

And between them, held up almost solely by her children, was Amanda Cardinal.

Lou had not taken her gaze from her mother from the moment Oz had led her down the hallway and into the bedroom, where her mother was lying in bed, her eyes wide open, tears running from them, her shaky arms finally reaching out to her children, her trembling lips forming a joyous smile.

Neither could Cotton take his gaze from the woman. Still, he had unfinished business before the court.

In a cracking, halting voice he said, "Your Honor, I would like to present to you Amanda Cardinal. The rightful and true guardian of her children."

The sea of now-silent people parted and allowed Cotton to walk slowly over to mother and her children, his legs stumbling along, as though they had forgotten the proper motions. His face was smirched with tears.

"Mrs. Cardinal," he began, "my name is—"

Amanda reached out a hand and touched him on the shoulder. Her body was very weak, yet her head was held high, and when she spoke her words were soft but clear. "I know who you are, Mr. Longfellow. I've listened to you often."

TODAY

THE TALL WOMAN WALKS ALONG A FIELD of bluegrass slowly curving in the wind. The line of mountains sweeps across in the background. Her hair is silver and hangs to her waist. She holds a pen and a paper tablet and sits on the ground and begins to write.

Maybe the wishing well did work. Or perhaps it was the unwavering faith of a little boy. Or maybe it was as simple as a little girl telling her mother she loved her. The important thing was our mother came back to us. Even as our beloved Louisa Mae left us. We had Louisa but a minute, yet we came close to having her not at all.

The woman rises, walks along, and then stops at two granite tombstones with the names Cotton Longfellow and Amanda Cardinal Longfellow engraved upon them. She sits and continues writing.

My mother and Cotton were married a year later. Cotton adopted Oz and me, and I showed equal love and affection to him and my mother. They spent over four wonderful decades together on this mountain and died within a week of one another. I will never forget Cotton's great kindness. And I will go to my own grave knowing that my mother and I made the most of our second chance.

My little brother did grow into those big feet, and developed an even bigger arm. And on a glorious autumn day, Oz Cardinal pitched and won a World Series for the New York Yankees. He's now a schoolteacher there, with a well-deserved reputation for helping timid children thrive. And his grandson has inherited that immortal bear. Some days I want nothing more than to be holding that little boy again, running my fingers through his hair, comforting him. My cowardly lion. But children grow up. And my little brother became a fine man. And his sister is truly proud of him.

Eugene went on to have his own farm and family and still lives nearby. He remains to this day one of my best friends in the world. And after his performance in that courtroom so long ago, I never heard anyone ever again refer to him as Hell No.

And me? Like my father, I left the mountain. But unlike Jack Cardinal, I came back. I married and raised a family here in a home I built on the land Louisa Mae left us. Now my own grandchildren come and visit every summer. I tell them of my life growing up here. About Louisa Mae, Cotton, and my dear friend Diamond Skin-

ner. *And also about others who touched our lives. I do so because I believe it important for them to know such things about their family.*

Over the years I had read so many books, I started to write one of my own. I loved it so much, I wrote fourteen more. I told stories of happiness and wonder. Of pain and fear. Of survival and triumph. Of the land and its people. As my father had. And while I never won the sorts of awards he did, my books tended to sell a little better.

As my father wrote, one's courage, hope, and spirit can be severely tried by the happenstance of life. But as I learned on this Virginia mountain, so long as one never loses faith, it is impossible to ever truly be alone.

This is where I belong. It is a true comfort to know that I will die here on this high rock. And I fear my passing not at all. My enthusiasm is perfectly understandable, you see, for the view from here is so very fine.

SHETLAND LIBRARY
WITHDRAWN

ACKNOWLEDGMENTS

I would be remiss in not thanking various people who helped with this project. First, all the fine folks at Warner Books, and especially my dear friend Maureen Egen, who was wonderfully supportive of my trying something different, and who performed a marvelous editing job on the novel. And thanks also to Aaron Priest and Lisa Vance for all their help and encouragement. They both make my life far less complicated. And to Molly Friedrich, for taking the time from her extraordinarily busy schedule to read an early draft of the novel and provide many insightful comments. And to Frances Jalet-Miller, who brought her usual superb editing skills and heartfelt enthusiasm to the story. And to my cousin Steve for reading all the words as usual. And to Jennifer Steinberg for her help.

To Michelle for all she does. It is a well-known fact that I would be utterly lost without her.

And to Spencer and Collin, for being my Lou and Oz.

And to my dear friend Karen Spiegel for all her help and encouragement with this work. You really helped make it better, and maybe one day we'll see it on the big screen.

And to all the fine people at the Library of Virginia in Richmond for allowing me use of its archives, providing a quiet place to work and think, and for pointing me in the direction of numerous treasure troves: remembrances penned by mountain folks; oral histories documented by diligent WPA staff in the 1930s; pictorial histories of rural counties in Virginia; and the first state publication on midwifery.

A very special thanks to Deborah Hocutt, the Executive Director of the Virginia Center for the Book at the Library of Virginia, for all her assistance with this project, and also with the many other endeavors I'm involved with in the Commonwealth.

POCKET
B O O K S

Saving Faith
David Baldacci

Washington lobbyist Danny Buchanan has made a
fortune peddling influence for his cash-rich client companies, and now he's attempting to do the same to help
the world's poor. He works tirelessly and in secret to
establish a network of politicians who can be bribed to
vote the right way on matters concerning international
aid – until the CIA want in on the illegal strategy.

Danny's partner, the tough-minded, independent and
fiercely loyal Faith Lockhart senses danger and reveals
all to the FBI in exchange for her and Danny's immu-
nity. But she doesn't anticipate the ruthlessness of the
CIA, a diminished and directionless organization at
the helm of which is a renegade obsessive who's determined to take out Faith and anyone remotely connected
to her...

ISBN 0 7434 1526 4

PRICE £6.99

POCKET
B O O K S

The Simple Truth
David Baldacci

A heart-stopping story of an evil conspiracy at the core of the American legal system . . .

As a young soldier, Rufus Harms was jailed for the brutal killing of a schoolgirl. Yet, after twenty-five years of incarceration, a letter from the US Army reveals new facts about the night of the murder – and the evil secret shared by some of Washington's most powerful men. Rufus turns to the only man who can help: ex-cop turned criminal attorney, John Fiske.

But for both men time is already running out. Their enemy is buried deep within the system and is completely ruthless in protecting the truth . . .

ISBN 0 671 03307 7

PRICE £6.99

POCKET
B O O K S

The Winner
David Baldacci

LuAnn Tyler is a twenty-year-old unwed mother striving to escape an abusive relationship and a life of endless poverty. Suddenly, a mysterious Mr Jackson makes her an offer no one can refuse: a guarantee to be the winner of the $100 million national lottery. But with it comes the condition that she leave the country for ever.

Ten years later, LuAnn secretly returns to the United States to begin a new life. But before long her peace is shattered. A canny reporter has picked up her trail, as have the FBI – and Jackson, a man she knows not to cross.

ISBN 0 7434 0848 9

PRICE £6.99

POCKET
B O O K S

Total Control
David Baldacci

Jason Archer is a rising young executive at Triton Global, the world's leading technology conglomerate. Determined to give his family the best of everything, Archer has secretly entered into a deadly game of cat and mouse. He is about to disappear – leaving behind a wife who must sort out his lies from his truths and a FBI agent who wants to know it all.

Soon the startling truth behind Jason Archer's disappearance explodes into a sinister plot with the murder of the country's single most powerful individual. And Archer's wife, Sidney, is plunged straight into the violence that is leaving behind a trail of dead bodies and shocking, exposed secrets . . .

ISBN 0 7434 0847 0

PRICE £6.99

POCKET
B O O K S

This book and other **David Baldacci** titles are available from your bookshop or can be ordered direct from the publisher.

☐ 0 7434 0846 2 **Absolute Power** £6.99
☐ 0 7434 0848 9 **The Winner** £6.99
☐ 0 671 03307 7 **The Simple Truth** £6.99
☐ 0 7434 0847 0 **Total Control** £6.99
☐ 0 7434 1526 4 **Saving Faith** £6.99

Please send cheque or postal order for the value of the book, free postage and packing within the UK; OVERSEAS including Republic of Ireland £1 per book.

OR: Please debit this amount from my

VISA/ACCESS/MASTERCARD ....

CARD NO ....

EXPIRY DATE ....

AMOUNT £ ....

NAME ....

ADDRESS ....

....

SIGNATURE ....

Send orders to SIMON & SCHUSTER CASH SALES
PO Box 29, Douglas, Isle of Man, IM99 1BQ
Tel: 01624 675137, Fax 01624 670923
www.bookpost.co.uk
Please allow 14 days for delivery.
Prices and availability subject to change without notice.